A TOUGH AUDIENCE

"I regret the intrusion," the holographic image of Broghuilio began. He spoke stiffly, in the manner of somebody performing a duty that demanded a greater show of feeling than he could muster readily. "We have just received news of the most serious nature. All traces of the *Shapieron* have disappeared from our tracking data. We can only conclude that it has been destroyed." He paused a moment. "I know that this could be the news you were hoping for, but it must be dismissed."

The Thuriens stared at him for what seemed a long time. They did not show any concern or dismay . . . or even surprise. The first glimmer of uncertainty crept into Broghuilio's eyes as he searched the Ganymean faces for a reaction. This was not going as he had anticipated.

One of the other two humans, dressed somberly in dark blue and black, with icy blue eyes, slicked-back silver hair, and a florid face, seemed not to have read the signs. "We tried to warn you," Wylott said, spreading his hands imploringly in a good imitation of sharing the anguish that the Thuriens were presumably supposed to be feeling at that moment. "We told you that Earth would never allow the *Shapieron* to reach Thurien."

"Really?" Calazar responded after a pause. He sounded neither convinced nor impressed. "Your concern is most touching, Secretary Wylott. You almost sound as if you believe your own lies."

By James P. Hogan

THE TWO WORLDS

TWO GIANTS NOVELS

JAMES P. HOGAN

BAEN

THE TWO WORLDS

This is a work of fiction. All the characters and events portrayed in this book are fictional, and any resemblance to real people or incidents is purely coincidental.

A Baen Books Original

Baen Publishing Enterprises
P.O. Box 1403
Riverdale, NY 10471
www.baen.com

ISBN 10: 1-4165-3725-2
ISBN 13: 978-1-4165-3725-0

Cover art by Allan Pollack

First Baen paperback printing, September 2007

Distributed by Simon & Schuster
1230 Avenue of the Americas
New York, NY 10020

Printed in the United States of America

10 9 8 7 6 5 4 3 2 1

CONTENTS

years that have elapsed since, and been translated into many languages.

1977 was also the year that I moved from the UK to Massachusetts, still with DEC, to manage specialist sales training for their laboratory and scientific computing division. It is sometimes said that writing is not so much a hobby or a profession as an incurable disease. By the time I finished *Inherit the Stars* I had been bitten sufficiently by the bug to launch into two new novels virtually simultaneously. (This was during the period between the last ice age and the invention of the PC, when e-mail was unknown and private trans-Atlantic phone calls were rarities typically indulged in on birthdays and at Christmas. I found that a beginning writer needs a lot of editorial contact, and having two books going in parallel avoided wasting time while waiting for responses via the three-week communications loop to New York.) These next novels were *The Genesis Machine*, and *The Gentle Giants of Ganymede*. Discerning readers may have noticed that they were released in consecutive months, April and May, 1978—six months or so after I arrived in the U.S.A.

In *Inherit the Stars*, I had shamelessly stolen Arthur's premise of a mystery discovered in the course of twenty-first-century lunar exploration, sufficient to arouse the excitement of a goodly portion of the scientific community. Instead of an obelisk, however, the mystery took the form of a space-suited corpse, fully human in all anatomical detail, which further examination reveals to have been there for 50,000 years. The scientific detective story that follows establishes "Charlie" to have belonged to a race christened the "Lunarians," from the planet Minerva, that once existed between Mars and Jupiter. They were descended from hominid ancestors who had been transported from Earth by an extinct race of alien giants known as the Ganymeans, Minerva's original natives, named after Jupiter's moon Ganymede, where the first evidence of their existence came to light. When changing conditions rendered the Solar System uninhabitable, the "Giants" migrated to another star system. In the millions of years that followed, the

Introduction

My first book, *Inherit the Stars*, was published by Ballantine Del Rey in May, 1977. I was living in the UK then, having graduated as an electrical and electronics engineer from the Royal Aircraft Establishment, Farnborough, and Reading Technical College, and then worked for some years on digital control and instrumentation systems, and then in real-time computer sales with Honeywell and Digital Equipment Corporation. The sortie into writing occurred while I was at DEC, after seeing the movie of Arthur Clarke's *2001*. I liked it in many ways but didn't understand the ending, and my subsequent remonstrations to that effect in the office were met with the retort that if I thought I could write something that made more sense why didn't I? This led to an office bet at five pounds a head that I couldn't write a science fiction novel and get it published. The upshot was that I did, and it was, and I made fifty pounds on top of the publisher's advance. *Inherit the Stars* has been in print continuously throughout the thirty

Lunarians emerged on Minerva as a technically advanced but divided human culture that carried its militarization out into space. In a final, cataclysmic war, Minerva was destroyed. The survivors came to Earth at the time of the Neanderthals, multiplied and prevailed over them, and are finally recognized as the direct ancestors of modern man.

The *Gentle Giants of Ganymede* picks up at this point, with researchers at the scientific base on Ganymede continuing their investigations of an ancient Ganymean starship discovered deep beneath the ice fields, which provided most of the evidence from which the story of pre-Lunarian Minerva was reconstructed. When the Terrans begin experimenting with equipment recovered from the vessel, a device that they succeed in reactivating turns out to be a signal beacon that attracts a live, functioning Ganymean starship that was sent on an interstellar mission millions of years ago. Through a quirk of relativity physics that came into play following an accident, it has been existing under conditions of extended time-dilation since the era when their kind inhabited Minerva. But their home planet no longer exists. They come to Earth, where they create a sensation, are made welcome, and for six months lead a harmonious existence. It is assumed that the two races will now continue to share the world and a common future. However, that ends when the the Giants depart once more to seek out their own race at a star called the Giants' Star, where the Ganymeans from the Minerva of long ago are believed to have migrated. Many think the story of the migration is a myth. Even if it were true, there is no guarantee that any descendants will still be found there. But the Giants feel compelled to try.

These two books, *Inherit the Stars*, and *The Gentle Giants of Ganymede*, were the first two titles in what has since developed into the "Giants" series. In April, 2006, Baen Books re-released them in a single-volume combined omnibus edition entitled *The Two Moons*. In the Introduction, I promised that there would be a companion volume containing the third and fourth titles in the series. It is *The Two Worlds*, the book that you are now holding. The two titles that it contains were both written during the 1980s, after I had left DEC to become a full-time writer, been granted permanent residency of the United States, and was free to live and work where and when and how I chose.

I had written two more books during the time I was still with DEC: *The Two Faces of Tomorrow* and *Thrice Upon a Time*. After those were done, my thoughts turned back once more to the Giants. *The Gentle Giants of Ganymede* had ended with a hint that the Giants' Star is not a myth but indeed real and very alive, giving a clear indication of an intended further story to follow. At the end of 1979 I found myself single again, in possession of a car, two suitcases, and a portable typewriter, heading south from Boston for New York, where I was thinking of relocating. I had almost settled on an apartment in a former hotel overlooking Central Park, when I ran into a character called Al, heading the other way—to take a position with my former employer Honeywell, as it turned out—who had lived in what sounded like an identical place, except that it also had a pool, health club, and tennis courts, in Orlando, Florida, for about one sixth the rent. The 2-3 day drive took me about three months; strange things can happen when you're loose, exploring a wonderland like America was—to me, anyway—in the early 1980s. By the time I took an apartment in Altamonte Springs, I had the first draft of *Giants' Star* finished. It was written in people's kitchens, people's spare rooms, back porches, and motel rooms down the east coast and along the Gulf, and at various circuitous places between. It would be inappropriate to give away too much about it here. Suffice it to say that the Ganymeans who left Earth arrive at the Giants' Star a lot sooner than they expected, and find a thriving civilization on a planet called Thurien. The subsequent opening of direct contact between Thurien and Earth reveals the existence of another branch of the Lunarian race descended from other survivors who were removed to Thurien after Minerva's destruction. Still seeing Terrans as rivals, the "Jevlenese" have been meddling in Earth's history for millennia in anticipation of an eventual day of reckoning, but are exposed through the joint efforts of the Terrans and the Thuriens, with delivery of due come-uppances.

The fourth book in the series, *Entoverse*, was written at the latter end of the decade, by which time I was married again, raising three children again—three sons this time, in contrast to the three daughters from my first marriage—and living in California, in the foothills of the Sierra Nevada, about three hours drive inland from San Francisco. The team that we have gotten to know in the first three books arrives at Jevlen, the planet that the Thuriens entrusted to the Jevlenese as their own world, to help investigate a strange craziness that has affected much of the population and resulted in social malaise and general decline. I'll say no more here than that it turns out to be due to one of the strangest alien invasions ever. Along with *Giants' Star*, it makes up *The Two Worlds*.

The fifth Giants novel, *Mission to Minerva*, was released in May, 2005. Since then I have received many appreciative comments, along with inquiries as to if and when we can expect a sixth. So, although there is nothing definite in the works yet, perhaps we'll see a further title. It certainly appears that we need one to make up a third two-book omnibus to complete what would be a handsome set. In the meantime, I hope that this latest addition to the collection will help keep the Giants alive on the shelves for many more years to come, and introduce them to many new readers.

James P. Hogan
County Leitrim, Ireland
May, 2007

Giants' Star

To Jackie

Prologue

B y the beginning of the fourth decade of the twenty-first
century, it seemed that the human race was finally beginning to learn to live together and that it was on its way to the
stars. Having abandoned the crippling arms race and disbanded
the bulk of their strategic forces, the superpowers were instead
pouring their billions into a massive transfer of Western technology and know-how to the nations of the Third World. With
the increased wealth and living standards that came universally with global industrialization, and the security and variety
that accompanied more affluent life-styles, population became
self-limiting, and hunger, poverty, along with most of mankind's
other traditional age-old scourges, at last looked as if they were
on the brink of being eradicated permanently. While the U.S.-
U.S.S.R. rivalry transformed itself into a war of wits and
diplomacy for economic and political influence among the
stabilizing nation-states, Man's adventure lust found its expression in a revitalized, multinational space program, which burst
outward across the solar system in a new wave of exploration
and expansion coordinated under a specially formed UN Space
Arm. Lunar development and exploitation proceeded rapidly,

permanent bases appeared on Mars and in orbit above Venus, and a series of large-scale manned missions reached the outer planets.

But probably the greatest revolution of the times was the upheaval in science that had followed some of the discoveries made on the Moon and out at Jupiter in the course of these explorations. In the space of just a few years, a series of astonishing discoveries had toppled beliefs unquestioned since the beginnings of science, forced a complete rewriting of the history of the solar system itself, and culminated in Man's first encounter with an advanced alien species.

A hitherto unknown planet, christened Minerva by the investigators who unraveled its story, had once occupied the position between Mars and Jupiter in the solar system as originally formed, and had been inhabited by an advanced race of eight-foot-tall aliens who came to be known as the "Ganymeans" after the first evidence of their existence came to light on Ganymede, largest of the Jovian moons. The Ganymean civilization, which flourished up until twenty-five million years before the present, vanished abruptly. Some of Earth's scientists believed that deteriorating environmental conditions on Minerva might have forced the "Giants" to migrate to some other star system, but the matter had not been settled conclusively. Much later—some fifty thousand years prior to the current period in Earth's history—Minerva was destroyed. The bulk of its mass, thrown outward into an eccentric orbit on the edge of the solar system, became Pluto. The remainder of the debris was dispersed by Jupiter's tidal effect and formed the Asteroid Belt.

While the pieces of this puzzle were still being fitted together, a starship from the ancient Ganymean civilization returned. Having undergone a relativistic time dilation that was compounded by a technical problem in the vessel's space-time-distorting drive system, the net result was that an elapsed time of twenty-odd years for the ship corresponded to the passing of something on the order of a million times that number on Earth. The *Shapieron* had departed from Minerva before the onset of whatever had befallen the rest of the

Ganymean race, and its occupants were therefore unable to either confirm or refute the theories of the terrestrial researchers involved with the subject. The Giants stayed for six months, combining their efforts with those of Earth's scientists in a search for more clues and mingling harmoniously into Earth's society. Mankind had found a friend, and the remnants of the Ganymean race had, it was assumed, found a home.

But it was not to be. Investigations uncovered a hint that the Ganymean civilization had migrated to a star located near the constellation of Taurus—a star that came to be called the "Giants' Star"; there was no guarantee, but there was hope. Shortly afterward the *Shapieron* departed, leaving behind a sad, but in many ways wiser, world.

Radio observatories on lunar Farside beamed a signal toward the Giant's Star to forewarn of the *Shapieron*'s coming. Though the signal would take years to cover the distance, it would still arrive well ahead of the ship. To the astonishment of the scientists who composed the transmission, a reply purporting to have come from the Giants' Star and confirming that it was indeed the new home of the Ganymeans was received only hours after they first began sending. But by that time the *Shapieron* had already left, and news of the message could not be relayed to it because of the space-time distortion induced around the craft by its drive, which prevented electromagnetic signals from being received coherently. There was nothing more that the scientists on Earth could do; the *Shapieron* had vanished back into the void from whence it had come, and many more years of uncertainty would pass before the Ganymeans aboard it would know whether or not their quest was in vain.

The transmitters on lunar Farside continued sending intermittently during the three months that followed, but no further reply was evoked.

Chapter One

D r. Victor Hunt finished combing his hair, buttoned on a clean shirt, and paused to contemplate the somewhat sleepy-eyed but otherwise presentable image staring back at him from the bathroom mirror. He detected a couple of gray strands here and there among his full head of dark brown waves, but somebody would have had to be looking for them to notice them. His skin had an acceptably healthy tone to it; the lines of his cheeks and jaw were solid and firm, and his belt still rested loosely on his hips to serve its intended purpose of keeping his pants up and not to keep his waistline in. All in all, he decided, he wasn't doing too badly for thirty-nine. The face in the mirror frowned suddenly as the ritual reminded him of a typical specimen of middle-age male wreckage in a TV commercial; all it wanted now was for the mentally defective, bottle-brandishing wife to appear in the doorway behind to deliver the message on baldness cures, body deodorants, remedies for bad breath, or whatever. Shuddering at the thought, he tossed the comb into the medicine cabinet above the sink, closed the door, and ambled through into the apartment's kitchen.

"Are you through in the bathroom, Vic?" Lyn's voice called from the open door of the bedroom. It sounded bright and cheerful, and should have been illegal at that time in the morning.

"Go ahead." Hunt tapped a code into the kitchen terminal to summon a breakfast menu onto its screen, studied the display for a few seconds, then entered an order to the robochef for scrambled eggs, bacon (crisp), toast with marmalade, and coffee, twice. Lyn appeared in the hallway outside, Hunt's bathrobe hanging loosely on her shoulders and doing little to hide her long, slim legs and golden-tanned body. She flashed him a smile, then vanished into the bathroom in a swirl of the red hair that hung halfway down her back.

"It's coming up," Hunt called after her.

"The usual," her voice threw back from the doorway.

"You guessed?"

"The English are creatures of habit."

"Why make life complicated?"

The screen presented a list of grocery items that were getting low, and Hunt okayed the computer to transmit an order to Albertson's for delivery later that day. The sound of the shower being turned on greeted him as he emerged from the kitchen and walked through into the living room, wondering how a world that accepted as normal the nightly spectacle of people discussing their constipation, hemorrhoids, dandruff, and indigestion in front of an audience of a million strangers could possibly find something obscene in the sight of pretty girls taking their clothes off. "There's now't so strange as folk," his grandmother from Yorkshire would have said, he thought to himself.

It wouldn't have needed a Sherlock Holmes to read the story of the night before from the scene that confronted him in the living room. The half-filled coffee cup, empty cigarette pack, and the remains of a pepperoni pizza surrounded by scientific papers and notes strewn untidily in front of the desk terminal told of an evening that had begun with the best and purest of intentions to explore another approach to the Pluto problem. Lyn's shoulder bag on the table by the door, her coat draped across one end of the couch, the empty Chablis bottle, and the white cardboard box containing traces of a beef-curry dinner-to-go all added up to an interruption in the form of an unexpected but not exactly unwelcome arrival. The crumpled cushions and the two pairs of shoes lying where they had fallen between the couch and the coffee table said the rest. Oh well, Hunt told himself, it wouldn't make much difference to the rest of the world if the solution to how Pluto had wound up where it was had to wait an extra twenty-four hours.

He walked over to the desk and interrogated the terminal for any mail that might have come in overnight. There was a draft of a paper being put together by Mike Barrow's team at Lawrence Livermore Labs, suggesting that an aspect of Ganymean physics that they had been studying implied the possibility of achieving fusion at low temperatures. Hunt scanned it briefly and rerouted it to his office for closer reading there. A couple of bills and statements of account . . . file away and present again at the end of the month. Videorecording from Uncle William in Nigeria; Hunt entered a command for a replay and stood back to watch. Beyond the closed door the shower noises stopped, then Lyn sauntered back into the bedroom.

William and the family had enjoyed having Vic over on vacation recently and had especially liked hearing his personal account of his experiences at Jupiter and later back on Earth with the Ganymeans . . . Cousin Jenny had gotten an admin job at the nuclear steelmaking complex that was just going into operation outside Lagos. . . . News from the family in London was that all were well, except for Vic's older brother, George, who had been charged with threatening behavior after an argument about politics at his local pub. . . . The postgraduate students at Lagos University had been enthralled by Hunt's lecture about the *Shapieron* and were sending on a list of questions that they hoped he'd find time to reply to.

Just as the recording was finishing, Lyn came out of the bedroom wearing her chocolate blouse and ivory crepe skirt from the night before, then disappeared again into the kitchen. "Who's that?" she called, to the accompaniment of cupboard doors being opened and closed and plates being set down on a working surface.

"Uncle Billy."

"The one in Africa that you visited a few weeks ago?"

"Uh huh."

"So how are they doing?"

"He looks fine. Jenny's got herself fixed up at the new nuplex I told you about, and brother George is in trouble again."

"Uh-oh. What now?"

"Doing his pub lawyer act by the sound of it. Somebody didn't agree that the government ought to guarantee paychecks to anybody on strike."

"What is he—some kind of nut?"

"Runs in the family."

"You said it, not me."

Hunt grinned. "So never say you weren't warned."

"I'll remember that. . . . Food's ready."

Hunt flipped off the terminal and walked into the kitchen. Lyn, perched on a stool at the breakfast bar that divided the room in two, had already started eating. Hunt sat down opposite her, drank some coffee, then picked up his fork. "Why the rush?" he asked. "It's still early. We're not pushed for time."

"I'm not coming straight in. I ought to go home first and change."

"You look okay to me—fact, not a bad piece of womanry at all."

"Flattery will get you anywhere you like. No . . . Gregg's got some special visitors coming down from Washington today. I don't want to look 'groped' and spoil the Navcomms image." She smiled and mimicked an English accent. "One must maintain standards, you know."

Hunt snorted derisively. "It needs more practice. Who are the visitors?"

"All I know is they're from the State Department. Some hush-hush stuff that Gregg's been mixed up with lately . . . lots of calls coming in on secure channels, and couriers showing up with for-your-eyes-only things in sealed bags. Don't ask me what it's about."

"He hasn't let you in on it?" Hunt sounded surprised.

She shook her head and shrugged. "Maybe it's because I associate with crazy, unreliable foreigners."

"But you're his personal assistant," Hunt said. "I thought you knew about everything that happens around Navcomms."

Lyn shrugged again. "Not this time . . . at least, not so far. I've got a feeling I might find out today, though. Gregg's been dropping hints."

"Mmm . . . odd . . ." Hunt returned his attention to his plate and thought about the situation. Gregg Caldwell, Executive Director of the Navigation and Communications Division of the UN Space Arm, was Hunt's immediate chief. Through a combination of circumstances, under Caldwell's direction Navcomms had played a leading role in piecing together the story of Minerva and the Ganymeans, and Hunt had been intimately involved in the saga both before and during the Ganymeans' stay on Earth. Since their departure, Hunt's main task at Navcomms had been to head up a group that was coordinating the researches being conducted in various places into the volume of scientific information bequeathed by the aliens to Earth. Although not all the findings and speculations had been made public, the working atmosphere inside Navcomms was generally pretty frank and open, so security precautions taken to the extreme that Lyn had described were virtually unheard of. Something odd was going on, all right.

He leaned against the backrest of the bar chair to light a cigarette, and watched Lyn as she poured two more coffees. There was something about the way her gray-green eyes never quite lost their mischievous twinkle and about the hint of a pout that was always dancing elusively around her mouth that he found both amusing and exciting—"cute," he supposed an American would have said. He thought back over the three months that had elapsed since the *Shapieron* left, and tried to pinpoint what had happened to turn somebody who had been just a smart-headed, good-looking girl at the office into somebody he had breakfast with fairly regularly at one apartment or the other. But there didn't seem to be any particular where or when; it was just something that had happened somehow, somewhere along the line. He wasn't complaining.

She glanced up as she set the pot down and saw him looking at her. "See, I'm quite nice to have around, really. Wouldn't the morning be dull with only the vi-screen to stare at." She was at it again . . . playfully, but only if he didn't want to take it seriously. One rent made more sense than two, one set of utility bills was cheaper, et cetera, et cetera, et cetera.

"I'll pay the bills," Hunt said. He opened his hands appealingly. "You said it yourself earlier—Englishmen are creatures of habit. Anyhow, I'm maintaining standards."

"You sound like an endangered species," she told him.

"I am—chauvinists. Somebody's got to make a last stand somewhere."

"You don't need me?"

"Of course not. Good Lord, what a thought!" He scowled across the bar while Lyn returned an impish smile. Maybe the world could wait another forty-eight hours to find out about Pluto. "What are you up to tonight—anything special?" he asked.

"I got invited to a dinner party over in Hanwell . . . that marketing guy I told you about and his wife. They're having a big crowd of people in, and it sounded as if it could be fun. They told me to bring a friend, but I didn't think you'd be all that interested."

Hunt wrinkled his nose and frowned. "Isn't that the ESP-and-pyramid bunch?"

"Right. They're all excited because they've got a superpsychic going there tonight. He predicted everything about Minerva and the Ganymeans years ago. It has to be true—*Amazing Supernature* magazine said so."

Hunt knew she was teasing but couldn't suppress his irritation. "Oh for Christ's sake . . . I thought there was supposed to be an educational system in this bloody country! Don't they have any critical faculties at all?" He drained the last of his coffee and banged the mug down on the bar. "If he predicted it years ago, why didn't anybody hear about it years ago? Why do we only hear about it after science has told him what he was supposed to predict? Ask him what the *Shapieron* will find when it gets to the Giants' Star and make him write it down. I bet that never gets into *Amazing Supernature* magazine."

"That would be taking it too seriously," Lyn said lightly. "I only go there for the laughs. There's no point in trying to explain Occam's Razor to people who believe that UFOs are timeships from another century. Besides, apart from all that, they're nice people."

He was becoming too serious, he decided, and dismissed the matter with a wave of his hand and a grin. "Come on. We'd better do something about sending you on your way."

Lyn headed for the living room to collect her shoes, bag, and coat, then met him again at the front door of the apartment. They kissed and squeezed each other. "I'll see you later, then," she whispered.

"See you later. Watch out for those crazies."

He waited until she had disappeared into the elevator, then closed the door and spent five minutes clearing the kitchen and restoring some semblance of decency to the rest of the place. Finally he put on a jacket, stuffed some items from the desk into his briefcase, and left in an elevator heading for the roof. Minutes later his airmobile was at two thousand feet and climbing to merge into an eastbound traffic corridor with the rainbow towers of Houston gleaming in the sunlight on the skyline ahead.

chapter two

Ginny, Hunt's slightly plump, middle-aged, meticulous secretary, was already busy when he sauntered into the reception area of his office, high in the skyscraper of Navcomms Headquarters in the center of Houston. She had three sons, all in their late teens, and she hurled herself into her work with a dedication that Hunt sometimes thought might represent a gesture of atonement for having inflicted them on society. Women like Ginny always did a good job, he had found. Long-legged blondes were all very nice, but when it came to getting things done properly and on time, he'd settle for the older mommas any day.

"Good morning, Dr. Hunt," she greeted him. One thing he had never been able to persuade her to accept fully was that Englishmen didn't expect, or really want, to be addressed formally all the time.

"Hi, Ginny. How are you today?"

"Oh, just fine, I guess."

"Any news about the dog?"

"Good news. The vet called last night and said its pelvis isn't fractured after all. A few weeks of rest and it should be fine."

"That's good. So what's new this morning? Anything panicky?"

"Not really. Professor Speechan from MIT called a few minutes ago and would like you to call back before lunch. I'm just finishing going through the mail now. There are a couple of things I think you'll be interested in. The draft paper from Livermore, I guess you've already seen."

They spent the next half-hour checking the mail and organizing the day's schedule. By that time the offices that formed Hunt's section of Navcomms were filling up, and he left to update himself on a couple of the projects in progress.

Duncan Watt, Hunt's deputy, a theoretical physicist who had transferred from UNSA's Materials and Structures Division a year and a half earlier, was collecting results on the Pluto problem from a number of research groups around the country. Comparisons of the current Solar System with records from the *Shapieron* of how it had looked twenty-five million years before established beyond doubt that most of what had been Minerva had ended up as Pluto. Earth had been formed originally without a satellite, and Luna had orbited as the single moon of Minerva. When Minerva broke up, its moon fell inward, toward the Sun, and by a freak chance was captured by Earth, about which it had orbited stably ever since. The problem was that so far no mathematical model of the dynamics involved had been able to explain how Pluto could have acquired enough energy to be lifted against solar gravitation to the position it now occupied. Astronomers and specialists in celestial mechanics from all over the world had tried all manner of approaches to the problem but without success, which was not all that surprising since the Ganymeans themselves had been unable to produce a satisfactory solution.

"The only way you can get it to work is by postulating a three-body reaction," Duncan said, tossing up his hands in exasperation. "Maybe the war had nothing to do with it. Maybe what broke Minerva up was something else passing through the Solar System."

Thirty minutes later and a few doors farther along the corridor, Hunt found Marie, Jeff, and two of the students on loan from Princeton, excitedly discussing the set of partial-differential tensor functions being displayed on a large mural graphics screen.

"It's the latest from Mike Barrow's team at Livermore," Marie told him.

"I've already seen it," Hunt said. "Haven't had a chance to go through it yet, though. Something about cold fusion, isn't it?"

"What it seems to be saying is that the Ganymeans didn't have to generate high thermal energies to overcome proton-proton repulsion," Jeff chipped in.

"How'd they do it then?" Hunt asked.

"Sneakily. They started off with the particles being neutrons so there wasn't any repulsion. Then, when the particles were inside the range of the strong force, they increased the energy gradient at the particle surfaces sufficiently to initiate pair production. The neutrons absorbed the positrons to become protons, and the electrons were drawn off. So there you've got it—two protons strongly coupled. Pow! Fusion."

Hunt was impressed, although he had seen too much of Ganymean physics by that time to be astounded. "And they could control events like that down at that level?" he asked.

"That's what Mike's people reckon."

Shortly afterward, an argument developed over one of the details, and Hunt left the group as they were in the process of placing a call to Livermore for clarification.

It seemed as if the information left by the Ganymeans was all starting to bear fruit at once, causing something new to break out every day. Caldwell's idea of using Hunt's section as an international clearinghouse for the research into Ganymean sciences was starting to produce results. When the first clues concerning Minerva and the Ganymeans were coming to light, Caldwell had set up Hunt's original pilot group to do exactly this kind of thing. The organization had proved well suited to the task, and now it formed a ready-made group for tackling the latest studies.

Hunt's last call was on Paul Shelling, whose people occupied a group of offices and a computer room on the floor below.

One of the most challenging aspects of Ganymean technology was their "gravitics," which enabled them to deform space-time artificially without requiring large concentrations of mass. The *Shapieron*'s drive system had utilized this capability by creating a "hole" ahead of the ship into which it "fell" continuously to propel itself through space; the "gravity" inside the vessel was also manufactured, not simulated. Shelling, a gravitational physicist on a sabbatical from Rockwell International, headed up a mathematical group which had been delving into Ganymean field equations and energy-metric transforms for six months. Hunt found him staring at a display of isochrons and distorted space-time geodesies, and looking very thoughtful.

"It's all there," Shelling said, keeping his eyes fixed on the softly glowing colored curves and speaking in a faraway voice. "Artificial black holes . . . just switch 'em on and off to order."

The information did not come as a big surprise to Hunt. The Ganymeans had confirmed that the *Shapieron*'s drive had in fact achieved this, and Hunt and Shelling had talked about its theoretical basis on many occasions. "You've figured it out?" Hunt asked, slipping into a vacant chair and studying the display.

"We're on our way, anyhow."

"Does it get us any nearer instant point-to-point transfers?" That was something the Ganymeans had not achieved, although the possibility was implicit in their theoretical constructs. Black holes distantly separated in normal space seemed to link up via a hyperrealm within which unfamiliar physical principles operated, and the ordinary concepts and restrictions of the relativistic universe simply didn't apply. As the Ganymeans had agreed, the promises implied by this were staggering, but nobody knew how to turn them into realities yet.

"It's in there," Shelling answered. "The possibility is in there, but there's another side to it that bothers me, and it's impossible to separate out."

"What's that?" Hunt asked.

"Time transfers," Shelling told him. Hunt frowned. Had he been talking to anybody else, he would have allowed his skepticism to show openly. Shelling spread his hands and gestured toward the screen. "You can't get away from it. If the solutions admit point-to-point transfers through normal space, they admit transfers through time too. If you could find a way of exploiting one, you'd automatically have a way of exploiting the other as well. Those matrix integrals are symmetric."

Hunt waited for a moment to avoid appearing derisive. "That's too much, Paul," he said. "What happens to causality? You'd never be able to unscramble the mess."

"I know . . . I know the theory sounds screwy, but there it is. Either we're up a dead end and none of it works, or we're stuck with both solutions."

They spent the next hour working through Shelling's equations again but ended up none the wiser. Groups at Cal Tech, Cambridge, the Ministry of Space Sciences in Moscow, and the University of Sydney, Australia, had found the same thing. Obviously Hunt and Shelling were not about to crack the problem there and then, and Hunt eventually left in a very curious and thoughtful mood.

Back in his own office, he called Speehan at MIT, who turned out to have some interesting results from a simulation model of the climatic upheavals caused fifty thousand years earlier by the process of lunar capture. Hunt then took care of a couple of other urgent items that had come in that morning, and was just settling down to study the Livermore paper when Lyn called from Caldwell's suite at the top of the building. Her face was unusually serious.

"Gregg wants you in on the meeting up here," she told him without preamble. "Can you get up right away?"

Hunt sensed that she was pushed for time. "Give me two minutes." He cut the connection without further ado, consigned Livermore to the uncharted depths of the Navcomms data bank, told Ginny to consult Duncan if anything desperate developed during the rest of the day, and left the office at a brisk pace.

Chapter Three

From the web of communications links interconnecting UNSA's manned and unmanned space vehicles with orbiting and surface bases all over the solar system, to the engineering and research establishments at places such as Houston, responsibility for the whole gamut of Navcomms activities ultimately resided in Caldwell's office at the top of the Headquarters Building. It was a spacious and opulently furnished room with one wall completely of glass, looking down over the lesser skyscrapers of the city and the ant colony of the pedestrian precincts far below. The wall opposite Caldwell's huge curved desk, which faced inward from a corner by the window, was composed almost totally of a battery of display screens that gave the place more the appearance of a control room than of an office. The remaining walls carried a display of color pictures showing some of the more spectacular UNSA projects of recent years, including a seven-mile-long photon-drive star probe being designed in California and an electromagnetic catapult being constructed across twenty miles of Tranquillitatis to hurl lunar-manufactured structural components into orbit for spacecraft assembly.

Caldwell was behind his desk and two other people were sitting with Lyn at the table set at a T to the desk's front edge when a secretary ushered Hunt in from the outer office. One of them was a woman in her mid- to late forties, wearing a high-necked navy dress that hinted of a firm and well-preserved figure, and over it a wide-collared jacket of white-and-navy check. Her hair was a carefully styled frozen sea of auburn that stopped short of her shoulders, and the lines of her face, which was not unattractive in a natural kind of way beneath her sparse makeup, were clear and assertive. She was sitting erect and seemed composed and fully in command of herself. Hunt had the feeling that he had seen her somewhere before.

Her companion, a man, was smartly attired in a charcoal three-piece with a white shirt and two-tone gray tie. He had a fresh, clean-shaven look about him and jet-black hair cut short and brushed flat in college-boy fashion, although Hunt put him at not far off his own age. His eyes, dark and constantly mobile, gave the impression of serving an alert and quick-thinking mind.

Lyn flashed Hunt a quick smile from the side of the table opposite the two visitors. She had changed into a crisp two-piece edged with pale orange and was wearing her hair high. She looked distinctly un-"groped."

"Vic," Caldwell announced in his gravelly bass-baritone voice, "I'd like you to meet Karen Heller from the State Department in Washington, and Norman Pacey, who's a presidential advisor on foreign relations." He made a resigned gesture in Hunt's direction. "This is Dr. Vic Hunt. We send him to Jupiter to look into a few relics of some extinct aliens, and he comes back with a shipful of live ones."

They exchanged formalities. Both visitors knew about Hunt's exploits, which had been well publicized. In fact Vic had met Karen Heller once very briefly at a reception given for some Ganymeans in Zurich about six months earlier. Of course! Hadn't she been the U.S. Ambassador to—France, wasn't it, at the time? Yes. She was representing the U.S. at the UN now, though. Norman Pacey had met some Ganymeans too, it turned out—in Washington—but Hunt hadn't been present on that occasion.

Hunt took the empty chair at the end of the table, facing along the length of it toward Caldwell's desk, and watched the head of wiry, gray, close-cropped hair while Caldwell frowned down at his hands for a few seconds and drummed the top of his desk with his fingers. Then he raised his craggy, heavily browed face to look directly at Hunt, who knew better than to expect much in the way of preliminaries. "Something's happened that I wanted to tell you about earlier but couldn't," Caldwell said. "Signals from the Giants' Star started coming in again about three weeks ago."

Even though he should have known about such a development if anyone did, Hunt was too taken aback for the moment to wonder about it. As months passed after the sole reply to the first message transmitted from Giordano Bruno at the time of the *Shapieron*'s departure, he had grown increasingly suspicious that the whole thing had been a hoax—that somebody with access to the UNSA communications net had somehow arranged a message to be relayed back from some piece of UNSA hardware located out in space in the right direction. He was open-minded enough to admit that with an advanced alien civilization anything could be possible, but a hoax had seemed the most likely explanation for the fourteen-hour turnaround time. If Caldwell were right, it made so much nonsense of that conviction.

"You're certain they're genuine?" he asked dubiously when he had recovered from the initial shock. "It couldn't all be a sick joke by a freak somewhere?"

Caldwell shook his head. "We have enough data now to pinpoint the source interferometrically. It's way out past Pluto, and UNSA does not have anything anywhere near it. Besides, we've checked every bit of traffic through all our hardware, and it's clean. The signals are genuine."

Hunt raised his eyebrows and exhaled a long breath. Okay, so he'd been wrong on that one. He shifted his gaze from Caldwell to the notes and papers lying along the middle of the table in front of him, and frowned as another thought occurred to him. Like the original message from Farside, the reply from the Giants' Star had been composed in the ancient Ganymean language and communications codes from the time of the *Shapieron.* After the ship's departure, the reply had been translated by Don Maddson, head of the linguistics section lower down in the building, who had made a study of Ganymean during the aliens' stay. That had required considerable effort, short though the reply had been, and Hunt knew of no one else anywhere who could have handled the more recent signals that Caldwell was talking about. As a rule Hunt didn't have much time for protocol and formality, but if Maddson was in on this, Hunt sure-as-hell should have known about it too. "So who did the translating?" he asked suspiciously. "Linguistics?"

"There wasn't any need," Lyn said simply. "The signals are coming through in standard datacomm codes. They're in English."

Hunt slumped back in his chair and just stared. Ironically that said definitely that it was no hoax; who in their right mind would forge message from aliens in English? And then it came to him. "Of course!" he exclaimed. "They must have intercepted the *Shapieron* somehow. Well, that's good to—" He broke off in surprise as he saw Caldwell shake his head.

"From the content of the dialogue over the last few weeks, we're pretty certain that's not the case," Caldwell said. He looked at Hunt gravely. "So if they haven't talked to the Ganymeans who were here, and they know our communication codes and our language, what does that say to you?"

Hunt looked around and saw that the others were watching him expectantly. So he thought about it. And after a few seconds his eyes widened slowly, and his mouth fell open in undisguised belief. "*Je-sus!*" he breathed softly.

"That's right," Norman Pacey said. "This whole planet must be under some kind of surveillance . . . and has been for a long time." For the moment Hunt was too flabbergasted to offer any reply. Little wonder the whole business had been hushed up.

"That supposition was backed up by the first of the new

signals that came in at Bruno," Caldwell resumed. "It said in no uncertain terms that nothing whatsoever relating to the contact was to be communicated via lasers, comsats, datalinks, or any kind of electronic media. The scientists up at Bruno who received the message went along with that directive, and told me about it by sending a courier down from Luna. I passed the word up through Navcomms to UNSA Corporate in the same way and told the Bruno guys to carry on handling things locally until somebody got back to them."

"What it means is that at least part of the surveillance is in the form of tapping into our communications network," Pacey said. "And whoever is sending the signals, and whoever is running the surveillance, are not the same . . . 'people,' or whatever. And the ones who are talking to us don't want the other ones knowing about it." Hunt nodded, having figured that much out already.

"I'll let Karen take it from there," Caldwell said and nodded in her direction.

Karen Heller leaned forward to rest her arms lightly along the edge of the table. "The scientists at Bruno established fairly early on that they were indeed in contact with a Ganymean civilization descended from migrants from Minerva," she said, speaking in carefully modulated tones that rose and fell naturally and made listening easy. "They inhabit a planet called Thurien, in the planetary system of the Giants' Star, or 'Gistar,' to use the contraction that seems to have been adopted. While this was going on, UNSA in Washington referred the matter to the UN." She paused to look over at Hunt, but he had no questions at that point. She went on, "A special working party reporting to the Secretary General was formed to debate the issue, and the ruling finally came out that a contact of this nature was first and foremost a political and diplomatic affair. A decision was made that further exchanges would be handled secretly by a small delegation of selected representatives of the permanent-member nations of the Security Council. To preserve secrecy, no outsiders would be informed or involved for the time being."

"I had to hold things right there when that ruling came

down the line," Caldwell interjected, looking at Hunt. "That was why I couldn't tell you about any of this before." Hunt nodded. Now that it had been explained, at least he felt a little better on that score.

He was still far from completely happy, however. It sounded as if there had been a typical bureaucratic overreaction to the whole thing. Playing safe was all very well up to a point, but surely this supersecrecy was taking things too far. The thought of the UN keeping everybody out of it apart from a handful of select individuals who had probably had few, if any, dealings with Ganymeans was infuriating.

"They didn't want *anybody* else included?" he asked dubiously. "Not even a scientist or two—somebody who knows Ganymeans?"

"*Especially* not scientists," Caldwell said, but volunteered nothing further. The whole thing was beginning to sound nonsensical.

"As a permanent member of the Council, the U.S.A. was informed from high up in the UN and applied sufficient pressure to be represented on the delegation," Heller continued. "Norman and myself were assigned that duty, and for most of the time since then we've been at Giordano Bruno, participating in the exchange of signals that has been continuing with the Thuriens."

"You mean everything is being handled locally from there?" Hunt asked.

"Yes. The ban on communicating anything to do with it electronically is being strictly adhered to. The people up there who know what's going on are all security-cleared and reliable."

"I see." Hunt sat back and braced his arms along the table in front of him. So far there was a mystery and some reason for being uncomfortable, but nothing that had been said so far explained what Heller and Pacey were doing in Houston. "So what's been going on?" he asked. "What have you been talking to Thurien about?"

Heller motioned with her head to indicate a lockable document folder lying by her elbow. "Complete transcripts of everything received and sent are in there," she told him. "Gregg has a full set of copies, and since you'll no doubt be involved from now on, you'll be able to read them for yourself shortly. To sum up, the first messages from Thurien asked for information about the *Shapieron*—its condition, the well-being of its occupants, their experiences on Earth, and that kind of thing. Whoever was sending the messages seemed concerned . . . as if they considered us a threat to it for some reason." Heller paused, seeing the look of noncomprehension that was spreading across Hunt's face.

"Are you saying they didn't know about the ship before we beamed that first signal out from Farside?" he asked.

"So it would appear," Heller replied.

Hunt thought for a moment. "So again, whoever is handling the surveillance isn't talking to whoever is sending these messages," he said.

"Exactly," Pacey agreed, nodding. "The ones handling the surveillance could hardly have not known about the *Shapieron* while it was here if they have any access to our communications network. There were enough headlines about it."

"And that's not the only strange thing," Heller went on. "The Thuriens that we have been in contact with seem to have formed a completely distorted picture of Earth's recent history. They think we're all set for World War III only this time interplanetary, with orbiting bombs everywhere, radiation and particle-beam weapons commanding the surface from the Moon . . . you name it."

Hunt had been growing even more bemused as he listened. He could see now why it looked as if the *Shapieron* couldn't have been intercepted—at least not by the Thuriens who were talking to Earth; the Ganymeans from the ship would have cleared up any misunderstandings like that straight away. But even if the Thuriens who were doing the talking hadn't intercepted the *Shapieron*, they had an impression of Earth nonetheless, which meant that they could only have obtained it from the Thuriens who were handling the surveillance. The impression they had obtained was wrong. Therefore, either the surveillance wasn't very effective, or the story being passed on was being distorted. But if the messages had been coming in composed in English, the surveillance methods had to be pretty effective, which therefore implied that the Thuriens passing on the story weren't passing it on straight.

But that didn't make a lot of sense, either. Ganymeans didn't play Machiavellian games of intrigue or deceive one another knowingly. Their minds didn't work that way; they were far too rational . . . unless the Ganymeans who now existed on Thurien had changed significantly in the course of the twenty-five million years that separated them from their ancestors aboard the *Shapieron*. That was a thought. A lot of changes could have taken place in that time. He couldn't arrive at any definite conclusions now, he decided, so the information was simply filed away for retrieval and analysis later.

"It sounds strange, all right," Hunt agreed after he had sorted that much out in his head. "They must be pretty confused by now."

"They were already," Caldwell said. "The reason they reopened the dialogue is that they want to come to Earth physically—I guess to straighten out the whole mess. That's what they've been trying to get the UN people to arrange."

"Secretly," Pacey explained in answer to Hunt's questioning look. "No public spectacles or anything like that. What it seems to add up to is that they're hoping to do some quiet checking up without the outfit that's running the surveillance knowing about it."

Hunt nodded. The plan made sense. But there was a note in Pacey's voice that hinted of things not having gone so smoothly. "So what's the problem?" he asked, shifting his eyes to glance at both Pacey and Heller.

"The problem is the policy that's been handed down from the top levels inside the UN," Heller replied. "To put it in a nutshell, they're scared of what it might mean if this planet simply opens up to a civilization that's millions of years ahead of us . . . our whole culture could be torn up by the roots; our civilization would come apart at the seams; we'd be avalanched with technology that we're not ready to absorb . . . that kind of thing."

"But that's ridiculous!" Hunt protested. "They haven't said

they want to take this place over. They just want to come here and talk." He made an impatient throwing-away motion in the air. "Okay, I'll accept that we'd have to play it softly and exercise some caution and common sense, but what you're describing sounds more like a neurosis."

"It is," Heller said. "The UN's being irrational—there's no other word for it. And the Farside delegation is following that policy to the letter and operating in go-slow, stall-stall-stall mode." She waved toward the folder she had indicated earlier. "You'll see for yourself. Their responses are evasive and ambiguous, and do nothing to correct the wrong impressions that the Thuriens have got. Norman and I have tried to fight it, but we get outvoted."

Hunt caught Lyn's eye as he sent a despairing look around the room. She sent back a faint half-smile and a barely perceptible shrug that said she knew how he felt. A faction inside the UN had fought hard and for the same reasons to prevent the Farside transmissions being continued after the first, unexpected reply had come in, he remembered, but had been overruled after a deafening outcry from the world's scientific community. That same faction seemed to be active again.

"The worst part is what we suspect might be behind it," Heller continued. "Our brief from the State Department was to help move things smoothly toward broadening Earth's communications with Thurien as fast as developments allowed, at the same time protecting this country's interests where appropriate. The Department didn't really agree with the policy of excluding outsiders, but had to go along with it because of UN protocols. In other words, the U.S. has been trying to play it straight so far, but under protest."

"I can see the picture," Hunt said as she paused. "But that just says that you're becoming frustrated by the slow progress. You sounded as if there's more to it than that."

"There is," Heller confirmed. "The Soviets also have a representative on the delegation—a man called Sobroskin. Given the world situation—with us and the Soviets competing everywhere for things like the South Atlantic fusion deal, industrial-training franchises in Africa, scientific-aid programs, and so on—the advantage that either side could get from access to Ganymean know-how would be enormous. So you'd expect the Soviets to be just as impatient to kick some life into this damn delegation as we are. But they aren't. Sobroskin goes along with the official UN line and doesn't bitch about it. In fact he spends half his time throwing in complications that slow things down even further. Now when those facts are laid down side by side, what do they seem to say?"

Hunt thought over the question for a while, then tossed out his hands with a shrug. "I don't know," he said candidly. "I'm not a political animal. You tell me."

"It could mean that the Soviets are planning to set up their own private channel to fix a landing in Siberia or somewhere so that they get exclusive rights," Pacey answered. "If that's so, then the UN line would suit them fine. If the official channel stays clogged up, and the U.S. plays straight and sticks with the official channel, then guess who walks off with the bonanza. Think of the difference it would make to the power balance if a few heads of select governments around the world were quietly tipped off that the Soviets had access to lots of know-how that we didn't. You see—it all fits with the way Sobroskin is acting."

"And an even more sobering thought is the way in which the UN's policy fits in with that so conveniently," Heller added. "It could mean that the Soviets have ways that we don't even know about of pulling all kinds of strings and levers right inside the top levels of the UN itself. If that's true, the global implications for the U.S. are serious indeed."

The facts were certainly beginning to add up, Hunt admitted to himself. The Soviets could easily set up another long-range communications facility in Siberia, up in orbit, out near Luna maybe, and operate their own link to whatever was intercepting Farside's signals out beyond the edge of the solar system. Any reply coming back would probably be in the form of a fairly wide beam by the time it got to Earth, which meant that anybody could receive it and know that somebody somewhere other than the UN was cheating. But if the replies were in a prearranged code, nobody would be able to interpret them or know for whom they were intended. The Soviets might be accused, in which case they would deny the charge vehemently . . . and that would be about as much as anybody would be able to do about it.

He thought he could see now why he had been brought in on all this. Heller had given herself away earlier when she said that the U.S. had been trying to play it straight, *"so far."* As insurance the State Department had decided that it needed its own private line too, but nothing crude enough to be detected anywhere within a few hundred thousand miles of Earth. So who would they have sent Heller and Pacey to talk to? Who else but someone who knew a lot about Ganymeans and Ganymean technology, somebody who had also been among the first people to receive them on Ganymede?

And that was another point—Hunt had spent a lot of time on Ganymede, and he still had many close friends among the UNSA personnel there with the Jupiter Four and Jupiter Five missions. Jupiter was a long, long way from the vicinity of Earth, which meant that no receivers anywhere near Earth would ever know anything about a beam aimed toward Jupiter from the fringe of the solar system, whether the beam diverged appreciably or not. And, of course, the *J4* and *J5* command ships were linked permanently to Earth by laser channels . . . which Caldwell and Navcomms just happened to control. It couldn't possibly be all just a coincidence, he decided.

Hunt looked up at Caldwell, held his eye for a second, then turned his head to gaze at the two people from Washington. "You want to set up a private wire to Gistar via Jupiter to arrange a landing here, without any more messing around, before the Soviets get around to doing something," he told them. "And you want to know if I can come up with an idea for telling the people at Jupiter what we want them to do, without the risk of any Thuriens who might be bugging the laser link finding out about it. Is that right?" He turned his eyes back toward Caldwell and inclined his head. "What do I get, Gregg?"

Heller and Pacey exchanged glances that said they were impressed.

"Ten out of ten," Caldwell told him.

"Nine," Heller said. Hunt looked at her curiously. There was a hint of laughter in her expression. "If you can come up with something, we'll need all the help we can get handling whatever comes afterward," she explained. "The UN might have decided to try going it alone without their Ganymean experts, but the U.S. hasn't."

"In other words, welcome to the team," Norman Pacey completed.

Chapter Four

Joseph B. Shannon, Mission Director of *Jupiter Five*, orbiting two thousand miles above the surface of Ganymede, stood in an instrumentation bay near one end of the mile-and-a-quarter-long ship's command center. He was watching a large mural display screen from behind a knot of spellbound ship's officers and UNSA scientists. The screen showed an undulating landscape of oranges, yellows, and browns as it lay cringing beneath a black sky made hazy by a steady incandescent drizzle falling from somewhere above, while in the far distance half the skyline was erupting in a boiling column of colors that exploded upward off the top of the picture.

It had been fifty-two years before—the year that Shannon was born—when other scientists at the Jet Propulsion Laboratory in Pasadena had marveled at the first close-ups of Io to be sent back by the *Voyager I* and *II* probes, and dubbed the extraordinary disk of mottled orange "the great pizza in the sky." But Shannon had never heard of any pizza being cooked in the way this one had.

Orbiting through a plasma flux of mean particle energies corresponding to 100,000° Kelvin sustained by Jupiter's magnetic field, the satellite acted as an enormous Faraday generator and supported internal circulating currents of five million amperes with a power dissipation of a thousand billion watts. And as much energy again was released inside it as heat from tidal friction, resulting from orbital perturbations induced as Europa and Ganymede lifted Io resonantly up and down through Jupiter's gravity. This amount of electrically and gravitationally produced heat maintained large reservoirs of molten sulfur and sulfur compounds below the moon's surface, which eventually penetrated upward through faults to explode into the virtually zero-pressure of the outside. The result was a regular succession of spectacular volcanoes of solidifying sulfur and sulfur-dioxide frost that ejected at velocities of up to a thousand meters per second, and sometimes reached heights of 300 kilometers or more.

Shannon was looking at a view of one of those volcanoes now, sent back from a probe on Io's surface. It had taken the mission's engineers and scientists more than a year of back-to-the-drawing-board experiences to devise an instrumentation package and shielding method that would function reliably under Jupiter's incessant bombardment of radiation, electrons, and ions, and Shannon had felt an obligation to be present in person to observe the results of their eventual success. Far from being the chore he had expected, the occasion had turned out an exhilaration and served as a reminder of how easy it was for supreme commanders of anything to allow themselves to become remote and lose touch with what was happening in the trenches. In future, he thought to himself, he would make a point of keeping more up to date on the progress of the mission's scientific projects.

He remained in the command center discussing details of the probe for a full hour after he was officially off duty, and then at last excused himself and retired to his private quarters. After a shower and a change of clothes he sat down at the desk in his stateroom and interrogated the terminal for a listing of the day's mail. One item that had come in was qualified as a text message from Vic Hunt at Navcomms Headquarters. Shannon was both pleasantly surprised and intrigued. He had

had many interesting talks with Hunt during the latter's stay on Ganymede, and didn't perceive him as being somebody with much time for idle socializing, which suggested that something interesting was afoot. Curious, he keyed in a command for Hunt's message to be displayed. Five minutes later he was still sitting there staring at the message, his brows knitted in a mystified frown. It read:

> Joe,
> To avoid any further cross words on this subject, I looked for some clues in the book you mentioned and came across some references on pages 5, 24, and 10. When you get down to sections 11 and 20, it all makes more sense.
> How they got 786 is still a puzzle.
> Regards
> Vic

Not a word of it meant anything to him. He knew Hunt well enough to be reasonably sure that something serious was behind the message, and all he could think of was that Hunt was trying to tell him something highly confidential. But why would Hunt go to this kind of trouble when UNSA possessed a perfectly adequate system of security codes? Surely it wasn't possible that somebody could be eavesdropping on the UNSA net, somebody equipped with enough computer power to render its protective measures unreliable. On the other hand, Shannon reflected soberly, the Germans had thought exactly that in World War II, and the British, with their "Turing Engine" at Bletchley, had been able to read the complete radio traffic between Hitler and his generals, frequently even before the intended recipients. Certainly this message would mean nothing to any third party even though it had come through in plain English, which made it appear all the more innocuous. The problem was that it didn't mean anything to Shannon, either.

✻   ✻   ✻

Shannon was still brooding about the message early the next morning when he sat down for breakfast in the senior officers' dining quarters. He liked to eat early, before the captain, the first navigation officer, and the others who were usually on early shift appeared. It gave him time to collect his thoughts for the day and keep up with events elsewhere by browsing through the *Interplanetary Journal*—a daily newspaper beamed out from Earth by UNSA to its various ships and installations all over the solar system. The other reason he liked to be early was that it gave him an opportunity to tackle the *Journal's* crossword puzzle. He'd been an incurable addict for as long as he could remember, and rationalized his addiction by claiming that an early-morning puzzle sharpened the mental faculties in preparation for the demands of the day ahead. He wasn't really sure if that were true, and didn't care all that much either, but it was as good an excuse as any. There was nothing sensational in the news that morning, but he skimmed dutifully through the various items and arrived gratefully at the crossword page just as the steward was refilling his coffee cup. He folded the paper once, then again, and rested it against the edge of the table to scan through the clues casually while he felt inside his jacket for a pen. The heading at the top read: JOURNAL CROSSWORD PUZZLE NUMBER 786.

Shannon stiffened, his hand still inside his jacket, as the number caught his eye. *"How they got 786 is still a puzzle"* replayed itself instantly in his mind. Every word of Hunt's mysterious message had become firmly engraved by that time. *"786"* and *"puzzle"* . . . both appearing in the same sentence. It couldn't be a coincidence, surely. And then he remembered that Hunt had been a keen crossword solver too in his rare moments of free time; he had introduced Shannon to the particularly cryptic puzzles contained in the London *Times*, and the two of them had spent many a good hour solving them over drinks at the bar. Suppressing the urge to leap from his chair with a shout of *Eureka!* he pushed the pen back into his pocket and felt behind it for the copy of the message tucked inside his wallet. He drew out the sheet of paper, unfolded it, and smoothed it flat on the table between the *Journal* and his coffee cup. He read it once again, and the words took on a whole new light of meaning.

Right there in the first line it said *"cross words,"* and a little farther on, *"clues."* Their significance was obvious now. What about the rest of it? He had never mentioned any book to Hunt, so that part had to be just padding. Presumably the numbers that followed meant something, though. Shannon frowned and stared hard at them: 5, 24, 10, 11, and 20. . . . The sequence didn't immediately jump out and hit him for any reason. He had already tried combining them in various ways and gotten nowhere, but when he read through the message again in its new context, two of the phrases that he had barely noticed before did jump out and hit him: ". . . came *across* . . ." associated with 5, 24, and 10, and immediately after: ". . . get *down* . . ." associated with 11 and 20, had obvious connotations to do with crosswords: they referred to the across and down sets of clues. So presumably whatever Hunt was trying to say would be found in the answers to clues 5, 24, and 10 across, and 11 and 20 down. That had to be it.

With rising excitement he transferred his attention to the *Journal.* At that moment the captain and the first navigation officer appeared in the doorway across the room, talking jovially and laughing about something. Shannon rose from his seat and picked up the *Journal* in one movement. Before they were three paces into the room he had passed them, walking briskly in the opposite direction and tossing back just a curt "Good morning, gentlemen," over his shoulder. They exchanged puzzled looks, turned to survey the doorway through which the Mission Director had already vanished, looked at each other again and shrugged, and sat down at an empty table.

Back in the privacy of his stateroom, Shannon sat down at his desk and unfolded the paper once more. The clue to 5 across read, "Find the meaning of a poem to Digital Equipment Corporation (6)." The company name was well known among UNSA and scientific people; DEC computers were used for everything from preprocessing the datastreams that poured incessantly through the laser link between Jupiter and Earth to controlling the instruments contained in the robot landed on Io. "*DEC*"! Those letters had to be part of the solution. What about the rest of the clue? "Poem." A list of synonyms paraded through Shannon's head: "verse" . . . "lyric" . . . "epic" . . . "elegy." They were no good. He wanted something of three letters to complete the single-word answer of six letters indicated in the parentheses. "*Ode*"! Added to "DEC" it gave "DECODE," which mean, "Find the meaning of." Not too difficult. Shannon penned in the answer and shifted his attention to 24 across.

"Dianna's lock causes heartache (8)." "Dianna's" was an immediate giveaway, and after some reflection Shannon had succeeded in obtaining Di's tress (lock of hair), which gave heartache in the form of "DISTRESS."

10 across read, "A guiding light in what could be a confused voyage (6)." The phrase "could be a confused voyage" suggested an anagram of "voyage," which comprised six letters. Shannon played with the letters for a while but could form them into nothing sensible, so moved on to 11 down. "Let's fit a date to reorganize the experimental results (4,4,4)." Three words of four letters each made up the solution. "Reorganize" looked like a hint for an anagram again. Shannon searched the clue for a combination of words containing twelve letters and soon picked out "Let's fit a date." He scribbled them down randomly in the margin of the page and juggled with them for a few minutes, eventually producing "TEST DATA FILE," which his instinct told him was the correct answer.

The clue for 20 down was, "Argon beam matrix (5)." That didn't mean very much, so Shannon began working out some of the other clues to obtain some cross-letters in the words he had missed. The "guiding light" in 10 across turned out to be "BEACON," which was *in* the remainder of the clue and staring him in the face all the time as it had said: ". . . could *be a con*-fused . . ." The suggestion of an anagram had been made deliberately to mislead. He wondered what kind of warped mentality was needed to qualify as a crossword compiler. Finally the "argon beam" was revealed as "Ar" (chemical symbol) plus "ray" (beam), to give "ARRAY," i.e., a matrix. Interestingly the answer to the first clue of all, 1 across, was "SHANNON," a river in Ireland, presumably slipped in as a confirmation to him personally.

JOURNAL CROSSWORD PUZZLE NUMBER 786
(Compiler: D. Maddson, Navcomms HQ, Houston)

ACROSS

1 Watery Irish flower (6)
5 Find the meaning of a poem to Digital Equipment Corporation (6)
9 Guilty of having no money after the pub? Quite the opposite (8)
10 A guiding light in what could be a confused voyage (6)
12 Writer, jumping into action, arrives at a profound conclusion (4,3)
13 The ultimate in text remedies (7)
14 Oriental rule changed by Swiss mathematician (5)
16 Wild riot about the point of a short preamble, colloquially speaking (5)
17 Expert loses two-thirds but takes back art for something more (5)
18 A separated piece (9)
20 Continental one-fan car, maybe (7)
21 Ringing around to abolish a right (7)
23 Keep the elephant's head and tail in the rain (6)
24 Dianna's lock causes heartache (8)
25 After six months, men and I find a type of Arab (6)
26 Surrounds North Carolina with ease, to a point (7)

DOWN

1 Win in a sled, perhaps? It's not fair! (7)
2 But the arms this noted lady was advised to get wouldn't have been much good to Venus (5)
3 Powerful response, right from the heart (7,8)
4 Possibly did on gin? Can't—it's not habit-forming (3,9)
6 A wave from a charge of the Light Brigade (15)
7 Hydrogen makes harmony in turbulent star-core (9)
8 Norman's head in the lake? No—some other guy (5)
11 Let's fit a date to reorganize the experimental results (4,4,4)
15 It sounds like a lumberjack's musical number (9)
19 Hoover, initially in trust over the South, urges progress (7)
20 Argon beam matrix (5)
22 Deposit nothing in the smaller amount (5)

The complete message with the words placed in the same order as the numbers that Hunt had given now read:

DECODE DISTRESS BEACON TEST-DATA-FILE ARRAY.

Shannon sat back in his chair and studied the final result with some satisfaction, although it so far still told him far from everything. It was evident, however, that it had something to do with the Ganymeans, which tied in with Hunt's being involved.

Some time before the *Shapieron* appeared out of the depths of space at Ganymede, the UNSA missions exploring the Jovian moon system had discovered the wreck of an ancient Ganymean spaceship from twenty-five million years back entombed beneath Ganymede's ice crust. In the process of experimenting with some of the devices recovered from the vessel, Hunt and a group of engineers at Pithead—one of the surface bases on Ganymede—had managed to activate a type of Ganymean emergency transmitter that utilized gravity waves since the propulsive method used by Ganymean ships precluded their receiving electromagnetic signals while under main drive; that was what had attracted the *Shapieron* to Ganymede after reentering the Solar System. Shannon remembered that there had been a suggestion to use that same device to relay the news of the surprise reply from the Giants' Star on to the *Shapieron* after its departure, but Hunt had grown suspicious that the reply was a hoax and had vetoed the idea.

That had to be the "Distress Beacon" in Hunt's message. So what was the "Test-Data-File Array" that Shannon was supposed to decode? The Ganymean beacon had been shipped to Earth along with many other items that various institutions had wanted to experiment with firsthand, and the researchers conducting those experiments usually made a point of sending their results back to Jupiter via the laser link to keep interested parties there informed. The only thing that Shannon could think of was that Hunt had somehow arranged for some information to be sent over the link disguised as a file of ordinary-looking experimental test data purportedly relating to the beacon and probably consisting of just a long list of numbers. Now that Shannon's attention had been drawn to the file, the way the numbers were supposed to be read would hopefully, with close enough scrutiny, make itself clear.

If that was it, the only people likely to know anything about unusual files of test data coming in from Earth would be the engineers down at Pithead who had worked on the beacon after it was brought up from beneath the ice. Shannon activated the terminal on his desk and entered a command to access the *Jupiter Five* personnel records. A few minutes later he had identified the engineering project leader in charge of that work as a Californian called Vincent Carizan, who had joined J5 from UNSA's Propulsion Systems and Propellants Division, where he had worked for ten years after obtaining a master's degree in electrical and electronic engineering at Berkeley.

Shannon's first impulse was to put a call through to Pithead, but after a minute or two of further reflection he decided against it. If Hunt had taken such pains to avoid any hint of the subject being interpretable from what went over the communications network, anything could be happening. He was still pondering on what to do when the call-tone sounded from the terminal. Shannon cleared the screen and touched a key to accept. It was his adjutant officer calling from the command center.

"Excuse me, sir, but you are scheduled to attend the Operations Controller's briefing in G-327 in five minutes. Since nobody's seen you this morning, I thought maybe a reminder might be called for."

"Oh . . . thanks, Bob," Shannon replied. "Look, something's come up, and I don't think I'm going to be able to make it. Make excuses for me, would you."

"Will do, sir."

"Oh, and Bob . . ." Shannon's voice rose suddenly as a thought struck him.

The adjutant looked up just as he had been about to cut the call. "Sir?"

"Get here as soon as you've done that. I've got a message that I want couriered down to the surface."

"Couriered?" the adjutant appeared surprised and puzzled.

"Yes. It's to go to one of the engineers at Pithead. I can't explain now, but the matter is urgent. If you don't waste any time, you should be able to make the nine o'clock shuttle down to Main. I'll have it sealed and waiting by the time you get here. Treat this as grade *X-ray.*"

The adjutant's face at once became serious. "I'll be there right away," he said, and the screen went blank.

Shannon received a brief call from Pithead shortly before lunch, advising that Carizan was on his way up to *Jupiter Five* via Ganymede Main Base. When Carizan arrived, he brought with him a printout of a file of data, supposedly relating to tests performed on the Ganymean beacon, that had materialized in the computers at Pithead that very morning after coming in from Earth over the link and being relayed down to the surface. The engineers at Pithead had been puzzled because the file header was out of sequence and contained references that didn't match the database indexing system. And nobody had known anything about any tests being scheduled of the kind that the header mentioned.

As Shannon had anticipated, the file contained just numbers—many groups of numbers, each group consisting of a long list of pairs; it was typical of the layout of an experimental report giving readings of interrelated variables and would have meant nothing more to anybody who had no reason not to accept it at face value. Shannon called together a small team of specialists whose discretion could be trusted, and it didn't take them long to deduce that each group of pairs formed a set of datapoints defined by x-y coordinates in a 256-by-256 matrix array; the hint had been there in the crossword. When the sets of points were plotted on a computer display screen, each set formed a pattern of dots that looked just like a statistical scattering of test data about a straight-line function. But when the patterns of dots were superposed they formed lines of words written diagonally across the screen, and the words formed a message in English. The message contained pointers to other files of numbers that had also been beamed through from Earth and gave explicit instructions for decoding them, and when this was done the amount of information that they yielded turned out to be prodigious.

The result was a set of detailed directions for *Jupiter Five* to transmit a long sequence of Ganymean communications coding groups not into the UNSA net but outward, toward coordinates that lay beyond the edge of the solar system. The contents of any replies received from that direction were, the directions said, to be disguised as experimental data in the way that had thus been established and communicated to Navcomms via the laser link.

Shannon was weary and red-eyed due to lack of sleep by the time he sat down at the terminal in his stateroom and composed a message for transmission to Earth, addressed to Dr. Victor Hunt at Navcomms Headquarters, Houston. It read:

> Vic,
> I've talked to Vince Carizan, and it's all a lot clearer now. We're running some tests on it as you asked, and if anything positive shows up I'll have the results sent straight through.
> Best wishes,
> Joe

Chapter Five

Hunt lounged back in the pilot's seat and stared absently down at the toytown suburbs of Houston while the airmobile purred along contentedly, guided by intermittent streams of binary being directed up at it from somewhere below. It was interesting, he thought, how the patterns of movement of the groundcars, flowing, merging, slowing, and accelerating in unison on the roadways below seemed to reveal some grand, centrally orchestrated design—as if they were all parts of an unimaginably complex score composed by a cosmic Bach. But it was all an illusion. Each vehicle was programmed with only the details of its own destination plus a few relatively simple instructions for handling conditions along the way; the complexity emerged as a consequence of large numbers of them interacting freely in their synthetic environment. It was the same with life, he reflected. All the magical, mystical, and supernatural forces invoked through the ages to explain it were inventions that existed in the minds of misled observers, not in the universe they observed. He wondered how much untapped human talent had been wasted in futile pursuit of the creations of wishful thinking. The

Ganymeans had entertained no such illusions, but had applied themselves diligently to understanding and mastering the universe as it was, instead of how it seemed to be or how they might have wanted it to be. Maybe that was why the Ganymeans had reached the stars.

In the seat next to him, Lyn looked up from the half-completed crossword in the *Interplanetary Journal* of a few days earlier. "Got any ideas for this—'It sounds like a lumberjack's musical number.' What do you make of that?"

"How many letters?" Hunt asked after a few moments of thought.

"Nine."

Hunt frowned at the flight-systems status summaries being routinely updated on the console display in front of him. "Logarithm," he said after another pause.

Lyn thought about it, then smiled faintly. "Oh, I see . . . sneaky. It sounds like 'logger rhythm.' "

"Right."

"It fits okay." She wrote the word in on the paper resting on her lap. "I'm glad that Joe Shannon had fewer problems with it than this."

"You and me both."

Shannon's confirmation that the message was understood had arrived two days earlier. The idea had occurred to Hunt and Lyn one evening while they were at Lyn's apartment, solving a puzzle in one of Hunt's books of London *Times* crosswords. Don Maddson, the linguistics expert at Navcomms who had studied the Ganymean language, was one of the regular compilers of the *Journal* puzzles and also a close friend of Hunt's. So with Caldwell's blessing, Hunt had told Maddson as much as was necessary about the Gistar situation, and together they had constructed the message transmitted to Jupiter. Now there was nothing to do but wait and hope that it produced results.

"Let's hope Murphy takes a day off," Lyn said.

"Never hope that. Let's hope somebody remembers Hunt's extension to the Law."

"What's Hunt's extension?"

" 'Everything that can go wrong, will . . . unless somebody makes it his business to do something about it.' "

The stub wing outside the window dipped as the airmobile banked out of the traffic corridor and turned to commence a shallow descent. A cluster of large white buildings standing to attention on a river bank about a mile away moved slowly around until they were centered in the windshield and lying dead ahead.

"He must have been an insurance salesman," Hunt murmured after a short silence.

"Who?"

"Murphy. 'Everything's going to screw up—sign the application now.' Who else but an insurance salesman would have thought of saying something like that?"

The buildings ahead grew to take on the smooth, clean lines of the Westwood Biological Institute of UNSA's Life Sciences Division. The vehicle slowed to a halt and hovered fifty feet above the roof of the Biochemistry building, which with Neurosciences and Physiology formed a trio facing the elongated bulk of Administration and Central Facilities across a plaza of colorful mosaic paving broken up by lawns and a bevy of fountains playing in the sun. Hunt checked the landing area visually, then cleared the computer to complete the descent sequence. Minutes later he and Lyn were checking in at the reception desk in the building's top-floor lobby.

"Professor Danchekker isn't in his office," the receptionist informed them as she consulted her screen. "The route-through code entered against his number is for one of the basement labs. I'll try there." She keyed in another code, and after a short delay the characters on the screen vanished in a blur of colors which immediately assembled themselves into the features of a lean, balding man wearing a pair of anachronistic gold-rimmed spectacles perched at the top of a thin, somewhat aquiline nose. His skin gave the impression of having been stretched over his bones as an afterthought, with barely enough left over to cover his defiant, outthrust chin. He didn't seem too pleased at the interruption.

"Yes?"

"Professor Danchekker, top lobby here. I have two visitors for you."

"I am extremely busy," he replied curtly. "Who are they and what do they want?"

Hunt sighed and pivoted the display around to face him. "It's us, Chris—Vic and Lyn. You're expecting us."

Danchekker's expression softened, and his mouth compressed itself into a thin line that twitched briefly upward at the ends. "Oh, of course. I do apologize. Come on down. I'm in the dissecting lab on Level E."

"Are you working alone?" Hunt asked.

"Yes. We can talk here."

"We'll see you in a couple of minutes."

They walked on through to the elevator bank at the rear of the lobby. "Chris must be working with his animals again," Lyn remarked as they waited.

"I don't think he's come up for air since we got back from Ganymede," Hunt said. "I'm surprised he hasn't started looking like some of them."

Danchekker had been with Hunt on Ganymede when the *Shapieron* reappeared in the Solar System. In fact Danchekker had made the major contribution to piecing together what was probably the most astounding part of the whole story, the more sensitive details of which still had not been cleared for publication to an unsuspecting and psychologically unprepared world.

Not surprisingly, the Ganymeans had made visits to Earth during the period that their civilization had flourished on Minerva—twenty-five million years before. Their scientists had predicted an epoch of deteriorating environmental conditions on Minerva in the form of an increasing concentration of atmospheric carbon dioxide, for which they had only a low inherent tolerance, so one of the reasons for their interest in Earth had been to assess it as a possible candidate for migration. But they soon abandoned the idea. The Ganymeans had evolved from ancestors whose biochemistry had precluded the emergence of carnivores, thus inhibiting the development of aggressiveness and ruthlessness together with most of the related traits that had characterized the survival struggle on Earth. The savagery that abounded in the environment of late-Oligocene, early-Miocene Earth made it altogether too inhospitable for the placid Ganymean temperament, and the notion of settling there unthinkable.

These visits to Earth did, however, have one practical outcome in addition to satisfying the Ganymeans' scientific curiosity. In the course of their studies of the forms of animal life they discovered, they identified a totally new, gene-based mechanism for absorbing CO_2, which gave terrestrial fauna a far higher and more adaptable inherent tolerance. It suggested an alternative approach to solving the problem on Minerva. The Ganymeans imported large numbers of terrestrial animal species back to their own planet to conduct genetic experiments aimed at transplanting the functional terrestrial coding groups into their own species, thereafter to be inbred automatically into their descendants. Some well-preserved specimens of these early terrestrial animals had been recovered from the wrecked ship on Ganymede, and Danchekker had brought many of them back to Westwood for detailed studies.

The experiments were not successful, and soon afterward the Ganymeans disappeared. The terrestrial species left on Minerva rapidly wiped out the virtually defenseless native forms, adapted and radiated to flourish across the planet, and continued to evolve. . . .

Almost twenty-five million years later—around fifty thousand years before the current period on Earth—an intelligent, fully human form had established itself on Minerva. This race was named the "Lunarians" after the first traces of their existence came to light in the course of lunar explorations being conducted in 2028, which was when Hunt had first gotten involved and moved from England to join UNSA. The Lunarians were a violent and warlike race who developed advanced technology rapidly and eventually polarized into two superpowers, Cerios and Lambia, which clashed in a final, cataclysmic war fought across the entire surface of Minerva and beyond. In the violence of this conflict Minerva had been destroyed, Pluto and the Asteroids born, and Luna orphaned.

A few survivors were left stranded on the lunar surface at the end of these events. Somehow, when at last the Moon stabilized in orbit around Earth after being captured, some of these survivors succeeded in reaching the only haven left for them in the entire solar system—the surface of Earth itself. For millennia they clung precariously to the edge of extinction, reverting to barbarism for a period and in the process losing the thread that traced their origins. But in time they grew strong and spread far and wide. They supplanted the Neanderthals, who were descended from the primates that had continued to evolve undisturbed on Earth, and eventually came to dominate the entire planet in the form of Modern Man. Only much later, when at last they rediscovered the sciences and ventured back into space, did they find the evidence to reconstruct the story of their origins.

They found Danchekker attired in a stained white lab smock, measuring and examining parts taken from a large, brown, furry carcass lying on the dissection table. It was powerfully muscled, and its fearsome, well-developed carnivore's teeth were exposed where the lower jaw of the snout had been removed. Danchekker informed them that it was an intriguing example of a relative to *Daphoenodon* of the Lower Miocene. Despite its evidently distinct digitigrade mode of locomotion, moderately long legs, and heavy tail, its three upper molars distinguished it as an ancestor of *Amphicyon* and through it of all modern bears—unlike *Cynodesmus,* of which Danchekker also had a specimen, whose upper dentition of two molars put it between *Cynodictis* and contemporary Canidae. Hunt took his word for it.

Hunt had practically insisted to Caldwell that if they succeeded in arranging a landing for a ship from Thurien, Danchekker would have to be included in the reception patty; he probably knew more about Ganymean biology and psychology than anybody else in the world's scientific community. Caldwell had broached the subject confidentially with the Director of the Westwood Institute, who had agreed and advised Danchekker accordingly. Danchekker had not needed very much persuading. He was far from happy at the manner in which the eminent personages responsible for managing Earth's affairs had been handling things, however.

"The whole situation is preposterous," Danchekker declared irritably while he was loading the instruments he had been using into a sterilizer on one side of the room. "Politics, cloak-and-dagger theatrics—this is an unprecedented opportunity for the advancement of knowledge and probably for a quantum leap in the progress of the whole human race, yet here we are having to plot and scheme as if we were dealing in illicit narcotics or something. I mean, good God, we can't even talk about it over the phone! The situation's intolerable."

Lyn straightened up from the dissecting table, where she had been curiously studying the exposed innards of *Daphoenodon*. "I guess the UN feels it has an obligation to humanity to play safe," she said. "It's a contact with a whole new civilization, and they figure that up front it ought to be handled by the professionals."

Danchekker closed the sterilizer lid with a bang and walked over to a sink to rinse his hands. "When the *Shapieron* arrived at Ganymede, the only representatives of *Homo sapiens* there to meet it were, as I recall, the scientific and engineering personnel of the UNSA Jupiter missions," he pointed out coolly. "They conducted themselves in exemplary fashion and had established a perfectly civilized relationship with the Ganymeans long before the ship came to Earth. That was without any 'professionals' being involved at all, apart from sending inane advice from Earth on how the situation should be managed, and which those on the spot simply laughed at and ignored."

Hunt looked across from a chair by a desk that stood in one corner of the lab, almost surrounded by computer terminal equipment and display screens. "Actually there is something to be said for the UN line," he said. "I don't think you've thought yet just how big a risk we might be taking."

Danchekker sniffed as he came back around the table. "What are you talking about?"

"If the State Department wasn't convinced that if we don't go it alone and fix a landing the Soviets will, we'd be a lot more cautious too," Hunt told him.

"I don't follow you," Danchekker said. "What is there to be cautious about? The Ganymean mind is incapable of conceiving anything that could constitute a threat to our, or anybody else's, well-being, as you well know. They simply have not been shaped by the factors that have conditioned *Homo sapiens* to be what he is." He waved a hand in front of his face before Hunt could reply. "And as for your fears that the Thuriens may have changed in some fundamental way, you may forget that. The fundamental traits that determine human behavior were established, not tens but hundreds of millions of years ago, and I have studied Minervan evolution sufficiently to be satisfied that the same may safely be said of Ganymeans also. On such timescales, twenty-five million years is scarcely significant, and quite incapable of giving rise to changes of the magnitude that your suggestion implies."

"I know that," Hunt said when he could get a word in. "But you're going off at a wrong tangent. That's not the problem. The problem is that we might not be talking to Ganymeans at all."

Danchekker seemed taken aback for a moment, then frowned as if Hunt should have known better. "That's absurd," he declared. "Who else could we be talking to? The original transmission from Farside was encoded in Ganymean communications format and understood, was it not? What reason is there to suppose its recipients were anything else?"

"They're talking in English now, but it's not coming from London," Hunt replied.

"But they are talking from Gistar," Danchekker retorted. "And isn't that where, from independently derived evidence, we deduced that the Ganymeans went?"

"We don't *know* that those signals are coming from Gistar," Hunt pointed out. "They say they are, but they've been saying all kinds of other strange things as well. Our beams are being aimed *in the direction of* Gistar, but we've no idea what's out there past the edge of the solar system picking them up. It could be some kind of Ganymean relay that transforms signals that our physics knows nothing about into electromagnetic waves, but then again it might not."

"Surely it's obvious," Danchekker said, sounding a trifle disdainful. "The Ganymeans left some kind of monitoring device behind when they migrated to Gistar, probably to detect and alert them to any signs of intelligent activity."

Hunt shook his head. "If that were the case, it would have been triggered by early radio over a hundred years ago. We'd have known about it long before now."

Danchekker thought about it for a moment, then showed his teeth. "Which proves my point. It responded only to Ganymean codes. We've never sent anything out encoded in Ganymean before, have we? Therefore it must be of Ganymean origin."

"And now it's talking English. Does that mean it was made by Boeing?"

"Obviously the language was acquired via their surveillance operation."

"And maybe they learned Ganymean the same way."

"You're being absurd."

Hunt threw out his arms in appeal. "For Christ's sake, Chris, all I'm saying is let's be open-minded for now and accept that we might be letting ourselves in for something we didn't expect. You're saying they have to be Ganymeans, and you're probably right; I'm saying there's a chance they might not be. That's all I'm saying."

"You said yourself that Ganymeans don't play cloak-and-dagger games and twist facts around, Professor," Lyn injected in a tone that she hoped would calm things a little. "But whoever it is seems to have some funny ideas about how to open up interplanetary relations. . . . And they've got some pretty weird ideas on how Earth is coming along these days, so somebody hasn't been talking straight to somebody somewhere. That hardly sounds like Ganymeans, does it?"

Danchekker snorted but seemed hard-pressed for a reply. The terminal on a side table by the desk saved him by emitting a call-tone. "Excuse me" he muttered, leaning past Hunt to accept. "Yes?" Danchekker inquired.

It was Ginny, calling from Navcomms HQ. "Hello, Professor Danchekker. I believe Dr. Hunt is with you. I have an urgent message for him. Gregg Caldwell said to find him and let him know right away."

Danchekker moved back a pace, and Hunt rolled his chair forward in front of the screen. "Hi, Ginny," he acknowledged. "What's new?"

"A message has come in for you from *Jupiter Five*." She looked down to read something below the edge of the screen. "It's from the Mission Director—Joseph B. Shannon. It reads, " 'The lab tests worked out just as you hoped. Complete file of results being assembled for transmission now. Good luck.' " Ginny looked up again. "Is that what you wanted to know?"

Hunt's face was radiating jubilation. "It sure is, Ginny!" he said "Thanks . . . a lot." Ginny nodded and tossed him a quick smile; the screen blanked out.

Hunt swiveled his chair around to find two awed faces confronting him. "I guess we can stop arguing about it," he told them. "It looks as if we'll know for sure before very much longer."

Chapter Six

The main receiver dish at Giordano Bruno was like a gigantic Cyclopean eye—a four-hundred-foot-diameter paraboloid of steel latticework towering into the starry blackness above the lifeless desolation of lunar Farside. It was supported by twin lattice towers moving in diametric opposition around the circular track that formed the most salient surface feature of the observatory and base. As it stood motionless, listening to whispers from distant galaxies, the lines of its lengthening shadow lay draped as a distorted mesh across the domes and lesser constructions huddled around it, spilling over on one side to become indistinct and lost among the boulders and craters scattered beyond.

Karen Heller stood gazing up at it through the transparent wall of an observation tower protruding from the roof of the two-story Main Block. She had gone there to be alone and re-compose herself after yet another acrimonious meeting of the eleven-person UN Farside delegation, which had gotten nowhere. Their latest scare was that the signals might not be coming from Ganymeans at all, which was her own fault for ill-advisedly introducing the thought that Hunt had voiced when she was in Houston a week earlier. She wasn't sure even now why she had brought that possibility up at all, since with hindsight it provided an opportunity for procrastination that they were bound to latch on to. As she had commented to a surprised Norman Pacey afterward, it had been a badly calculated attempt at a shock tactic to spur any positive reaction, and had misfired. Perhaps in her frustration she hadn't been thinking too clearly at the time. Anyway it was done now, and the latest transmission sent out toward Gistar had discounted the possibility of any landing in the immediate future and instead talked reams of insignificant detail to do with rank and protocol. Ironically this in itself should have said clearly enough that the aliens, Ganymean or not, harbored no hostile intentions; if they did, they would surely have just arrived, if that was what they wanted to do, without waiting for a cordial invitation. It all made the UN policy more enigmatic and reinforced her suspicions, and the State Department's, that the Soviets were setting themselves up to go it alone and were manipulating the UN somehow. Nevertheless the U.S. would continue to follow the rules until Houston succeeded in establishing a channel via Jupiter—assuming Houston succeeded. If they did, and if none of the efforts to speed things up at Bruno had borne fruit by that time, the U.S. would feel justified in concluding that its hand had been forced.

As she gazed up at the lines of metal etched against the blackness by the rays of the setting sun, she marveled at the knowledge and ingenuity that had created an oasis of life in a sterile desert a quarter of a million miles from Earth and built instruments such as this, which even as she watched might be silently probing the very edges of the universe. One of the scientific advisors from NSF had told her once that all of the energy collected by all the world's radio telescopes since the beginnings of that branch of astronomy almost a century earlier was equivalent to no more than that represented by the ash from a cigarette falling through a distance of several feet. And somehow the whole fantastic picture painted by modern cosmology—of collapsed stars, black holes, X-ray-emitting binaries, and a universe consisting of a "gas" of galaxy "molecules"—had all been reconstructed from the information contained in it.

She had ambivalent views about scientists. On the one hand, their intellectual accomplishments were baffling and at times like this awesome; on the other, she often felt that at a deeper level their retreat into the realm of the inanimate represented an abdication—an escape from the burdens of the world of human affairs within which the expression of knowledge acquired meaning. Even biologists seemed to reduce life to terms of molecules and statistics. Science had created the tools to solve humanity's problems a century ago, but had stood by helplessly while others took the tools and forged them into means of attaining other ends. It was not until the 2010s, when the UN emerged as a truly coherent global influence to be reckoned with, that strategic disarmament had become fact and the resources of the superpowers were at last mobilized toward building a safer and better world.

It was all the more tragic and inexplicable that the UN—until so recently the epitome of the world's commitment to meaningful progress and the realization of the full potential of the human race—should be the obstacle in the road along which the arrow of that progress surely pointed. It seemed a law of history for successful movements and empires to resist further change after the needs that had motivated them into promoting change had been satisfied. Perhaps, she reflected, the UN was already, in keeping with the universally accelerating pace of the times, beginning to show the eventual senility symptoms of all empires—stagnation.

But the planets continued to move in their predicted orbits, and the patterns being revealed by the computers connected to the instruments at Giordano Bruno didn't change. So was her "reality" an illusion built on shifting sands, and had scientists shunned the illusion for some vaster, unchanging reality that was the only one of permanence that mattered? Somehow she couldn't picture the Englishman Hunt or the American she had met in Houston as fugitives who would idle their lives away tinkering in ivory towers.

A moving point of light detached itself from the canopy of

stars and enlarged gradually into the shape of the UNSA surface transporter ship due in from Tycho. It came to a halt above the far side of the base, and after pausing for a few seconds sank slowly out of sight between Optical Dome 3 and a clutter of storage tanks and laser transceivers. Aboard it would be the courier with the latest information from Houston via Washington. The experts had decreed that if Ganymean technology was behind the surveillance of Earth's communications anything was possible, and the ban on using even supposedly secure channels was still being rigidly enforced. Heller turned away and walked across the floor of the dome to call an elevator at the rear wall. A minute or two later she stepped out into a brightly lit, white-walled corridor three levels below the surface and began walking in the direction of the central hub of Bruno's underground labyrinth.

Mikolai Sobroskin, the Soviet representative on Farside, came out of one of the doors as she passed and turned to walk with her in the same direction. He was short but broad, completely bald, and pink-skinned, and he walked with a hurried, jerking gait, even in lunar gravity, that made her feel for a moment like Snow White. From a dossier that Norman Pacey had procured, however, she knew that the Russian had been a lieutenant-general in the Red Army, where he had specialized in electronic warfare and countermeasures, and a counter-intelligence expert for many years after that. He came from a world about as far removed from Walt Disney's as it was possible to get.

"I spent three months in the Pacific conducting equipment trials aboard a nuclear carrier many years ago," Sobroskin remarked. "It seemed that it was impossible to get from anywhere to anywhere without interminable corridors. I never did find out what lay in between half those places. This base reminds me of it."

"I'd say the New York subway," Heller replied.

"Ah, but the difference is that these walls get washed more regularly. One of the problems with capitalism is that only the things that pay get done. So it wears a clean suit which conceals dirty undershorts."

Heller smiled faintly. At least it was good that the differences that erupted across the table in the conference room could be left there. Anything else would have made life intolerable in the cramped, communal atmosphere of the base. "The shuttle from Tycho just landed," she said. "I wonder what's new."

"Yes, I know. No doubt some mail from Moscow and Washington for us to argue about tomorrow." The original UN charter had ruled against representatives receiving instructions from their national governments, but nobody at Farside kept up any pretenses about that.

"I hope not too much," she sighed. "We should be thinking of the future of the whole planet. National politics shouldn't come into this." She glanced sideways as she spoke, searching his face for a hint of a reaction. Nobody in Washington had yet been able to decide for sure if the UN stance was being dictated from the Kremlin, or if the Soviets were simply playing along with something they found expedient to their own ends. But the Russian remained inscrutable.

They came out of the corridor and entered the "common room"—normally the UNSA Officers' Mess, but assigned temporarily for off-duty use by the visiting UN delegation. The air was warm and stuffy. A mixed group of about a dozen UN delegates and permanent residents of the base was present, some reading, two engrossed in a chess game, and the others talking in small groups around the room or at the small bar at the far end. Sobroskin continued walking and disappeared through the far door, which led to the rooms allocated for office space for the delegation. Heller had intended going the same way, but she was intercepted by Niels Sverenssen, the delegation's Swedish chairman, who detached himself from a small group standing near where they had entered.

"Oh, Karen," he said, catching her elbow lightly and steering her to one side. "I've been looking for you. There are a few points from today's meeting that we ought to resolve before finalizing tomorrow's agenda. I was hoping to discuss them before it's typed up." He was very tall and lean, and he carried his crown of silver hair with a haughty uprightness that always made Heller think of him as the last of the true blue-blooded European aristocrats. His dress was always impeccable and formal, even at Bruno where practically everyone else had soon taken to more casual wear, and he gave the impression somehow of looking on the rest of the human race with something approaching disdain, as if condescending to mix with them only as an imposition of duty. Heller was never able to feel quite at ease in his presence, and she had spent too much time in Paris and on other European assignments to attribute it simply to cultural differences.

"Well, I was on my way to check the mail," she said. "If the discussion can wait for an hour or so, I could see you back here. We'll go through it over a drink maybe, or use one of the offices. Was it anything important?"

"A few questions of procedure and some definitions that need clarifying under one or two headings." Sverenssen's voice had fallen from its public-address mode of a moment earlier, and as he spoke he moved around as if to shield their conversation from the rest of the room. He was looking at her with a curious expression—an intrigued detachment that was strangely intimate and distant at the same time. It made her feel like a kitchen wench being looked over by a medieval lord-of-the-manor. "I was thinking of something perhaps a little more comfortable later," he said, his tone now ominously confidential. "Possibly over dinner, if I might have the honor."

"I'm not sure when I'll be having dinner tonight," she replied, telling herself that she was getting it all wrong. "It might be late."

"A more companionable hour, wouldn't you agree," Sverenssen murmured pointedly.

It was getting to her again. His words implied that the honor would be his, but his manner left no doubt that she should consider it hers. "I thought you said that you needed to talk before the agenda gets typed," she said.

"We could clear that matter up in an hour as you suggest. That would make dinner a far more relaxing and enjoyable occasion . . . later."

Heller had to swallow hard to maintain her composure. He

was propositioning her. Such things happened and that was life, but the way this was happening wasn't real. "I think you must have misjudged something," she told him curtly. "If you have business to discuss, I'll talk to you in an hour. Now would you excuse me please?" If he left it at that, it would all soon be forgotten.

He didn't. Instead he moved a pace closer, causing her to back away a step instinctively. "You are an extremely intelligent and ambitious, as well as an attractive, woman, Karen," he said quietly, dropping his former pose. "The world has so many opportunities to offer these days—especially to those who succeed in making friends among its more influential circles. I could do a lot for you that you would find extremely helpful, you know."

His presumption was too much. "You're making a mistake," Heller breathed harshly, striving to keep her voice at a level that would not attract attention. "Please don't compound it any further."

Sverenssen was unperturbed, as if the routine were familiar and mildly boring. "Think it over," he urged, and with that turned casually and rejoined the group he had left. He'd paid his dollar and bought a ticket. It was no more than that. The fury that Heller had been suppressing boiled up inside as she walked out of the room, managing with some effort to keep her pace normal.

Norman Pacey was waiting for her when she reached the U.S. delegate's offices a few minutes later. He seemed to be having trouble in containing his excitement over something. "News!" he exclaimed without preamble as she entered. Then his expression changed abruptly. "Hey, you're looking pretty mad about something. Anything up?"

"It's nothing. What's happened."

"Malliusk was here a little while ago." Gregor Malliusk was the Russian Director of Astronomy at Bruno and one of the privileged few among the regular staff there who knew about the dialogue with Gistar. "A signal came in about an hour ago that isn't intended for us. It's in some kind of binary numeric code. He can't make anything out of it."

Heller looked at him numbly. It could only mean that somebody else, either somewhere on Earth or in its vicinity, had begun transmitting to Gistar and wanted the reply kept private. "The Soviets?" she asked hoarsely.

Pacey shrugged. "Who knows? Sverenssen will probably call a special session, and Sobroskin will deny it, but I'd stake a month's pay."

His voice didn't carry the defeat that it should have, and what he had said didn't account for the jubilant look that Heller had caught on his face as she entered. "Anything else?" she asked, praying inwardly that the reason was what she thought it might be.

Pacey's face split into a wide grin that he could contain no longer. He scooped up some papers from a wad lying in front of the opened courier's bag on a table beside him and waved them triumphantly in the air. "Hunt got through!" he exclaimed. "They've done it via Jupiter! The landing is already fixed for a week from now, and the Thuriens have confirmed it. It's all arranged for a disused airbase in Alaska. It's all fixed up!"

Heller took the papers from him and smiled with relief and elation as she scanned rapidly down the first sheet. "We'll do it, Norman," she whispered. "We'll beat those bastards yet!"

"You've got a recall to Earth from the Department so you can be there as planned. You'll be getting space-happy with all these lunar flights." Pacey sighed. "I'll be thinking about you while I'm holding the fort up here. I only wish I was coming too."

"You'll get your chance soon enough," Heller said. Everything looked bright again. She lifted her face suddenly from the papers in her hand. "I'll tell you what—tonight we'll both have a special dinner to celebrate . . . a kind of farewell party until whenever. Champagne, a good wine, and the best poultry the cook here's got in his refrigerator. How does that sound?"

"Sounds great," Pacey replied, then frowned and rubbed his chin dubiously. "Although . . . would it really be a good idea? I mean, with this unidentified signal coming in only an hour ago, people might wonder what the hell we're celebrating.

Sverenssen might think it's us, not the Soviets, who are being underhanded."

"Well we are, aren't we?"

"Yeah, I guess so—but for a good reason. That's different."

"So let them. If the Soviets think the heat's on us, they might get a false sense of security and not move too fast." A look of grim satisfaction came into Heller's eyes as she thought of something else. "And let Sverenssen think anything he damn well likes," she said.

Chapter Seven

C lad in a standard-issue UNSA arctic jacket, quilted over-
trousers, and snowboots, Hunt stood in the center of a
small group of muffled figures stamping their feet and
breathing frosty clouds of condensation into the air on the concrete apron of McClusky Air Force Base, situated in the
foothills of the Baird Mountains one hundred miles inside the
Arctic Circle. The ground fog of the previous day had thinned
somewhat to become a layer of overcast through which the
washy blob of the sun was just able to impart a drab mix of off-
white and grays to the texture of the surrounding landscape.
Most of the signs of life among the huddle of semiderelict
buildings behind them were concentrated around the former
mess hall, which had been hastily patched up and windproofed
to provide makeshift accommodation and a command post for
the operation. A gaggle of UNSA aircraft and other vehicles
parked among a litter of supplies and equipment along the
near edge of the apron, and a team of handpicked UNSA
personnel positioned in the background with cameras and
microphone booms set up ready to record the impending event,
completed the scene. The command post had landline links

into the area radar net, and a homing beacon had been set up for the Ganymean ship. A strangely tense silence predominated, broken only by the intermittent cries of kittiwakes wheeling and diving above the frozen marshes beyond the perimeter fence, and the humming of a motor generator supplying power from one of the parked trailers.

McClusky was about as far from population centers and major air-traffic lanes as it was possible to get without going outside the U.S., but like every other point on the Earth's surface it was still subject to satellite scrutiny. In an attempt to mask the landing, UNSA had given notice that tests of a new type of reentry vehicle would be conducted in the area during that week, and had requested airlines and other organizations to reroute flights accordingly until further notice. To accustom the region's radar controllers to an abnormal pattern of activity, UNSA had also been staging irregular flights over Alaska for several days and altering their announced flight plans at short notice. Beyond that there was little they could do. How anything like the arrival of a starship could be kept secret from terrestrial observers, never mind an advanced alien surveillance system, was something nobody was quite sure of. Whoever was sending the messages through Jupiter had seemed satisfied with the arrangements, however, and had stated that they would take care of the rest.

The last message to go out via Jupiter had given the names of the persons who would make up the reception party, their positions, and a brief summary of what they did and why each was included. The aliens had reciprocated with a reply advising that three of their members would be prominent in conducting their dealings with Earth. The first was "Calazar," who was described as personifying the government of Thurien and its associated worlds—the figure nearest to a "president" that the planet seemed to possess. Accompanying him would be Frenua Showm, a female "ambassador" whose function had to do with affairs between the various sectors of Thurien society, "and Porthik Eesyan, who was involved with policies of scientific, industrial, and economic importance. Whether or not more than just these three would be involved, the aliens hadn't said.

"This is all a striking contrast to the *Shapieron*'s arrival on this planet," Danchekker muttered, surveying the scene around them. That event on the shore of Lake Geneva had been witnessed by tens of thousands and shown live over the news grid.

"It reminds me of Ganymede Main," Hunt replied. "All we need is helmets on and a few Vegas around. What a way to start a new era!"

On Hunt's other side, Lyn, looking lost in the outsize, fur-trimmed hood pulled closely around her face, thrust her hands deeper into her jacket pockets and ground down a block of slush with her foot. "They're about due," she said. "I hope they've got good brakes." Assuming all was on schedule, the ship would have left Thurien, over twenty light-years away, just about twenty-four hours earlier.

"I don't think we need entertain any fears of ineptitude on the part of the Ganymeans," Danchekker said confidently.

"*If* they turn out to be Ganymeans," Hunt remarked, even though by this time he no longer had any real doubts about the matter.

"Of *course* they're Ganymeans," Danchekker snorted impatiently.

Behind them Karen Heller and Jerol Packard, the U.S. Secretary of State, stood motionless and silent. They had persuaded the President to go ahead with the operation on the strength of the implication that the aliens, Ganymean or not, were friendly, and if they were wrong they could well have committed their country to the worst blunder in its history. The President had hoped to be present in person, but in the end had accepted reluctantly the advice of his aides that the absence of too many important people at the same time without explanation would be inviting undesirable attention.

Suddenly the voice of the operations controller inside the mess hall barked over the loudspeaker mounted on a mast at the rear. "Radar contact!" The figures around Hunt stiffened visibly. Behind them the team of UNSA technicians hid their nervousness behind a frenzied outbreak of last-minute preparations and adjustments. The voice came again: "Approaching due west, range twenty-two miles, altitude twelve thousand feet, speed six hundred miles per hour, reducing." Hunt swung his head around instinctively to peer upward along with all the others, but it was impossible to make out anything through the overcast.

A minute went by in slow motion. "Five miles," the controller's voice announced. "It's down to five thousand feet. Visual contact any time now." Hunt could feel the blood pumping solidly in his chest. Despite the cold, his body suddenly felt clammy inside his heavy clothing. Lyn wriggled her arm through his and pulled herself closer.

And then the wind blowing down from the mountains to the west brought the first snatch of a low moaning sound. It lasted for a second or two, faded away, then came back again and this time persisted. It swelled slowly to a steady drone. A frown began forming on Hunt's face as he listened. He turned and glanced back, and saw that several of the UNSA people were exchanging puzzled looks too. There was something wrong. That sound was too familiar to be from any starship. Mutterings started breaking out, then ceased abruptly as a dark shape materialized out of the cloud base and continued descending on a direct line toward the base. It was a standard Boeing 1227 medium-haul, transonic VTOL—a model widely used by domestic carriers and UNSA's preferred type for general-purpose duties. The tension that had been building up around the apron released itself in a chorus of groans and curses.

Behind Heller and Packard, Caldwell, his face dark with fury, spun around to confront a bewildered UNSA officer. "I thought this area was supposed to have been cleared," he snapped.

The officer shook his head helplessly. "It was. I don't understand. . . . Somebo—"

"Get that idiot out of here!"

Looking flustered, the officer hurried away and disappeared through the open door of the mess hall. At the same time voices from the control room inside began pouring out over the loudspeaker, evidently left inadvertently live in the confusion.

"I can't get anything out of it. It's not responding."

"Use the emergency frequency."

"We've already tried. Nothing."

"For Christ's sake what's happening in here? Caldwell just chewed my balls off outside. Find out from Yellow Six who it is."

"I've got 'em on the line now. They don't know, either. They thought it was ours."

"Gimme that goddam phone!"

The plane leveled out above the edge of the marshes about a mile away and kept coming, heedless of the volley of brilliant red warning flares fired from the top of McClusky's control tower. It slowed to a halt above the open area of concrete in front of the reception party, hung motionless for a moment, and then started sinking toward the ground. A handful of UNSA officers and technicians ran forward making frantic crossed-arms signals over their heads to wave it off, but fell back in disarray as it came on down regardless and settled. Caldwell strode ahead of the group, gesticulating angrily and shouting orders at the UNSA figures who were converging around the nose and making signs up at the cockpit.

"Imbeciles!" Danchekker muttered. "This kind of thing should never happen."

"It looks as if Murphy's back from vacation," Lyn said resignedly in Hunt's ear. But Hunt only half heard. He was staring hard at the Boeing with a strange look on his face. There was something very odd about that aircraft. It had landed in the middle of a sea of watery snow and slush churned up by the activity of the last few days, yet its landing jets hadn't thrown up the cloud of spray and vapor that they should have. So maybe it didn't have any landing jets. If that were so it might have looked like a 1227, but it certainly wasn't powered like one. And there didn't seem to be much response from the cockpit to the antics of the people below. In fact, unless Hunt's eyes were deceiving him, there wasn't anybody in the cockpit at all. Suddenly his face broke into a wide grin as the penny dropped.

"Vic, what is it?" Lyn asked. "What's funny?"

"What's the obvious way to hide something in the middle of an airfield from a surveillance system?" he asked. He gestured toward the plane, but before he could say any more a voice that could have belonged to a natural-born American boomed out across the apron from its direction.

"Greetings from Thurien to Earth, et cetera. Well, we made it. Too bad about the lousy weather."

All movement around the craft ceased instantly. A total silence fell. One by one the heads on every side jerked around and gaped at each other as the message percolated through.

This was a starship? The *Shapieron* had stood nearly half a mile high. It was like having a little old lady show up at Tycho on a bicycle.

The forward passenger door opened, and a flight of steps unfolded itself to the ground. All eyes were riveted to the open doorway. The UNSA people up front drew back slowly while Hunt and his companions, with Heller and Packard a pace behind, moved forward to close in behind Caldwell and then slowed to a halt again uncertainly. Behind them the expectant cameras focused unwaveringly on the top of the steps.

"You'd better come on in," the voice suggested. "No sense in catching colds out there."

Heller and Packard exchanged bemused glances; none of their talks and briefings in Washington had prepared them for this. "I guess we just ad-lib as we go," Packard said in a low voice. He tried to summon up a reassuring grin, but it died somewhere on its way to his face.

"At least it's not happening in Siberia," Heller murmured.

Danchekker was fixing Hunt with a satisfied look. "If those utterances are not indicative of Ganymean humor at work, I'll accept creationism," he said triumphantly. The aliens could have warned them about the ship's disguise, Hunt agreed inwardly, but apparently they had been unable to resist making a mild joke out of it. And they obviously had little time for pomp and formality. It sounded like Ganymeans, all right.

They began moving toward the steps with Caldwell in the lead while the UNSA people opened up to let them pass through. Hunt was a couple of paces behind Caldwell as Caldwell was about to step onto the first stair. Caldwell emitted a startled exclamation and seemed to be lifted off the ground. As the others froze in their tracks, he was whisked upward over the stairway without any part of his body seeming to touch it, and deposited on his feet inside the doorway apparently none the worse for wear. He seemed a trifle shaken when he turned to look back down at them, but composed himself rapidly. "Well, what are you waiting for?" he growled. Hunt was obviously next in line. He drew a long, unsteady breath, shrugged, and stepped forward.

A strangely pleasant and warm sensation enveloped him, and a force of some kind drew him onward, carrying his weight off his legs. There was a blurred impression of the steps flowing by beneath his feet, and then he was standing beside Caldwell, who was watching him closely and not without a hint of amusement. Hunt was finally convinced—this was not a 1227.

They were in a fairly small, bare compartment whose walls were of a translucent amber material and glowed softly. It seemed to be an antechamber to whatever lay beyond another door leading aft, from which a stronger light was emanating. Before Hunt could take in any more of the details, Lyn sailed in through the doorway and landed lightly on the spot he had just vacated.

Then Danchekker's voice shouted in sudden alarm from outside. "What in God's name is happening? Do something with this infernal contraption!" They looked back down. He was hanging a foot or two above the stairway, flailing his arms in exasperation after having apparently come to a halt halfway through the process of joining them. "This is ridiculous! Get me down from here!"

"You're crowding the doorway," the voice that had spoken before advised from somewhere around them. "How about moving on through and making more room?" They moved toward the inner doorway, and Danchekker appeared behind somewhat huffily a few seconds later. While Heller and Packard were following, Hunt and Lyn followed Caldwell into the body of the craft.

They found themselves in a short corridor that ran twenty feet or so toward the tail before stopping at another door, which was closed. A series of partitions extending from floor to ceiling divided the space on either side into a half-dozen or so narrow cubicles facing inward from left and right. As they moved along the corridor, they found that all the cubicles were identical, each containing some kind of recliner, upholstered in red, facing inward toward the corridor and surrounded by a metal framework supporting panel inlays of a multicolored crystalline material and a bewildering layout of delicately constructed equipment whose purpose could have been anything. There was still no sign of life.

"Welcome aboard," the voice said. "If you'd each take a seat, we can begin."

"Who's doing the talking?" Caldwell demanded, looking around and overhead. "We'd appreciate the courtesy of your identifying yourself."

"My name is VISAR," the voice replied. "But I'm only the pilot and cabin crew. The people you're expecting will be here in a few minutes."

They were probably through the door at the far end, Hunt decided. It seemed odd. The voice reminded him of his first meeting with the Ganymeans, inside the *Shapieron* shortly after it had arrived in orbit over Ganymede. On that occasion, too, contact with the aliens had been through a voice functioning as interpreter, which turned out subsequently to belong to an entity called ZORAC—a supercomputer complex distributed through the ship and responsible for the operation of most of its systems and functions. "VISAR," he called out. "Are you a computer system built into this vehicle?"

"You could say that," VISAR answered. "It's about as near as we're likely to get. A small extension is there. The rest is scattered all over Thurien plus a whole list of other planets and places. You've got a link into the net."

"Are you saying this ship isn't operating autonomously?" Hunt asked. "You're interacting between here and Thurien in realtime?"

"Sure. How else could we have turned around the messages from Jupiter?"

Hunt was astounded. VISAR's statement implied a communications network distributed across star systems and operating with negligible delays. It meant that the point-to-point transfers, at least of energy, that he had often talked about with Paul Shelling at Navcomms were not only proved in principle, but up and running. No wonder Caldwell was looking stunned; it put Navcomms back in the Stone Age.

Hunt realized that Danchekker was now immediately behind him, peering curiously around, with Heller and Packard just inside the door. Where was Lyn? As if to answer his unvoiced equation, her voice spoke from inside one of the cubicles. "Say, it feels great. I could stand this for a week or two, maybe." He turned and saw that she was already lying back in one of the recliners and apparently enjoying it. He looked at Caldwell, hesitated for a moment, then moved into the adjacent cubicle, turned, and sat down, allowing his body to sink back into the recliner's yielding contours. It felt right for human rather than Ganymean proportions, he noted with interest. Had they built the whole craft in a week specifically for the occasion? That would have been typical of Ganymeans too.

A warm, pleasant feeling swept over him again and made him feel drowsy, causing his head to drop back automatically into the concave rest provided. He felt more relaxed than he could ever remember and suddenly didn't care if he never had to get up again. There was a vague impression of the woman—he couldn't recall her name—and the Secretary of something-or-other from Washington floating in front of him as if in a dream and gazing down at him curiously. "Try it. You'll like it," he heard himself murmuring distantly.

Some part of his mind was aware that he had been thinking clearly only moments before, but he was unable to remember what or really to care why. His mind had stopped functioning as a coherent entity and seemed to have disassembled into separate functions that he could observe in a detached kind of way as they continued to operate as isolated units instead of in concert. It should be troubling him, part of himself told the rest casually, and the rest agreed . . . but it wasn't.

Something was happening to his vision. The view of the

upper part of the cubicle collapsed suddenly into meaningless blurs and smears, and then almost as quickly reassembled itself into an image that swelled, shrank, then faded and finally brightened once again. When it stabilized all the colors were wrong, like those of a false-color, computer-generated display. The colors reversed into complementary tones for a few insane seconds, overcorrected, and then suddenly were normal.

"Excuse these preliminaries," VISAR's voice said from somewhere. At least Hunt thought it was VISAR's; it was barely comprehensible, with the pitch sliding from a shrill whine through several octaves to finish in an almost inaudible rumble. "This process . . ." something completely unintelligible followed, ". . . one time, and after that there will be no . . ." a confusion of telescoped syllables, ". . . will be explained shortly." The last part was free from distortion.

And then Hunt became acutely conscious of the pressure of the recliner against his body, of the touch of his clothes against his skin, and even of the sensation of air flowing through his nostrils as he breathed. His body started to convulse, and he felt a sudden spasm of alarm. Then he realized that he was not moving at all; the impression was due to rapid variations in sensitivity taking place all over his skin. He felt hot all over, then cold, itchy for a moment, prickly for a moment, and then completely numb—and then suddenly normal once more.

Everything was normal. His mind had reintegrated itself, and all his faculties were in order. He wriggled his fingers and found that the invisible gel that had been immersing him was gone. He tried moving an arm, then the other arm; everything was fine.

"Feel free to get up," VISAR said. Hunt climbed slowly to his feet and stepped back into the corridor to find the others emerging and looking as bewildered as he felt. He looked past them at the door blocking the far end, but it was still closed.

"What do you suppose may have been the object of that exercise?" Danchekker asked, for once looking at a loss. Hunt could only shake his head.

And then Lyn's voice sounded from behind him. "Vic." It was just one word, but its ominous tone of warning spun him around instantly. She was staring along the corridor toward the door through which they had entered. He turned his head farther to follow her gaze.

Filling the doorway was the huge frame of a Ganymean, clad in a silvery garment that was halfway between a short cape and a loose jacket, worn over a trousered tunic of dark green. The deep, liquid violet, alien eyes surveyed them for a few seconds from the elongated, protruding face while they watched silently, waiting for a first move. Then the Ganymean announced, "I am Bryom Calazar. You are the people we have been expecting, I see. Please step this way. It's a little too crowded in here for introductions." With that he moved out of sight toward the outer door. Danchekker thrust out his jaw, drew himself up to his full height, and went back into the antechamber after him. After a moment's hesitation Lyn followed.

"This is absurd." Danchekker's voice reached Hunt just as he was stepping through behind Lyn. The statement was uttered in the tone of somebody clinging obstinately to reason and flatly denying that what his senses were reporting could be real. A split second later Lyn gasped, and an instant after that Hunt could see why. He had assumed that Calazar had come from another compartment leading forward from the antechamber, but there was no such compartment. There didn't need to be. The other Ganymeans were outside.

For McClusky Air Force Base, Alaska, and the Arctic had all gone. Instead he was looking out at a completely different world.

Chapter Eight

The plane, starship, or whatever the vessel was no longer stood in the open at all. Hunt found himself staring out at the interior of an enormous enclosed concourse formed by a mind-defying interpenetration of angled planes and flowing surfaces of glowing amber and shades of green. It seemed to be the hub of an intricate, three-dimensional dovetailing of thoroughfares, galleries, and shafts extending away up, down, and at all angles through a conjunction of variously oriented spaces that baffled the senses. He felt as if he had stepped into an Escher drawing as he fought to extract some shred of sense from the contradictions of the same surfaces serving as floors here, walls there, and transforming into roofs overhead elsewhere, while all over the scene dozens of Ganymean figures went unconcernedly about their business, some in inverted subsets of the whole, others perpendicular, with one merging somehow into the other until it was impossible to tell which direction was what. His brain balked and gave up. He couldn't take in any more of it.

A group of about a dozen Ganymeans was standing a short distance back from the doorway, with the one who had introduced himself as Calazar positioned a few feet ahead. They seemed to be waiting. After a few seconds Calazar beckoned. In a complete daze and with his mind only barely able to register what was happening, Hunt felt himself being pulled almost hypnotically through the door and was aware only vaguely that he was stepping out at floor level.

Everything exploded around him. The whole scene burst into a spinning vortex of color that whirled around him on every side to destroy even the sense of orientation of his immediate surroundings that he had retained. The noise of a thousand banshees was crushing him. He was trapped inside a shrieking avalanche of light.

The vortex became a spinning tunnel into which he was hurtling helplessly at increasing speed. Shapes of light hurled themselves out of the formlessness ahead and exploded away into fragments only inches from his face. Never in his life had he known true panic, but it was there, clawing and tearing, paralyzing any ability to think. He was in a nightmare that he could neither control nor wake up from.

A black void opened up at the tunnel end and rushed at him. Suddenly it was calm. The blackness was . . . space. Black, infinite, star-studded space. He was out in space, looking at stars.

No. He was inside somewhere, looking at stars on a large screen. His surroundings were shadowy and indistinct—some kind of control room with vague suggestions of figures around him . . . human figures. He could feel himself shaking and perspiration drenching his clothes, but part of the panic had let go and was allowing his mind to function.

On the screen a bright object was enlarging steadily as it appeared to be approaching from the background of stars. There was something familiar about it. He felt as if he were reliving something he had experienced a long time ago. Part of a large metallic structure loomed in the foreground to one side of the view, highlighted by an eerie reddish glow coming from offscreen. It suggested part of whatever place the view was being captured from—a spacecraft of some kind. He was aboard a spacecraft watching something approaching on a screen, and he had been there before.

The object continued to enlarge, but even before it became recognizable he knew what it was: It was the *Shapieron*. He had gone back almost a year in time and was back inside the command center of *Jupiter Five* watching the arrival of the *Shapieron* as he had been when it first appeared over Ganymede. He had watched this sequence replayed from UNSA's archives many times since then and knew every detail of what was coming next. The ship slowed gradually and maneuvered to come to relative rest standing five miles off in parallel orbit, swinging around to present a side view of the graceful curves of its half-mile length of astronautic engineering.

And then something happened that he was completely unprepared for. Another object, moving fast and blazing white at the tail curved into the screen from one side, passed close by the *Shapieron*'s nose, and exploded in a huge flash a short distance beyond. Hunt stared at it, stunned. That wasn't the way it had happened.

And then a voice sounded from the screen—an American voice, speaking in the clipped tones of the military. "Warning missile launched. Attack salvo primed and locked on target. T-beams being directed in near-miss pattern, and destroyers moving in to take up close-escort formation. Orders are to fire for effect if alien attempts evasion."

Hunt shook his head and looked wildly from side to side, but the shadow figures around him paid no heed to his presence. "No!" he shouted. "It wasn't like that! This is all wrong!" The shadows remained heedless.

On the screen a flotilla of black, sinister-looking vessels moved into view from all directions to take up position around the Ganymean starship. "Alien is responding," the voice announced neutrally. "Commencing descent into parking orbit."

Hunt shouted out again in protest and leaped forward, at the same time wheeling around to appeal for a response from the shadow figures. But they had gone. The command center had gone. All of *Jupiter Five* had gone.

He was looking down on a huddle of metal domes and buildings standing beside a line of Vega ferries amid an icy wilderness that lay naked beneath the stars. It was Main Base on the surface of Ganymede. And on an open area to one side of the complex, dwarfing the Vegas behind, stood the awesome tower of the *Shapieron.* He had advanced by several days and was witnessing again the moment when the ship had just landed.

But instead of the simple but touching welcoming scene that he remembered, he saw a column of forlorn Ganymeans being herded across the ice from their ship between lines of impassive, heavily armed combat troops, under the muzzles of heavy weapons being trained from armored vehicles positioned farther back. And the base itself had acquired defense works, weapons emplacements, missile batteries, and all kinds of things that had never existed. It was insane.

He couldn't tell whether he was inside one of the domes and looking out over the scene as he had been at the time, or whether he was somehow floating disembodied at some other viewpoint. Again his immediate surroundings were indistinct. He swung around, moving in a dreamlike way in which his body had lost its substance, and found that he was alone. Even surrounded by ice and endless empty space he felt clammy and claustrophobic. The terror that had gripped him when he first stepped out of the alien vessel was still there, gnawing insistently and stripping away his powers of reason. "What is this?" he demanded in a voice that choked somewhere at the back of his throat. "I don't understand. What does this mean?"

"You don't remember?" the voice boomed deafeningly from nowhere and everywhere.

Hunt looked wildly in every direction, but there was nobody. "Remember what?" he whispered. "I remember none of this."

"You do not remember these events?" the voice challenged. "You were there."

An anger surged up inside him suddenly—a delayed-action reflex to protect him from the merciless assault on his mind and senses. "*No!*" he shouted. "Not like *that*! They never happened like that. What kind of lunacy is this?"

"How, then, did they happen?"

"They were our friends. They were welcomed. We gave

gifts." His anger boiled over into a quivering rage. "Who are you? Are you mad? Show yourself."

Ganymede vanished, and a series of confused impressions poured by in front of his eyes, which inexplicably his mind assembled together into coherent meaning. There was a vision of the Ganymeans being taken into captivity by a stern and uncompromising American military . . . being allowed to repair their ship only after agreeing to divulge details of their technology . . . being taken to Earth to keep their side of the bargain . . . being dispatched ignominiously back into the depths of space.

"Was it not so?" the voice demanded.

"For Christ's sake, NO! Whoever you are, you're insane!"

"What parts are untrue?"

"All of it. What is the—"

A Soviet newscaster was talking hysterically. Although it was in Russian, Hunt somehow understood. The war had to start now, before the West could turn its advantage into something tangible . . . speeches from a balcony; crowds chanting and cheering . . . launchings of U.S. MIRV satellites . . . propaganda from Washington . . . tanks, missile transporters, marching lines of Chinese infantry . . . high-power radiation weapons hidden in deep space across the solar system. A race that had gone insane was marching off to doomsday with bands playing and flags waving.

"NO-O-O-O!" He heard his own voice rise to a shriek that seemed to come from all sides to engulf him, and then die somewhere far off in the distance. His strength evaporated abruptly, and he felt himself collapsing.

"He speaks the truth," a voice said from somewhere. It was calm and decisive, and sounded like a lone rock of sanity amid the maelstrom of chaos that had swept him out of the universe.

Collapsing . . . falling . . . blackness . . . nothing.

Chapter Nine

Hunt was dozing in what felt like a soft and very comfortable armchair. He was relaxed and refreshed, as if he had been there for some time. The memory of his experience was still vivid, but it lingered only as something that he regarded in a detached, almost academically curious, kind of way. The terror had gone. The air around him smelled fresh and slightly scented, and subdued music was playing in the background. After a few seconds it registered as a Mozart string quartet. What kind of insanity was he part of now?

He opened his eyes, straightened up, and looked around. He was in an armchair, and the chair was part of an ordinary-looking room, furnished in contemporary style with another, similar chair, reading desk, a large wooden table in the center, a side table near the door set with an ornate vase of roses, and a thick carpet of dark brown pile that blended fairly well with the predominantly orange and brown decor. There was a single window behind him, covered by heavy drapes that were closed and billowing gently in the breeze coming through from the outside. He looked down at himself and found that he was wearing a dark blue, open-necked shirt and light gray slacks. There was nobody else in the room.

After a few seconds he got up, found that he felt fine, and strolled across the room to part the drapes curiously. Outside was a pleasant, summery scene that could have been part of any major city on Earth. Tall buildings gleamed clean and white in the sun, familiar trees and open green spaces beckoned, and Hunt could see the curve of a wide river immediately below, an older-style bridge with a railed parapet and rounded arches, familiar models of groundcars moving along the roadways, and processions of airmobiles in the sky. He let the drapes fall back as they had been and glanced at his watch, which seemed to be working normally. Less than twenty minutes had passed since the "Boeing" touched down at McClusky. Nothing made sense.

He turned his back to the window and thrust his hands into his pockets while he thought back and tried to remember something that had been puzzling him even before he stepped out of the spacecraft. It had something trivial, something that had barely registered in the few moments that had elapsed between Calazar's brief appearance inside the craft and Hunt's first glimpse of the stupefying scene that had greeted him outside just before everything went crazy. It had been something to do with Calazar.

And then it came to him. In the *Shapieron*, ZORAC had interpreted between Ganymeans and humans by means of earpiece and throat-mike devices that provided normal-sounding synthesized voices, but which did not synchronize with the facial movements of the original speakers. But Calazar had spoken without any such aids, and apparently quite effortlessly. What made it all the more peculiar was that the Ganymean larynx produced a low, guttural articulation and was utterly incapable of reproducing a human pitch even approximately. So how had Calazar done it, and without looking like a badly dubbed movie at that?

Well, he wasn't going to get nearer any answers by standing here, he decided. The door looked normal enough, and there was only one way to find out whether it was locked or not. He was halfway toward it when it opened and Lyn walked in, looking cool and comfortable in a short-sleeved pullover top and slacks. He stopped dead and stared at her while part of him braced itself instinctively for her to hurl herself across the room and throw her arms around his neck while sobbing in true heroine tradition. Instead she stopped just inside the door and stood casually inspecting the room.

"Not bad," she commented. "The carpet's too dark, though. It should be a more red rust." The carpet promptly changed to a more red rust.

Hunt stared at it for a few seconds, blinked, and then looked up numbly. "How the hell did you do that?" he asked, looking down again to make sure that he hadn't imagined it. He hadn't.

She looked surprised. "It's VISAR. It can do anything. Haven't you been talking to it?" Hunt shook his head. Lyn's face became puzzled. "If you didn't know, how come you're wearing different clothes? What happened to your Nanook outfit?"

Hunt could only shake his head. "I don't know. I don't know how I got here, either." He stared down at the red rust carpet again. "Amazing . . . I think I could use a drink."

"VISAR," Lyn said in a slightly raised voice. "How about a scotch, straight, no ice?" A glass half filled with an amber liquid materialized from nowhere on the table beside Hunt. Lyn picked it up and offered it to him nonchalantly. He reached out hesitantly to touch with it a fingertip, at the same time half hoping that it wouldn't be there. It was. He took the glass unsteadily from her hand and tested it with a sip, then downed a third of the remainder in one gulp. The warmth percolated smoothly down through his chest and after a few moments had worked a small miracle of its own. Hunt drew a long breath, held it for a few seconds, then exhaled it slowly but still shakily.

"Cigarette?" Lyn inquired. Hunt nodded without thinking. A cigarette, already lit, appeared between his fingers. Don't even ask about it, he told himself.

It all had to be some kind of elaborate hallucination. How, when, why, or where he didn't know, but it seemed that he had little choice for the moment but to go along with it. Perhaps this whole preliminary interlude had been staged by the Thuriens to provide a period of adjustment and familiarization or something like that. If so, he could see their point. This was like dumping an alchemist from the Middle Ages into the middle of a computerized chemical plant. Thurien, or wherever this was, was going to take some getting used to, he realized. Having decided that much, he felt that probably he was over the biggest hurdle already. But how had Lyn managed to adapt so quickly? Maybe there were disadvantages to being a scientist that he hadn't thought about before.

When he looked up and studied her face, he could see now that her superficial calm was being forced in order to control an underlying bemusement not far short of his own. Her mind was temporarily blocking itself off from the full impact of what it all meant. He could detect no sign of her having been through anything as traumatic as he had. At least that was something to be thankful for.

He moved over to one of the chairs and turned to perch himself on an arm. "So . . . how did you get here?" he asked.

"Well, I was right behind you on the gravity conveyor, or whatever you'd call it, from that crazy place that we all walked out into from the planet, and then . . ." She broke off as she caught the perplexed expression creeping across Hunt's face. "You don't know what I'm talking about, do you?"

He shook his head. "What gravity conveyor?"

Lyn frowned at him uncertainly. "We all walked out of the plane? . . . There was this big bright place with everything upside down and sideways? . . . Something like whatever lifted us up the stairs picked us all up and took us off along one of the tubes—a big yellow-and-white one? . . ." She was listing the items slowly and intoning them as questions, all the while watching his face intently as if trying to help him identify the point at which he had lost the thread, but it was obvious already that she had experienced something quite different right from the beginning.

He waved a hand in front of his face. "Okay, skip the details. How did you get separated from the others?"

Lyn started to reply and then stopped suddenly and frowned, as if realizing for the first time that her own recollections were by no means as complete as she had thought. "I'm not sure . . ." She hesitated. "Somehow I ended up . . . I don't know where it was. . . . There was this big organization chart—colored boxes with names in them, and lines of who reports to who—that had to do with some crazy kind of United *States* Space *Force*." Her face grew more confused as she replayed the memory in her mind. "There were lots of UNSA names on it that I knew, but with ranks and things that didn't make any sense. Gregg's name was there as a general, and mine was right underneath as a major." She shook her head in a way that told Hunt not to bother asking her to explain it.

Hunt remembered the transcripts he had read of the Thurien messages received at Farside, which had been baffling in their suggestion of a militarized Earth divided in an East-West lineup that was strangely reminiscent of the reconstructions of how Minerva had been—just before the final, cataclysmic Cerian-Lambian war. And the grilling that he had just gone through, if that was the right word for it, had echoed the same theme. There had to be a connection. "What happened then?" he asked.

"VISAR started talking and asked me if that was an accurate representation of the outfit I worked for," Lyn replied. "I told it that most of the names were right, but the rest was garbage. It asked some questions about a couple of weapons programs that Gregg was supposed to be mixed up with. Then it showed me some pictures of a surface-bombardment satellite that this U.S.S.F. was supposed to have put in orbit, and a big radiation projector on the Moon that never existed. I told VISAR it was out of its mind. We talked about it for a bit, and in the end we got quite friendly."

All that hadn't happened in ten minutes, Hunt thought. There must have been some kind of time-compression process involved. "There wasn't anything . . . 'high-pressure' about all this?" he inquired.

Lyn looked at him, surprised. "No way. It was all very civilized and nice. That was when I mentioned that I felt strange wearing those clothes indoors, and suddenly—*zap!*" She gestured down at herself. "Instant outfit. Then I found out more about VISAR's tricks. How long do you think it'll be before IBM gets one on the market?"

Hunt stood up and began pacing across the room, noting absently as he moved that his cigarette didn't seem to be accumulating any ash to be disposed of. It was some kind of interrogation procedure, he decided. The Thuriens had obviously gotten confused over the situation on today's Earth, and for some reason it was important to them to have the correct story. If that was the case, they certainly hadn't wasted any time over it. Perhaps Hunt's experience had been a shock tactic designed to guarantee straight answers at the optimum moment when he had been totally unprepared and too disoriented to have fabricated anything. If so, it had certainly worked, he reflected grimly.

"After that I asked where you were. VISAR directed me out through a door and along a corridor, and here I am," Lyn completed.

Hunt was about to say something more when the phone rang. He looked around and noticed it for the first time. It was a standard domestic datagrid terminal and went so naturally with the surroundings that it hadn't registered previously. The call-tone sounded again.

"Better answer it," Lyn suggested.

Hunt walked over to the corner, pulled up a chair, sat down, and touched a key on the terminal to accept. His jaw dropped open in disbelief as he found himself staring at the features of the operations controller at McClusky.

"Dr. Hunt," the controller said, sounding relieved. "Just a routine check to see if everything's okay. You people have been in there for a while now. Any problems?"

For what seemed a long time, Hunt could only stare back blankly. He'd never heard of phone calls from the real world intruding into hallucinations before. It had to be part of the hallucination too. What was somebody supposed to say to hallucinatory operations controllers? "How are you talking to us?" he managed at last, succeeding with some effort in making his voice almost normal.

"We got a transmission from the plane a while ago saying it would be okay for us to use a low-power, narrow beam aimed straight at it," the controller replied. "We set it up and waited, but when nothing came through we thought we'd better try calling you."

Hunt closed his eyes for a moment, then opened them again and glanced sideways at Lyn. She didn't understand it, either. "Are you saying that plane is still out there?" he asked, looking back at the screen.

The controller looked puzzled. "Why . . . sure . . . I'm looking right at it out the window." Pause. "Are you sure everything's okay in there?"

Hunt sat back woodenly, and his mind jammed up. Lyn stepped past him and stooped in front of the screen. "Everything's okay," she said. "Look, we're a bit busy right now. Call you back in a few minutes, okay?"

"Just as long as we know. Okay, talk to you later." The controller vanished from the screen.

Lyn's composure evaporated with the picture. She looked down at Hunt, visibly worried and frightened for the first time since entering the room. "It's still out there. . . ." Her voice was coming unevenly as she struggled to keep it under control. "Vic—what's happening?"

Hunt scowled around the room as the indignation that he had been suppressing at last came surging up inside. "VISAR," he called on impulse. "Can you hear me?"

"I'm here," the familiar voice answered.

"That plane that landed at McClusky—it's still there. We just talked to them on the phone."

"I know," VISAR agreed. "I put the call through."

"Isn't it about time you told us what the hell's going on?"

"The Thuriens were intending to explain it when you meet them very shortly," VISAR replied. "You are due an apology, and they want to make it to you personally, not second-hand through me."

"Then would you mind telling us where the hell we are?" Hunt said, not feeling very mollified by the statement.

"Sure. You're in the *perceptron*, which as you've just told me is still on the apron at McClusky." Hunt caught Lyn's eye in a mute exchange of baffled looks. She shook her head weakly and sank down into one of the chairs. "You don't look very convinced," VISAR commented. "A small demonstration, perhaps?"

Hunt felt his mouth opening and closing, and heard sounds coming out. But he wasn't making it happen. He was moving like a puppet to the pulls of invisible strings. "Excuse me," his mouth said as his head turned itself toward Lyn. "Don't worry about this—VISAR will explain. I'll be back in a few minutes."

And then he was lying back on something yielding and soft.

"*Voila!*" VISAR's voice pronounced from somewhere overhead.

He opened his eyes and looked around, but a few seconds went by before he realized where he was.

He was back in the recliner inside one of the cubicles in the ship that had landed at McClusky.

Everything seemed very quiet and still. He rose to his feet and moved out into the corridor to peer into the adjacent cubicle. Lyn was still there, lying back in the recliner looking relaxed, her eyes closed and her face serene. He looked down and noticed for the first time that, like her, he was wearing UNSA arctic clothing again. He moved along to inspect the other cubicles and found all the others were there too, looking much the same.

"Take a walk outside and check it out," VISAR's voice suggested. "We'll still be here when you get back."

Hunt made his way to the door at the forward end of the corridor, stopped for a moment and braced himself for anything, and stepped through into the antechamber. McClusky and Alaska were back again. Through the open outer door he could see figures stirring and starting to move forward as they saw him. He moved toward the door, and seconds later was on his feet at the bottom of the access stairway. The figures converged around him, and excited questions assailed him from all sides as he began walking across the apron toward the mess hall.

"What's happening in there?"

"Are there Ganymeans inside?"

"Are they coming out?"

"How many of them are there?"

"Just . . . talking so far. What? Yes . . . well, sort of. I'm not sure. Look, give me a few minutes. I need to check something."

Inside the mess hall he made straight for the control room, set up in one of the front rooms. The controller and his two operators had watched Hunt through the window that looked out across the apron and were waiting expectantly. "Vic, how's it going?" the controller greeted as he came in the door.

"Fine," Hunt murmured absently. He stared hard at the consoles and screens set up around the room and forced his mind to go back over what had happened since they entered the craft. What he was seeing right now was real. Everything around him was real. The phone call had been part of something that hadn't been real. Obviously it couldn't have worked the other way around; reality couldn't communicate into the realm of the hallucinatory via radio. Obviously?

"Have you had any contact from that plane since we went inside?" he asked, turning to glance at the control-room crew.

"Why . . . yes." The controller looked suddenly worried. "You talked to us yourself a few minutes ago. You're sure everything's . . . all right?"

Hunt brought a hand up to massage his brow and give the confusion boiling inside his head time to die down a little. "How did you get through?" he asked.

"We got a signal from it earlier telling us we could couple in via a low-power beam, like I told you. I just asked for you by name."

"Do it again," Hunt said.

The controller moved in front of the supervisory console, tapped a command, and spoke toward the two-way audio grille above the main screen. "McClusky Control to alien. Alien vessel, come in please."

"Acknowledged," a voice answered.

"VISAR?" Hunt said, recognizing it.

"Hi again. Convinced now?"

Hunt's eyes narrowed thoughtfully as he stared at the blank screen. At last the wheels of his brain felt as if they were sorting themselves out and lining themselves up on the right axles again. There was one obvious thing for him to try. "Put me through to Lyn Garland," he said.

"One moment."

The screen came to life, and a second later Lyn was looking out at him, framed by the background of the room he had recently been in. It must have been equally clear that Hunt was calling from McClusky, but her face did not register undue surprise. VISAR must have been doing some explaining.

"You sure get around," she commented drily.

A shadow of a smile formed on Hunt's face as the first glimmer of light began showing through it all. "Hi," he said. "Question: What happened after I last talked to you?"

"You vanished into thin air—just like that. It gave me a bit of a fright, but VISAR's been straightening me out about a lot of things." She held up a hand and wriggled her fingers in front of her face, at the same time shaking her head wonderingly. "I can't believe I'm not really doing this. It's all happening inside my head? It's incredible!"

Right at that moment she probably knew more about what was going on than he did, Hunt reflected. But he thought he had the general idea now. An instant communications link to Thurien . . . miracles worked to order . . . Ganymeans talking in English. . . . And what had VISAR called that vessel—the *perceptron*? The pieces started dropping into place.

"Just keep talking to VISAR," he said. "I'll be back in a few minutes." Lyn smiled the kind of smile that said she knew everything would work out okay; Hunt winked, then cut off the screen.

"Would you mind telling us what's going on?" the controller asked. "I mean . . . we're only supposed to be running this operation."

"Just give me a second," Hunt said, entering the code to reactivate the channel. He turned his face toward the grille. "VISAR?"

"You rang?"

"That place we walked out of the perceptron into—does it exist, or did you invent it?"

"It exists. It's part of a place called Vranix, which is an old city on Thurien."

"Did we see it the way it is right now?"

"Yes, you did."

"So you have to be relaying instantly between here and Thurien."

"You're getting the idea."

Hunt thought for a second. "What about the room with the carpet?"

"I invented that. A special effect—faked. We thought that maybe some familiar-looking surroundings would help you get used to how we do things. Figured the rest out yet?"

"I'll try a long shot," Hunt said. "How about total sensory stimulation and monitoring, plus an instant communications link. We never went to Thurien; you brought Thurien here. And Lyn never answered any phone call. You pumped it straight into her nervous system along with everything else she thinks she's doing, and you manufactured all the appropriate AV data to send through the local beam. How's that?"

"Pretty good," VISAR replied, managing to inject a strong note of approval into its voice. "So are you ready to rejoin the party? You're due to meet the Thuriens in a few minutes."

"I'll talk to you later," Hunt said, and cut the connection.

"Now would you mind telling us what the hell this is all about?" the controller invited.

Hunt's expression was distant, his voice slow and thoughtful. "That's just a flying phone booth out there on the apron. It's got equipment inside that somehow couples directly into the perceptual parts of the nervous system and transfers a total impression from a remote place. What you saw on the screen a minute ago was extracted straight out of Lyn's mind. A computer translated it into audiovisual modulations on a signal beam and directed it into your antenna. It processed the transmission from here in the opposite direction."

Ten minutes later Hunt reentered the perceptron and sat

down in the same recliner that he had occupied before. "What do I say—'Home, James'?" he asked aloud.

This time there were no preliminary sensory disturbances. He was instantly back in the room with Lyn, who seemed to have been expecting him to reappear; VISAR had evidently forewarned her. He looked around the room curiously to see if he could detect any hint of its being a creation manufactured by a computer, but there was nothing. Every detail was authentic. It was uncanny. As with VISAR's command of English and the data needed to disguise the perceptron as a Boeing, all the information must have been extracted from Earth's communications links; practically everything necessary had been communicated electronically from somewhere at some time or another. No wonder the Thuriens had been particular about keeping everything connected with this business out of the network!

He reached out and ran a finger experimentally down Lyn's arm. It felt warm and solid. The whole thing was exactly what he had said to VISAR—a *total* sensory stimulation process, probably acting on the brain centers directly and bypassing the neural inputs. It was astounding.

Lyn glanced down at his hand, then looked up and eyed him suspiciously. "I don't know if it's that authentic, either," she told him. "And right now I'm not that curious. Forget it."

Before Hunt could reply, the phone rang again. He answered it. It was Danchekker, looking ready to commit mayhem.

"This is monstrous! Outrageous!" The veins at his temples were throbbing visibly. "Have you any idea of the provocation to which I have been subjected? Where are you in this computerized lunatic asylum? What kind of—"

"Hold it, Chris. Calm down." Hunt held up a hand. "It's not as bad as you think. All that's—"

"*Not as bad?* Where in God's name are we? How do we get out of it? Have you talked to the others? By what right do these alien creatures presume to—"

"You're not anywhere, Chris. You're still on the ground at McClusky. So am I. We all are. What's happened is—"

"Don't be preposterous! It's quite evident that—"

"Have you talked to VISAR? It'll explain it all far better than I can. Lyn's with me and—"

"No I have not, and what's more I have no intention of doing anything of the kind. If these Thuriens do not possess the common courtesy to—"

Hunt sighed. "VISAR, take the professor home and straighten him out, could you. I don't think I'm up to dealing with him right now."

"I'll handle it," VISAR replied, and Danchekker promptly vanished from the screen leaving an empty room in the frame.

"Amazing," Hunt murmured. There were times, he thought, when he would have liked to be able to pull that stunt with Danchekker himself.

A knock sounded lightly on the door. Hunt and Lyn's heads jerked around to look at it, turned back to meet each other's questioning looks, then stared at the door again. Lyn shrugged and moved across the room toward it. Hunt switched off the terminal and looked up to find the eight-foot-tall figure of a Ganymean straightening up after ducking through the doorway. Lyn stood speechless with surprise as she held the door open.

"Dr. Hunt and Miss Garland," the Ganymean said. "First, on behalf of all of us, I apologize for the somewhat bizarre welcome. It was necessary for some very important reasons, which will be explained when we all get together very shortly. I hope that our leaving you on your own like this hasn't seemed too bad-mannered, but we thought that perhaps a short period of adjustment might be beneficial. I am Porthik Eesyan—one of those you were expecting to meet."

Chapter Ten

Eesyan was subtly different in form from the Ganymeans of the *Shapieron*, Hunt noticed as they walked. He had the same massive torso lines beneath his loose-fitting yellow jerkin and elaborately woven shirt of red and amber metallic threads, and the same six-fingered hands, each with two thumbs, but his skin was darker than the grays that Hunt remembered—almost black—and seemed smoother in texture; his build was lighter and more slender, his height slightly less than would have been normal, and his lower face and skull, though still elongated significantly, had receded and broadened into a more rounded head that was closer to the human profile.

"We can move objects from place to place instantaneously by means of artificially generated spinning black holes," Eesyan told them. "As your own theories predict, a rapidly spinning black hole flattens out into a disk, and eventually becomes a toroid with the mass concentrated at the rim. In that situation the singularity exists across the central aperture and can be approached axially without catastrophic tidal effects. The aperture affords an 'entry port' into a hyperrealm described by laws

95

not subject to the conventional restrictions of ordinary space-time. Creating such an entry port also gives rise to a hypersymmetric effect that appears as a projection elsewhere in normal space, and which functions as a coupled exit port. By controlling the dimensions, spin, orientation, and certain other parameters of the initial hole, we can select with considerable accuracy the location of the exit up to distances in the order of several tens of light-years."

With Eesyan between Vic and Lyn, they were walking along a broad, enclosed, brightly illuminated arcade of soaring lines, gleaming sculptures, and vast openings, which led into other spaces. There were more Escher-like distortions and inversions here and there in the scene, but nothing as overwhelming as the sight they had first seen from the perceptron. Apparently Ganymean gravitic engineering tricks came with the architecture on Thurien. For this was Thurien. They had emerged from the room and walked through a series of galleries and a huge domed space bustling with Ganymeans, eventually to this place, the illusory blending so smoothly into reality that Hunt had missed the point along the way at which the switch from one to the other had taken place. The meeting between the two worlds was about to take place, Eesyan had informed them, and he had been assigned to escort them there personally. No doubt VISAR could have transferred them there instantly, Hunt thought, but this seemed a more natural way while they were still "acclimatizing." And having an opportunity to get to know at least one of the aliens informally in advance helped the process further. Probably that was the idea.

"That must be how you got the perceptron to Earth," Hunt said.

"Almost to Earth," Eesyan told him. "A black hole large enough to take a sizable object creates a significant gravitational disturbance over a large distance. Therefore we don't project things like that into the middle of planetary systems; it would disrupt clocks and calendars and so on. We exited the perceptron outside the Solar System, and it had to make the last lap in a more conventional way."

"So a round trip needs four conventional stages," Lyn commented. "Two one way, and two the other?"

"Correct."

"Which explains why it took something like a day to make it from Thurien to Earth," Hunt said.

"Yes. Instant planet-to-planet hopping is out. But *communications* is another matter entirely. We can send messages by beaming a gamma frequency microlaser into a microscopic black-hole toroid that can be generated in equipment capable of operating on planetary surfaces without undesirable side effects. So instant planet-to-planet datalinks are practicable. What's more, generating the microscopic black holes needed for them doesn't require the enormous amount of energy that holes big enough to send ships through do. So we don't do a lot of instantaneous people-moving unless we have to; we prefer moving *information* instead."

It fitted in with what Hunt already knew: he and Lyn were really at McClusky, and all the information they were perceiving was being transmitted there through VISAR. "That explains how the information gets sent," he said. "But what's the input to the system? How is it originated in the first place?"

"Thurien is a fully 'wired' planet," Eesyan explained. "So are most of the other planets in the portions of the Galaxy where we have spread. VISAR exists all over those worlds, and in other places between, as a dense network of sensors located inside the structures of buildings and cities, distributed invisibly across mountains, forests, and plains, and in orbit above planetary surfaces. By combining and interpolating between its data inputs, it is able to compute and synthesize the complete sensory input that would be experienced by a person located at any particular place.

"VISAR bypasses the normal input channels to the brain and stimulates symbolic neural patterns directly with focused arrays of high-resolution spatial stress-waves. Thus it can inject straight into the mind all the information that would be received by somebody physically present at whatever place is specified. Also it monitors the neural activity of the voluntary motor system and reproduces faithfully all the feedback sensations that would accompany muscular movements and so forth. The net result is to create an illusion of actually being at a remote location which is indistinguishable from the real thing. Physically transporting the body would add nothing."

"Star travel the easy way," Lyn murmured. She gazed around as they came to the end of the arcade and turned off to begin walking across a curved, sweeping surface that had looked like a wall a minute ago, but now seemed to be pivoting slowly as they moved onto it and lifting the whole of the arcade and the structures connected to it up at an increasing angle behind them. "This is all real and twenty light-years away?" she said, still sounding disbelieving. "I really haven't come here?"

"Can you tell the difference?" Eesyan asked her.

"How about you, Porthik?" Hunt asked as a new thought struck him. "Are you actually here . . . there . . . whatever, in Vranix, or what?"

"I'm on an artificial world twenty million miles from Thurien," Eesyan replied. "Calazar is on Thurien, but six thousand miles from Vranix at a place called Thurios—the principal city of Thurien. Vranix is an old city that we keep preserved for sentimental and traditional reasons. Frenua Showm, whom you were also expecting to meet and will very shortly, is on a planet called *Crayses*, which is in a star system about nine light-years from Gistar."

Lyn was looking puzzled. "I'm not quite sure I get this," she said. "How do we all manage to get consistent impressions when we're in different places? How do I see you there, Vic next to you, and all this around us when it's scattered all over the Galaxy?" Hunt was still too boggled by what Eesyan had said a moment earlier to be able to ask anything.

"VISAR manufactures composite impressions from data originated in different places and delivers them as a total package," Eesyan replied. "It can combine visual, tactile, audile, and other details of an environment with data synthesized from monitoring the neural activity of other persons linked into the system, and provide each individual with a complete, personalized impression of being in that environment and interacting physically and verbally with the others. Hence we can visit other worlds, travel among other cultures, convene for meetings in other star systems, and make visits to artificial worlds out in space . . . and be home in an instant. We do move around physically to some degree, of course, for example in recreation or for activities that require physical presence, but for the most part our long-range business and travel is conducted via electronics and gravitics."

The surface continued curving over and brought them out into a wide circular gallery that looked down over a railed parapet on a fairly busy plaza of some kind a level below. Between the flowing curves and surfaces enclosing the space from above, they could see part of the floor of the arcade that they had been walking along a few minutes earlier. At least, it had seemed like a floor at the time. But by now they were beginning to get used to that kind of thing.

"When we first sat down inside that planet at McClusky, all my senses went haywire for a while," Lyn said as she thought back. "What was that all about?"

"VISAR tuning in to your personal cerebral patterns and activity levels," Eesyan told her. "It was making adjustments until it obtained correct feedback responses. They vary somewhat from individual to individual. The process is a one-time thing. You could think of it as somewhat like fingerprinting."

"Porthik," Hunt said after they had continued for some distance in silence. "That stunt you pulled on me right at the beginning—you've been getting some mixed-up stories about Earth, and you needed to check them out. Right?"

"It was extremely important, as Calazar will explain," Eesyan answered.

"But was it necessary?" Hunt queried. "If VISAR can access neural patterns directly, why couldn't it have simply pulled whatever it wanted to know straight out of my memory? That way there wouldn't have been any risk of wrong answers."

"Technically that would be possible," Eesyan agreed. "However, for reasons of privacy such things are not permitted under our laws. VISAR is programmed in a way that restricts it to supplying primary sensory inputs to the brain and monitoring motor and certain other terminal outputs only. It communicates only what would be seen, heard, felt, and so on; it does not read minds."

"How about the others?" Hunt inquired. "Do you have any idea how they're getting along? I wouldn't exactly recommend your welcoming ceremonies as the best way of making friends."

Eesyan's mouth puckered in the way that Hunt had long ago recognized as the Ganymean equivalent of a smile. "You needn't worry. They haven't all been getting to the bottom of VISAR as quickly as you did, so some of them are still a little confused, but apart from that they're fine."

The confusion had been intentional, Hunt realized suddenly. It was a deliberate measure calculated to defuse any animosity left lingering as a result of the initial shock tactics. Eesyan's showing up to escort them to wherever they were going was no doubt part of the plan too. "It didn't seem quite like that when I talked to Chris Danchekker on the phone a few minutes before you arrived," he said, grinning to himself as he caught the expression on Lyn's face.

"As a matter of fact, you and Professor Danchekker did have comparatively hard rides," Eesyan admitted. "We're sorry about that, but the two of you were unique in that you both possessed firsthand knowledge of certain events connected with the *Shapieron* that we were particularly anxious to obtain. The experiences of your companions were more in the nature of discussions concerning their various specialized fields. Their accounts corroborated one another's perfectly. It was very illuminating."

"What happened with you and Chris?" Lyn asked, looking across at Hunt.

"I'll tell you about it later," he replied. What they did might have been unconventional, but it had certainly worked, he told himself. In those first few minutes the Ganymeans had obtained and verified more information than they could have in days of talking. If it was that important, he could hardly blame them after the way they had been messed around by the UN at Farside. He wondered if Caldwell and the others saw things the same way. It wouldn't be long before he found out, he saw as he looked ahead of them. They seemed to have arrived at their destination.

They were walking down a shallow, fan-shaped ramp that was taking them through a final arch out into the open. They emerged into a descending arrangement of interlocking geometric forms, terraces, and esplanades that formed one side of a large circular layout echoing the same theme. The lowermost, central part, directly ahead of them, consisted of a forum of seats set in tiers and facing one another from all four sides of a rectangular floor. The whole place was a vast composition of color and form set among pools of liquid fluorescence fed by slow-motion rivers and fountains of shimmering light. A number of figures were assembled on three sides of the floor, all Ganymean. They were standing and seemed to be waiting. At the front and in the center of a raised section of seats on one side was Calazar, recognizable by his dark green tunic and silvery cape.

And then Hunt saw Caldwell's stocky frame emerge from another entrance on the far side of an open area to his right, accompanied by a Ganymean . . . and beyond Caldwell, Heller and Packard appeared with another Ganymean, Heller walking calmly and with assurance, Packard staring from side to side and looking bewildered. Hunt turned his head the other way in time to see Danchekker walking through an archway, waving his arms and remonstrating to a Ganymean on either side; evidently it was taking two of them to handle him. The arrivals had been synchronized perfectly. It couldn't have been accidental.

Suddenly Lyn gasped and stopped, her face raised to stare at something overhead. Hunt followed her gaze . . . and stopped . . . then gasped.

From three sides beyond the raised rim of the place they were in, three slim spires of pink ivory converged upward above their heads for an inestimable distance before blending into an inverted cascade of terraces and ramparts that broadened and unfolded upward and away for what must have been miles. Above it—it didn't make sense, but above it, where the sky should have been, the scene mushroomed out into a mind-defying fusion of structures of staggering dimensions that marched away as far as the eye could see in one direction, and fringed a distant ocean in the other. It had to be the city of Vranix. But it was all hanging miles over their heads and upside down.

And then the realization hit him. They had walked out into the sky. The three pink spires "rising" from around them in fact surmounted an enormous tower that projected upward from the city, supporting a circular platform that held the place they were in. But they had come out on the *underside* of it! Their senses had become sufficiently disoriented in the Ganymean labyrinth for them to have inverted without realizing it, and they had walked outside in some locally generated gravity effect to find themselves gazing down over the surface of Thurien stretching away over their heads.

Caldwell and the others had seen it too, and were just standing, staring. Even Danchekker had stopped talking and was looking upward, his mouth hanging half open. It was the Ganymeans' final trump card and master stroke, Hunt realized. Even if any of his companions had been harboring any lingering resentments, they would be too overwhelmed by this—timed precisely to hit them minutes before the meeting was due to begin—to protest very strongly. He liked these aliens, he decided, strange though the thought seemed in some ways at that particular moment. He always enjoyed seeing professionals in action.

One by one the dazed figures of the Terrans came slowly back to life and began moving again, down toward the central forum where the Ganymeans were waiting.

Chapter Eleven

"We owe you an apology," Calazar said bluntly as soon as the introductions had been completed. "I know that's not supposed to be the best way of starting a meeting by Earth's customs, but I've never really understood why. If it needs saying, let's say it and get it out of the way. As you no doubt appreciate by now, we needed to check some facts that are important to us, and to you too I would imagine. It seems just as well that we did." It was going to be a far less formal affair than he had been half prepared for, Hunt noted with relief. He wondered if what he was nearing was an accurate translation of Calazar's words or a liberal interpretation concocted by VISAR. He had assumed that an opening on this note would be unavoidable, and was ready for some fireworks there and then. But as he looked around he could see that the Ganymean defusing tactics appeared to be having their desired effect. Caldwell and Heller seemed in command of themselves and were looking purposeful as if by no means ready to let the matter just go at that, but at the same time they were subdued sufficiently to wait and see what developed before making an issue out of anything. Danchekker had obviously come in spoiling for a fight, but the psychological left hook that the Ganymeans had delivered out of the blue—literally—at the last moment had temporarily knocked it out of him. Packard appeared to be in some kind of trance; in his case the tranquilizer had, perhaps, worked too well.

After pausing, Calazar continued, "On behalf of our entire race, we welcome you to our world and to our society. The threads that have traced the evolution of our two kinds, and which have remained separated until now, have at last crossed. We hope that from this point on they will continue to remain entwined for the benefit and greater learning of all of us." With that he sat down. It was simple, Hunt thought, and seemed a good way of getting things moving.

The Terran faces turned toward Packard, who was officially the most senior in rank and therefore the designated spokesman. It took him a few seconds to realize that the others were looking at him. Then he looked uncertainly from side to side, gripped the sides of his chair, moistened his lips, and rose slowly and somewhat unsteadily to his feet. "On behalf of the . . . government of . . ." The words dried up. He stood swaying slightly and staring dumbstruck at the rows of alien countenances arrayed before him, and then raised his head and shook it disbelievingly at the spectacle of the tower falling away into the metropolis of Vranix and the panorama of Thurien stretching off on every side beyond. For an instant Hunt thought he was going to collapse. And then he vanished.

"I regret that the Secretary of State appears to be temporarily indisposed," VISAR informed the assembly.

That was enough to break the spell. At once Caldwell was on his feet, his eyes steely and his mouth clamped in a downturned line. Heller had also started to rise, but she checked herself and sank back into her seat as Caldwell beat her to it by a split second. "This has gone too far," Caldwell grated, fixing his eyes on Calazar. "Save the niceties. We came here in good faith. You owe us an explanation."

Instantly everything changed. The forum, the tower, Vranix, and the overhead canopy of Thurien were gone. Instead they were all indoors in a fairly large but not huge room with a

domed ceiling, which contained a wide, circular table of irides-
cent crystal and a centerpiece. The principal participants were
placed around it in the same relative positions as before with
Caldwell still standing; the other Ganymeans who had been
present earlier were looking on from raised seats behind. Compared to the previous setting this one felt protective and secure.

"We underestimated the impact," Calazar said hastily. "Perhaps this will be closer to what you are used to."

"Never mind the Alice-in-Wonderland effects," Caldwell
said. "Okay, you've made your point—we're impressed. But
we came here at your request and somebody just flipped out
as a consequence. We don't find it amusing."

"That was not intentional," Calazar replied. "We have
already expressed our regrets. Your colleague will be back to
normal very soon."

The exchange did not have the connotations that it would
have if this confrontation were taking place on Earth, Hunt
knew as he listened. Because of their origins Ganymeans simply
didn't seek to intimidate nor did they respond to intimidation.
They didn't think that way. Calazar was simply stating the facts
of the matter, no more and no less. The standards and conditioning of human culture did not apply to this situation.
Caldwell knew it too, but somebody had to be seen to set the
limits.

"So let's get down to some straight questions and answer,"
Caldwell said. "You said that our two races have evolved sepa-
rately until now. That's not entirely true—the two lines come
together a long way back in the past. Since the story you've
been getting about us seems to have become confused somewhere, it might help clear up a lot of uncertainty and save us
some time if I sum up what we already know." Without waiting
for a response he went on, "We know that your civilization
existed on Minerva until around twenty-five million years ago,
that you shipped a lot of terrestrial life there, possibly to attempt
a genetic-engineering solution to the environmental problems,
and that the Lunarians evolved from ancestors included among
them after you left. We also know about the Lunarian war of
fifty thousand years ago, about the Moon being captured by

Earth, and about ourselves having descended from Lunarian survivors that came with it. Are we talking the same language so far?"

A ripple of murmurings broke out among the Ganymeans. They seemed surprised. Evidently the Terrans knew a lot more than they had expected. That could put an interesting new perspective on things, Hunt thought.

Frenua Showm, the female ambassador of Thurien, who had been introduced at the commencement of the proceedings, replied. "If you already know about the Lunarians, you shouldn't have any difficulty in finding the answer to one of the questions that you have no doubt been asking," she said. "Earth has been under surveillance because of our concern that it might go the way of its Lunarian ancestors and become a technically advanced, belligerent planet. The Lunarians destroyed themselves before they spilled out of the Solar System. Earth might not have. In other words we saw in Earth a potential threat to the other parts of the Galaxy, and perhaps, one day, to all of it." Showm gave the impression that she was far from convinced, even now, that it wasn't so. Definitely not a Terranophile, Hunt decided. The reason did not come as a surprise. With the Ganymeans being the way they were and the Lunarians having been the way they had, it had to be something like that.

"So why all the secrecy?" Heller asked from beside Caldwell. Caldwell sat down to allow her to take it from there. "You claim to represent the Thurien race, yet it's obvious that you don't speak for everybody. You don't want this dialogue brought to the attention of whoever is responsible for the surveillance. So are you what you say you are? If so, why do you need to conceal your actions from your own people?"

"The surveillance is operated by an autonomous . . . shall we say, 'organization' within our system," Calazar replied. "We had reason to suspect the accuracy of some of the information being reported. It became necessary for us to verify it . . . but discreetly, in case we were wrong."

"Suspect the accuracy!" Hunt repeated, spreading his hands in an imploring gesture around the table. "You're making it sound like just a minor aberration here and there. Christ . . . they didn't even tell you that the *Shapieron* had returned and was on Earth at all—your own ship with your own people in it! And the picture you got of Earth wasn't just inaccurate; it was systematically distorted. So what the hell's been going on?"

"That is an internal affair of Thurien that we will now be in a position to do something about," Calazar assured him. He seemed a little off balance, perhaps as a result of his having been unprepared for the Terrans knowing as much as Caldwell had revealed.

"It's not just an internal affair," Heller insisted. "It concerns our whole planet. We want to know who's been misrepresenting us, and why."

"We don't know why," Calazar told her simply. "That's what we're trying to find out. The first step was to get our facts straight. My apologies again, but I think we have now achieved that."

Caldwell was scowling. "Maybe you ought to let us talk to this 'organization' direct," he rumbled. "We'll find out why."

"That's not possible," Calazar said.

"Why?" Heller asked him. "Surely we've got a legitimate interest in all this. You've carried out your discreet checking of facts now, and you've got your answers. If you in fact represent this planet, what's to stop you acting accordingly?"

"Are you in a position to make such demands?" Showm challenged. "If our interpretation of the situation is correct, you do not constitute an officially representative group of the whole of Earth's society, either. That function surely belongs rightfully to the United Nations, does it not?"

"We've been communicating with them for weeks," Calazar said, taking Showm's point. "They have done nothing to dispel any wrong impressions of Earth that we may have, and they seem disinclined to meet us. But your transmissions were directed from another part of the Solar System entirely, suggesting perhaps that you did not wish our replies to become general knowledge, and therefore that you are equally concerned with preserving secrecy."

"What is the reason for the UN's curious attitude?" Showm

asked, looking from one to another of the Terrans and allowing her eyes to rest finally on Heller.

Heller sighed wearily. "I don't know," she admitted. "Perhaps they're wary of the possible consequences of colliding with an advanced alien culture."

"And so it might be with some of our own race," Calazar said. It seemed unlikely since Earth was hardly advanced by Thurien standards, but strange things were possible, Hunt supposed.

"So maybe we should insist on talking to that organization directly," Showm suggested pointedly. There was no response to that.

There was still something Hunt didn't understand when he sat back and tried to reconstruct in his mind the probable sequence of events as the Thuriens would have perceived them. For some time they had been building up a picture of a belligerent and militarized Earth from the accounts forwarded by the mysterious "organization," none of which had mentioned the *Shapieron.* Then a signal, coded in Ganymean, had suddenly come in direct to Calazar's side of the operation, advising that the ship was on its way home. After that, the further transmissions from Farside would have accumulated to hint of an Earth significantly different from that which the surveillance reports had described. But why had it been so important for the Thuriens to establish which version was correct? The measures that they had employed to find out said very clearly that the issue had been taken much more seriously than could be explained by mere academic curiosity or the need to straighten out some internal management problems.

"Let's start at the beginning with this relay device—or whatever you'd call it—that you've got outside the Solar System," he suggested when he had that much clear in his head.

"It's not ours," Eesyan said at once from his position next to Calazar, opposite Showm. "We don't know what it is, either. You see, we didn't put it there."

"But you must have," Hunt protested. "It uses your instant communications technology. It responded to Ganymean protocols."

"Nevertheless it's a mystery," Eesyan replied. "Our guess is that it must be a piece of surveillance hardware, not operated by us but by the organization responsible for that activity, which malfunctioned in some way and routed the signal through to our equipment instead of to its intended destination."

"But you replied to it," Hunt pointed out.

"At the time we were under the impression it was from the *Shapieron* itself," Calazar answered. "Our immediate concern was to let its people know that their message had been received, that they had correctly identified Gistar, and that they were heading for the right place." Hunt nodded. He would have done the same thing.

Caldwell frowned in a way that said he still wasn't clear about something. "Okay, but getting back to this relay—why didn't you find out what it was? You can send stuff from Thurien to Earth in a day. Why couldn't you send something to check it out?"

"If it was a piece of surveillance hardware that had gone faulty and given us a direct line, we didn't want to draw attention to it," Eesyan replied. "We were getting some interesting information through it."

"You didn't want this—'organization' to know about it?" Heller queried, looking puzzled.

"Correct."

"But they already knew about it. The reply from Gistar was all over Earth's newsgrid. They must have known about it if they run the surveillance."

"But they weren't picking up *your* signals to the relay," Eesyan said. "We would have known if they were." Suddenly Hunt realized why Gistar hadn't responded to the Farside transmissions that had continued for months after the *Shapieron*'s departure: the Thuriens didn't want to reveal their direct line via Earth's news network. That fitted in with their insistence on nothing being communicated via the net when at last they had elected to reopen the dialogue.

Heller paused for a moment and brought her hand up to her brow while she collected her thoughts. "But they couldn't have left it at that," she said, looking up. "From what they had picked up out of the newsgrid, they would have known that you knew about the *Shapieron*—something they hadn't been telling you about. They couldn't have just done nothing . . . not without arousing suspicion. They'd have to tell you about it at that point, because they knew if they didn't you'd be going to them and asking some awkward questions."

"Which is exactly what they did," Calazar confirmed.

"So didn't you ask them why they hadn't gotten around to it earlier?" Caldwell asked. "I mean—hell, the ship had been there for six months."

"Yes, we did," Calazar replied. "The reason they gave was that they were concerned for the *Shapieron's* safety, and feared that attempts to interfere with the situation might only jeopardize it further. Rightly or wrongly, they had come to the decision that it would be better for us to know only after it was out of the Solar System."

Caldwell snorted, obviously not impressed by the mysterious "organization's" excuse. "Didn't you ask to see the records they had acquired through their surveillance?"

"We did," Caldwell answered. "And they produced ones that had every appearance of justifying their fears for the *Shapieron* completely."

Now Hunt knew where the phony depictions that he had witnessed of the *Shapieron's* arrival at Ganymede had come from: the "organization" had faked them just as they had been faking their reports of Earth all along. Those were the versions that Calazar's people had been shown. If those scenes with their frighteningly authentic blending of reality and fantasy were typical of what had been going on, it was no wonder that the deception had gone unsuspected for years.

"I've seen some of those records," Hunt said. He sounded incredulous. "How did you ever come to suspect that they might not be genuine? They're unbelievable."

"We didn't," Eesyan told him. "VISAR did. As you may be aware, the drive method of the *Shapieron* creates a space-time deformation around the ship. It is most pronounced when main drive is operating, but exists to some extent even under auxiliary drive—sufficient to displace the apparent positions of background stars close to the vessel's outline by a measurable amount. VISAR noticed that the predicted displacements were present in some of the views we were shown, but completely missing from others. Hence the reports of the *Shapieron* were suspect."

"And not only those," Calazar said. "By implication, every other report that we had ever received of Earth was in doubt too, but we had no comparable way of testing them." He moved his eyes solemnly along the row of Terran faces. "Perhaps now you can see why we were concerned. We had two conflicting impressions of Earth, and no way of knowing how much of each might be true. But suppose that Earth was as aggressive and as irrational as we had been led to believe for years, and that the occupants of the *Shapieron* had indeed been received and treated in the ways described to us. . . ." He left the sentence unfinished. "Well, in our position what might you have thought?"

A silence descended around the table. The Thuriens wouldn't have known what to believe, Hunt conceded inwardly. Their only way to check the facts would have been to reopen the dialogue with Earth secretly and establish face-to-face contact, which was precisely what they had done. So why had it been so important?

Suddenly Lyn's mouth dropped open, and she stared wide-eyed at Calazar. "You were afraid that we might have bombed the *Shapieron* or something!" she gasped, horrified. "If we were the way those stories said, we'd never have let that ship get to Thurien to tell anybody about it." The shocked looks coming from around her said that it suddenly all made sense to the others too. Even Caldwell seemed deflated for the moment. It was a shame about Jerol Packard, but nobody could blame the Thuriens for acting as they had.

"But you didn't have to wait to find out," Hunt said after a few seconds. "You can project black-hole ports across light-years. Why didn't you simply intercept the snip and get it here fast? Surely they'd have been the obvious people to check your surveillance reports with; they had been on Earth for six months."

"Technical reasons," Eesyan replied. "A Thurien vessel can clear a planetary system in about a day, but only because it carries on-board equipment that interacts with the transfer port and keeps the gravitational disturbance relatively localized. Naturally the *Shapieron* does not have such equipment. We needed to give it months if we were to avoid perturbing your planetary orbits. That would have been embarrassing if our fears were groundless. But we've been taking a risk. We finally reached the point where we had to know whether or not that ship was safe—*now*, without any further delays and obstructions."

"We had decided to go ahead anyway when it became clear that we were not making progress with the UN," Calazar told them. "Only when your messages from Jupiter started coming in did we decide to leave it a little longer. We had the necessary ships and generators ready then, and they have been standing by ever since. All they needed was one signal from us to commence the operation."

Hunt sank back in his chair and released a long breath. It had been a close thing. If Joe Shannon on *Jupiter Five* had not been thinking too clearly for a day or two, all of Earth's astronomical tables would have needed to be worked out all over again from square one.

"You'd better send the signal."

The voice sounded suddenly from one end of the Terran group. Everyone looked round, surprised, and found Danchekker directing a challenging look from one part of the table to another as if inviting them to make some obvious deduction. A score of Terran and Ganymean faces stared back at him blankly.

Danchekker removed his spectacles, polished them with a handkerchief, and then returned them to his nose in the manner of a professor allowing a class of slow students time to reflect upon some proposition he had put to them. There was no reason why VISAR would make lenses that existed only in somebody's head go cloudy, Hunt thought to himself; the ritual was just an unconscious mannerism.

At last Danchekker looked up. "It seems evident that this,

er, 'organization' responsible for the surveillance activities, whatever its nature, would not see its interests served by the *Shapieron* reaching Thurien." He paused to let the full implication sink in.

"And now let me conjecture as to what might be my disposition now, were I in the position of the leaders of that organization," he resumed. "I assume that I know nothing about this meeting or that any dialogue between Thurien and Earth is taking place at all since my source of information would be the terrestrial communications network, and all references to such facts have been excluded from that system. Therefore I would have no reason to believe that my falsified accounts of Earth have been questioned. Now, that being so, if the *Shapieron* were to encounter an unfortunate, shall we say, accident, somewhere in the void between the stars, I would have every reason to feel confident that, if perchance the Thuriens should suspect foul play, Earth would top their list as the most likely culprit." He nodded and showed his teeth briefly as the appalled expressions around the table registered the impact of what he was driving at.

"Precisely!" he exclaimed, and looked across at Calazar. "If you have at your disposal the means of extracting that vessel from its present predicament, I would strongly advise that you proceed with such action without a moment of further delay!"

Chapter Twelve

N iels Sverenssen lay propped against the pillows in his
executive-grade quarters at Giordano Bruno, watching
the girl dress by the vanity on the far side of the room. She was
young and quite pretty, with the clear complexion and open
features typical of many Americans, and her loose black hair
cut an intriguing contrast against her white skin. She should
use the sunray facilities provided in the gymnasium more often,
he thought to himself. As with most of her sex, her superficial
layer of college-applied pseudointellectualism went no deeper
than the pigment in her skin; beneath it she was as facile as
the rest of them—a regrettably necessary but not unpleasant
diversion from the more serious side of life. "You only want
my body," they had cried indignantly down through the ages.
"What else can you offer?" was his reply.

She finished buttoning her shirt and turned toward the
mirror to run a comb hurriedly through her hair. "I know it's a
strange time to be leaving," she said. "Trust me to be on early
shift this morning. I'm going to be late again as it is."

"Don't worry about it," Sverenssen told her, putting more
concern into his voice than he felt. "First things must come first."

She picked her jacket up off the back of a chair next to the vanity and slung it over her shoulder. "Have you got the cartridge?" she asked, turning back to face him.

Sverenssen opened the drawer of the bedside unit, reached inside, and took out a matchbook-size, computer micromemory cartridge. "Here. Remember to be careful."

The girl walked over to him, took the cartridge and folded it inside a tissue, then slipped it into one of the pockets of her jacket. "I will. When will I see you again?"

"Today will be very busy. I'll have to let you know."

"Don't make it too long." She smiled, stooped to kiss him on the forehead, and left, closing the door softly behind her.

Professor Gregor Malliusk, the Director of Astronomy at the Giordano Bruno observatory, was not looking pleased when she arrived in the main-dish control room ten minutes later. "You're late again, Janet," he grumbled as she hung her jacket in one of the closets by the door and put on her white working coat. "John had to leave in haste because he's going to Ptolemy today, and I've had to cover. I've got a meeting in less than an hour and things to do beforehand. This situation is becoming intolerable."

"I'm sorry, Professor," she said. "I overslept. It won't happen again." She walked quickly across to the supervisory console and began going through the routine of calling up the night's status logs with deft movements of her fingers.

Malliusk watched balefully from beside the equipment racks outside his office, trying not to notice the firm, slim lines of her body outlined by the white material of her coat and the raven black curls tumbling carelessly over her collar. "It's that Swede again, isn't it," he growled before he could stop himself.

"That's my business," Janet said without looking up, making her voice as firm as she dared. "I've already said—it won't happen again." She compressed her mouth into a tight line and stabbed savagely at the keyboard to bring another screen of data up in front of her.

"The check correlation on 557B was not completed yesterday," Malliusk said icily. "It was scheduled for completion by fifteen hundred."

Janet hesitated from what she was doing, closed her eyes momentarily, and bit her lip. "Damn!" she muttered beneath her breath, then louder, "I'll skip break and get it done then. There's not a lot of it left."

"John has already completed it."

"I'm . . . sorry. I'll do an extra hour off his next shift to make up."

Malliusk scowled at her for a few seconds longer, then turned on his heel abruptly and left the control room without saying anything more.

When she had finished checking the status logs, she switched off the screen and walked over to the transmission auxiliary processor cabinet, opened a cover panel, and inserted the cartridge that Sverenssen had given her into an empty slot. Then she moved around to the front of the system console and ran through the routine of integrating the contents of the cartridge into the message buffer already assembled for transmission later that day. Where the transmission was intended for she didn't know, but it was part of whatever had brought the UN delegation to Bruno. Malliusk always took care of the technical side of that personally, and he never talked about it with the rest of the staff.

Sverenssen had told her that the cartridge contained some mundane data that had come in late from Earth for appending to the transmission that had been already composed; everything that went out was supposed to be approved formally by all of the delegates, but it would have been silly to call them all together merely to rubber-stamp something as petty as this. But a couple of them could be touchy, he had said, and he cautioned her to be discreet. She liked the feeling of being confided in over a matter of UN importance, even if it had only to do with some minor point, especially by somebody so sophisticated and worldly. It was so deliciously romantic! And, who knew? From some of the things that Sverenssen had said, she could be doing herself a really big favor in the long run.

"He is a guest here, like the rest of you, and we have done our best to be accommodating," Malliusk told Sobroskin later that morning in the Soviet delegate's offices. "But this is interfering with the observatory's work. I do not expect to have to be accommodating to the point of having my own work disrupted. And besides that, I object to such conduct in my own establishment, particularly from a man in his position. It is not becoming."

"I can hardly intervene in personal matters that are not part of the delegation's business," Sobroskin pointed out, doing his best to be diplomatic as he detected more than merely outraged propriety beneath the scientist's indignation. "It would be more appropriate for you to try talking to Sverenssen directly. She is your assistant, after all, and it *is* the department's work that is being affected."

"I have already done that, and the response was not satisfactory," Malliusk replied stiffly. "As a Russian, I wish my complaint to be conveyed to whichever office of the Soviet Government is concerned with the business of this delegation, with the request that they apply some appropriate influence through the UN. Therefore I am talking to you as the representative here of that office."

Sobroskin was not really interested in Malliusk's jealousies, and he didn't particularly want to stir up things in Moscow over something like this; too many people would want to know what the delegation was doing on Farside in the first place, and that would invite all kinds of questions and poking around. On the other hand, Malliusk obviously wanted something done, and if Sobroskin declined there was no telling whom the professor might be on the phone to next. There really wasn't a lot of choice. "Very well," he agreed with a sigh. "Leave it with me. I'll see if I can talk to Sverenssen today, or maybe tomorrow."

"Thank you," Malliusk acknowledged formally, then marched out of the office.

Sobroskin sat there thinking for a while, then reached behind himself to unlock a safe, from which he took a file that an old friend in Soviet military intelligence had sent up to Bruno unofficially at his request. He spent some time thumbing through its contents to refresh his memory, and as he thought further, he changed his mind about what he was going to do.

There were a number of strange things recorded in the file on Niels Sverenssen—the Swede, supposedly born in Malmo in 1981, who had vanished while serving as a mercenary in Africa in his late teens and then reappeared ten years later in Europe with inconsistent accounts of where he had been and what he had been doing. How had he suddenly reemerged from obscurity as a man of considerable wealth and social standing with no record of his movements during that time that could be traced? How had he established his international connections without it being common knowledge?

The pattern of womanizing was long and clear. The affair with the German financier's wife was interesting . . . with the rival lover who had publicly sworn vengeance and then met with a skiing accident less than a month later in dubious circumstances. A lot of evidence implied people had been bought off to close the investigation. Yes, Sverenssen was a man with connections he would not like to see aired publicly and the ruthlessness to use them without hesitation if need be, Sobroskin thought to himself.

And more recently—within the last month, in fact—why had Sverenssen been communicating regularly and secretly with Verikoff, the space-communications specialist at the Academy of Sciences in Moscow who was intimately involved with the top-secret Soviet channel to Gistar? The Soviet Government did not comprehend the UN's apparent policy but it suited them, and that meant that the existence of the independent channel had to be concealed form the UN more than from anybody else; the Americans had doubtless deduced what was happening, but they were unable to prove it. That was their loss. If they insisted on tying themselves down with their notions of fair play, that was up to them. But why was Verikoff talking to Sverenssen?

And finally, in years gone by Sverenssen had always been a prominent figure in leading the UN drive for strategic disarmament, and a champion of world-wide cooperation and increased productivity. Why was he now vigorously supporting a UN policy that seemed opposed to seizing the greatest opportunity the human race had ever had to achieve those very things? It seemed strange. Everything to do with Sverenssen seemed strange.

Anyhow, what was he going to do about Malliusk's assistant? She was 'an American girl, Malliusk had said. Perhaps there was a way in which he could clear this irritating business up without inviting Sverenssen's close attention at a time when he was particularly anxious to avoid it. Their national loyalties aside, he admired the way in which Pacey had continued battling to promote his country's views after Heller left, and he had got to know the American quite well socially. In fact it was a shame in some ways that over this particular issue the U.S.S.R. and the U.S.A. were not together on the same side of the table; at heart they seemed to have more in common with each other than with the rest of the delegation. Very probably it wouldn't make much difference for a lot longer anyway, he admitted to himself. As Karen Heller had said on one occasion, it was the future of the whole race they should be thinking about. As a man he tended to agree with her; if the contact with Gistar meant what he thought it meant, there would be no national differences to worry about in fifty years' time, nor maybe even any nations. But that was as a man. In the meantime, as a Russian, he had a job to do.

He nodded to himself as he closed the file and returned it to the safe. He would talk to Norman Pacey and see if Pacey would talk to the American girl quietly. Then, with luck, the whole thing would resolve itself with no more than a few ripples that would soon die away.

Chapter Thirteen

Framed in the screen that took up most of one wall of the room was the image of a planet, captured from several thousand miles out in space. Most of its surface was ocean blue or stirred into spirals of curdled clouds through which its continents varied from yellowy browns and greens at its equator to frosty white at the poles. It was a warm, sunny, and cheerful world, but the image failed to re-create the sense of wonder at the energy of the life teeming across its surface that Garuth had felt at the time the image was captured months earlier.

As Garuth, commander of the long-range scientific mission ship *Shapieron*, sat in his private stateroom staring at the last view to be obtained of Earth, he pondered on the incredible race of beings that had greeted the return of his ship from its long exile in the mysterious realm of compoundly dilated time. Twenty-five million years before, although only a little over twenty by the *Shapieron*'s clocks, Garuth and his companions had left a flourishing civilization on Minerva to conduct a scientific experiment at a star called Iscaris; if the experiment had gone as planned, they would have been gone for twenty-three years of elapsed time back home, having lost less than five years from their own lifetimes. But the experiment had not gone as planned, and before the *Shapieron* was able to return, the Ganymeans had vanished from Minerva; the Lunarians had emerged, built their civilization, split into opposing factions, and finally destroyed themselves and the planet; and *Homo sapiens* had returned to Earth and written several tens of thousands of years of history.

And so the *Shapieron* had found them. What had been a pathetically deformed mutant left by the Ganymeans to fend for itself against hopeless odds in a harsh and uncompromising environment had transformed itself into a creature of pride and defiance that had not only survived, but laughed its contempt at every obstacle that the universe had tried to throw in its path. The Solar System, once the exclusive domain of the Ganymean civilization, had become rightfully the property of the human race. And so the *Shapieron* had departed once more into the void on a forlorn quest to reach the Giant's Star, the supposed new home of the Ganymeans.

Garuth sighed. Supposed for what reasons? Speculations based upon nothing that even the most elementary student of logic would accept as evidence; a frail straw of possibility clutched at to rationalize a decision taken in reality for reasons that only Garuth and a few of his officers knew about; a fabrication in the minds of Earthmen, whose optimism and enthusiasm knew no bounds.

The incredible Earthmen . . .

They had persuaded themselves that the myth of the Giants' Star was true and gathered to wish the Ganymeans well when the ship departed, believing, as most of Garuth's own people still believed, the reason he had stated—that Earth's fragile civilization was still too young to withstand the pressures of coexistence with an alien population that would have grown in numbers and influence. But there must have been a few, like the American biologist Danchekker, and the Englishman Hunt, who had guessed the real reason—that long ago the Ganymeans had created the ancestors of *Homo sapiens*. The human race had survived and flourished in spite of all the handicaps that the Ganymeans had inflicted upon them. Earth had earned its right to freedom from Ganymean interference; the Ganymeans had already interfered enough.

And so Garuth had allowed his people to believe the myth and follow him into oblivion. The decision had been hard, but they deserved the comfort of hope, at least for a while, he told himself. Hope had sustained them through the long voyage from Iscaris; they trusted him again now as they had then. Surely it was not wrong to allow them that until the time came when they would have to know what only Garuth and a select few knew at present, and probably what Earthmen like Danchekker and Hunt already knew. But he would never be certain how much those two friends from that astounding race of impetuous and at times aggressively inclined dwarves had really known. He would never see them again.

Garuth had stared silent and alone at this image many times since the ship's departure from Earth, and at the star maps showing its distant destination, still many years away and gleaming as just another insignificant pinpoint among millions. There was a chance, of course, that the scientists of Earth had been right. There was always a shred of hope that. . . . He checked himself abruptly. He was allowing himself to slip into wishful thinking. It was all nothing but wishful thinking.

He straightened up in his chair and returned from his reverie. There was work to do. "ZORAC," he said aloud. "Delete the image. Inform Shilohin and Monchar that I would like to see them later today, immediately after this evening's concert if possible." The image of Earth disappeared. "Also I'd like to have another look at the proposal for revising the Third Level Educational curriculum." The screen came to life at once to present a table of statistics and some text. Garuth studied it for a while, voiced some comments for ZORAC to record and append, then called up the next screen in the sequence. Why was he worried at all about an educational curriculum that was nothing more than part of a pattern of normality that had to be preserved? Condemned by his decision along with the rest of his people, the children were destined to perish ignominiously and unmourned in the emptiness between the stars, knowing no home other than the *Shapieron*. Why did he concern himself with details of an educational curriculum that would serve no purpose?

He pushed the thought from his mind and returned his attention fully to the task.

Chapter Fourteen

"Look, I know I don't have any right to interfere in your private life, and I'm not trying to," Norman Pacey said from an armchair in his private room at Bruno some hours after Sobroskin had talked to him about Janet. He tried to make his voice reasonable and gentle, but at the same time firm. "But when it gets to the point where I get dragged in and it affects the delegation's business, I have to say something."

From the chair opposite, Janet listened without changing expression. There was just a trace of moisture in her eyes, but whether that was due to remorse, anger, or to a sinus condition that had nothing to do with either, Pacey couldn't tell. "I suppose it was a bit silly," she said at last in a small voice.

Pacey sighed inwardly and did his best not to show it. "Sverenssen should have known better anyway," he said, hoping that it might be a consolation. "Hell—look, I can't tell you what to do, but at least be smart. If you want my advice for what it's worth, I'd say forget the whole thing and concentrate on your job here. But it's up to you. If you decide not to, then keep things so that they don't give Malliusk anything to come bitching about to us. There—that's as frank as I can be."

Janet stroked her lip with a knuckle and smiled faintly. "I'm not sure if that would be possible," she confided. "If you want the real reason why it's bugging him, it's because he's had this thing about me ever since I came up here."

Pacey groaned under his breath. He had felt himself slipping into a father role, and her responding to it. Now her whole life story was about to come pouring out. He didn't have the time. "Oh Jesus . . ." He spread his hands appealingly. "I really don't want to get too involved in your personal life. I just felt there was an aspect that I ought to say something about purely as the U.S. member of the delegation. Suppose we simply leave it at that and stay friends, huh?" He pushed his mouth into a grin and looked at her expectantly.

But she had to explain everything. "I guess it was just that everything here was so strange and different . . . you know . . . out here on the back of the Moon." She looked a little sheepish. "I don't know . . . I suppose it was nice to meet someone friendly."

"I understand." Pacey half-raised a hand. "Don't imagine you're the first—"

"And he was such a different kind of man to talk to. . . . He understood things too, like you." Her expression changed suddenly, and she looked at Pacey in a strange way, as if unsure about voicing something that was on her mind. Pacey was about to stand up and bring the matter to a close before she turned the room into a private confessional, but she spoke before he could move. "There's something else I've been wondering about . . . whether I ought to mention it to somebody or not. It seemed okay at the time, but . . . oh, I don't know—it's been kind of bothering me." She looked at him as if waiting for a signal to go on. Pacey stared back without the slightest indication of interest. She went on anyway. "He gave me some micromemories with some additional data in for appending to the transmissions that Malliusk has been handling. He said it was just some extra trivial stuff, but . . . I don't know . . . there was something strange about the way he said it." She released her breath sharply and seemed relieved. "Anyhow, there—now you know about it."

Pacey's posture and manner had changed abruptly. He leaned forward and stared at her, a shocked look on his face. Her eyes widened in alarm as she realized that what she said was more serious than she thought. "How many?" he demanded crisply.

"Three . . . The last was early this morning."

"When was the first?"

"A few days ago . . . more maybe. It was before Karen Heller left."

"What did they say?"

"I don't know." Janet shrugged helplessly. "How would I know that?"

"Aw, come on." Pacey waved a hand impatiently. "Don't tell me you weren't curious. You've got the equipment to read a memory onto a screen."

"I tried to," she admitted after a few seconds. "But they had a lockout code that wouldn't permit a read from the console routine. They must have had a built-in, one-time activating sequence from the transmission call. They'd self-erased afterward."

"And that didn't make you suspicious?"

"At first I thought it was just some kind of routine UN security procedure. . . . Then I wasn't so sure. That was when it started bothering me." She looked across at Pacey nervously for a few seconds, then added timidly, "He did say it was only some trivial additions." Her tone said she didn't believe that now, either. Then she lapsed into silence while Pacey sat back with a distant expression on his face, gnawing unconsciously at the knuckle of his thumb while his mind raced through the possible meaning of what she had said.

"What else has he said to you?" he asked at last.

"What else?"

"Anything. Try and remember anything strange or unusual that he might have done or talked to you about—even things that sound stupid. This is important."

"Well . . ." Janet frowned and stared at the wall behind him. "He told me about all the work he did for disarmament and how he was mixed up in turning the UN into an efficient global power since then . . . all the people in high places that he knows all over."

"Uh huh. We know about that. Anything else?"

A smile flickered on Janet's mouth for a second. "He gets mad because you seem to give him a hard time at the delegation meetings. I get the impression he thinks you're a mean bastard. I can't think why, though."

"Yes."

Her expression changed suddenly. "There was something else, not long ago. . . . Yesterday, it was." Pacey waited and said nothing. She thought for a moment. "I was in his quarters—in the bathroom. Somebody else from the delegation came in the front door suddenly, all excited. I'm not sure which one it was. It wasn't you or that little bald Russian guy, but somebody foreign. Anyhow, he couldn't have known I was in there and started talking straight away. Niels shut him up and sounded really mad, but not before this other guy had said something about some news coming in that something out in space a long way off would be destroyed very soon now." She wrinkled her brow for a moment, then shook her head. "There wasn't anything else : . . not that I could make out, anyway."

Pacey was staring at her incredulously. "You're sure he said that?"

Janet shook her head. "It sounded like that . . . I can't be sure. The faucet was running and . . ." She let it go at that.

"You can't remember hearing anything else?"

"No . . . sorry."

Pacey stood up and walked slowly over to the door. After pausing for a while he turned and came back, halting to stand staring down in front of her. "Look, I don't think you realize what you've got yourself into," he said, injecting an ominous note into his voice. She looked up at him fearfully. "Listen hard to this. It is absolutely imperative that you tell nobody else about this. Understand? *Nobody!* If you're going to start being sensible, the time is right now. You must *not* let one word of what you've told me go a step further." She shook her head mutely. "I want your word on that," he told her.

She nodded, then after a second or two asked, "Does that mean I can't see Niels?"

Pacey bit his lip. The chance to learn more was tempting, but could he trust her? He thought for a few seconds, then replied, "If you can keep your mouth shut about what you heard and what you've said. And if anything else unusual happens, let me know. *Don't* go playing at spies and looking for trouble. Just keep your eyes and ears open, and if you see or hear anything strange, let me know and nobody else. And don't write anything down. Okay?"

She nodded again and tried to grin, but it didn't work. "Okay," she said.

Pacey looked at her for a moment longer, then spread his arms to indicate that he was through. "I guess that's it for now. Excuse me, but I've got things waiting to get done."

Janet got up and walked quickly to the door. She was just about to close it behind her when Pacey called, "And Janet . . ." She stopped and looked back. "For Christ's sake try to get to work on time and stay out of the hair of that Russian professor of yours."

"I will." She managed a quick smile, and left.

Pacey had noted for some time that, like himself, Sobroskin seemed excluded from the clique that revolved around Sverenssen, and he had come to believe increasingly that the Russian was playing a lone game on behalf of Moscow and merely finding the UN policy expedient. If so, Sobroskin would not be a party to whatever information Janet had caught a snippet of. Unwilling to break radio silence on Thurien-related matters with Earth, he decided to risk playing his hunch and arranged to meet the Russian later that evening in a storage room that formed part of a rarely frequented section of the base.

"Obviously I can't be sure, but it could be the *Shapieron*," Pacey said. "There seem to be two groups of Thuriens who aren't exactly on open terms with each other. We've been talking to one group, who appear to have the best interests of the ship at heart, but how do we know that other people back here haven't been talking to the other group? And how do we know that the other group feels the same way?"

Sobroskin had been listening attentively. "You're referring to the coded signals," he said. As expected, everybody had denied having anything to do with them.

"Yes," Pacey answered. "We assumed it was you because we know damn well it isn't us. But I'm willing to concede that we might have been wrong about them. Suppose the UN has set up this whole thing at Bruno for appearance's sake while it plays some other game behind the scenes. They could be stalling both of us while all the time they're talking behind our backs to . . . I don't know, maybe one Thurien side, maybe the other, or maybe even both."

"What kind of game?" Sobroskin asked. He was obviously fishing for ideas, probably through having few of his own to offer just then.

"Who knows? But what I'm worried about is that ship. If I'm wrong about it I'm wrong, but we can't just do nothing and hope so. If there's reason to suppose that it might be in danger, we have to let the Thuriens know. They might be able to do something." He had thought for a long time about risking a call to Alaska, but in the end decided against it.

Sobroskin thought deeply for a while. He knew that the coded signals were coming in in response to the Soviet transmissions, but there was no reason to say so. Yet another oddity had come to light concerning the Swede, and Sobroskin was anxious to follow it through. Moscow wished for nothing other than good relations with the Thuriens, and there was nothing to be lost by cooperating in warning them by whatever means Pacey had in mind. If the American's fears proved groundless, no permanent harm would result that Sobroskin could see. Either way, there was no time to consult with the Kremlin. "I respect your confidence," he said at last, and meant it, as Pacey could see he did. "What do you want me to do?"

"I want to use the Bruno transmitter to send a signal," Pacey replied. "Obviously it can't go through the delegation, so we'd have to go to Malliusk directly to take care of the technical side. He's a pain, but I think we could trust him. He wouldn't respond to an approach from me alone, but he might from you."

Sobroskin's eyebrows raised a fraction in surprise. "Why did you not go to the American girl?"

"I thought of it, but I'm not convinced she's reliable enough. She's too close to Sverenssen."

Sobroskin thought for a moment longer, then nodded. "Give me an hour. I'll call you in your room then, whatever the news." He sucked his teeth pensively as if weighing up something in his mind and then added, "I would suggest taking things easy with the girl. I have reports on Sverenssen. He can be dangerous."

They met Malliusk in the main-dish control room after the evening shift was over and while the astronomers booked for the night were away having coffee. Malliusk agreed to their request only after Sobroskin had consented to sign a disclaimer stating that the action was requested by him, acting in his official capacity as a representative of the Soviet Government. Malliusk locked the statement among his private papers. He then closed the control-room doors and used the main screen of the supervisory console to compose and transmit the message that Pacey dictated. Neither of the Russians could understand why Pacey insisted on appending his own name to the transmission. There were some things that he was not prepared to divulge.

Chapter Fifteen

M onchar, Garuth's second-in-command, was visibly tense when Garuth arrived in response to the emergency call to the *Shapieron*'s Command Deck. "There's something we've never seen before affecting the stressfield around the ship," he said in answer to Garuth's unvoiced question. "Some kind of external bias is interfering with the longitudinal node pattern and degrading the geodesic manifolds. The gridbase is going out of balance, and ZORAC can't make sense of it. It's trying to recompute the transforms now."

Garuth turned to Shilohin, the mission's chief scientist, who was in the center of a small group of her staff, taking in the information appearing on a battery of screens arrayed around them. "What's happening?" he asked.

She shook her head helplessly. "I've never heard of anything like this. We're entering some kind of space-time asymmetry with coordinates transforming inversely into an exponential frame. The whole structure of the region of space that we're in is breaking down."

"Can we maneuver?"

"Nothing seems to work. The divertors are ineffective, and

the longitudinal equalizers can't compensate even at full gain."

"ZORAC, what's your report?" Garuth called in a' louder voice.

"Impossible to construct a gridbase that couples consistently into normal space," the computer replied. "In other words I'm lost, don't know where we are, where we're going, or even if we're going anywhere, and don't have control anyway. Otherwise everything's fine."

"System status?" Garuth inquired.

"All sensors, channels, and subsystems checked and working normally. No—I'm not sick, and I'm not imagining it."

Garuth stood nonplussed. Every face on the Command Deck was watching and waiting for his orders, but what order could he give when he had no idea what was happening and what, if anything, could be done about it. "Call all stations to emergency readiness and alert them to stand by for further instructions," he said, more to satisfy expectations than for any definite reason. A crewman to one side acknowledged and turned toward a panel to relay the order.

"Total stressfield dislocation," Shilohin murmured, taking in the latest updates on the screens. "We're dissociated from any identifiable reference." The scientists around her were looking grim. Monchar nervously gripped the edge of a nearby console.

Then ZORAC's voice sounded again. "The trends reported have begun reversing rapidly. Coupling and translation functions are reintegrating to a new gridbase. References are rotating back into balance."

"We might be coming out of it," Shilohin said quietly. Hopeful mutterings broke out all around. She studied the displays again and appeared to relax somewhat.

"Stressfield not returning to normal," ZORAC advised. "The field is being externally suppressed, forcing reversion to subgravitic velocity. Full spatial reintegration unavoidable and imminent." Something was slowing the ship down and forcing it to resume contact with the rest of the universe. "Reintegration complete. We're in touch with the universe again . . ." An unusually long pause followed. "But I don't know which part. We seem to have changed our position in space." A spherical display in the middle of the floor illuminated to show the starfield surrounding the ship. It was nothing like that visible from the vicinity of the Solar System, which should not have altered beyond recognition since the *Shapieron*'s departure from Earth.

"Several large, artificial constructions are approaching us," ZORAC announced after a short pause. "The designs are not familiar, but they are obviously the products of intelligence. Implications: we have been intercepted deliberately by a means unknown, for a purpose unknown, and transferred to a place unknown by a form of intelligence unknown. Apart from the unknowns, everything is obvious."

"Show us the constructions," Garuth commanded.

Three screens around the Command Deck displayed views obtained in different directions of a number of immense craft, the like of which Garuth had never seen, moving slowly inward from the background of stars. Garuth and his officers could only stand and stare in silent awe. Before anybody could find words, ZORAC informed them, "We have communications from the unidentified craft. They are using our standard high-spectrum format. I'm putting it on the main monitor." Seconds later, the large screen overlooking the floor presented a picture. Every Ganymean in the Command Deck froze, stupefied by what they saw.

"My name is Calazar," the face said. "Greetings to you who went to Iscaris long ago. Soon you will arrive at our new home. Be patient, and all will be explained."

It was a Ganymean—a slightly modified Ganymean, but a Ganymean sure enough. Elation and joy mixed with disbelief surged in the confused emotions exploding in Garuth's head. It could only mean that . . . the signal that the Earthmen had beamed outward from their Moon had been received. Suddenly his heart went out to the impetuous, irrepressible, unquenchable Earthmen. They had been right after all! He loved them, every one.

Gasps of wonder were erupting on every side as one by one the others realized what was happening. Monchar was turning circles and waving his arms in the air in an uncontrollable release of emotion, while Shilohin had sunk into an empty seat and was just gaping wide-eyed and speechless up at the screen. Then ZORAC confirmed what they already knew. "I've matched the starfield with extrapolations from records and fixed our location. Don't ask me how, but it seems that the voyage is over. We're at the Giants' Star."

Less than an hour later, Garuth led the first party of Ganymeans out of the lock of one of the *Shapieron*'s daughter vessels and into a brilliantly lit reception bay in one of the craft from Thurien. They approached the line of figures that were waiting silently, and went through a short welcoming ritual in which the dam finally broke and all the pent-up anguish and hope that the wanderers had carried with them burst forth in a flood of laughter and not a few tears. It was over. The long exile was over, and the exiles were finally home.

Afterward the new arrivals were conducted to a side chamber and required to recline on couches for a few minutes. The purpose of this was not explained. The Ganymeans experienced a strange sequence of sensory disturbances, after which all was normal again. They were then told that the process was complete. Minutes later, Garuth left the side chamber with his party to reenter the area where the Thuriens were assembled . . . and suddenly stopped dead in his tracks, his eyes popping in disbelief.

Slightly ahead of the Thuriens, grinning unashamedly at the Ganymeans' bemusement, stood a small group of familiar pink dwarves. Garuth's mouth fell open, hung limply for a moment, and then closed again without making any sound. For the two figures moving toward him, ahead of the other humans, were none other than—

"What kept you, Garuth?" Hunt asked cheerfully. "Did you miss a sign somewhere along the way?"

"Do forgive my amusement at your expense," Danchekker said, unable to suppress a chuckle. "But I'm afraid the expression on your face is irresistibly provocative."

Behind them Garuth could see another familiar figure—stocky and broad, with wiry hair streaked with gray and deeply etched features; it was Hunt's superior from Houston, and next to him was the red-haired girl who also worked there. Beside them were another man and woman, neither of whom he recognized. Garuth forced his feet to move again, and through his daze saw that Hunt was extending a hand in the customary manner of greeting of Earth. Garuth shook hands with him warmly, then with the others. They were not optical images of some kind; they were real. The Thuriens must have brought them from Earth for this occasion by methods unknown at the time of Minerva.

As he stood back to allow his companions to surge forward toward the Terrans, Garuth spoke quietly into the throat microphone that still connected him with the *Shapieron*, riding not far away from the Thurien vessel. "ZORAC, I am not dreaming? This is really happening?" ZORAC could monitor visual scenes via the miniaturized TV-camera headbands that Ganymeans from the ship wore most of the time.

"I don't know what you mean," ZORAC's voice replied in the earpiece that Garuth was also wearing. "All I can see is a ceiling. You're all lying in chairs of some kind in there, and you haven't moved for almost ten minutes."

Garuth was at a loss. He looked around and saw Hunt and Calazar making their way toward him through the throng of Ganymeans and Terrans. "Can't you see them?" he asked, mystified.

"See who?"

Before Garuth could answer, another voice said, "Actually that wasn't ZORAC. It was me, repeating and imitating ZORAC. Allow me to introduce myself—my name is VISAR. Perhaps it's time we explained a few things."

"But not in the lobby," Hunt said. "Let's go on through into the ship. There's quite a lot that needs explaining." Garuth was even more perplexed. Hunt had heard and understood the exchange even though he was not wearing communications accessories and the exchange had been in Ganymean.

Calazar stood waiting until the rest of the welcomes and introductions had been completed. Then he beckoned and led the mixed group of Ganymeans and Terrans into the body of the huge spacecraft from Thurien, now only a matter of hours away.

Chapter Sixteen

Hunt and Danchekker were somewhere out in the vastness of space. Around them was a large, darkened area made up of walled enclosures that looked like booths and interconnecting stretches of open floor, extending away beneath pools of subdued local lighting into the shadows on all sides. The dominant light was a soft, ghostly whiteness coming from the stars overhead, every one bright and unblinking.

After the reception of the *Shapieron* some distance outside the system of Gistar, Jerol Packard, by then his normal self once more, had decided to leave the two groups of Ganymeans alone for some time without Terran intrusion. The others had agreed. They seized the opportunity thus presented to make some instant "visits," courtesy of VISAR, to experience other parts of the Thurien civilization. Packard and Heller went to Thurios to learn more of the system of social organization while Caldwell and Lyn were taken on a tour of light-years between stops to observe more of Thurien space engineering in action. Hunt and Danchekker, intrigued after following the operation that had been mounted to intercept the *Shapieron*, were curious about how the energy had been generated to form the enormous black-hole toroid thrown in the ship's path, and how it was hurled across such an immense distance. VISAR had offered to show them a Thurien power plant, and an instant later they had found themselves here.

They were beneath a huge, transparent blister that formed part of some form of construction hanging in space. But what scale of construction was this? To left and right outside the blister, and in front and behind, the external parts of the structure swept away and upward in four gently curving arms of intricately engineered metal architecture that shrank into the distance to give an impression of immensity that was almost frightening. They seemed to be standing at the crossover point of two shallow crescents meeting at right angles like sections of the equator and a longitude line drawn on a globe. The tips of the four crescent arms carried four long, narrow, cylindrical forms whose axes seemed to converge on some distant point like those of four gigantic gun barrels trained to concentrate fire on a remote target. How far away they were was impossible to guess since there was nothing familiar to give any visual cue of size.

Farther away and to one side, positioned almost edge-on to their vantage point, was another structure identical to the one they were in, comprising a similar cruciform of two crescents and carrying its own quadruplet of cylinders, details of its far side losing themselves in foreshortening and distance. And on the other side of the view was another, also edge-on, and another above, and yet another below. The whole set of them, Hunt realized as he looked, was positioned symmetrically in space around a common center to form sections of an imaginary spherical surface like parts of an engineer's exploded drawing, and the gun barrels were pointing inward radially. And far away at the focus of this configuration, an eerie halo of blurred, scrambled starlight was hanging in the void, tinted with a dash of violet.

After giving them some time to take in the scene VISAR informed them, "You are now something like five hundred million miles outside the system of Gistar. You're standing in something called a *stressor*. There are six of them, and together they define a boundary around a spherical volume of space. Each of the arms outside is of the order of five thousand miles long. That's how far away those cylinders are, which should give you some idea of their size."

Danchekker looked at Hunt dumbfounded, raised his head again to take in the scene above, then looked at Hunt once more. Hunt just stared back glassy-eyed.

VISAR continued, "The stressors induce a zone of enhanced space-time curvature that increases in intensity toward the center until, right at the focus, it collapses into a back hole." A bright red circle, obviously superposed on their visual inputs by VISAR, appeared from nowhere to surround the hazy region. "The hole is in the center of the circle," VISAR told them. "The halo effect is distorted light from background stars—the region acts like a gravitic lens. The hole itself is about ten thousand miles from you, and the space you're in is actually highly distorted. But I can censor confusing data, so you feel and act normal.

"Behind the shell defined by the stressors are batteries of projectors that create intense beams of energy by matter annihilation and direct them between the sensors and into the hole. From there the energy is redirected and distributed through a higher-order dimension grid and extracted back into ordinary space wherever it's needed. In other words this whole arrangement forms the input into an h-space distribution grid that delivers to anywhere you like, instantaneously, and over interstellar distances. Like it?"

A while went by before Hunt found his voice. "What kinds of things hook on the other end?" he asked. "I mean, would this feed a whole planet . . . or what?"

"The distribution pattern is very complex," VISAR replied. "Several planets are being fed from Garfalang, which is what the place you're at is called. So are a number of high-energy projects that the Thuriens are engaged in at various places. But you can hook smaller units into the grid wherever they happen to be, such as spacecraft, other vehicles, machines, dwellings—anything that uses power. The local equipment needed to tap into the grid is not large in size. For instance the perceptron that we landed in Alaska was powered from the grid on the conventional stage from its exit port to Earth. It would have had to be much larger if it carried its own on-board propulsion source. Hardly any of our machines have local, self-contained power sources. They don't need them. The grid feeds everything from large centralized generators and redirectors, like the one you're in, located far out in space."

"This is unbelievable," Danchekker breathed. "And to imagine, fifty years ago people were frightened of their energy sources being exhausted. This is stupefying . . . quite stupefying."

"What's the prime source?" Hunt asked. "You said the input beams were produced by matter annihilation. What gets annihilated?"

"Mainly the cores of burned-out stars," VISAR answered. "Part of the energy generated is tapped off to drive a network of transfer ports for conveying material from the remote sites, where the cores are dismantled, to the annihilator batteries. The net production of useful energy fed into the grid from Garfalang is equivalent to about one lunar mass per day. But there's plenty of fuel around. We're a long way from any crisis. Don't worry about it."

"And you can concentrate the energy from here across light-years of space through some kind of . . . hyperdimension and create a transfer toroid remotely," Hunt said. "Is it always as elaborate as the operation we watched?"

"No. That was a special case that required exceptionally precise control and timing. An ordinary transfer is pretty simple by comparison, and just routine."

Hunt fell silent while he took in more of the spectacle overhead, and went back in his mind over the details of the operation he had witnessed.

Calazar had decided to go ahead with the interception of the *Shapieron* without further delay when a baffling message, signed personally by Norman Pacey, came in from Bruno to warn of a possibility that the ship could be in some kind of danger. How Pacey could have known about a risk that had been recognized on Thurien only with the benefit of information that Pacey couldn't possibly have possessed was a mystery.

Apparently the "organization" possessed equipment capable of tracking the *Shapieron* just as Calazar's people did, and Calazar had been unwilling to reveal his actions by simply allowing the ship to vanish from the course it had been following. Therefore he had called upon Eesyan's engineers to modify the operation to cover not only the fishing of a vessel out of the void twenty light-years away, but also the substitution of a dummy object constructed to give identical readings on the "organization's" tracking instruments. There was a risk that the gravitational disturbance produced in the process might itself be detected, but since continuous monitoring was not practicable for technical reasons, there was a good chance that the substitution could be made invisible provided the operation was pulled off in minimum time. As planned, the switch had gone quickly and smoothly, and if all had gone well the "organization" would by now be receiving tracking-data updates originating from the decoy while the *Shapieron* was in fact light-years away and almost at Thurien. Time would no doubt tell if the switch had gone quickly and smoothly enough.

Hunt didn't know what to make of this game of deception and counterdeception between two, possibly rival, groups of Ganymeans. As Danchekker had maintained from the beginning, the response simply did not fit with the way Ganymean minds worked. Hunt had tried several times to squeeze a hint of what was behind it all out of VISAR, but the machine, evidently acting under a directive not to discuss the matter, merely reaffirmed that Calazar would broach the subject himself at the appropriate time.

But whatever the reasons, the *Shapieron* had not been attacked or interfered with in whatever way Pacey had feared, and it was now in safe hands. The only conclusion Hunt could draw was that Pacey had misinterpreted something and over-reacted, which seemed strange for the kind of person Hunt had judged Pacey to be. To be fair, Hunt conceded as he thought about it again, Pacey hadn't actually said for certain that it was the *Shapieron* that was threatened; what he had said was that he had reason to believe that *something* well out in space was in danger of destruction, and he had expressed concern that it might be the *Shapieron*. Calazar had decided not to take any chances, and Hunt couldn't blame him for that. What the warning did seem to indicate was that Pacey had been hopelessly wrong about something. Or had he? Hunt wondered.

Suddenly Hunt realized he was feeling physically uncomfortable. Surely not, he thought. Surely the package of sensations that made up his computer-simulated body couldn't be that complete. What would be the point?

He looked around him instinctively and discovered he was back in his own body in the recliner inside the perceptron. "Facing you at the back end of the corridor," VISAR's voice informed him. Hunt sat up, shaking his head in wonder. As always, the Ganymeans had thought of everything. So *that* was what the mysterious door was for.

He was back at Gistar a few minutes later, and found Danchekker waiting for him wearing a grave expression. "Some alarming news has come through while you were absent," the professor informed him. "It appears that our friend at Giordano Bruno was not quite as mistaken as we had supposed."

"What's happened?" Hunt asked.

"The device that has been relaying the communications between Farside and Thurien has ceased operating. According to VISAR, indications are that something destroyed it."

Chapter Seventeen

How could Norman Pacey, isolated and incommunicado on lunar Farside, have known that the relay was about to be destroyed? His only source of information from outside the solar system was the signals coming in from the Thuriens at Gistar, and the Thuriens themselves hadn't known about it. And why had Pacey apparently acted independently of the official UN delegation on Farside in sending the warning? Furthermore, how had he gained access to the equipment there, and how had he been able to operate it? In short, just what was going on at Farside?

Jerol Packard requested from the Thuriens a complete set of their versions of all the messages that had been exchanged with Earth since the whole business began. Calazar agreed to supply them, and VISAR hard-copied them through to McClusky by means of equipment contained in the perceptron. When the team there compared the Thuriens' transcripts with their own, some peculiar discrepancies emerged.

The first set comprised one-way traffic from Earth and were from the period immediately following the *Shapieron*'s departure, when scientists at Bruno had resisted UN pressure and continued transmitting in the hope of renewing the dialogue that the first brief, unexpected signal from the Giants' Star had initiated. These messages contained information regarding Earth's civilization and state of scientific progress that over the months had begun adding up to form a picture which was not at all consistent with that reported to the Thuriens for years by the still mysterious and undefined "organization." Perhaps these inconsistencies had been the cause of the Thuriens becoming suspicious about the reports in the first place. In any event, the two sets of transcripts of these messages matched perfectly.

The next group of exchanges dated from the time that Thurien began talking again, and the UN stepped in to handle Earth's end. At this point the tone of the transmissions from Farside took on a distinctly different flavor. As Karen Heller had told Hunt at his first meeting with her in Houston, and as he had verified for himself since, the messages became negative and ambivalent, doing little to dispel the Thuriens' notions of a militarized Earth and rejecting their overtures for a landing and direct talks. Among these transmissions the first discrepancies appeared.

Every one of the communications sent during the period in which Heller was on Farside was reproduced faithfully in the Thuriens' records. But there were two additional ones—identifiable by their format and header conventions as having undoubtedly originated from Bruno—that she had never seen before. What made these even more mysterious was that their contents were overtly belligerent and hostile to a degree that the UN delegation would never have condoned even with its negative attitude. Some of the things they said were simply untrue, the gist of them being that Earth was capable of managing its own affairs, didn't want and wouldn't tolerate alien interference, and would respond with force if any landing was attempted. More inexplicable still was the fact that some of the details correlated with and reinforced the falsified picture of Earth that Hunt and the others had learned of only after meeting the Thuriens. How could anyone at Bruno have known anything about that?

Then Hunt's signals had started coming in from Jupiter—coded in Ganymean, welcoming the suggestion for a landing, suggesting a suitable location, and projecting a different image completely. No wonder the Thuriens had been confused!

After that came the Soviet signals, complete with details of the security code to be used for replies. Packard had persuaded Calazar to include them by playing up the grilling that the Terrans had been put through and especially its effect on him personally. The Soviets, too, had expressed interest in a landing, though in a manner distinctly more cautious than Hunt's messages from Jupiter. This theme traced consistently through most of the Soviet signals, but again there were some, in this case three, that stood out as exceptions and conveyed similar sentiments to those of the "unofficial" transmissions from Bruno. And even more amazingly, they tallied in some significant details with the Bruno exceptions in ways that couldn't have been coincidental.

How could the Soviets have known about unofficial signals from Bruno that even Karen Heller hadn't known about when she was there? The only way, surely, was if the Soviets were responsible for them. Did that mean that the Kremlin was so dominating the UN that the whole Bruno operation had been simply a sham to distract the U.S. and other prominent nations that knew about Gistar, and that the delegation's ostensibly mild but nevertheless counterproductive actions had been secretly derailed, presumably by somebody put there for the purpose—perhaps in the form of Sobroskin? That the Director of Astronomy at Bruno was also a Russian gave further credibility to the thought, but against it was the unavoidable fact that the Soviets' own effort had been sabotaged in exactly the same manner. Again nothing made sense.

Later a third unofficial message from Bruno, sent after Karen Heller had left, reached a new peak of aggressiveness, announcing that Earth was severing relations and had taken steps to insure that the dialogue would be discontinued permanently. Finally there was Norman Pacey's warning of something about to be destroyed out in space, and shortly afterward the relay had ceased operating.

The answers to these riddles would not be found in Alaska. Packard waited until a State Department courier arrived at McClusky with the official news that communications with Gistar had ceased and the UN delegation was returning to Earth, and then left for Washington with Caldwell. Lyn went with them for the purpose of returning to McClusky with an update as soon as they had talked to Pacey.

Hunt and Danchekker stood on the apron at McClusky, watching the UNSA jet that had just lifted off to take Packard, Caldwell, and Lyn to Washington turn and begin climbing away steeply toward the south. Not far from them, a ground crew was busy shoveling snow over the holes in the concrete left by the landing gear of the perceptron, which had moved itself into line with the other UNSA aircraft parked along one side of the apron in order to provide a more natural scene for the "organization's" surveillance instruments. Although the black hole contained in the vessel's communications system was microscopic, it still had the equivalent mass of a small mountain; McClusky's apron hadn't been designed for that.

"It's funny when you think about it," Hunt remarked as the plane shrank to a dot above the distant ridgeline. "It's twenty light-years from Vranix to Washington, but the last four thousand miles take all the time. Maybe when we get this business cleared up, we could think about wiring a few parts of this planet into VISAR."

"Maybe." Danchekker's voice was noncommittal. He had been noticeably quiet since breakfast.

"It would save Gregg a lot of charges from Transportation Services."

"I suppose so."

"How about wiring up Navcomms HQ and Westwood? Then we'd be able to go straight to Thurien from the office and be back for lunch."

"Mmm . . ."

They turned and began walking back toward the mess hall. Hunt glanced sideways to give the professor a curious look, but Danchekker appeared not to notice and kept walking.

Inside they found Karen Heller hunched over a pile of communications transcripts and notes she had made while at Bruno. She pushed the papers away and sat back in her chair as they entered. Danchekker moved over to a window and stared silently out at the perceptron; Hunt turned a chair around and straddled it to face the room from a corner. "I just don't know what to make of this," Heller said with a sigh. "There just isn't any way that some of this information could have been known to anybody here or on the Moon except us—unless they've been in contact with Calazar's 'organization.' Could that be possible?"

"I wondered the same thing," Hunt replied. "How about the coded signals? Maybe Moscow wasn't transmitting to Calazar's bunch at all."

"No, I've checked." Heller gestured toward the papers around her. "Every one that we picked up was sent by Calazar's aide. They're all accounted for."

Hunt shook his head and folded his arms on the backrest of the chair. "It's got me beat too. Let's wait and see what they find out from Norman when he gets back." A silence descended. Lost in thoughts of his own, Danchekker continued staring out through the window. After a while Hunt said, "You know, it's funny—sometimes when things become so confusing that you think you'll never make any kind of sense out of them, it just needs one simple, obvious thing that everybody's overlooked to make everything come together. Remember a couple of years back when we were trying to figure out where the Lunarians came from. Nothing added up until we realized that the Moon must have moved. Yet looking back, that should have been obvious all along."

"I hope you're right," Heller said as she collected papers and returned them to their folders. "Something else I don't understand is all this secrecy. I thought Ganymeans weren't supposed to be like that. Yet here we are with one group doing one thing, another doing something else, and neither wanting to let the other know anything about it. You know them better than most people. What do you make of it?"

"I don't know," Hunt confessed. "And who bombed the

relay? Calazar's bunch didn't, so it must have been the other bunch. If so, they must have found out about it despite all the precautions, but why would they want to bomb it, anyway? It's definitely a strange way for Ganymeans to be carrying on, all right . . . or at least, it is for the kind of Ganymeans that existed twenty-five million years ago." He turned his head unconsciously and directed his last words at Danchekker, who still had his back to them. Hunt had not yet been convinced that such a span of time couldn't have been sufficient to bring about some fundamental change in Ganymean nature, but Danchekker had remained intractable. He thought that Danchekker hadn't heard, but after a few seconds the professor replied without moving his head.

"Perhaps your original hypothesis deserved more consideration than I was prepared to give it at the time."

Hunt waited for a few seconds, but nothing further happened. "What hypothesis?" he asked at last

"That perhaps we are not dealing with Ganymeans at all." Danchekker's voice was distant. A short silence fell. Hunt and Heller looked at each other. Heller frowned; Hunt shrugged. Of course they were dealing with Ganymeans. They looked back at Danchekker expectantly. He wheeled around to face them suddenly and brought his hands up to clasp his lapels. "Consider the fact," he invited. "We are confronted by a pattern of behavior that is totally inconsistent with what we know to be true of the Ganymean nature. That pattern concerns the relationship between two groups of beings. One of these groups we have met and know to be Ganymean. The other group we have not been permitted to meet, and the reasons that have been offered, I have no hesitation in dismissing as pretexts. A logical conclusion to draw, therefore, would be that the second group is *not* Ganymean—would it not?"

Hunt just stared back at him blankly. The conclusion was so obvious that there was nothing to be said. They had all been assuming that the "organization" was Ganymean, and the Thuriens had said nothing to change their minds. But the Thuriens had never said anything to confirm it either.

"And consider this," Danchekker went on. "The structural

organizations and patterns of neural activity at the symbolic level in human and Ganymean brains are quite dissimilar. I find it impossible to accept that equipment designed to interact in a close-coupled mode with one form would be capable of functioning at all with the other. In other words, the devices inside that vessel standing out on the apron cannot be standard models designed for use by Ganymeans, which, purely by good fortune, happen to operate effectively with human brains too. Such a situation is impossible. The only way in which those devices could operate as they do is by virtue of having been *specifically constructed to couple with the human central nervous system in the first place*! Therefore the designers must have been intimately familiar with the most detailed inner workings of that system—far more so than they could have been by any amount of study of contemporary terrestrial medical science through their surveillance activities. Therefore that knowledge could only have been acquired on Thurien itself."

Hunt looked across at him incredulously. "What are you saying, Chris?" he asked in a strained voice, although it was already plain enough. "That there are *humans* on Thurien as well as Ganymeans?"

Danchekker nodded emphatically. "Exactly. When we first entered the perceptron, VISAR was able, in a matter of mere seconds, to adjust its parameters to produce normal levels of sensory stimulation and to decode the feedback commands from the motor areas of our nervous systems. But how did it know what stimulation levels were normal for humans? How did it know what patterns of feedback were correct? The only possible explanation is that VISAR already possessed extensive prior experience in operating with human organisms." He looked from one to the other to invite comment.

"It could be," Karen Heller breathed, nodding her head slowly as she digested what he had said. "And maybe that explains why the Ganymeans haven't exactly been rushing themselves to tell us about it until they've got a better feel for how we might react—especially with the accounts they've been getting of what we're like. And it could make sense that if they *are* human, they got the job of running a surveillance program to keep an eye on Earth." She thought over what she had said and nodded again to herself, then frowned as something else occurred to her. She looked up at Danchekker. "But how could they have gotten there? Could they be from some independent family of evolution that already existed on Thurien before the Ganymeans got there . . . something like that maybe?"

"Oh, that's quite impossible," Danchekker said impatiently. Heller looked mildly taken aback and opened her mouth to object, but Hunt shot her a warning glance and gave a barely perceptible shake of his head. If she got Danchekker into a lecture on evolution, they'd be listening all day. She signaled her acceptance with a slight raising of an eyebrow and let it go at that.

"I don't think we have to search very far for the answer to that question," Danchekker informed them airily, drawing himself upright and tightening his hold on his lapels. "We know that the Ganymeans migrated to Thurien from Minerva approximately twenty-five million years ago. We also know that by then they had acquired numerous species of terrestrial life, including primates as advanced as any of the period. Indeed we discovered some of them ourselves in the craft on Ganymede, which we have every reason to believe was involved in that very migration." He paused for a moment as if doubting that the rest needed spelling out, then continued. "Evidently they took with them some representatives of early prehuman hominids, the descendants of which have since evolved and increased to become a human population enjoying full cocitizenship within the society of Thurien, as is evidenced by the fact that VISAR accommodates both them and Ganymeans equally." Danchekker dropped his hands to clasp them behind his back and thrust his chin out with evident satisfaction. "And that, Dr. Hunt, unless I am very much mistaken, would appear to be the simple and obvious missing factor that you were looking for," he concluded.

Chapter Eighteen

Norman Pacey held up his hand in a warning gesture and closed the door to cut off the room from the secretary giving directions to two UNSA privates who were loading boxes onto a cart in the outer office. Janet watched from a chair that she had cleared of a stack of papers and document holders waiting to be packed in preparation for the delegation's departure from Bruno. "Now start again," he told her, turning away from the door.

"It was last night, maybe early this morning . . . I'm not sure what time." Janet fiddled awkwardly with a button on her lab coat. "Niels got a call from somebody—I think it was the European, Daldanier—about something they needed to discuss right away. He started saying something about somebody called Verikoff, it sounded like, but Niels stopped him and said he'd go and talk to him at his place. I pretended I was still asleep. He got dressed and slipped out . . . kind of creepily, as if he were being careful not to wake me up."

"Okay," Pacey said with a nod. "Then what?"

"Well . . . I remembered he'd been looking at some papers earlier when I came in. He put them away in a holder, but I

150

was sure he hadn't locked it. So I decided to take a chance and see what they were about."

Pacey clenched his teeth in the effort not to let his feelings show. That was exactly the kind of thing he had told her *not* to do. But the outcome sounded interesting. "And," he prompted.

Janet's face took on a mystified look. "There was a folder among the things inside. It was bright red around the edges and pink inside. What made me notice it was that it had your name on the front."

Pacey's brows creased as he listened. What Janet had described sounded like a standard UN-format document wallet that was used for highly confidential memoranda. "Did you look inside it?"

Janet nodded. "It was weird . . . the report criticized the way you'd been obstructing the meeting here and stated in a *Conclusions* section that the delegation would have made more progress if the U.S. had shown a more cooperative attitude. It didn't sound like you at all, which was why I thought it was weird." Pacey was staring at her speechlessly. Before he could find words to reply, she shook her head as if feeling a need to disclaim responsibility for what she was going to say next. "And there was this part about you and—Karen Heller. It said that you two were . . ." Janet hesitated, then raised a hand with her index and second fingers intertwined, ". . . like that, and that such—how was it put?—such 'blatant and indiscreet conduct was not becoming to a mission of this nature, and possibly had some connection with the counterproductive contribution of the United States to the proceedings.'" Janet sat back and shook her head again. "I knew the report simply wasn't true . . . And coming from him, well . . ." She let the sentence trail away and left it at that.

Pacey sat down on the edge of a half-filled packing case and stared at her incredulously. A few seconds went by before he found his voice. "You actually saw all this?" he asked at last.

"Yes . . . I can't give you all of it word for word, but that was what it said." She hesitated. "I know it's crazy, if that helps. . . ."

"Does Sverenssen know you saw this report?"

"I don't see how he could. I put everything back exactly the way it was. I guess I could have got you more of it, but I didn't know how long he'd be away. As it turned out, he was gone quite a while."

"That's okay. You did the right thing not risking it." Pacey stared down at the floor for a while, feeling totally bewildered. Then he looked up again and asked, "How about you? Has he been acting strange now that we're leaving? Anything . . . ominous, maybe?"

"You mean sinister warnings to keep my mouth shut about the computer?"

"Mmm . . . yes, maybe." Pacey looked at her curiously.

She shook her head and smiled faintly. "Quite the opposite as a matter of fact. He's been very gentlemanly and said what a shame it is. He even hinted that we could get together again sometime back on Earth—he could fix me up with a job that pays real money, all kinds of interesting people to meet . . . stuff like that."

A smarter move, Pacey thought to himself. High hopes and treachery had never gone together. "Do you believe him?" he asked, cocking an eyebrow.

"No."

Pacey nodded in approval. "You *are* growing up fast." He looked around the office and massaged his forehead wearily. "I'm going to have to do some thinking now. I'm glad you told me about it. But you've got your coat on, which says you probably have to get back to work. Let's not start upsetting Malliusk again."

"He's off today," Janet said. "But you're right—I do have to get back." She stood up and moved toward the door, then turned back as she was about to open it. "I hope it was okay. I know you said to keep this away from the delegation offices, but it seemed important. And with everybody leaving . . ."

"Don't worry about it. It's okay. I'll see you again later."

Janet departed, leaving the door open in response to Pacey's waved request. Pacey sat for a while and began turning what she had told him over again in his mind, but was interrupted by the UNSA privates coming in to sort out the boxes ready for moving. He decided to go and think about it over a coffee in the common room.

＊　　＊　　＊

The only people in the common room when Pacey entered a few minutes later were Sverenssen, Daldanier, and two of the other delegates, who were all together at the bar. They acknowledged his arrival with a few not overfriendly nods of their heads and continued talking among themselves. Pacey collected a coffee from the dispenser on one side of the room and sat down at a table in the far corner, wishing inwardly that he had picked somewhere else. As he studied them surreptitiously over his cup, he listed in his mind the unanswered questions that he had collected concerning the tall, immaculately groomed Swede who was standing in the center of the vassals gathered around him at the bar.

Perhaps Pacey's fears about the *Shapieron* had been misplaced. Could what Janet had overheard have been connected with the communications from Gistar ceasing so abruptly? It had happened suspiciously soon afterward. If so, how could Sverenssen and at least one other member of the delegation have known about it? And how were Sverenssen and Daldanier connected with Verikoff, whom Pacey knew from CIA reports to be a Soviet expert in space communications? If there were some conspiracy between Moscow and an inner clique of the UN, why had Sobroskin cooperated with Pacey? Perhaps that had been part of some even more elaborate ruse. He had been wrong to trust the Russian, he admitted to himself bitterly. He should have used Janet and kept Sobroskin and Malliusk out of it.

And last of all, what was the motive behind the attempt to character-assassinate him personally, compromise Karen Heller, and misrepresent the role they had played at Bruno? It seemed strange that Sverenssen had expected the plan to work, because the document Janet had described would not be substantiated by the official minutes of all the delegation's meetings, a copy of which would also be forwarded to UN Headquarters in New York. Furthermore, Sverenssen knew that as well as anybody; and whatever his other faults, he was not naive. Then a sick feeling formed slowly in his stomach as the truth dawned on him—he had no way of being certain that the minutes which *he* had read and approved, which had recorded the debates verbatim, would be the versions that would go to New York at all. From what Pacey had glimpsed of whatever strange machinations were in progress behind the scenes, anything was possible.

"In my opinion it would be a good thing if the South Atlantic deal did go to the Americans," Sverenssen was saying at the bar. "After the way the United States almost allowed its nuclear industry to be wrecked just before the turn of the century, it's hardly surprising that the Soviets gained a virtual monopoly across most of Central Africa. An equalizing of influence in the general area and the stiffening of competition it would produce could only be in the better long-term interests of all concerned." The three heads around him nodded obediently. Sverenssen made a casual throwing-away motion. "After all, in my position I can hardly allow myself to be swayed by mere national politics. The longer-term advancement of the race as a whole is what is important. That is what I have always stood for and shall continue to stand for."

After everything else this was too much. Pacey choked down his mouthful of coffee and slammed his cup down hard on the table. The heads at the bar turned toward him in surprise. "Hogwash!" he grated across the room at them. "I've never heard such garbage."

Sverenssen frowned his distaste for the outburst. "What do you mean?" he asked coldly. "Kindly explain yourself."

"You had the biggest opportunity ever for the advancement of the race right in your hand, and you threw it away. That's what I mean. I've never listened to such hypocrisy."

"I'm afraid I don't follow you."

Pacey couldn't believe it. "Goddammit, I mean this whole farce we've been having here!" He heard his voice rising to a shout, knew it was bad, but couldn't stop himself in his exasperation. "We were talking to Gistar for weeks. We said nothing, and we achieved nothing. What kind of 'standing for advancement' is that?"

"I agree," Sverenssen said, maintaining his calm. "But I find it strangely inappropriate that *you* should protest in this extra-ordinary fashion. I would advise you instead to take the matter up with your own government."

That didn't make any sense. Pacey shook his head, momentarily confused. "What are you talking about? The U.S. policy was always to get this moving. We wanted a landing from the beginning."

"Then I can only suggest that your efforts to project that policy have been singularly inept," Sverenssen replied.

Pacey blinked as if unable to believe that he had really heard it. He looked at the others, but found no sympathy for his predicament on any of their faces. The first cold fingers of realization as to what was going on touched at his spine. He shifted his eyes rapidly across their faces in a silent demand for a response, and caught Daldanier's gaze in a way that the Frenchman couldn't evade.

"Let us say it has been apparent to me that the probability of a more productive dialogue would have been improved considerably were it not for the negative views persistently advanced by the representative of the United States," Daldanier said, avoiding the reference to Pacey by name. He spoke in the reluctant voice of somebody who had been forced to offer a reply he would have preferred left unsaid.

"Most disappointing," Saraquez, the Brazilian, commented. "I had hoped for better things from the nation that placed the first man on the Moon. Hopefully the dialogue might be resumed one day, and the lost time made good."

The whole situation was insane. Pacey stared at them dumbfounded. They were all part of the plot. If that were the version that was going to be talked about back on Earth, backed by documentary records, nobody would believe his account of what had happened. Already he wasn't sure if he believed it himself, and he hadn't left Bruno yet. His body began shaking uncontrollably as a rising anger took hold. He got up and moved forward around the table to confront Sverenssen directly. "What is this?" he demanded menacingly. "Look, I don't know who you think you are with the high-and-mighty act and the airs and graces, but you've been making me pretty sick ever since I arrived here. Now let's just forget all that. I want to know what's going on."

"I would strongly advise you to refrain from bringing personal issues into this," Sverenssen said, then added pointedly, "*especially* somebody of your inclination toward the . . . indiscreet."

Pacey felt his color rising. "What do you mean by that?" he demanded.

"Oh, come . . ." Sverenssen frowned and looked away for an instant like somebody seeking to avoid a delicate subject. "Surely you can't expect your affair with your American colleague to have escaped notice completely. Really . . . this kind of thing is embarrassing and uncalled for. I would rather we dropped the matter."

Pacey stared at him for a moment in frank disbelief, then turned his gaze toward Daldanier. The Frenchman turned to pick up his drink. He looked at Saraquez, who avoided his eyes and said nothing. Finally he turned to Van Geelink, the South African, who had only been listening so far. "It was very unwise," Van Geelink said, almost managing to sound apologetic.

"*Him!*" Pacey gestured in Sverenssen's direction and swept his eyes over the others again, this time offering a challenge. "You let *him* stand there and spew something like that? Him of all people? You can't be serious."

"I'm not sure that I like your tone, Pacey," Sverenssen said. "What are you trying to insinuate?"

The situation was real. Sverenssen was actually brazening it out. Pacey felt his fist bunch itself against his side but resisted the urge to lash out. "Are you going to try and tell me I dreamed that too?" he whispered. "Malliusk's assistant—it never happened? Are these puppets of yours going to back you up on that too?"

Sverenssen made a good job of appearing shocked. "If you are suggesting what I mink you are suggesting, I would advise you to retract the remark at once and apologize. I find it not only insulting, but also demeaning to somebody in your position. Pathetic fabrications will not impress anybody here, and are hardly likely to do anything to restore the doubtlessly somewhat tarnished image that you will have made for yourself on Earth. I would have credited you with more intelligence."

"Bad, very bad," Daldanier shook his head and sipped his drink.

"Unheard of," Saraquez muttered.

Van Geelink stared uncomfortably at the floor, but said nothing.

At that moment a call from the speaker concealed in the ceiling interrupted. "Calling Mr. Sverenssen of the UN Delegation. Urgent call holding. Would Mr. Sverenssen come to a phone, please."

"You must excuse me, gentlemen," Sverenssen sighed. He looked sternly at Pacey. "I am prepared to attribute this sad exhibition to an aberration occasioned by your having to acclimatize to an extraterrestrial environment, and will say no more about it." His voice took on a more ominous note. "But I must warn you that should you persist in repeating such slanderous accusations when we leave the confines of this establishment, I will be obliged to take a far more serious view. If so, you would not find the consequences beneficial either to your personal situation or to your future prospects professionally. I trust I make myself clear." With that he turned and conveyed himself regally from the room. The other three drank up quickly and left in rapid succession.

That night, his last at Bruno, Pacey was too bewildered, frustrated, and angry to sleep. He stayed up in his room and paced about the floor going over every detail of all that had happened and examining the whole situation first from one angle and then from another, but he could find no pattern that fitted everything. Once again he was tempted to call Alaska, but resisted.

It was approaching 2 A.M. local time when a light tap sounded on the door. Puzzled, Pacey rose from the chair in which he had been brooding and went over to answer it. It was Sobroskin. The Russian slipped in quickly, waited until Pacey closed the door, then reached inside his jacket and produced a large envelope that he passed over without speaking. Pacey opened it. Inside was a pink wallet with a bright red border. The title label on the front read:

CONFIDENTIAL. REPORT
238/2[G/NTS/FM]. NORMAN H. PACEY—
PERSONAL PROFILE AND NOTES.

Pacey looked at it incredulously, opened it to ruffle quickly through the contents, then looked up. "How did you get this?" he asked in a hoarse voice.

"There are ways," Sobroskin said vaguely. "Did you know of it?"

"I . . . had reason to believe that something like it might exist," Pacey told him guardedly.

Sobroskin nodded. "I thought you might wish to put it somewhere safe, or perhaps burn it. There was only one other copy, which I have already destroyed, so you may rest with knowledge that it will not get to where it was supposed to go." Pacey looked down at the wallet again, too stunned to reply. "Also, I came across a very strange volume of minutes of the delegation's sessions—nothing at all like what I remembered. I substituted a set of the copies that you and I both saw and approved. Take my word for it that those are the ones that will reach New York. I resealed them myself in the courier's bag just before it was taken to Tycho."

"But . . . how?" was all Pacey could say.

"I have not the slightest intention of telling you." The Russian's voice was curt, but his eyes were twinkling.

Suddenly Pacey grinned as the message at last got through that not everybody in the world was his enemy. "Perhaps it's about time we sat down and compared notes," he said. "I guess I don't have any vodka in the place. How about gin?"

"Precisely the conclusion that I have come to also," Sobroskin said, extracting a sheaf of notes from an inside pocket. "Gin would be fine—I'm very partial to it." He hung his jacket by the door and sat down to make himself comfortable in one of the armchairs while Pacey went into the next room for some glasses. While he was there he checked to make sure the ice maker was well stocked. He had a feeling it was going to be a long night.

Chapter Nineteen

Garuth had spent twenty-eight years of his life with the *Shapieron*.

A group of scientists on ancient Minerva had advocated a program of extensive climatic and geological engineering to control the predicted buildup of carbon dioxide. The project would have been extremely complicated, however, and simulation models revealed a high risk of rendering the planet uninhabitable sooner rather than later by disrupting the greenhouse effect that enabled Minerva to support life at its considerable distance from the Sun. As an insurance against this risk, another group proposed a method for increasing the Sun's radiation output by modifying its self-gravitation, the idea being that the climatic-engineering program could go ahead, and if instabilities did set in to the point of destroying the greenhouse effect, the Sun could be warmed up to compensate. Thus, overall, Minerva would be no worse off.

As a precaution, the Minervan government decided to test the latter idea first by dispatching a scientific mission aboard the *Shapieron* to conduct a full-scale trial on a sunlike star called Iscaris, whose planets supported no life of any kind. It was as well that they did. Something went wrong that caused Iscaris to go nova, and the expedition had been forced to flee without waiting for completion of the repairs to the ship's main-drive system, which were in progress at the time. Hurled to maximum speed and with its braking system inoperative, the *Shapieron* returned to the vicinity of the solar system and circled for over twenty years by its own clocks under conditions of compounded time dilation while a million times that amount sped by in the rest of the Universe. And so, eventually, the ship had come to Earth.

As Garuth stood in the doorway of one of the lecture theaters of the ship's school and gazed across the rows of empty seats and scratched worktops to the raised dais and array of screens at the far end, his mind recalled those years. Many who had left Minerva with him had not survived to see this day. At times he had believed that none of them would ever see it. But, as was the pattern of life, a new generation had replaced those who were gone—a generation born and raised in the emptiness of space, who, apart from the brief stay on Earth, had known no other home than the inside of the ship. In many ways Garuth felt like a father to all of them. Although his own faith had wavered at times, theirs had not, and as they had never thought to doubt, he had brought them home. What would happen to them now? he wondered.

Now that the day had arrived, he found he had mixed feelings. The rational part of him was joyful, naturally, that the long exile of his people was over, and they were at last reunited with their kind; but at a deeper level, another part of him would miss this miniature, self-contained world, which for so long now had been the only one he had known. The ship, its way of life, and its tiny, close-knit community were as much part of him as he was part of them. Now all that was over. Would he ever be able to belong in the same way in the mind-defying, overwhelming civilization of Thurien with technologies that bordered on magic and a population of hundreds of billions flung across light-years of stars and space? Could any of them? And if not, could they ever belong anywhere again?

After a while he turned away and began walking slowly

through the deserted corridors and communications decks toward an access point into a transfer tube that would take him back to the ship's command section. The floors were worn by years of treading feet, the corners of the walls abraded and smoothed by the passings of innumerable bodies. Every mark and score had its own tale to tell of some event that had occurred somewhere in the course of all those years. Would all that now be forgotten?

In some ways he felt that it already had been. The *Shapieron* was in high orbit over Thurien, and most of its occupants had been taken down to accommodations prepared for them on the surface. There had been no public celebrations or welcoming ceremonies; the fact that the ship had been intercepted still had to be concealed. Only a handful of Thuriens were aware that Garuth and his people existed at all.

Shilohin was waiting on the Command Deck when he arrived, studying information on one of the displays. She looked around as he approached. "I had no idea just how complex the operation to intercept the ship was," she said. "Some of the physics is quite remarkable."

"How so?" Garuth inquired.

"Eesyan's engineers created a composite hyperport—a dual-purpose toroid that functioned as an entry port in one direction and an exit in the other at the same time. That was how they made the substitution so quickly: the dummy came out of one side as we went into the other. But to control it, they had to get their timing down to picoseconds." She paused and gave him a searching look. "You seem sad. Is something wrong?"

He gestured vaguely in the direction he had just come from. "Oh, it's just . . . walking through the ship . . . empty, with nobody around. It takes some getting used to after so long."

"Yes, I know." Her voice fell to an understanding note. "But you shouldn't feel sad. You did what you promised. They will all have their own lives to live again soon. It will be for the better."

"I hope so," Garuth said.

At that moment ZORAC spoke. "I've just received another message through VISAR: Calazar is free now and says he'll see you as soon as you're ready. He suggests meeting at a planet called Queeth, approximately twelve light-years from here."

"We're on our way," Garuth said. He shook his head wonderingly at Shilohin as they left the Command Deck. "I'm not sure I'll ever get used to this."

"The Earthpeople seem to be adapting well," she replied. "The last time I talked to Vic Hunt, he was trying to find a way of getting a coupler installed in his office."

"Earthpeople can adapt to anything," Garuth said with a sigh.

They entered the room in which the Thuriens had installed a row of four portable percepto-coupling cubicles, which represented the only means of using the Thurien system since the *Shapieron* was not wired for VISAR; hence Calazar could not "visit" the ship. Had the ship not been in orbit and therefore in free-fall, the weight of the microtoroid contained in the communications module of the equipment would have buckled the deck at best. Garuth entered one of the cubicles as Shilohin selected another, and he settled back in the recliner to couple his mind into VISAR. An instant later he was standing alongside Calazar in a large room that was part of an artificial island floating fifty miles above the surface of Queeth. Shilohin appeared next to him a few seconds later.

"Terrans are shrewder than you give them credit for," Garuth stated after the three of them had been talking for some time. "We lived among them for six months, and we know. What is difficult for the Ganymean mind to grasp is that deception and the recognition of deception are parts of their way of life. They have a natural feel for it and will soon get to the truth. Trying to conceal it any longer will only make the situation more embarrassing for all of us when they do. You should be frank with them now."

"And besides, this is not the Ganymean way," Shilohin said. "We have told you the true situation on Earth and how we were made welcome and helped there in every way possible. Your earlier doubts were justified because of the lies reported to you by the Jevlenese, but that no longer holds. You owe it to the Terrans, and to us, to tell them the whole truth now."

Calazar moved away a short distance and turned to stand with his hands clasped behind his back while he considered what they had said. The room they were in formed an oval projection hanging from the underside of the island. Its interior comprised a sunken floor surrounded by a continuous, sloping transparent wall that looked down over the purple, cloud-flecked surface of Queeth in every direction. Outside the wall and above, the mass of the island loomed in a series of metallic contours, blisters, and prominences converging together as they curved away out of sight overhead. "So . . . we won't be able to keep the truth from them," Calazar said at last without turning his head.

"Remember it was the Terrans who first recognized the risk that the Jevlenese could have planned to destroy the *Shapieron* with Earth set up to take the blame," Garuth reminded him. "The Thuriens would never have thought of it. Let's be honest—Terran and Jevlenese minds think very much alike, and Ganymean minds think very differently. We are not predators, and we have not evolved the art of sensing predators."

"And for the same reason you might well find you *need* the Terrans to help get to the bottom of exactly what the Jevlenese are up to," Shilohin added. "Are you any nearer to finding out why they have been systematically falsifying their reports of Earth for years?"

Calazar turned from the viewing wall and faced them again. "No," he admitted.

"Years," Garuth repeated pointedly. "And you suspected nothing until you began receiving the communications from Farside."

Calazar thought for a while, then sighed and nodded in resignation. "You are right—we suspected nothing. Until recently we believed the Jevlenese had integrated well into our society as enthusiastic students of our science and culture. We saw them as cocitizens who would spread outward with us to other worlds. . . ." He gestured behind him and downward. "This one, for example. We even helped them to establish their own autonomously administered and completely self-governed planet as the cradle of a new civilization that would cross the Galaxy in partnership with our own."

"Well, something has obviously gone badly wrong somewhere," Shilohin commented. "Maybe it needs a Terran mind to fathom out what and why."

Calazar looked at them for a moment longer, then nodded again. "Officially Frenua Showm is responsible for our dealings with Earth," he said. "We should talk to her about this. I'll see if I can get her here now." He turned his face away and called in a slightly raised voice, "VISAR, find out if Frenua Showm is available. If she is, show her a replay of our conversation here and ask if she'd join us when she has seen it."

"I'll see to it," VISAR acknowledged.

After a short silence Shilohin remarked, "She didn't strike me as being overfond of Earthpeople in the replay of the Vranix meeting."

"She has never trusted the Jevlenese," Calazar answered. "Her sentiments apparently extend to include Terrans also. Maybe it's not surprising." After another silence he commented, "Queeth is an interesting world, with an emergent intelligent race spread across much of its surface. The Jevlenese have cooperated in bringing many similar planets into our system in the past. They seem to possess a natural aptitude for dealing with primitive races in a way that would not come easily to Ganymeans. I'll show you an example of what I mean. VISAR, let's have another view of the place I was looking at earlier."

A solid image appeared above the open area in the center of the floor. It was of a view looking down on a township in which blocks of hewn rock or baked clay had been built into crude buildings of strangely curved designs. They were huddled around the base of a larger and more imposing edifice of ramps and columns set at the top of an arrangement of broad flat steps ascending on all of its six sides. As Garuth looked at the structure, it reminded him in a vague way of the depictions of ancient temples that he had seen while he was on Earth. The space at the foot of the steps on one side was densely packed with figures.

"Queeth is not integrated into VISAR yet," Calazar informed them as they watched. "Therefore we can't go down there. The view is being captured under high resolution from orbit and injected into your visual cortexes."

The view narrowed, and the magnification increased. The crowd consisted of beings who were bipeds with two arms and a head, but the parts not covered by their roughly cut clothes seemed to be formed from what looked like a pink, glinting crystal rather than skin. Their heads were elongated vertically and covered with reddish mats on top and behind, their limbs were long and slender, and they moved with a flowing grace that Garuth found strangely captivating.

What made his eyes open wider in surprise was the group of five figures posing above the crowd at the top of the steps, standing motionless and erect in flowing garments and high, elaborate headdresses. They seemed aloof and disdainful. And then Garuth realized suddenly what the movements of the slender, pink aliens meant. The movements were signaling supplication and reverence—worship, almost. The starship commander turned his head sharply to direct a questioning look at Calazar.

"The Queeths think that the Jevlenese are gods," Calazar explained. "They come down from the sky in magic vessels and work miracles. The Jevlenese have been experimenting with the technique for some time as a means of pacifying primitive races and instilling respect and trust in them before moving them from barbarism toward civilization. Apparently they got the idea from Earth—from their surveillance observations of long ago."

Shilohin seemed concerned. "Is it wise?" she asked. "How could a race hope to advance toward rational methods and effective control of its environment if its foundations are built on such unreason? We know what happened on Earth."

"I was wondering if you'd say something like that," Calazar said. "I myself have been wondering the same thing. Perhaps, before these recent developments, we have been altogether too trusting of the Jevlenese." He nodded soberly. "I think we will see some big changes in the not-too-distant future."

Before either of the others could reply, VISAR informed them, "Frenua Showm will join you now."

"We don't need the view anymore," Calazar said. The image of Queeth vanished, and a second or two later Showm was standing by Calazar.

"I don't like it," she said frankly. "The Terrans will want a confrontation with the Jevlenese, and that would mean all kinds of problems. The whole situation is complicated enough as it is."

"But we did set the Jevlenese up to handle the surveillance of Earth," Calazar pointed out. "Why shouldn't we expect to accept the consequences?"

"We didn't set them up," Showm said. "They argued and pressed demands until the Thurien administration of the time conceded. They practically took it over." She shook her head apprehensively. "And the idea of the Terrans getting involved in our investigations makes me nervous. I don't like the thought of them gaining access to Thurien-level technology. Remember what happened to the Lunarians. And look at what the Jevlenese have been doing since they acquired their own version of VISAR. It's simply a fact with all their kind—if they get their hands on advanced technology, they abuse it." She glanced at Garuth and Shilohin and then looked back at Calazar. "Our concern was for the *Shapieron*. It is now safely at Thurien. If the rest were up to me alone, I'd break off contact with Earth now and leave them out of it completely while we straighten out the situation with the Jevlenese. We don't need Terrans. They've served their purpose."

"I must protest!" Garuth exclaimed. "We regard them as close friends. If it hadn't been for their help, we would never have reached Thurien at all. We cannot simply disregard them. It would be an insult to every Ganymean on the *Shapieron*."

Before Calazar could reply, VISAR interrupted with another announcement. "Excuse me again, but Porthik Eesyan is asking to join you. He says it's urgent."

"Well, we're not going to resolve this in minutes," Calazar said. "Very well, VISAR. We will receive him."

Eesyan materialized at once. "I've just left Hunt and

Danchekker at Thurien," he said. The Thuriens took VISAR so much for granted that they never bothered with preliminaries. "I was half expecting it—they've found out about the Jevlenese. They're demanding to talk to us all about them."

Calazar stared at him in astonishment. The others looked equally taken aback. "How?" Calazar asked. "How could they? VISAR has been censoring all references to them from the datastream beamed to Earth. They couldn't have witnessed one scene with a single Jevlenese in it."

"They've deduced that humans are here," Eesyan replied, modifying his previous statement. "They've worked out that the surveillance has to have been run by humans. We'll have to do something. I don't think I can stall them much longer—especially Danchekker."

Garuth turned toward Calazar and Showm, at the same time spreading his hands wide. "I hate to say I told you so, but it is as I said—you *can't* keep secrets from Terrans. Now you've got to talk to them." Calazar looked inquiringly at Showm.

Showm searched her mind for an alternative but couldn't find one. "Very well," she agreed wearily. "If it must be. Let's bring them here while we're together and tell them the facts."

"What about Karen Heller, VISAR?" Calazar asked. "Is she coupled into the system at this moment too?"

"She's at Thurien examining surveillance reports from earlier years," VISAR replied.

"In that case invite her to join us," Calazar instructed. "Then bring them all here as soon as they're ready."

"One second." A short pause followed. Then, "She's just finishing hardcopying some notes through to McClusky. She'll be here in half a minute." Simultaneously Hunt and Danchekker materialized in the middle of the floor.

"I still say I'll never get used to this," Garuth muttered to Shilohin.

Chapter Twenty

"**W**e have conducted surveillance of Earth since the beginning of human civilization," Calazar declared. "For most of that time the operation has been entrusted to a race within our society known as the Jevlenese, which until now we have not brought to your attention. As you appear to have deduced for yourselves already, the Jevlenese are fully human in form."

"*Homo sapiens* are somewhat . . . volatile," Frenua Showm added, as if feeling that some additional explanation was called for. "Humans possess an intense instinct for rivalry. We felt that the issue was potentially sensitive. It could always be revealed tomorrow, but never unsaid again once said today."

"You see," Danchekker pronounced, looking toward Hunt with some evident satisfaction from where he was standing on the far side of Karen Heller. "As I maintained—an independent hominid line descended from ancestral primates taken to Thurien at the time of the migration from Minerva."

"Er . . . no," Calazar said apologetically.

Danchekker blinked and stared at the alien as if he had just uttered a blasphemy. "I beg your pardon."

"The Jevlenese are far more closely related to *Homo sapiens* than that. In fact they are descended from the same Lunarian ancestors as yourselves—of fifty thousand years ago." Calazar glanced anxiously at Showm, then looked back at the Terrans to await their reactions. Garuth and Shilohin waited in silence; they knew the whole story already.

Hunt and Danchekker looked at each other, equally confused, and then at the Ganymeans again. The Lunarian survivors had reached Earth from the Moon; how could any of them have got to Thurien? The only possible way was if the Thuriens had taken them there. But where could the Thuriens have taken them from? There couldn't have been any survivors on Minerva itself. All of a sudden so many questions began boiling inside Hunt's head that he didn't know where to begin. Danchekker seemed to be having the same problem.

Eventually Karen Heller said, "Let's go back to the start of it all and check some of the basics." She was still looking at Calazar and directing her words to him. "We've been assuming that the Lunarians evolved on Minerva from terrestrial ancestors that you left behind when you went to Thurien. Is that correct, or have you been leaving out something?"

"No, that is correct," Calazar replied. "And by fifty thousand years ago they had developed to the level of a fairly advanced technological civilization very much as you supposed. Up to that point all was as you reconstructed."

"That's good to know, anyhow." Heller nodded and sounded relieved. "So why don't you take the story from there and fill in what happened after that, in the order it happened," she suggested. "That'll save a lot of questions."

"A good idea," Calazar agreed. He paused to collect his thoughts, then looked from side to side to address all three of them, and went on, "When the Ganymeans migrated to Thurien, they left behind an observation system to monitor developments on Minerva. At that time they did not possess the sophisticated communications that we have today, so the information they received was somewhat sporadic and incomplete. But it was enough to give a reasonably complete account of what took place. Perhaps you would like to see Minerva as captured by the sensors operating at that time." He gave an instruction to VISAR, moved back a few paces, and looked expectantly at the center of the floor. A large image appeared, looking solid and real enough to touch. It was an image of a planet.

Hunt knew every coastal outline and surface feature of Minerva by heart. One of the most memorable discoveries of recent years—in fact the one that had started off the investigations which had culminated in proof of Minerva's and the Ganymeans' existence even before the *Shapieron* appeared—had been that of "Charlie," a space suit-clad Lunarian corpse uncovered in the course of excavations on the Moon. From maps found on Charlie, the researchers at Navcomms had been able to reconstruct a six-foot-diameter model of the planet. But the image that Hunt was examining now did not exhibit the enormous ice caps and narrow equatorial belt that Hunt remembered from the model. The two land masses were there, though changed appreciably in outline, but as parts of a more extensive system of continents that stretched north and south to ice caps much smaller—not much larger than those of contemporary Earth. For this was not the Minerva of the Lunarians of fifty thousand years back; it was the Minerva of twenty-five million years before the Lunarians existed. And it was captured live, as it had been; it was no mere model reconstructed from maps. Hunt looked around at Danchekker, but the professor was too spellbound to respond.

For the next ten minutes they watched and listened as Calazar replayed a series of close-ups captured from orbit that showed the imported terrestrial animal species evolving and spreading, extinguishing the native Minervan forms, adapting and radiating at the rate of over two million years per minute, until eventually the first social man-apes emerged from a line that had begun with an artificially modified type of the originally imported primates.

The pattern was very much as had been conjectured for many years on Earth, except that until 2028 it had all been assumed to have taken place on the wrong planet, or at least the fossils discovered from the pre-fifty-thousand-less-a-bit years B.C. period had been attributed to the wrong hominid family. But there was a completely unexpected phase that had never appeared in the story put together by the anthropologists on Earth: early in the man-ape era, the species had returned for a period to a semiaquatic environment, mainly as a consequence of not being equipped physically to deal with predators on land. Thus they had commenced the path that whales and other aquatic mammals had taken, but they reversed it and came out of the water again when their increasing intelligence provided them with other means of protecting themselves, which happened before any significant physical adaptations had developed. This phase accounted for their upright posture, loss of body hair, rudimentary webbing between thumb and index finger, the salt-excreting function of their tear ducts, and several other peculiarities that experts on Earth had been arguing about for years. Danchekker would have spent the rest of the week talking about that alone, but Hunt persuaded him to take it up again with Eesyan at some other time.

After that came the discovery of tools and fire, tribalization, and the sequence of evolving social order that led from primitive hunter-gatherer economies through agriculture and city-building to the discovery of the sciences and the beginnings of industrialization. And there was something about this part of their history too that set them apart from terrestrial humans in Hunt's eyes: the practical and realistic approach that the Lunarians had adopted to everything they did. They had exploited their resources and talents efficiently, without drifting off into fruitless reliance on superstitions and magic to solve their problems as had so many millennia of Earth people. For the early hunters, better weapons and greater skill decided success, not the whims of imaginary gods who needed to be placated. For the crop growers, better knowledge of plants, the land, and the elements improved yields; rituals and incantations did not, and were soon abandoned. And not very long afterward it was measurement, observation, and the powers of reason that uncovered the laws governing the universe and opened up new horizons for the harnessing of energy and the creation of wealth. As a result the Lunarian sciences and industries had mushroomed almost overnight in comparison with the halting, faltering groping toward enlightenment that had come later when the same general pattern repeated itself on Earth.

The scientists on Earth who had recovered the information on the Lunarians had pictured them as an incurably aggressive and warlike breed whose discoveries of advanced technology had inevitably spelled their eventual self-destruction. Hunt and the others now learned that this picture was not really accurate. There had been some feuding and fighting in the earlier periods of Lunarian history, it was true, but by the time of the early industrial period such things had become rare. A greater common cause had united the Minervan nations. Their scientists recognized the deteriorating conditions that were descending with the coming Ice Age, and the whole race embarked on a feverish development of the sciences that would enable them to move to a warmer planet in the centuries ahead. The astronomers of the time singled out Mars and Earth as the most promising candidates. The stakes were survival, and there were no resources to be squandered on internal conflicts, until . . .

About two hundred years before the final, catastrophic war, something happened to change all that. Calazar explained, "It could have been a result of extreme genetic instabilities still inherent in the race. At about the time they had learned to harness steam and were just beginning to explore electricity, a superbreed of Lunarians appeared quite suddenly and advanced a quantum leap ahead of anything else in existence anywhere on the planet. Exactly where or when they appeared we don't know. Numerically they were few to begin with, but they spread and consolidated rapidly."

"Was that when the planet started to polarize?" Heller asked.

"Yes," Calazar replied. "The superbreed became the Lambians. They were totally ruthless. They militarized and formed a totalitarian regime that imposed itself by force on a large portion of the planet before the other nations could muster the strength to resist. Their aim was to gain control of Minerva's industrial and technical capabilities totally and exclusively to guarantee their own move to Earth, which meant taking over the nations that had been pursuing that goal collectively. Submission would have meant extinction. The other nations had no choice but to unite, arm, and defend their security. They became the Cerians. The course was set irrevocably toward a struggle to the death between the two factions."

Hunt watched more scenes showing the gradual transformation of Minerva into one enormous military and manufacturing machine dedicated to preparations for war. The tragedy of what had happened appalled him. There had been no need for it. More effort had gone into armaments than would have been needed to move the whole Lunarian race to Earth twice over. If the Lambians hadn't appeared on the scene when they did, the people on Minerva would have done it. After millennia they had gotten to within two hundred years of achieving the goal that would have saved them from extinction and preserved their civilization, and then they had thrown it all away.

VISAR began showing scenes from the war itself. A world quaked under the shocks of miles-high fireballs that vaporized cities; oceans boiled, and forests flared into carpets of sterile ash writhing and twisting in an atmosphere in turmoil. Then blankets of smoke and dust blotted out the surface and turned the planet into a murky ball of black and brown. Spots of red and slowly pulsating yellow appeared, isolated and glowing dimly at first, but becoming brighter and spreading, then merging as continents ruptured and the planet's interior exploded through and hurled fragments of crust into the void. The asteroids were being born, and what would eventually become Pluto was being carved into a tombstone for a whole race, destined to drift forever far from the Sun. Although Garuth and Shilohin had watched these scenes before, they became very quiet; they alone among all those present had known Minerva as home.

Calazar waited a while for the mood to lighten, then resumed, "The Ganymeans had long been troubled by their consciences over their genetic interference with the early Lunarian ancestors. Therefore their policy toward Minerva had been one of nonintervention in its affairs. You've just seen the result of that. After the calamity a few survivors were left stranded on the Moon with no hope of survival. By that time Thurien had perfected the black-hole technology that made instant communications and transfers of objects possible, so the Ganymeans were aware of events in real time, and they were in a position to intervene. After witnessing the results of their policy, they could not simply stand aside and allow the survivors to perish. Accordingly, they organized a rescue mission and sent several large vessels to the close vicinity of Luna and Minerva."

It took Hunt a few seconds to see the implications of what Calazar had just said. He stared at the Ganymeans in sudden surprise. "Not outside the Solar System?" he queried. "I thought you said you didn't establish large toroids inside planetary systems."

"It was an emergency," Calazar replied. "The Ganymeans decided to forget their rules for once. They didn't have any time to spare."

Hunt's eyes opened wider as the implication hit him: *that* was how Pluto had gotten to where it was! And *that* was what had broken the gravitational coupling between Minerva and its moon. One simple statement had put half his people at Navcomms out of business.

"So the Lunarian ancestors of the human race never came to Earth with the Moon at all," Karen Heller said. "They were *taken* here—by the Ganymeans. The Moon only showed up later."

"Yes," Calazar replied simply.

That answered another mystery. All the math models of the process had required a long transit time for the Moon to get from Minerva to the orbit of Earth. A lot of doubt had been expressed that a handful of Lunarian survivors could have lasted for any length of time at all, let alone with the resources necessary to reach Earth. But with Ganymean intervention added into the equation, all that changed. With some Ganymean help that handful would have established a secure settlement for themselves and been able to make a viable start at rebuilding their culture. So why had they plunged back into a barbarism that had taken tens of thousands of years to recover from? The only answer could be the upheavals caused by Luna being captured later. The truth was so ironic, Hunt thought: if they hadn't been stabbed in the back by their own Moon, they could have been back into space by 45,000 B.C., if not sooner.

"But not all were taken to Earth," Danchekker concluded. "Another group was taken back to Thurien, and have since become the Jevlenese."

"It was so," Calazar confirmed.

"Even after all that had happened," Showm explained, "the Cerians and the Lambians were unmixable. Since the Lambians had been the cause of the trouble, the Ganymeans of that time considered that more good would come out of the Lambians being taken to Thurien and—it was hoped—being integrated into Ganymean ways and society. The Cerians were taken to Earth at their own request. They were offered ongoing aid to rebuild, but they declined. So a surveillance system was set up instead to keep an eye on them—as much for their own protection as anything." Hunt was surprised. If the surveillance system had been in place that long, the Ganymeans would have known about the collapse of the colony which they themselves had helped found. Why had they let it happen?

"So how did the others make out—the Lambians?" Heller asked. "They couldn't have been running the surveillance that far back. How did they get their hands on it?"

Calazar emitted a heavy sigh. "They caused a lot of problems for the Thuriens of that time, so much so that when Luna came to be captured by Earth and caused widespread catastrophes that demolished the fragile beginnings of the new Cerian society that had started to take root there, it was decided to leave things be. With troubles of their own at home, the Thuriens were not eager to see another human civilization rushing headlong toward advancement, perhaps to repeat the Minervan disaster." He shrugged as if to say that right or wrong, that was the way it had been, then resumed, "But as time went by and further generations of Lambians came and went, the situation seemed to improve. Signs appeared that they could be integrated fully into Ganymean society, so the Ganymean leaders adopted a policy of appeasement in an attempt to accelerate the process. As a result the Jevlenese, as the descendants of the Lambians were called by then, acquired control of the surveillance program."

"A mistake," Showm commented. "They should have been exiled."

"With hindsight, I think I agree," Calazar said. "But that was long before either my time or yours."

"How about telling us something about this system," Hunt suggested. "How does it work?"

Eesyan answered. "Mostly from space. Until about a century ago, it was comparatively simple. Since Earth entered its electronics and space era, the Jevlenese have had to be more careful. Their devices are very small and virtually undetectable. Most of their information comes from intercepting and retransmitting your communications, such as the laser links between Jupiter and Earth. At one time in the early years of your space program they manufactured instrument packages to resemble pieces of your own space debris, but they had to stop when you started clearing things up. That experiment had its uses though; that was where we got the idea of building a perceptron that looked like a Boeing."

"But how could they fake the reports as well as they did?" Hunt asked. "They must have something of their own like VISAR. No Mickey Mouse computer did that."

"They have," Eesyan told him. "Long ago, when there seemed reason to feel optimistic about the Jevlenese, the Thuriens helped them establish their own autonomous world. It's called Jevlen, on the fringe of our developed region of space, and it's equipped with a system known as JEVEX, which is VISAR-like but independent of VISAR. Like VISAR, JEVEX operates across its own system of many stars. The surveillance system from Earth is coupled into JEVEX, and the reports that we receive are transmitted indirectly from JEVEX through VISAR."

"So it isn't difficult to understand how the fabrications and distortions were engineered," Showm said. "So much for philanthropy. They should never have been allowed to operate such a system."

"But why did they do it?" Karen Heller asked. "We still don't have an answer. Their reports were pretty accurate up until about the time of World War II. The problems of the late twentieth century were somewhat exaggerated, but for the last thirty years it's turned into pure fiction. Why would they want you to think we were still heading for World War III?"

"Who can understand the contortions of human minds?" Showm asked, using the general term unconsciously.

Hunt just caught the look that she flashed involuntarily at Calazar as she spoke. There was something more behind it all, he realized—something that the Thuriens were not divulging even now. Whatever it was, he was just as certain in that same split second that Garuth and Shilohin didn't know about it, either. But he didn't feel this was the time to force a confrontation. Instead he steered the discussion back into technicalities as he remembered something else. "What kind of archives does JEVEX have?" he asked. "Do they go all the way back to the Ganymean civilization on Minerva, like VISAR's?"

"No," Eesyan replied. "JEVEX is of much more recent vintage. There was no need to load it with VISAR's complete archives, which concerned only Ganymeans." He studied Hunt curiously for a few seconds. "Are you thinking about the anomalies in the displacements of background stars that VISAR noticed in the shots of the *Shapieron*?"

Hunt nodded. "That explains it, doesn't it. JEVEX couldn't have known about the displacements. VISAR had access to the original design data for the ship; JEVEX didn't."

"Correct," Eesyan said. "There were a few other anomalies too, but all similar—all to do with an old Ganymean technology that JEVEX couldn't have known very much about. That was when we became suspicious." At which point everything that had ever come from JEVEX would be suspect, Hunt saw. But there would have been no way of checking any of the rest without bypassing the Jevlenese completely and going straight to the source of the information—Earth. And that was precisely what the Thuriens had done.

Calazar seemed anxious to move them away from the whole topic. When a lull presented itself, he said, "Garuth wanted me to show you another sequence that he thought you would find interesting. VISAR, show us the Ganymean landing at Gorda."

Hunt jerked his head up in surprise. The name was familiar. Danchekker was looking incredulous as well. Heller was looking from one to the other of the men with a puzzled frown; she was less conversant with Charlie's story than they were.

Don Maddson's linguistics team at Navcomms had eventually succeeded in deciphering a notebook of Charlie's that had remained a mystery for a long time. It gave a day-to-day account of Charlie's experiences as one member of a rapidly diminishing band of Cerian survivors making a desperate trek across the lunar surface to reach a base that offered their last hope of escape from the Moon, if any hope remained at all. The account had covered events up to the point of Charlie's arrival at the place at which he had been found, by which time attrition of various kinds had reduced his band to just two—him, and a companion whose name had been Koriel. Charlie had collapsed there from the effects of a malfunctioning life-support system, and Koriel had left on a lone bid to reach the base. Apparently he had never returned. The base was called Gorda.

A new image appeared above the center of the floor. It was of a wilderness of dust and boulders etched harshly beneath a black sky thick with stars. The landscape had been seared and churned by forces of unimaginable violence to leave just the twisted and mutilated wreckage of what could once have been a vast base. Amid the desolation stood a single structure that appeared to have survived almost intact—a squat, armored dome or turret of some kind, blown open on one side. Its interior was in darkness.

"That was all that was left of Gorda," Calazar commented. "The view you are seeing is from a Thurien ship that had landed a few minutes before."

A small vehicle, roughly rectangular but with pods and other protuberances cluttering its outside, moved slowly into view from behind the camera, flying twenty feet or so above the ground. It landed near the dome, and a group of Ganymeans wearing space suits emerged and began moving cautiously through the wreckage toward the opening. Then they stopped suddenly. There were movements in the shadows ahead of them.

A light came on from somewhere behind to light up the opening. It revealed more figures, also in suits, standing in front of what looked like an entrance leading down to an underground section of whatever the dome had been part of. Their suits were different, and they stood a full head and shoulders shorter than the Ganymeans facing them from a few yards away. They were carrying weapons, but they appeared unsure of themselves as they looked nervously at one another and at the Ganymeans. None of them seemed to know what to do or what to expect. None of them, except one . . .

He was standing in front of the others in a blue space suit that was plastered with dust and grotesquely discolored by scorch marks, his feet planted firmly astride, and a rifle-like weapon held unwaveringly in one hand to cover the leading Ganymean. With his free arm he made a gesture behind him to wave the others forward. The movement was decisive and commanding. They obeyed, some moving up to stand on either side of him, others moving out to cover the aliens from protected positions among the surrounding debris. He was taller than the others and heavy in build, and the lips of the face behind his visor were drawn back in a snarl to reveal white teeth that contrasted sharply with his dark, unshaven chin and cheeks. Something unintelligible came through on audio. Although the words meant nothing, the tone of challenge and defiance was unmistakable.

"Our surveillance methods were not as comprehensive then," Calazar commented. "The language was not known.'"

In the scene before them, the Ganymean leader was replying in his own tongue, evidently relying on intonation and gesture to dispel alarm. As the exchange continued, the tension seemed to ease. Eventually the human giant lowered his weapon, and the others who had taken cover began emerging again. He beckoned for the Ganymeans to follow, and as the ranks behind him opened to make way, he turned away to lead them down into the inner entrance.

"That was Koriel," Garuth said.

Hunt had already guessed that. For some reason he felt very relieved.

"He succeeded!" Danchekker breathed. Elation was showing on his face, and he swallowed visibly. "He *did* get to Gorda. I'm—I'm glad to know that."

"Yes," Garuth said, reading the further question written across Hunt's face. "We have studied the ship's log. They did return, but Koriel's companion had already died. They left him as they found him. They did manage to rescue some of the others who had been left strung out along the way, however."

"And after that?" Danchekker queried. "Another thing we have often wondered is whether or not Koriel was among those who finally reached Earth. It seems now that he may well have been. Do you happen to know if he in fact was?"

In reply Calazar called up another image. It was a view of a settlement formed from a dozen or so portable buildings of unfamiliar design, situated on a river bank against a background of semitropical forest with the hazy outline of mountains rising in the distance beyond. On one side was what looked like a supply dump, with rows of stacked crates, drums, and other containers. A crowd of two or three hundred figures was assembled in the foreground—human figures, dressed mainly in simple but serviceable-looking shirts and pants, and many of them carrying weapons either holstered at the waist or slung across the shoulder.

Koriel was standing ahead of them, huge, broad-shouldered, with dense, black hair, unsmiling features, and his thumbs hooked loosely in his belt. Two lieutenants were standing on either side and a pace behind him. Some of the arms in the crowd began rising in a farewell salutation.

Then the view began to fall away and tilt. The settlement shrank quickly and lost itself among a carpet of treetops, which in turn faded to become just a hazy area of green on a patchwork of colors taking form as the scale reduced and more of the surrounding landscape flowed into view from the sides. "The last view from the ship as it departed from Earth to return to Thurien," Calazar said. A coastline that was recognizable as part of the Red Sea moved into the picture and shrank to become part of a familiar section of Middle East geography despite being distorted at the periphery by perspective. Finally the edge of the planet itself appeared, already looking distinctly curved.

They watched in silence for a long time. Eventually Danchekker murmured, "Imagine . . . the whole human race began with that tiny handful. After all that they had endured, they conquered a whole world. What an extraordinary race they must have been."

This was one of the few occasions on which Hunt had seen Danchekker genuinely moved. And he felt it too. He thought back again to the scenes from the Lunarian war and the visions that the Jevlenese had created of Earth stampeding toward exactly the same catastrophe. And yet it had almost come true. It had been close—far too close. If Earth had not changed course when it did, just two or three decades more would have made that come true. And then Charlie, Koriel, Gorda, the efforts of the Thuriens, the struggles of the handful of survivors that he had just seen—and all that they endured after that—would have been for nothing.

It brought to mind Wellington's words after Waterloo: "It was a close-run thing, a damned close-run thing—the closest-run thing you ever saw in your life."

Chapter Twenty-one

After hearing Norman Pacey's account of the events at Bruno, Jerol Packard lodged a confidential request with an office of the CIA for a compendium of everything that had accumulated in its files over the years concerning Sverenssen and, for good measure, the other members of the UN Farside delegation as well. Clifford Benson, the CIA official who had dealt with the request, summarized the findings a day later at a closed-door session in Packard's State Department office.

"Sverenssen reappeared in Western Europe in 2009 with a circle of social and financial contacts already established. How that happened is not clear. We can't find any authenticated traces of him for about ten years before then—in fact from the time he was supposed to have been killed in Ethiopia." Benson gestured at a section of the summary charts of names, photographs, organizations, and interconnecting arrows pinned to a wallboard. "His closest ties were with a French-British-Swiss investment-banking consortium, a big part of which is still run by the same families that set up a network of financial operations around Southesast Asia in the nineteenth century to launder the revenues from the Chinese opium trade. Now here's an interesting thing—one of the biggest names on the French side of that consortium is a blood relative of Daldanier. In fact the two names have been connected for three generations."

"Those people are pretty tightly knit," Caldwell commented. "I don't know if I'd attach a lot of significance to something like that."

"If it were an isolated case, I wouldn't, either," Benson agreed. "But look at the rest of the story." He indicated another part of the chart. "The British and Swiss sides control a sizable part of the world's bullion business and are connected through the London gold market and its mining affiliations to South Africa. And look what name we find prominent among the ones at the end of that line."

"Is that Van Geelink of the same family as Sverenssen's cohort?" Lyn asked dubiously.

"It's the same," Benson said. "There are a number of them, all connected with different parts of the same business. It's a complicated setup." He paused for a moment, then resumed, "Up until around the first few years of this century, a lot of Van Geelink-controlled money went into preserving white dominance in the area by undermining the stability of black Africa politically and economically, which is one reason why nobody seemed interested in backing resistance to the Cuban and Communist subversions that were going on from the '70s through '90s. To maintain their own position militarily in the face of trade embargoes, the family organized arms deals through intermediaries, frequently South American regimes."

"Is this where the Brazilian guy fits in?" Caldwell asked, raising an eyebrow.

Benson nodded. "Among others. Saraquez's father and grandfather were both big in commodity financing, especially to do with oil. There are links from them as well as from the Van Geelinks to the prime movers behind the destabilization of the Middle East in the late twentieth century. The main reason for that was to maximize short-term oil profits before the world went nuclear, which also accounts for the orchestrated sabotage of public opinion against nuclear power at around the same time. A side effect that worked in the Saraquezes' interests was that it boosted the demand for Central American oil." Benson shrugged and tossed out his hands. "There's more, but you can see the gist of it. The same kind of thing shows up with a few more who were on that delegation. It's one happy family, in a lot of cases literally."

Caldwell studied the charts with a new interest once Benson had finished. After a while he sat back and asked, "So what does it tell us? What's the connection with what went on at Farside? Figured that out yet?"

"I just collect facts," Benson replied. "I leave the rest to you people."

Packard moved to the center of the room. "There is another interesting side to the pattern," he said. "The whole network represents a common ideology—feudalism." The others looked at him curiously. He explained, "Cliff's already mentioned their involvement in the antinuclear hysteria of thirty or forty years ago, but there's more to it than that." He waved a hand at the charts that Benson had been using. "Take the banking consortium that gave Sverenssen his start as an example. Throughout the last quarter of the 1900s they provide a lot of behind-the-scenes backing for moves to fob the Third World off with 'appropriate technologies,' for various antiprogress, antiscience lobbies, and that kind of thing. In South Africa we had another branch of the same net pushing racism and preventing progressive government, industrialization, and comprehensive education for blacks. And across the ocean we had a series of right-wing fascist regimes protecting minority interests by military takeovers and at the same time obstructing general advancement. You see, it all adds up to the same basic ideology—preserving the feudal privileges and interests of the power structure of the time. What it says, I guess, is that nothing's changed all that much."

Lyn appeared puzzled. "But it has, hasn't it?" she said. "That's not the way the world is these days. I thought this guy Sverenssen and the rest were committed to just the opposite—advancing the whole world all over."

"What I meant was that the same people are still there,"

Packard replied. "But you're right—their underlying policy seems to have shifted in the last thirty years or so. Sverenssen's bankers provided easy credit for Nigerian fusion and steel under a gold-backed standard that couldn't have worked without the cooperation of people like the Van Geelinks. South American oil helped defuse the Middle East by leading the changeover to synthetic hydrocarbon liquid substitutes, which was one of the things that made disarmament possible." He shrugged. "Suddenly everything changed. The backing was there for things that could have been done fifty years earlier."

"So what about their line at Bruno?" Caldwell asked again, looking mystified. "It doesn't fit."

There was a short silence before Packard proceeded. "How's this for a theory? Controlling minorities never have anything to gain from change. That explains their traditional opposition to technology all through history, unless it offered something to advance their interests. That meant it was okay as long as they controlled it. Hence we get the traditional stance of their kind through to the end of the last century. But by that time it was becoming obvious from the way the world was going that if something didn't change soon, somebody was going to start pressing buttons, and then there wouldn't be any kind of pond left to be a fish in. The only choice was nuclear reactors or nuclear bombs. So this revolution they made happen, and they managed to maintain control in the process—which was neat.

"But Thurien and everything it could mean was something else. This group would have been swept away by the time the dust from that kind of revolution finally settled. So they cornered the UN handling of the matter and put up a wall until they got some ideas about where to go next." He threw out his hands and looked around the room to invite comment.

"How did they find out about the relay?" Norman Pacey asked from a corner. "We know from what Gregg and Lyn said that the coded signals had nothing to do with it. And we know Sobroskin wasn't mixed up with it."

"They must have been involved with getting rid of it," Packard replied. "I don't know how, but I can't think of anything else. They could have used some personnel of UNSA who they knew wouldn't talk, or maybe a government or commercial outfit that operates independently to send a bomb or something out there . . . probably as soon as the first signal from Gistar came in months ago. So what they've been doing is stalling things until it got there."

Caldwell nodded. "It makes sense. You've got to hand it to them—they almost had it tied up. If it wasn't for McClusky . . . who knows?"

A solemn silence descended and persisted for a while. Eventually Lyn looked inquiringly from one man to another. "So what happens now?" she asked.

"I'm not sure," Packard replied. "It's a complicated situation all around."

She looked at him uncertainly for a second. "You're not saying they might get away with it?"

"It's a possibility."

Lyn stared as if she couldn't believe her ears. "But that's ridiculous! You're telling us that for . . . I don't know how many years, people like this have been keeping whole nations backward, sabotaging education, and supporting all kinds of idiot cults and propaganda to stay on top of the pile, and there's nothing anybody can do? That's crazy!"

"I didn't put the situation as definitely as that," Packard said. "I said it's complicated. Being pretty sure of something and being able to prove it are two different things. We're going to have to do a lot more work to make a case out of it."

"But, but . . ." Lyn searched for words. "What else do you need? It's all wrapped up. Bombing that relay outside Pluto has to be enough on its own. They weren't acting for the whole planet when they did that, and certainly not in its interests. There has to be enough in that to nail them."

"We don't have any way of *knowing* for sure that they did it," Packard pointed out. "It's pure speculation. Maybe the relay just broke down. Maybe Calazar's organization did it. You couldn't pin anything on Sverenssen that'd stick."

"He knew it was going to happen," Lyn objected. "Of course he was mixed up in it."

"Knew on whose say-so?" Packard countered. "One little girl at Bruno who thinks she might have overheard something that she didn't understand, anyway." He shook his head. "You heard Norman's story. Sverenssen could produce witnesses lined up all down the hall to state that he never had anything to do with her. She became infatuated, then went running to Norman with a silly story to get even when Sverenssen wasn't interested. Such things happen all the time."

"What about the fake signals he got her to send?" Lyn persisted.

"What fake signals?" Packard shrugged. "All part of the same game. She made up that story. They never existed."

"But the Thurien records say they did," Lyn said. "You don't have to tell the whole world about Alaska right now, but when the time's right you can wheel in a whole planet of Ganymeans to back you up."

"True, but all they confirm is that some strange signals came in that weren't sent officially. They don't confirm where they came from or who sent them. The header formats could have been faked to resemble Farside's." Packard shook his head again. "When you think it through, the evidence is not anywhere near conclusive."

Lyn turned an imploring face toward Caldwell. He shook his head regretfully. "He's got some good points. I'd like to see them all go down just as much as you would, but it doesn't look as if the case to do it is there yet."

"The problem is you can never get near them," Benson said, coming back into the conversation. "They don't make many slips, and when they do you're never around. Now and again you get something leaking out like what happened at Bruno, but it's never enough to be a clincher. That's what we need—something to clinch it. We need to put somebody on the inside, close to Sverenssen." He shook his head dubiously. "But something like that needs a lot of research and planning, and it takes a long time to select the right person for the job. We'll start working on it, but don't hold your breath waiting for results."

❊   ❊   ❊

Lyn, Caldwell, and Pacey were all staying at the Washington Central Hilton. They ate dinner together that evening, and over coffee Pacey talked more about what they had learned in Packard's office.

"You can trace the same basic struggle right down through history," he told them. "Two opposed ideologies—the feudalism of the aristocracies on one side, and the republicanism of the artisans, scientists, and city-builders on the other. You had it with the slave economies of the ancient world, the intellectual oppression of the Church in Europe in the Middle Ages, the colonialism of the British Empire, and, later on, Eastern Communism and Western consumerism."

"Keep 'em working hard, give 'em a cause to believe in, and don't teach 'em to think too hard, huh?" Caldwell commented.

"Exactly." Pacey nodded. "The last thing you want is an educated, affluent, and emancipated population. Power hinges on the restriction and control of wealth. Science and technology offer unlimited wealth. Therefore science and technology have to be controlled. Knowledge and reason are enemies; myth and unreason are the weapons you fight them with."

Lyn was still thinking about the conversation an hour later when the three of them were sitting around a small table in a quiet alcove that opened off one end of the lobby. They had opted for a last drink before calling it a night, but the bar had seemed too crowded and noisy. It was the same war that Vic, consciously or not, had been fighting all his life, she realized. The Sverenssens who had almost shut down Thurien stood side by side with the Inquisition that had forced Galileo to recant, the English nobility who would have ruled the Americans as a captive market, and the politicians on both sides of the Iron Curtain who had seized the atom to hold a world to ransom with bombs. She wanted to contribute something to his war, even if only a token gesture to show that she was on his side. But what? She had never felt so restless and so helpless at the same time.

Eventually Caldwell remembered an urgent call that he needed to make to Houston. He excused himself and stood up, saying he would be back in a few minutes, then disappeared into the arcade of souvenir and menswear shops that led to the elevators. Pacey lounged back in his seat, put his glass down on the table, and looked across at Lyn. "You're being very quiet," he said. "Eat too much steak?"

She smiled. "Oh . . . just thinking. Don't ask what about. We've talked too much shop today already."

Pacey stretched out an arm to pick up a cracker from the dish in the center of the table and popped it into his mouth. "Do you get up to D.C. much?" he asked.

"Quite a bit. I don't stay here very often, though. I usually put up at the Hyatt or the Constitution."

"Most UNSA people do. I guess this is one of the two or three favorite places for political people. It's almost like an after-hours diplomatic club at times."

"The Hyatt's pretty much like that for UNSA."

"Uh huh." Pause. "You're from the East Coast, aren't you?"

"New York originally—upper East Side. I moved south after college to join UNSA. I thought I was going to be an astronaut, but I ended up flying a desk." She sighed. "Not complaining though. Working with Gregg has its moments."

"He seems quite a guy. I imagine he'd be an easy boss to get along with."

"He does what he says he's going to do, and he doesn't say he's going to do what he can't. Most of the people in Navcomms respect him a lot, even if they don't always agree with him. But it's mutual. You know, one of the things he always—"

A call from the paging system interrupted. "Calling Mr. Norman Pacey. Would Norman Pacey come to the front desk, please. There is an urgent message waiting. Urgent message for Norman Pacey at the front desk. Thank you."

Pacey rose from his chair. "I wonder what the hell that is. Excuse me."

"Sure."

"Want me to order you another drink?"

"I'll do it. You go ahead."

Pacey made his way across the lobby, which was fairly busy with people coming and going and parties assembling for late dinner. One of the clerks at the desk raised his eyebrows inquiringly as he approached. "My name is Pacey. You paged me just now. There should be a message here somewhere."

"One moment, sir." The clerk turned to check the pigeonholes behind him, and after a few seconds turned back again holding a white envelope. "Mr. Norman Pacey, Room 3527?" Pacey showed the clerk his key. The clerk passed over the envelope.

"Thanks." Pacey moved a short distance away to open the envelope in a corner by the Eastern Airlines booth. Inside was a single sheet of paper on which was handwritten:

Important that I talk to you immediately. Am across lobby. Suggest we use your room for privacy.

Pacey frowned, then looked up and from side to side to scan the lobby. After a few seconds he picked out a tall, swarthy man in a dark suit watching him from the far side. The man was standing near a group of half a dozen noisily chattering men and women, but he appeared to be alone. He gave a slight nod. Pacey hesitated for a moment, then returned it. The man glanced casually at his watch, looked around, and sauntered toward the arcade that led through to the elevators. Pacey watched him disappear, and then walked back to where Lyn was sitting.

"Something just came up," he told her. "Look, I'm sorry about this, but I have to meet somebody right away. Give Gregg my apologies, would you."

"Want me to tell him what it's about?" Lyn asked.

"I don't know myself yet. I'm not sure how long it'll take."

"Okay. I'll be fine just watching the world go by. See you later."

Pacey walked back across the lobby and entered the arcade just in time to miss a tall, lean, silver-haired and immaculately dressed figure turning away from the reception desk after collecting a room key. The man moved unhurriedly to the center of the lobby and stopped to survey the surroundings.

❀   ❀   ❀

The swarthy man was waiting a short distance from the elevators when Pacey emerged a minute or so later on the thirty-fifth floor. As Pacey approached him, he turned silently and led the way to 3527, then stood aside while Pacey unlocked the door. Pacey allowed him to enter first, then followed and closed the door behind them as the other turned on the light. "Well?" he demanded.

"You may call me Ivan," the swarthy man said. He spoke in a heavy European accent. "I am from the Soviet Embassy here in Washington. I have a message that I have been instructed to deliver to you in person: Mikolai Sobroskin wishes to meet with you urgently concerning matters of some considerable importance which, I understand, you are aware of. He suggests that you meet in London. I have the details. You may convey your response back to him through me." He watched for a few seconds while Pacey stared back uncertainly, not knowing what to make of the message, then reached inside his jacket and drew out what looked like a folded sheet of stiffened paper. "I was told that if I gave you this, you would be satisfied that the message is genuine."

Pacey took the sheet and unfolded it. It was a blank sample of the pink, red-bordered document wallet used by the UN for confidential information. Pacey stared at it for a few seconds, then looked up and nodded. "I can't give you an answer on my own authority right at this moment," he said. "I'll have to get in touch with you again later tonight. Could we do that?"

"I had expected as much," Ivan said. "There is a coffee shop one block from here called the Half Moon. I will wait there."

"I may have to take a trip somewhere," Pacey warned. "It could take a while."

Ivan nodded. "I will be waiting," he said, and with that, he left.

Pacey closed the door behind him and spent a few minutes walking thoughtfully back and forth across the room. Then he sat down in front of the datagrid terminal, activated it, and called Jerol Packard's private home number.

❀   ❀   ❀

Downstairs in the alcove to one side of the lobby, Lyn was thinking about Egyptian pyramids, medieval cathedrals, British dreadnoughts, and the late-twentieth-century arms race. Were they all parts of the same pattern too? she wondered. No matter how much more wealth per capita improving technology made possible, always there had been something to soak up the surplus and condemn ordinary people to a lifetime of labor. No matter how much productivity increased, people never seemed to work less, only differently. So if they didn't reap the fruits, who did? She was beginning to see lots of things in ways she hadn't before.

She didn't really notice the man in the seat that Pacey had vacated a few minutes earlier until he started speaking. "May I sit with you? It is so relaxing to do nothing for a few minutes at the end of a hectic day and just watch the human race going about its business. I do hope you don't mind. The world is so full of lonely people who insist on making islands of themselves and a tragedy of life. It always strikes me as such a shame, and so unnecessary."

Lyn's glass nearly dropped from her hand as she found herself looking at a face that she had seen only hours before on one of the charts that Clifford Benson had hung on the wall in Packard's office. It was Niels Sverenssen.

She downed the rest of her drink in one gulp, almost choking herself in the process, and managed, "Yes . . . it is, isn't it?"

"Are you staying here, if you don't mind my asking?" Sverenssen inquired. She nodded. Sverenssen smiled. There was something about his aristocratic bearing and calculated aloofness that set him apart from the greater part of the male half of the race in a way that many women find alluring, she admitted to herself. With his silver hair and well-tanned noble features, he was. . . . well, not exactly handsome by *Playgirl* standards, but intriguing in some undeniable way. And the distant look in his eyes made them almost hypnotic. "On your own?" he asked.

She nodded again. "Sort of."

Sverenssen raised his eyebrows and motioned his head in the direction of her glass. "I see you are empty. I was on my way to have an unwinder myself in the bar. It seems that, temporarily at least, we are both islands in a world of nine billion people—a most unfortunate situation, and one which I am sure we could do something to correct. Would you consider it an impertinence if I invited you to join me?"

Pacey stepped into the elevator and found Caldwell there, evidently on his way back down to the lobby.

"It took longer than I thought," Caldwell said. "There's a lot of hassle going on at Houston about budget allocations. I'm going to have to get back there pretty soon. I've been away too long as it is." He looked at Pacey curiously. "Where's Lyn?"

"She's downstairs. I got called away." Pacey stared at the inside of the doors for a second. "Sobroskin's been in touch via the Soviet Embassy here. He wants me to meet him in London to talk about something."

Caldwell raised his eyebrows in surprise. "You're going?"

"I'll know later. I just called Packard, and I'm going to his place right now to tell him about it. I've arranged to meet somebody later tonight to let them know." He shook his head. "And I thought this would be a quiet night."

They came out of the elevator and walked through the arcade to where Pacey had left Lyn. The alcove was empty. They looked around, but she was nowhere in sight.

"Maybe she went to the little girls' room," Caldwell suggested.

"Probably."

They stood for a while talking and waiting, but there was no sign of Lyn. Eventually Pacey said, "Maybe she wanted another drink, couldn't get served out here, and went into the bar. She might still be in there."

"I'll check it out," Caldwell said. He about-faced and stumped away across the lobby.

A minute later he returned, wearing the expression of somebody who had been hit from behind by a tramcar while minding his own business in the middle of the Hilton. "She's in there," he announced in a dull voice, slumping down into one of the empty seats. "She's got company. Go see for yourself, but stay back from the door. Then come back and tell me if it's who I think it is."

A minute later Pacey thudded down into the chair opposite. He looked as if he had been hit by the same tram on its return trip. "It's him," he said numbly. A long time seemed to pass. Then Pacey murmured, "He's got a place up in Connecticut somewhere. He must have stopped off in D.C. for a few days on his way back from Bruno. We should have picked some other place."

"How'd she look?" Caldwell asked.

Pacey shrugged. "Fine. She seemed to be doing most of the talking, and looked quite at home. If I hadn't known any better, I'd have said it was some guy swallowing a line and well on his way to ending up a few hundred poorer. She looks as if she can take care of herself okay."

"But what the hell does she think she's trying to do?"

"You tell me. You're her boss. I hardly know her."

"But we can't just leave her there."

"What can we do? She walked in there, and she's old enough to drink. Anyhow, I can't go in there because he knows me, and there's no point in making problems. That leaves you. What are you going to do—make like the boss who can't see when he's being a wet blanket, or what?" Caldwell scowled irritably at the table but seemed stuck for a reply. After a short silence Pacey stood up and spread his hands apologetically. "Look, Gregg, I know this sounds kind of bad, but I'm going to have to leave you to handle it in whatever way you want. Packard's waiting for me right now, and it's important. I have to go."

"Yeah, okay, okay." Caldwell waved a hand vaguely. "Call me when you get back and let me know what's happening."

Pacey left, using a side entrance to avoid crossing the lobby in front of the bar. Caldwell sat brooding for a while, then shrugged, shook his head perplexedly, and went back up to his room to catch up on some reading while he waited for a call from Pacey.

Chapter Twenty-two

Danchekker gazed for a long time at the two solid images being displayed side by side in a laboratory in Thurien. They were highly magnified reproductions of a pair of organic cells obtained from a species of bottom-dwelling worm from an ocean on one of the Ganymean worlds, and showed the internal structures color-enhanced for easy identification of the nuclei and other components. Eventually he shook his head and looked up. "I'm afraid I am obliged to concede defeat. They both appear identical to me. And you are saying that one of them does not belong to this species at all?" He sounded incredulous.

Shilohin smiled from a short distance behind him. "The one on the left is a single-cell microorganism that contains enzymes programmed to dismantle the DNA of its own nucleus and reassemble the pieces into a copy of the host organism's DNA," she said. "When that process is complete, the whole structure is rapidly transformed into a duplicate of whatever type of cell the parasite happens to be residing in. From then on the parasite has literally become a part of the host, indistinguishable from the host's own naturally produced cells and therefore immune to its antibodies and rejection mechanisms. It evolved on a planet subject to intense ultraviolet radiation from a fairly hot, blue star, probably from a cell-repair mechanism that stabilized the species against extreme mutation. As far as we know it's a unique adaptation. I thought you'd be interested in seeing it."

"Extraordinary," Danchekker murmured. He walked across to the device of gleaming metal and glass from which the data to generate the image originated, and stooped to peer into the tiny chamber containing the tissue sample. "I would be most interested in conducting some experiments of my own on this organism when I get back. Er . . . do you think the Thuriens might let me take a sample of it?"

Shilohin laughed. "I'm sure you'd be welcome to, Professor, but how do you propose carrying it back to Houston? You're forgetting that you're not really here."

"Tch! Stupid of me." Danchekker shook his head and stepped back to gaze at the apparatus around them, the function of most of which he still failed to comprehend. "So much to learn," he murmured half to himself. "So much to learn . . ." He thought for a while, and his expression changed to a frown. Eventually he turned to face Shilohin again. "There's something about this whole Thurien civilization that has been puzzling me. I wonder if you can help."

"I'll try. What's the problem?"

Danchekker sighed. "Well . . . I don't know . . . after twenty-five *million* years, it should be even *more* advanced than it is, I would have thought. It is far ahead of Earth, to be sure, but I can't see Earth requiring anywhere near that amount of time to reach a level comparable to Thurien's today. It seems . . . strange."

"The same thought occurred to me," Shilohin said. "I talked to Eesyan about it."

"Did he offer a reason?"

"Yes." Shilohin paused for a long time while Danchekker looked at her curiously. Then she said, "The civilization of Thurien came to a halt for a very long time. Paradoxically it was as a result of its advanced sciences."

Danchekker blinked uncertainly through his spectacles. "How could that be?"

"You have studied Ganymean genetic-engineering techniques extensively," Shilohin replied. "After the migration to Thurien, they were taken even further."

"I'm not sure I see the connection."

"The Thuriens perfected a capability that they had been dreaming of for generations—the ability to program their own genes to offset the effects of bodily aging and wasting . . . indefinitely."

A moment or two went by before Danchekker grasped what she was saying. Then he gasped. "Do you mean immortality?"

"Exactly. For a long time it seemed that Utopia had been achieved."

"Seemed?"

"Not all the consequences were foreseen. After a while all their progress, their innovation, and their creativity ceased. The Thuriens became too wise and knew too much. In particular they knew all the reasons why things were impossible and why nothing more could be achieved."

"You mean they ceased to dream." Danchekker shook his head sadly. "How unfortunate. Everything that we take for granted began with somebody dreaming of something that couldn't be done."

Shilohin nodded. "And in the past it had always been the younger generations, too naive and inexperienced to recognize the impossible when they saw it, who had been foolish enough to make the attempt. It was surprising how often they succeeded. But now, of course, there were no more younger generations."

Danchekker was nodding slowly as he listened. "They turned into a society of mental geriatrics."

"Exactly. And when they realized what was happening, they went back to the old ways. But their civilization had stagnated for a very long time, and as a result most of their spectacular breakthroughs have occurred only comparatively recently. The instant-transfer technology was developed barely in time for them to be able to intervene at the end of the Lunarian war.

And things like the h-space power-distribution grid, direct neural coupling into machines, and, eventually, VISAR came much later."

"I can imagine the problem," Danchekker murmured absently. "People complain that life is too short for the things they want to do, but without that restriction perhaps they would never do anything. The pressure of finite time is surely the greatest motivator. I've often suspected that if the dream of immortality were ever realized, the outcome would be something like that."

"Well, if the Thuriens' experience was anything to go by, you were right," Shilohin told him.

They talked about the Thuriens for a while longer, and then Shilohin had to return to the *Shapieron* for a meeting with Garuth and Monchar. Danchekker remained in the laboratory to observe some more examples of Thurien biological science presented by VISAR. After spending some time at this he decided he would like to discuss some of what he had seen with Hunt while the details were fresh in his mind, and asked VISAR if Hunt was currently coupled into the system.

"No, he's not," VISAR informed him. "He boarded a plane that took off from McClusky about fifteen minutes ago. If you want, I could put you through to the control room there."

"Oh, er . . . yes, if you would," Danchekker said.

An image of a communications screen appeared in mid-air a couple of feet in front of Danchekker's face, framing the features of the duty controller at McClusky. "Hello, Professor," the controller acknowledged. "What can I do for you?"

"VISAR just told me that Vic has left for somewhere," Danchekker replied. "I wondered what was happening."

"He left a message for you saying he's gone to Houston for the morning. It doesn't go into any details, though."

"Is that Chris Danchekker? Let me talk to him." Karen Heller's voice sounded distantly from somewhere in the background. A few seconds later the controller moved off one side of the screen, and she came into view. "Hello, Professor. Vic got fed up waiting for Lyn to get back from Washington with some news, so he called Houston. Gregg is back there, but

Lyn isn't. Vic's gone to find out what's going on. That's really about all I can tell you."

"Oh, I see," Danchekker said. "How strange."

"There was something else that I wanted to talk to you about," Heller went on. "I've been doing a lot of looking into some parts of Lunarian history with Calazar and Showm, and it's becoming rather interesting. We've some questions I'd like your answers to. How soon do you think you'll be back?"

Danchekker muttered under his breath and looked wistfully around the Ganymean laboratory, then realized that he was getting signals through VISAR that his body was getting hungry again. "Actually, I'll be coming back now," he replied. "Perhaps I could talk to you in the canteen, ten minutes from now, say?"

"I'll see you there," Heller agreed and disappeared with the image of the screen.

Ten minutes later Danchekker was demolishing a plate of bacon, eggs, sausage, and hash browns at McClusky while Heller talked over a sandwich from the opposite side of the table. Most of the UNSA people were busy refitting one of the other buildings to afford more permanent storage facilities, and apart from some clatterings and bangings from the adjoining kitchen there were no signs of life in their immediate vicinity.

"We've been analyzing the rates of development of the Lunarian civilization and Earth's," she said. "The difference is staggering. They were into steam power and machines in a matter of a few thousand years after starting to use stone tools. We took something like ten times as long. Why do you think that was?"

Danchekker frowned while he finished chewing. "I thought that the factors responsible for the accelerated advancement of the Lunarians were already quite obvious," he replied. "For one thing, they were closer chronologically to the original Ganymean genetic experiments. Therefore they possessed a great genetic instability, and with it a tendency to a more extreme form of mutation. The sudden emergence of the Lambians is doubtless a case in point."

"I'm not convinced that it explains it," Heller replied slowly. "You've said yourself a few times that tens of thousands of years isn't enough to make a lot of difference. I got VISAR to do some calculations based on human genetic data that ZORAC acquired when the *Shapieron* was on Earth. The results seem to bear it out. And the pattern was already established long before the Lambians appeared. That was only two hundred years before the war."

Danchekker sniffed as he buttered a piece of toast. Politicians had no business playing at being scientists. "The Lunarians would have found a profusion of remnants of the earlier Ganymean civilization on Minerva," he suggested. "The knowledge gained from sources of that nature gave them a flying start over Earth."

"But the Cerians who came to Earth were from a civilization that was already advanced," Heller pointed out. "So that balances. What else made the difference?"

Danchekker wrinkled his nose up and scowled. *Female* politicians playing at being scientists were intolerable. "The Lunarians' culture developed during the deteriorating environmental conditions of the approaching Ice Age," he said. "That provided additional pressures."

"The Ice Age was here when the Cerians arrived, and it lasted for a long time afterward," Heller reminded him. "So that balances too. So again—what caused the difference?"

Danchekker stabbed his fork into his meal in a show of exasperation. "If you wish to doubt my word as a biologist and an anthropologist, you have of course every right to do so, madam," he said airily. "For my part, I see no justification whatsoever for elaborating any hypothesis beyond the simple minimum required to account for the facts. And what we already know is perfectly adequate for that purpose."

Heller seemed to have been expecting something like that, and didn't react. "Maybe you're thinking too much like a biologist," she suggested. "Try looking at it from a sociological angle, and asking the question the other way around."

Danchekker's expression said that there couldn't be any other way around. "What do you mean?" he demanded.

"Instead of telling me what speeded the Lunarians up, try asking what slowed Earth down."

Danchekker stared darkly down at his plate for a few seconds, then raised his head and showed his teeth. "The upheavals caused by the Moon's capture," he pronounced.

Heller looked at him in open disbelief. "And regressed them to a point that needed tens of thousands of years to recover from? No way! A few centuries at the most, maybe, but not *that* much. I couldn't buy it. Neither could Showm. Neither could Calazar."

"I see." Danchekker looked a bit taken aback. He attacked his bacon in silence for a while and then said, "And what alternative explanation, if any, are you offering, might I ask?"

"Something you haven't mentioned so far," Heller answered. "The Lunarians developed rational, scientific thinking early on, and relied on it totally from the beginnings of their civilization. By contrast Earth went off into thousands of years of believing that magic, mysticism, Santa Claus, the Easter Bunny, and the Tooth Fairy would solve its problems. It only started to change comparatively recently, and even today there's still a lot of that around. We got VISAR to estimate the effects, and it eclipses all the other factors put together. *That's* what caused the difference!"

Danchekker thought about it for a while, then replied a trifle grudgingly, "Very well." He thrust his chin out defensively. "But I fail to see the need for any melodramatic suggestion that it poses a different question. It's as valid to argue that the early adoption of rational methods accelerated one race as it is to say that its absence retarded the other. What *point* are you making?"

"I've been thinking a lot about it since I talked to Calazar and Showm, and asking what the reason was. Vic says everything has to have a reason, even if it takes some digging to find it. So what would the reason be for a whole planet clinging obstinately to a lot of nonsense and superstitions for thousands of years when even a little bit of observation and common sense should have shown it doesn't work?"

"I think perhaps you underestimate the complexities of scientific method," Danchekker told her. "It takes centuries . . .

scores of generations to evolve the techniques necessary to distinguish reliably between facts and fallacies, and truth and myth. Certainly it couldn't happen overnight. What else did you expect?"

"So why didn't that stop the Lunarians?"

"I have no idea. Have you?"

"That was the question I was leading up to." Heller leaned forward to look at him intently across the table. "What do you think of this for a suggestion: The reason that belief in myths and magic became so deeply rooted in Earth's cultures and persisted for so long could be that, in the earliest stage of our first civilizations, it *did* work?"

Danchekker gagged over the mouthful of food that had been about to swallow and colored visibly. "*What?* That's preposterous! Are you suggesting that the laws of physics that dictate the running of the Universe could have changed in the last few thousand years?"

"No, I'm not. All I'm—"

"I've never heard such an absurd suggestion. This whole matter is already complicated enough without introducing attempts to explain it by astrology, ESP, or whatever other inanities you have in mind." Danchekker looked about him impatiently and sighed. "Really, it would take far too long to explain why if you are unable to distinguish between science and the banalities dispensed in adolescent magazines. Just take my word that you are wasting your time . . . mine too, I might add."

Heller maintained her calm with some effort. "I am *not* suggesting anything of the kind." An edge of strain had crept into her voice. "Kindly listen for two minutes." Danchekker said nothing and eyed her dubiously across the table as he continued eating. She went on, "Think about this scenario. The Jevlenese have never forgotten that they're Lambians, and we're Cerians. They still see Earth as a rival and always have. Now put them in the situation where they've been taken to Thurien and are making the most of the opportunity to absorb all that Ganymean technology, and the rivals on Earth have been slowed down by the Moon showing up. They've gained control of the surveillance operation, and probably by this time they can do their own instant moving of ships and whatever around the Galaxy because they've got their own independent computer, JEVEX, on their own independent planet. Also they're *human* in form—physically indistinguishable from their rivals." Heller sat back and looked at Danchekker expectantly, as if waiting for him to fill in the rest himself. He stopped with his fork halfway to his mouth and gaped at her incredulously.

"They could have *made* magic and miracles work," Heller went on after a few seconds. "They could have put their own, shall we say, 'agents' into our culture way back in its ancient history and deliberately instilled systems of beliefs that we still haven't entirely recovered from—beliefs that were guaranteed to make sure that the rival would take a long, long time to rediscover the sciences and develop the technologies that would make it an opponent worth worrying about again. Meanwhile the Jevlenese have bought themselves a lot of time to become established on their own system of worlds, expand JEVEX, milk off more Ganymean know-how, and whatever else they've been up to." She sat back, spread her hands, and looked at Danchekker expectantly. "What do you think?"

Danchekker stared at her for what seemed a long time. "Impossible," he declared at last.

Heller's patience finally snapped. "Why? What's wrong with that theory?" she demanded. "The facts are that something slowed Earth's development down. This accounts for it, and nothing that you came up with does. The Jevelenese had the means and the motive, and the answer fit the evidence. What more do you want? I thought science was supposed to be open-minded at least."

"Too farfetched," Danchekker retorted. He became openly sarcastic. "Another principle of science, which you appear to have overlooked, is that one endeavors to test one's hypotheses by experiment. I have no idea how you intend testing this far-flung notion of yours, but for suggestions I recommend that you might try consulting the illustrators of *Superman* comics or the authors of the articles one finds in those housewives' journals found on sale in supermarkets." With that he returned his attention fully to his meal.

"Well if that's your attitude, enjoy your lunch." Heller rose indignantly to her feet. "I heard that Vic had a hell of a time getting you to accept that the Lunarians existed at all. I can see why!" She turned and marched out of the room.

Karen Heller was still fuming thirty minutes later as she stood by one of the buildings on the edge of the apron watching a UNSA crew installing a more permanent generator facility. Danchekker came out of the door of the mess hall some distance away, saw her, then walked slowly off in the opposite direction, his hands clasped behind his back. He stopped at the perimeter fence and stood for a long time staring out across the marshes, turning his head every now and then to glance back at where Heller was standing. Eventually he turned and paced thoughtfully back to the door of the mess hall. When he was almost there he stopped, looked across at her again, hesitated for a few seconds, then changed direction and came over to her.

"I, er—I apologize," he said. "I think you may have something. Certainly your conclusions warrant further investigation. We should contact the others and tell them about it as soon as possible."

Chapter Twenty-three

"**S**he what?!"

Hunt caught Caldwell's arm and drew him to a halt halfway along the corridor leading toward Caldwell's office at the top of the Navcomms Headquarters Building.

"He told her to give him a call next time she was in New York to see her mother," Caldwell said. "So I told her to take some vacation and go see her mother." He lifted Hunt's fingers from the sleeve of his jacket and resumed walking.

Hunt stood rooted to the spot for a second, then came to life once more and caught up in a few hurried paces. "What in hell? . . . You can't do that! She happens to be very special to me."

"She also happens to be my assistant."

"But . . . what's she supposed to do when she sees him— read poetry? Gregg, you can't do that. You've got to get her out of it."

"You're sounding like a maiden aunt," Caldwell said. "I didn't do anything. She set it up herself, and I didn't see any reason not to use the chance. It might turn up something useful."

"Her job description never said anything about playing Mata

Hari. It's a blatant and inexcusable exploitation of personnel beyond the limits of their contractual obligations to the Division."

"Nonsense. It's a career-development opportunity. Her job description stresses initiative and creativity, and that's what it is."

"What kind of career? That guy's only got one track in his head. Look, it may come as kind of a surprise, but I don't go for the idea of her being another boy-scout badge for him to stitch on his shirt. Maybe I'm being old-fashioned, but I didn't think that that was what working for UNSA was all about."

"Stop overreacting. Nobody said a word about anything like that. It could be a chance to fill in some of the details we're missing. The opportunity came out of the blue, and she grabbed it."

"I've heard enough details already from Karen. Okay, we know the rules, and Lyn knows the rules, but he doesn't know the rules. What do you think he's going to do—sit down and fill out a questionnaire?"

"Lyn can handle it."

"You can't let her do it."

"I can't stop her. She's on vacation, seeing her mother."

"Then I want to take some special leave, starting right now. I've got personal emergency matters to attend to in New York."

"Denied. You've got too much to do here that's more important."

They fell silent as they passed through the outer office and into Caldwell's inner sanctum. Caldwell's secretary looked up from dictating a memo to an audiotranscriber and nodded a greeting.

"Gregg, this is going too far," Hunt began again when they got inside. "There's—"

"There's more to it than you think," Caldwell told him. "I've heard enough from Norman Pacey and the CIA to know that the opportunity was worth seizing when it presented itself. Lyn knew it too." He draped his jacket on a hanger by the door, walked around the other side of his desk, and dumped the briefcase that he had been carrying down on top of it. "There's a hell of a lot about Sverenssen that we never dreamed of, and a lot more we don't know that we'd like to. So stop being neurotic, sit down and listen for five minutes, and I'll give you a summary."

Hunt emitted a long sigh of capitulation, threw out his hands in resignation, and slumped down into one of the chairs. "We're going to need a lot more than five minutes, Gregg," he said as Caldwell sat down facing him. "You wait till you hear about the things we found out yesterday from the Thuriens."

Four and a half thousand miles from Houston, Norman Pacey was sitting on a bench by the side of the Serpentine lake in London's Hyde Park. Strollers in open-necked shirts and summery dresses making the best of the first warm days of the year added a dash of color to the surrounding greenery topped by distant frontages of dignified and imposing buildings that had not changed appreciably in fifty years. That was all they had ever wanted, he thought to himself as he took in the sights and sounds around him. All that people the world over had ever wanted was to live their lives, pay their way, and be left alone. So how had the few with different aspirations always been able to command the power to impose themselves and their systems? Which was the greater evil—one fanatic with a cause, or a hundred men free enough not to care about causes? But caring about freedom enough to defend it made it a cause and its defenders fanatics. For ten thousand years mankind had wrestled with the problem and not found an answer.

A shadow fell across the ground, and Mikolai Sobroskin sat down on the bench next to him. He was wearing a heavy suit and necktie despite the fine weather, and his head was glistening with beads of perspiration in the sunlight. "A refreshing contrast to Giordano Bruno," he commented. "What an improvement it would be if the *maria* were really seas."

Pacey turned his head from staring across the lake and grinned. "And maybe a few trees, huh? I think UNSA has got its work cut out for a while with the proposals for cooling down Venus and oxygenating Mars. Luna's way down the list. Even if it weren't, I'm not sure that anybody has come up with any good ideas for what they could do about it. But who knows? One day, maybe."

The Russian sighed. "Perhaps we had such knowledge in the palm of our hand. We threw it away. Do you realize that we have witnessed what could be the greatest crime in human history? And perhaps the world will never know."

Pacey nodded, waiting for a second to assume a more businesslike manner, and asked, "So? . . . What's the news?"

Sobroskin drew a handkerchief from his breast pocket and dabbed his head. "You were right about the coded signals from Gistar when you suspected that they were in response to an independent transmitting facility established by us," he replied.

Pacey nodded without showing surprise. He knew that already from what Caldwell and Lyn Garland had revealed in Washington, but he couldn't say so. "Have you found out how Verikoff and Sverenssen fit in?" he asked.

"I think so," Sobroskin said. "They seem to be part of a global operation of some sort that was committed to shutting down communications of any kind between this planet and Thurien. They used the same methods. Verikoff is a member of a powerful faction that strongly opposed the Soviet attempt to open another channel. Their reasons were the same as the UN's. As it turned out, they were taken by surprise before they could organize an effective block, and some transmissions were sent. Like Sverenssen, Verikoff was instrumental in causing additional messages to be sent secretly, designed to frustrate the exercise. At least we think so. . . . We can't prove it."

Pacey nodded again. He knew that too. "Do you know what they said?" he inquired out of curiosity, although he had read Caldwell's transcripts from Thurien.

"No, but I can guess. These people knew in advance that the relay to Gistar would deactivate. That says to me that they must have been responsible. Presumably they arranged it months ago with an independent launching organization, or maybe a part of UNSA that they knew they could trust . . . I don't know. But my guess is that their strategy was to delay the proceedings via both channels until the relay was put out of action permanently."

Pacey stared across the lake to an enclosed area of water on the far side in which crowds of children were swimming and playing in the sun. The sounds of shouting and laughter drifted across intermittently on the breeze. Apart from the confirmation of Verikoff's involvement, he hadn't learned anything new so far. "What do you make of it?" he asked without turning his head.

After a long, heavy silence, Sobroskin replied, "Russia had a tradition of tyranny through to the early years of this century. Ever since it threw off the yoke of Mongol subjugation in the fifteenth century, it was obsessed with preserving its security to the point that the security of other nations became a threat that could not be tolerated. It expanded its borders by conquest and held on to its acquired territories by oppression, intimidation, and terror. But the new lands in turn had borders, and there was no end to the process. Communism changed nothing. It was merely a banner of convenience for rallying gullible idealists and rationalizing sacrifice. Apart from a few brief months in 1917, Russia was no more Communist than the Church of the Middle Ages was Christian."

He paused to fold his handkerchief and return it to his pocket. Pacey waited without speaking for him to continue. "We thought that all that began to change in the early decades of this century with the end of the threat of thermonuclear war and a more enlightened view of the internationalism. And superficially it did. Many like myself dedicated themselves to creating a new climate of understanding and common progress with the West as it emerged from its own style of tyranny." Sobroskin sighed and shook his head sadly. "But the Thurien affair has revealed that the forces that plunged Russia into its own Dark Age did not go away, and their purpose has not changed." He looked at Pacey sharply. "And the forces that brought religious terror and economic exploitation to the West have not gone away, either. On both sides they have merely modified their stance to avert what would have guaranteed their destruction along with everything else. There is a web across this whole planet that connects many Sverenssens with many Verikoffs. They pose behind banners and slogans that call for liberation, but the liberation they seek is their own, not that of the people who follow them."

"Yes, I know," Pacey said. "We've uncovered some of it too. What's the answer?"

Sobroskin raised an arm and gestured at the far side of the lake. "Those children might have grown up to see other worlds under other suns. But the price of that would have been knowledge, and knowledge is the enemy of tyranny in any disguise. It has freed more people from poverty and oppression than all of the ideologies and creeds in history put together. Every form of serfdom follows from serfdom of the mind."

"I'm not sure what you're saying," Pacey said. "Are you saying you want to come over to us or something?"

The Russian shook his head. "The war that matters has nothing to do with flags. It is between those who would set the minds of children free, and those who would deny them Thurien. The latest battle has been lost, but the war will continue. Perhaps one day we will talk to Thurien again. But in the meantime another battle is looming in Moscow for control of the Kremlin, and that is where I must be." He reached behind him for a package that he had placed on the bench behind him and passed it to Pacey. "We have a tradition of ruthlessness in handling our internal affairs that you do not share. It is possible that many people will not survive the next few months, and I could be one of them. If so, I would like to think that my work has not been for nothing." He released the package and withdrew his arm. "That contains a complete record of all that I know. It would not be safe with my colleagues in Moscow since their future, like my own, is full of uncertainties. But I know that you will use the information wisely, for you understand as well as I do that in the war that really matters we are on the same side." With that he stood up. "I am glad that we met, Norman Pacey. It is reassuring to see that on both sides, bonds exist that are deeper than the colors on maps. I hope that we meet again, but in case that is not to be . . ." He let the words hang and extended a hand.

Pacey stood up and grasped it firmly. "We will. And things will be better," he said.

"I hope so." Sobroskin released his grip, turned, and began walking away along the side of the lake.

Pacey's finger tightened around the package as he stood watching the short, stocky figure marching jerkily off to keep its appointment with fate, possibly to die so that children might laugh. He couldn't let him, he realized. He couldn't let him walk away without knowing. "Mikolai!" he called.

Sobroskin stopped and looked back. Pacey waited. The Russian retraced his steps.

"The battle was not lost," Pacey said. "There's another channel to Thurien operating right now . . . in the United States. It doesn't need the relay. We've been talking to Thurien for weeks. That was why Karen Heller returned to Earth. It's okay. All the Sverenssens in the world can't stop it now."

Sobroskin stared at him for a long time before the words seemed to register. At last he moved his head in a slow, barely perceptible nod, his eyes expressionless and distant, and murmured quietly, "Thank you." Then he turned away and began walking again, this time slowly, as if in a trance. When he had covered twenty yards or so he stopped, stared back again, and raised his arm in a silent salutation. Then he turned away and began walking once more, and after a few steps his pace lightened and quickened.

Even at that distance Pacey had seen the exultation in his expression. Pacey watched until Sobroskin had vanished among the people walking by the boathouses farther along the shoreline, then turned away and walked in the opposite direction, toward the Serpentine bridge.

Chapter Twenty-four

Niels Sverenssen's ten-million-dollar home was situated in Connecticut, forty miles from New York City, on the shore side of a two-hundred-acre estate of parkland and trees overlooking Long Island Sound. The house framed two sides of a large, clover-leaf pool set among terraced banks of shrubs. A tennis court on one side and outbuildings on the other completed the pool's encirclement. The house was fashionably contemporary, spacious, light, and airy, with sections of roof sweeping in clean, unbroken planes from crest almost to ground level in some places to give the complete structure the lines and composition of an abstract sculpture, and drawing back in others to reveal vertical faces and slanted panels of polished brownstone, tiled mosaic, or glass. The imposing central structure rose two levels and contained the larger rooms and Sverenssen's private quarters. One wing fell to single level and comprised six extra bedrooms and additional living space to accommodate the guests of his frequent weekend parties and other functions. The other was two-storied, though not as high as the central portion; it contained offices for Sverenssen and a secretary, a library, and other rooms dedicated to his work.

There was something odd about the history of Sverenssen's house.

Lyn had flown up to New York accompanied by one of Clifford Benson's agents, who had introduced her to a local office of the CIA to examine their records for additional information on Sverenssen. It turned out that his house had been built for him ten years previously by the construction division of Weismand Industries, Inc., a large, diversified corporation. The company was a builder of industrial premises, not private dwellings, which was no doubt why they had called in several outside architects and designers as consultants. What made the project even stranger was that Weismand was based in California; why would Sverenssen have used them when any number of qualified firms existed in the area?

Further checks revealed that Weismand Industries stock was held mainly by a Canadian insurance consortium that was closely linked to the same British banking fraternity that, along with its French and Swiss connections, had launched Sverenssen's spectacular career upon his sudden return from obscurity. Had Sverenssen simply been repaying a favor, or were there other reasons why he felt it necessary to build his house using a company with which he had close, and presumably confidential, connections?

Lyn asked herself the question again as she reclined in a bikini on a chaise by the pool and studied the house through the intervening flower beds and shrubs. Sverenssen, wearing sunglasses and clad in a pair of scarlet bathing trunks, was sitting a few feet away at an umbrellaed table, drinking iced lemonade and talking with a man he had introduced as Larry. A blonde named Cheryl was basking face-down and naked on another chaise a short distance away, while two other girls, Sandy and Carol, were laughing and shouting in the pool with a Mediterranean-looking character by the name of Enrico. Sandy was topless, and the object of the melee in progress was evidently to render her bottomless as well. Another couple had been around earlier, but had been gone for the last hour or so. It was Friday afternoon, and more people were expected to arrive as the evening wore on, plus a few the next morning.

Sverenssen had described the occasion as "a pleasant get-together of some interesting friends" when Lyn called him on Thursday morning.

The only thing that seemed even slightly unusual about the house was the office wing, she decided as she looked at it. Sverenssen had stressed that it was not open to visitors when he showed her around earlier. That seemed reasonable enough, but something *was* different about it, she realized. This part of the building wasn't built to the same airy and open design as the rest of the place, with yards of plate-glass windows and sliding glass doors that led through to the inside. Instead it was solid, with small windows set high off the ground. They looked thick and seemed more suited to keeping sunlight out, along with everything else. As she looked closer, she was sure that what had seemed at first to be ornamental trim across the windows was in fact carefully disguised bars guaranteed to exclude any possibility of entry—not just by burglars, but by a tank. There were no doors to the outside at all; the only access to the wing was from inside the house. If she hadn't been looking specifically, she would never have noticed it, but the office wing, beneath its veneer of tiled designs and paintwork to match the rest of the house, was virtually a fortress.

The noise from the pool rose to a crescendo that culminated in a shriek as Enrico emerged from a flurry of water and bodies waving the lower half of Sandy's swimsuit triumphantly over his head. "One down, one to go," he yelled.

"Not fair!" Sandy screamed. "I was drowning. That's an unfair advantage."

"Carol's turn," Enrico shouted.

"Like hell," Carol laughed. "That's inequality. Sandy, give me a hand and let's get the bastard." The commotion started all over again.

"It sounds as if they could use some help," Sverenssen said, turning his head to look across at Lyn. "Go ahead and join in. There aren't any restrictions on how you enjoy yourself here, you know."

She let her head fall back on the raised end of the chaise

and forced a smile. "Oh, sometimes spectator sports are just as much fun. Anyway, they seem to be managing okay. I'll be the reserve division."

"She's being smart and saving her energy," Larry said, speaking to Sverenssen and sending Lyn a broad wink. She did a good job of pretending not to notice.

"Very wise," Sverenssen said.

"The real fun starts later," Larry explained, grinning. Lyn managed a half-smile, at the same time wondering how she was going to handle that. "We'll find you lots of new friends. They're great people here."

"I can't wait," Lyn said drily.

"Isn't she charming," Sverenssen said, glancing at Larry and looking approvingly back at Lyn. "I met her in Washington, you know—a most fortunate encounter. She has people that she visits here in New York." It made her feel like a piece of merchandise, which was probably a pretty close assessment of her situation.

"I get to Washington a lot," Larry said. "You work there or something?"

Lyn shook her head. "Uh uh. I'm with the Space Arm in Houston—computers, lasers, and people who talk numbers all day . . . but it's a living."

"Ah, but we're going to change that, aren't we, Lyn," Sverenssen said. He looked at Larry. "As a matter of fact I was thinking of something in Washington that would suit her perfectly, and prove far more interesting, I'm sure. Do you remember Phil Grazenby? I had lunch with him one day while I was there recently, and he wants somebody bright and attractive to manage the new agency he's opening. And he is talking about really worthwhile money."

"We'll have to get together there if you make it," Larry said to Lyn. He made a face. "Aw, but that's business, and it's a long time away. Why wait until Washington? We can get to know each other right here. Are you here alone?"

"Yes, she's free," Sverenssen murmured.

"That's great!" Larry exclaimed. "Me too, and I'm the perfect guy for introducing new faces around here. Believe me, honey, you've made the right choice. You must have good taste. Tell you what—you can partner me in one of the games later. So we've got a deal, right?"

"I live for the present," Lyn said. "Suppose we let later take care of itself later, okay?" She stretched to squint up at the sun, then looked at Sverenssen. "Right now all I'm going to be good for is a case of radiation sickness if I don't cover up. I'm going to go inside in the shade and put on something else until it cools down a bit. I'll see you later?"

"By all means, my dear," Sverenssen said. "The last thing we want is for you to end up on the casualty list." Lyn unfolded herself from the chaise and walked toward the house. "I think you may have a little game of playing hard to get to win before—" she heard Sverenssen murmur. The rest was drowned out by another burst of screaming from the pool.

Cheryl raised her head and watched as Lyn disappeared between the shrubs. "You've got nothing to offer, Larry," she said. "Now *I* could show her a good time that's really different."

"So what's wrong with both of us?" Larry asked.

Lyn's room contained twin king-size beds and was as luxuriously furnished and fitted as every other part of the house. She was supposed to be sharing it with somebody called Donna, who hadn't arrived yet. Inside, she took off her bikini and put on a shirt and shorts. Then she stood by the window thinking for a while.

There was a datagrid screen in the room, but she didn't want to make any calls since there was a good chance it was bugged. Anyway she didn't need to if she wanted to get out because Clifford Benson's people had already anticipated that. Inside her shoulder bag in the closet was a microelectronic transmitter that looked like a powder compact but would send out a signal when she unlocked a safety catch and pressed a disguised button. If she pressed it once, a CIA agent would call the house within seconds, posing as a brother with news of a family emergency and stating that a cab was on its way to collect her. If she pressed it three times, the two agents in the airmobile parked a mile down the road from the front gate would arrive in under half a minute, but that option was for use only if she got into real trouble. But she didn't want to get out just yet. The house was empty and quieter than it would be at any time for the rest of the weekend. There would never be another chance like this for a look around the place with little risk of being disturbed. She sure-as-hell wasn't going to chicken out after a couple of hours with nothing to report, she told herself.

She took a deep breath, bit her lip nervously, walked over to the door, inched it open, and listened. Everything seemed still. As she let herself out into the passage a half-stifled giggle came from behind the door opposite. She stopped for a second; there was no other sound, and she moved quietly on toward the central part of the house.

The passage led through a small den into a large, central, open room that rose the full height of the building, one side a sloping wall of glass panels facing the rear of the house. The room was elbow-shaped, thickly carpeted, and had a sunken floor in front of a large fireplace of brickwork, with areas of raised floors around it angling away to openings and stairways which gave access to other parts of the house.

Muffled voices and kitchen noises were coming from one of the corridors, but she didn't detect any sign of Sverenssen's domestic staff in her immediate vicinity. She slowly examined the furnishings, ornaments, the pictures on the walls, and the fittings overhead, but found nothing that looked out of place. After pausing to replay her mental model of the layout, she picked out a narrow corridor that seemed to lead toward the office wing and followed it.

Eventually, after exploring the system of rooms that the corridor brought her to, most of which she had already seen in the course of the quick tour that Sverenssen had given her, she came back to what seemed to be the only door anywhere that opened through into the office wing. She tried the handle gently, but it was locked, as she had expected. When she tapped it with a knuckle, the sound it produced was flat and solid, even from the parts that looked like ordinary wood panels. They might have been wood on the surface, but there was a lot of something else underneath; that door had been put there to keep out a lot more than just drafts. Without a rock drill or an army demolition squad, she wasn't going to get any farther in that direction, so she turned to go back to the center part of the house. As she began moving, she recalled one of the sculptures that she had seen in the central room. It hadn't really struck her at the time, but now as she thought about it again, she realized that there had been something vaguely familiar about it. Surely not, she thought as she tried to visualize it again in her mind. There was no way it could be possible. She frowned and her pace quickened a fraction.

The piece was standing in an illuminated recess of one side of the brick fireplace—an abstract form rendered in some kind of silver and gold translucent crystal, about eight inches high and mounted on a solid black base. At least, when she glanced over it casually a few minutes earlier she had thought it to be abstract. But now as she picked it up and turned it slowly over in her hands, she became more convinced than ever that its form couldn't be simply a coincidence.

Its lowermost part was a composition of surfaces and shapes that could have meant anything, but projecting up from the center to form the main body of the design was a tapering column of finely carved terraces, levels, and intervening buttresses flowing upward in distinctive curves. Could it represent a tower? she wondered. A tower that she had seen not long ago. Three slim spires continued upward from the top of the main column—three spires supporting a circular disk just below their apexes. A platform? The disk had more finely cut details on its surface. She turned the sculpture over . . . and gasped. There were more details, defining a readily discernible pattern of concentric rings—on the *underside* of the platform! She was looking at a representation of the central tower of the city of Vranix. It couldn't possibly be. But it couldn't be anything else.

Her hand was shaking as she carefully replaced the sculpture in its recess. What the hell had she gotten herself into? she asked herself. Her first urge was to go back to her room, collect her things, and get out fast; but as she forced herself to calm down and her mind to think more clearly, she fought back the feeling. The opportunity to learn more was unique, and it would never present itself again. If there were more, nobody might ever know unless she found it now. She closed her eyes for a second and took a deep breath to summon up her reserves of nervous energy to see it through.

She had to find out more about the office wing, but there seemed no way to get inside. Maybe she could get nearer in some other way . . . under it, perhaps? A house like this would surely have cellars. There would probably be stairs somewhere in the direction of the kitchen. She moved across to the end of the corridor leading that way; voices were still audible, but they sounded closed off. Two doors proved to be closets. The third that she tried revealed a flight of wooden stairs going down. She entered, eased the door shut behind her, and descended.

The cellar that she found herself in looked ordinary, with a bench and some tool racks, a storage space, and lots of pipes and conduits. Machinery of some kind, probably a central air conditioner, was humming behind a louvered door to one side. Two other cellars opened off from this one, one in each direction of the two arms of the house; she moved on into the one leading toward the office wing. It was another storage area, full of boxes and leftover decorating materials. A partition wall with a gap in its center screened off the far end. Lyn crossed the area and peered through the gap. The cellar did not continue on beneath the office wing, but ended at a bare wall on the far side of the small space behind the partition. As Lyn looked around and studied the surroundings, she realized that the part of the cellars she had entered was strangely different from the rest structurally, particularly the blank wall facing her.

The line where the wall and ceiling met was formed by a steel girder that must have measured fifteen inches across the flange at least, and it was supported by two more, equally massive members running down the corners and terminating in what looked like solid concrete foundations partly visible along the lower part of the walls and going down into the floor.

The ceiling, too, was reinforced with girders and cross ties gusseted at the angles. All was painted white to blend in with the general background of the other cellar rooms, and the casual visitor would probably never have noticed; but to somebody who was looking for the unusual and who had a special interest in that end of the house, the heavy structures stood out unmistakably.

So the office wing itself was not over any part of the cellars but was built on solid ground, and she was looking at one side of its foundation and underpinning. It was built from materials and in a fashion that would have supported a battleship. What could there be upstairs that would have crushed the foundations of an ordinary house and had made all this necessary? she wondered.

And then she remembered the holes she had seen punched through the concrete at McClusky.

A Thurien interstellar communications system contained a microscopic, artificially generated, black-hole toroid when it was switched on and operating.

But that idea was even more insane. The house had been built ten years before. Nobody had heard of the Ganymeans, let alone Thurien, in 2021.

She backed slowly away from the partition and turned dazedly back toward the stairs.

At the top of the stairs she stopped for a while to give the thumping in her chest time to slow down and to bring her reeling mind under some kind of control. Then she opened the door a fraction and brought her eye close to it just in time to catch a glimpse of Sverenssen moving out of sight behind an angle in the wall back near the corner room. He had been turning his head from side to side as he moved, as if he were looking for something . . . or somebody. Lyn immediately erupted into a new spasm of shaking and shivering. Suddenly Navcomms and Houston seemed very far away. If she ever got out of this, she'd never want to leave the coziness of her own office again.

If Sverenssen was looking for her, he would already have tried knocking on the door of her room. The part of her that felt guilty told her that she needed a reason for not being there.

She thought for a few seconds, then let herself out into the corridor and went the other way, into the kitchen. A minute later she reemerged holding a cup of coffee and began making her way back to the guest section of the house.

"Oh, *there* you are." Sverenssen's voice sounded from behind her when she was halfway across one of the raised floors around the periphery of the corner room. She froze; had she done anything else, the coffee and the cup would have been all over the carpet. Sverenssen came out of one of the side rooms as she turned to face him. He was still wearing his bathing trunks, but had put sandals on his feet and thrown a shirt loosely over his shoulder. He was eyeing her uncertainly, as if he were mildly suspicious about something but not sufficiently sure of himself to be direct.

"I went to get some coffee," she said, as if it weren't obvious. Immediately she felt like the classic dumb broad; but at least she managed to stop herself from following up her statement with an inane laugh. She was certain that Sverenssen was looking past her shoulder at the sculpture in its recess. She could picture it in her mind's eye with a neon sign in six-inch letters above shouting, "I HAVE BEEN MOVED." Somehow she resisted the compulsion to turn her head.

"I wouldn't have thought that somebody from Houston would be bothered by the sun," he remarked. "Especially somebody with a tan like yours." His voice was superficially casual, but had an undertone that invited an explanation.

For a second or two she felt trapped. Then she said, "I just wanted to get away for a while. Your friend . . . Larry, was starting to come on a bit strong. I guess I need time to get used to this."

Sverenssen looked at her dubiously, as if she had just confirmed his fears about something. "Well, I do hope you manage to loosen up a little before too much longer," he said. "I mean, the whole idea of being here is to enjoy oneself. It would be such a shame if one person allowed her inhibitions to ruin the atmosphere for everyone else, wouldn't it."

Despite her confusion, Lyn couldn't keep a sharp edge out of her voice. "Look . . . I didn't exactly come here expecting this," she told him. "You never said anything about playing musical people."

A pained expression came over Sverenssen's face. "Oh dear, I do hope you're not going to start preaching any middle-class morals. What did you expect? I said I would be entertaining some friends, and I expect them to be entertained and made to feel welcome in a manner appropriate to their tastes."

"*Their* tastes? That's very nice of you. They must love you for it. What about my tastes?"

"Are you suggesting that *my* acquaintances fail to come up to *your* standards? How amusing. You've already made your tastes quite plain—you aspire to luxury and the company that goes with it. Well, you have them. Surely you don't expect anything in this life to come free."

"I didn't expect to be treated like a piece of candy to be dangled in front of those overgrown kids out there."

"You're talking like an adolescent. Do I not have a right to expect you, as my guest, to behave sociably in return for my hospitality? Or did you imagine that I was some kind of a philanthropist who opens his home to the world for reasons of pure charity? I can assure you that I am nothing of the kind, and neither is anybody else who has the intelligence to understand the realities of life."

"Who said anything about charity? Doesn't respect for people come into it anywhere?"

Sverenssen sneered. Evidently it didn't. "Another middle-class opiate. All I can say to you is that whatever fantasies you have been harboring appear to have been sadly unfounded." He sighed and shrugged, apparently having already dismissed the matter as a lost cause. "The opportunity is yours to enjoy a life quite free from worries financial or otherwise, but seizing it requires that you throw off a lot of silly protective notions left over from childhood and make a pragmatic assessment of your situation."

Lyn's eyes blazed, but she managed to keep her voice under control. "I think I just made it." Her tone said the rest.

Sverenssen appeared indifferent. "In that case I suggest that you call yourself a cab without further delay and return to your world of misplaced romanticism and unfulfillable dreams," he said. "It really makes no difference to me. I can get some-body else here within the hour. The choice is entirely yours."

Lyn stood absolutely still until she had fought down the urge to hurl her coffee in his face. Then she turned away and, mustering the effort to maintain her calm, walked off in the direction of her room. Sverenssen followed her coldly with his eyes for a few seconds, then shrugged contemptuously and hurried out through a side door to rejoin the others at the pool.

Two hours later Lyn was sitting in a Washington-bound plane beside the CIA agent who had accompanied her to New York. Around them sat families, couples, people alone, and people together; some were dressed in business suits, some in jackets, and others in casual shirts, sweaters, and jeans. They were talking, laughing, reading, and sleeping—just ordinary, sane, civilized people, minding their own business. She wanted to hug every one of them.

Chapter Twenty-five

In the illusory world of VISAR's creations, Karen Heller was half a billion miles tall and floating in space. A loosely coupled binary system of Ping-Pong-ball-size stars, one yellow and one white, was revolving slowly in front of her while a myriad more glowed as pinpoints of light in the blackness stretching away on every side. The center of mass of the two stars was located at one of the foci of a highly elongated ellipse, superposed on the view by VISAR, tracing the orbit of the planet Surio.

Hanging in space beside Heller and looking like some cosmic god contemplating the material universe as if it were a plaything, Danchekker extended an arm to point at the planet sliding along its trajectory in VISAR's speeded-up simulation. "The conditions that Surio encounters at opposite ends of the ellipse are completely different," he said. "At one end it's in close proximity to both its suns and therefore very hot; at the other it's remote from them and therefore quite cool. Its year alternates between a long oceanic phase during the cool period, and an equally long hot phase during which Surio possesses practically no hydrosphere at all. Eesyan tells me it's unique among the worlds that the Thuriens have discovered so far."

"It's fascinating," Heller said, enthralled. "And you're saying that life has emerged there despite those conditions. It sounds impossible."

"I thought so too," Danchekker told her. "Eesyan had to show me this before I'd believe otherwise. That was what I wanted to show you. Let's go down and take a closer look at the planet itself."

They seemed to be rushing toward Surio as VISAR responded to the verbal cue. The stars vanished away behind them, and the planet grew rapidly and swelled into a sphere that flattened out beneath them as they descended from the sky. It was in a cool, oceanic phase, and as they plunged downward they shrank in size so that the sea stretching from horizon to horizon looked normal. Then they were underwater, with strange alien life forms swimming and twisting the ocean around them.

A black, fishlike creature, vaguely reminiscent of some shark species, seemed to single itself out, their viewpoint moving progressively as they followed it. Then, as VISAR altered the content of the information being injected into their visual systems, the body and soft tissues of the creature became a translucent haze to reveal clearly the structure of its skeleton. The light filtering through the water from above went out suddenly, then came on again, then continued to flicker steadily like a slow-motion stroboscope. The image of the fish remained motionless in front of them. "Day and night cycles," Danchekker explained in answer to Heller's questioning look. "VISAR is speeding them up and freezing this image artificially so that we can observe it. Have you noticed yet that the intensity of the daylight periods is increasing?"

Heller had. She also noticed that the creature's skeleton was beginning to change subtly. Its spine was shortening and getting thicker, and the bones inside its fins were elongating and differentiating into clearly discernible jointed segments. Also, the fins were slowly migrating toward the creature's underside. "What's happening there?" she asked, pointing.

"It's an adaptation that I thought you might be interested

in seeing," Danchekker replied. "The year is growing warmer, and the oceans around us have begun evaporating rapidly." VISAR obligingly raised them high above the surface again to confirm the statement. The face of the planet had already changed beyond recognition since their arrival. The oceans had retreated to a series of steep-sided basins, uncovering broad shelves that now connected into vast land masses what had previously been scattered islands, and minor continents. Carpets of vegetation were creeping outward behind the receding shorelines and upward into what had been barren mountainous regions. A dense cloud blanket had formed, from which continuous rains were drenching the highlands.

They watched the surface transformation continue for a while, and then descended once more to follow local events in a shallow estuary formed where a river draining water from the rainy areas inland had carved a trench across the exposed continental shelf to one of the diminishing ocean basins. The creature that they had studied previously was now an amphibian living on the mud flats, with rudimentary legs already functioning and a fully differentiated mobile head. "It dissolves its bones by means of specially secreted fluids triggered by environmental cues, and grows a new skeleton more suited to an existence in its changed environment," Danchekker commented. "Quite remarkable."

To Heller this seemed an overly drastic solution. "Couldn't it stay a fish and simply move out into the oceans?" she asked.

"Very soon there won't be any oceans," Danchekker told her. "Wait and see."

The oceans shrank into isolated pools surrounded by mud, and then dried up completely. As the climate grew hotter the rivers from the highlands became trickles as they flowed downhill, finally evaporating away before reaching the basins, and what had been the seabeds turned into deserts. The vegetation receded across the shelves until it had been reduced to scattered oases of life clinging doggedly to the highest plateaus and mountain peaks. The creature had migrated upward and was now a fully adapted land dweller with a scaly skin and prehensile forelimbs, not unlike some of the earliest terrestrial reptiles. "Now it's in its fully transformed state," Danchekker said. "As Surio goes through a year, the animal cycles are repeated from one extreme of morphology to the other. An amazing example of how tenacious life can be under adverse conditions, wouldn't you agree."

The day lengthened as light periods from the two suns over-lapped, and then shortened again as Surio came around the tip of its orbit and began its long swing outward into another cold phase. The vegetation began advancing down the mountainsides, the creature's limbs commenced reducing, and the whole sequence went slowly into reverse. "Do you think intelligence could ever emerge in a place like this?" Heller asked curiously.

"Who can say?" Danchekker replied. "A few days ago I would have said that what we have just witnessed was unthink-able."

"It's fantastic," Heller murmured in awe.

"No, it's reality," Danchekker said. "Reality is far more fan-tastic than anything that unaided human imagination could ever devise. The mind could not, for example, visualize a new color, such as infrared or ultraviolet. It can only manipulate combinations of elements that it has already experienced. Everything that is truly new can only come from the Universe outside. And uncovering the truth that lies out there is, of course, the function of science."

Heller looked at him suspiciously. "If I didn't know you better, I'd think you were trying to start an argument," she teased. "Let's get back before this conversation goes any fur-ther and see if Vic's called in yet."

"I agree," Danchekker said at once. "VISAR, back to McClusky, please."

He got up from the recliner, moved out into the corridor of the perceptron, and waited for a moment until Heller emerged from one of the other cubicles. They exited through the ante-chamber, were conveyed down to ground level, and a few seconds later were walking along the side of the apron toward the mess hall.

"I'm not going to let you get away with that," Heller began

after a short silence. "I started out in law, which has a lot to do with uncovering the truth too, you know. And its methods are just as scientific. Just because you scientists need computers to do your work for you, that doesn't give you a monopoly on logic."

Danchekker thought for a moment. "Mmm . . . very well. If one is hampered by mathematical illiteracy, law does provide something of an alternative, I suppose," he conceded loftily.

"Oh really? I would say it demands far more ingenuity. What's more, it taxes the intellect in ways that scientists never have to bother about."

"What an extraordinary statement! And how would that be, might I ask?"

"Nature is often complex, but never dishonest, Professor. How often have you had to contend with deliberate falsification of the evidence, or an opponent with as much vested interest in obscuring the truth as you have in revealing it?"

"Hmph! And when was the last time that you had to subject your hypotheses to the test of rigorous proof by experiment, eh? Answer me that," Danchekker challenged.

"We do not enjoy the luxury of repeatable experiments," Heller responded. "Not many criminals will oblige by recommitting their crimes under controlled laboratory conditions. So, you see, we have to keep our wits sharp enough to be right the first time."

"Hmm, hmm, hmm . . ."

They had timed their return to McClusky well. Hunt called just as they entered the control room. "How quickly can you get back here?" Danchekker asked him. "Karen has had some remarkable thoughts which after some reflection I find myself forced to agree with. We need to discuss them at the earliest opportunity."

"Gregg and I are leaving right away," Hunt told him. "We've just heard about John's visit to the city. It puts a whole new light on everything. We need to talk to the board ASAP. Can you fix it?" It meant that Packard's report of Pacey's meeting with Sobroskin had arrived in Houston, and a meeting with

Calazar and the Thuriens was urgently called for.

"I'll see to it immediately," Danchekker promised.

An hour later, while Hunt and Caldwell were still on their way and after Danchekker had made arrangements with Calazar, Jerol Packard called from Washington. "Hold everything," he instructed. "Mary's back. We're putting her on a plane up to you right now. Whatever you think you already know, I guarantee it's not half of it. She just blew our minds here. Don't do anything until she's talked to you."

"I'll see to it immediately," Danchekker sighed.

Chapter Twenty-six

For Imares Broghuilio, Premier of the Federation of Jevlenese Worlds and head of the Thurien civilization's Jevlenese component, the past few months had been beset with unexpected crises that had threatened to disrupt the carefully laid plans of generations.

First there had been the sudden and completely unpredictable reappearance of the *Shapieron* on Earth. The Thuriens had known nothing about that until the signal sent out by the Terrans at the time of the ship's departure was somehow relayed directly to VISAR without going through JEVEX. How that had happened had been, and still was, a mystery. Broghuilio had been left with no choice but to preempt awkward questions by going to Calazar first with the Jevlenese account of what had transpired, namely that the Jevlenese had felt apprehensive at the thought of inviting Thurien intervention in a situation already made precarious by the belligerence and instability of the Terrans and therefore, rightly or wrongly, had decided to postpone announcing any news until the ship was safely clear of Earth. The explanation had by necessity been hastily contrived, but at the time Calazar had seemed to accept it. The device that had relayed the signal was not something that the Thuriens had placed near the solar system, Calazar had insisted in response to Broghuilio's accusation; the Thuriens had not broken their agreement to leave Earth surveillance to the Jevlenese. Privately, however, Broghuilio's experts had been able to suggest no other explanation for the relay. It seemed possible, therefore, that the Thuriens were, after all, more prudent than he had given them credit for.

This suspicion had been reinforced some months later when the Thuriens secretly reopened their dialogue with Earth for the unprecedented purpose of double-checking information supplied by JEVEX. Broghuilio had been unable to challenge this development openly since doing so would have revealed the existence of information sources on Earth that the Thuriens could not be allowed to discover, but with some fast footwork he had neutralized the attempt, at least for the time being, by securing control of the Earth end of the link. His bid to counter the surprise Soviet move of opening a second channel had not proved as successful, and he had been forced to resort to more desperate measures by having the link put out of action—something which he had avoided until that point because of the risk of the Thuriens electing to continue the dialogue by more direct means. He had calculated that they would hesitate for a long time before breaking their agreement in so open a fashion.

The Thuriens had not chosen to divulge their contact with Earth by mentioning the incident. Broghuilio's advisors had interpreted this as confirmation that the measures taken to persuade the Thuriens that Earth was responsible for the destruction of the relay had succeeded. A further implication was that the image that had been created of a hostile and aggressive Earth had survived intact, which, it was felt, would suffice to dissuade the Thuriens from taking things further by contemplating a landing.

After some anxious moments, therefore, the gamble appeared to have paid off. The only remaining problem was the *Shapieron*, outward bound from the solar system and already beyond the point where an interception could be staged with only a moderate risk of disturbing planetary orbits. Broghuilio had guessed that the Thuriens, being the cautious breed that they were, would play safe and allow an ample safety margin. Accordingly he had put the relay first in order of priority, using it as a test of how easily the Thuriens would accept a suggestion of an overtly hostile act on the part of the Terrans. If they did accept it, then the odds would be acceptable they would hold Earth responsible for the destruction of the *Shapieron* as well. The Thuriens had passed the test, and now only a matter of minutes stood between Imares Broghuilio and the elimination of the last element of a problem that had been plaguing him for too long.

He felt a deep sense of satisfaction at a difficult challenge met as he stood at one end of the War Room, deep below a mountain range on Jevlen, surrounded by his entourage of advisors and military strategists, following the reports coming in through JEVEX from the instruments tracking the *Shapieron* many light-years away. As he looked slowly around at the ranks of generals in the all-black uniforms of the Jevlenese military and at the arrays of equipment bringing information from and carrying his directions to every corner of his empire, he felt a deep and stirring anticipation of fulfillment at the approaching appointment that destiny had set for him. It was a manifestation of the Jevlenese superiority and iron willpower of which he was both the last in a long succession of architects and the ultimate personification, and which would soon assert itself across the Galaxy.

The uniforms were not yet worn openly, and this place was not known to the Ganymeans who visited Jevlen and on occasion remained for protracted periods for various reasons. Organization, planning, and training operations were still conducted in secret, but already an embryonic officer corps was ready to emerge with an established command chain to a nucleus of trained active units upon which a carefully worked-out recruitment program could begin building at short notice. The factories hidden deep beneath the surface of Uttan, one of the remote worlds controlled by Jevlen, had been steadily accumulating weapons and munitions for several years, and the plans to switch the whole Jevlenese industrial and economic machine fully to a war footing were in an advanced stage.

But the time was not yet quite right. On one or two occasions the events of the past few months had almost prompted him into being swayed by the overreactions and panickings of his lesser aides and acting prematurely. But by thinking clearly and with courage and sheer willpower he had steered them through the obstacles and annihilated the problems one by one until finally only the matter of the *Shapieron* remained. And that would be disposed of very soon now. He had been tested and found not to be lacking, as the Cerians would discover for themselves as soon as the inhibiting yoke of Thurien had been cast off. But not yet . . . not quite yet.

"Target closed to within one scan period," JEVEX announced. The atmosphere in the room was tensely expectant. The *Shapieron* was approaching the device that had been transferred into its path via a toroid projected several days earlier in order for the gravitational disturbance to be outside the range of any Thurien tracking instruments following the ship at the time. The device itself, packing a nucleonic punch of several gigatons and programmed to detonate automatically on proximity, was gravitationally passive and would not register on the Thurien tracking system, which operated by computing the spatial location of the stressfield produced by the ship's drive. JEVEX's statement meant that the bomb would go off before the tracking system delivered its next update.

Garwain Estordu, one of Broghuilio's scientific advisors, seemed nervous. "I don't like it," he muttered. "I still say we should have diverted the ship and interned it at Uttan or somewhere. This . . ." He shook his head. "It's too extreme. If the Thuriens find out, we'll have no defense."

"This is a unique opportunity. The Ganymeans are psychologically ready to blame Earth," Broghuilio declared. "Such an opportunity will not come again. Such moments are to be seized and exploited, not wasted by timidity and indecision." He looked at the scientist disdainfully. "That is why I command and you follow. Genius is knowing the difference between acceptable risk and rashness, and then being willing to play for high stakes. Great things were never achieved by half-measures." He snorted. "Besides, what could the Thuriens do? They cannot match strength with strength. Their heritage has left them sadly ill-equipped to deal with the realities of the Universe on the terms that the Universe dictates."

"They have survived for a long time, nevertheless," Estordu observed.

"Artificially, because they have never faced the test of opposition," General Wylott declared, taking up the party line from one side of Broghuilio. "But trial by strength is the Universe's natural law. When the more natural course of events unfolds, they will not prevail. They are not tempered to spearhead the advance into the unknowns of the Galaxy."

"There speaks a soldier," Broghuilio said, scowling balefully at Estordu and the rest of the scientists. "You bleat like Ganymean sheep while you are in the safety of the fold, but who will protect you when you go out onto the mountain to face the lions?"

At that moment JEVEX spoke again: "Latest update now analyzed." A hush fell at once across the Jevlenese War Room. "Target no longer registering in scan data. All traces have vanished. Destruction effected with one-hundred-percent success. Mission accomplished."

The tension lifted abruptly, and a flurry of relieved murmurings broke out on all sides. Broghuilio permitted a grim smile of satisfaction as he drew himself up to his full height to acknowledge the congratulations being directed toward him from around the floor. His chest swelled with the feeling of power and authority that his uniform symbolized. Wylott turned and threw his arm out in a crisp Jevlenese salute acknowledging the leader. The rest of the military followed suit.

Broghuilio made a perfunctory return, waited a few moments for the excitement to subside, then raised an arm. "This is but a small foretaste of what is to come," he told them, his voice booming to carry to the far corners of the room. "Nothing will stand in our path when Jevlen marches forward to its destiny. The Thuriens will be wisps of straw lost in the hurricane that will sweep across first the solar system, and then the Galaxy. DO YOU DARE TO FOLLOW ME?"

"WE DARE!" came the response.

Broghuilio smiled again. "You will not be disappointed," he promised. He waited for the room to quiet and then said in a milder tone, "But in the meantime we have our good *duty* to perform for our Ganymean masters." His mouth writhed in sarcasm as he wrung out the final word, causing grins to appear on the faces of some of his followers. He raised his head a fraction. "JEVEX, contact Calazar through VISAR and request that Estordu, Wylott, and I see him at once on a matter of gravest urgency."

"Yes, Excellency," JEVEX acknowledged. A short delay followed. Then JEVEX reported, "VISAR informs me that Calazar is currently in conference and asks if the matter can wait."

"I have just received news of the most serious nature," Broghuilio said. "It cannot wait. Convey my apologies to Calazar and inform VISAR that I must insist on going to Thurien immediately. Tell VISAR we have reason to believe that the *Shapieron* has met with a catastrophe."

A minute or two went by. Then JEVEX announced, "Calazar will receive you immediately."

Chapter Twenty-seven

At Houston, Caldwell had described to Hunt the network of real power that had lain hidden across the world possibly for centuries, operating to preserve privilege and promote self-interest by opposing and controlling scientific progress. The attempt first to frustrate and then to shut down communications with Thurien had seemed consistent with such a power structure and policy.

Then Danchekker had called in a visibly excited state from McClusky with the news that Karen Heller had opened up a completely new dimension to the whole situation. On arriving in Alaska hours later, Hunt and Caldwell learned of the evidence for supposing that the Jevlenese had been interfering with Earth's technological development since the dawn of its history while they grew in numbers, reorganized, and profited from their access to Ganymean knowledge. This notion had proved so astonishing that nobody made the connection between the two sets of information until Lyn arrived from Washington with the staggering announcement that not only was Sverenssen in communication with the Jevlenese, as he apparently had been for many years, but that, from the evidence of the sculpture, the Jevlenese were still staging physical visits to Earth, at least intermittently. In other words the Jevlenese had not been interfering merely way back in early times; what Pacey and Sobroskin had started to uncover parts of right now was a Jevlenese-controlled operation.

This news immediately threw up a host of whole new questions. Was Sverenssen simply a native Terran working as a collaborator, or was he actually a Jevlenese agent injected into Earth's society and using the identity of a Swede killed in Africa years before? Whatever the answer, how many more like him were there and who were they? Why had the Jevlenese been distorting their reports to make Earth appear warlike? Could the reason be that they wanted a pretext to justify to the Ganymeans their maintaining a military strength of their own as an "insurance" against the possibility of future terrestrial aggression beyond the solar system? If so, who had the Jevlenese been intending to direct the military strength against—the Thuriens, to end what was seen as an era of Ganymean domination; or Earth, to settle an account that went back fifty thousand years? If Earth, had the activities of Sverenssen's network to promote strategic disarmament and peaceful coexistence during recent decades been a deliberate ploy calculated to render Earth defenseless and set it up to be taken over as a going industrial and economic concern instead of the ball of smoking rubble that would have been left had it been able to offer resistance? And if this were true, how had the Jevlenese then intended to deal with the Thuriens, who would hardly have just sat and done nothing while it all happened?

There had been more than enough reasons to talk straight away to the Ganymeans, so Calazar had called everybody together at Thurios—including Garuth, Shilohin, and Monchar from the *Shapieron*. After the ensuing debate had droned on for over two hours, VISAR interrupted to announce that something had just destroyed the object substituted for the *Shapieron*. Minutes later Imares Broghuilio, Premier of the Jevlenese group of worlds, contacted Calazar to request an immediate appointment.

Sitting off to one side of a room in the Government Center at Thurios with the others from McClusky, Hunt waited tensely for the confrontation with the first Jevlenese they would meet face to face, who were due to appear at any second. Garuth and his two companions from the *Shapieron* formed another small group on the far side; and Calazar, Eesyan, Showm, and a few more Thuriens were clustered at one end. The Ganymeans were still somewhat shaken by what they had learned of deception and subterfuge that went beyond their wildest imaginings. Even Frenua Showm had conceded that without the apparently uniquely human ability to penetrate such deviousness, it was doubtful that the Ganymeans would ever have reached the bottom of it. It seemed that being suspicious of another's motives was something that came with the conditioning of predatorial thinking, and Ganymeans simply were not predators. "On Earth they say you must set a thief to catch a thief," Garuth had remarked. "It appears just as true that to catch a human you must set a human."

"They might be great scientists, but they'd make lousy lawyers," Karen Heller murmured in Danchekker's ear. Danchekker snorted and said nothing.

Calazar was curious to see how far the Jevlenese would go in their fabrications if fed sufficient rope; also, there was more that he hoped to learn from them before exposing just how much he knew. For these reasons he did not want to confront them immediately with the presence of the Terrans and the *Shapieron* Ganymeans. He therefore instructed VISAR to edit out of the datastream sent to JEVEX, and hence to the participants on Jevlen, all information pertaining to those two groups. It meant that Hunt, Garuth, and their companions would, after a fashion, be there, but remain completely invisible to the Jevlenese. Such a tactic was a flagrant violation of good manners and Thurien law, and unprecedented throughout the many centuries for which VISAR had been in use. Nonetheless Calazar decreed that by their own actions the Jevlenese had warranted making this occasion an exception. Hunt was looking forward to the consequences.

"Premier Broghuilio, Secretary Wylott, and Scientific

Adviser Estordu," VISAR announced. Hunt stiffened. Three figures materialized at the end of the room opposite Calazar and
the Thuriens. The one in the center had to be Broghuilio, Hunt
decided at once. He stood six-foot-three at least, and had dark
eyes that blazed fiercely from a face made all the more intimi-
dating by a mane of thick, black hair and a pugnacious mouth
surrounded by a short, cropped beard. His body was clad in a
short coat of gold sheen worn over a mauve tunic covering a
barrel-like chest and powerful torso.

"What of the *Shapieron*?" Calazar demanded in an unusually
clipped voice. Hunt would have expected that for one of
Broghuilio's rank some form of opening formality would have
been appropriate. The flicker of surprise that he caught on
the faces of the other two Jevlenese seemed to say so too. One
of them looked directly at where Hunt was sitting and stared
straight through. It was a strange feeling.

"I regret the intrusion," Broghuilio began. His voice was
deep and harsh, and he spoke stiffly, in the manner of somebody performing a duty that demanded a greater show of
feeling than he could muster readily. "We have just received
news of the most serious nature: all traces of the ship have
disappeared from our tracking data. We can only conclude that
it has been destroyed." He paused and cast his eyes around
the room for effect. "The possibility that this could be the result
of a deliberate act cannot be dismissed."

The Thuriens stared back in silence for what seemed a long
time. They did not attempt playacting any show of concern or
dismay . . . or even surprise. The first glimmer of uncertainty
crept into Broghuilio's eyes as he searched the Ganymean faces
for a reaction. Evidently this was not going as he had anticipated.

One of the other two, also tall, dressed somberly in dark
blue and black, with icy blue eyes, slicked-back silver hair, and
a florid face that tended toward puffiness, seemed not to have
read the signs. "We tried to warn you," he said, spreading his
hands imploringly in a good imitation of sharing the anguish
that the Thuriens were presumably supposed to be feeling at
that moment. "We urged you to intercept the ship before now."

That was hardly true; possibly he placed a lot of faith in his powers of suggestion. "We told you that Earth would never allow the *Shapieron* to reach Thurien."

Across the room Garuth's eyes turned steely, and his expression was about as close to malevolence as that of a Ganymean could get. "Patience, Garuth," Hunt called out. "You'll get your shots in before long."

"Luckily Ganymeans possess plenty of that," Garuth replied. The Jevlenese didn't hear a thing. It was uncanny.

"Really?" Calazar responded after a pause. He sounded neither convinced nor impressed. "Your concern is most touching, Secretary Wylott. You almost sound as if you believe your own lies."

Wylott froze with his mouth hanging half open, obviously taken completely aback. The third Jevlenese, who had to be Estordu, was a lean, thin-faced man with a hooked nose, wearing an elaborate two-piece garment of light green embroidered with gold over a yellow shirt. He threw up his hands in shock. "Lies? I don't understand. Why do you say that? You have been tracking the ship yourselves. Hasn't VISAR confirmed the data?"

Broghuilio's expression darkened. "You have insulted us," he rumbled ominously. "Are you telling us that VISAR does not corroborate what we have said?"

"I'm not disputing the data," Calazar told him. "But I would advise you to think again about your explanation for it."

Broghuilio drew himself up to his full height to face the Thuriens squarely. Evidently he was going to brazen it out. "Explain yourself, Calazar," he growled.

"But we are waiting for *you* to explain yourself," Showm said from one side of Calazar. Her voice was low, little more than a whisper, but it held the tension of a tightly wound spring. Broghuilio jerked his face around to look at her, his eyes darting suspiciously from side to side as a sixth sense told him he had walked into a trap. "Let's forget the *Shapieron* for a moment," Showm went on. "How long has JEVEX been falsifying its reports of Earth?"

"What?" Broghuilio's eyes bulged. "I don't understand. What is the—"

"How long?" Showm asked again, her voice rising suddenly to cut the air sharply. Her tone and the expressions of the other Thuriens spelled out clearly that any attempt at a denial would have been futile. The hue of Broghuilio's face deepened to purple, but he seemed too stunned to form a reply.

"What grounds do you have for such an accusation?" Wylott demanded. "The department that conducts the surveillance is responsible to me. I consider this a personal attack."

"Evidence?" Showm uttered the word offhandedly, as if the demand were too absurd to take seriously. "Earth disarmed strategically in the second decade of its current century and has pursued peaceful coexistence ever since, but JEVEX has never mentioned it. Instead JEVEX has reported nucleonic weapons deployed in orbit, radiation projectors sited on Luna, military installations across the solar system, and a whole concoction of fictions that have never existed. Do you deny it?"

Estordu was thinking frantically as he listened. "Corrections," he blurted suddenly. "Those were corrections, not falsifications. Our sources led us to believe that Earth's governments had discovered the surveillance, and they had conspired to conceal their warlike intentions. We instructed JEVEX to apply a correction factor by extrapolating the developments that would have taken place if the surveillance had not been discovered, and we presented these as facts in order to insure that our protective measures would not be relaxed." The stares coming from the Thuriens were openly contemptuous, and he finished lamely, "Of course, it is possible that the corrections were . . . somewhat exaggerated unintentionally."

"So I ask you again, how long?" Showm said. "How long has this been practiced?"

"Ten, maybe twenty years . . . I can't remember."

"You don't know?" She looked at Wylott. "It's your department. Have you no records?"

"JEVEX keeps the records," Wylott replied woodenly.

"VISAR," Calazar said. "Obtain the records from JEVEX for us."

"This is outrageous!" Broghuilio shouted, his face turning black with anger. "The surveillance program is entrusted to us by long-standing agreement. You have no right to make such a demand. It has been negotiated."

Calazar ignored him. A few seconds later VISAR informed them, "I can't make any sense of the response. Either the records are corrupted, or JEVEX is under a directive not to release them."

Showm did not seem surprised. "Never mind," she said, and looked back at Estordu. "Let's give you the benefit of the doubt and say twenty years. Therefore anything reported by JEVEX before that time will not have been altered. Is that correct?"

"It might have been more," Estordu said hastily. "Twenty-five . . . thirty, perhaps."

"Then let's go back farther than that. The Second World War on Earth ended eighty-six years ago. I have examined some of the accounts of events during that period as reported by JEVEX at the time. Let me give you some examples. According to JEVEX, the cities of Hamburg, Dresden, and Berlin were devastated not by conventional saturation bombing but by nuclear weapons. According to JEVEX, the Korean conflict in the 1950s escalated into a major clash of Soviet and American forces; in fact, nothing of the kind took place. Neither were tactical nuclear devices used in the Middle East wars of the '60s and '70s, nor was there an outbreak of Sino-Soviet hostilities in the 1990s." Showm's voice became icy as she concluded, "And neither was the *Shapieron* taken into captivity by a United States military garrison on Ganymede. The United States has never had a military garrison on Ganymede."

Estordu had no answer. Wylott remained immobile, staring straight in front of himself. Broghuilio seemed to swell with indignation. "We asked for *evidence!*" he thundered. "That is not evidence. Those are allegations. Where is your proof? Where are your witnesses? Where is your justification for this intolerable behavior?"

"I'll take it," Heller said, rising to her feet beside Caldwell. There was no way she was going to let him beat her to it this time. From where Hunt was sitting nothing appeared to change, but the way the three Jevlenese heads snapped around to gape at her left no doubt that VISAR had suddenly put her on stage.

Before any of them could say anything, Calazar spoke. "Allow me to introduce somebody who might satisfy your requirement—Karen Heller, Special Envoy to Thurien from the State Department of the United States."

Estordu's face had turned white, and Wylott's mouth was opening and closing ineffectively without producing any sound. Broghuilio was standing with his fists clenched and paroxysms of rage sweeping in visible tremors through the length of his body. "We have many witnesses," Calazar said. "Nine billion of them, in fact. But for now, a few representatives will suffice." The Jevlenese's eyes opened wider as the remainder of the Terran delegation became visible. None of them glanced in the opposite direction, indicating that Calazar had not yet instructed VISAR to reveal Garuth and the others from the *Shapieron.*

Karen Heller had compiled a long list of suspicions concerning Jevlenese manipulations of events on Earth, none of which she could prove. The opportunity for bluffing the confirmation from the Jevlenese would never again be quite what it was at that moment, and she plunged ahead without giving them a second's respite. "Ever since the Lambians were taken from Luna to Thurien after the Minervan war, they have never forgotten their rivalry with the Cerians. They have always seen Earth as a potential threat that would one day have to be eliminated. In anticipation of that day, they took advantage of their access to Ganymean sciences and devised an elaborate scheme to insure that their rival would be held in a state of backwardness and prevented from reemerging to challenge them until they had absorbed the last ounce of the knowledge and technologies that they thought would make them invincible." She was unconsciously addressing her words to Calazar and the Thuriens as if they were judge and jury, and the proceedings were a trial. They remained silent and waiting as she paused for a moment to shift to a different key.

"What is knowledge?" she asked them. "*True* knowledge, of reality as it is, as opposed to how it might appear to be or how one might wish it to be? What is the only system of thought that has been developed that is effective in distinguishing fact from fallacy, truth from myth, and reality from delusion?" She paused again for a second and then exclaimed, "*Science!* All the truths that we *know*, as opposed to beliefs which some choose blindly to adopt as if the strength of their convictions could affect facts, have been revealed by the rational processes of applied *scientific method*. Science alone yields a basis for the formulation of beliefs whose validity can be *proved* because they predict *results* that can be *tested*. And yet . . ." Her voice fell, and she turned her head to include the Terrans sitting around her. "And yet, for thousands of years the races of Earth clung persistently to their cults, superstitions, irrational dogmas, and impotent idols. They refused to accept what their eyes alone should have told them—that the magical and mystical forces in which they trusted and which they aspired to command were fictions, barren in their yield of results, powerless in prediction, and devoid of useful application. In a word, they were *worthless*, which of course made any consequences *harmless*. And this, from the Lambian, or Jevlenese, viewpoint, constituted a remarkably convenient situation. It was too convenient to be just a coincidence." Heller turned her head to look coldly at the Jevlenese. "But we know that it was not merely a coincidence. Far from it."

Danchekker turned an astonished face to Hunt, leaned closer, and whispered, "How extraordinary! I'd never have believed I'd hear *her* make a speech like that."

"I'd never have believed it, either," Hunt muttered. "What have you been doing to her?"

Still looking at the Jevlenese, Heller went on, "We know that the early beliefs in the supernatural were established by miracle workers whom *you* recruited and trained, and injected as agents to found and popularize mass movements and countercultures based on myth, and to undermine and discredit any tendencies toward the emergence of the rational systems of thought that could lead to advanced technology, mastery over the environment, and a challenge to your position. Can you deny it?" She could read on their faces that her bluff had succeeded. They were standing rigid and unmoving, too numbed with shock to respond. Feeling more confident, Heller looked over at the Thuriens and resumed, "The superstitions and religions of Earth's early cultures were carefully contrived and implanted. The beliefs of the Babylonians, the Mayas, the ancient Egyptians, and the early Chinese, for example, were based on notions of the supernatural, magic, legend, and folklore, to sap them of any potential for developing logical methods of thought. The civilizations that grew upon those foundations built cities, developed arts and agriculture, and constructed ships and simple machines, but they never evolved the sciences that could have unlocked true power on any significant scale. They were harmless."

Low mutterings and murmurs were rippling among the Thuriens as some of them only began to realize for the first time the full extent of what the Terrans had uncovered. "And what of Earth's later history?" Calazar asked, mainly for the benefit of those Thuriens who had not been as involved in everything as he.

"The same pattern traces through to modern times," Heller replied. "The saints and apparitions who created legends by conveying messages and performing miracles were agents sent from Jevlen to reinforce and reassure. The cults and movements that perpetuated beliefs in spiritualism and the occult, in paranormal sciences and other such nonsenses that were in vogue in Europe and North America in the nineteenth century, were manufactured in an attempt to dilute the progress of true science and reason. And even in the twentieth century, the so-called popular reactions against science, technology, positive economic growth, nuclear energy, and the like were in fact carefully orchestrated."

"Your answer?" Calazar demanded curtly, staring at Broghuilio.

Broghuilio folded his arms, drew a long breath, and turned slowly to face directly toward where Heller was standing. He seemed to have recomposed himself and was apparently far from conceding defeat yet. He glared defiantly at the Terrans for a few seconds and then turned his head toward Calazar.

"Yes, it was so. The facts are as stated. The motive, however, was not as described. Only a *Terran* mind could conceive of such motives. They are projecting into us their own evils." He threw out an arm to point at the Terrans accusingly. "You know the history of their planet, Calazar. All the violence and blood-thirstiness that destroyed Minerva is preserved today on Earth. I do not have to repeat to you their unending history of quarrels, wars, revolutions, and killing. And that, mark you, was *despite* our efforts to contain them! Yes, we planted agents to steer them away from the sciences and from reason. Do you blame us? Can you imagine the holocaust that would be sweeping across the Galaxy today if they had been allowed to return into space tens of thousands of years ago? Can you imagine the threat that it would have posed to you as well as to us?" He looked again at where the Terrans were sitting, and scowled distastefully. "They are primitives. Insane! They always will be. We kept their planet backward for the same reason that we would not give fire to children—to protect them as well as ourselves, and you too. We would do the same again. I have no apologies to offer."

"Your actions betray your words," Frenua Showm retorted. "If you believed that you had pacified a warlike planet, you would have been proud of the achievement. You would not have concealed the fact. But you did the opposite. You presented a falsified picture of Earth that showed it as warlike when in fact it was moving in exactly the direction that you should have considered desirable. You successfully delayed its advancement until its Minervan inheritance had been diluted sufficiently for it to advance wisely. But not only did you conceal that fact, you distorted it. How do you explain that?"

"A temporary aberration," Broghuilio replied. "Underneath nothing has changed. We altered the more recent developments so that you would not be misled. A final solution to the problem was still called for."

Heller was thinking rapidly as she listened. The "final solution" had to mean that the Jevlenese had used Earth's belligerence as an excuse to maintain their own military forces as she had suspected. It seemed to support another line of thought that her researches had caused her to wonder about, and here was an opportunity to test it. But to do so she would have to resort to bluff again. "I challenge that explanation," she said. "What I have described so far is only part of what the Jevlenese have been doing." All the heads in the room turned toward her. "By the time of the nineteenth century, it was obvious that Western civilization was rapidly spreading science and industrial technology across the globe in spite of all their efforts. At that point the Jevlenese changed their tactics. They actually began to stimulate and accelerate scientific discovery by leaking information in various quarters that precipitated major breakthroughs." She turned her head a fraction. "Dr. Hunt. Would you like to comment, please?"

Hunt had been expecting the question. He stood up and said, "The sharp discontinuities and nonlinearities that attended the major breakthroughs in physics and mathematics in the late nineteenth and early twentieth centuries have been a mystery for a long time. In my opinion, such conceptual revolutions could not have happened in the time they did without some external influence."

"Thank you," Heller said. Hunt sat down. She looked back at the Thuriens, more than a few of whom appeared puzzled. "Why would the Jevlenese do such a thing when their policy up until then had been to retard their rival? Because they were forced to accept the fact that they would not be able to keep Earth back any longer. Therefore, if Earth was about to become a high-technology planet anyway, the Jevlenese decided to use their already established infrastructure of influence to steer that advancement in such a direction that their rival would eliminate itself. In other words they set out to engineer events in such a way that the sciences which they themselves had helped develop would be used not to eradicate the scourges that had plagued mankind throughout history, but to wage war on a global scale and with unprecedented ferocity." She watched Broghuilio carefully as she spoke, and saw that she had hit the mark. Now was the moment to go for the kill.

"Deny that it was Jevlenese agents who infiltrated the European nobility at the end of the nineteenth century and created the rash of internecine jealousies that culminated in the horrors of the First World War," she challenged in a suddenly loud and cutting voice. "Deny that it was a Jevlenese-controlled organization that seized control of Russia after the 1917 revolution and developed the prototype for the totalitarian police state. And deny that you set up a Jevlenese group in the wreckage of postwar Germany to resurrect the hatreds that the League of Nations was formed to resolve by peaceful means. They were led by some very carefully selected and trained individuals, weren't they? What happened to the real Adolf Hitler? Or perhaps you operated from behind the throne—Alfred Rosenberg, perhaps?" The three Jevlenese did not have to say anything. Their frozen postures and stunned expressions provided all the confirmation needed. Heller turned her head toward the Thuriens and explained, "World War II was supposed to be nuclear. The necessary scientific, political, social, and economic prerequisites had all been taken care of. It didn't quite work as planned, but it came frighteningly close."

A new wave of mutterings broke out among the Thuriens. Heller waited for it to subside and then concluded in a quieter voice, "The tensions continued for over half a century, but despite the continuing Jevlenese efforts, the global catastrophe that they sought never quite took place." The next part was pure guesswork, but she continued without any change of tone. "They concluded that one day they would have to confront their rival themselves, and so embarked on a program of exaggerating Earth's wars and armament developments to justify to the Thuriens their creation of a 'protective' strength of their own. At the same time they reversed their policy on Earth and used their network to defuse tensions, promote disarmament, and permit its people to develop their talents and resources creatively in the ways they had always wanted to. The object of this, of course, was to turn Earth into a defenseless target. To maintain the justification for increasing their own armed forces, they supplied the Thuriens with what gradually became a total fantasy manufactured inside JEVEX."

Heller paused again, but this time there was no sound. She

wheeled around to point at the Jevlenese, and her voice rose to an accusing shout. *"They* accuse *us* of killing each other, when all the time they know full well that *their agents* have orchestrated the worst episodes of havoc and bloodshed in Earth's history. *They* have murdered more people than all the leaders of planet Earth put together." Her voice fell to an ominous whisper. "But the unexpected arrival of the *Shapieron* threw all those plans into confusion. Here was a group of Ganymeans who would expose the lie if they were allowed to make contact with Thurien. Now we see the *real* reason why its existence was never disclosed." The color was draining from Broghuilio's face. Wylott had turned scarlet and seemed to be having difficulty breathing, while on Broghuilio's other side Estordu was dripping with perspiration and shaking visibly. Across the room Garuth, Shilohin, and Monchar were sitting forward tensely as they sensed the moment approaching for them to reveal themselves.

"And now we come to the question of the *Shapieron,*" Heller said. Her tone was almost soft, but menace was glittering in her eyes as she fixed them upon the Jevlenese. "We heard earlier a suggestion that Earth had sabotaged it. The suggestion is based on what we have seen to be lies. The *Shapieron* was never in any jeopardy at any time during the six months it was on Earth. On the contrary, our relationship with the Ganymeans was very friendly. We have ample records to prove that." She paused for a second. "But we do not have to rely on those records to prove that Earth did nothing to harm that ship or its occupants. We have far more convincing evidence than that." Across the room Garuth and his companions stiffened. Calazar was about to give the instruction to VISAR.

And the Jevlenese vanished.

The floor where they had been standing was suddenly empty. Surprised murmurs broke out on all sides. After a few seconds VISAR announced, "JEVEX is cutting all its links. I have no access to it at all. It is ignoring requests to reconnect."

"What do you mean?" Calazar asked. "You have no communications to Jevlen at all?"

"The whole planet is isolating itself," VISAR replied. "All the

Jevlenese worlds are disconnecting. JEVEX has detached and become an independent system. No further communications or visits within its operating zone are possible."

The consternation breaking out among the Thuriens meant that something very unusual was happening. Hunt turned to meet an inquiring look from Danchekker and shrugged. "It looks as if JEVEX has broken off diplomatic relations," he said.

"What do you suppose it means?" Danchekker asked.

"Who knows? It sounds like a siege. They're inside their own zone controlled by JEVEX, and JEVEX isn't talking to anyone. So I guess that short of sending ships in there's no way anyone can get at them now."

"It might not be that easy," Lyn said from Hunt's other side. "If they've been setting themselves up as a Galactic police force, there could be a problem there."

A strange silence fell over the Thuriens. Calazar and Showm looked uneasily at each other; Eesyan looked down and fiddled awkwardly with his knuckles. The Terrans and the *Shapieron* Ganymeans looked at them curiously. Eventually Calazar looked up with a sigh. "Your demonstration of how to get truth from the Jevlenese was remarkable. You were wrong on one of your assumptions, however. We have never agreed to any proposal by the Jevlenese that they maintain a military force either to counter possible aggressive expansionism by Earth or for any other reason."

Heller didn't seem too reassured by the statement as she sat down. "You know now what they're like," she said. "How can you be certain that they haven't been secretly arming themselves."

"We can't," Calazar admitted. "If they have, the implications of the situation that would confront both of our civilizations are serious."

Caldwell was puzzled. He frowned for a moment as if to check over what was going through his mind, stared at Heller for a second, then looked across at Calazar. "But we assumed that was why they invented the phony stories," he said. "If that wasn't the reason, then what was?"

The Thuriens looked even more uncomfortable. Showm turned to Calazar and spread her hands as if conceding there was something that couldn't be concealed any longer. Calazar hesitated, then nodded. "It is clear to us now why the Jevlenese falsified their reports," Showm said, turning her head to address the whole room. An expectant hush fell as she paused. She took a long breath and resumed, "There is more to this, which up until now we have felt it wiser not to talk about . . ." She turned her head momentarily sideways to glance at Garuth and his colleagues, ". . . to any of you." They waited. She went on, "For a long time the Ganymeans have been haunted by the specter of Minerva repeating itself, and this time possibly spilling out into the Galaxy. Just under a century ago, the Jevlenese persuaded our predecessors that Earth was on the verge of doing just that, and urged a solution to contain Earth's expansion permanently. The Thuriens commenced working on a contingency plan accordingly. Because of the false picture that we were given by the Jevlenese, we have continued with the preparations to implement that plan. If we had known the true situation on Earth, we would have abandoned the idea. Clearly the Jevlenese were misleading us in order to harness our technology to contain their rival permanently and eliminate it from competing with them across the Galaxy in times to come. That was what Broghuilio meant when he referred to the final solution."

The Terrans needed a few seconds to digest what Showm was saying. "I'm not sure I follow what you mean," Danchekker said at least. "Contained Earth's expansion by what means? You don't mean by force, surely."

Calazar shook his head slowly. "That would not be the Ganymean way. We said contain, not oppose. The choice of word was deliberate."

Hunt frowned as he tried to fathom what Calazar was driving at. Contain Earth? It was too late for that; mankind's civilization had already spread a long way beyond Earth. Then it could only mean . . . His eyes widened suddenly in disbelief. Surely not even Thurien minds could think on a scale as vast as that. "Not the Solar System!" he gasped, staring at Calazar in awe. "You're not telling us you were going to shut in the whole solar system."

Calazar nodded gravely. "We devised a scheme for using our gravitic science to create a shell of steepened gravitational gradient that nothing—not Earthmen, nor Earthmen's aggression, nor even light itself, would escape from. Inside the shell conditions would be normal, and Earth would be free to pursue whatever way of life it chose. And beyond the shell, so would we." Calazar looked around and took in the appalled stares coming back at him. "That was to have been our final solution," he told them.

Chapter Twenty-eight

And so for the first time in the long history of their race the Ganymeans found themselves at war, or at least in a situation so akin to war that the differences were academic. Their response to the Jevlenese was swift and devastating. Calazar ordered VISAR to withdraw all its services from the Jevlenese who were physically present on Thurien and the other Ganymean-controlled worlds. A whole population who throughout their lives had taken for granted the ability to communicate or travel instantly anywhere at any time, to have information of every description available on request, and who had relied completely on machines for every facet of their existence, found themselves suddenly cut off from the only form of society that they knew how to function in. They were isolated, powerless, and panic-stricken. Within hours they had been reduced to helplessness and were speedily rounded up and detained, as much for their own safety and sanity as to keep them out of any unlikely mischief, until the Ganymeans decided what to do with them. The whole Jevlenese contingent scattered across all the Ganymean worlds had thus been eliminated in a single lightning blow that left no survivors.

That left the enemy headquarters planet of Jevlen together with its system of allied worlds, which were serviced by JEVEX and not by VISAR. This, it turned out, was going to be a far harder nut to crack since it was unassailable by simply sending in ships as Hunt had thought of doing earlier.

The problem was that Jevlen was light-years away from Gistar, and the only way of getting ships there was through black-hole toroids projected by VISAR. But when VISAR attempted to project a few test beams into JEVEX's operating zone, it found that JEVEX was able to disrupt the beams easily; evidently the Jevlenese had been planning to break from Thurien for some time. Neither was it feasible for VISAR to transfer ships through toroids projected to just beyond the fringe of JEVEX's effective jamming radius to make their own way to Jevlen from there. The problem in this case was that all the Thurien vessels relied on power, as well as navigational and control signals, beamed through the Thurien h-grid from centralized generating and supervisory centers, and JEVEX could disrupt those beams just as easily. In other words, nothing could get into the Jevlenese system as long as JEVEX was operating, and the only way to stop it from operating was to send something in. It was a deadlock.

More serious was the possibility that the Jevlenese might have been amassing weapons secretly for a long time, and, in anticipation of exactly the kind of situation that now existed, building vessels to transport them that operated with self-contained propulsion and control capability. If so, they would be in a position to move their forces with impunity into VISAR-controlled regions and proceed unopposed with whatever threats or actions they had been planning. Time was crucial. The events at Thurios had clearly forced the Jevlenese to make their break sooner than they had intended, and the more swiftly the Thuriens reacted, the better the chances would be of catching the Jevlenese at a disadvantage with their preparations incomplete. But what kind of reaction was possible from a race that had no experience of resisting an armed opponent, possessed no weaponry to react with even if they had, and couldn't get near their opponent anyway? Nobody had any solution to offer until a day after the confrontation in Thurios, when Garuth, Shilohin, and Eesyan requested a private audience with Calazar.

"No disrespect, but your experts are missing the obvious," Garuth said. "They've taken advanced Thurien technology for granted for so long that they can't think in any other terms."

Calazar raised his hands protectively. "Calm down, stop waving your arms about, and tell me what you're trying to say," he suggested.

"The way to get in at Jevlen is in orbit over Thurien right now," Shilohin said. "The *Shapieron*! It might be obsolete by your standards, but it's got its own on-board power, and ZORAC flies it perfectly well without any need for anybody's h-grid."

For a few seconds Calazar stared mutely back at them in astonishment. What they had said was true—none of the scientists who had been debating the problem without a break since JEVEX had severed its connections had even considered the *Shapieron*. It seemed so obvious that Calazar was convinced there had to be a flaw. He looked questioningly at Eesyan.

"I can't see why not," Eesyan said. "As Shilohin says, there's no way JEVEX could stop it."

There was something deeper behind this proposal, Calazar sensed as he searched Garuth's face. What was equally obvious, and had not been said, was that even if JEVEX could not prevent the *Shapieron* from physically entering its operating zone, it might well have plenty of other means at its disposal for stopping the ship once it got in there. Garuth had been itching to confront the Jevlenese yesterday, and had been frustrated at the last moment. Was he now ready to risk himself, his crew, and his ship in recklessly settling something that he saw as a personal vendetta against Broghuilio? Calazar could not permit that. "The *Shapieron* would still be detected," he pointed out. "The Jevlenese will have sensors and scanners all over their star system. You could be walking into anything. A ship on its own, isolated from any communications with Thurien, with no defensive equipment of any kind? . . ." He let the sentence hang and allowed his expression to say the rest.

"We think we have an answer to that," Shilohin said. "We could fit the ship's probes with low-power h-link communicators that wouldn't register on JEVEX's detectors and deploy them as a covering screen twenty miles or so out from the *Shapieron*. That would give them, effectively, faster-than-light communications back to the ship's computers. ZORAC would be able to generate cancellation functions that the probes would relay outward as out-of-phase signals added to the optical and radar wavelengths reflected from the ship so that the net readings registered at a distance in any direction would be zero. In other words it would be electromagnetically invisible."

"It would still show up on h-scan," Calazar objected. "JEVEX could detect its main-drive stressfield."

"We don't have to use main drive at all," Shilohin countered. "VISAR could accelerate the ship in h-space and eject it from the exit port with sufficient momentum to reach Jevlen passively in a day. When it got near, it could retard and maneuver on its auxiliaries, which radiate below detection threshold."

"But you'd still have to project an exit port outside the star system," Calazar said. "You couldn't hide that scale of disturbance from JEVEX. It would know that something was going on."

"So we send another ship or two as decoys . . . unmanned ships," Shilohin replied. "Let JEVEX jam those and think that's all there is to it. In fact that would be a good way of diverting its attention from the *Shapieron*."

Calazar still didn't like the proposal. He turned away, clasped his hands behind his back, and paced slowly across the room to stare at the wall while he thought it over. He was not a technical expert, but from what he knew, the scheme was workable theoretically. Thurien ships carried on-board compensators that interacted with a projected toroid, compacting it and minimizing the gravitational disturbance created around it. That was why Thurien ships could travel out of a planetary system and transfer into h-space after only a day of conventional cruising. The *Shapieron* had not been built with such compensators, of course, which was why months had been necessary for it to clear the solar system. But even as the thought struck him, Calazar realized there was a simple answer to that too: the

Shapieron could be equipped with a Thurien compensator system in a matter of days. Anyway, if there were serious technical difficulties, Eesyan would already have found them.

Calazar did not have to ask what the purpose of the exercise would be. JEVEX consisted of a huge network similar to VISAR, and in addition to its grid of h-communications facilities possessed a dense mesh of conventional electromagnetic signal beams that it employed for local communications over moderate distances around Jevlen. If the Thuriens could intercept one, or preferably several, of those beams, simulating regular traffic in order to be inconspicuous, there was a chance that they might be able to gain access to the operating nucleus of JEVEX and crash the system from the inside. If they succeeded, the whole Jevlenese operation would come down with it, and the same thing would happen to the whole empire that had happened on a smaller scale to the Thurien Jevlenese a day earlier. But the problem was how to get the necessary hardware physically into a position to intercept the beams. Eesyan's scientists had been debating it for over a day and so far had produced no usable suggestions.

At last Calazar wheeled around to face the others again. "Very well, you seem to have that side of it all figured out," he conceded. "But tell me if I'm missing something. There's something else that you haven't mentioned: the kind of computing power you'd need to bring down a system like JEVEX would be phenomenal. ZORAC could never do it. The only system in existence that would stand a chance is VISAR, but you couldn't couple VISAR into ZORAC because that would require an h-link, and you couldn't close an h-link while JEVEX is running."

"That's a gamble," Eesyan admitted. "But ZORAC wouldn't have to crash the whole JEVEX system. All it would have to do is open up a channel to let VISAR in. Our idea is to equip the *Shapieron* and a set of its daughter probes with h-link equipment that VISAR can couple in through, and disperse them to intercept a number of channels into JEVEX. Then if ZORAC can just get far enough into JEVEX to block its jamming capability, we can throw the whole weight of VISAR in behind ZORAC and hit JEVEX from all directions at once. VISAR would do the rest."

There was a chance, Calazar admitted to himself. He didn't know what the plan's odds of success were, but it was a chance; and Garuth's idea was more than anybody else had been able to come up with. But the vision in his mind's eye of the *Shapieron* venturing alone into a hostile region of space, unarmed and defenseless, and the tiny ZORAC pitting itself against the might of JEVEX, was chilling. He walked slowly back to the center of the room while the other three Ganymeans watched him intently. It was clear from their expressions what they wanted him to say. "You realize, of course, that this could mean subjecting your ship to what could be a considerable risk," he said gravely, looking at Garuth. "We have no idea what the Jevlenese have waiting there. Once you are in, there will be no way for us to get to you if you encounter difficulties. You would not even be able to contact us without revealing your presence, and even then the channel would immediately be jammed. You would be entirely on your own."

"I know that," Garuth answered. His expression had hardened, and his voice was uncharacteristically tense. "*I* would go. I would not ask any of my people to follow. It would be for them to decide individually."

"I have already decided," Shilohin said. "A full crew would not be necessary. More would come forward than would be needed."

Inside, Calazar was beginning to yield to the irrefutable logic of their argument. Time was precious, and the effectiveness of anything that could be done to thwart the Jevlenese ambitions would be amplified by an enormous factor with every day saved. But Calazar knew, too, that Garuth's scientists and ZORAC would not possess the knowledge of Thurien computing techniques viably to wage a war of wits with JEVEX; the expedition would have to include some expertise from Thurien as well.

Eesyan seemed to read his mind. "I will go too," he said quietly. "And there will also be more volunteers among my experts than we will require. You can count on it."

After a long, heavy silence, Shilohin said, "Gregg Caldwell has a method that he uses sometimes when he has to make a difficult decision quickly: forget the issue itself and consider the alternatives; if none of them is acceptable, the decision is made. It fits this situation well."

Calazar drew a long breath. She was right. There were risks, but doing nothing and having to face at some later date what the Jevlenese had been preparing anyway, with their plans correspondingly more advanced, might be taking a greater risk in the long run. "Your opinion, VISAR?" he said.

"Agreed on all points, especially the last," VISAR replied simply.

"You're confident about taking on JEVEX?"

"Just let me at it."

"You could operate effectively with access only through ZORAC? You could neutralize JEVEX on that basis?"

"Neutralize it? I'll tear it apart!"

Calazar's eyebrows lifted in surprise. It sounded as if VISAR had been talking with Terrans too much. His expression grew serious again as he thought for a few seconds longer, then nodded once. The decision was made. At once his manner became more businesslike. "The most important thing now is time," he told them. "How much thought have you given to that? Do you have a schedule worked out yet?"

"A day to select and brief ten of my scientists, five days to equip the *Shapieron* with entry compensators for it to clear Gistar in minimum time, and five days to fit the ship and probes with h-link and screening hardware," Eesyan replied at once. "But we can stage those jobs in parallel and conduct testing during the voyage. We'll need a day to clear Gistar and another to make Jevlen from the exit port, plus an extra day to allow for Vic Hunt's Murphy Factor. That means we could be leaving Thurien in six days."

"Very well," Calazar said, nodding. "If we are agreed that time is vital, we must not waste any. Let us begin immediately."

"There is one more thing," Garuth said, then hesitated.

Calazar waited for a few seconds. "Yes, Commander?"

Garuth spread his hands, then dropped them to his sides again. "The Terrans. They will want to come too. I know them.

They will want to use the perceptron to come physically to Thurien to join us." He looked appealingly at Shilohin and Eesyan as if for support. "But this . . . war will be fought purely with advanced Ganymean technologies and techniques. The Terrans would be able to contribute nothing. There is no reason why they should be allowed to place themselves at risk. On top of that, we have been helped enormously so far by information from Earth, and we might well be again. In other words we cannot afford to be without the communications channel to McClusky at a time like this. They have a more valuable function to perform there. Therefore I would rather we deny any such request . . . for their own good as much as anything else."

Calazar looked into Garuth's eyes and saw again the hardness that he had glimpsed at the moment when Broghuilio had announced the *Shapieron's* destruction. It was as Calazar had suspected—a personal score to be settled with Broghuilio. Garuth wanted no outsiders, not even Hunt and his colleagues. It was a strange reaction to find in a Ganymean. He looked at Shilohin and Eesyan and could see that they had read it too. But they would not offend Garuth's pride and dignity by saying so. And neither would Calazar.

"Very well," he agreed, nodding. "It will be as you request."

Chapter Twenty-nine

Night surrounded the Soviet military jet skimming northward over the ice between Franz Josef Land and the Pole. The clash that had occurred inside the Kremlin and throughout the ruling hierarchy of the Soviet Union was still far from resolved, and the loyalties of the nation's forces were divided; the flight was therefore being made secretly to minimize risks. While Verikoff sat rigidly between two armed guards at the back of the darkened cabin and the half-dozen other officers dozed or talked in lowered voices in the seats around him, Mikolai Sobroskin stared out at the blackness through the window beside him and thought about the astounding events of the past forty-eight hours.

The aliens didn't stand up very well under interrogation, he had discovered. At least, the alien Verikoff hadn't. For that was what Verikoff was—a member of a network of agents from the fully human contingent of Thurien that ran the surveillance operation, and who had been infiltrating Earth's society all through history. Niels Sverenssen was another. The demilitarization of Earth had been engineered in preparation for their emergence as a ruling elite to be established by the Jevlenese,

261

with Sverenssen as planetary overlord. Earth would eventually be deindustrialized to provide a playground for the aristocracy of Jevlen and extensive rural estates as rewards for its more faithful servants. How a planet reduced to this condition would support the portion of its population not required for labor and services had not been explained.

Once this much had been established, the value of Verikoff's skin had fallen markedly. To save it he had offered to cooperate, and to prove his credibility he had divulged details of the communications link between Jevlen and its operation on Earth, located at Sverenssen's home in Connecticut and installed by Jevlenese technicians employed by a U.S. construction company set up as a front for some of the Jevlenese's other activities. Through this link Sverenssen had been able to report details of the Thurien attempt to talk to Earth secretly via Farside and had received his instructions for controlling the Earth end of the dialogue. Sobroskin had detected no hint that Verikoff knew anything about the U.S. channel that Norman Pacey had mentioned. Despite the elaborate Jevlenese information-gathering system, therefore, Sobroskin had concluded that at least that secret had been kept safe.

Sobroskin had decided that the first step toward breaking up the network would have to be the severing of the link through Connecticut while its discovery was still unknown, and the Jevlenese were therefore off guard and vulnerable. Obviously that could only be accomplished with the help of somebody in Washington, and since nobody, not even Verikoff, knew the full extent of the network or who might be among its members, that had meant Norman Pacey. Sobroskin had called "Ivan" at the Soviet embassy and, using a prearranged system of innocuous-sounding phrases, conveyed a message for relaying to Pacey. A call from the U.S. State Department to an office in Moscow eight hours later, stating that hotel reservations had been made for a group of visiting Russian diplomats, confirmed that the message had been received and understood.

"Five minutes to touchdown," the pilot's voice sounded from an intercom in the darkness overhead. A low light came on in the cabin, and Sobroskin and the other officers began collecting the cigarette packages, papers, and other items strewn around them, then put on heavy arctic coats in preparation for the cold outside.

Minutes later the plane descended slowly out of the night and settled in the center of a dim pool of light that marked the landing area of an American scientific research base and arctic weather station. A U.S. Air Force transport stood in the shadows to one side with its engines running and a small group of heavily muffled figures huddled in front of it. The door forward of the cabin swung open, and a set of steps telescoped downward. Sobroskin and his party descended and walked quickly across the ice with Verikoff and the two officers escorting him making up the middle of the group. They halted briefly in front of the waiting Americans.

"You see, it wasn't such a long time, after all," Norman Pacey said to Sobroskin as they shook hands through the thick gloves they were wearing.

"We have much to talk about," Sobroskin said. "This whole thing goes further than your wildest imaginings."

"We'll see," Pacey replied, grinning. "We haven't exactly been standing still, either. You may have some surprises coming too."

The group began boarding while behind them the engine note of the Soviet jet rose, and the plane disappeared back into the night. Thirty seconds later the American transport lifted off, its nose swinging northward onto the course that would take it over the Pole and down across eastern Canada to Washington, D.C.

It was late evening at McClusky. The base was quiet. A short distance from the line of parked aircraft brooding silently in the subdued orange glow cast by lamps spaced at intervals along the perimeter fence, Hunt, Lyn, and Danchekker were staring in the direction of the constellation Taurus.

They had argued, inveigled, and protested that the business was as much Earth's as anybody's, and that if Garuth and Eesyan were risking themselves, honor and justice demanded that Earthpeople should also be there to share whatever consequences were in store, but to no avail; Calazar had been adamant that the perceptron could not be moved. They had not dared call in higher authority in the form of the UN or the U.S. Government to back their case because there was no way of knowing who might be working for the Jevlenese. Therefore they could do nothing but resign themselves to hoping and waiting.

"It's crazy," Lyn said after a while. "They've never fought a war in their history, and now they're going in on a commando raid to try and take out a whole planet. I never knew Ganymeans were like that. Do you think Garuth has flipped out or something?"

"He just wants to fly his ship one more time," Hunt murmured and snorted humorlessly. "You'd think that after twenty-five million years of it he'd have had enough." The thought had also crossed Hunt's mind that perhaps Garuth had decided to go down with it like the proverbial captain. He didn't say so.

"A noble gesture, nevertheless," Danchekker said. He shook his head with a sigh. "But I feel uneasy. I don't see why the perceptron had to remain here. That sounded like an excuse. Even if we could not have contributed anything technically, we could still contribute something else which I fear Garuth and his friends might well find themselves in need of if they encounter difficulties."

"How do you mean?" Lyn asked.

"I'd have thought it was obvious," Danchekker answered. "We have seen already how differently Ganymean and human minds function. The Jevlenese may possess some talent for intrigue and deception, but they are not the masters of the art that they appear to imagine. It requires a human insight, however, to recognize and exploit their blunders."

"They've only had Ganymeans to deal with," Hunt said. "We've had a few thousand years of practice handling one another."

"My point entirely."

A short period of silence elapsed, then Lyn said absently,

"You know what I'd like to see? If those Jevlenese guys think they're so smart, I'd like to see them come up against some real professionals and find out what deception is all about. And with VISAR on our side, we ought to have the right equipment to do it with, too."

Hunt looked at her and frowned. "What are you talking about?"

"I'm not sure really." She thought for a moment and shrugged. "I was just thinking that with JEVEX faking all that information for years and feeding it to the Thuriens, it would be kind of nice if we did something like that to them . . . just for the hell of it."

"Did something such as what?" Hunt asked, still puzzled.

Lyn looked back up at the night sky with a distant expression. "Well, imagine this as a for-instance. JEVEX must have all those stories about weapons and bombs and things that it's been inventing stored away someplace in its records, right? And someplace else in its records, it must have all the genuine information about Earth that it's collected through its surveillance system—in other words, all the stuff about Earth that it knows is true. But how does it know which is which? How does it know which records are real and which are phony?"

"I don't know." Hunt shrugged and reflected for a second. "I suppose it'd have to tag them with some kind of header-label system."

"That's what I thought," Lyn said, nodding. "Now suppose VISAR did manage to get inside JEVEX, and it scrambled those labels around so that JEVEX couldn't tell the difference anymore. It would make JEVEX really believe all those stories were true. Imagine what would happen if it started saying things like that. See what I mean—it'd be nice to watch."

"What a delightful thought," Danchekker murmured, intrigued. An evil smile crept across his face as he pictured it. "How unfortunate that we never mentioned it to Calazar. War or not, the Ganymeans would have been unable to resist it."

Hunt was smiling distantly too as he thought about it. The idea could be taken a lot farther than Lyn had suggested. If

VISAR got into JEVEX's memory system sufficiently to change the labels, it would only be a short step from there for it to add in some extra fiction of its own devising. For example, if it could gain access to the part of JEVEX that handled the incoming surveillance data from Earth, VISAR could probably make JEVEX think anything it wanted about what was happening on Earth—such as a whole armada being readied to blow Jevlen out of the Galaxy. As Danchekker had said, a delightful thought.

"You could fake an agreement with Thurien to use their toroids to transport a strike force to Jevlen," Hunt said. "That way you could have JEVEX saying it would arrive in days. And if you'd already scrambled its records from way back, that would be fully consistent with what it would think it had been reporting for years. The Jevlenese would know it hadn't . . . but then if they've never questioned it all their lives, maybe they wouldn't know what to think. What do you think Broghuilio would make of that?"

"He'd have a heart attack," Lyn said. "What do you think, Chris?"

Danchekker turned serious all of a sudden. "I have no idea," he replied. "But this is an example of precisely the kind of thing I was referring to. The idea of finding ways to bewilder a foe is something that comes naturally to humans but not to Ganymeans. They are going to attempt the straightforward approach of simply crashing JEVEX—direct, logical, and without any thought of deviousness. But suppose that the Jevlenese have prepared themselves by providing backup systems capable of operating autonomously even without JEVEX. If so, the *Shapieron* could still find itself exposed to considerable dangers when it reveals itself by bringing down JEVEX, assuming it succeeds. I trust you see my point." Danchekker directed a solemn stare at the other two, then continued: "But on the other hand, if their plan had been to *control* JEVEX rather than disable it, and to disorient the Jevlenese by subterfuge of the kind you have been describing, then perhaps all manner of opportunities to exploit and exacerbate the resulting situation further might have presented themselves, which as things stand will never be created." He looked up at the sky again and shook his head sadly. "I can't for a moment imagine our Ganymean friends adopting such a tactic, I'm afraid."

The amusement of a few minutes earlier had drained from Hunt's face as he listened. He had tried, Caldwell had tried, and Heller had tried, but still he couldn't escape the lingering discomfort that perhaps they could have tried harder still. Now that Danchekker had voiced them, he recognized the same thoughts that he had been suppressing. "We should have gone with them," he said in a heavy voice. "We should have made Gregg bully them into it."

"I doubt that it would have made any difference," Danchekker said. "Couldn't you see that Garuth had a personal score to settle with Broghuilio? He didn't want anybody else involved as a matter of principle. Calazar knew it too. Nothing we could have said would have made any difference."

"I guess you're right." Hunt sighed. He looked toward Taurus again, stared at it for a while, then suddenly snapped out of his reverie and looked from side to side at the others. "It's getting cold," he said. "Let's go inside and get some coffee."

They turned and began walking slowly back across the apron toward the mess hall.

Many light-years away, the *Shapieron* slipped quietly out of orbit above Thurien. For a little over a day VISAR tracked it to beyond the Gistar system and monitored its transfer through h-space to a point just outside JEVEX's zone of control on the fringe of the Jevlenese star system. The power and control beams to the two unmanned decoy ships sent with it were promptly jammed, and while they drifted helplessly on the edge of JEVEX-space, the *Shapieron* continued moving inward and vanished from the view of VISAR's instruments into the cloak of impenetrability that surrounded the enemy star.

Chapter Thirty

The construction floating in space was in the form of a hollow square. It measured over five hundred miles along a side. From each of its corners a bar, twenty miles thick, extended diagonally inward to support the two-hundred-mile-diameter sphere held in the center. The surfaces of the outer square bristled with angular protuberances, sections of ribbing, and domed superstructures, all etched harshly in black and shades of metallic gray, and immense winding girded parts of the central sphere and its supporting members. Receding away into space behind it, a line of identical objects spaced at two-thousand-mile intervals diminished in size with distance until they were lost in the background of stars.

Imares Broghuilio, formerly Premier of the Jevlenese faction of Thurien and now Overlord of the recently proclaimed Independent Protectorate of Jevlenese Worlds, stood in his black Supreme Military Commander's uniform, his arms folded across his chest, and scowled out at the scene from inside a blisterdome on the hull of a spacecraft riding several thousand miles off. Low to one side, the dark, rugged sphere of the planet Uttan hung as a crescent against the blackness, appearing the size of a tennis ball held at arm's length. Wylott and a number of generals from various commands of the Jevlenese military were standing behind him with Estordu and a handful of civilian advisors. To one side, not looking very happy, were Niels Sverenssen and Feylon Turl, technical coordinator of the quadriflexor construction program.

Broghuilio waved an arm at the scene outside. "*We* have been forced to revise *our* timetables just as drastically and in just as little time," he said curtly, glaring at Turl. "I expect you to do at least as well."

"But engineering on this scale can't be accelerated by that kind of factor simply by ordering it to be," Turl protested. "We are still short by fifty units. It will take two years at least, even with round-the-clock shifts in all critical—"

"Two years is unacceptable," Broghuilio said flatly. "I've given you our requirement, and I want your confirmation, today, that it will be met as stipulated. Tell me what *can* be done for a change. The Protectorate is now operating on a war economy, and whatever resources are needed will be made available."

"It isn't simply a question of production resources," Turl insisted. "The power to transfer that number of quadriflexors to the target won't be available for two years. Crallort's latest estimates show that—"

"Crallort has been removed," Broghuilio informed him. "That office is now under military control. The generator battery will be expanded under an emergency program that is already in effect, and the power requirement will be met as stipulated."

"I—" Turl began, but Broghuilio cut him off with an impatient motion of his hand.

"You have until twenty-four hours from now to discuss the revisions with your staff. I shall expect you at the Directorate of Strategic Planning on Jevlen at that time to report. I will *not* expect to hear lame excuses. Do I make myself understood?"

"Yes, Excellency," Turl mumbled.

Subvocally Broghuilio instructed JEVEX to remind him later

in the day to review possible candidates for Turl's replacement at Uttan, then turned his eyes contemptuously toward Sverenssen. "And it appears that my 'able lieutenant' who was supposed to have had the situation on Earth 'well under control' is equally incompetent," he sneered. "Well, what have you been able to find out? How did the Thuriens manage to communicate with Terrans right under your noses? Where is their facility located? What is your plan to eliminate it? How did they penetrate your operation? Who has been betraying it? I hope you have good answers, Sverenssen."

"I must protest," Sverenssen said in a shocked voice. "Yes, I admit that the Thuriens did establish a link somehow. But the accusation that we have allowed our operation to be penetrated is without foundation. There is no evidence to—"

"Then you are either blind or stupid!" Broghuilio spat. "I was there, in Thurios. You were not. I tell you they knew everything. The Terrans must have turned half the imbeciles in your organization and had them working against us for years. How long have they had a link on Earth direct into VISAR?"

"We . . . have not been able to ascertain that yet, Excellency," Sverenssen admitted.

"Obviously since long before they started anything on Farside," Broghuilio said. "The whole Bruno operation was a façade to fool you and keep you occupied, and you swallowed every inch of it." He screwed up his face and mimicked a fawning tone. " 'We have gained complete control, Excellency,' I was told. Pah!" Broghuilio slammed a fist into his other palm. "Control! They were manipulating you like a puppet. They probably have been for years. Overlord of Earth? You'd be a laughingstock trying to govern a kindergarten." Sverenssen paled, and his jaw strained, but he said nothing.

Broghuilio raised his arms in front of the rest of the company as if inviting them to witness his predicament. "You see what I have to contend with—imbecile engineers and imbecile agents. And what of you? Clearly the enemy will not sit idly by and do nothing while we complete our preparations. But we are told that it will take two years. Thus we have a problem situation that demands some form of action now, while we retain the initiative. What are your plans?"

Some of the generals looked uncertainly at one another. Eventually Wylott replied hesitantly, "We are still analyzing the latest developments. The situation calls for a complete revision of every—"

"Never mind your academic analyses and evaluations. Do you have firm *plans* drawn up for offensive *action, now,* to secure our position while the quadriflexor program is being completed?"

"No, but we've never—"

"The general does not have a plan," Broghuilio told the rest of them. "You see—on all sides I have to deal with imbeciles. But fortunately for all of us, I do have a plan. Our weapons production program here at Uttan has begun showing results, has it not? We have ships, armaments, and sufficient generating capacity to transfer them to Gistar at once, while the Thuriens have nothing. It is a time for boldness."

Wylott seemed worried. "That is not the way we have always intended," he said. "Our plans have never included launching an unprovoked assault on Thurien. The weapons were to be used against the Cerians. We would find it hard to justify such an action to the people. It would not be popular."

"Did I say anything about attacking Thurien?" Broghuilio asked. "Can you conceive of no methods other than brute force and clumsiness? Have you no sense of subtlety?" He turned his head to address all present. "War is as much a matter of psychology as it is of weapons, and in particular of understanding the psychology of one's enemy. Study the history of Earth, or even of Minerva. Many great victories have been won by seizing an opportune psychological moment. And such a moment presents itself to us now."

"What are you proposing?" Estordu asked uneasily. "That we might intimidate Thurien into submission?"

Broghuilio looked at him in surprise and with unconcealed approval. "For a scientist you are thinking quickly for once," he said. He raised his voice. "You hear? The scientist is thinking more like a general than any of you. The Thuriens have no taste for war, nor even any concept of it. At this moment they believe that we have retreated into a shell and will not trouble them for a long time to come. They feel secure for the time being, and that is why they are vulnerable."

He strode slowly to one side of the dome and stared out at the distant ball of Uttan for a few seconds. Then he came back to the center and resumed, "I will tell you what the Thuriens are thinking at this moment. They realize that we present a threat which they do not have the stomach to face, but which the Terrans do. On the other hand they possess the technology necessary to counter that threat, whereas the Terrans do not. So what will be their obvious strategy?"

Wylott was beginning to nod slowly. "To arm and equip the Terrans as proxy troops," he said. "Thurien will enlist Earth to fight on its behalf."

"Exactly!" Broghuilio exclaimed. "But Earth is demilitarized and not competent to match us technically anyway, and at this moment the Thuriens have nothing to arm them with." He looked around with a triumphant glint in his eyes. "In other words their solution will require *time*. But we do not need time because right now we have something, and they have nothing. Our forces might be small compared to what they will be in times to come, but that situation gives us a ratio of something to zero, which equates to infinite superiority. That advantage will not exist indefinitely, and it will never again be in our favor to the extent that it is now. And *that* is why the time to act is *now*, and not later."

Wylott's eyes gleamed as he began to see what Broghuilio was driving at. "With self-powered ships we can send a task force in and issue an ultimatum to the Thuriens to place VISAR under our control," he said. "Being Ganymeans, they will have no choice. Then they'd be helpless, and we would assume full control of the combined empires of JEVEX and VISAR."

"And the Terrans will be deprived of their armorers," Broghuilio completed. "In two years they could never hope to match us without the Thuriens. Thus we will have bought the time we need to complete our preparations for dealing with Earth, and for neutralizing Thurien permanently." He turned to confront Wylott squarely, folded his arms across his chest, and stuck out his chin. "That, General, is the plan—*my* plan." ·

"A stroke of genius," Wylott declared. A chorus of murmurs from the ranks behind endorsed the statement. "We will commence detailed preparations at once."

"See to it," Broghuilio ordered. He turned and glowered at Sverenssen. "And you, if you think you have the ability to redeem yourself, go back to Earth. I want every one of the traitors in your organization uncovered, tracked down, and dealt with. All except Rank B2 and above. *Those* are to be held while we arrange a landing to bring them back to Jevlen. I will deal with *them* personally." His voice fell to an ominous growl, and his eyes smoldered. "And if you fail in this, Sverenssen, *you* will certainly be brought back, even if I have to come physically to Earth myself to do it."

Chapter Thirty-one

S everal days went by without news from the *Shapieron*. VISAR analyzed all the available data on the design of JEVEX and gave ZORAC a five-percent chance of electronically lock-picking its way through the layers of security checks and access restrictions protecting the enemy system. The problem was that JEVEX's Ganymean-designed molecular circuits worked at subnanosecond speeds, enabling an enormous amount of self-checking to be interleaved with its regular operations. The odds were overwhelming that any chink in JEVEX's armor that ZORAC managed to slip a wedge into would be detected and closed before VISAR could be brought in to drive the wedge home. In other words JEVEX could scan its own internal processes too rapidly, or as Hunt put it to Caldwell, "It's got too much instant-to-instant awareness of what's going on inside itself. If we could distract its attention somehow, even for a few seconds, at the speeds those machines work at, ZORAC might be able to neutralize the jamming system and let VISAR in." But how could they distract JEVEX when the only channel they had to it was through ZORAC, and ZORAC couldn't get in until JEVEX had been distracted?

And then VISAR reported a series of gravitational disturbances outside Gistar's planetary system, followed by a steady accumulation of objects that seemed to be ships of some kind being transferred through from somewhere. Shortly afterward, the objects began moving toward Thurien. VISAR could detect no h-grid power or control beams and was unable to check their progress. They were self-powered, heavily armed Jevlenese war vessels, and there were fifty of them. As they fanned out to maneuver into positions around Thurien, JEVEX reopened contact briefly with VISAR to deliver the Jevlenese ultimatum: the Thuriens had forty-eight hours to place their entire world system under Jevlenese control. If at the end of that period they had not agreed, obliteration of Thurien cities one at a time would commence, starting with Vranix. Those were the terms. There was nothing to discuss.

The atmosphere inside the Government Center at Thurios was strained and tense. All of the Terran group from McClusky were present with Calazar, Showm, and a selection of engineering and technical experts that included Eesyan's deputy, Morizal. They were already six hours into the ultimatum period.

"But there must be something you can do," Caldwell protested, stamping backward and forward across the center of the room in frustration. "Couldn't you try using remote-controlled ships to ram them? Couldn't VISAR make a few black holes to suck them into or something? There has to be a way."

"I agree," Showm said, looking at Calazar. "We should try. I know it's distasteful, but the Jevlenese have made the rules. Have you considered the alternatives?"

"They could pick off ramships long before they even got near," Morizal said. "And they could detect a black hole forming and evade it long before it could trap them. And even then you could only hope to get a few at the most. The rest would incinerate Thurien then and there without waiting for the deadline."

"And besides, that's not the way," Calazar said at last, throwing up his hands. "Ganymeans have never sought solutions by war or violence. I couldn't condone anything like that. We will not descend to the level of Jevlenese barbarism."

"You've never faced this kind of threat before," Karen Heller pointed out. "What other way is there to meet it?"

"She's right," Showm said. "The Jevlenese force is not large. There's a good chance that it's all they possess right now. Six months from now that could change. Earth's logic is harsh, but nevertheless realistic in this kind of situation: losing some people now could buy the time to save many more later. It's a lesson they have learned, and we may have to as well."

"It's not the way," Calazar said again. "You've seen Earth's history. That kind of logic always leads to escalation without limits. It's insane. I won't allow us to start down that road."

"Broghuilio is insane," Showm insisted. "There's no other way."

"There must be. We need time to consider."

"We don't have any time."

A heavy silence descended. On one side of the room, Hunt caught Lyn's eye and shrugged hopelessly. She raised her eyebrows and sighed. There was nothing to say. The situation didn't look good. A short distance away Danchekker was becoming restless. He removed his spectacles, squinted through them while he twisted them first this way and then that in front of his face, then replaced them and began pinching his nose with his thumb and forefinger. Something was going through his mind. Hunt watched him curiously and waited.

"Suppose . . ." Danchekker began, thought for a second longer, then swung his head toward Calazar and Morizal. "Suppose we could induce the Jevlenese to postpone their offensive intentions and switch their force to the defensive . . . in other words take it back to Jevlen," he said. "That would gain us some time."

Calazar looked at him, puzzled. "Why should they do that? To defend against what? We have nothing to threaten any attack against them with, and neither have you."

"Agreed," Danchekker said. "But perhaps there is a way in which we could persuade them that we do." The Ganymeans stared back at him nonplussed. He explained, "Lyn and Vic were talking recently about an idea to *simulate* an all-out assault on Jevlen inside VISAR and inject it into JEVEX, assuming ZORAC gains access of course. And by suitably manipulating JEVEX's internal records, VISAR could, perhaps, then instill in JEVEX the conviction that the existence of such forces was consistent with what it has been observing for years. You see my point? Such a ruse might create enough confusion inside the Jevlenese camp for them to withdraw their forces. And given a sufficient level of uncertainty, they would probably not risk firing upon Thurien until they had determined the true situation. What we would do then I have no idea, but it would at least gain us some respite from the current predicament."

Showm was listening with a strange look on her face. "That would be almost identical to what they did to us," she murmured. "We'd be turning their own tactic right back at them."

"Yes, it does have a certain appeal of that nature about it," Danchekker agreed.

In response to some questions from Morizal, Danchekker went on to describe the idea in greater detail. When he had finished, the Ganymeans looked at one another dubiously, but none of them could pick out a fatal flaw in the argument. "What do you say, VISAR?" Calazar asked after they had talked for some time.

"It might work, but it still rests on a five-percent probability at best," VISAR replied. "It's still the same problem: the only way I could get into JEVEX is if ZORAC can switch off its jamming system, and so far ZORAC doesn't seem to be having much luck. I still haven't heard a thing from it."

"What else can you suggest?" Calazar asked.

A few seconds went by. "Nothing," VISAR admitted. "I could get to work and manufacture the information with some help from the Terrans and have it ready to beam through on the off-chance ZORAC does get me in, but its still five percent. In other words don't bank on it."

A faraway look had been coming into Hunt's eyes while the discussion was going on. One by one the heads in the room turned toward him curiously as they noticed. "It's this problem about distracting JEVEX's attention again," he said, "isn't it? If we could just freeze its self-checking functions for the couple of seconds ZORAC would need to switch off the jamming routines and open an h-link, VISAR would be able to hold that link open permanently and do the rest."

"True, but what's the point?" VISAR said. "We've already been through all this. We can't do anything like that because the only way in is through ZORAC in the first place."

"I think maybe we can," Hunt said in a distant voice. The room became very still. His eyes cleared suddenly as he gazed around at the others. They waited. "We can't create a diversion through ZORAC because ZORAC is outside the system trying to get in," he said. "But we've got another channel that goes straight through to the *inside*—direct into the core of JEVEX."

Caldwell shook his head and looked puzzled. "What are you talking about? What channel? Where?"

"In Connecticut," Hunt told them. He glanced at Lyn for a second and then looked back at the others. "I'm betting that what's inside Sverenssen's house is a complete communications facility into JEVEX—probably one with its own neural coupler. What else could it be? We could get at it through that."

A few seconds elapsed before what he had said registered fully. Morizal seemed mystified. "Get at it and do what?" he asked. "How would you use it?"

Hunt shrugged. "I haven't really thought about it yet, but there has to be something. Maybe we could use it to tell JEVEX all the things that VISAR's inventions will corroborate—Earth is fully armed and has been for years; an attack is on its way to wipe Jevlen out now . . . supporting evidence, that kind of thing. That ought to shake it up for a second or two."

"That's the craziest thing I ever heard." Caldwell shook his head helplessly. "Why would it believe you? It wouldn't even know who you were. And anyhow, would you sit down in that thing and let JEVEX inside your head?"

"No, I wouldn't," Hunt said. "But JEVEX knows Sverenssen. And it would believe what he told it. That would really shake it up."

"Why would Sverenssen ever do something like that?" Heller asked. "What makes you think he'd want to cooperate?"

Hunt shrugged. "We put a gun to the bastard's head and make him," he replied simply.

Silence fell once again. The suggestion was so outrageous that nobody had a ready comment to offer. The Ganymeans were looking at each other in amazement, all except Frenua Showm, who seemed ready to go along with the scheme without further ado. "How would you get in?" Caldwell asked dubiously at last. "Lyn said it'd take an army."

"So use the Army," Hunt said. "Jerol Packard and Norman Pacey must know some people who could pull it off."

The idea was taking root as they thought about it. "But how do you know you could force him to do something like that without JEVEX knowing you were there doing it?" Heller asked. "I mean, VISAR can see somebody in the perceptron at McClusky even before they sit down in a recliner. How do you know Sverenssen's place isn't the same?"

"I don't," Hunt conceded. He spread his hands appealingly. "It's a risk. But it's a hell of a lot less of a risk than the one you were asking Calazar to take. And besides, the Ganymeans have taken enough of the risks already."

Caldwell nodded curtly as soon as Hunt said this. "I agree. Let's do it."

"VISAR?" Calazar inquired, still somewhat dazed by the sudden turn of events.

"I've never heard of anything like it," VISAR declared. "But if it increases the odds above five percent, it's worth a try. How soon can I start working on the movies?"

"Right away," Caldwell said. He moved to the center of the group and suddenly felt the old, familiar feeling of being in command once again. "Karen and I will stay here to help out with that side of it. You'd better stay too, Chris, to explain the whole idea again. Vic needs to go to Washington to tell Packard what we want, and Lyn had better go with him because she knows the layout of the house."

"It sounds as if we should consider you in charge of this operation," Calazar said.

"Thanks." Caldwell nodded and looked around the room. "Okay," he said. "Let's go through the whole thing in detail from the beginning and work out as much as we can to synchronize the two ends of it."

●   ●   ●

Hunt and Lyn arrived in Washington late that afternoon. Caldwell had already called Packard from Alaska, so they were expecting to find Packard, Pacey, and Clifford Benson of the CIA waiting for them. What they were not expecting to find was a contingent of Soviet military officers there too, headed by Mikolai Sobroskin. To their further and total amazement they learned that a Jevlenese defector in the form of the scientist Verikoff was also present in another part of the building.

Most of the Russians were too stunned by what they heard from Hunt and Lyn to be capable of contributing very much to the proceedings. Sobroskin, however, digested their story quickly and confirmed—from what Verikoff had already told him—that the office wing of Sverenssen's house did indeed contain a full communications system into JEVEX, including a neural coupler. In fact Verikoff himself had used it on numerous occasions to make quick visits to Jevlen. This led Sobroskin to propose a means of simplifying considerably the plan that Hunt and Lyn had described. "As you say, the big risk in forcing Sverenssen to do it is that JEVEX might be able to observe what is happening," he said. "But perhaps there is no need for that at all. If we could just gain access to the device, Verikoff might be persuaded to do what is required voluntarily. JEVEX already knows Verikoff. It would have no reason to see anything amiss."

Ten minutes later they all left the room and descended one story of the building to enter a door that had two armed guards stationed outside it. Verikoff was inside with two more of Sobroskin's officers. At Sobroskin's request, Verikoff sketched a plan of Sverenssen's house on a mural display, indicating the location of the communications room and the access door into the wing in which it was located, as well as describing the building's protective features. "What's your verdict?" Pacey asked, looking at Lyn, when Verikoff had finished.

She nodded. "One-hundred-percent accurate. That's it, just the way it is."

"He seems to be telling the truth," Packard said, sounding

satisfied. "And everything else he told Sobroskin checks with what Vic Hunt has told us. I think we can trust him."

Verikoff's eyes widened in surprise. He waved a hand at the sketch he had drawn, and then at Lyn. "She knows this already? How could that be? How could she know about the coupler?"

"It would take too long to explain," Sobroskin said. "Tell us what kind of visual sensors JEVEX has around the house. Are there some in all rooms, outside, inside the communications room, or what?"

"Only inside the communications room itself," Verikoff answered. He was looking from side to side uncomprehendingly.

"So JEVEX would not know about anything that was happening in the rest of the house outside that room," Sobroskin said.

Verikoff shook his head. "No."

"How about conventional intruder alarms around the grounds?" Pacey inquired. "Is the place equipped with anything like that? Would it be possible to get in over the walls and fences without being detected?"

"It's extensively wired," Verikoff replied. His expression became alarmed as he realized the implication of the questions. "Detection would be certain."

"Is the place watched from orbit by Jevlenese surveillance?" Hunt asked. "Could it be assaulted without it being reported?"

"As far as I know it is checked periodically, but not continuously."

"How frequently?"

"I don't know."

"How about Sverenssen's domestic staff?" Lyn asked. "Are they Jevlenese too, or just help that he hires locally? How much do they know?"

"Specially picked Jevlenese guards—all of them."

"How many?" Sobroskin demanded. "Are they armed? What armaments do they have?"

"Ten of them. There are always at least six in the house. They are armed at all times. Conventional Terran firearms."

Packard looked over at the others. One by one they returned slow nods. "It looks as if we could be in with a chance," he said. "It's time to bring in the professionals and see what they think."

Verikoff suddenly seemed apprehensive. "What is this talk of an assault?" he asked. "You are going in there?"

"*We* are going in there," Sobroskin told him.

Verikoff started to protest but stopped when he saw the menace in Sobroskin's eyes. He licked his lips and nodded. "What do you want me to do?" he asked.

An hour later a VTOL personnel carrier flew the whole party across the Potomac to the army base at Fort Myer. They were met by a Colonel Shearer, who commanded a Special Forces antiterrorist unit that had already been called to alert and was standing by. The planning and briefing session that followed went on until the early hours of the morning. The first gray light of dawn was showing in the east as an Air Force transport took off from Fort Myer and followed the coast toward New England. It landed with a whisper less than thirty minutes later at an out-of-the-way military supply depot situated among wooded hills twenty miles or so outside Stamford, Connecticut.

Chapter Thirty-two

The Jevlenese were still tapping into Earth's communications net. Earth knew they were, and the Jevlenese knew that Earth knew. Therefore, Caldwell reasoned, the Jevlenese would expect any high-level communications between Earth's governments, especially anything to do with an impending attack on Jevlen, to be encoded by methods that were generally thought to be unbreakable; anything else would not look authentic. But if the codes were indeed unbreakable, little purpose would be served by planting authentically encoded information in JEVEX since JEVEX wouldn't be able to unravel what it said.

At Caldwell's request the scientists at McClusky beamed details of the coding algorithms currently used for high-security terrestrial communications through to the perceptron. VISAR studied them and announced that JEVEX would have no problem. The scientists were skeptical. As a test VISAR invited them to compose an encoded message and send it over the beam, which they did. VISAR returned the plaintext translation less than a minute later. The stunned scientists decided that they still had a lot to learn about algorithms. But the implication was satisfactory: JEVEX could be led plausibly to believe that it was eavesdropping on Earth's highest-level secure communications.

Since then VISAR had been busy manufacturing a revised history of the last few decades on Earth in which the superpowers had not disarmed but gone on to escalate their strategic forces to insane levels of overkill capability, concluding with an account of Earth's leaders meeting secretly and agreeing to a hasty alliance to hurl their combined strength at Jevlen with the Thuriens transporting the force to within striking distance. Its latest creation, being previewed in the Government Center in Thurios, showed a conference hookup in which some of the senior officers engaged in the joint planning of the operation were delivering a preliminary briefing to their staffs. A General Gearvey, whom VISAR had already appointed as the American Supreme Commander, began speaking.

"We are about to engage an enemy who possesses a technology incalculably ahead of our own, and of unknown strength and retaliatory capability. But against that we have two factors in our favor that could redress the balance—*time* and *preparedness*. We are in a position to move now, while all our intelligence from the Thuriens leads us to believe that the enemy is not. Our strategy is therefore based on exploiting these factors to the fullest. We will forgo detailed planning and rely heavily on the initiative of local commanders in order to move fast and aim at total devastation of the enemy in a single, surprise, all-out, lightning strike with no compromises. This is not a time to ponder about morality. We might not have a second chance."

A Russian general leaned forward and took it from there. "The opening phase of the assault is designated OXBOW. Fifteen long-range radiation projectors will commence area-obliteration of selected targets on Jevlen, firing from one million miles standoff behind screens of destroyers and close-support tactical units. Five more will be held in reserve at ten million miles. The bombardment is intended to draw and engage the defensive forces while the spearheads move in to commence operations around the planet itself."

A European Air Force chief continued, "Phase BANSHEE will begin with a high-level sweep of Jevlenese nearspace to clear it of all enemy hardware. This will be followed immediately by rapid deployment of a mixed-strike orbital system to neutralize major military installations and observed ground concentrations. A secondary force will concentrate on population centers and administrative focal points to dislocate the defenses by creating panic and disrupting communications. Simultaneously, lower-altitude intercept units and killsats will contest Jevlenese air space, with carrier-based tactical groups operating in selective ground-strike and counterfire roles. Our objective here is to gain complete control above the surface within twelve hours of the spearheads going in. The codeword CLAYMORE will be issued upon the successful completion of this phase."

A Chinese general summed up the last part. "When CLAYMORE is declared, conditions will have been established to permit the seizure of bridgeheads on the surface. This phase is designated DRAGON. The first descents will be made by remote-controlled decoy landers to enable surviving defensive installations to be identified and destroyed by a portion of the orbital bombardment groups held in reserve for that purpose. The remaining orbiting groups will redeploy to provide close-support fire for the landings, and the carrier groups assigned to ground suppression will commence launching aircraft. When descent corridors have been cleared, the ground forces will be landed initially at twelve strategic points. Details of those operations are currently being finalized with the respective bridgehead commanders. Strategic bombardment from high level will continue throughout to prevent the defenses from concentrating on the landing areas."

"That concludes the overview," Gearvey said. "Individual unit assignments, timetabling, and call signs will follow immediately. Remain on standby."

"What do you think?" Caldwell asked as the image cut out.

"I'm impressed," Heller said. "It'd sure scare the hell out of me."

"Horrifying," Calazar pronounced numbly. "It is just as well that you did not go with the *Shapieron*. We would never have conceived anything like that."

Danchekker did not seem completely happy. "It still doesn't contain the sense of urgency that we have to convey," he said. "It doesn't mention any specific dates."

"I did that on purpose," Caldwell told him. "If we're going to be credible, we'd have to allow Earth ships months to get out of the solar system. The best thing seemed to be to leave it uncertain. What other way is there?"

"I don't know, but I still don't like it," Danchekker said.

Nobody spoke for a few seconds, then Morizal said, "Well, we've already got the Thuriens providing the transfer ports outside the Solar System. We could take it a step further and have the Terran vessels fitted with Thurien-supplied h-grid boosters. That way we could get them out of the solar system in a day."

"A whole fleet?" Heller said dubiously. "Could a whole fleet be fitted out that quickly?"

"Conceivably yes," Morizal replied. "It's quite a simple job. With unlimited assistance from Ganymean engineers, it would be feasible."

"How does that sound?" Caldwell asked, looking at Danchekker.

"It sounds more like what we want," Danchekker agreed, nodding.

"Suppose I change the last part to this," VISAR offered. The image reappeared and showed General Gearvey again, just about to sum up.

"That concludes the overview," he said. "There are no major revisions to the schedule to report. The h-beam boosters are currently being fitted by the Thuriens, and the first assault elements should commence moving out from Earth, on time, at eighteen hundred hours today. Current indications are that the full force will complete its assembly outside the enemy star system three days from now as planned. The force will then reenter h-space and be accelerated to reexit into normal space at a velocity that will move it to Jevlen in twenty-two hours. Therefore we should be going into action four days from now. Good luck to you all. Individual unit assignments, timetabling, and call signs will follow immediately. Remain on standby." The image vanished.

"Excellent," Danchekker murmured.

"The next thing I need to start working on is some surveillance data from Earth to back it all up," VISAR said. "But first I need some reference information on contemporary Terran military hardware and installations. Can you get it beamed in through McClusky?"

"Give me a line," Caldwell said. "I'll get something moving right away." He turned his head away and stared grimly for a few seconds at another view, constructed from VISAR's locally collected data, of the pattern of Jevlenese warships positioned around Thurien. "Any news about the *Shapieron* yet?" he asked.

"Nothing," VISAR told him. Its tone was neutral.

An image in the form of a frame enclosing the features of the controller at McClusky appeared in the air a few feet in front of Caldwell's face. Caldwell turned his head away from the view of the Jevlenese threat and returned his attention to the matter at hand.

Chapter Thirty-three

"**D**amn! Damn! Damn!" Niels Sverenssen hammered savagely at the touchboard of the datagrid terminal, then brought his fist down heavily on top of the unit as the screen remained dead. He turned away and marched furiously toward the L-shaped central room. "Vickers!" he shouted. "Where are you, for God's sake? I thought those confounded dataphone people were supposed to be here by now."

Vickers, the heavily built and swarthy chief of Sverenssen's domestic staff, appeared from one of the passages. "I only returned ten minutes ago. They said they'd be right over."

"Well, why aren't they?" Sverenssen demanded irritably. "I have calls waiting that must be made immediately. The service *must* be restored at once."

Vickers shrugged. "I already told 'em that. What else was I supposed to do?"

Sverenssen began massaging a fist with his other hand and pacing to and fro, cursing beneath his breath. "Why do such things always have to happen at a time like this? What kinds of buffoon are unable to maintain a simple communications service competently? Oh, the whole thing is intolerable!"

The first faint hum of an approaching aircar drifted in from the direction of the window. Vickers cocked his head to listen for a second, then walked over to peer out through one of the sliding glass panels that formed part of a wall. "It's a cab," he said over his shoulder, "coming down over the roof." They heard the cab land on the other side of the house, in the front driveway. The door chime sounded shortly afterward, followed by the footsteps of one of the maids as she hurried to the front hallway. He heard a muted exchange of female voices, and a few moments later the maid ushered in a smiling Lyn Garland. Sverenssen's' mouth dropped open in a mixture of surprise and dismay.

"Niels!" she exclaimed. "I tried to call you, but you seem to be having problems with the line. I thought you wouldn't mind me showing up, anyway. I've been thinking about what you said. You know, maybe you were right. I thought maybe we could patch things up a little." Her hand was resting casually on the top of her shoulder bag as she spoke. Sverenssen was not inside the communications room, which was the one thing Colonel Shearer had insisted on before he could move in. Inside the top of the bag, Lyn's finger found the button on the microtransmitter and pressed it three times.

"Oh, not now!" Sverenssen groaned. "You should know better than to barge in like this. I am an extremely busy man, and I have things to attend to. Anyway, I thought I made myself perfectly clear on the not-so-memorable occasion of our last meeting. Good day. Vickers, kindly show Miss Garland back to her cab."

"This way," Vickers said, taking a step forward and nodding his head toward where the maid was still hovering.

"Oh, but you did," Lyn said, looking at Sverenssen and ignoring Vickers. "You made it very clear. And I was being so silly, wasn't I, just like you said. But now I've had a chance to think about it, it sounds so—"

"Get her out of here," Sverenssen muttered, turning away. "I don't have time to waste listening to any inane female prattling today." Vickers gripped Lyn's upper arm and steered her firmly back along the corridor to the front hall while the maid ran on ahead to hold the door open. The cab was still there. Just as they reached the door, a Southern New England Dataphones repair truck rounded the bend in the driveway and drew up in front of the house, halting so close to the cab that the ladders slung on its side overhung and blocked its ascent path.

The cabbie wound down his window and leaned out to yell in the direction of the front end of the truck. "Hey, asshole! Who taught ya ta drive dat thing? How the hell am I supposed to get outa here?" Two repairmen had jumped out of the passenger-side door of the truck, and another was emerging from the rear. The truck's engine came to life again in a series of laboring electric whines, then shuddered and died.

"I've got problems," a voice shouted through the open driver's window of the truck. "The same thing happened just now when we left the office."

"Well, do something with the goddam thing, willya. I've got a living ta make."

Vickers had released Lyn's arm and was growling profanities beneath his breath. With what was going on in the driveway, neither he nor the maid noticed her backing quietly away across the hall.

"Back up for Chrissakes. What's the matter? Don't you know how to reverse a cab?"

"How can I back up? Don't those look like flowers behind me to you? You need lenses or sump'n?"

Another technician was coming out of the back of the truck. There were already more of them than would have been sent on a simple domestic repair job, but Vickers and the maid were too preoccupied with the argument to register the fact for a few vital seconds. Also they failed to notice the sound of air engines growing steadily louder from beyond the treetops flanking the driveway.

When Lyn reappeared in the corner room Sverenssen was on the far side at one of the windows, peering out and upward as sound deluged the house suddenly, seemingly from all directions. All in the same moment, two Army assault landers dropped into sight from above and came down on the terrace by the pool with khaki-clad figures already bursting from their doors, explosions and the sounds of shattering glass came from the upper part of the house, and there was a brief glimpse of Vickers and the maid being bowled over by more figures pouring into the front hall before additional concussions followed by clouds of smoke blotted out the view along the corridor.

Lyn snatched the respirator from her bag, clamped it over her face and eyes, and snapped its retaining band into position behind her head just as the barrage of stun grenades and gas bombs crashed in through the ground-floor windows of the house. Detonations and smoke were everywhere, punctuated by shouting, splintering glass, the thuds of doors being smashed down, and a few scattered shots. One of the domestics appeared in the archway that led through to the main stairs, gesticulating frantically upward and behind him. "They're on the roof! There's soldiers coming in off the roof! They're—" The rest was drowned by more explosions, and he was engulfed by a cloud of smoke and gas erupting behind him.

Sverenssen had recoiled from the window, and Lyn could see him clawing at his eyes in the middle of the room as he tried to get his bearings. Whatever happened, he couldn't be allowed to get to the communications room now. She began picking her way cautiously around the wall to get between him and the passageway leading to the office wing. He saw the movement through the smoke and came nearer. *"You!"* His face twisted into a mask of fury as he recognized her, made even more grotesque by the watery streaks cutting through the smoke grime on his cheeks. Lyn's heart did a backflip in her chest. She backed away, but kept moving toward the passageway. Sverenssen's shape came looming through the smoke, straight at her.

Then barked military commands sounded inside the house, seemingly from not far away in the direction of the guest annex. Sverenssen threw a glance back over his shoulder and hesitated. Shadowy figures were struggling in the corridor outside the kitchen, and there was more movement on the side of the house facing the pool. He changed direction and made a bolt toward the office wing. Without realizing what she was doing,

Lyn scooped up a wicker chair and hurled it across the floor at his legs. Sverenssen went down heavily and struck his head on the wall as he sprawled full-length on the floor.

But through the smoke Lyn could see he was still moving. She looked around desperately, picked up a large vase from a side table. Swallowing hard and trying to stop her hands from shaking, she forced herself to move nearer. Sverenssen was half sitting up, one hand clutching at his head, a small trickle of blood oozing through his fingers. He braced a foot beneath himself, stretched out an arm to steady himself against the wall, and started to haul himself up. Lyn raised the vase high with both hands. But Sverenssen's legs had turned to jelly. He swayed for a second, groaned aloud, and then collapsed back against the baseboard. Lyn was still standing paralyzed in the same position when the first figures wearing respirators and Army combat uniforms and carrying assault rifles materialized out of the fumes around her. One of them took the vase lightly from her hands. "We'll take care of him," a gruff voice told her. "Are you okay?" She nodded mutely while in front of her two Special Forces troopers lifted Sverenssen roughly to his feet.

"Bloody good show that," an English voice commented from somewhere behind her. "You know, if you worked at it, you might even get a job with the SAS." She turned and found Hunt looking at her approvingly. Shearer stood next to him. Hunt moved beside her, slipped an arm around her waist, and squeezed reassuringly. She pressed the side of her head against his shoulder and clung tightly as the tension released itself in a spasm of trembling. Talking could wait until later.

Around them the noise had subsided, and the smoke was clearing to reveal Sverenssen's domestic staff being brought into the corner room to be searched and relieved of their weapons before they were herded away into the guest annex. As the assault troops and the others already inside the house removed their respirators, a knot of American and Soviet officers came in through the wreckage. They were accompanied by men wearing civilian clothes beneath combat jackets. Sverenssen's eyes bulged in disbelief as they refocused. "Hi,"

Norman Pacey said, with a trace of deep satisfaction. "Remember us?"

"For you the war is over, my friend," Sobroskin informed him. "In fact, everything is over. It's a shame that you did not find Bruno up to your standards. It's quite luxurious compared to where you will be going." Sverenssen's face withered with anger, but he still seemed too dazed to make any reply.

A sergeant crossed the room, saluted, and reported to Shearer. "No casualties, sir. Just some cuts and bruises, mainly on the other side. None of them got away. The whole house is secured."

Shearer nodded. "Start getting them out right away. Let's get those landers away before they're spotted by the surveillance. Where are Verikoff and the CIA people?" Even as he spoke, another group of figures pushed into the room. Sverenssen's head jerked around, and his jaw dropped as he heard the name. Verikoff halted a few feet away from him and stood eying him defiantly.

"So, it's you . . ." Sverenssen hissed. "You . . . *traitor*!" He lunged forward instinctively and was promptly doubled over by a sharp blow delivered to the solar plexus by a rifle butt. As he sagged two of the troopers caught him and held him.

"He carries the key to the facility on him at all times," Verikoff said. "It should be on a chain around his neck." Shearer ripped open the front of Sverenssen's shirt, found the key, removed it, and passed it to Verikoff.

"You'll pay for these atrocities, Colonel," Sverenssen wheezed weakly. "Mark my words. I've ruined bigger men than you."

"Atrocities?" Shearer turned his head aside quizzically. "Do you know what he's talking about, Sergeant?"

"I've no idea, sir."

"Did you see anything?"

"Didn't see a thing, sir."

"Why do you think this man is holding his stomach?"

"Probably indigestion, sir."

As Sverenssen was hustled away to join his staff, Shearer turned to Clifford Benson. "I'm pulling my men out right away, apart from ten that I'll leave as guards for the house. I guess it's ready for you to take over."

"You did a fine job, Colonel," Benson acknowledged. He turned to the others. "Well, time's precious. Let's get on with it."

They stood aside while Verikoff led the way into the passage toward the office wing, and followed a few paces behind. At the end of the passage he came to a large, solid-looking, wooden door. "I am not sure how far JEVEX's visual field extends," he called to them. "It would be better if you kept well back." The others fell back into a small dense huddle with Hunt, Sobroskin, Lyn, Benson, and Pacey together at the front. "I need a minute to compose myself," Verikoff told them. They waited while he brushed a few specks of soot from his clothes, smoothed his hair, and wiped his face with a handkerchief. "Do I look as if all is normal?" he asked them.

"Fine," Hunt called back.

Verikoff nodded, turned to face the door, and unlocked it. Then he drew a deep breath, grasped the handle, and pushed the door open. The others caught a glimpse of elaborate instrumentation panels and banks of gleaming equipment, and then Verikoff stepped inside.

chapter thirty-four

The strain on the Command Deck of the *Shapieron* had been hovering around breaking point for days. Eesyan was standing in the center of the floor gazing up at the main display screen, where an enormous web of interconnected shapes and boxes annotated with symbols showed the road map into JEVEX that ZORAC had laboriously pieced together from statistical analyses and pattern correlations of the responses it had obtained to its probe signals. But ZORAC was not getting through to the nucleus of the system, which it would have to penetrate if it was going to disrupt JEVEX's h-jamming capability. Its attempts had been repeatedly detected by JEVEX's constantly running self-checking routines and thwarted by automatically initiated correction procedures. The big problem now was trying to decide how much longer they could allow ZORAC to try before the tables of fault-diagnostic data accumulating inside JEVEX alerted its supervisory functions that something very abnormal was happening. Opinions were more or less evenly divided between Eesyan's scientists from Thurien, who already wanted to call the whole thing off, and Garuth and his crew, who seemed willing to risk almost anything to pursue what was beginning to look, the more Eesyan saw of it, like some kind of death wish.

"Probe Three's function directive has been queried for the third time," one of the scientists announced from a nearby station. "Header response analysis indicates we've triggered a veto override again." He looked across at Eesyan and shook his head. "It's too dangerous. We'll have to suspend probing on this channel and resume regular traffic only."

"Activity pattern correlates with a new set of executive diagnostic indexes," another scientist called. "We've initiated a high-level malfunction check."

"We have to shut down on Three," another, standing by Eesyan, pleaded. "We're too exposed as it is."

Eesyan stared grimly up at the main screen as a set of mnemonics unrolled down one side to confirm the warning.

"What's your verdict, ZORAC?" he asked.

"I've reduced interrogation priority, but the fault flags are still set. It's tight, but it's the nearest we've come so far. I can try it one more time and risk it, or back off and let the chance go. It's up to you."

Eesyan glanced across to where Garuth was watching tensely with Monchar and Shilohin. Garuth clamped his mouth tight and gave an almost imperceptible nod. Eesyan drew a long breath. "Give it a try, ZORAC," he instructed. A hush fell across the Command Deck, and all eyes turned upward toward the large screen.

In the next second or two a billion bits of information flew back and forth between ZORAC and a Jevlenese communications relay hanging distantly in space. Then, suddenly, a new set of boxes appeared in the array. The symbols inside them were etched against bright red backgrounds that flashed rapidly. One of the scientists groaned in dismay.

"*Alarm condition,*" ZORAC reported. "General supervisor alert triggered. I think we just blew it." It meant that JEVEX knew they were there.

Eesyan looked down at the floor. There was nothing to say. Garuth was shaking his head dazedly in mute protest as if refusing to accept that this could be happening. Shilohin moved a step nearer and rested a hand on his shoulder. "You tried," she said quietly. "You had to try. It was the only chance."

Garuth was staring around him as if he had just awakened from a dream. "What was I thinking?" he whispered. "I had no right to do this;"

"It had to be done," Shilohin told him firmly.

"Two objects a hundred thousand miles out, coming this way fast," ZORAC reported. "Probably defensive weapons coming to check out this area." It was serious. The screen hiding the *Shapieron* would never stand up to probing at close range.

"How long before we register on their instruments?" Eesyan asked hoarsely.

"A couple of minutes at most," ZORAC replied.

In the Jevlenese War Room, Imares Broghuilio stood gazing at a display showing the deployment of his task force in the vicinity of Thurien. Although the ships were in VISAR-controlled space, VISAR had not jammed their communications beams to Jevlen. No doubt the Thuriens had guessed that the force had standing orders to commence offensive action automatically if it was interfered with in any way. At least, they hadn't risked it, which was precisely the kind of reaction he had expected from a timid and overcautious race like the Ganymeans. Again his instincts had proved infallible. Exposed at last for what they were, the Thuriens had shown again that they had nothing with which to oppose the combination of nerve, strength, and willpower that he had forged. A deep sense of satisfaction and fulfillment swept through him with the realization that the issue was already as good as decided.

If a response had not been received by a certain time, the plan called for some selected uninhabited areas of Thurien's surface to be devastated as a demonstration that the ultimatum was serious. That time had now arrived, and Broghuilio's aides were waiting with a tense expectancy. "Report the current status of the fleet," he instructed curtly.

"No change," JEVEX replied. "Bombardment squadron standing by and awaiting orders. Secondary beams unlocked and primed for area saturation. Coordinates programmed for targets as selected."

Broghuilio gazed around his circle of generals to savor the moment for a while longer, then opened his mouth to issue the command. At that instant JEVEX spoke again. "I have to interrupt, Excellency. A channel has just opened from Earth, top priority. Your response is requested at once."

The smirk vanished from Broghuilio's face. "I have nothing to talk to Sverenssen about. He has his instructions. What does he want?"

"It isn't Sverenssen, Excellency. It's Verikoff."

Broghuilio's expression changed to an angry frown. "Verikoff? What business does he have there at this time? He should be handling the situation in Russia. What does he mean by ignoring protocols in this fashion?"

JEVEX seemed to hesitate for a moment. "He . . . says he has an ultimatum to deliver to you personally, Excellency."

Broghuilio looked as if he had suddenly been punched in the face. He stood absolutely motionless for a few seconds while an ominous tide of deep purple crept slowly upward behind his beard, starting at his collar and eventually finding its way to his scalp. The generals around him were exchanging shocked, uncomprehending looks. Broghuilio licked his lips, and his fist opened and closed by his sides. "Get him here," he growled. "And JEVEX, do *not* disconnect him until *I* say so."

"I regret that is impossible, Excellency," JEVEX replied. "Verikoff is not coupled neurally into the system. I have audio and visual contact only." A screen on one wall of the room came to life to show Verikoff standing in the center of Sverenssen's communications room, evidently having thought better of committing himself to the recliner that was partly visible behind him. Something had happened to him since he had entered the room. He was staring out from the screen with his arms folded solidly across his chest, and he looked calm and assured.

"Behold, the textbook warlord," Verikoff allowed his lip to curl contemptuously. "You should not have sent us to Earth, Broghuilio. It has been an honor and an education to meet *real* warriors. Believe my words—you would be even more of a fool than the fool you are to pit your rabble of amateurs against the Terrans. If you do, they will destroy you. That is my message."

Broghuilio's eyes widened. The veins at the sides of his neck began pulsating. "*You* are the traitor!" he spat. "Now we see the vermin exposing himself at last. What is this talk of an ultimatum?"

"Traitor? No." Verikoff remained unperturbed. "Merely a question of calculating the winning odds, which after all is your own dictum. You have set us up well to assume control of Earth very soon, and we thank you for it, but unfortunately for you that puts us on the winning side. Which do you think we'd rather be—caretakers of an outpost of your empire, or rulers of our own? The answer should not be difficult."

"What do you mean by *we*?" Broghuilio demanded. "How many of you are behind this?"

"All of us, of course. We manipulate all of Earth's major national governments and therefore have control over its strategic forces. And we have enjoyed the cooperation of the Thuriens for a long time now. How else do you think they've been able to talk to the Terrans without your knowing anything about it? They know that you, not the Terrans, are the real threat to the Galaxy, and we have persuaded them to allow us a free hand to deal with it. So we command a fully armed planet, backed by Thurien technology. It's all over, Broghuilio. All you have left to save now is your skin."

A short distance back from the open door through which Verikoff was speaking, Hunt turned an astounded face toward Lyn and leaned close to whisper in her ear. "I didn't think he had it in him. The guy deserves an Oscar." Beside them, Sobroskin, looking as if he didn't really believe it either, had lowered the automatic with which he had been covering Verikoff from the passageway.

Broghuilio was looking bewildered. "Strategic forces? What strategic forces? Earth doesn't have any strategic forces."

Then JEVEX interrupted again. "We have an alarm condition in Sector Five. Something unidentified is attempting to penetrate the net. Two destroyers have been detached from station and sent to investigate."

"Don't bother me with such things now," Broghuilio raged, waving his arms impatiently. "Delegate to Sector Control and report later." He looked back at Verikoff again. "Earth demilitarized years ago."

"Is that what you believe?" Verikoff leered openly. "You poor simpleton. You don't really imagine we'd allow Earth to disarm when we knew this day was coming, do you? That story was purely for your consumption. Ironically you almost changed it back into the truth. It has given the Thuriens a lot of amusement."

Broghuilio still couldn't make any sense out of it. "Earth has disarmed," he insisted. "Our surveillance . . . JEVEX has shown us—"

"JEVEX!" Verikoff scoffed. "VISAR has been pumping fairy tales into JEVEX for years." His expression became hard and threatening. "Listen to me, Broghuilio, for I am in no mood to repeat myself. This demonstration at Thurien has taken things too far. The Ganymeans have seen now what you represent, and they are not of a mind to hold us back by scruples. So this is our ultimatum to you: either you withdraw from Thurien now, and agree to place your entire military command under our jurisdiction unconditionally, or the Thuriens will transfer through to Jevlen a combined Terran force that will blow you to stardust—you, your whole planet, and that laughable aggregation of scrap that you call a computer network."

Somewhere deep inside JEVEX something hiccuped. A million tasks that had been running inside the system froze in the confusion as directives coming down from the highest operating levels of the nucleus redefined the whole structure of priority assignments to force an emergency analysis of the new data. And in the middle of it all, the routines that had been scanning for inquisitive probes through h-space faltered. It was only for a few seconds, but . . .

On Thurien, VISAR spoke suddenly to end a long vigil that had been dragging silently by for hours. "Something's happened! I've got a link to ZORAC!" Even as Caldwell was jumping to his feet, and Heller and Danchekker were looking up with startled faces on the other side of the room, streams of binary were pouring across the gulf to the *Shapieron*, light-years away, and VISAR had begun analyzing the patterns assembled by ZORAC.

"What's the situation?" Calazar asked tensely. "Is the ship all right? How far into JEVEX have they penetrated?"

"They've got problems," VISAR said after a short delay. "Give me a few more seconds. This is going to need some fast footwork."

On the Command Deck of the *Shapieron*, a familiar voice that had not been heard for several days spoke suddenly to break the silence that had fallen with despair. "Say, you're in a bit of a mess here. Sit tight. I'll handle this."

Eesyan's jaw dropped in disbelief. Garuth looked up speechlessly from where he had sunk down into a chair at one of the empty crew stations. Around them a score of other dazed Ganymeans had heard it too, but didn't believe it, either. "VISAR?" Eesyan whispered, as if half fearing an aural hallucination. "ZORAC, was that VISAR?"

"It's busy," ZORAC's voice answered. "Don't ask me what's happened, but yes it was. Something deactivated the self-checking functions, and I've switched off the jamming routine. We're through to Thurien."

While ZORAC was speaking, VISAR decoded the access passwords into JEVEX's diagnostic subsystem, erased a set of data that it found there, substituted new data of its own, and reset the alarm indicators. Inside the Jevlenese Defense Sector Five control center, a display screen changed to announce a false alarm caused by a malfunctioning remote communications relay. Far off in space, the two destroyers turned away to return to their stations and resume routine patrolling. Already VISAR was pouring volumes of information into JEVEX that it had no time to explain, not even to ZORAC. At the same time it broke its way into JEVEX's communications subsystem and gained control of the open channel to Earth.

A voice that Verikoff recognized as VISAR's spoke suddenly in the communications room in Sverenssen's house. "Okay, we've done it. If Vic Hunt and the others are there somewhere, you can bring them in to watch what happens next. I can edit them out of the datastream to Jevlen on a one-way basis. Get off the line now as quick as you can."

Somehow Verikoff kept his astonishment from showing. Behind him Hunt and the others had heard and were slowly moving in through the door, too astounded to say anything. Broghuilio, obviously unaware of them, was still staring dumbstruck from one of the screens. Verikoff pulled himself together and reacted swiftly. "You have one hour to give your reply, Broghuilio," he said. "And hear this—if one of those ships at Thurien makes so much as anything that even looks like a hostile move, we will attack under an order that will be irrevocable once issued. You have one hour."

Nothing changed on the screen, but VISAR announced, "Okay, you're off the air." At once a bewildered Verikoff was assailed by congratulations and backslapping from all sides. Pacey and Benson were watching incredulously from the doorway, while just inside the room Sobroskin slipped his automatic surreptitiously back inside his jacket.

Another screen came to life to show the Command Deck of the *Shapieron* as VISAR continued to integrate the communications functions of JEVEX that it was taking over into its own network. A few seconds later another screen brought the view from the Government Center in Thurios. It had to be the most bizarre computer hookup ever, Hunt thought as his eyes jumped from side to side to take it all in. Caldwell, Heller, and Danchekker were physically in Alaska, yet he was seeing them through a link that extended from Connecticut to a Jevlenese star light-years away, back to the *Shapieron* and from there to a second star, and from Gistar back to the perceptron at McClusky.

"You . . . apparently believe in cutting things close," Eesyan said from the *Shapieron,* still looking distinctly shaken.

"You worry too much," Caldwell told him, addressing a point offscreen. "We know how to manage a business." He shifted his gaze to look straight out of the screen in Connecticut. "How'd it go? Is everybody okay? Where's Sverenssen?"

"We had a change of plans," Hunt replied. "I'll tell you about it later. Everybody's fine here."

On the screen that showed the Jevlenese War Room, Broghuilio had demanded a report from JEVEX on its current surveillance intercepts from Earth. JEVEX responded by producing accounts of Earth's leaders meeting secretly to agree on details of a combined attack on Jevlen. That was already historical, JEVEX declared in answer to questions from a completely stunned Broghuilio. Currently the plans for the assault were complete, and preparations were well advanced. JEVEX's latest intercept was a briefing from the senior officers of the joint Terran command staff, which it proceeded to replay. Broghuilio grew more perplexed and more flustered as he listened.

"Explain this, JEVEX," he demanded in a strangled voice. "What forces were those primitives talking about? What were those weapons?"

"My respect, Excellency, but it would appear to be self-explanatory," JEVEX answered. "The strategic forces that Earth has been building for some time. The weapons referred to are typical of those deployed by the various nations of Earth at the present time."

Broghuilio's brow knotted, and his beard quivered. He scowled at the nervous faces around him as if seized by the sudden suspicion that only he among all of them might be sane. "Typical of what weapons deployed by Earth at the present time? You have never informed us of such weapons."

Invisible fingers raced through JEVEX's memory, interchanging hundreds of thousands of record descriptors in a fraction of a second. "I regret that I must dispute the statement, Excellency. I have reported the details consistently."

The color of Broghuilio's face darkened even further. "What are you talking about? Reported details of what?"

"The sophisticated interplanetary offensive and defensive capabilities that Earth has been developing for several decades," JEVEX informed him.

"JEVEX, WHAT ARE YOU TALKING ABOUT?" Broghuilio exploded. "Earth disarmed years ago. You have reported *that* consistently. Explain this."

"There is nothing to explain. I have always reported what I have just said."

Broghuilio brought his hands up to massage his eyes, then wheeled around suddenly to throw out his hands in an imploring gesture to those around him. "Am I going mad, or is that idiot machine having some kind of a fit?" he demanded. "Will somebody tell me that I have been seeing and hearing what I think I have been seeing and hearing for all these years. Have I been imagining things? Were we told that Earth had disarmed, or were we not? Do those weapons that we just heard about exist, or do they not? Am I the only sane person in this room, or am I not? Somebody tell me what's happening."

"JEVEX reports the facts," Estordu said lamely, as if that explained everything.

"HOW CAN IT BE REPORTING FACTS?" Broghuilio shouted. "It's contradicting itself. Facts are facts. They can't contradict."

"I have contradicted nothing," JEVEX objected. "My records all indicate that—"

"Shut up! Speak when you are spoken to."

"My apologies, Excellency."

"What Verikoff said about VISAR must be true," Estordu muttered in a worried voice. "VISAR could have been manipulating JEVEX when they were coupled together, before JEVEX disconnected—for years, maybe. Now that JEVEX is isolated, possibly we're receiving the truth for the first time." A ripple of alarmed voices ran around the War Room.

Broghuilio licked his lips and looked suddenly less sure of himself. "JEVEX," he commanded.

"Excellency?"

"Those reports—they were received direct from the surveillance system?"

"Of course, Excellency."

"Those weapons exist? They are being mobilized now?"

"Yes, Excellency."

Wylott was looking uncertain. "How can we be sure?" he objected. "JEVEX says first one thing and then another. How do we know what is true?"

"So, do we do nothing?" Broghuilio asked him. "Would you just sit there and hope that the Terran assault force doesn't exist? What would it take to convince you—a hundred thousand of them coming for your throat? And what would you do then? Imbecile!" Wylott fell silent. The others around the War Room looked at one another with apprehension.

Broghuilio clasped his hands behind his back and began pacing slowly. "We still have a card up our sleeve," he said after a few seconds. "We have decoded their top-level secure communications, and we know their plans. We may have fewer weapons, but we are immeasurably ahead of Earth technically. We command a vastly superior firepower." He looked up, and his eyes began to gleam. "You heard those primitives—the main advantage they were counting on was surprise. Well, they no longer have that advantage. So, Verikoff calls us a rabble, does he? Let him send in his horde of Terran primitives. We will be waiting for them. He will find out who are the rabble when they come up against *Jevlenese* weapons."

Broghuilio turned back to face Wylott. "The operation at Thurien must be suspended for the time being," he declared. "Recall our forces at once and redeploy them for defense of Jevlen, This is not a time to be concerned about upsetting orbits at Gistar. Project the transfer ports in to where the ships are now, and get them back here as soon as possible. I want them in position by this time tomorrow."

New orders went out to the commanders of the task force at Thurien, who prepared their vessels for immediate transfer back. But they were in VISAR-controlled space, and JEVEX reported that its attempts to project entry ports into that region were being jammed; the ships could not be brought back without getting clear of Gistar first. Broghuilio had no choice but to extend his deadline by an extra day and order his force to get away under its own power. An hour later it was streaming in full flight back toward the edge of the Thurien planetary system.

"Phase One completed successfully," Caldwell announced with satisfaction from Thurios as he watched the data displays being presented inside the Government Center. "We've got the bastards on the run. Now let's make sure we keep things going that way."

chapter thirty-five

The transfer ports were ready and waiting outside the system of Gistar as arranged, and the Jevlenese warships peeled out of formation to enter them in relays with crisp, disciplined, military precision. What they didn't know was that by then VISAR was controlling the transfer system, not JEVEX, and such were VISAR's manipulations of JEVEX's internal functions that JEVEX didn't know it, either. Upon exiting back into normal space, one squadron found itself at Sirius, another at Aldebaran, and another near Canopus, while the rest reappeared strewn in ones and twos across Arcturus, Procyon, Castor, Polaris, Rigel, and assorted other stars in between. Thus they were out of harm's way for the time being and could be rounded up later. That completed Caldwell's Phase Two.

With a cigarette in one hand and a cup of black coffee in the other, Hunt stood on the patio outside Sverenssen's house, watching a protesting group of people in brightly colored garb being herded into an Air Force personnel carrier by the pool while a vigilant semicircle of Special Forces troopers looked on from a short distance back. The most recent captives had arrived at Sverenssen's expecting a party, but had found the CIA waiting instead. With VISAR controlling the surveillance there was no longer any need to conceal the activity around the house from orbital observation, but Clifford Benson had decided to maintain a low profile all the same, mainly to take advantage of just this kind of opportunity to extend further his suspect list of Sverenssen's acquaintances. But that was really just a precaution to identify any collaborators that might have been recruited locally. VISAR had found included among JEVEX's records a complete organizational chart of the Jevlenese operation on Earth, and with that information now in Benson's and Sobroskin's hands, the rest of the network would soon be mopped up.

A concentration of Ganymean spacecraft had been building up on the periphery of the Jevlenese planetary system, and at that point it would have been possible for VISAR to shut off all of JEVEX's services from the Jevlenese in the same way that it had done with the Jevlenese element across the Thurien-administered worlds. The problem, however, was that the Jevlenese had clearly been preparing for a war situation for some time, and there was no way of telling what other standalone and backup systems they might possess that were capable of operating without JEVEX. Hunt and Caldwell therefore decided that simply pulling the plug, sending in the Ganymeans, and hoping for the best was not the way to go. Instead they opted to continue applying pressure until either they obtained the unconditional surrender that Verikoff had demanded, or the Jevlenese operation somehow fell apart from the inside. Also they hoped that the reactions they observed inside the Jevlenese War Room would reveal whether or not, and if so to what degree, the Jevlenese could in fact carry on without JEVEX.

Behind Hunt, a flap opened in the plastic sheeting with which the back of the house had been temporarily repaired, and Lyn stepped out through what had been a glass-panel wall of the corner room. She moved over to where he was standing and slipped an arm lightly through his. "I guess this place is off the list for the party rounds from now on," she said, looking across at the VTOL down by the pool.

"Just my luck," Hunt murmured. "As soon as some of the girls I've been hearing about show up, they take 'em away again. Who ever deserved a life like this?"

"Is that all you were worried about?" she asked. Her eyes were twinkling, and there was an elusive, playfully challenging note in her voice.

"And to see pal Sverenssen off on his way, of course. What else?"

"Oh, really," Lyn said softly and mockingly. "That wasn't exactly the way I heard it from Gregg."

"Oh." Hunt frowned for a moment. "He, er . . . he told you about that, huh?"

"Gregg and I work pretty well together. You should know that." She wriggled her arm more tightly inside his. "It sounded to me like somebody was pretty upset."

"Principles," Hunt said stiffly after a pause. "Fancy me being stuck up in a place like McClusky while somebody else was down here in the sun, getting all that action. It was the principle of it. I have very strong principles."

They walked back into the house. Sobroskin was standing nearby with a couple of his officers, and Verikoff was sitting on a couch on the far side of the room, talking with Benson and a mix of CIA officials and more Soviets. Norman Pacey was nowhere in sight; probably he was still in the communications room where Hunt had left him a while earlier. Hunt caught Sobroskin's eye and inclined his head slightly in Verikoff's direction. "That guy's done a good job, and he's trying hard," he muttered in a low voice. "I hope he gets a big remission."

"We'll see what we can do," Sobroskin said. His tone was noncommittal, but there was something deep down in it that Hunt found reassuring.

"WHAT?" A voice that sounded like Broghuilio's shrieked distantly from the direction of the passageway that led through to the communications room. "YOU'VE MANAGED TO LOCATE THEM WHERE?"

"Oh-oh. I think somebody's just found his fleet," Hunt said, grinning. "Come on. Let's go and watch the fun." They moved across toward the passageway, and all around the room figures began standing up and converging behind them. Nobody, it seemed, wanted to miss the excitement.

"There must have been a malfunction in JEVEX," the Supreme Commander of the Jevlenese task force pleaded, cringing as Broghuilio advanced menacingly toward him. "Everything has been premature. There was no time to test the transfer system thoroughly."

"It's true," a white-faced Wylott said from behind. "There wasn't enough time. An interplanetary operation could not be organized on such a schedule. It was impossible."

Broghuilio whirled around and pointed a finger at a screen showing the latest details of the Terran order of battle. "WELL THEY'VE DONE IT!" he raged. "Every bicycle and bedpan factory on the planet is making weapons." He turned to appeal to the whole room. "And what do my *experts* tell me? Two years to complete the quadriflexor program! Twelve months to bring the extra generators on line! 'But we have the overwhelming technical superiority, Excellency,' I'm told." He turned purple and raised his clenched fists over his head. "WELL WHERE IS IT? Do I have all the imbeciles in the Galaxy on my side? Give me a dozen of those Earthmen and I'd conquer the Universe." He wheeled upon Estordu. "Get them back here. Even if you have to exit them here in the middle of the planetary system, get them back here today."

"It . . . seems that it isn't quite that simple," Estordu mumbled bleakly. "JEVEX is reporting difficulties in controlling the transfer system."

"JEVEX, what is this oaf babbling about?" Broghuilio snapped.

"The central beam synchronization system is not responding, Excellency," JEVEX answered. "I am confused. I have not been able to interpret the diagnostic reports."

Broghuilio closed his eyes for a moment and fought to keep control of himself. "Then do it without JEVEX," he said to Estordu. "Use the standby transfer facility at Uttan."

Estordu swallowed. "The Uttan system is not general purpose," he pointed out. "It was only set up to handle supply transfers to Jevlen. The fleet is scattered across fifteen different stars. Uttan would have to recalibrate for every one. It would take weeks."

Broghuilio turned away in exasperation and began pacing furiously back and forth across the floor. He halted suddenly in front of the commanding general of the local defense system. "They've got their attack planned all the way down to who will dig the latrines after they've wiped out the last imbecile in your army. You have a direct line into their communications network, and you can decode their signals. You know their intentions. Where is your defense plan?"

"What? I . . ." the general faltered helplessly. "How do you—"

"YOUR PLAN OF DEFENSE. WHERE IS IT?"

"But . . . we have no weapons."

"You have no reserves? What kind of a general are you?"

"A few robot destroyers only, all controlled by JEVEX. Can they be relied upon? The reserves were sent to Thurien." That had been at Broghuilio's insistence, but nobody chose to remind him of the fact.

A deathly silence enveloped the Jevlenese War Room. At last Wylott said firmly. "A truce. There is no alternative. We must sue for a truce."

"What?" Broghuilio looked toward him. "The Protectorate has barely been declared, and already you are saying we should crawl to primitives? What kind of talk is this?"

"For time," Wylott urged. "Until Uttan is in full production and the stockpiles are built up. Give the army time to be brought up to strength and trained. Earth has been geared to war for centuries. We have not, and there is the difference. The break from Thurien was forced too soon."

"It looks as if it may be the only chance we have, Excellency," Estordu said.

"JEVEX has reopened a channel," VISAR announced. "Broghuilio wishes a private audience with Calazar." Calazar had been expecting the call and was sitting alone on one side of the room in the Government Center waiting for it, while Caldwell, Danchekker, Heller, and the Thuriens watched from the far side.

A head-and-shoulders image of Broghuilio appeared in a frame before Calazar. Broghuilio looked surprised and uncertain. "Why are we talking like this? I asked to come to Thurien."

"I do not feel that the intimacy of proximity would be appropriate," Calazar replied. "What did you wish to discuss?"

Broghuilio swallowed and forced his words with a visible effort. "I have had an opportunity to consider the recent . . . developments. On reflection, it seems that perhaps we were disoriented by the arrogance of the Terrans. Our reactions were, perhaps, a little . . . hasty. I would like to propose a debate to reconsider the relationship between our races."

"That is no longer an affair that concerns me," Calazar told him. "I have agreed with the Terrans to leave the matter to be settled between yourselves. They have given you their terms. Do you accept them?"

"Their terms are outrageous," Broghuilio protested. "We have to negotiate."

"Negotiate with the Terrans."

Alarm showed on Broghuilio's face. "But they are barbarians . . . savages. Have you forgotten what leaving them to settle things their way will mean?"

"I choose not to. Have you forgotten the *Shapieron*?"

Broghuilio paled. "That was an inexcusable error. Those responsible will be punished. But this . . . this is different. You are Ganymeans. We stood beside you for millennia. You can't stand aside and abandon us now."

"You deceived us for millennia," Calazar replied coldly. "We wanted to keep Lunarian violence from spreading into the Galaxy, but it is loose in the Galaxy already. Our attempts to change you have failed. If the only solution left lies with the Terrans, then so be it. The Ganymeans can do no more."

"We must discuss this, Calazar. You can't allow this."

"Will you accept the Terran terms?"

"They cannot be serious. There must be room for negotiation."

"Then negotiate with the Terrans. I have nothing more to say. Excuse me now, please." The image of Broghuilio vanished.

Calazar turned to confront the approving faces across the room. "How did I do?" he asked.

"Terrific," Karen Heller told him. "You should apply for a seat in the UN."

"How does it feel to be hard-nosed, Terran-style," Showm asked curiously.

Calazar stood up, drew himself up to his full height, and filled his lungs with air while he considered the question. "Do you know, I find it rather . . . invigorating," he confessed.

Caldwell turned his head toward an image showing the observers on Earth. "It's not looking so bad," he said. "They can't get their ships back, and they don't seem to have a lot else. We could pull the rug out now. What do you think?"

Hunt was looking dubious. "Broghuilio's shaky, but he hasn't cracked yet," he replied. "He might have enough there to turn nasty with, especially if only unarmed Thurien ships show up. I'd like to see him a bit more unhinged first."

"So would we," Garuth said from the *Shapieron*. His tone left no room for doubt about the matter.

Caldwell thought for a second, then nodded. "I'll go along with that." He stroked his chin and cocked an eye at Hunt. "And VISAR has done a helluva job preparing all this material. It'd be a shame to waste it, wouldn't it."

"A terrible shame," Hunt agreed solemnly.

Chapter Thirty-six

The scene being presented inside the Jevlenese War Room was a view of the combined Terran battle fleet forming up as it moved from Earth. In the foreground a formation of destroyers, sleek, gray, and menacing, was moving into position to become part of an unfolding armada that extended away as far as the eye could see. As the first shrank into the distance to merge into the array, more formations slid majestically inward from the sides of the view and were absorbed in turn into the growing panorama. The first groups carried the Red Star of the Soviet Union, the next ones the Stars and Stripes of the U.S.A., and after those came the emblems of U.S. Europe, Canada, Australia, and the Republic of China. Farther away, moving slowly behind the vessels maneuvering and turning in the foreground, were lines of immense warships, their stark, solid contours broken by sinister weapon housings and ominous clusters of externally mounted missile pods. And behind them were the task groups and supply convoys—carriers, bombardment platforms, battle cruisers, interceptor mother ships, ground-suppression orbiters, shuttle launchers, troop and armor carriers, transports, all attended by swarms of support and escort craft—diminishing away to become pinpoints that seemed to be hardly moving at all against the stars. But appearances were deceiving. The whole awesome constellation was speeding silently and relentlessly away from Earth—toward the Ganymean transfer ports.

JEVEX'S comments came through on audio. "The first wave, moving out from its forming-up area near Luna. Measured acceleration is consistent with the arrival time that the Terrans have indicated."

Broghuilio turned a shade paler. "First wave?" he gasped. "There's more?"

In response the scene changed to show a view looking down on what appeared to be a huge base of some kind, enclosed by a perimeter fence and surrounded by desolate, sandy terrain. Lines of dots along one side expanded rapidly as the view enlarged, and resolved themselves into rows of surface shuttles in the process of being loaded. The area in front of them was packed with lines of tanks, artillery, personnel carriers, and thousands of troops waiting in neat, geometric groupings. "Chinese regular divisions embarking to be ferried up for the second wave now assembling in orbit," JEVEX announced.

The view changed again to show a similar scene, but this time set among thickly forested hills. "Conventional low-level supersonic bombers and high-altitude interceptors being loaded in Siberia."

And another view. "Missile batteries and antitank laser units embarking in the western U.S.A. There're more coming in from all over. Contingency plans are being drawn up for a third wave."

Perspiration was showing on Broghuilio's face. He closed his eyes, and his lips moved soundlessly as he struggled to remain calm. "Might I suggest, Excellency, that—" Wylott began, but Broghuilio cut him off with a sharp wave of his hand.

"Quiet. I need time to think." Broghuilio brought his hand up to his chin and began tugging at his beard nervously. He clenched his other fist behind his back and paced to the far end of the War Room. Then he turned to face back again. "JEVEX."

"Excellency?"

"VISAR must have a link into the Terran communications

net through the Thurien facility there. Get me a channel into
it through VISAR. I want to talk to the President of the United
States of America, the Soviet Premier, or anybody else in high
authority that VISAR can get hold of. Do it immediately."

"How do you want me to play it?" VISAR asked in the Government Center at Thurios.

"We can't let the plan bog down," Caldwell said. "Unconditional surrender has to be his only way out. Fix it so that he
thinks he's cut off from everybody except Verikoff."

Anxious and impatient, Broghuilio had started pacing again.
Then JEVEX announced, "VISAR is denying the request. It has
been directed to conform to Thurien policy, which is to disso-
ciate itself from Terran-Jevlenese affairs."

Broghuilio's legs almost buckled beneath him. "The
Thuriens are transferring those warships here to wipe us out!"
he shouted. "What kind of dissociation policy is that? Tell VISAR
I insist."

"VISAR has instructed me to advise you, with respect, Excellency, to go to hell."

Broghuilio was too numbed with shock to react violently.
"Then tell VISAR to connect me to Calazar again," he choked.

"VISAR refuses."

"Then connect VISAR through to me."

"VISAR has severed all connections. I am unable to obtain
further responses."

Broghuilio had begun trembling with a mixture of rage and
fear. He spun his head wildly from side to side, his eyes white
and staring. "Verikoff is your only choice," Wylott said. "You
have to accept the ultimatum."

"*Never!*" Broghuilio shouted. "I'll never surrender my force
intact. We still have two days. We can evacuate the entire officer
corps, our scientists, our best engineers, and consolidate at
Uttan. We will make our stand there. Uttan has permanent
defenses that the Terrans will find themselves hard put to
match. They will still have some surprises in store for them if
they try to follow us there." He looked at Wylott. "Work out a

schedule with JEVEX to evacuate the maximum of value from Jevlen in two days. Begin at once. Ignore all other tasks."

"I think we ought to try the switch," Hunt said, watching. "They're just about ready."

"Are you really going to try that?" Shilohin asked from the *Shapieron*. She sounded skeptical. "It's too illogical, surely."

"What do you think, Chris?" Caldwell asked, glancing over his shoulder.

"They have been conditioned to accept contradictions now," Danchekker said. "At this moment there is a good chance that they will be incapable of thinking sufficiently clearly to question it."

"And they are close to panic," Sobroskin observed from beside Hunt. "Panic and logic are impossible companions."

"I'm still not sure I understand this phenomenon you call panic," Eesyan said from the *Shapieron*.

"Let's see if we can show you," Caldwell said, and gave an instruction to VISAR.

"Pardon, Excellency," JEVEX queried. "But your figure of two days appears irrelevant."

"What?" Broghuilio stopped dead in his tracks. "What do you mean, irrelevant?"

"I don't understand why you have specified two days," JEVEX answered.

Broghuilio shook his head, nonplussed. "It's obvious, isn't it? The Terran attack will begin two days from now, will it not?"

"I don't follow, Excellency."

Broghuilio sent a puzzled frown around the room. His aides stared back at him equally bemused. "The attack is due in two days, is it not?" he said again.

"There has been no postponement, Excellency. The attack is still expected today, twelve hours from now."

Nothing happened for a few seconds.

Then Broghuilio brought his hand up to his face and beat it slowly and deliberately several times against his brow. "JEVEX," he said. His voice was quiet as his effort to control himself overcompensated. "You have just told us that the first wave is only now in the process of leaving Earth."

"Pardon, Excellency, but I have no record of saying any such thing."

It was too much. Broghuilio's voice began to rise and shake uncontrollably. "How can the Terrans be less than a day away?" he demanded. "Are they or are they not departing from Earth now?"

"They began departing from Earth two days ago," JEVEX replied. "They have entered Jevlenese planetary space and will commence their attack in twelve hours' time."

Broghuilio's color was deepening rapidly. "Those surveillance reports that you just presented. Were they or were they not live from Earth as of this moment, as you stated?"

"They were records obtained two days ago, as I stated."

"YOU DID NOT SAY THAT!" Broghuilio screamed.

"I did. My records confirm it. Shall I replay them?"

Broghuilio turned to appeal to the rest of the room. "You all heard it. What did that idiot machine say? Were those views live or were they not?" Nobody was listening. One of the aides was rushing back and forth and jabbering incoherently, another was clutching at his face and moaning, while among the rest consternation was breaking out on every side.

"They couldn't be from two days ago."

"How do you know? How do you know what's happening and what isn't? How do you know anything?"

"JEVEX said so."

"It said the opposite too."

"Maybe JEVEX is mad."

"But JEVEX said—"

"JEVEX doesn't know what it's saying. We can't trust anything."

"The Terrans are coming! They're only hours away!"

On one side of the room the scientist, Estordu, quietly vanished. In the confusion, nobody noticed.

Broghuilio was waving his arms and shouting above the clamor. "Twelve hours. *Twelve hours!* And you tell me you have no weapons! They'll be coming straight in for the kill because they don't know what opposition to expect. . . . AND WE HAVE NO OPPOSITION TO OFFER! A shipful of children could walk in and take us over, and the Terrans don't even know it. And what do I have to stop them? Imbecile generals, imbecile scientists, and an imbecile computer!"

Wylott shouldered his way through to where Broghuilio was standing. "There is no choice," he insisted. "You have to accept Verikoff's terms. At least that way there will come another day." Broghuilio turned his head and glowered, but the inevitability of what Wylott had said was written in his eyes. But still he could not bring himself to give the order. Wylott waited for a few seconds, then raised his head to call above the commotion still going on around them. "JEVEX. Call Earth via your own channel to Sverenssen. Get Verikoff on the line."

"At once, General," JEVEX acknowledged.

In the communications room in Connecticut, Hunt turned his head toward Verikoff, who was watching from the doorway. "You'd better come on in. It looks as if you'll be on again in a few seconds to accept the surrender. It's just about all over." Verikoff moved to the center of the room while the others fell back to clear a small circle around him. On the screen showing the Jevlenese War Room, Wylott and Broghuilio had turned to look directly out at the room and were waiting expectantly for JEVEX to make the connection. Verikoff folded his arms and assumed a domineering posture in readiness.

And suddenly the screen went blank.

Puzzled looks appeared all around the room. "VISAR?" Hunt said after a few seconds. "VISAR, what's happened?" There was no reply. The screens that had been connecting them to Thurien and the *Shapieron* had gone blank as well.

Verikoff moved quickly over to a bank of equipment on one side of the room and ran rapidly through a sequence of tests. "It's dead," he announced, looking up at the others. "The whole system is dead. We don't have any channels to anywhere, and I can't open any. Something has cut us off from JEVEX completely."

In the Government Center at Thurios, Caldwell was equally bewildered. "VISAR, what's happened?" he demanded. "Where did the views from Earth and Jevlen go? Have you lost them or something?"

A few seconds went by, then VISAR answered. "It's worse than that. I haven't only lost Connecticut and the War Room, I've lost everything from JEVEX. I don't have anything into it at all. The whole system has switched off."

"Don't you know anything that's happening at Jevlen at all?" Morizal asked, aghast.

"Nothing," VISAR said. "The only channel I've got to anywhere in the whole of the JEVEX-controlled world-system is the one through to the *Shapieron*. JEVEX seems to be dead. The whole system has just gone down."

Broghuilio found himself reclining in his private quarters deep underground in the complex that housed the Directorate of Strategic Planning. He sat up sharply, unsure of what had happened. A moment before he had been in the War Room with Wylott, waiting for a connection to Verikoff. Even as he remembered, he saw again in his mind's eye the armada from Earth, at that moment sweeping inward toward Jevlen. He looked around wildly. "JEVEX?"

No response.

"JEVEX, answer me."

Nothing.

Something cold and heavy turned over deep in his stomach. He leaped to his feet, fumbled his way into a robe to cover his shorts and undershirt, and hurried into the next room to check the status indicators of the suite's monitor panel. Lighting, air conditioning, communications, services . . . everything had reverted to emergency backup mode. JEVEX was not operating. He tried activating the communications console, but the only thing he could raise on the screen was a message stating that all channels were saturated. It meant that the condition was general and not due simply to some local failure; the complex was in panic. He rushed through into his bedroom and began frantically tearing clothes out of a closet.

He was still buttoning his tunic when a tone sounded from the outside door in the hallway. Broghuilio hastened out and pressed his thumb against a printlock plate to dematerialize the door. Estordu was there with two other aides. The sounds of shouting and commotion came in from behind them.

"What's happened?" Broghuilio demanded. "The whole system is dead."

"I deactivated it," Estordu told him. "I threw the manual override breakers in the master nucleus control room. I've shut JEVEX down totally."

Broghuilio's beard quivered, and his eyes widened. "You *what*—" he began, but Estordu waved a hand impatiently to silence him. The gesture was so out of character that Broghuilio just stared.

"Can't you see what's happened?" Estordu said, speaking rapidly and urgently. "JEVEX was not functioning coherently. Something was affecting it from the *inside*. It could only have been VISAR. Somehow VISAR gained access to it. That meant that the Thuriens could have been watching every move we made. We still have twelve hours, and if we move quickly we can still get away. We still have emergency communications channels to Uttan, and the standby transfer system can project an entry port to Jevlen. With JEVEX inoperative and VISAR therefore blind, we can make our arrangements without risking interference from the Thuriens or the Terrans. The nearest Terran ships are still twelve hours away. By the time they get here we can be gone, and they'll have no way of knowing where to. By the time they think of looking for us at Uttan, we will be well prepared. Don't you see? It was the only way. With JEVEX running we couldn't have planned a move without them knowing."

Broghuilio thought rapidly as he listened. There was no time for arguing, and anyway, Estordu was right. He nodded. "Everyone with their wits about them will go physically to the War Room," he said. He looked at Estordu. "Find Lantyar and tell him I want five reliable crews mustered and brought to Geerbaine by eighteen hundred hours today. You . . ." He directed his gaze at one of the two aides standing behind Estordu. "Contact the operations commander at Geerbaine and tell him I want five E-class transports ready for launch not one minute later than then, and power standing by on-line at Uttan to project ports as soon as the transports clear Jevlen." He gestured to the other aide. "And you, find General Wylott and tell him to mobilize four companies of guards and organize air transportation from here to Geerbaine, ready to leave by seventeen thirty hours. I'll need capacity for two thousand persons. Commandeer it from wherever you need to, and don't hesitate to use force. Do you understand?" Broghuilio straightened his collar and went back through to the bedroom to buckle on his belt and sidearm. "I am going to the War Room now," he called out to them. "The three of you will report to me there not later than one hour from now. Do as I say, and this time tomorrow we will all be on Uttan."

Chapter Thirty-seven

The *Shapieron* had moved closer to Jevlen to await the arrival of the Ganymean ships from Thurien, which had begun moving inward from the edge of the planetary system but were still many hours away. The main screen on the Command Deck was showing views of Jevlen's surface being sent back from probes at lower altitudes. The planet seemed to be in chaos. Nothing was flying anywhere, but in many places people had begun leaving the cities on foot and in disorderly streams of ground vehicles that had soon jammed solid on highway systems never intended for more than minor local or recreational traffic. Disturbances and rioting had broken out in a few places, but in most the populations were merely assembling in the open spaces, leaderless and bewildered. Communications traffic from the surface was garbled and revealed no organization for maintaining order or vital services. In short, the Ganymeans were going to have a big job on their hands putting the pieces of the mess together again.

Garuth was tense and apprehensive as he stood in the center of the Command Deck taking in the reports. VISAR had not crashed JEVEX, so the culprit had to have been the Jevlenese themselves. Somehow they had discovered they were the unwitting objects of surveillance through JEVEX, and had shut down the system to blind VISAR to what they were doing. In other words they were up to something, and there was no way of knowing what. Garuth didn't like it.

The other thing that was bothering him at a deeper level was the feeling that he had failed. Despite the reassurances of Eesyan, Shilohin, Monchar, and the others that his bringing the *Shapieron* to Jevlen had saved Thurien, Garuth was acutely conscious of how near to disaster he had brought them, and that only the fast action of Hunt and the others on Earth had saved things. He had risked his crew and Eesyan's scientists irresponsibly, and others had bailed him out. Yes, the threat to Thurien had been removed; but Garuth didn't feel he deserved very much credit for that. He would have liked to have contributed more and the congratulations that had poured through from Thurien had only added to his discomfort.

On a smaller screen to one side, Hunt was talking over his shoulder to the others who were crowded into the room in the Connecticut house that had been the headquarters of the Jevlenese operation to infiltrate Earth. "Can you imagine the problems we might have created for lots of people on this planet in years to come?"

"What do you mean?" the voice of Norman Pacey, the American government representative, asked from somewhere in the background.

Hunt half turned to wave at the screen in front of him. "One day people might be sending their kids to college on Thurien. Suppose the kids figure out this stunt for themselves and start calling home collect."

After JEVEX had gone off the air and shut down the communications facility, the group in Connecticut had reestablished contact by the simple expedient of telephoning the control room at McClusky and linking back into VISAR via the databeam to the perceptron. They had called on two lines from the datagrid terminals in Sverenssen's office, next door to the communications room, and had one screen to the *Shapieron* and another to the Government Center at Thurios.

"I still don't believe it," the CIA official, Benson, said from a chair by a window, partly visible over Hunt's shoulder. "When I see somebody picking up the phone and calling talking computers in an alien spaceship out at some other star, I don't believe it." Benson turned his head to address somebody offscreen. "*Jeez!* The CIA should have had something like this years ago. We could even have tuned into what you guys were talking about in the men's room inside the Kremlin."

"I think the days of that kind of thing will very soon be over, my friend," a voice replied from somewhere in an accent that Garuth assumed was Russian.

It would have made no difference if they were physically present in the *Shapieron*, he thought to himself. They would banter and laugh in the same way whatever the risks and whatever the unknowns. They could try, fail, forget, laugh, and try again—and probably succeed. The thought that they had been within a hair's breadth of disaster didn't trouble them. They had won the round, now it was dismissed and in the past, and their only thoughts now were for the next. Sometimes Garuth envied Earthmen.

ZORAC spoke suddenly. Its tone was urgent. "Attention please. There is a new development. Probe Four has detected ships rising fast from the surface on the far side of Jevlen— five of them in tight formation." At the same instant the view on the main screen changed to show the curving, cloud-blotched surface of the planet with five dots creeping across the mottled background.

On the auxiliary screen Hunt was leaning forward while others crowded behind him. They had stopped talking. An adjacent screen showed Calazar and the observers at Thurios, all equally tense.

"It has to be Broghuilio and his staff," Calazar said after a few seconds. "They must be making a break for Uttan. Estordu said they've got a standby transfer system that operates between Jevlen and Uttan. That's what they've been planning! We should have thought of it."

Eesyan had joined Garuth in the center of the Command Deck. Shilohin, Monchar, and some of the scientists were gathering around from the sides of the room. "They have to be stopped," Eesyan said, sounding worried. "They could have Uttan prepared and defended as a fallback base. If they reach it and regroup, they could decide to fight it out. It would only be a matter of time before they realized that we don't have anything to challenge them with. With Uttan in their hands, we'd be in real trouble."

"What is Uttan?" Hunt asked from the screen.

Eesyan turned away from Garuth and answered in a faraway voice as he tried to think. "An airless, waterless ball of rock on the fringe of Jevlenese space, but very rich in metals. The Jevlenese were granted it long ago as a source of raw materials to build up their industries. It's obviously where their weapons came from. But if what we suspect is right, they've turned the whole planet into a fortified armaments factory. We've got to prevent Broghuilio's getting there."

While Eesyan was speaking to Hunt, Garuth quickly reviewed what he could recollect of the Thurien h-transfer system. VISAR or JEVEX could jam h-beams projected into their respective regions of space by virtue of the dense networks of sensors they possessed, which enabled them to monitor the field parameters of a transfer toroid just beginning to form, and disrupt the energy flow through from h-space. Without the sensors, jamming wouldn't work. But the only sensors that existed in the vicinity of Jevlen were JEVEX's and VISAR would not be able to use them since it could only do so through JEVEX, and JEVEX was dead. Hence a beam from Uttan couldn't be disrupted by VISAR. So *that* was why the Jevlenese had shut down the system.

"There's nothing we can do," Calazar was saying from the other screen. "We haven't got anything near there. Our ships are still eight hours away at least."

An agonized silence fell on the Command Deck. Calazar was looking helplessly from one side to another about him, while to one side of him Hunt and the Terrans on Earth had frozen into immobility. On the main screen the five Jevlenese vessels had cleared the edge of the planet's disk.

A feeling of composure and confidence that he had not

known for a long time flowed slowly into Garuth's veins as the situation unfolded in sudden crystal clarity. There was no doubt about what he had to do. He was himself again, in control of himself and in command of his ship. "We are right here."

Eesyan stared for a second, then turned his head to gaze uncertainly at the five dots on the main screen, now diminishing rapidly into the starry background of space. "Could we catch them?" he asked dubiously.

Garuth smiled grimly. "Those are just Jevlenese planetary transports," he said. "Have you forgotten? The *Shapieron* was built as a starship." Without waiting for a response from Calazar, he raised his head and called in a louder voice, "ZORAC, dispatch Probe Four in pursuit immediately, recover deployed probes, lift the ship into high orbit, charge all onboard probes for maximum range, and bring the main drives up to full-power readiness. We're going after them."

"And what will you do then?" Calazar asked.

"Worry about that later," Garuth replied. "The first thing is not to lose them."

"Tally ho!" ZORAC cried, mimicking a flawless English accent.

Hunt sat up and blinked in astonishment on one of the screens. "Where the hell did it pick that up?" he asked.

"Documentaries of World War II British fighter pilots," ZORAC announced. "That was for your benefit, Vic. I thought you'd appreciate it."

Chapter Thirty-eight

B roghuilio stood on the bridge of the Jevlenese flagship
and scowled while the technicians and scientists clustered around a battery of datascreens in front of him took in
the details of the report coming through from the long-range
scanning computers. Gasps of disbelief sounded among the
rising murmur of voices. "Well?" he demanded as his patience
finally exhausted itself.

Estordu turned from the group. His eyes were wide with
shock. "It can't be possible," he whispered. He made a vague
gesture behind him. "But it's true . . . there's no doubt about
it."

"What is it?" Broghuilio fumed.

Estordu swallowed. "It's . . . the *Shapieron*. It's pulling away
from Jevlen and turning this way."

Broghuilio stared at him as if he had just gone insane, then
snorted and pulled two of the technicians out of the way to see
the screens for himself. For a second his mouth clamped tight,
and his beard quivered as his mind refused to accept what his
eyes were seeing. Then another screen came to life to show a
magnified view from the long-range optical imagers that left

no room for dissent. Broghuilio spun around to glare at Wylott, who was watching numbly from a few feet back. "HOW DO YOU EXPLAIN THIS?" he shouted.

Wylott shook his head in protest. "It can't be. It was destroyed. I *know* it was destroyed."

"THEN WHAT IS THAT COMING AT US RIGHT NOW?" Broghuilio whirled to the scientists. "How long has it been at Jevlen? What is it doing here? Why didn't any of you know about it?"

The captain's voice came from the raised section of the bridge above them. "I've never seen acceleration like it! It's vectoring straight after us. We'll never outrun it."

"They can't do anything," Wylott said in a choking voice. "It's not armed."

"Fool!" Broghuilio snapped. "If it wasn't destroyed, it must have been transferred to Thurien. And Terrans could have been transferred to Thurien. So it could have Terrans on board it with Terran weapons. They could blow us apart, and after your bungling, the *Shapieron*'s crew won't lift a finger to stop them." Wylott licked his lips and said nothing.

"Stressfield around the *Shapieron* building up rapidly," the long-range surveillance operator called from one of the stations above. "We're losing radar and optical contact. H-scan shows it's maintaining course and acceleration."

Estordu was thinking furiously. "We may have a chance, Excellency," he said suddenly. Broghuilio jerked his head around and thrust his chin out demandingly. Estordu went on, "The Ganymean ships from that period did not possess stressfield transmission correction, and h-scan equipment was unknown. In other words they have no means of tracking us while they're under main drive. They'll have to aim blind to intercept our predicted course and slow down at intervals to correct. We might be able to lose them by changing course during their blind periods."

At that instant another operator called out, "Gravitational anomaly building up astern and starboard, range nine eighty miles, strength seven, increasing. Readings indicate a Class Five exit port. H-scan shows conformal entry-port mapping to vicinity of *Shapieron*." The tension on the bridge rocketed. It meant that VISAR was projecting two beams to create a linked pair of transfer ports—a "tunnel" through h-space from the *Shapieron* to the Jevlenese vessels. A Class Five port would admit something relatively small. The operator's voice came again, rising with alarm. "An object has emerged at this end. It's coming this way, fast!"

"*A bomb!*" somebody screamed. "*They've exited a bomb!*" Consternation broke out around the bridge. Broghuilio was wide-eyed and sweating profusely. Wylott had collapsed onto a chair.

The operator's voice came again. "Object identified. It's one of the *Shapieron*'s robot probes . . . matching us in course and speed. The exit port has dissolved."

And the long-range surveillance operator: "*Shapieron* closing and still accelerating. Range two-twenty thousand miles."

"Get rid of it," Broghuilio barked up at the level above. "Captain, shake that thing off."

The captain gave a set of course-correction instructions, which the computers acknowledged and executed.

"Probe matching," came the report. "Evasion ineffective. *Shapieron* has corrected to a new vector and is still closing."

Broghuilio turned a furious face toward Estordu. "You said they'd be blind! They're not even slowing down." Estordu spread his hands and shook his head helplessly. Broghuilio looked at the rest of the group of scientists. "Well, how are they doing it? Can't any of you work it out?" He waited for a few seconds, then pointed a finger angrily at the screens showing the tracking data of the *Shapieron*. "Some genius on *that* ship has thought of something." He began pacing back and forth across the bridge. "How does this happen? They have all the geniuses, and I have all the imbeciles. Give me—"

"The probe!" Estordu groaned suddenly. "They must have fitted the probe and the *Shapieron* with h-links. The probe will be able to monitor every move we make and update the *Shapieron*'s flight-control system through VISAR. We'll never lose it now."

Broghuilio glared at him for a second, then looked across at the communications officer. "We have to make the jump to Uttan now," he declared. "What's the status there?"

"The generators are up to power and standing by," the officer told him. "Their director is locked onto our beacon, and they can throw a port here immediately."

"But what if that probe transfers through with us?" Estordu said. "VISAR would locate it when it reenters at Uttan. It would reveal our destination."

"Those geniuses will have guessed our destination already," Broghuilio retorted. "So what could they do? We can blow anything that comes near Uttan to atoms."

"But we're still too close to Jevlen," Estordu objected, looking alarmed. "It would disrupt the whole planet . . . chaos everywhere."

"So would you rather stay here?" Broghuilio sneered. "Hasn't it occurred to you yet that the probe was just a warning? The next thing they tunnel through at us *will* be a bomb." He sent a stare around the bridge that defied anybody to argue with him. Nobody did. He raised his head. "Captain. Transfer now, to Uttan."

The command was relayed to Uttan, and within seconds huge generators were pouring energy into a tiny volume of space ahead of the five Jevlenese ships. The fabric of space-time wrinkled, then buckled, heaved, and fell in upon itself to plummet out of the Universe. A spinning vortex began growing to open up the gateway to another realm, first as a faint circle of curdled starlight against the void, then getting stronger, thicker, and sharper, and expanding slowly to reveal a core of featureless, infinite blackness.

And then a counterspinning pattern of refractions materialized inside the first. The resultant composite of vortices shimmered and pulsated as filaments of space and time writhed in a tangle of knotted geodesies. Something was wrong. The port was going unstable. "What's happening?" Broghuilio demanded.

Estordu was turning his head frantically from side to side to take in the displays and data reports. "Something is deforming the configuration . . . breaking up the field manifolds. I've never seen anything like this. It can only be VISAR."

"That's impossible," one of the other scientists shouted. "VISAR can't jam. It has no sensors. JEVEX is shut down."

"That's not jamming," Estordu muttered. "The port began to form. It's doing something else. . . ." His eye caught the view of the *Shapieron* again. "The probe! VISAR is using the probe to monitor the entry-port configuration. It couldn't jam the beam, so it's trying to project a complementary pattern from Gistar to cancel out the toroid from Uttan. It's trying to neutralize it."

"It couldn't," the other scientist protested. "It couldn't get enough resolution through a single probe. It would be aiming virtually blind from Gistar."

"The Gistar and Uttan beams would interact constructively in the same volume," another pointed out. "If an unstable resonance developed, anything could happen."

"That *is* an unstable resonance," Estordu shouted, pointing at the display. "I tell you, that's what VISAR's doing."

"VISAR would never risk it."

Ahead of the ships, a maelstrom of twisting, convulsing, multiple-connected relativity was boiling under the clash of titanic bolts of energy materializing and superposing from two points, each light-years away. The core shrank, grew again, fragmented, then reassembled itself. And still they were heading directly for its center.

Broghuilio had listened enough. He turned his head up to where the captain was watching him, waiting. Then at the last second, something about Estordu pulled his attention away.

Estordu was standing absolutely still with a strange look on his face as he stared at the view of the *Shapieron*. He was mumbling to himself, and seemed to have forgotten everything going on around him. "H-links through the probes," he whispered. "That was how VISAR got into JEVEX." His eyes opened wider, and his face became ashen as the full realization hit him. "That was how . . . *everything* got into JEVEX! It never existed, any of it. They were doing it through the *Shapieron* all the time. . . . We're running away from a single unarmed ship."

"What is it?" Broghuilio snapped. "Why are you looking like that?"

Estordu looked at him with a bleak stare. "It doesn't exist. . . . The Terran strike force doesn't exist. It never did. VISAR wrote it into JEVEX through the *Shapieron*. The whole thing was a fabrication. There was nothing there but the *Shapieron* all the time."

The captain leaned over from above. "Excellency, we have to . . ." He stopped as he saw that Broghuilio was not listening, hesitated for a second, then turned away to call to somewhere behind him. "Disengage forward compensators. Cut in emergency boost and reverse at full power. Compute evasion function and execute immediately."

"*What?—What did you say?*" Broghuilio turned to face the semicircle of cowering figures behind him. "Are you telling me the Terrans have been making fools out of all of you?"

From above the synthetic voice of a computer came tonelessly: "Negative function. Negative function. All measures ineffective. Ship accelerating on irreversible gradient. Corrective action now impossible. Repeat: Corrective action now impossible."

But Broghuilio didn't hear, even as the craft plunged into the knot of insanely tangled space-time looming around them. "You imbeciles!" he breathed. His voice rose and began shaking uncontrollably as he lifted his fists high above his head. "*Imbeciles! IMBECILES! You IM-BE-CILES!!*"

"My God, they're going straight into it!" Hunt gasped from a screen on the Command Deck of the *Shapieron*. The view on the main screen was being sent back from the probe two hundred thousand miles away, still clinging doggedly to the heels of the Jevlenese ships. A horrified silence had fallen all around.

"What's happening?" Eesyan whispered from the center of the floor.

"An oscillating instability is coupling positively to an h-frequency alias caused by discrepancies in the beam spectra," VISAR answered. "The properties of the region created are beyond analysis."

On another screen Calazar, openmouthed with shock, was shaking his head in protest. "I never intended this," he said in a strangled voice. "Why didn't they turn away? I just wanted to deny them the port."

"ZORAC, cut the main drives and decelerate," Garuth instructed in a voice that was clipped and expressionless. "Present an optical scan of the area as soon as we reintegrate."

A background of turbulent light and blackness now filled the entire main screen. The five dots grew smaller in front of it . . . and were suddenly swallowed up in the chaos. The turmoil seemed to rush out as the probe followed in after them, and then the view changed abruptly as the *Shapieron*'s stressfield dispersed and ZORAC switched through the long-range image from the ship's own scanners. "The instability is breaking down," VISAR reported. "The resonances are degenerating into turbulence eddies. If there was a tunnel there, it's caving in." On the screen the patterns broke up into swirling fragments of light that spiraled rapidly inward, at the same time growing smaller, dimmer, and redder. They faded, and then died. The region of the starfield that was left shimmered for a few seconds to mark where the upheaval had been, and then all was normal just as if nothing had happened.

For a long time an absolute silence gripped the Command Deck, and nobody moved. The faces on the screens showing Earth and Thurien were grim.

And then VISAR spoke again. There was a distinct note of disbelief in its voice. "I have a further report. Don't ask me how right now, but it looks as if they got through. The probe was still transmitting when the tunnel closed in behind it, and its last signal indicates that it reentered normal space." While surprise was still evident all over the Command Deck, the view on the main screen changed to show the last image transmitted by the probe. The five Jevlenese ships were hanging in ragged formation in what looked like ordinary space sure enough, studded with what looked like ordinary stars. And up near one corner was a larger speck that could have been a planet. The image froze at that point. "The transmission ceased there," VISAR said.

"They survived that?" Eesyan stammered. "Where is it? Where in space did they emerge?"

"I don't know," VISAR answered. "They must have been trying for Uttan, but anything could have happened. I'm trying to match the starfield background with projections from Uttan now, but it could take a while."

"We can't risk waiting," Calazar said. "Even though Uttan might be defended, I'll have to send in the reserve ships from Gistar to try and cut Broghuilio off before he reaches that planet." He waited for a few seconds, but nobody could disagree. His voice became heavier. "VISAR, connect me to the reserve-squadron commander," he said.

"There is nothing more for us to do here," Garuth said in a voice that had become very quiet and very calm. "ZORAC, return the ship to Jevlen. We will await the arrival of the Thuriens there."

While the *Shapieron* was turning to head back, a set of toroids opened up briefly some distance outside the planetary system of Gistar, and the squadron of Thurien vessels that had been held in reserve there transferred into h-space, then reemerged outside the system of Uttan. The Jevlenese long-range surveillance instruments detected them as a series of objects hurtling inward at a speed not much below that of light. The commander at Uttan decided that a portion of the Terran strike force had been diverted, and within minutes every emergency signal band was carrying frantic offers of unconditional surrender. The Thuriens arrived at Uttan some hours later and took over without opposition.

That result had been unexpected. The reason for it was even more unexpected: Broghuilio's ships had not, after all, appeared at Uttan, or anywhere near it. Uttan control had lost contact when they vanished from the vicinity of Jevlen, and had been unable to relocate them. Without their leaders, the defenders at Uttan opted to capitulate without a fight.

So where had the five Jevlenese ships gone? VISAR reported that they had not rematerialized anywhere inside the regions of space that it controlled, and when it projected small transfer ports to the scores of worlds previously run by JEVEX and sent search probes bristling with sensors and instruments, the ships were not to be found at any of those places, either. They seemed to have vanished entirely from the explored portion of the Galaxy.

The Thuriens did find something else at Uttan, however—something that left them shaken and mystified. Hanging in space, all at various stages of construction, they found lines of immense engineering structures. Each was in the form of a hollow square that measured five hundred miles along a side, and carried at its center a two-hundred-mile-diameter sphere supported by bars extending diagonally inward from the corners.

Chapter Thirty-nine

"I don't understand this," Calazar said as he stared out from one of the Thurien vessels floating near Uttan. "Those are full-scale quadriflexors, exactly as we designed them. The Jevlenese have been building hundreds of them."

"I don't know," Showm replied, shaking her head beside him. "It makes no sense."

Heller, Caldwell, and Danchekker looked at each other. "What's a quadriflexor?" Caldwell asked.

Calazar sighed. There was no point in being evasive. "They are the devices with which we were going to enclose the Solar System," he said. "They were to be positioned at a considerable distance outside Pluto at points defining a quasispherical surface around the system. Every quadriflexor would couple through h-fields to the four adjacent to it in the grid, and collectively they would create a cumulative deformation of space-time at that boundary which would equate to an escape-proof gravitic gradient.

"We performed preproduction testing on some scaled-down prototypes, and we did in fact begin building some of the full-size versions, but we are still a long way from being in a position to implement the final plan." Calazar waved at the view outside the ship. "But the Jevlenese have obviously been copying our designs in secret, and their program was far more advanced. I can't understand why."

Danchekker was blinking behind his spectacles and frowning to himself while he wrestled with the riddle. Somehow he had the feeling that the last layer of the enigmatic onion that seemed to surround everything connected with the Jevlenese was about to be peeled away. By at first exaggerating Earth's aggressiveness and later manufacturing false evidence, the Jevlenese had persuaded the Thuriens that Terran expansion had to be checked, and nothing short of physical containment would check it. The Thuriens had, until very recently, been convinced, and had set the necessary preparations in motion accordingly. But the Jevlenese had embarked on an identical venture and concealed the fact from the Thuriens. Why? What did it mean?

Danchekker looked over at the images that VISAR was presenting of the Command Deck of the *Shapieron* and Sverenssen's office in Connecticut, but there were no suggestions forthcoming from those directions. The Ganymeans in the *Shapieron* were preoccupied with something that was happening on the main screen inside the ship, while in the other view he could see only the backs of Hunt and the others as they crowded around the terminal on the other side of the room, which connected them to the *Shapieron*. A lot of excited talking was going on in both places, but what it was about was obscure.

"Could they have been planning to do the same thing themselves?" Karen Heller said at last.

"For what reason?" Calazar asked. "We were already working on it. What could they have stood to gain?"

"Time?" Caldwell offered.

Calazar shook his head. "If time was so critical to them, they could have persuaded us to accelerate our own program with a fraction of the effort that they must have put into this. Certainly we have the resources to have been able to beat any schedule they could have been aiming at."

Frenua Showm was looking thoughtful. "And yet it's

strange," she mused. "On several occasions when we wanted to speed up our program, the Jevlenese actually seemed to play down the risks of Terran expansion. It was if they were trying to keep our research moving, but weren't in a hurry to see us move into production."

"They were milking off the know-how," Caldwell grunted. "Making sure that their program stayed well ahead of yours." He paused for a few seconds, then asked, "Could those things be used for shutting in anything else apart from a star system?"

"Hardly," Calazar replied, then added, "Well, I suppose they could be used to close in anything of comparable size . . . or something smaller, come to that."

"Mmm . . ." Caldwell lapsed back into thought.

Heller shrugged and turned up her hands. "If they weren't going to enclose the solar system, they must have been planning to enclose some other . . ." Her voice trailed away as the answer suddenly became plain, to her and to everybody else at the same time.

Calazar and Showm stared speechlessly at each other for a few seconds. "*Us?*" Calazar managed at last in a strained voice. "*The Thuriens? They were going to shut in Gistar?*" Showm brought her hand up to her brow and shook her head as she struggled to take in the implication of it. Caldwell and Heller were standing dumbstruck.

The whole thing slowly became clear in Danchekker's mind. "*Yes!*" he exclaimed. He moved forward to the center of the group and stood for a moment checking his thoughts, then began nodding his head vigorously. "Yes!" he said again. "Surely it's the only acceptable explanation." He looked excitedly from one to another of the others as if he expected them to agree with something there and then. They stared back at him blankly. Nobody knew what he was talking about. He waited for a moment and then elaborated. "I have never been able to accept fully that the obsessive Lambian-Cerian rivalry could have persisted in the minds of the Jevlenese for all that time, especially with their exposure to Ganymean influence. Did it never strike you as strange? Didn't any of you ever feel that there had to be something more behind it than just that?" He looked at the others questioningly again.

After a few seconds Caldwell said, "I guess not, Chris. Why? What are you getting at?"

Danchekker moistened his lips. "It's an interesting thought, wouldn't you agree, that there was one entity that was always there at the back of things, permanent and unchanging while generations of Jevlenese came and went."

There was a moment of silence. Then Heller stared at him and gasped. "JEVEX? Are you saying the computer was behind the whole thing?"

Danchekker nodded rapidly. "JEVEX was established a long time ago. Is it completely inconceivable that its basic design and programming couldn't somehow have embodied as some kind of innate driving instinct the ruthlessness and ambitions of its creators—the descendants of the original Lambians? And to realize those ambitions, could it not have harnessed the Jevlenese elite as its instruments? But if that were so, it would have found itself confronted by a serious obstacle in the form of the restraints imposed on it by the Thuriens."

Caldwell was beginning to nod. "It would have had to get the Thuriens out of the way somehow," he agreed.

"Precisely," Danchekker said. "But not too quickly. There was a lot that it wanted to learn from them first. And the really cunning part was that at the end of it all, the Thuriens' own ingenuity and technology would provide the means whereby the Jevlenese would get rid of them. Then, armed with stolen Ganymean science and with JEVEX as their leader, the Jevlenese would have had the Galaxy at their mercy. Think of all those developing worlds . . . and a technology that could cross light-years in moments: They would become the masters of every part of explored space, poised to expand their empire without limit, and the only potential opposition would be safely locked up inside a gravitic shell that nothing could get out of." Danchekker gripped his lapels and turned from side to side to take in the astounded expressions around him. "So now at last we see what was behind it all—the ultimate design that they had been working on, probably ever since Minerva. And how near they came to succeeding!"

"So the weapons at Uttan . . ." Calazar said falteringly, still struggling to grasp the enormity of it all. "They were never intended to be used against Thurien at all?"

"I doubt it," Danchekker said. "I suspect that they were for afterward, to add teeth to their expansion when the time came."

"Yes, and guess who'd have been first on the list," Heller said. "They were Lambians, and we were Cerians."

"Of course!" Showm whispered. "Earth would have been defenseless. *That* was why they concealed your demilitarization from us." She nodded slowly in grudging admiration. "It was neatly worked out. First they work to retard Earth's advancement while they grow strong and learn. Then they accelerate Earth's rate of discovery suddenly, engineer the results into a threat which they enlist Thuriens aid to eliminate. And finally they remove the threat to themselves but conceal the fact from the Thuriens, and use the very technique that they have induced the Thuriens to develop as the means of eliminating the Thuriens instead. That would have left them in a position to settle the old score with the Cerians without interference, and with the odds overwhelmingly in their favor."

"We wouldn't have stood a chance," Caldwell breathed, for once genuinely staggered.

"And the Jevlenese would have repossessed the solar system, which I suspect has always been their first goal," Danchekker said. "I would imagine they have always considered it rightly theirs. And they would no longer have had to play second fiddle to the Thuriens, a position they clearly have never been able to come to terms with gracefully."

"It all makes sense," Calazar said in a resigned voice. "Why they were so insistent about administering their own, autonomous group of worlds . . . why they needed a system independent of VISAR, controlling its own volume of space." He looked at Showm and nodded. "A lot of things are beginning to make sense now."

He fell silent for a few seconds. When he spoke again his voice was lighter. "If all this is true, then our problem of what to do next could be eased considerably. If the roots of it all lay not so much in the Jevlenese people but in JEVEX, then maybe there is hope for them after all. Distasteful punitive measures may not be necessary."

A distant look came into Showm's eyes. "Ye-es," she said slowly, and began nodding. "Perhaps, given the right help, they might rebuild their civilization upon a new model and emerge from it all as a mature and benign race. All may not be lost yet."

"It does give us a positive goal to aim at and a task to accomplish," Calazar said, sounding more enthusiastic. "Despite all the setbacks, things might work out to a successful conclusion. As you say, all is not lost."

"Er, at present this is merely a hypothesis, you understand," Danchekker said hastily. "But there might be a way to test it. If the whole thing did in fact begin with JEVEX, it might be possible to trace the origins of some of the things we've been talking about back to conceptual subnets of some form buried in JEVEX's older archives." He looked at Calazar. "I assume that once your people are fully in control of Jevlen, it would be possible to reactivate parts of JEVEX in a controlled fashion and allow VISAR to examine its records thoroughly."

Calazar was already nodding. "I would have thought so. Eesyan is really the person we should talk to about that." He looked across at the view coming from the Command Deck of the *Shapieron*. "Isn't he free yet? What's happening there?"

Consternation was breaking out among the Ganymeans crowded below the main screen in the image. At the same time a chorus of shouts erupted from the other image, showing the view from Earth, in which Hunt and the others were bumping into each other in their haste to get back across the room to the terminal that connected them to the Thurien ship at Uttan. Danchekker, Calazar, and the others with them forgot their conversation of a few moments earlier and stared in astonishment. Hunt was almost incoherent with excitement as he got to the screen. "We've found them! ZORAC reprocessed the planet. We know where they went. It's impossible!"

Danchekker blinked at him. "Vic, what are you babbling about? Kindly calm down, and simply say whatever it is that you're trying to say."

Hunt recomposed himself with some effort. "The five Jevlenese ships. We know what happened to them." He paused for a second to get his breath back, then turned his head away to call over the people behind him to the terminal connecting them to the *Shapieron*. "ZORAC, pass that shot over to VISAR, would you. Tell VISAR to display it at Uttan." In the ship where Danchekker was, an image appeared of the final shot of the Jevlenese vessels sent back by the *Shapieron's* probe just before the tunnel caved in. "Have you got it?" Hunt asked.

Danchekker nodded. "Yes. What about it?"

"The spot in the upper right-hand corner is a planet," Hunt said. "We asked ZORAC if there was any way it could reprocess that part of the image and enhance it to give us a better look at it. It did. We know what planet it is."

"Well?" Danchekker asked, puzzled, after a second or two. "Where is it?"

"A better question would be *when*?" Hunt told him.

Danchekker frowned and looked around him only to be met by expressions as confused as his own. "Vic, what are you talking about?" he asked.

"VISAR, show them," Hunt said in reply.

The speck enlarged in an instant to become a full disk occupying the whole frame. It was a world shining brightly against the stars with cloud formations and oceans. The resolution was not good, but there were continental outlines discernible on its surface. Calazar and Showm froze. A split second later, Danchekker realized why.

What he was looking at was not unfamiliar. Like Hunt, he had studied every island, isthmus, estuary, and coastline sandwiched between the two enormous ice caps of that planet many times—at Houston, in the course of the Lunarian investigations over two years earlier. He looked away. Calazar and Showm were still staring in silent awe, and now Caldwell too was wide-eyed with disbelief. Danchekker slowly turned his head to follow their gaze once again. It was still there. He hadn't imagined it.

The planet was Minerva.

Chapter Forty

Nobody could say for certain exactly how it had come about in those final few seconds as VISAR and the projector at Uttan fought for control of the same speck of space-time light-years away, and many believed that nobody ever would. But Hunt was forced at last to accept the truth of the claim that Paul Shelling had made at Houston on the day that Karen Heller and Norman Pacey had come to talk to Caldwell: the Ganymean physical equations that described the possibility of point-to-point transfers through space had solutions that admitted transfers through time too. Or both. For somehow the five Jevlenese ships had been hurled across light-years of space and backward through tens of thousands of years of time to emerge in the solar system when Minerva was still in existence. In fact, by careful measurement of the positions of background stars, the Ganymean scientists determined to a high degree of accuracy when; it came out to be about two hundred years before the final Lunarian war.

And that, of course, explained where the superbreed of Lambians, who had emerged seemingly overnight with a technology far in advance of anything else anywhere on the planet, had come from. And it explained why a planet that had, by and large, mended its warlike ways and commenced working constructively and cooperatively toward an eventual migration to Earth became divided into the two rival factions that in the end had destroyed each other. The Cerians were native, having evolved from the terrestrial primates transported to Minerva twenty-five million years earlier by the Ganymeans, while the Lambians were from Jevlen and fifty thousand years in the future. The Lambians never emerged at all; they *arrived*.

There were more than enough riddles in this for the scientists to argue over for many years to come. How, for example, could the Lambians have been the descendants of their own descendants? Their greed and power lust were seen at last as characteristic of them as a group rather than of the human race as a whole, but that being so, where had those characteristics originated? The Jevlenese had inherited them from the Lambians, who had inherited them from the Jevlenese that had landed on Minerva. So where and when had it started? Danchekker speculated that their passage through the zone of dislocated space-time might have induced some form of psychological aberration that had started the whole thing off, but the suggestion was not very satisfying since the meaning of the word "started" in this context was obscure to say the least.

Another enigma arose from the knowledge of subsequent events that the Jevlenese would presumably have taken back to Minerva with them. If they knew about the next two hundred years, the war, the millennia after that with the Thuriens, and their own eventual defeat at the hands of VISAR, why would they have allowed those very things to happen? Had they been powerless to change the sequence? Surely not. Had a whole new history somehow been written into the timeloop to erase and replace something else that had existed there "before," whatever that meant? Or had they perhaps taken few hard records with them in their haste and suffered some kind of stress-induced amnesia such that they arrived not knowing who they were or where they had come from, thus dooming themselves to launch again into an endless, unaltering cycle?

The Thuriens didn't know the answers to these questions either, which raised issues that were on the fringes of their own theoretical researches. Possibly, one day, future generations of Ganymean and Terran mathematicians and physicists would deduce the strange logic within which such things could happen. Then again, possibly no one would ever know.

But one mystery was solved that had been perplexing the Terrans, the Ganymeans, and the Jevlenese alike—the mystery of the device out beyond Pluto that had responded to that first message beamed from Farside in ancient Ganymean code, and relayed it directly to VISAR. The Thuriens had assumed it was something that the Jevlenese had positioned, the Jevlenese had assumed it was something that the Thuriens had emplaced, and because of the circumstances neither side had ever been able to challenge the other. And now that it had been destroyed, there was no way of investigating it. So what had it been, and how had it gotten there?

The answer could only be the probe that had gone through the tunnel on the heels of the Jevlenese ships. Naturally it had been programmed to respond to the communications protocols used by its own mother ship, and it had been fitted with an h-link to Thurien. By analyzing the log of messages exchanged during those last few seconds, Shilohin's scientists established that, just before the tunnel closed behind it, the probe had been in a passive mode awaiting its next command from the *Shapieron*. Apparently it had waited for a long time. After exiting near Minerva under the impetus that VISAR had imparted in accelerating it in pursuit of the Jevlenese ships, it climbed away from the Sun and eventually stabilized in a distant orbit out beyond Pluto. And it waited. And eventually it heard a command that it understood, and relayed it to VISAR because that was what its instructions told it to do. It didn't know that fifty thousand years had gone by in the meantime.

And so the full circle that linked Minerva and the early Ganymeans, the Lunarians both Lambian and Cerian, Charlie and Koriel, Earth and *Homo sapiens*, and the Giants' Star, was complete. It had begun with its own ending, and in the process JEVEX, Broghuilio, and the Lambians had become locked in an unbreakable loop that was firmly and permanently embedded in the past. Ironically their prison was even more escape-proof than the one that they themselves had devised.

Deprived of their corrupt element, the people of Jevlen turned out to be not so unlike human beings anywhere else after all, and set themselves to the task of rebuilding their society with a new mood of cooperation and optimism. This would require a great deal of physical hard work as well as social and political reforms because of the widespread damage, mainly from flooding, that had been caused by the gravitational upheaval of Broghuilio's spectacular departure, so Calazar installed Garuth as temporary planetary governor to supervise and coordinate the operation. Jevlen would be on probation for a while to come, and for some time there would be no planet-wide system after the pattern of JEVEX; planning and other functions would require extensive information-processing capacity nevertheless, and fortunately a machine of just the right size presented itself in the form of ZORAC. The *Shapieron* was permanently based at Jevlen, and ZORAC became the nucleus of a new pilot network that one day would assume interplanetary dimensions and be merged into VISAR.

Furthermore the temporarily decomputerized world of Jevlen would provide an ideal environment for Garuth's people from the *Shapieron*, displaced twenty-five million years from their own civilization, to recuperate and readjust to the ways of the Thuriens. At the same time they would be able to play a key role in helping Garuth rebuild the planet and inaugurate a new system of Jevlenese government. So Garuth, his people, and ZORAC had a worthwhile job to do, a challenging future ahead, and a home of their own once again.

On Earth, Mikolai Sobroskin became the Soviet Foreign Minister under the new order that emerged from the wreckage of the previous regime. Through some machinations inside the Kremlin that would never be fully disclosed, Verikoff ended up as an advisor on extraterrestrial sciences, having made history as the first alien ever to apply for and be granted Terran citizenship.

In the U.S. State Department, Karen Heller and Norman

Pacey headed a team assigned by Packard to draft a policy aimed at breaking down the barriers of East-West suspicions that had festered for over a century, and forging an era of universal prosperity from the combined economic and industrial might of the U.S. and Soviet giants, and the material and human resources of the emerging Third World. Already the international web that had precipitated World War I, financed both the Bolshevik Revolution and the rise of Hitler, manufactured the Middle East and Southeast Asian crises of later years, contrived for a whole world to fund its own blackmail through the nuclear arms race, and been behind a long list of other interesting things found recorded in great detail inside JEVEX, was well on its way to being broken up for good.

The UN, purged of the influences that would have manipulated it into a focal point of global power to be delivered wholesale into the hands of the Jevlenese, would be remolded into the instrument through which Earth would take its place in the interstellar community. And it would have an important role to play in that community—a role in which people like Clifford Benson, Colonel Shearer, and Sobroskin's generals would still have a place. For despite their sciences and their technology, the Ganymeans had learned the wisdom of preserving a strong right arm; there was no telling how many more Broghuilios might be waiting in the unexplored reaches of the Galaxy.

Such days would come, but they were still far in the future. In the meantime there were preparations to be made—a whole planet to reeducate, and a whole system of natural sciences to be revised and brought up to date. UNSA drew up tentative plans for merging Navcomms into a new superdivision under Caldwell, who would move to Washington to begin the mammoth task of rewriting the long-range plans for the space program in the light of Ganymean technology and initiate studies for integrating selected parts of Earth's communications net into VISAR. Hunt would become Deputy Director of the new organization, and Danchekker, fired by the vision of unlimited access to scores of alien worlds each with its own alien biology and alien evolution, accepted an offer to go too as Director of Alien Life Sciences. At least, that was why Danchekker said he wanted to move to Washington. Caldwell reserved a box in the organization chart for Lyn too, of course.

But the real hero of the war, for which neither anybody nor anything else in existence anywhere could conceivably have substituted, was VISAR. Calazar agreed that VISAR would take over Uttan and run the planet exclusively, to enjoy its own measure of independence, and in the process be free to evolve further its own brand of intelligence in its own way and to its own design. But VISAR's ties to its creators would not be broken, and in the years and centuries ahead, the expansion into the Galaxy would manifest the same alliance of human and Ganymean, organic and inorganic instincts and abilities that had already proved to be a formidable combination.

Epilogue

The procession of black limousines drew slowly to a halt before the military guard of honor and lines of foreign ambassadors standing by the side of the field of Andrews Air Force Base, Maryland, a few miles from Washington, D.C. The day was sunny and clear, and the thousands filling the area outside the boundary fence all around were strangely quiet.

Feeling somewhat odd and formal in his black pinstripe three-piece suit, stiffened cuffs and collar, and tightly knotted necktie, Hunt stepped out of the second car back from the one flying the presidential pennant on its hood, and helped Lyn out after him while the chauffeur held the door. Danchekker, similarly attired though nothing seemed to fit exactly as it was supposed to, came next, followed by Caldwell and a group of senior UNSA executives.

Hunt looked around and picked out the perceptron among a line of aircraft parked some distance away in the background. "It's not really like home, is it," he commented. "There aren't any windows boarded up, and it needs some snow and a few mountains around."

"I never thought you were sentimental," Lyn said. She looked up. "Blue sky, and lots of green. I'll stick with this."

"Not a romantic who hankers for old times, I perceive," Danchekker said.

Lyn shook her head. "After the amount of flying that I did back and forth to that place, I don't care if I never see McClusky again."

"We might be sending you a lot farther than that before very much longer," Caldwell grunted.

The Soviet Premier and his delegation had not yet emerged from the car immediately in front of them, but ahead of that the U.S. President and his entourage were assembling. Karen Heller and Norman Pacey detached themselves from the group and walked back. "Well, get used to it," Pacey said, making a sweeping gesture with his arm. "It's going to be your new home for a while. I've got a feeling this place will get to feel like your own private airport. You people are going to be pretty busy."

"We were just talking about it," Lyn said. "Vic seems to prefer McClusky."

"When will you be moving up to D.C.?" Heller inquired.

"It'll be a few months yet at least," Caldwell said.

She looked at Danchekker. "The first thing we'll have to do is have dinner somewhere, Chris. It'll make up for all those canteen meals in Alaska."

"An admirable suggestion," Danchekker replied. "And one with which I concur fully." Lyn nudged Hunt in the ribs. Hunt looked away and grinned.

Pacey glanced at his watch and looked over his shoulder. Sobroskin was leading the Soviet party from the car ahead. "It's almost time," he said. "We'd better move on up." They walked forward to join the Soviet contingent, all of whom they had already met individually in the Executive Lounge earlier, and the whole group moved on to join the President and his party at the front of the cavalcade of limousines. Sobroskin moved closer to Pacey as they came to a halt. "The day has arrived, my friend," he said. "The children will see other worlds under other stars."

"And I told you you'd see it happen," Pacey said.

Packard was looking at Pacey curiously. "What did that mean?" he asked.

Pacey smiled. "It's a long story. I'll have to tell you about it sometime."

Packard turned his head toward Caldwell. "Well, at least I know what to expect this time, Gregg. You know, I don't think I'll ever live that down."

"Don't worry about it," Caldwell told him. "The rest of us were only a few seconds behind you."

They moved toward the open area of the base and came to a halt again, arranged in orderly rectangular groups with the McClusky team, including Jerol Packard, at the front, the U.S. and Soviet leaders alongside each other behind them with Pacey and Sobroskin standing ahead of their respective national delegations, and the UNSA and other groups from the remaining cars arrayed at the back. Every head was turned upward, waiting. And suddenly, sensed rather than heard, a wave of excitement rippled across the entire base and through the crowds packed outside.

The ship was already visible as a faint dot enlarging in the flawless blue above. As it grew larger, it took on a brilliant silvery sheen that glinted with reflected highlights in the sun, and resolved into a slender wedge with gracefully curved leading edges flaring to merge into two needle-pointed nacelles at the tips. And still it was getting larger.

Hunt's mouth dropped open as the raised bulges along its hull, ancillary housings swelling from its underside, fairings, pods, blisterdomes, and turrets gradually revealed themselves in a steadily unfolding hierarchy of detail to give the first real hint of the craft's awesome size. Gasps of wonder were coming from either side of him and behind, and the crowd outside seemed paralyzed. It must have been miles in length . . . tens of miles; there was no way of telling. It expanded above their heads to fill half the sky like some huge, mythical bird that seemed to be hanging over the entire state of Maryland. And still it might have been in the stratosphere, or even beyond that.

He had seen the Thurien power generators and been told

they were thousands of miles across, but that had been out in empty space where there were no references. His senses had been spared the impact of direct confrontation, leaving only his imagination to grapple with what the numbers had meant. This was different. He was standing on Earth, surrounded by trees, buildings, and everything else that made up the world of the familiar and the .unquestioned, in which intrusions like this were forbidden. Even the distance from one horizon to another, which he sensed unconsciously although it was not visible directly, set a perspective that defined the permissible, imposed rules, and forced limits. The Thurien spaceship had no place in that scheme. It belonged to a different order of magnitude, breaking every known rule and making nonsense of the usual limits. He felt like an insect that had just grasped the meaning of the toe-nail in front of it, or a microbe that had glimpsed an ocean. His mind had no model to accommodate it. His senses rebelled from taking in the totality of what he was seeing. His brain fought to reconcile it with something that was manageable within a lifetime's stored experiences, couldn't, and gave up.

At last a light moving across his field of view against the underside of the ship broke the hypnotic trance that had taken hold of him. The figures that had been frozen into immobility around him began stirring as they saw it too. Something was coming down, and was already much nearer than the ship; it had to have been descending for some time, and had only just become visible. It moved swiftly and silently on a direct line toward the center of the base and turned into a flattened, highly elongated ellipsoid of pure gold, completely smooth except for two low, sharply swept fins projecting from its upper surface. It landed without a sound a short distance away, its nose pointing to where Hunt and the others were standing. For perhaps ten seconds not a sound or a movement disturbed the total stillness that had enveloped the base.

And then the forward section of the underside hinged slowly downward to form a broad, shallow ramp leading down to the ground. The point where the ramp entered the body was lost in a glow of brilliant yellow light. Lyn's fingers found Hunt's

and squeezed as the first eight-foot-tall shapes appeared a
dozen or so abreast out of the light and began moving down
the ramp. At the bottom of the ramp, they halted to survey the
waiting lines of Terrans.

In the center was Calazar, easily recognizable even without
his familiar short silver cape and green tunic, and on one side
of him were Frenua Showm, Porthik Eesyan, and Eesyan's
deputy, Morizal. Garuth was at Calazar's other side, with
Shilohin, Monchar, and other Ganymeans from the *Shapieron*
whose light gray skins set them apart as a group from the darker,
less heavily built Thuriens. The team that had gone to
McClusky had been waiting a long time for this moment. For
the first time since the perceptron's landing and their first hesi-
tant entry into it, they were not seeing the Thuriens via neural
stimulations transmitted from light-years away. This time the
Thuriens were real.

Massed bands had begun playing in the background. The
crowd, still overwhelmed by the spectacle filling the sky above
their heads, was quiet. Then with orderly, unhurried dignity
the Ganymeans started moving again, and Caldwell stepped
forward to lead the McClusky team to meet them at the halfway point.

"It was a bit scary at times, but I think Earth has made it,"
Lyn whispered as they began moving.

"You're making it sound as if it's all over," Hunt murmured
beside her. "This is just the start of it."

And it was. For the Ganymeans, it was the end of a task
they had been working on for millennia; for the inhabitants of
Jevlen, it was a change of heart and direction; and for VISAR, it
was a new phase of existence.

But for *Homo sapiens*, it was a whole new beginning.

The heirs to the stars were about to claim their inheritance.

Appendix

ANSWERS TO CROSSWORD

ACROSS

1 SHANNON—Irish river, (flow-er, not flower).

5 DECODE—find the meaning of. "Ode" (poem) added to "DEC."

9 INNOCENT—opposite of "guilty." "0" (zero) "cent" (money) *after* "inn" (pub).

10 BEACON—guiding light. Literally *in* "could *(be a con)*-fused."

12 DEEP END—profound conclusion. "Pen" (writer) jumping into (hint) "deed" (action).

13 EXTREME—ultimate. Literally *in* "*t*" *(ext reme)* dies.

14 EULER—Swiss mathematician. "E" (east, i.e., oriental) plus *changed* (anagram of) "rule."

16 INTRO—colloquial *short* form of "introduction," i.e., preamble. *Wild* (anagram of) "riot" *about* (around) "N" (compass point):

17 EXTRA—something more. "Ex" ("expert" less four letters of six) plus "tra," i.e., "art" *back*(ward).

18 APART—separated. A-part (piece).

354

20 AFRICAN—continental. *Maybe* (anagram of) "i" (one) "fan car."

21 ANNULAR—ring-shaped, around. Annul (abolish) a "r" (right).

23 RETAIN—keep. "E" and "T" (head and tail of "elephant") *in*(side) "rain."

24 DISTRESS—heartache. Di's (Dianna's) tress (lock of hair).

25 YEMENI—type of Arab. "Men" and "I" *after* "ye" (half of "year," i.e., six months).

26 ENCASES—surrounds. "Ease" *surrounding* (double use) "NC" added *to* "S" (compass point).

DOWN

1 SWINDLE—something not fair. "Win" *in*(side) *perhaps* (anagram of) "sled."

2 ANNIE—noted (musical) lady. Advised to get a gun (arms).

3 NUCLEAR REACTION—powerful reaction (response) from nucleus (heart). Extra hint: "r" (right) taken *from* "heart" gives "heat."

4 NON-ADDICTING—not habit-forming. *Possibly* (anagram of) "did on gin can't."

6 ELECTROMAGNETIC—a (kind of) wave. Generated *from* charges of the kind (brigade) that produce light (i.e., accelerating electric ones).

7 ORCHESTRA—something that makes harmony. "H" (chemical symbol for hydrogen) in(side) *turbulent* (anagram of) "star core."

8 ERNIE—man's name. "N" (head of "Norman") *in*(side) "Erie" (lake).

11 TEST DATA FILE—experimental results. *Reorganized* (anagram of) "let's fit a date."

15 LOGARITHM—type of number. Phonetically similar to "logger" (lumberjack) "rhythm" (music).

19 THRUSTS—urges progress (mechanically, not politically). "H" (*initial* or "Hoover") *in*(side) "trust," *over* (literally) "S" (South).

20 ARRAY—matrix. "Ar" (chemical symbol for argon) plus "ray" (beam).

22 LOESS—geological deposit. "0" (nothing) *in*(side) "less" (smaller amount).

Entoverse

**TO
ELEANOR WOOD,
WHOSE IDEA IT WAS**

—and because a good agent deserves
to be mentioned in the final
product.

Prologue

It had taken until the fourth decade of the twenty-first century for humanity to get its act together and learn to resolve or live with its differences, and begin the migration outward as one species toward the stars. In the process, many of the prejudices and irrationalities that had underlain the strife of ages at last withered or were swept away. The core of beliefs that survived would form a solid foundation for the continuing expansion of human knowledge—for surely with the wealth of modern observational data and the sophistication of experimental method, the universe had little left to offer in the way of further reserves of facts to seriously challenge them.

Or so, for a short, comforting while, it seemed.

And then a series of unforeseen and utterly unprecedented events not only added a new dimension to the history of the solar system, but forced a complete rewriting of the origins of humankind itself.

When Man, under the thrust of the revitalized, international space program that arose from redirection of defense industries, finally reached the regions of the outer planets, he discovered that others had been there before him and had surpassed all that he had achieved. Twenty-five million years in the past, a civilization of eight-foot-tall, benevolently disposed giants—called the Ganymeans, after the first traces of them came to light on Ganymede, largest of the Jovian moons—had flourished on a planet Minerva, occupying the position between Mars and Jupiter.

And more astonishing still, while generations of work by anthropologists, geneticists, comparative anatomists, and others had correctly reconstructed the abrupt transformation responsible for the emergence of Homo sapiens from an arena of early-hominid contenders, it turned out that—understandably, in the circumstances—they had assigned the event to the wrong place. Modern Man hadn't evolved on Earth at all!

Despite Minerva's greater distance from the Sun, an effective natural greenhouse mechanism had maintained generally cool but Earthlike conditions there. But by the time the Ganymean civilization reached its advanced stage, the climate was altering in a direction that their constitution would have been unable to tolerate. As was to be expected, their own voyages of discovery across the early solar system brought them to Earth, and from there they transported back to Minerva numerous plant and animal forms representative of life on late-Oligocene, early-Miocene Earth in connection with large-scale bioengineering researches aimed at combating the problem. These efforts were in vain, however, and the Ganymeans migrated to what later came to be called the Giants' Star, some twenty light-years from Earth in the direction of the constellation of Taurus.

In the millions of years that followed, the imported terrestrial animals eclipsed and replaced the native Minervan forms, which, owing to a peculiarity of early Minervan biology that had precluded the emergence of land-dwelling carnivores, had evolved no prey-predator adaptations and were unable to compete. These terrestrial types included a population of genetically modified primates as advanced as anything that existed on Earth at the time. Almost twenty-five million years later, fifty thousand years before the present, while the various hominid lines that had been developing on Earth were just yielding the first crude beginnings of stone-using cultures, a second advanced, spacegoing race had already developed on Minerva: the first version of modern Man, subsequently given the name Lunarians when the first evidence of their existence was found in the course of early twenty-first-century exploration of Earth's moon.

At the time of the Lunarians' emergence, the solar system was entering the most recent ice age. Conditions on Minerva were deteriorating, and the Lunarian sciences and industrial technologies developed rapidly as part of a long-term stratagem to move their civilization to the warmer and more hospitable world of Earth.

But such was not to be.

When the Lunarians were practically within reach of the goal toward which they had been working constructively for generations, they embarked on a course of ruinous military rivalries that culminated in a cataclysmic war between two superpowers, Cerios and Lambia, in the course of which the planet Minerva was destroyed.

The Ganymeans by that time had established a thriving interstellar civilisation centered on the planet Thurien of the Giants' Star system. They had never felt comfortable with what they regarded as their abandonment of a genetic mutant that they expected would have no chance of survival, and they had followed the progress of the Lunarians with a mixture of increasing guilt and awe. But when they saw it all end in catastrophe, the Ganymeans forgot their previous policy of nonintervention and appeared in time to save the last few survivors from the war. Gravitational upheavals caused by the emergency methods used to transport the Ganymean rescue mission threw what remained of Minerva into an eccentric outer orbit to become Pluto, while the smaller debris dispersed under Jupiter's tidal effects as the Asteroids. Minerva's orphaned moon fell inward toward the Sun and was later captured by Earth.

Despite their experience, the surviving Lunarians remained hostile and immiscible. The Lambians went back with the

Ganymeans and were installed on a world called Jevlen, eventually to become a fully integrated, human component of the Thurien civilization. The Cerians were returned, at their own request, to the world of their origins: Earth, where they were almost overwhelmed shortly afterward by climatic and tidal upheavals caused by the arrival of Minerva's moon. For thousands of years they reverted to barbarism, struggling on the edge of extinction, and the knowledge of their origins was lost. Only in modern times, when they at last climbed outward once more toward the stars and found the traces of what had gone before, were they able to piece the story together.

The Jevlenese never ceased regarding the people of Earth as Cerians. As part of a plan for one day settling the score with their ancient rivals, they inaugurated a campaign to retard Earth's progress toward rediscovery of the sciences and advanced civilization, while they themselves absorbed Thurien technology and gained autonomy over their own affairs. From its beginnings, they altered the course of Earth's history by infiltrating agents, fully human in form, to spread beliefs in magic and superstition, and to found irrational mass movements that would keep Earth impotent by diverting its energies away from the path by which real knowledge is acquired.

As the confidence and arrogance of the Jevlenese leaders grew, so did their resentment of the restraint to their ambitions posed by the Ganymeans, whose nonviolent ways merely aroused their contempt. Taking advantage of the innate Ganymean inability to suspect motives, the Jevlenese gained control of the surveillance operation set up to keep a watch over Earth's development; while preserving outward appearances of being model protégés of the Ganymeans, they fed the Ganymeans falsified accounts of a militarized Earth about to burst out from the solar system, and used this as a pretext for inducing the Ganymeans to prepare countermeasures. What the Jevlenese planned to do was seize control of the countermeasures themselves, eliminate their Terran rivals and repossess the solar system, and then sweep outward in a wave of acquisition and conquest across the galaxy, unchecked and unopposed.

But the reappearance of a lost starship from the ancient Ganymean civilization on Minerva changed everything.

The Ganymean scientific mission ship *Shapieron*, returning after a twenty-five-million-year time dilation compounded by a fault in the vessel's space-time-distorting drive method, came back to the solar system to find Minerva gone and a new, terrestrial race spacefaring among the planets. The "Giants" remained on Earth for six months and mingled harmoniously. But the most significant outcome of the pooling of the Terran proclivity for intrigue with alien technical ability was the establishing of the first direct contact between Earth and Thurien, bypassing the Jevlenese and the millennia-old surveillance system. The alliance led to a confrontation in which the deceit and scheming of the Jevlenese was exposed, revealing the network of infiltrators by which they had endeavored to subvert modern-day Earth after the attempts to block its technological advancement failed.

The encounter that followed came to be known as the Pseudowar. In it, the supercomputing entity JEVEX, which managed all of the communications, information handling, and other vital functions of the Jevlenese worlds, was penetrated and defeated by a fictional interstellar attack force consisting entirely of computer-generated imagination. The just-proclaimed "Federation," by which the Jevlenese proposed bringing their plans to fruition, collapsed, JEVEX was shut down, and Jevlen put on a period of probation. The Ganymeans of the *Shapieron*, displaced from their own home and time and needing an interval of respite to adapt to their new circumstances, were installed on Jevlen to take charge of the rehabilitation. Earth, rid of the corrupt element responsible for practically all of the more sordid side of its turbulent history, looked forward to assuming its rightful place in the interstellar community.

So, once again, after a few more old beliefs had been toppled, what remained was surely fact, resting on solid foundations. The future could be faced with assurance.

Nothing more could go wrong, now . . .

Chapter One

N ieru, the god of darkness, was descending in the west after his nightly domination of the sky, his cloak wrapped about him in a glowing purple spiral. Overhead, Cassona, the goddess who created weather, had become the dawn star. The three lesser stars of her daughters, the Cassoneids, which oscillated about her—Peria, Isthucis, and Dometer, the spirits of wind, rain, and cloud—were very close, almost in alignment, which meant that it was early summer. Compared to the splendor that the night sky had once been, the stars were few and feeble.

Cassona had once been capricious and vindictive, liable to cleave mountains with a lightning bolt or send storms to devastate an entire countryside on a whim. Today, however, she was placid. The morning was clear, and the first light revealed that the peaks at the far end of the valley outside Orenash had receded unusually far during the night, with the rooftops within the city walls and the patches of woodland on the slopes beyond noticeably lengthened in proportion. During the night, Gralth, the gods' baker, who kneaded the world as if it were dough, stretched all dimensions in the east-west direction; he would compress them back to their evening minima as the day wore on. But so visible an extension at daybreak presaged an uneventful day ahead.

From an upper window of his uncle's house below the rock upon which stood the temple of Zos, Thrax brooded to himself, confused and afraid with the bemusement of a youth whose world was running down just as he was approaching manhood and thought he had made sense of it.

But these days, everyone was confused and afraid. The old ways were ceasing to work, and the old wisdom had no answers. Priests prayed, seers beseeched, and people redoubled their sacrifices. But the force-currents waned, and life-power ebbed. No signs came; the oracles remained mute. And as the gods died, their stars were going out.

Some thought that a great war had been waged in the sky, that new gods had defeated the old, and different laws were coming into being to rule the world. Mystics spoke of having seen a higher realm that they called Hyperia, beyond the everyday plane of existence, where perpetual serenity reigned and impossible happenings were commonplace.

Perhaps, a few of the more hopeful reasoned, the breaking down of the old laws portended a transition of their world into a phase that would be governed by the new kinds of laws glimpsed in the world beyond. They experimented in unheard-of ways to prepare themselves, striving to grasp strange notions and unfamiliar concepts . . .

"Hold it, Thrax. I think it needs a bit more play here." Thrax's uncle Dalgren poked inside the contraption standing on the stone slab in his basement workshop and adjusted a clamp. "And probably this one opposite, too."

It consisted essentially of two pairs of legs, each pair set one behind the other in an arrangement of vertical slides that allowed either pair to protrude below the other. In addition, whichever pair was raised could move lengthwise along a horizontal guide and descend at varying displacements with respect to the lower. Each leg had a foot in the form of a rocker that was tipped at one end by the metal mobilium, which was "apathetic" to most kinds of rock and slid easily over them, and at the other by frictite crystal, which bound when in contact. It was a fact of nature that all materials possessed an affinity for each other to a greater or lesser degree, determining how strongly they were attracted or repelled; thus, depending on the position of the rocker, the foot would either grip the surface or be repulsed. The whole thing was an attempt at artificially mimicking the sliding-planting-lifting-sliding of the leg movements of an animal, such as a *drodhz.*

Nobody had ever conceived such an idea before—carts and other vehicles had always been hauled along on skids of mobilium or something similar. The mystics who had seen Hyperia told of indescribable, magical devices capable of performing motions of complexities that defied imagination. They even spoke of constructions that spun.

"There. Try it now, Thrax," Dalgren said, stepping back.

Thrax pushed one of the operating rods projecting from the assembly. While one pair of legs remained anchored to the bench, the other lifted, slid forward one half of a leg-pitch, and then descended in a new position. Then the rocker mechanism operated, locking the legs that had advanced, and releasing the pair that had remained stationary. As Thrax pulled the activating rod back again, the rearmost pair of legs moved past the others in turn, and reanchored themselves to complete the cycle.

"Yes, that did the trick!" Dalgren exclaimed. "Keep going!"

Thrax moved the rod slowly back and forth several times, and the contrivance walked its way jerkily across the slab. As it approached the edge, however, its motion became stiffer and slower, and Thrax had to push harder on the rod to keep it moving. "It's starting to jam," he said. "I can feel it."

"Hmm." Dalgren stooped to peer at the horizontal guides. "Ahah, yes, I think I can see why. The main guide is expanding and starting to jam." He sighed and sat down on a stool. "I'm not sure how we get around it. It may need an additional compensating liner."

Every problem solved seemed to introduce a new complication. They had adjusted the device for correct operation early in the morning, but as the world shrank from east to west under Gralth's kneading, the mechanism's dimensions had changed. Automatically, Thrax began mentally composing a prayer to Gralth. Then he checked himself, remembering that those were old methods that had to be set aside firmly if the new ones were ever to be understood. At the same time, he felt an inner twinge of discomfort at such defiance of all his years of conditioning.

As if echoing his doubts, a voice spoke accusingly from the doorway. "Sorcerers! Blasphemy! These things belong to a higher realm. They are not *meant* to be meddled with here in the world of Waroth. That is why the powers are failing. Just as you are abandoning faith, so are the gods abandoning us."

It was Keyalo, a foster son of Dalgren and Thrax's aunt, Yonel. He was a couple of years older than Thrax and had resented Thrax's intrusion into the household ever since Thrax's own family had been lost when Vandros, the underworld god whose blood ran as rivers of light, punished the Dertelians by consuming five villages in a lake of fire.

"No one can be sure of that, Keyalo," Dalgren replied. His voice was curt. Keyalo had never expressed gratitude for being taken in, and there was little liking between the two of them either way. The fact that he had come down to the basement at all indicated that he was out to cause trouble.

"The priests *know*!" Keyalo retorted. "The gods are putting us to a test. And we shall all be judged by the failures of those who deny them, such as *you*."

"Appeasing the gods, angering the gods . . ." Dalgren shook his head. "I'm beginning to suspect that it's all in the mind. The world runs according to its own rules, and what we think they influence is all our imagination. When has anyone ever—"

Without warning, Keyalo stepped forward and shot out an arm in the manner of a Master casting a firebolt, pointing at the mechanism on the slab. The tip of his finger swelled and glowed faintly for an instant—most people could achieve that— and then returned to normal without discharging. Keyalo stared at it in anger and surprised disappointment.

Perhaps he had thought that a concentrated moment of

belief and will would induce a god to favor him.

Keyalo's problem was that he was lazy. He hung around the disciples and the Masters, and sometimes attended the ceremonies, and even a few of the lessons, occasionally; but he could never have mustered the concentration and discipline to enter one of the orders and train into an adept. Probably that was why he was so jealous of Thrax, whom he knew had the potential. But in Keyalo's eyes Thrax not only abused his ability but, what was worse, misdirected it upon heresy.

"We are busy," Dalgren said in a tight voice. "Your words are wasted here, Keyalo. Leave us alone."

"It is those like you who are bringing destruction on all of us," Keyalo hissed. Then, white-faced with rage, he turned and left the room.

Dalgren took the rods and walked the device back across the slab in silence while the mood cleared. "They say there are devices in Hyperia that propel themselves," he murmured absently. "Imagine, Thrax, a chariot without a *drodhz*. What form of propulsion could move it, I wonder?"

"They say there are devices that fly, too," Thrax pointed out, his voice registering the obvious impossibility of such a notion. "The stories become exaggerated with telling and retelling."

Dalgren's expression remained serious. "But why not?" he asked. "It simply involves the same way of looking at things: Instead of jumping to the conclusion that *it can't work because*, try saying, *it could work, if* . . . You've only got to open your eyes to see that the world is filled with animals that propel themselves and creatures that fly. If we can make other objects do whatever they do, then why shouldn't they behave in the same way?"

Thrax nodded, but his expression remained unconvinced. "Maybe I'll believe it when I've seen a *drodhz*less carriage," he said. "You know, Uncle, it wouldn't surprise me if you start talking about spinning objects next."

Dalgren let go the rods and straightened up. "Spinning objects?" he repeated. "Now you are getting fanciful. I couldn't even imagine how to begin."

Thrax stared out at the patch of sky visible through the top of the basement window. "It's the same seers who tell of them," he pointed out.

"Ah yes. But if it's true, it's something that can only exist in Hyperia. Our animals prove that at least the *concepts* of objects propelling themselves and objects flying are possible in Waroth. The precedents exist. But we don't have a precedent for what you're talking about. If it's possible at all, space itself must be different from what we know in this world. And quite beyond my ability to contemplate."

Thrax continued to stare up at the window. "Another universe, beyond our wildest imaginings," he said distantly.

"I think I know how to compensate for the daily contraction, now," Dalgren muttered, returning his attention to the mechanism.

"Where objects spin . . ." Thrax went on dreamily, more to himself.

"Then we'll have to think about getting it to turn corners."

"And inhabited by strange beings."

"We'd need two more slides at the top."

"What kind of beings could they be? . . ."

Chapter Two

D r. Victor Hunt closed the starter circuit, and the turbine hybrid engine of the GM Husky groundmobile standing in the driveway outside the garage kicked into life. As Hunt eased the throttle valve open with a screwdriver, the pitch rose, then settled at a smooth, satisfying whine. He held the position steady and cocked an inquiring eye at his neighbor, Jerry Santello, who was on the far side of the opened hood, tapping at buttons and watching the screen of a portable test unit connected to the vehicle's drive processor.

"It's looking better, Vic. Try it a few revs higher . . . Now gun it a few times . . . Yup, I think we've cracked it."

"How about the burn on idle?" Hunt ran the turbine down to a murmur while Jerry inspected the panel; then Hunt speeded it back up a little and repeated the process several times.

"Good," Jerry pronounced. "I reckon that's it. It had to be the equalizer. Shut it down now, and let's have that beer."

"That sounds like one of the better ideas I've heard today." Hunt turned the valve fully back, operated a cutout, and the engine died.

Jerry unplugged the test lead, which rewound itself into the case. He closed the lid, gathered together the tools they had been using, and returned them to their box. "How is it with you English guys? Is it right, you drink it warm? Am I supposed to put it in the cooker or something?"

"Oh, don't believe everything they tell you, Jerry."

Jerry looked relieved. "So it's okay normal?"

"Sure."

"Hang on there while I get a couple from inside. We can sit out here and take in the sun."

"Even better."

While Jerry's swarthy, mustached form, clad in beach shorts and a navy sweatshirt, flip-flopped its way eupeptically up the shallow, curving steps flanking the rockery by the side of the apartment, Hunt walked around the front of the Husky to toss a few more items into the toolbox. Then he sat down on a grassy hump below the wall separating Jerry's driveway from his own and fished a pack of Winstons from his shirt pocket.

Around him, the other apartment units of Redfern Canyons clustered in comfortable, leafy seclusion on terraced slopes divided by steep ravines climbing from a central valley. The main valley contained a common access road running alongside a creek that widened at intervals into pools fringed by rocky shelves and overhangs. Although the name was more than a little forced in the middle of Maryland less than a dozen miles north of the center of Washington, D.C., and the artificiality of the pseudo-Californian contouring went without saying, on the whole it had all been pleasingly accomplished. The effect worked. After the months that he had spent inside the cramped, miniature metal cities of the UN Space Arm's long-range mission ships and at its bases down on the ice fields beneath the methane haze of Ganymede, Hunt wasn't complaining.

He lit a cigarette and exhaled, smiling faintly to himself as the vista of Redfern Canyons brought to mind the two directors from an Italian urban development corporation who had approached him several days previously. Could the Ganymean "gravitic" technology—which enabled gravitational fields to be generated, manipulated, and switched on and off at will as readily as familiar electrical and magnetic effects—be somehow engineered into a piece of mountainous terrain, they had wanted to know, in such a way as to render it gravitationally flat? The idea was to create high-income habitats, or even entire townships, in places that would offer all the visual aesthetics of the Dolomites, and yet be as easy to walk around as Constitution Gardens. Ingenious, Hunt had conceded.

And typical of human adaptability.

It was hardly a year since mankind had made the first contact with intelligent aliens and brought them back to Earth; and as if that weren't enough, the discovery of an interstellar alien culture, and Earth's opening what promised to become a permanent relationship with it, had followed less than half as long since, with all the promise which that portended of unimaginable gains to human knowledge and the greatest single upheaval ever to occur in the history of the race. The whole edifice of science could crash and have to be rebuilt afresh; every philosophic insight might be demolished to its foundations—but people only became seriously affected when they thought they saw a way of making a buck or two. The human alacrity for getting back to business-as-usual would never cease to amaze him, Hunt thought. Ganymeans had often marveled at the same thing.

Jerry came ambling back down from the house with a six-pack of Coors, a large bag of potato chips, and a tub of onion-flavored dip. He perched himself on one of the rocks lining the foot of the bank that Hunt was sprawled on and passed him a can. "I thought you guys were supposed to drink it warm," he said again.

"English beer is heavier," Hunt said. "If it's too cold you lose the taste. It's better at room temperature, that's all—which in a pub means cellar temperature, usually a bit less than the bar. Nobody actually warms it."

"Oh."

"And the lighter lager stuff, which is closer to yours, they prefer chilled, just like you do. So we're not really so alien, after all."

"That's nice to know, anyhow. We've had enough aliens

showing up around here recently." Jerry flipped open his own can and tilted his head back to take a swig; then he wiped his mustache with the back of a hand. "Hell, what am I telling you for? You must get tired of people asking about them."

"Sometimes, Jerry. It depends on the people."

"There's a couple I know across in Silver Spring—old friends—with this kid who's about five. Last time I was over there, he wanted to know what planet Australians come from."

"What planet?"

Jerry nodded. "Yeah, see: Austr-alians. It was the way he heard it. He figured they had to be from someplace else."

"Oh, I get it." Hunt grinned. "Smart kid."

"I never thought about it that way in over thirty years."

"Kids don't have the ruts yet that adults have carved into their minds. They're born logical. Crooked thinking has to be taught."

"It doesn't work that way in your area, though—science? That right?" Jerry said.

"Oh, don't believe that myth. If anything, it's worse. You always have to wait for a generation of entrenched authority to die off before anything new happens. It's not like revolutions in your business. At least in politics you can get rid of the obstructions yourself and move things along."

"But at least you always know you've got a job," Jerry pointed out.

"There is that side to it, I suppose," Hunt agreed.

Although still officially an employee of the CIA at Langley, Jerry had been on extended leave for three months. With the residual Soviet-Western rivalry transforming into economic competition, and the global development of nuclear technology spelling an end to the dependence of advanced nations on oil-rich, medieval dictator-states and sheikhdoms, the world had been on its way to resolving the twentieth century's legacy of political absurdities even before the first Ganymean contact. That had shaken things up enough, even though it involved only a single shipload of time-stranded aliens. But after the meeting with the Thuriens, immediately following that event, nobody knew what the next ten years would hold in store. Few doubted, however, that there was little in the realm of human affairs that would stand unaffected.

"Although, I don't know . . . with all those new worlds out there, you never know what we might find," Hunt said. "It's your line of business that the Ganymeans can't compete in, not mine. I wouldn't think of turning my badge in just yet if I were you."

Jerry seemed unconvinced as he took another draft, but there was nothing to make an issue over. "Let's hope you're right," he replied. After a pause he went on. "So I guess it's all keeping you pretty busy over at Goddard, eh? I hear you coming and going at all hours of the day and night."

"We're up to our ears there," Hunt agreed. He snorted lightly. "And the funny thing is that at the beginning of the last century it was the scientists who were talking about handing their badges in—half of them, anyway—because they didn't think there was anything worthwhile left to discover. So maybe you can take some heart from that."

"Are you mixed up with that thing that's been in orbit up there for the last couple of weeks?" Jerry asked. "I saw on the news that a bunch of 'em from there were down at Goddard." A gigantic Thurien space vessel, named the *Vishnu* by Terrans, after the Hindu deity that was able to cross the universe in two strides, was currently visiting Earth, having brought delegations to meet with representatives of various nations, institutions, corporations, and other organizations for all manner of purposes as the scope of dealings between the two cultures grew.

"Yes, I talk to some of them," Hunt said, nodding.

"What kind of thing do you do there exactly?" Jerry asked curiously.

Hunt drew on his cigarette and stared out at the central valley between the green, terraced slopes. A glint of metallic bronze appeared briefly as a car rounded a bend a short distance away on the road below. "I used to be with UNSA's Navcomms division down in Houston—that was how I got to go on the Jupiter Five mission. So I was out at Ganymede and mixed up with the Ganymeans right from the start."

"Okay." Jerry nodded.

"Well, now this business with Thurien is all happening, one of the things we need to find out is what sense we can make of their sciences, and how much of our own needs to go in the trash can. UNSA moved me up to Goddard to head up a team that's looking into some parts of that."

"And they do things like travel around between stars and remodel whole planets?" Jerry thought about it for a moment. "That could be pretty hair-raising."

Hunt nodded. "They've got power plants out in space that turn eight lunar masses of material a day into energy and beam it instantly to wherever you need it, light-years away. Sometimes I feel like a scribe from an old monastery would have, trying to unravel what goes on inside IBM."

"Wasn't there a woman who used to visit sometimes, when you first moved here?" Jerry asked. "Kinda red hair, not bad-looking . . ."

Hunt nodded. "That's right. Lyn."

"I talked to her once or twice. Said she'd moved up from Houston, too. So was she with UNSA as well?"

"Right."

"Haven't seen her around lately."

Hunt made a vague gesture with the can he was holding, and stubbed his cigarette in a tin lid that he had found in the toolbox. "An old flame from her college days breezed in out of nowhere, and the next thing I knew it was serious and they got married. They're over in Germany now. She's still with UNSA—coordinating some program with the European side."

"Just like that, eh?"

"Oh, it was just as well, Jerry. She'd been sending domestication signals my way for a while. You know how it is."

"Not really your scene, huh?"

"No . . . Probably a great institution, mind you, Jerry. But I don't think I'm ready for an institution yet."

Jerry seemed more at ease, as if back on ground that he understood. He raised his beer. "I'll drink to that."

"Never tried it?" Hunt asked.

"Once. That was enough."

"Not exactly a happy affair?"

Jerry pulled a face. "Oh, no, there's no such thing as an unhappy marriage. They're all happy—you only have to look at the wedding pictures. It's the living together afterward that does it." He crumpled his empty can and dropped it into the carton, then pulled out another, peeled back the tab, and settled back comfortably until he was half lying against a tree standing behind the rock.

Hunt stretched back on the grassy bank and clasped his hands behind his head. "Anyhow, life's full and exciting right now. I don't need any of that kind of complication. A whole alien civilization. A revolution in science—profound things that need concentration."

"You need all your time," Jerry agreed solemnly. "Can't afford the distraction."

"To tell you the truth, life has never been simpler and more exhilarating."

"A good way for it to be."

Hunt lay back in the sun and closed his eyes. "Oh, you don't have to worry about that. All the complications are three thousand miles away now, in Germany, and that's about where I intend to keep them."

At the sound of a car coming to a halt, he opened his eyes and sat up again. The metallic bronze car that he had glimpsed approaching a minute or two before had come up the access road and was standing outside the gateway where the driveways from the two apartments merged. It was a newish-looking Peugeot import, sleek in line, but with just the right note of restraint in dark brown upholstery and trim to set it apart from pretentiousness.

The same could be said of the woman who was driving it. She was in her early to mid-thirties, with a sweep of raven hair framing an open face with high cheeks, a slightly pouting, well-formed mouth, rounded, tapering chin, and a straight nose, just upturned enough to add a hint of puckishness. She was wearing a neatly cut, sleeveless navy dress with a square white collar, and the tanned arm resting along the sill of the open window bore a light silver bracelet.

"Hi," she said. Her voice was easy and natural. She inclined her head slightly to indicate the still-open hood of Jerry's Husky. "Since you're relaxing, I assume you got it fixed."

Jerry detached himself from the tree and straightened up. "Yes. It's fine now. Er . . . can we help you?"

Her eyes were bright and alive, with a deep, intelligent quality about them that gave the impression of having taken in everything of note in the scene in a brief, first glance. Her gaze flickered over the two men candidly, curiously, but with no attempt at beguiling. Her manner was neither overly assertive nor defensive, intrusive nor apologetic, or calculated to impress. It was just, simply and refreshingly, the way that strangers everywhere ought to be able to be with each other.

"I think I'm in the right place," she said. "The sign at the bottom said there were only these two places up here. I'm looking for a Dr. Hunt."

Chapter Three

The planet Jevlen possessed oceans that were rich in chloride and chlorate salts. Molecules of these found their way high aloft via circulating winds and air currents, where they were readily dissociated by a sun somewhat bluer and hotter than Earth's, and therefore more active in the ultraviolet. This mechanism sustained a population of chlorine atoms in the upper atmosphere, which resulted in a palish chartreuse sky illuminated by a greeny-yellow sun. The atmosphere also had a high neon content, which with its relatively low discharge voltage added an almost continual background of electrical activity that appeared in the form of diffuse, orange-red streaks and streamers.

This was where, fifty thousand years previously, after the destruction of Minerva, the Thurien Ganymeans installed the survivors of the Lambian branch of protohumanity, when the Cerian branch elected to be returned to Earth. Thereafter, the Jevlenese were given all the benefits of Thurien technology and allowed to share the knowledge gained through the Thurien sciences. The Thuriens readily conferred to them full equality of rights and status, and in time Jevlen became the center of a quasi-autonomous system of Jevlenese-controlled worlds.

As the Thuriens saw things, a misguided worldview resulting from the Lunarians' predatorial origins had been the cause of the defects that drove them to the holocaust of Minerva. It wasn't so much that the limited availability of resources caused humans to fight over them, as most Terran conventional wisdom supposed; rather, the instinct to fight over anything led to the conclusion that what was fought over had to be worth it, in other words, of value, and hence in scarce supply.

But once the Lunarians absorbed the Ganymean comprehension that the resources of the universe were infinite in any sense that mattered, all that would be changed. Unrestricted assimilation into the Thurien culture and access to all the bounties that it had to offer would allay aggression, relieve insecurities and fears, curb the urge for domination and conquest, and build in their place a benign, homogeneous society founded on grateful appreciation. Freed, like the Thuriens, from want, doubt, and drudgery, the Jevlenese would unlock the qualities that were dormant inside them like the potential waiting to be expressed in a seed. No longer fettered by time or space, nor constrained to the things that one mere planet had to offer, they would radiate outward in a thousand lifestyles spread across as many worlds to complete the upward struggle that had begun long before in Earth's primeval oceans, and thence become whatever they were capable of.

At least, that was the way the Thuriens had imagined it would be.

But in all those millennia the Thuriens had learned less about human perversity than Garuth, former commander of the Ganymean scientific mission ship *Shapieron*, from ancient Minerva, had in six months on Earth.

For self-esteem could only be earned, not given. Dependence bred feelings of inadequacy and resentment. The results were apathy, envy, surliness, and hate.

The more ambitious minority who gained control of Jevlenese affairs had lied, schemed, and eventually gained control of the surveillance operation set up by the Thuriens for monitoring developments on Earth. They had intervened covertly to keep Earth backward while they built up a secret military capability, and almost succeeded in a plan that would have enabled them to overthrow the Thuriens. Although Thurien technology had been indispensable in thwarting the Jevlenese, what had actually saved the situation had been the Thuriens' decision to open direct contact with the Terrans— when the *Shapieron*'s story from Earth contradicted the Jevlenese version—and thus involve other minds capable of working at comparable depths of deviousness.

But the circumstances of the greater mass of Jevlenese were very different from those of the minority who rose to take charge. For them, the society that grew under the Thurien guidance became a protective incubator cocooning them until the grave. Smothered by largesse to the point where nothing they did or didn't do could make any difference that mattered to their lives, they abandoned control of their affairs to impenetrable layers of nameless administrators and their computers, and either sank into lethargy or escaped, into empty social rituals of acting out roles that no longer signified anything, or into delusion.

Under the collective name JEVEX—the processing and networking totality serving the system of Jevlenese-controlled worlds—the computers ran the factories and farms, mining and processing, manufacturing, distribution, transportation, and communications, along with all the monitoring to keep track of what was going on. JEVEX kept the records, stocked the warehouses, scheduled the repairs; it directed the robots that built the plants, serviced the machines, delivered the groceries, and hauled the trash. And it created the dreams into which the people escaped from a system that didn't require them to be people anymore.

And that, the Thurien and Terran leaders had concluded after the three-day Pseudowar that ended the self-proclaimed Jevlenese Federation, had been the problem. JEVEX had been modeled on the larger and more powerful Thurien complex, VISAR, which, while equipping JEVEX admirably for catering to *Ganymean* temperaments and needs, had done nothing to satisfy the very human compulsions to seek challenge and to compete.

So, the thinking had gone, the key to remedying the situation would be to switch off all but JEVEX's essential services for a time. By compelling the Jevlenese to take charge of their own affairs—and at the same time leaving them less opportunity for making mischief—they would stimulate them into learning to become human again. And the Ganymeans from the *Shapieron* had agreed gamely to oversee and administer the rehabilitation program with its period of probationary decomputerization.

Garuth was only now beginning to realize what they had taken on.

He sat with Shilohin, a female Ganymean who had been the mission's chief scientist, in his office in the Planetary Administration Center on Jevlen, the former headquarters of the local Jevlenese government at a city called Shiban. Before them an image floated, seemingly hanging in midair in the room. It was being transmitted from Barusi, another city situated several thousand miles away on the coast of one of Jevlen's southern continents, with three towers of its central composition rising more than a mile into the pale green sky. But the scene that Garuth and Shilohin were watching was set against a background of drabness, the buildings shabby and most of the machines idle. A lot of the populace had moved into shanty camps thrown up around the city's outskirts, where the simpler routines of living that they had been obliged to revert to were more easily organized—even an act like collecting and preparing food could turn out to be unexpectedly complicated when removed from the context of what had been a totally automatic, self-adapting environment.

The view, taken from the Civic Center housing the Ganymean prefect and his staff responsible for the Barusi district, looked down over the tiered expanse of Sammet Square. A procession of Jevlenese numbering several thousand was spilling in from an avenue leading east out of the city, adding to a comparable number who had been gathering there through the afternoon. Virtually all of them had contrived to be wearing something of purple, and the bands spread at intervals through the parade came to the front as they entered, massing behind banners carrying the device of a purple spiral in a black circle on a red ground.

The focus of all the activity was a figure waiting behind the speaker's rostrum atop the steps facing the square, backed by a huge, hanging sign showing the purple spiral. As soon as the noise of the bands ceased, he launched into his harangue. His name was Ayultha. He wore a dark blue tunic with a purple cloak, and his face had a fierce, intense look, accentuated by heavy, dark brows and a short beard, which he directed this way and that at the crowd with sharp motions of his head as he spoke, punctuating his words with abrupt gestures of appeal and frequent drivings of a fist into the other palm. His amplified voice boomed across the sea of eager faces to sustained outbursts of roared approval.

"Was it not *we* who believed in the Ganymeans? Was it not we who trusted them and came with them across light-years of space, willing to join their culture and learn their ways? It was the *Terrans* who spurned their offer and chose to go their own way." A pause, with appealing looks to left and right, and a dramatic lowering of voice at the crucial point. "Perhaps the Cerians saw more even in those early days than we credited them for." A sudden rise to crescendo. "It was not them who were betrayed!"

Cries of outrage; shakings of fists. The speaker waited, glaring, until the noise abated.

"I say again, *betrayed*! There was an agreement—a solemn covenant honored by us not just through a hundred years, not through centuries, even, but for millennia!" He was referring to the surveillance watch that had been kept over the developing Earth, which the Thuriens had entrusted to the Jevlenese. "*We* performed our duties faithfully. *We* fulfilled our obligation." Another pause. Expectations were almost audible with the buildup of tension. Then, the explosive release: "*The Ganymeans broke that covenant!*"

Thunderous ovation, unfurlings of banners, waves of upthrust hands.

In the foreground to one side of the image, watching from inside the Barusi Civic Center, stood several more Ganymeans:

angular, gray-hued, eight-foot-tall figures, with lengthened, narrowish heads compared to the vaulted human cranium, and protruding lower faces with skulls elongated behind. The nearest, whose name was Monchar, swung around to look out at the two Ganymeans watching from Shiban. Monchar had been second-in-command of the *Shapieron* mission that Garuth had led.

"But he's completely distorting what happened!" Monchar protested. "Yes, in the end the Thuriens opened a dialogue with Earth directly. But that was only after things they knew to be fact contradicted what the Jevlenese were telling them. The Jevlenese had been lying for centuries. They systematically falsified their reporting!"

"The Thuriens were being betrayed long before they thought to question anything," one of the other Ganymeans said.

Monchar motioned with an arm to indicate the crowd outside. "But those people down there *know* all this. They have been acquainted with the facts. How can they react like this to what he's telling them? Don't they possess any critical faculties at all?"

"I think we're still a long way from comprehending the human ability to see and hear what they want to," another Ganymean replied. "Facts don't come into it."

Below, Ayultha was thundering, "But merely keeping bad faith was not enough. They deceived us by intercepting the *Shapieron* and bringing it secretly to Thurien after it left Earth, and then overwhelmed us through trickery."

"But they would have destroyed the *Shapieron*!" Monchar exclaimed, aghast. "If it weren't for the Thuriens, we would all have been killed." He turned back to look at Garuth again. "What are we supposed to do? They change the past to what they think it should have been, and then remember it as having happened. They can't distinguish their myths from reality."

Beside Garuth, Shilohin shook her head. Even a year after meeting them, she was still bewildered by the politics of these strange, pink, brown, yellow, and black, aggressively inclined, alien dwarves. "Yet they're human," she said. "We got to know many humans well while we were on Earth. They can be excitable, I agree, but they're not irrational. We know that."

"They can accept reason or not as it suits them," Monchar said.

In the square, Ayultha shouted, "And now they use the disruption caused by their own trickery as a pretext to impose this alien rule upon us, violating the most fundamental of our rights: the right of any people to determine their own affairs. They try to tell us that we would be unable to function without them. But we functioned well enough before JEVEX was withdrawn. And who withdrew JEVEX? *They* did themselves! So was not this whole situation planned and contrived with the Terrans all along, because *they*—they who break their covenant; they who deceive and betray; they who use trickery to impose themselves—*they* saw the Jevlenese Federation as a threat . . . A threat because of anything we had threatened? No! Because of anything we had done? No! But because we had committed no other crime than to exist!"

At that moment, a group to one side of the crowd suddenly tore off their purple garments, produced green sashes that they had concealed about them, and began waving them as they broke into some kind of chant. Some of the purple-wearers who were nearest began jostling them and grabbing at the sashes. Squads of Barusi police who were lining the square waded in and made for the trouble spot, and a general scuffle broke out.

In Shiban, Garuth stared at the scene in consternation. He had watched scenes like this on old Terran newsfilms during the time the *Shapieron* was on Earth and, more recently, on numerous occasions after taking up his present appointment, in the faint hope of getting some guidance on how to deal with the situations that had been arising on Jevlen. But he was at a loss . . . And trusting to the Jevlenese police and civic authorities to handle it wasn't any answer. Human though they might be, it had already become clear that their loyalty was lukewarm at best; and in any case, initiative wasn't one of their greater strengths.

"There," Monchar pronounced, watching. "Look, it's started. I don't understand it. Can they be so irrational? What good to anybody can come from it?"

As the unrest spread, Garuth watched, then turned to Shilo-hin. "If this kind of thing starts breaking out all over Jevlen, people are going to get hurt," he murmured. "Maybe killed. We couldn't deal with it. It would need a different kind of response."

He meant with force—or the credible threat of being able to resort to force if necessary. That would mean replacing the Ganymeans with a Terran military occupation, since Gany-means were psychologically unsuited to applying that kind of solution. Garuth didn't like it any more than another of his kind would have; but enough history had shown that it was the only way to contain humans once they started running amok.

Shilohin thought silently for a while. "Suppose it isn't just irrationality?" she said at last. "Suppose it's precisely what some-body wants?"

"Who? Surely it couldn't be in the interests of any of the Jevle-nese," Garuth replied.

"I don't think half the Jevlenese are capable of knowing what's in their interests," Shilohin said.

"JPC rejected such a policy when it was proposed," Garuth pointed out.

"And now some of the Terran members are urging them to change their minds."

The Joint Policy Council, consisting of both Thuriens and Terrans, had been established following the Pseudowar and the collapse of the Jevlenese Federation to formulate the program that Garuth was attempting to implement. At that time, some of the Terran representatives, particularly from the West, had predicted problems of the kind that were now appearing and proposed setting up a Terran security force on Jevlen for Garuth to be able to call upon. JPC, however, heady with the euphoria of the moment and swayed by Thurien ideals, had turned the suggestion down. Garuth was beginning to worry that if dem-onstrations of the kind now breaking out were to get sufficiently out of hand, JPC, instead of merely installing an auxiliary force to supplement the Ganymean presence as had first been pro-posed, would order the Ganymeans to be replaced completely.

And if that happened, all their work on trying to understand the Jevlenese problem would probably have been in vain, just when it seemed that they were onto something important. For Garuth was convinced that there was more to account for in the Jevlenese condition than just apathy and reality-withdrawal caused by overdependence on JEVEX. Something more serious was going on, and had been for a long time. Something about JEVEX had been sending the Jevlenese insane.

Garuth slumped back in his chair wearily. "Fortunately, we do have some friends in political circles on Earth," he said. "Perhaps we can find out from them what's happening."

"I'm not so sure it's their political people that we should be going to," Shilohin answered in a distant voice.

"No?"

Shilohin shook her head. "Their affairs are so convoluted that none of us understand them. I was thinking, more, of somebody whom we know we can communicate with and trust—in fact, one of the very first of the Terrans that we met."

Garuth sat back, his face thoughtful and his eyes illuminated suddenly by a questioning light that seemed to ask why the idea had not occurred to him sooner. "You mean direct? We just forget about 'proper channels' and all that official business in between?"

Shilohin shrugged. "Why not? It's what he'd do."

"Hmm . . . And he *does* know them better . . ." Garuth thought about it, then looked at Shilohin and grinned. It was the first time she had seen him smile all day.

"As you said yourself, people might start getting killed if we don't," she said. "We wouldn't want to risk that."

"Of course not." Garuth raised his voice slightly and addressed the computer-control intelligence built into the *Shapieron*. "ZORAC."

"Commander?"

With JEVEX suspended, ZORAC had been coupled into the planetary net to monitor its operations and provide a connection to the Thuriens' VISAR system.

"Connect a channel into Earthnet for us, right away," Garuth instructed.

Chapter Four

H er name was Gina Marin. She was from Seattle, and she
wrote books.

"What kind?" Hunt asked. "Anything I might have read?"

Gina pulled a face. "If only you knew how tired writers get
of hearing that question."

He shrugged unapologetically. "It comes naturally. What
else are we supposed to say?"

"Not any blockbusters that you'd know as household names,"
she told him candidly. Then she sighed. "I guess I have a habit
of getting into those controversial things where whatever line
you take will upset somebody." She managed not to sound very
remorseful about it. "Taking sides probably isn't the smart thing
to do if you want to be popular." She shrugged. "But those are
the things that make life interesting."

Hunt grinned faintly. "Isn't there a German proverb about
people preferring a popular myth to an unpopular truth?"

"Right. You've got it. Exactly."

They were sitting drinking coffee in the lounge of his apartment, she on a couch by the picture window, he sprawled in
the leather recliner by the fireplace. Alongside his recliner

was the cluttered surface that served as a desk, elbow-distance bookshelf, breakfast bar, and workbench for a partly disman- tled device of peculiar design and fabrication, which he had informed her was from the innards of a Ganymean gravitic communications modulator. The rest of the room was a casual assortment of easygoing bachelordom mixed with the trappings of a theoretical scientist's workplace. A framed photograph of Hunt with a couple of grinning colleagues and a group of Ganymeans posing in front of a backdrop of the *Shapieron* was propped on top of the frame of a four-foot wallscreen showing a contour plot of some kind of three-dimensional wave function; a tweed jacket, necktie, and bathrobe hung all together on a cloakroom hook fixed to the endpiece of a set of overloaded bookshelves; there was a reproduction of a Beethoven symphonic score affixed to the wall next to several feet of a program listing hanging above a pile of American Physical Society journals.

"So, you take up unpopular causes," Hunt said. "Not exactly a creature of the herd, I take it."

Gina made a brief shake of her head to forestall any misun- derstanding. "Don't get me wrong. It's not something that I set out to do deliberately, just to be different or anything like that. It's just that I get interested in things that seem to mat- ter." She paused. "When you start taking the trouble to find out about things, it's amazing how often they turn out not to be the way 'everyone knows' at all. But once you're into it that far, you have to go with what's true as you see it."

Hunt pursed his lips for an instant. "Why worry? People are going to carry on believing what they want to, anyway. They don't want truth; they want certainty. You won't change that. Why burn your life away at both ends trying to?"

She returned a short, resigned nod. "I know. I'm not trying to change anybody. It's more for me, really—you've got to be true to yourself. I'm just curious about the way the world really is. If it turns out to be not the way a lot of people think, then that's just too bad. They won't change reality, either."

Hunt raised his coffee mug and regarded her over the rim. At least she wasn't launching into one of the standard recitations that he had heard so often of how people rationalize their being at odds with the world. If she was a misfit, she had come to terms with the fact and was fully at ease with herself. Whatever the subject was that had brought her here, he decided that he had the time and the inclination to listen.

After a few seconds he said, "Maybe you're in the wrong job. You're beginning to sound as if *you* should have been a scientist."

"You mean, to seek out what objective reality really is? That's what scientists do, right?" Her impish raising of an eyebrow and the tongue pushing lightly in her cheek were just quizzical enough to stop short of skepticism.

"Okay . . . well, they're supposed to, anyway."

Gina's eyes widened in mock surprise. "Oh, but they *do*. You only have to read the textbooks."

Hunt grinned. He liked this kind of company. "I thought we were talking about reality," he said.

"But isn't that what you do?" Gina asked, maintaining the pretense. "Uncover reality?"

"Of course I do. Every scientist knows that *he's* different."

"So you know what's really out there?"

"Sure."

Gina moved her legs and sat forward to rest her chin on her hand, staring at him in a play of fascination. "Go on then, tell me. What's really out there?"

"Photons."

"That's it?"

Hunt turned a palm upward. "That's all that physics can tell you. Everything that's out there reduces to photons interacting with atoms in nerve endings. That's it. There isn't anything else. Just wave packets of whatever, tagged with quantum numbers."

"Not too exciting," Gina commented.

"You did ask."

"So what about the rest of this interesting world that I see?"

"What else do you see?"

She shrugged and motioned vaguely with a hand. "Cabbages and kings. Oceans and mountains, colors and shapes. Places with people in them, doing things that mean something. Where does all that come from?"

"Emergent properties of relationships manifesting themselves at progressively higher levels in a hierarchy of increasing complexity," he told her, not really expecting her to make much out of it.

"Neural constructs," she supplied, parrying him. "I create it in my head."

Hunt raised his eyebrows and nodded his compliments. "Where else? We've already agreed what everything from outside is."

"In the same way that every book that might ever be written is built up from the same twenty-six-letter alphabet. The qualities that we think we perceive aren't out there in the symbols. The symbols are simply a coding system for triggering what a lifetime of living has written into our nervous systems."

"You've got the idea. Sometimes I think it's amazing that any two of us ever manage to perceive anything similar at all."

"I'm not always so sure that we do," Gina responded.

"Which from your point of view is just as well. If we all saw everything the same, you wouldn't have anything controversial to write about." He paused. "I don't exactly get the feeling that all this is especially new."

"I already told you, I get curious about things. And in any case, writers read a lot. It's compulsive. The real reason they write is that it gives them an excuse for doing the research."

Enough fencing, Hunt decided. She had held her own without getting defensive and turning the thing into a duel. He got up and took the mugs through to the kitchen, along with his breakfast dishes. "So what have you written that brought lynch mobs screaming out of the woodwork?" he asked over his shoulder as he loaded the dishwasher.

In the lounge, Gina rose from the couch and turned to study the view out of the picture window. She was a shade on the tall side of average, with a trim, firmly shaped figure that was right for the navy dress.

"Well, there was one I did awhile back about Earthguard

and the no-growth lobby," she said, without turning her head. "Have you had much to do with that?"

"Not a lot. I thought they went away years ago . . . Anyhow, haven't the Thuriens pretty much blown them out of the water for good?"

"I wrote it before the Thuriens showed up."

"Okay. So what were the doomsday brigade into this time?"

"Oh, our expansion out into the Solar System. Numbers were growing too fast, resources being depleted. Earth wouldn't be able to feed an unchecked spacegoing population, and off-planet alternatives were either inadequate or impractical, et cetera, et cetera."

Hunt poured coffee into two fresh mugs. "If we paid too much attention to that lot, we'd still be conserving flint for our grandchildren to make axes. I've got other things to do."

"The trouble is, a lot of people who matter do pay attention to them. And they're the ones who shape what everyone else thinks."

"Well, I think you'll find all that's changing."

"But look what it took," she said. "Yes, now at last, the world's beginning to realize that by all the measures that mean anything, growing populations are a sign of things getting better." She turned as Hunt came back into the lounge, carrying the mugs. "Everyone's got two hands and one mouth, right? People produce more than they consume."

"I had a grandmother from Yorkshire who used to say something like that: You should always listen twice as much as you talk. That's why God gave thee two ears an' one mouth, lad.'"

Gina frowned at him suspiciously. "Are you trying to tell me something?"

"No. What you said just reminded me of it. There's—" Hunt broke off and looked up at her suddenly as he set down the mugs. "Wait a minute. Was it you who wrote that book— something about people being precious?"

"*People, Priceless People,*" Gina confirmed, nodding. "Did you read it?"

"Not all of it. Someone I used to work with showed me some of it—about how the real cost of just about every natural resource has been falling over the last couple of centuries, wasn't it?"

"Which is a sign of a commodity that's getting more abundant, not scarcer."

"And how things like longer life expectancies and falling infant mortality add up to an environment that's getting better, not worse. Yes, I remember it." Hunt nodded and looked at her with greater interest. "What other heresies have you committed?"

"Oh . . . that the nuclear weapons of the twentieth century were the main thing that prevented World War III from happening on at least four occasions between 1945 and final disarmament. In other words, the Bomb and the Pentagon probably saved more lives than penicillin did."

"The Russians more or less admitted that," Hunt commented. "It ruled out major war as an option, and that was all they understood."

"But how much of the public knows that they admitted it? Most people still think it was the peace demonstrators that did it."

Hunt nodded. "That would stir up a few waves on the port beam. What about the starboard side of the ship? Did you start any storms there, as well?"

"Oh, yes . . . by suggesting that sex is probably better for teenagers than religion, and drugs aren't a problem. You know—the usual prime-time family-hour stuff."

"That'd do it, right enough. You've been busy." Hunt himself seemed comfortable enough with everything she had said. He sat down in the recliner and leaned back with his fingers interlaced behind his head. "But you never got to be a millionairess out of it, eh?"

"Not that I noticed, anyhow."

Hunt inclined his head to indicate the general direction outside, where her Peugeot was parked. "Not doing too badly, all the same, by the looks of things," he remarked.

"Rented." .

"Ah."

"From the airport."

"So you're just visiting."

"Right."

"Where are you staying?"

"At the Maddox—a small hotel on the east side of town."

"Uh-huh." Hunt watched her silently for a few seconds to let the preliminary talk fade into the background. "So," he said finally, "now that you're here, what can I do for you?"

"I'd like some help with a new book that I want to write." Gina drew back from the window, but instead of sitting back down on the couch, she crossed the lounge and turned, arms folded, propping herself against the table carrying the comnet terminal. "About the Jevlenese. You're one of the few original sources, and from what I've read, a pretty open and approachable one. So I'm approaching."

Hunt had already guessed that it would be something like that. Her directness about it was refreshing. The public was already being deluged with popular material, most of it second-hand information and wild speculation, being churned out in the rush to cash in by people who didn't know what they were talking about. Concocting plausible but unsubstantiated reasons why any historical figure that somebody disliked or disagreed with had been a Jevlenese agent had become something of a game in the popular media.

"There's some awful stuff out there," he agreed, anticipating her line. "People are being told all kinds of nonsense. So you decided to come to somebody who was in at the beginning." He nodded in a way that said he couldn't find anything to argue with in that.

But Gina shook her head. She went back to the chair that she had occupied before and sat down. "No, that isn't quite it. I'm more interested in some of the things they're *not* being told."

Hunt stroked the side of his nose with a finger and looked at her curiously. "Go on."

"Let's make sure I've got the background correct."

"Okay."

• "The Jevlenese and ourselves are both the same, equally human species, descended from the same ancestors, right?"

Hunt nodded. "The Lunarians, yes."

"But the civilization on Jevlen is more advanced, which isn't surprising since it grew up under the wing of the Thuriens. The early colony on Earth was almost wiped out and went back to barbarism."

"Yes," Hunt said, nodding again.

Gina leaned forward. "But before all that happened, the Lunarian civilization on Minerva also discovered the sciences rapidly and reached an advanced stage much faster than we did, without any Ganymean help. The reason we didn't do the same was that the Jevlenese retarded Earth's development by infiltrating agents to spread irrational belief systems and organize cults based on superstition and unreason. That's why it took us two thousand years to get from Euclid to Newton."

"It took the Lunarians closer to two hundred," Hunt said.

Gina's voice took on a curious, more distant tone. "Just think . . . nobody ever thought of Homer as a science writer before. The *Iliad* could all have been real—an authentic account of human contact with an alien race. Take Hesiod's account of the origins of the universe. First there was Chaos: just dark, empty space and proto-etements. Then Gaea, the fusion of Earth and Life, and Uranus, the star-filled heavens, were born from Eros, the force of attraction that causes all things to come together. Expressed in those terms, it does come interestingly close to the real thing, doesn't it?"

"You've been doing some homework," Hunt murmured.

"The gods that kept coming down and meddling in the Trojan War might actually have existed. Maybe the Biblical miracles really happened, and Velikovsky had a point after all. Is it any wonder that ideas of magic and the supernatural became so deeply rooted here? At one time, it really used to work."

Hunt wondered where she was leading. Everything she had said so far was more or less public knowledge.

She waited for a moment, then tossed out a hand lightly. "Speculating on which figures in history may or may not have been Jevlenese provocateurs has become a popular pastime these days. But what I'd like to see is something on a few of the obvious candidates that people *aren't* talking about."

Hunt stared at her for a second to be sure he had followed, then nodded. It was not a thought that had eluded him completely. "Christ," he muttered.

"Possibly. But probably not. My guess is that he was on the other side."

Hunt had not meant it as a response to her implied question; it had simply been his reaction to the prospect of the wrench that he could see her throwing into the works of cherished belief systems everywhere, going back thousands of years and forming the foundations of entire cultures. What she was inferring threatened, in short, the demolition of virtually all traditionalism and the systems of authority based on it. Hunt did not want to guess at the outrage and unlikely closings of ranks which that would be likely to provoke. Perhaps he had been avoiding thinking about it himself because he had unconsciously glimpsed the implications.

"I, ah . . . I see now what you meant about getting into controversial subjects where you always end up upsetting somebody," he said dryly.

"But you have to agree it gets interesting. Imagine—Euclid to Newton should have taken a couple of hundred years. How else might things have gone, do you think, if the Jevlenese had left us alone? Perhaps Newton would have formulated relativity. James Watt could have invented the nuclear reactor. The Wright brothers might have flown the first starship. But instead, we got headed off into the Dark Ages."

Hunt was staring at her with an intrigued expression. He had discussed such possibilities with colleagues often enough, but they were specialists, linked through their own circles. Gina had put the conclusions together independently.

She was about to continue, when the call-tone from the comnet terminal next to her interrupted. "Excuse me," Hunt said, getting up from the recliner and coming across to answer it. Gina stood up and moved aside. The screen activated to reveal a head-and-shoulders view of two longish, gray-hued countenances with deep blue eyes, large pupils, and dark, neck-length hair. Only someone who had been in a coma or a hermitage for the last year could have failed to recognize them as Ganymeans.

"Hello, Vic," the male said. His mouth movements did not synchronize with the voice, which had a natural human intonation. Ganymeans spoke at a deep, guttural pitch that was incapable of reproducing human speech faithfully. The voice was familiar to Hunt as one that ZORAC synthesized in its role as interpreter.

"Garuth. Good to see you," he replied. "And Shilohin."

"It's been awhile now," the female acknowledged.

Gina, intrigued, moved around to come closer to Hunt, which brought her into the lens angle. "Oh, I didn't realize you had company," Garuth said. "I should have asked."

"Don't worry about it. This is Gina, a friend of mine. She writes books. Gina, meet Garuth and Shilohin."

Gina was at a loss for a moment but recovered quickly. "Hello. I, er, I don't get to do this every day." The two Ganymeans inclined their heads in their customary greeting.

There were currently a number of Ganymeans at various places on Earth for various reasons, and Hunt guessed that Gina was assuming the two faces on the screen to be among them. Although it was no secret that the Thurien communications network managed by VISAR had been extended to Earth, only a few, select locations, such as Goddard, had connections into it. It would hardly have occurred to Gina that Hunt might have wrangled himself a private home extension. He made no mention of the fact, however, and asked casually, "So, how are things on Jevlen these days?"

A hand flashed for an instant in front of Garuth's face. "As a matter of fact, not too good. That's why we're calling. We need some help on a problem that's been developing here."

"Oh really?" Hunt said. "What kind of—" The abrupt movement of Gina passing a hand across her brow made him look away.

"Wait a minute," Gina whispered.

"Would you excuse us for a second?" Hunt said to Garuth.

"But of course. We intruded."

Hunt looked inquiringly at Gina, his face an expression of

forced innocence. She shook her head as if to clear it.

"Did you say Jevlen?" she asked.

"Yes. Garuth is the *Shapieron*'s commander. Shilohin is the chief scientist."

"Those people are on Jevlen—right now?"

"Of course," Hunt said, maintaining his nonchalant air. "That's where the *Shapieron* is."

Gina sat down on the arm of the couch, shaking her head bemusedly. "This isn't real. I've known this guy for an hour. The phone rings, and it's aliens calling from another star system? What happens next?"

"Oh, stick around and we'll find out," Hunt answered cheerfully. "Who knows? If you're not burned at a stake in the meantime, or exiled to Pluto or somewhere, it might be the beginnings of a new book."

Chapter Five

The Thuriens were a rational, nonquarrelsome race of beings to whom the benefits of a society that based itself upon mutual cooperation were too self-evident to require much pondering, let alone debate. As a consequence, the Thurien institution of government was a modest, service-oriented affair concerned mainly with resolving disputes and disagreements, and managing the comparatively few functions that it was felt preferable to consign to public agencies. It certainly had nothing to do with projecting power over individuals, enforcing policies that were none of anybody else's business, or bestowing upon a few the right to decide how the many should be compelled to live.

Having no concept of any alternative, they established the same system—or lack of one, in the opinion of many Terrans—on Jevlen in the period following the destruction of Minerva. So instead of producing the authoritarian institutions that were the inevitable outcome of the ferocious power struggles and ideological collisions characteristic of social evolution on Earth, Jevlenese society developed as a kind of patronized anarchy, secure in the guarantee of unlimited goods and products indefinitely, and the total absence of threats. Hence, survival had never played any great role as a shaper of individual or collective behavior; therefore, the rationality that human survival ultimately depends on had received little incentive to bloom.

Over the years, many popular political and quasireligious cults had come to flourish on Jevlen. They appealed by catering to the needs of individuals to discover some purpose and to affirm their identity in a risk-free, unstructured society, and to the fascination of the uncritical for peculiar beliefs. One of the largest and most militant of them called itself the Axis of Light. Its symbol was a green crescent. The leader, whose real name was Eubeleus, had been well connected with the previous regime responsible for the short-lived Federation, and went by the public title of Deliverer.

The Deliverer's followers numbered millions. Their faith was a conviction that the key to opening up latent, mystical human powers lay in the supercomputer, JEVEX. Their indignation at the Ganymeans' shutting down of JEVEX, therefore, stemmed not merely from material deprivations or fears of a political tactic to encourage dependency, but from what they saw as a persecution of their beliefs.

One of the most commonly used methods of interfacing to Thurien networking systems—JEVEX and VISAR—was by direct coupling into the user's neural centers, bypassing the normal sensory apparatus. The central dogma that the Deliverer taught was that the close-coupled interaction between the inner processes of the human psyche and the more remote levels of supercomputing complexity could unlock the mind to new dimensions of reality. Thus stimulated, the believer would be enabled to conquer the ultimate reaches of time and space. He would come to know his full self in all the dimensions of its existence, and gain access to the powers encompassed by them.

All heady stuff. The followers were suitably impressed. For his part, it was clear that the Deliverer, Eubeleus, held JEVEX in extraordinary awe and reverence, with an unswerving belief in its abilities that bordered on fanatical. But such loyalty was really to be expected: He believed himself to be a physically incarnate extension of JEVEX.

✳   ✳   ✳

The day after Garuth's call to Hunt, Eubeleus met with a man called Grevetz at the latter's walled villa and estate in a forested valley known as Cerberan, located among hills not far from the city of Shiban. Grevetz was the regional boss of the local Jevlenese criminal syndicate that had been making the most of the new black-market opportunities created by the surges in wants that the withdrawal of JEVEX had brought about. With them was a lieutenant of Grevetz's, Scirio, who ran the operation in a part of Shiban.

Eubeleus had influence because the size of his following translated into a substantial inflow of cash, a hefty block of political leverage, and when the occasion demanded, a guaranteed turnout to add physical pressure to rhetoric and persuasion on the streets. But the greatest benefit that he brought to Grevetz's organization was a result of the demand for the services of JEVEX itself. For although the primary operating functions of JEVEX had been suspended, a residual core capability had been left ticking to support certain maintenance and housekeeping functions, and to monitor faults and sustain system integrity; also, Thurien analysts were exploring parts of the records accumulated over centuries in an endeavor to uncover exactly what the Jevlenese had been up to. Through connections that existed somewhere in the planet's communications grid, Eubeleus could provide access into that core system of JEVEX. He had not told anybody how he did it.

"*I* am the one who is endowed with the vision," Eubeleus told the other two on the fronded patio, bordered with shrubs, at the rear of the villa. "My mind touches deep into JEVEX's soul. I know the things that must come to be. The design that is prepared has been revealed to me. That is why you must heed my words all the more closely when I say that this man is an instrument of forces that lie beyond the bounds of your present awareness of things. An obstacle that must be removed"—Eubeleus picked up an imaginary stone from in front of him and tossed it aside—"from the path."

He had a lean yet large-boned frame, and was tall in build,

with yellow hair that curled at the back of his neck, and piercing, electric blue eyes, which the word among the faithful held to be a manifestation of the paraphysical forces that operated through him. He was clean-shaven, which was unusual for Jevlenese cult gurus and mystagogues, but the countenance thus displayed was perhaps even more striking. It comprised angled cheekbones and hollowed features that objectified resilient austerity; a straight, undeviating nose that gave him a line along which to look downward unwaveringly on the lesser species of creation; a mobile, expressive mouth, and a hard, tapering jaw, obstinately set in a line that had never felt a need of questioning or known the twinges of self-doubt. He was dressed in a loose, two-piece tunic of orange with green-crescent devices on the lapels, topped by a green cape. His manner as he spoke was grandly imperious, an oration, even in private, his sonorously modulated phrases emphasized by dramatic bodily poses and flourishes of his hands and fingers . . .

But Grevetz and Scirio, used to that from somebody who thought he was a walking extension of a computer, reacted impassively.

The subject of Eubeleus's wrath was a document lying on the table at which Grevetz and Scirio were sitting. It was a report from Obayin, the deputy chief of the Shiban police, to Garuth, head of the Ganymean administration headquartered at the Planetary Administration Center, on the facilities for illicit access into JEVEX that had been uncovered both in that region of Jevlen and elsewhere. And it reported them straight, without playing things down. That kind of overzealousness could lose the Axis a lot of followers—not to mention cost Grevetz a lot of lost revenue from his own clients—if the authorities started taking serious action. A deputy chief of police who was any use would have *known* that. And there were longer-term plans that Eubeleus had chosen not to divulge yet that were far more important and stood to be disrupted even more. The risk was intolerable.

"So what if we do get rid of him?" Grevetz asked. "Do you have anybody in particular in mind to take over?"

"Whom do you have prepared?" Eubeleus threw back.

Grevetz looked at Scirio. "What are we paying Langerif these days?"

"Enough. It has to be. It's the second cut down, anyhow."

"We'd go for Langerif," Grevetz told Eubeleus.

The Deliverer nodded. "I shall have his record checked by my own sources. If it proves satisfactory, a word in the right quarters will assure his appointment." He tossed out an arm beneath his cape as if casting out an evil and moved a few paces away. "Then I can leave the more immediate aspect to you?" he said, turning and staring at Grevetz.

Grevetz looked across the table at Scirio. "He's on your turf. Reckon you can arrange a convenient accident or something for citizen Obayin?"

"It would take a little thought. He likes to be careful."

"I can arrange some suitable disturbances about the city," Eubeleus offered. "A turbulent and discordant background, against which all manner of the unlikely and the unexpected might happen?"

"It's the kind of thing that would get him out there," Grevetz agreed.

Scirio rubbed his chin and nodded. "Like I say, let me think about it from a few angles. I figure we should be able to come up with something."

Chapter Six

The window looked out over the bronzed-glass office towers, concrete experimental buildings, and tree-lined avenues of the UN Space Arm's Goddard Space Center. At the desk in front of it, a stockily built figure with a craggy face and close-cropped, steel gray hair drummed a tattoo on the leather top with his fingers. "What did they want?" Gregg Caldwell, director of UNSA's recently formed Advanced Sciences Division, demanded in his gravelly, bass-baritone voice.

The Thurien contact had made nonsense of all the plans for Man's expansion into space, just when those plans had at last begun taking shape as a united effort by the entire race. Accepting the pointlessness of preserving forms that even its bureaucrats were unable to deny now served no sensible purpose, UNSA had scrapped most of its previous organizational structure to clear the decks for the new challenges. This had included wrapping up Caldwell's former Navigation and Communications Division, which would have had about as much relevance to the changed circumstances as an astrolabe on the command deck of one of the Jupiter mission ships. Caldwell had moved to Washington to set up a new division charged with assimilating as much of the alien technology into Earth's space program as was practicable and desirable, and Hunt had moved with him to become deputy director.

Hunt answered from a leather-upholstered easy chair in front of a battery of display screens on the opposite wall. Caldwell had always liked big windows and lots of screens. His old office at Navcomms HQ in Houston had been fitted the same way.

"Garuth's realizing that he bit off more than he could chew when he agreed to take charge on Jevlen. Let's be frank, Gregg—it was a daft idea in the first place. Ganymeans aren't cut out to be planetary overlords. We should have put our foot down harder when Calazar and the rest of the Thuriens came up with it. Neither of us was happy about it at the time."

Caldwell shrugged. In the headiness of those times, everyone's judgment had been affected. Nothing could be done about it now. "You can't miss if you never shoot at anything," he replied. "What kind of problems are they having with the Jevlenese?"

"Nothing that would seem especially strange to us: civil disturbances and agitation. But to Ganymean minds it doesn't make any sense. They don't know how to handle the illogic of it."

"They still don't know what to make of people acting normal, eh?"

"I'm not sure they ever will—completely."

"What kind of illogic are we talking about? Give me a specific."

Hunt spread his hands for an instant. "Oh, keeping JEVEX shut down means that the Jevlenese can't function without Ganymean help—at least, so some of them say. Therefore the situation equates to forced subjugation and violates their rights of self-determination. And then the standard terrorist line: If we end up killing each other because we don't like it, it will be *your* responsibility."

"Which the Ganymeans buy, right?"

"They believe it, but they don't understand it."

"It sounds as if the leash is on the wrong way round, all right," Caldwell agreed.

"Yes . . . but what's making matters worse is the withdrawal symptoms of unhooking them from JEVEX, which it seems everyone underestimated. Garuth says the number of headworld junkies there was epidemic. You have to admit, it is the ultimate in escapism. People could get into it in a big way—even the Thuriens admit they sometimes have problems with it. But in the case of the Jevlenese, it's left half the population with no idea of how to cope. They've been conditioned to be totally, uncritically receptive, which makes them complete suckers for anyone with a message to put in their heads."

"Hmm." Caldwell drummed on the desk again for a second. "I thought the UN sent a bunch of sociologists and psychiatrists there who were supposed to know about how to deal with that kind of thing. How come they're not handling it?"

Hunt made a you-know-how-it-is gesture. "They're out-of-work social engineers looking for new places to take their theories now that people here are managing their own lives. Apparently the experts are producing lots of reports and statistics, but when anything serious happens they head for cover and leave it to the riot police."

"So why is Garuth coming to us? Our business is Ganymean physics, not Jevlenese psychology." Caldwell already had a pretty good idea of the reason; he just wanted to hear Hunt's reading of it.

"He's worried that if things get worse and JPC starts to panic, he might be pulled out and replaced by a Terran military administration. They've been putting in a lot of work there, Gregg."

Caldwell nodded. "Garuth doesn't want to see it all go to waste," he guessed, saving Hunt the need to spell it out. "Just when they might have been about to see some results?"

"That—and more." Hunt motioned briefly with a hand. "He sounded as if he thought they were close to discovering something important about what's screwing up the Jevlenese—more than their simply being JEVEX cabbages. But putting in a Colonel Blimp-style board of governors there would blow any chance of getting to the bottom of it." Hunt shook his head before

Caldwell could ask. "He didn't go into any more details."

Caldwell paused a shade longer than would have been natural before speaking—just enough to impart more currency into his question than its face value. "What do you think we should do?"

Properly speaking, there should have been no question. By all the formal rules and demarcation lines, it was none of Advanced Sciences' business. Hunt knew that, Caldwell knew that, and both of them knew that Garuth did, too. The department had close working relationships with plenty of influential figures in both political hemispheres, and all that the situation called for was a friendly word to refer the matter to them.

But as Hunt wasn't saying and Caldwell understood, there was more to it in reality. This was old friends appealing for help, and it couldn't be let go at that. The first encounter with Garuth and the Ganymeans at Jupiter had been, strictly speaking, a "political" problem, too; yet the UNSA scientists on the spot had achieved a common understanding without complications while the professional diplomats on Earth were still conferring about protocols and arguing over rivalries of precedence. That was why Hunt had raised the matter in the way he had. Caldwell was very good at interpreting his terms of authority creatively. Properly speaking, even before the Ganymeans appeared, getting involved with the Lunarian mystery when it had first surfaced should not have been any of Navcomms's business, either.

Hunt rubbed his chin and adopted an expression appropriate to weighing up a matter of considerable gravity. "You know, there could be a lot at stake here, Gregg . . . when you think about it. Our whole future relationship with what's shown itself to be an erratic and temperamental alien culture. Even with the best of intentions, the wrong people could get things into a big mess."

"I think so, too," Caldwell agreed, nodding solemnly.

Hunt shifted in the chair and recrossed his legs the other way. "It's not a time for taking risks with untried procedures. Tested methods would be safer, even if a little . . . irregular?"

"It ought to be played safe," Caldwell affirmed.

"It wouldn't be violating any precedent. In fact, it would be fully in accordance with the only precedent we've got."

"Exactly."

Hunt had wondered on and off whether Caldwell's promotion to Washington might spell the beginnings of a slow ossification into the role of dedicated administrator, and a waning of the dynamism that had helped fling humanity across the solar system. But as he stared back across the desk, he saw the old light that came with anticipation of a challenge, still there as bright as ever beneath the bushy brows. Hunt dropped the pretense. "Okay. What do you want me to do?"

Caldwell's manner became businesslike. "Garuth says he needs help. So see what you can do to help. Your job is to look into Ganymean science. Well, he's right in the middle of a whole civilization based on it. You'll find more there than you will from the scraps we've been sent here."

"There?" Hunt blinked. "You want me to go there—to Jevlen?"

Caldwell shrugged. "That's where the problem is. You don't expect Garuth to bring the planet here. The *Vishnu* will be going back to Thurien before very much longer, with a stop on the way at Jevlen. I'll get you a slot on board."

Hunt found himself with his usual feeling of already being left behind in seconds once Caldwell had made a decision. "Washington hasn't changed you, Gregg," he said resignedly.

"I know when you're curious, and I trust your instincts. You've never failed to come back with something better than we hoped for, yet. I sent you off to Ganymede to look into some relics of defunct aliens, and you came back with a shipload of live ones. You went up to Alaska to meet a starship, and discovered an interstellar civilization." Caldwell tossed out a hand. "Okay, I'll buy in again. I'm curious, too."

Caldwell wasn't missing any tricks of his own, either, Hunt realized. Already he had spotted territory for sending out feelers to explore growth potential for his new, embryonic empire. It was the old Gregg, as opportunistic as ever. And Hunt had one of his fuzzily defined, free-ranging assignments again.

"You'd better start giving some thought to who else you might need along," Caldwell said. He almost managed to sound as if Hunt had been dragging his heels over it.

"Well, Chris Danchekker for a start, I suppose—especially if it's going to involve alien psychology."

"I'd already assumed that."

"And Duncan's been agitating for a chance to do a spell off-planet. I think he should get it, too. He's been doing a great job." Hunt was referring to his assistant, Duncan Watt, who had moved with him from Houston. Duncan always ended up holding the fort whenever Hunt went away.

"Okay."

"Chris might want to bring one of his people, too."

"I'll let you take that up with him," Caldwell said.

Hunt sat back, rubbing his lower lip with a knuckle and eyeing Caldwell hesitantly. "There, er . . . there was one other small thing," he said finally.

"Oh, yes?" Caldwell sounded unsurprised, but in his preoccupation of the moment, Hunt missed it.

"It just occurred to me . . . There's a journalist that I happened to run into, who wants to write a book on some of the possible Jevlenese agents in history that people *aren't* talking about."

"Just occurred to you," Caldwell repeated.

"Well, sort of." Hunt made a vague circling motion in the air. "Anyhow, this business on Jevlen could provide a lot of valuable background to what happened here. So, if it looks as if we might end up getting involved in the Jevlenese situation, anyway . . ."

"Why not help the journalist out a little at the same time?" Caldwell completed.

"Well, yes. It occurred to me that . . ." Hunt's voice trailed away as he registered finally that Caldwell had not shown any sign that anything Hunt was saying was especially new. His manner became suspicious as an old, familiar feeling asserted itself. "Gregg, you're up to something. I can smell it. What's going on? Come on, give."

"Unusual kind of journalist, was it?" Caldwell asked nonchalantly. "From Seattle, maybe? Stimulating outlook: not programmed with the canned opinions that you seem to find in most people you meet these days. Quite attractive, too, if I remember." He grinned at the look on Hunt's face. Then his manner became more brisk, and he nodded. "She contacted me a little while back, and came here a few days ago."

Hunt got over his surprise and studied Caldwell with a frown. Gina, going straight to the top in what Hunt had already seen to be her direct, forthright fashion, had gotten in touch with Caldwell to ask if UNSA could help her with the book. And as Hunt thought it through, he could see why that might have posed problems. He knew from his own experience how many major publishers, TV companies, top-line writers, and others were wining and dining, wheeling and wheedling with UNSA's top executives to try and get a corner on the Jevlen story from the "inside." In that kind of climate it would have caused endless complications and ructions for UNSA to be seen as giving official backing to a relatively unheard-of free-lancer, and Caldwell was enough of a politician to stay out of it. But he could safely, if he chose to, turn a blind eye to something that Hunt chose to involve himself with privately.

But Gina had made no mention of having been referred to Hunt. That meant that she had let him make his own choice in the matter freely, without mentioning Caldwell's name, which would have carried the implication that Hunt was being prodded from above. She would have let the project go rather than resort to high-pressure tactics. Not many people would have done that. He felt relieved now that he had brought the matter back to Caldwell instead of burying it.

"I guess it wasn't something the firm could put its name on," Hunt said, nodding as it all became clearer. "But you thought she deserved a break all the same, eh?"

"She talks more sense than I hear from geniuses they put on TV screens for ten thousand bucks an hour," Caldwell replied. He pulled a cigar from a drawer in the desk. "But there's another side to it. Think of it this way. The kind of dealings that Garuth is talking about are going to require a certain amount of . . . let's call it 'discretion.' When you get there, situations will quite likely arise in which some kinds of irregularities might be acceptable, while others will not. Or to put it another way, things might need to be done that an independent free-lancer—and especially one with the kind of reputation that she's no doubt built up—might get away with, but which a deputy director of an UNSA division"—Caldwell pointed at Hunt with the cigar before putting it in his mouth—"couldn't be seen to do."

In other words, Hunt's team had an unofficial aide to help in potential politically sensitive situations where official UNSA action was precluded. And that, Hunt had to agree, could turn out to be very useful. What impressed him even more was that Caldwell had figured it out in the brief time that had gone by since his decision to send Hunt to Jevlen.

Caldwell was like a chess player, Hunt had noticed, building his winning positions from the accruing of many small advantages, none of them especially significant in itself to begin with, or created with any definite idea at the time of how it would eventually be used. In Gina's case, he could simply have told her that there was nothing he could do, and sent her away. But instead, he had invested the effort of doing her a small favor, which really had cost him nothing. And as things had turned out, the return had come a lot sooner than anyone could have guessed.

Caldwell read that Hunt had assessed everything accurately, and gave a satisfied nod. "How did you leave things with her?" he asked.

"I said I'd get back. She's still at the Maddox. I wanted to bring it up with you first."

"You talk to her, then, and tell her we want to send her to Jevlen. We'll work out some cover angle for public consumption." Caldwell waved in the direction of his outer office. "Mitzi has a line to the *Vishnu*. She'll fix the details. Then, that's it, unless you've got any other points for now."

Hunt started to rise, then looked up. "What are you expecting me to come back with this time, Gregg?" he asked.

"How do I know?" Caldwell spread his hands and made a face. "Lost planet, starship, interstellar civilization. What does that leave? The next thing can only be a universe."

"That's all? You know, you may have me there, Gregg," Hunt said, smiling. "There aren't too many of those left. Where am I supposed to find another universe?"

Caldwell stared at him expressionlessly. "I don't think anything you did could surprise me anymore," he replied.

Chapter Seven

The gods had turned away from the world of Waroth, and their stars had gone out. With the emptiness in the sky came changelessness upon the land. The currents of life, which brought storms and stirred the landscapes, died to a flicker, and sameness hung like a stupor everywhere from day to day and from place to place. Crops failed; orchards wilted. Sea monsters that devoured ships moved in close to the shores, and the fishermen were afraid to leave their harbors. Marauding bands roamed at large, plundering and burning. Sickness and pestilences came.

In the city of Orenash, the king and the council of rulers summoned the high tribunal of priests, who read from the signs that the reason the gods were abandoning the people was that the people were turning away from the gods by permitting sorcerers to meddle in knowledge that was not intended for this world. The currents and the stars would return when the people atoned and cleansed themselves by renouncing such arts and sacrificing to the gods those guilty of practicing them. Accordingly, the sorcerers were rounded up and brought in chains before the Grand Assembly. Thrax's uncle, Dalgren, was among them.

"They are not Seers. They have not seen Hyperia," the Holy Prosecutor thundered at the trial. "But they seek knowledge, here, now, of mysteries that the gods have seen fit not to unfold until the life that comes after Waroth. Thus they would exalt themselves and set themselves above the gods."

The Prosecutor glowered. "They speak of *laws*! Of processes constrained to predictability by strange powers of lawfulness beyond our comprehension. They are not Seers, mind you; but they feel able to tell us of the rules that govern Hyperia, which the Seers who have seen Hyperia have never seen. Is it *they*, then, are we to conclude—these sorcerers—who are to say what will be in Hyperia, rather than the gods?

"Their ambition spurred them to be as the gods. But, unable to expand their own powers to embrace the complexities of chaos that support the world, the sorcerers had to make the world simple enough to fit with what they could comprehend. They sought consistency across space and predictability over time—*laws* that would remain unchanged, making all objects stay the same no matter where or when they were observed.

"The gods granted them what they sought . . . and now they are letting us see the results of it. The currents that fed chaos are dying. *Lawfulness* is taking over the land, and the land, too, dies, stifled and crushed by sameness. For it is chaos that brings change, and change is life. Change is vigor. Change is the uncertainty that allows Good to vie with Evil, action to take meaning, and for the judgments of the gods to prevail."

He stabbed a finger in the direction of the accused, detaching a bolt of light that dispersed and vanished in a puff of expanding radiance. "The gods have shown us our folly. Now they must be paid the atonement that they demand . . ."

To determine the judgment, a year-old *uskiloy* was tethered inside a consecrated circle before the Assembly and thrice blessed. Then, seven Masters in unison prayed for a lightning stroke to appear and smite within the circle. A swirl of night and light gathered above the court before the temple, and when the flash came, the *uskiloy* was consumed. Thus, the verdict delivered was: Guilty.

Keyalo, the foster son of Dalgren, saw the verdict as

vindication of the uncompromising position that he himself had taken from the outset. Seeing an opportunity to win favor with the authorities and at the same time take care of the source of his resentment and jealousy, he went to the Holy Prosecutor's secretary-scribe and said, "The household of Dalgren is not cleansed yet of its stain. There is another there who also blasphemed against the teachings, an apprentice of the accursed arts."

"Who is this of whom you speak?" the Prosecutor's officer asked him.

"The nephew, whose name is Thrax. Many times have I seen him assisting in the fabrication of strange devices and performing unholy rites. And he, too, speaks of stealing the laws of Hyperia and bringing them to Waroth."

"Then he, too, shall stand accused" was the reply.

But Thrax had gone to consult a Seer outside the city, who touched the mind of Dalgren even while Dalgren sat chained in the Holy Prosecutor's dungeons. "He has a message for you, Thrax," the Seer announced. "He has seen the signs across the land and repented of his ways. Indeed, the ways that are of Hyperia are meant for Hyperia, and the ways that are of Waroth are meant for Waroth. The sorcerers have defied the teachings, and in their impudence and pride brought woe upon the world."

"Has he renounced the quest of lawfulness?" Thrax asked, seized with bewilderment as he listened.

"Aye," the Seer answered. "And he accepts his fate with fortitude and humility. The will of the gods and the way of life does indeed work through the whims of chaos. You have the ability, Thrax. Use it to learn the true wisdom."

"What would he have me do?"

"Begin again. Take thyself hence from the city and the plain. Find thee a Master who teaches, and learn from him the true way. Seek beyond for Hyperia; it can never be built in Waroth."

Thrax gasped. "He would have *me* become a Master?"

"Thus speaks the mind of Dalgren."

Seized by remorse and a new resolve, Thrax turned his back upon the city, and there and then, taking only the clothes that he stood in, he set off toward the wilderness. And it was as well for him that he did. For even as he fixed his gaze upon the distant mountains, the sheriff of the city was arriving at Dalgren's house with a troop of guards and a warrant from the Assembly to arrest him.

Chapter Eight

B efore joining UNSA, Hunt had been a theoretical physicist employed by the Metadyne Nucleonic Instrument
Company, a British subsidiary of the Intercontinental Data &
Control Corporation based in Portland, Oregon. IDCC's senior
physicist at that time was a man called Erwin Reutheneger, of
Hungarian extraction, well into his eighties, but with a mind
still sharper and more agile than most a quarter of his age. Hunt
remembered him talking once about the regrets that he felt,
looking back over life. The biggest, it turned out, wasn't that he
had not won a Nobel Prize for his contributions to nucleonic
science, or had a lecture series named after him at a major institution of learning, or otherwise made his mark in halls of fame
or rolls of honor in a way that would be recorded by posterity. It
was a missed opportunity with a petite, French philosophy grad-
uate from the Sorbonne whom he had met in the course of a
stay in Paris in 1968, which he was sure would have turned out
differently if he'd had a better idea at the time of what was going on. "Don't become a sad old man who missed his chances"
had been his advice. "Have plenty of memories to chuckle
about—even the ones that didn't work out the way you hoped."

Partly because of Hunt's nature, and partly because of the hardly orthodox life that he always seemed to find himself leading—as he had told his neighbor, Jerry, a settled domestic existence didn't go with things like year-long jaunts to Jupiter—it accorded well with his own philosophic disposition toward life. And since his work left little time for any creative precipitation of opportunity, the serendipitous incursions of good fortune that chose occasionally to infuse themselves into life's pattern were all the less to be sneered at.

Intelligence, he had always found, was the most potent aphrodisiac, and since inhibition did not seem to be one of Gina's problems, he had not bothered overly to disguise the fact. He had found himself intrigued by her questioning ways and curious to learn what else her peripatetic interests had led her to explore. She, for her part, had done nothing to hide her fascination for somebody who had crossed the solar system and who took calls at home from aliens at other stars. What happened next would develop in its own time, if it wanted to. Rushing the situation would be the worst thing to do, as well as not being in the best of taste. But a small helping hand while it was making its mind up wasn't the same thing at all, Hunt told himself.

Caldwell had stressed that Gina's involvement with the Jevlen mission had to be, as far as outward appearances went, a private matter, unconnected with UNSA. Therefore, Hunt reasoned, he could hardly invite her to Goddard to brief her on it. Accordingly, he called her at the Maddox later in the evening after his talk with Caldwell and told her that he had some news. Could they get together later somewhere and talk about it?

"How about meeting me here for a drink?" she suggested. "It's a bit small, but the bar's okay."

"Have you eaten?"

"Not yet."

"Well, why don't we make an evening of it and talk over dinner? There's a nice, quiet little place I happen to know over on that side of town."

"Uh . . . huh."

"I could pick you up there. This isn't really for bars, anyway."

Her pause was a study in amused suspicion.

"Sure. Why not?"

An hour and a half later, they were talking across a candlelit table by a penthouse window facing out across the illuminated towers of nighttime Washington. They had talked about Gina's approach to Caldwell and her handling of Caldwell's response, and Hunt had told her how he would be going to Jevlen.

"As a matter of fact, you couldn't have picked a better time to show up," he said, sipping from his wineglass over a plate of prime-rib special. Gina waited, watching his face curiously. He lowered his voice a fraction. "I'm going to let you in on something confidential. This business about going there to appraise the possibilities of Ganymean science is mostly a blind to fit in with my regular job. The real purpose is to find out more, firsthand, about Garuth's problem with the Jevlenese and see what we can do to help. The place to do that is on Jevlen, not here."

Gina's brow creased in puzzlement. "What is this guy Caldwell running, a scientific division of UNSA or a security agency?"

"The Ganymeans of the *Shapieron* are personal friends, who are in trouble. That's his first concern."

"Oh. I didn't realize that he sees it that way. I take it back."

"No, you're right. Essentially it is a political issue, and he should just hand it over. But he's always been a bit of an empire-builder. Besides the immediate aspect, the temptation to get a finger into what's going on at Jevlen is too much for him to resist."

"It sounds as if moving from Houston to Washington might have gotten him a little."

"Gregg's okay. He gets things done, and he doesn't mess around."

"Okay. So when do you leave?"

"In three days—with the *Vishnu*."

Gina raised her eyebrows and picked up her glass. "Well, what do I say? It sounds like a wonderful assignment. But it also means that you won't be around to give me any background on the book for some time. So why did you say I'd picked a good time? It sounds to me as if I couldn't have picked a worse one."

Hunt finished chewing before he replied. "There are a number of Earthpeople on Jevlen already for one reason or another. The situation there could be politically sensitive. We don't exactly know what to expect."

"All right . . ." Gina said slowly, nodding but not following.

"In particular, the job might call for some snooping around and talking to people that would look out of place for a scientist on a purely scientific assignment—the kind of thing that would invite unwelcome questions to be asked." Hunt held her eye steadily. "But a journalist—especially one known for being something of a maverick—wouldn't cause any eyebrows to be raised. It would be expected."

"Yes, I can see that."

"So officially you'd be there as a free-lancer collecting research for your book—but unofficially to help with the things that I couldn't go poking my own nose into too obviously."

It took Gina a few seconds to register what he was saying. She set her fork down on her plate and stared at him in disbelief. Hunt smirked back shamelessly at her befuddlement.

"Wait a minute," she muttered. "Am I hearing you correctly? Are you talking about *me* going to Jevlen, as well? Three days from now? Is that what you're saying?"

Hunt gestured to indicate the restaurant and the scene around them in general. "I said when I called you that I had news. All this isn't just to tell you, sorry, I'm going away, I can't help with the book."

Gina picked up her glass again and gulped from it unsteadily. She passed a hand over her brow and shook her head dazedly. Her voice choked when she finally managed to speak. "You . . . really are a guy for surprises. Or have I been living a sheltered life? You may not believe it, but this doesn't happen every time I get asked out on a dinner date."

"It's all Gregg's fault. I told you he doesn't mess around."

"I got that message." She paused. "You are serious, I suppose?"

"Of course. It'd make a pretty sick joke if I weren't." He watched her face for a few seconds. "So, do I take it that it's okay? You don't have a problem?"

"No . . . I don't think so." She thought it over, then sat back in her chair and laughed, momentarily intoxicated by the acceptance that the offer was real. "It's just that I still can't really believe it."

Hunt raised his glass. "Great."

Gina joined him in the unspoken toast, then set her glass down and looked serious again. "So, what am I supposed to do? I mean, if we don't want it to look as if I'm on an UNSA paycheck, I take it that I can't very well travel with you."

Hunt nodded. "That's right. If we happen to meet casually later, that's another matter."

"But how do I get a seat on an alien starship that's leaving in three days? Am I supposed to call a travel agent and ask to book a ticket?"

"There'll be a TWA shuttle going up from Vandenberg with some groups from the West Coast. That should give you enough time to get back to Seattle, pack a toothbrush, and sort out any notes and other stuff you need to bring along. I'll bump into you after you join the *Vishnu.*"

"All I have to do is book a flight with the shuttle?"

"Right."

Gina still looked perplexed. "But—what about getting on board the Thurien ship? Won't I need some kind of authorized place or something? How do I fix that?"

Hunt grinned. "You don't have a feel for Ganymeans yet, do you?" he said. "Most people don't. Ganymeans are the most informal beings, probably in the whole Galaxy. They have no concept of authorizations, passes, permits, ID checks, or any of the other hassles dreamed up by the makers of rules that we inflict on ourselves to make life difficult, or any clear notion why we imagine such things should be necessary."

"Oh, that life could be so simple," Gina said with a wistful sigh.

Hunt reached into his pocket and produced an envelope. "I just happen to have a number here at UNSA that can connect you through to the *Vishnu's* administration center. In short, you just ask. Your story is that you're a free-lancer working on a book, and you wonder if you can hitch a ride to Jevlen. There shouldn't be a problem. But if you get stuck, call me."

"Ask?" Gina looked nonplussed. "That's all? And they'll take you?"

"If they've got room. And there shouldn't be any shortage of that—the *Vishnu* is twenty miles long."

"So why isn't everyone doing it?"

"Because they don't know about it. They all assume nothing can be that simple—just like you did."

"What about when they find out? Won't the Thuriens have to make some rules then?"

"Who knows? Let's wait and see. They don't have much experience in dealing with people being unreasonable."

"But they couldn't let just anyone who wants to go there just move in, surely. It would get out of control."

"Ah, you see," Hunt said pointedly. "There you go, thinking like a Terran who assumes people have to be controlled. A Ganymean couldn't conceive why you should want to keep anyone out."

They ate in silence for a while. Hunt was content to enjoy the food and give Gina time to take in what had been said. At last she looked up again and asked, "Who else will be going?"

"Well, not too many on the short notice we've got," Hunt replied. "We're hoping to get a life-sciences specialist along, too, whom I've worked with before. His name's Chris Danchekker."

"I've read about him. He went to Jupiter with you, right?"

"That's him. He probably understands Ganymean psychology better than anybody. We haven't actually approached him about it yet, though. That's on the agenda for tomorrow."

"He sounds fascinating. I'd like to meet him."

"Oh yes, you have to meet Chris."

"Do you think he'll go?"

"Hopefully. He's been immersing himself in Jevlenese

biology lately, and I imagine he'd jump at a chance of going there. It would complete the cover of the whole thing as a scientific mission, too. Then there's my assistant from Goddard, a guy called Duncan Watt. And we're hoping Danchekker can get one of his people along, as well."

By the time they got to their coffees and brandies, Hunt had forgotten business matters and again found himself admiring the sweep of raven hair that framed one side of Gina's face, and trying to fathom the dancing, enigmatic light in her eye as she stared back over the rim of her glass. It was the kind of look in which it would have been possible to read anything one wanted to. But whether it was deliberately so or otherwise, he couldn't tell.

In the end, he decided that the situation had been given as much of a helping hand as was prudent, but he still wanted to think about it. He wondered if a Ganymean in a situation like this would simply ask.

Chapter Nine

On Jevlen there was a group of several large, tropical islands known as the Galithenes. Inland, they were mostly mountainous, but the wider valleys and the coastal plains supported dense canopies of rain forest that excluded all but a feeble twilight. And in the midday gloom of the two most northerly islands of the group, there lived a peculiar flying creature called the anquiloc.

About the size of a pigeon, it had strongly developed hind legs; modest, clawed forelegs with rudimentary grasping abilities, which it used, when at rest, to attach itself to vertical surfaces such as tree trunks; and black, scaly wings that glistened like wet asphalt. In its basic structure, it conformed to the general, bilaterally symmetric, triple-paired limb pattern of the Jevlenese animal classification corresponding roughly to terrestrial vertebrates.

The anquiloc's face had a narrow black snout that bulged at the end like the nose of a hammerhead shark, into an organ that luminesced in the infrared. Below its eyes were two large, forward-directed, concave areas, formed from a mixture of reflective and absorbent tissues that functioned both as variable-geometry focusing surfaces to produce a crudely directed beam that could be steered by moving the head, and as receivers tuned to the reflections. Thus, it navigated and hunted by means of its own system of self-contained, thermal radar.

The anquiloc's main prey was a small, wasplike octopod known as the chiff. The chiff possessed IR-sensitive antennae that evolution had shaped to operate in the same general range as the anquiloc's search frequencies, which gave rise to an unusual contest of ever-changing strategy and counterstrategy between the two species. The chiff's first, simple response on detecting a search signal was to fold its wings and drop out of the beam. The anquiloc countered by learning to dip its approach in anticipation when it registered a chiff. The chiff reacted by skewing its escape to the left; and when the anquiloc followed, the chiff switched to the right; when the anquiloc became adept at checking in both directions, the chiff reacted by climbing out of the beam instead of falling; or of going left, or maybe right. Whichever was adopted, all the possible ensuing variations would unfold in some order or other and then maybe revert to an earlier form, producing an ever-changing pattern in which new behaviors constantly appeared, lasted for as long as they were effective, and gave way to something else.

But what made the anquiloc more than just "peculiar" was the way it came preprogrammed with the right maneuvers to deal with the latest to have appeared from the chiff's repertoire of routines for evading it. And it was not simply a statistical effect, where newborn anquilocs possessing all possible varieties of behavior appeared equally, and only the ones that happened to be "right" at the time survived.

Newborn individuals exhibited the same response pattern as the latest that the parents had learned up to the time of conception. Since that pattern changed depending on the current mode of chiff behavior, the mechanism represented a clear case of inheriting a characteristic that had been acquired by the parent during life and not carried by the gene line—a flat contradiction of the principles determined by generations of researchers on Earth. Jevlenese and Ganymean scientists had long before settled the point by training anquilocs in certain tasks and testing their offspring for the ability after separating them at birth, and there was no doubt of it. Neither was it the only instance of the phenomenon that they had encountered in their probings of the nearby regions of the Galaxy.

But for the biologists of Earth it was a revelation that went against all the rules, throwing some of their most precious tenets into as much disarray as their colleagues from the physical sciences were already having to come to terms with.

Professor Christian Danchekker operated a tracker ball on the control panel of the molecular imager and peered at the foot-high hologram as it rotated in the viewing space in front of him. He tapped a command key to create a ghostly sphere of faint light, about the size of a cherry, and turned the ball again to guide the sphere until it enclosed a selected part of the image. Then he spoke in a slightly raised voice toward a grille in the panel to one side.

"Voice on. Magnify by ten." The part of the image that had been inside the sphere expanded to fill the viewing space and resolved itself into finer detail. "Reduce by five . . ." Danchekker rotated the image some more and repositioned the sphere slightly. "Magnify by ten . . . Increase contrast ten percent . . . Voice off."

For a few moments he sat back and contemplated the result with satisfaction tinged by a dash of undisguised amazement. He was tall and sparse in build, with a balding head and antiquated, gold-rimmed spectacles perched precariously on a hollowed, toothy face. The assistant seated on another chair called a set of neural mapping charts, onto one of the auxiliary display screens while she waited.

"There it is, Sandy," Danchekker murmured. "The base sequence has altered. Run a delta-sigma on the code and correlate it against the map. But I have no hesitation in predicting, now, that you'll find it embedded there. This is how it transfers."

Sandy Holmes leaned forward and studied the enhanced

section of the molecule's structure now being presented. "It's a cumulative progression from what we had before," she commented.

Danchekker nodded. "Which is what one would expect. As the learned routine is registered by the nervous system, the encoded representation impressed into the messenger increases. We're actually looking at transferable memory in action."

They had taught some anquilocs, brought from Jevlen, to adapt to artificial patterns of IR return signals resembling chiff evasion responses. The changes written into the configuration of circulating electrical currents in the brain as a permanent imprint of the learned behavior could then be identified and mapped by the established techniques of neutral psychoto-pography.

But the molecule that they were studying represented a step far outside the bounds of familiar terrestrial biology. It was created in specialized cells of the anquiloc's nervous system and carried a chemical encodement of the changes recorded in regular memory. Acting as a messenger, it transported the code to the reproductive cells, where it was copied into the animal's genetic control molecules as they replicated. Hence, it provided the equivalent of reprogrammable DNA.

Danchekker went on, "The possibilities of further evolutionary refinement of such an ability are intriguing. For example, can you imagine—" The call-tone from the terminal on a table by the far wall interrupted him. "Damn. Go and see to the wretched thing, would you, Sandy?" he muttered.

The girl got up, crossed the laboratory, and touched a key to accept the call. A woman's face appeared on the screen, mid-fortyish, perhaps, with hair tied straight back in a matronly fashion that added to her years. She had a long, sober face with beady dark eyes, high cheeks, and a large nose, and stared out with a commanding sternness.

"Is Professor Danchekker there, Ms. Holmes?" Her voice was shrill but firm, brooking no nonsense. "It is *most imperative* that I speak to him."

"Oh, God," Danchekker groaned, over by the imager console. It was Ms. Mulling, the personal secretary who had come with his appointment as director of Alien Life Sciences, calling from her domain in his outer office on the top floor, from where she ruled the building. Danchekker shook his head and made frantic to-and-fro motions with a hand to indicate that he had spontaneously evaporated off the planet.

But the movement in the background over Sandy's shoulder only caught Ms. Mulling's attention. "Ah! You are there, Professor. The budgetary review meeting is due to begin in M-6 in thirty minutes. I presumed that you would want reminding." She rolled the *r*s and spoke with as much of a hint of disapproval in her voice as a personal secretary with a strict sense of propriety could permit.

Danchekker rose from the console and advanced toward the terminal, stopping halfway across the floor as if wary of too close a proximity, even to an image. Sandy withdrew discreetly out of the viewing angle. "Can't Yamumatsu deal with it?" Danchekker asked irritably. "He understands convertible assets, depreciation ratios, and other such intricacies—*I* am only a scientist. I spoke to him this morning, and he said he'd be happy to substitute."

"It is customary for the departmental director to chair the quarterly review," Ms. Mulling replied in a tone as yielding as the hull armor of a battleship.

"How can it be customary?" Danchekker challenged. "The department is new. The division itself is barely six months old."

"The precedent derives from UNSA Corporate standard procedures, which predate the new organizational structure and have not been changed." Ms. Mulling's eyes moved up and down to take in his full length. "What on earth are you doing in *those*?" she demanded before Danchekker could respond. Following her gaze, he looked down at his feet. To save time getting to a black-tie dinner that evening which he had been unable to evade, he was already wearing evening dress underneath his lab coat—except for his shoes, which were of white, rubber-soled canvas.

"What do they look like?" he riposted. "They are popularly referred to, I believe, as sneakers."

"I know. But why are you wearing them with evening dress?"

"Because they are comfortable, of course."

"You can hardly appear at the Republican Society dinner like that, Professor."

The light glinted off Danchekker's spectacles and teeth. "Madam, I have no intention of doing so. I shall be changing them before I depart. Do you wish me to produce my patent leather pair from the closet and show them to you as proof?"

"That won't be necessary, thank you. But such a combination wouldn't be appropriate for the review meeting, I'm afraid. After all, both the deputy financial comptroller and the executive vice-president of planning will be attending."

Danchekker stood before the screen, seeming to crouch in the attitude of some scrawny bird of prey, his lab coat hanging from his hunched shoulders like a vulture's wings and his fingers curling by his sides like talons, as if he were about to pounce on the terminal and tear it to pieces.

"Very well," he granted, finally conceding. "Would you kindly arrange for the agenda, and whatever figures I might need, to be ready for me to collect?"

"I've already seen to it," Ms. Mulling replied.

Ten minutes later, Danchekker exploded through the door into Caldwell's office high up on the far side of the complex. "You've got to do something!" he insisted. "The creature isn't human. Can't you transfer her to one of the Martian bases or a deep-space mission probe? I cannot continue with my work under these conditions."

"Well, maybe it doesn't matter too much anymore," Caldwell said over his interlaced fingers. "Something else has come up, and—"

"*Doesn't matter!*" Danchekker stormed. "I'd sooner be married to one of the Gorgons. The possibility of retaining any modicum of sanity at all is utterly out of the question."

"I talked to Vic yesterday afternoon. He's probably been looking for you. There's—"

"The situation is preposterous. Now I'm even being subjected to dress inspections, for God's sake. I am adamant: She has to go."

Caldwell sighed. "Look, transferring her wouldn't be so simple. She was with Welland for thirteen years and came with his personal recommendation. He might be retired, but he still has a lot of pull through the old-buddy net. It could cause complications—especially at a time like this, when we've got all kinds of people looking for career opportunities and slices of the new action."

"I have no interest in the adolescent attention-seeking antics and Machiavellian inanities of other people. If this woman—"

The door opened and Solomon Cail from the public-relations office appeared. "Oh . . . excuse me, Gregg. I didn't realize. Mitzi thought you were alone."

"I was away for a couple of minutes," Mitzi's voice called from outside.

"It's all right, Sol," Caldwell said. "Chris just stopped by. Is it something urgent?"

"As a matter of fact, it was Chris that I wanted to talk about," Cail said.

"Me?" Danchekker looked suspicious. "What for?"

"Senator Greeling's wife has been onto us again. It's this women's discussion group that she runs. We've as good as promised them a tour of the alien-life-form labs, and she wants the director to look after them personally—mostly to impress her friends, I guess." Cail shrugged and showed a palm. "I know it's a drag and all that, Chris, but Greeling did a lot of work for us, getting the college sponsorship program through. We don't want to upset a friend like him if we can help it. She'd like an afternoon next month, maybe?"

"God help us," Danchekker moaned bleakly.

A call-tone sounded in the outer office. Mitzi answered, and a moment later Ms. Mulling's voice rang stridently through. "Is Professor Danchekker there, by any chance? He has an imminent appointment, and it is *most imperative* that I find him."

And then Hunt appeared in the doorway on the far side of Mitzi's desk, carrying a sheaf of papers in one hand and a cup of coffee in the other. "Hello, what's going on here? Ahah, Chris! Just the man."

"Sol, give us a minute, would you?" Caldwell said, at the

same time relieving Cail of any choice in the matter by rising and coming around the desk to steer him back toward the outer office. He waved Hunt in and closed the door behind him, holding up a hand to stay Danchekker before Danchekker could start talking again. "Yes, I've been aware of the problem for some time, Chris. But we needed a tactful solution that wouldn't create more hassles than it cured."

Danchekker shook his head and waved a hand impatiently. "I'm being turned into a club treasurer. We've got enough tally clerks and ledger keepers who can take care of that kind of thing. I was under the impression that this establishment was supposed to be dedicated to the advancement of the *sciences*. I've seen more—"

"I know, I know," Caldwell said, nodding and raising a hand. "But something's come up that—"

"Now they want to make me a tour guide for women's tea-party outings. The whole thing has become farcical. It's a—"

"Chris, shut up," Hunt interrupted calmly. "Delegate the lot. That's what being a director is all about. You haven't got time, now, anyway. Gregg's got an off-planet assignment for the two of us."

"And not only—" Danchekker stopped abruptly and sent Hunt a questioning look. "Off-planet? Us?"

Caldwell grunted and nodded at Hunt to continue.

"On Jevlen," Hunt said. "There's a Thurien ship in orbit that's due to go back there shortly. Just think of it: a whole planetful of alien biology, literally light-years away. I think that a director of life sciences should be breaking new ground in the field, don't you?" But it was clear already that Danchekker needed no further convincing. His expression had the rapture of a revivalist seeing light through the parting of the clouds.

They came out of Caldwell's office a few minutes later. "I think we're going to have to come up with some other arrangement," Caldwell said to Solomon Cail, who was still waiting. "Chris is going to be tied up on a priority project." He indicated the door of his office with a nod, and Cail disappeared inside.

Danchekker strode over to the terminal where Mitzi was still holding Ms. Mulling at bay. "Ah, *there* you are, Professor," the image on the screen began. "The review meeting—"

"Find Yamumatsu and get him there," Danchekker said. His voice rang with the newfound confidence of the reborn. "Also, contact the secretary of the Republican Society and give them my apologies, but I shall be unable to attend. Maybe Yamumatsu would like to stand in for me there, too."

For a few seconds Ms. Mulling was too shocked to reply; she stared back at him from the screen, open-mouthed, like a mother superior who had just heard the Pope proclaim his conversion to atheism. She recovered herself falteringly. "I don't understand . . . What's happened? Is something wrong?"

"Wrong?" Danchekker repeated lightly. "Not at all. Quite the contrary, in fact. Effective immediately, I shall be preoccupied with other matters. Have Brady come to my office, would you? Get out all the plans, charts, budgets, and other wastepaper that holds up the walls over there, and tell him he'll be deputized as from tomorrow morning. I"—Danchekker spread both hands in a careless throwing-away motion—"shall have flown."

Ms. Mulling looked confused. "What are you talking about, Professor Danchekker? There are urgent things to be attended to."

"I have no time for anything urgent. There are too many *important* things to be done, instead."

"But—where are you going?"

"To Jevlen. Where else can a science of alien life be practiced?" Danchekker lifted a leg to dangle a sneaker-shod foot in view of the screen and waggled it provocatively. "Far, far away, Ms. Mulling. Beyond the horizons of imagination of the entire Republican Society, the verbal compass of a gaggle of senators' wives, and even, if you are capable of comprehending such a thing, beyond the reaches of the sacred *UNSA Corporate Procedure Manual.*"

"Jevlen? Why? What are you going to do there?"

But Danchekker wasn't listening. Hunt and Mitzi could hear him singing tunelessly to himself as he ambled away down the corridor beyond the open door.

"Far, far away. Far, far away . . ."

Chapter Ten

E arth's physicists were having to do a lot of rethinking to accommodate the new facts brought by the Ganymeans. Some of the most far-reaching revelations had to do with the fundamental nature of matter itself.

As some Terran scientists had suspected and been investigating without conclusive result since the late twentieth century, the permanency of matter turned out to be just another illusion to be thrown overboard with such notions as classical predictability and absolute, universal time. For all forms of matter were continually decaying away to nothing, although at a rate immeasurably small by the techniques so far available on Earth—it would take ten billion years for a gram of water to vanish completely.

The fundamental particles of which matter was composed annihilated spontaneously, returning to a hyperrealm governed by laws different from those that operated in the familiar universe. It was the tiny proportion that was disappearing at any instant that gave rise to the gravitational effect of mass. Every annihilation event produced a minute gravity pulse, and the additive effect of large numbers of these pulses occurring every second gave the apparently steady field that was perceived macroscopically.

Hence, gravity ceased being a thing apart in physics, a static effect, passively associated with a mass, and fell instead into line along with other field phenomena as a vector quantity generated by the rate of *change* of something—in this case, the rate of change of mass. This principle, together with means of artificially inducing and controlling the process, formed the basis of early Ganymean gravitic engineering—the drive system used by the *Shapieron* was an example of its application.

Small though it sounded, such a rate of disappearance was not trivial on a cosmic time scale. The reason there was much of the universe left at all was that, throughout the entire volume of space, particles were constantly being created spontaneously, too. And in a converse way to that in which particle-annihilations induced gravity, particle-creations induced "negative gravity." Since a particle could only disappear from where it already existed, extinctions predominated inside masses and induced an attractive curvature into the local vicinity of space-time; but in the vast regions of empty space between galaxies, creations far outnumbered extinctions, and the resultant effect was a cosmic repulsion. It all made a rather tidy and symmetric, satisfying kind of sense.

A fundamental particle, therefore, appeared, lived out its allotted span in the observable dimensions of the known universe, and then vanished. Where it came from and where it returned to were questions that the scientists of Earth had never had to face, and which even the Ganymeans on Minerva at the time of the *Shapieron*'s departure had only begun delving into. It was their subsequent work in this direction that had given the Thuriens the technologies that made possible their interstellar civilization.

The hyperrealm that particles temporarily emerged from was the same domain that matter-energy entered when it disappeared into a black hole. That an object no longer continued to exist where it had when it entered a black hole, Terran physicists had known theoretically for some time. Therefore, it had to be either somewhere else in the known universe; or in another universe; or, conceivably, in some other time. Logic admitted no other alternatives. Remarkably, it turned out, all three were possible. The Thuriens had realized and applied the first two; they were still looking into and puzzling over the third.

An electrically charged, rapidly spinning black hole flattened into a disk and eventually became a toroid with the mass concentrated at the rim. In this situation, the singularity existed not as an impenetrably screened point, but as the central aperture itself, which could be approached axially without catastrophic tidal effects. Through a symmetric effect, creating such an "entry port" also gave rise to a coupled projection elsewhere in normal space, at which an object entering the aperture would appear instantaneously by traversing what had come to be known as "h-space." The location of the "exit port" depended on the dimensions, spin, orientation, and certain other parameters of the initial toroid and could be controlled up to distances of several tens of light-years. That was how the Thuriens moved their craft between stars.

The energy to create the toroids was directed through h-space by colossal generating systems located in space, consuming matter from the cores of burnt-out stars. However, to avoid causing orbital perturbations and all the attendant disruptions, the ports were never projected into planetary systems, but well away in the surrounding voids. To travel between planetary surfaces and the h-space ports, the Thurien ships used an advanced form of the more conventional gravitic drive pioneered by their ancestors on Minerva. Even so, a complete interstellar journey was typically measured in days.

Since the Thurien starships also drew power from the same h-space distribution grid that supplied the energy to create the transfer ports, they could be quite modest in size. Others were huge. The roughly globoid *Vishnu*, twenty miles across, was of intermediate size.

Three days after Hunt and Danchekker talked with Caldwell, they were part of a mixed group that boarded one of the *Vishnu*'s daughter craft at Andrews AFB, Maryland. Hunt's deputy, Duncan Watt, had joined the group as hoped, and so had Sandy Holmes from Danchekker's lab at Goddard.

It was all as simple and informal an affair as Hunt had expected. The Thurien crew offered them soft drinks or coffee and invited them to take a seat. Each of the arrivals was also issued with a communications device in the form of a small, flexible disk, about the size of a dime and looking like a Band-Aid, that self-attached behind the ear. It was a connection to VISAR, operating via relay from the mother ship orbiting twenty thousand miles overhead. By coupling directly into the wearer's sensory neural areas, the communicator could, upon command, convey to VISAR what was seen, heard, or spoken; in the reverse direction it could inject information from VISAR, which the wearer would experience as hearing and vision. It thus afforded not only instant access to the ship's system, but also person-to-person communications with other Terrans, as well as to Ganymeans through VISAR acting as interpreter.

"Welcome back," the computer's familiar voice said, seemingly speaking in Hunt's ear. "I take it you're getting restless again."

"Hello, VISAR. Well, you seem to be offering a more stylish service these days." The first vessel that the Thuriens had sent to make initial contact had landed at a disused Air Force base in Alaska and, to evade the Jevlenese-managed surveillance operation, had been built to resemble a conventional Terran aircraft.

"We like to keep the customers happy," VISAR said.

The ferry craft took off shortly afterward. Barely ten minutes later, it entered the immense composition of soaring hull structures and sweeping metallic surfaces curving away for miles on every side that made up the outer vista of the *Vishnu*. It entered a brightly lit cavern of projecting docking structures that looked like the Manhattan skyline stood on its side, and berthed alongside another of a fleet of daughter vessels of every size, shape, and description.

Some of the Thurien crew conducted the party through the access ramps and antechambers into a high space with wide corridors leading away on either side and overlooked by several levels of railed walkways. More Thuriens were waiting, scattered about. It seemed to be a terminal area for transportation links to other parts of the vessel, but exactly what one was supposed to do to get there was far from immediately obvious.

The starship manufactured its own internal gravity, creating "up," "down," and transitions between in whatever direction suited the purpose from place to place. The result was an Escherian confusion of corridors, shafts, intersecting planes and spaces, and surfaces that served as walls here, floors there, and elsewhere curved to transform from one into another. What had previously been below could unexpectedly appear overhead without one's experiencing any sense of having rotated, and through it all, streams of Ganymeans were being carried along in open conveyor shafts on directed g-field currents—rather like invisible elevators traversing the ship in all directions. Hunt and Danchekker had seen this kind of thing before, but the others around them were stopping and staring in bewilderment.

"Well, Chris, here we go again," Hunt said, looking around. "But this will be a darn sight quicker than last time."

"And a bit more comfortable when we get there, too," Sandy Holmes murmured in a slightly dazed voice as she struggled to take it all in. She had been with them on the UNSA *Jupiter Five* mission. When they had joined that ship, before its lift-out from lunar orbit, the voyage ahead of them had been six months, and the accommodation waiting at the other end of it had been cramped quarters in the subsurface part of a scientific base situated on Ganymede's ice sheets, with the constant vibration of machinery and an ever-present odor of hot oil.

"Yes," Danchekker agreed. "And I recollect being adamant at the termination of that escapade that I would never set foot inside one of these contraptions again." He sighed. "However, the designers responsible for this accomplishment would appear to have been from a different school from their terrestrial counterparts, whose imaginative limits one must suppose to have been set by experiences with submarines and tanks."

"And it will get you far, far away a lot faster," Hunt reminded him.

"Hmm, there is that."

Duncan Watt did a quick mental calculation. "Something like seventy million times faster, in fact," he said. He was thirty-two, with a ruddy, vigorous complexion and thick, jet black hair. He had the rugged kind of looks that made Hunt think of him as belonging more on a football field or in a boxing ring than in a mathematical physics lab.

Near Duncan were a man and a woman accompanying a group of teenagers, who at that moment were standing motionless in awe. "This is a unique moment in the history of the universe," the man muttered, moving a step closer and nodding his head to indicate his charges. "It's the first time ever that this bunch have all been quiet at the same time."

Duncan grinned. "Who are they?" he asked.

"A class of tenth-graders going on vacation. I'm still not really sure how it happened. Somebody at the school came up with the idea as a joke, and the Ganymeans said sure, no problem. Goddamnedest thing I ever heard of."

Then VISAR said to Hunt, "You have a reception committee waiting for you." From the change of expression on Danchekker's face, Hunt knew that VISAR was talking to him, too.

"Where?" Hunt asked.

"The two officers standing a bit to your left."

Hunt looked around and saw the Thuriens whom VISAR had indicated already moving forward. The millions of years that separated the Ganymeans of Minerva, as typified by the *Shapieron*'s complement, from the Thuriens had produced visible differences. Although of the same general pattern, the Thuriens were darker, almost black, more slender, and on average slightly shorter. The two who had been waiting were clad in loose-fitting green tunics, each with a halterlike embellishment of elaborately woven metallic threads hanging on either side from the neck to the waist.

"Dr. Hunt? Professor Danchekker?" one of them inquired.

"That's us," Hunt confirmed.

"My name is Kalor, and this is Merglis. We are here on behalf of Captain Fytom to welcome you aboard the *Vishnu*."

"It seemed fitting that you should be given a personal greeting," the other explained.

They shook hands—the Terran custom had come to be generally accepted. Hunt introduced Sandy and Duncan.

"The captain sends his compliments," Kalor informed them. "He is aware that your visit to Jevlen is to study Ganymean science. If any of the *Vishnu*'s specialists can be of assistance during our brief voyage, consider them at your disposal."

"Very considerate of him," Danchekker replied. "Convey our thanks. We will certainly bear his offer in mind."

"You are also invited to view the command center once we are under way," Kalor said. "But just at the moment things there are a bit hectic, as I'm sure you'll appreciate."

"Whenever is convenient. Yes, we'd like that very much," Hunt answered.

"Are we invited, too?" Sandy asked hopefully.

"But naturally," Kalor told her.

"I think we pick the right people to go traveling with," Duncan said.

"For now, we'll take you to the section that has been reserved for Terran accommodation," Kalor said. "Since it looks as if Terrans are going to become regular passengers on these trips, we're making it a permanent feature of the ship."

He led them over to a platform jutting out into a broad, elongated space, lower than the area they had just crossed, arched at intervals by sections of bulkhead that glowed with an internal amber light, and dividing to left, right, above, and below into smaller tunnels and shafts radiating away in all directions.

Sandy looked uncertainly at the platform as Kalor gestured. "What do I do?" she asked.

"To take a tube anywhere, just climb aboard," Merglis said. "VISAR will take you to your chosen destination." So saying, he stepped off the platform and hung suspended on an invisible cushion of force.

"It couldn't be simpler," Kalor said, gesturing again.

"Just what we need under New York," Hunt told her.

Sandy drew a breath, then shrugged resignedly and followed after Merglis, who was floating a few feet from the platform, waiting for them. One by one the others did likewise, with

Kalor bringing up the rear, and seconds later they found themselves being carried into the labyrinth as a group, close enough together to be able to talk easily. The field molded itself comfortably around their bodies. They entered a wide, vertical shaft walled by tiered galleries, which somehow transformed itself into an avenue of shining walls and huge windows of what seemed to be stores of every kind, amusement centers, offices, and eating places. It resembled an enclosed city street more than anything Hunt had ever pictured as a thoroughfare inside a spacecraft. Then they came out into a larger, open space like a plaza, but three-dimensional, with concourses and floors going off at all angles, and he completely lost what little sense of direction he had managed to retain. Like a bushman grappling with a modern-day city, he didn't have the conceptual knack for interpreting the geometry.

But when the party arrived at the Terran section of the ship, they found that the layout there confined itself to one recognizable plane where "up" was up and stayed that way, and everybody walked. There were reassuringly familiar sleeping cabins, a cafeteria modeled on the facilities in UNSA's mission ships, and a common mess area, complete with bar and white-jacketed bartender. And the chairs, tables, and other fittings were made to human proportions, not Ganymean.

Each of the passengers had a personal suite located along a corridor a short distance from the mess area and consisting of a bedroom, a sitting area with robot kitchen unit, and a bathroom, "I trust these will be comfortable enough for the two days," Kalor said, showing Hunt his quarters.

"They'd be comfortable for months," Hunt assured him.

"Very good. Then we'll be in touch later for you to meet Captain Fytom and his staff. Is there anything else we can do in the meantime?"

"I don't think so . . . is there, Chris?" Hunt looked at Danchekker.

"No—oh, there is some equipment that we'll be taking with us. But then I suppose that if it hasn't all arrived, there's not much that can be done about it now."

"If you think of anything, just let VISAR know," Kalor said.

He turned to Danchekker. "Your cabin is this way, Professor."

The door closed, leaving Hunt alone to unpack his few items of carry-on baggage and inspect the surroundings. The suite was spacious and comfortable. A bathrobe and slippers were provided. There was a dish of fruit on the table, including some strange forms that Hunt did not recognize as terrestrial, some candylike concoctions, and a box of his regular brand of cigarettes.

"Nothing to drink, VISAR?" he murmured, selecting one of the cigarettes. "Tch, tch. The service is slipping. I'd have expected a six-pack of Coors and a bottle of Black Label at least."

"In the cold compartment, below the autochef," VISAR replied.

Hunt sighed. As usual, the Ganymeans had thought of everything.

Chapter Eleven

Hunt was still in his cabin a little over an hour later, poring over an English translation of a Ganymean introductory text on the properties of i-space. In the realm beyond the transition boundary represented by the aperture of an entry port, the usual relationships of time and space were reversed: instead of three spatial dimensions and a unidirectional dimension of time, there existed three time dimensions in which it was possible to move freely, and a single spatial direction along which movement could only be one-way. Hunt was still struggling to visualize what that might mean when VISAR informed him that the TWA shuttle from the West Coast had docked. Shortly afterward, Gina called to say that she was aboard the *Vishnu*. VISAR presented her as a head and shoulders superposed into Hunt's visual system against the background of the cabin.

"Welcome aboard," Hunt greeted. "I see you've got your Thurien communicator."

"It's incredible."

"I didn't hear from you, so I assumed everything was going smoothly," Hunt said. In fact, Mitzi, Caldwell's secretary, had checked discreetly to make sure that Gina was booked on the flight.

"It was a busy couple of days, but it went the way you said. You didn't warn me that this would be like walking into a kaleidoscope."

"You get used to things like that with the Thuriens."

"Who else did you manage to get along, finally?"

"Chris Danchekker, as hoped. And we've got two others: Duncan Watt, my deputy from Houston that I mentioned; and the other is one of Chris's lab people, a girl called Sandy Holmes. She was with us on Ganymede."

"It didn't work out too badly after all, then?"

"Not badly at all, considering the time we had. But we can talk about all that when you get here."

"So where shall I meet you?"

"There's a lounge with a bar here, where the Terrans' quarters are. I'll see you there after you've gotten straightened out."

"How do I get there?"

"VISAR will take care of it."

"Fine." The face vanished.

Hunt spent a few more minutes grappling with Ganymean notions of dimensionality, then left the cabin and went along to the mess area. A good crowd had collected since he passed through with Danchekker and the others. He threaded his way through to the bar and ordered a Scotch. The bartender's name tag told him that the facility was provided by the Best Western hotels group.

"Tell me, Nick, how does your company come to have a bar installed in an alien starship?" Hunt asked as he watched the drink being poured.

"Oh, they figured there'll be a pretty regular traffic building up, I guess. Probably not too much volume right now, but the publicity's good."

"How did they get the franchise?"

"Just asked for it, as far as I know."

Even with his knowledge of Ganymeans, Hunt was surprised. "As easy as that? Wasn't there a big scramble with the competitors?"

"Not really. I don't think anyone else thought of it."

Hunt moved away, shaking his head. Snatches of conversation from around him caught his ear as he moved through the throng with his drink.

"Think how many people from Earth will be there, say, a year from now. I tell you it'll be a gold mine . . ."

"*Ja.* Unt der tourists, also dey vill be going. Ve haff plans."

"They just need to be told about Jesus."

"Just checkin' out the scene there, I guess. Shit, it's gotta be better'n Cleveland . . ."

Hunt found an empty table near a far corner and sat idly watching the company. He wondered how many more of them had also come to be there on no better authority or without any higher dispensation than just having asked. If that was a foretaste of things to come, then a large part of the meddlesome systems of rules and restrictions by which one half of the world made it its business to approve, regulate, license, and control how the other half lived could collapse in shambles or be laughed out of existence, he reflected.

It was funny, he thought as he watched, how many of the people talked too fast among themselves as they strove to act normally while suppressing what was probably the greatest excitement most of them had ever experienced. Appearances were so important to Terrans. Ganymeans had no defensive compulsion about maintaining images, and readily said how they felt about things. Their origins had given them no concept of domination by appearances, or any instinct for intimidation.

On one of the walls was a large display screen showing a view from the *Vishnu* of the flock of shuttles, transporters, and observer craft hanging in space around it, with Earth partly illuminated as a crescent in the background. They seemed to be drawing back, which suggested that the departure of the Thurien vessel was not far away.

"VISAR, how long now before we shove off?" Hunt inquired.

"A little under two hours."

Gina appeared in the doorway shortly afterward. Although it seemed slightly absurd and melodramatic, Hunt hoped she would play along with the act of running into him casually, as an old acquaintance. Some of the people whom Hunt had already identified in the room were among the last he would have wanted forming the notion that she was there at UNSA's instigation. To his relief, although he could tell from the glance she threw in his direction that she had seen him, she moved away toward the bar and ordered herself a drink.

He rested an elbow on the back of the seat next to him and stared at the mural display screen. A TWA shuttle, probably the one that Gina had arrived on, was pulling away, nudged by brief, intermittent pulses of its auxiliary thrusters. Its red-and-white design stood out vividly against the depthless black.

Then a man in a dark suit stopped on his way past Hunt's table, holding a glass in each hand. Hunt looked up inquiringly.

"Excuse, please. Is not the Dr. Hunt who goes to Ganymede, yes?" He sounded Eastern European.

"That's right," Hunt said.

"I hear through the grapetree that you go to Jevlen for UNSA, and recognize you from picture."

"News travels fast," Hunt commented.

The stranger bowed slightly. "Permit to introduce. My name is Alexis Grobyanin, from Volgograd Institute. Psychologist." He nodded to indicate a mixed group by the far wall. "We are sent by UN to advise Ganymeans on administering Jevlenese. Russians have much experience in handling troubleshooters."

"I got to know some Russians when the Pseudowar happened. Mikolai Sobroskin was one. Ever come across him?"

"Oh, yes. He is foreign minister now."

"That's him."

"You will be basing there in PAC?" Grobyanin asked.

"Yes, that's right."

"We, too. So maybe we see you there later. Excuse now. I must join my friends together."

"See you around," Hunt said, nodding. He leaned back again as the Russian moved away, smiling faintly as he recalled why Sobroskin had said Hunt would never have been a success in Russia. "You have too many good ideas," Sobroskin had said.

"You know what you used to get there for a good idea? At least five years."

Then another voice sounded suddenly from nearby, turning heads in the vicinity. "*Vic!*" It was Gina's. "What on Earth are *you* doing here?" Hunt had to force himself to hold a straight face until he had gone through the motions of looking up and about.

"I could say the same about you—except that 'Earth' is hardly appropriate."

"You show up in the most unexpected places."

"Who are you with?" Hunt asked loudly as she came across to his table.

"Just me," she answered, letting her voice fall to a more natural level. "I'm on a free-lance job. It's unreal . . . How about you?"

"Oh, I don't get any spare time to go gallivanting around. Regular UNSA assignment . . ." Hunt extended a hand to indicate the far side of the table. "Sit down and tell me all about it. When did you come on board?"

"Less than half an hour ago. I shuttled up from Vandenberg."

Gina settled herself in the chair opposite, and smiled warmly, just like an old friend. "It's an interesting bunch we've got here," she said, waving her hand.

"How do you mean?" Hunt asked.

"Did you know there's a bunch of kids here, going on a summer vacation from a school in Florida?"

"I didn't know they were from Florida."

"And there's a marketing group from Disney World, going to check out the tourism. Some Russians to help sort out the Jevlenese."

"I just met one of them."

"Even a holy man from Tibet or somewhere, who's heard the call of Jevlenese mysticism and came aboard this morning with some of his disciples."

"Tax problems?"

"Who knows?" she shrugged. "And directors from a corporation in Denver going to see about Jevlen for their next-year sales conference, a whole mix of ologists, a group making a movie, and a South American real-estate millionaire who's decided that Jevlen is where he wants to retire."

Hunt set his glass down and looked at her curiously. "You've only just arrived on board. How do you know so much already?"

"I took your advice and asked."

"Asked who?"

"VISAR. Apparently it doesn't occur to very many Earthpeople. VISAR thinks it's because we assume furtiveness everywhere."

Hunt had to smile. It would have come to her so naturally that he should have guessed—as naturally as calling Caldwell and saying she needed help with a book.

Gina finished her drink. "How'd I do?" she asked in a lowered voice.

"Terrific. I'm sure you've got another profession waiting if you find you've got tired of books."

"Is anyone still interested in us, do you think?"

Hunt shook his head. "We can just be natural now. If anyone gets curious later about how you got mixed up with the UNSA group, there were enough witnesses. So, forget any more Mata Hari stuff. Have you had lunch?"

"I'm still too excited about this whole business to have much of an appetite," Gina answered. "But this ship is fantastic! What do you think the chances would be of getting to see more of it while we're here?"

"Oh, pretty good, I should think." Hunt raised his voice slightly. "VISAR, could you take us on a tour around the *Vishnu*?"

"Be my guests," the machine replied.

They stood amidst stupefying constructions of gleaming metallic shapes, walls of light, and what looked like clean-cut massifs, as big as buildings, of internally glowing crystal. It was all too devoid of even a hint of anything recognizable for Hunt to form any coherent questions for VISAR of what it meant.

"You seem . . . impressed," Gina said, finding a tactful word to describe the look on Hunt's face.

His frown switched to a faint grin. "It is a bit much for one afternoon, isn't it?" he agreed. "This is all a long way past the ship from Minerva that we found on Ganymede. That was from the same era as the *Shapieron*. We thought it was pretty spectacular at the time. But compared to this it was like the boiler room of a tramp steamer."

"They produce some kind of 'stress wave,' or something, don't they?" Gina said. "A bubble of bent space-time around the ship. That's what moves through space, carrying the ship with it. Since the ship is at rest relative to the space inside the bubble, the usual speed limits don't apply."

"That's right. The rules for *space* propagating through space are different." Hunt shook his head wonderingly. "Is there anything you don't get interested in?"

"I told you, journalists are curious, like scientists."

Hunt nodded. "The *Shapieron* used a system that constrained superdense masses to move in closed paths at relativistic speeds, which generated high rates of change of gravitic potential and created a matter-annihilation zone that powered the stress field. The equipment to do it was colossal, but I don't see anything like it here. But there has to be something like it to get us out past Pluto, where the entry port will be projected for transfer to Jevlen. VISAR, how has it changed?"

"That's all done remotely now," VISAR replied. "The stress wave is generated by small converters located around the extremities of the ship and coupling into the Thurien h-space grid. The ship itself can be quite compact. Remember the one that landed in Alaska?"

"I take it this is the kind of thing you're finding out more about at Goddard," Gina said to Hunt.

"Trying to, anyway. There's a lot of it. Half the problem is getting the information organized."

"Have there been any big surprises so far—I mean, apart from the ones we've read about? You know: the universe is bigger than we thought, smaller than we thought; parallel universes are real; Einstein was wrong. Anything like that?"

Hunt looked around from the rail he was leaning on. "Well, it's funny you should mention Einstein," he said.

"You mean he *was* wrong?"

"Not wrong, exactly . . . but unnecessarily complicated, like Ptolemy's planetary orbits. It all works out a lot more simply and still agrees with the same experimental results if you take the velocity that matters as being not that with respect to the observer at all, but with respect to the local dominant energy field. The distortions of space that Einstein was forced to postulate turn out to be simply compensations for the breakdown of the inverse square law at high speeds, caused by the finite propagation speed of gravity. If you allow for that, then practically everything in relativity can be deduced by classical methods."

Gina stared at him as if unable to decide whether he was joking or being serious. "You mean everybody missed it?"

"Yes," Hunt answered, nodding. "Take the business with Mercury's perihelion, for instance. You know about that?"

"I thought that Einstein's answer works; Newton's doesn't."

"So do most people," Hunt agreed. He looked away and snorted. "But all the prestige and money for practically the last century has come for building more spectacular gadgets, not for going over the basics of physics. Do you know what VISAR found while it was browsing through some old European archives?"

"What?"

"The same formula that Einstein obtained through Riemannian geometry and gravitational tensors was derived classically by a German called Paul Gerber, in 1898, when Einstein was nine years old. It was there all the time, but everybody missed it."

The *Vishnu* was home for several hundred thousand Thuriens for periods that varied from short-term to permanent. They lived in baffling urban complexes that resembled their labyrinthine cities back home, amid simulations of external vistas beneath artificial skies, and in isolated spots enjoying the peculiarities of various landscapes, copied and contrived. Life aboard the ship combined all the functions of a complete social and professional infrastructure. The whole thing, Hunt began to realize, was more an elaborate, mobile space colony than anything conventionally thought of on Earth as a means of transportation.

"This is the kind of vessel typically sent out to explore local regions of the Galaxy," VISAR confirmed. "It might spend several years at a newly discovered planetary system."

Evidently the Thuriens liked to take their comforts with them.

Hunt and Gina sat on a boulder on a grassy slope overlooking a lake with a distinctly curved surface. There were boats on it, scattered among several islands, and on the opposite shore an intricate composition of terraced architecture that went up to the "sky." The sky was pale blue—like that of Thurien. The bushes around where they were sitting had broad, wedge-shaped, purple leaves that opened and folded like fans. According to VISAR, they could shed their roots and migrate downhill on bulbous pseudopods if the soil became too dry.

"How would you classify them?" Gina mused. "If animals move and plants don't, what are they?"

"Why does it matter what you call them?" Hunt said. "When people have problems with questions like that, it's usually because they're trying to make reality fit something from their kit of standard labels. They'd be better off thinking about rewriting the labels."

They contemplated the scenery in silence for a while.

"It's funny how evolution works," Gina said. "About ninety-five percent of all species were supposed to have been wiped out in a mass extinction that happened around two hundred million years ago. It didn't favor any particular kind of animal: large or small, marine or land-dwelling, complex or simple, or anything like that. Nothing can adapt for catastrophes on that kind of scale. So the survivors were simply the lucky five percent. Whole families vanished for no particular reason at all, and the few that were left determined the entire pattern of life subsequently." She looked at Hunt, as if asking him to confirm it.

"I don't know know too much about that side of things," he said. "Chris Danchekker's the one you ought to be talking to."

He stood up and offered her a hand. "Speaking of which, we ought to be getting back. It's about time you met the rest of the crew."

They walked down to the lakeside, where a path brought them to a transit conveyor. Soon they were being whisked back through the Escherian maze, and arrived shortly afterward at the Terran section. As they crossed the mess area, Hunt noticed that the wallscreen that had previously showed the view outside was blank. He knew that the stress wave surrounding a Ganymean vessel cut it off from electromagnetic signals, including light, when it was under full gravity drive.

"VISAR," he said aloud so that Gina could hear. "Is the ship under way already?"

"Since a little under fifteen minutes ago," the machine confirmed. Which would have been typical of the Ganymean way of doing things: no fuss or ceremony; no formal announcements.

"So where are we now?" Hunt asked.

"Just about crossing the orbit of Mars."

So UNSA might as well scrap all of its designs for the next fifty years, Hunt decided.

Chapter Twelve

At a lonely place high among the peaks of the Wilderness of Rinjussin, Thrax came to a large, flat rock where the path divided. A monk was floating in midair above the rock, absorbed in his meditations. His sash bore the purple-spiral emblem representing the cloak of the night god, Nieru. Thrax had heard that as an exercise in learning to attract and ride the currents, adepts would support themselves on currents that they generated themselves by prayer. He waited several hours until the monk descended back onto the rock and looked at him.

"What do you stare at?" Thrax asked him.

"I contemplate the world," the monk answered.

Thrax turned and looked back at the valley he had climbed, with its scene of barren slopes, shattered rock, and desolation. "Not much of a world to contemplate from here," he commented. "Do I take it, then, that your world is within?"

"Within, and without. For the currents that bring visions of Hyperia speak within the mind; yet they flow from beyond Waroth. Thus, Hyperia is at the same time both within and without."

"I, too, am in search of Hyperia," Thrax said.

"Why would you seek it?" the monk asked.

"It is taught that the mission of the adepts who rise on the currents and depart from Waroth is to serve the gods in Hyperia. Such is my calling."

"And what made you think that you would find it here, in Rinjussin?"

"I seek a Master known as Shingen-Hu, who, it is said, teaches in these parts."

"This is the last place that you should come looking for Shingen-Hu," the monk said.

Thrax reflected upon the statement. "Then my search has ended," he replied finally. "That means he must be here. For obviously he is to be found in the last place I would look, since why would I continue looking after I found him?"

"Many come seeking Shingen-Hu. Most are fools. But I see that you are not foolish," the monk said.

"So, can you tell me which path I must take?" Thrax asked.

"I can."

"Then, speak."

"One path leads to certain death. To know more, you must first ask the right question."

Thrax had expected having to give answers. But to be required to come up with the question itself put a different complexion on things. He looked perplexed from one to the other of the two trails winding away on either side of the rock.

Then he said, "But death is certain eventually, whichever path one takes. Which path must I take, therefore, to achieve the most that is meaningful along the way?"

"How do you judge what is meaningful?" the monk challenged.

"Let Shingen-Hu be the judge," Thrax answered.

"We are in troubled times. The currents that once shimmered and glinted across the night skies have become few and weak. Many come to learn, but few shall ride. Why, stranger, should Shingen-Hu choose you?"

"Again, let Shingen-Hu be the judge. I cannot give his reasons. Only mine."

The monk nodded and seemed satisfied. "You come to serve, and not to demand," he pronounced, climbing down from the rock. "Follow me. I will take you to Shingen-Hu."

Chapter Thirteen

The others had gone to take care of various chores, leaving Hunt and Gina together at the dinner table. They had all agreed to meet later in the mess area for a nightcap—or two, or maybe several.

Gina stared down at her coffee cup and unconsciously traced a question mark lightly on the tabletop with her finger. "Is it true that some of the animals on Jevlen have an uncanny resemblance to ones found in Earth's mythology?" she asked after a long silence.

Hunt had been watching her, thinking to himself that she was the most refreshing personality he had encountered in a long time. It wasn't just that she was curious about everything, which was an attraction in itself, and that she took the trouble to find out something about the things that intrigued her; she did it without making an attention-getting display of it, or taking it to the point of where it started to get tedious. Her judgment in knowing how far to go was just right, which was one of the first things in making people attractive to be around. In the course of the meal she had won the company's acceptance by refraining from thrusting herself on them, listening to

Danchekker's expositions without pandering like a student, putting Duncan at ease by not flaunting her femininity, and avoiding triggering rivalry vibes from Sandy. In fact, she and Sandy had gotten along instantly, like sisters.

"Do you know, you've never come back with a line that I expected, yet," Hunt replied.

"Seriously, I read about it somewhere. There's a kind of horned wolf with talons that's exactly like the Slavonic 'kikimora.' Another has parts of what look like a lion, a peacock, and a dog, just like the 'simurgh' of Iran. And would you believe a plumed, goggle-eyed reptile, practically identical to all those Mexican carvings?"

"I seem to remember something about it, but it isn't an area I've really looked at," Hunt said. "Why? What's the significance?"

"Oh, nothing earth-shattering. It just occurred to me that maybe that was where we got them from. Perhaps the Jevlenese agents that came to Earth in the past mixed ideas of their own animal forms into the belief systems that they spread."

"It's an intriguing thought," Hunt agreed. He stubbed his cigarette and looked across at her. "Doesn't it come into this new book that you're talking about?"

"Sure. That's why I'm interested in collecting opinions."

"When we talked back at my place, you said you thought Christ might have been one of them." Hunt paused and frowned. "No, wait a minute. It was the other way around, wasn't it. You said he was on the other side, right?"

"If he was Jevlenese, it was as a rebel working against their cause," Gina replied. "Or he could simply have been an exceptionally enlightened Terran. Either way, he wasn't working with them."

Hunt looked at her with interest as he refilled their cups from the coffeepot on the table. "What makes you say that?"

"Well, think about it. The operation that the Jevlenese set up was aimed at retarding Earth's development by implanting notions of the supernatural and starting mass movements based on irrationality. That's where early religions came from. The Lunarians didn't have anything like that."

"Yes, exactly." Hunt looked puzzled. "But isn't . . ."

Gina shook her head, reading the question. "No. He didn't. What people have been told for the best part of two thousand years is wrong. He didn't teach what the churches say he taught. What they daren't tell their followers is the one thing he *was* trying to say. You see—that's exactly the kind of thing I want to get into."

Hunt stared back curiously. "Go on," he said.

"He told people not to listen to the Pharisees, scribes, priests, or other self-important persons and institutions who were out to control them and exploit them. He taught, simply, that inner integrity and honesty were essential if you want to know yourself and the world. It didn't have anything to do with rituals and dogma, or rules for organizations. It was simply a prescription for a personal code of conduct and ethics aimed at coming to terms with one's nature and with reality. In other words, a philosophy of *individual* self-knowledge and responsibility, totally compatible with the notions of science and reason that were beginning to emerge at the time, despite all the efforts of the Jevlenese. And that, of course, made him dangerous. A threat to their whole operation." She looked pointedly at Hunt. His eyes widened. Gina nodded. "Exactly. So they got rid of him. Then they exterminated his followers, seized control of what he'd started, and rewrote the whole script."

"Giving us the Dark Ages," Hunt said, seeing the point.

"Right. Which stopped everything dead and put their program back on track. The medieval Church with its Inquisition, holy wars, land grabbing, and its involvements in European power politics had nothing to do with anything Christ taught. It was trying to stave off the Renaissance, which the Jevlenese could see coming. *Real* Christianity had been dead for centuries."

It fitted with the things Gina had said at his apartment on how things might have gone otherwise, Hunt recalled. She had done more work on it than he had realized. If a lot of powerful institutions had roots in those kinds of murky waters, he could understand why nobody was doing very much talking. At the same time, it was dawning on him just how devastating the book that she was proposing could be. Caldwell would have seen it, too. Small wonder, then, that Caldwell had declined to involve UNSA officially. The wonder was that Caldwell had been willing to have anything to do with her at all.

"Except, maybe, in one place," Gina said, making it sound like an afterthought.

"Uh?" Hunt returned abruptly from his thoughts.

"If my reading of history is right, there was one place where Christianity might have hung on long after it was stamped out across the rest of Europe," Gina said.

"Where?"

"Ireland."

Hunt's eyebrows lifted in surprise. "Begorrah!" he exclaimed.

Gina went on. "Even the Irish aren't told the true story. They're taught that Saint Patrick converted the island in the fifth century, and they've remained staunchly faithful ever since."

"That's what I always thought, too," Hunt said. "Not that it's a subject that I've ever had much reason to get involved in, especially."

"They didn't ally with the *Roman* Church until the sixteenth century—more than a thousand years later; and that was only as a gesture of defiance against the English after Henry VIII broke away. Roman Catholicism became a symbol of Irish nationalism. What Saint Patrick brought was Christianity."

"You mean the original?"

"Something a lot closer to it, anyhow. And it flourished because it fitted with the ways of the native culture. It spread from there through Scotland and England into northern Europe. But then it collided with the institutionalized Jevlenese counterfeit being pushed northward, and it was destroyed. The first *papal* mission didn't reach England until a hundred sixty-five years after Patrick died."

"How do you know all this?"

"My mother's side of the family comes from Wexford. I go there for vacations and lived there for a while once."

"When did Patrick die?" Hunt asked, realizing that he really had no idea.

"In the fifth century. He was probably born in Wales and carried across by pirates."

"So we're talking about a long time before that, then."

"Oh yes. In terms of literature and learning, they were unsurpassed anywhere in Western Europe long before Caesar crossed the Channel."

"Let me see, every English schoolboy knows that. Fifty-five B.C., yes?"

"Right. Their race was unique, descended from a mixture of Celts and a pre-Celtic stock from the eastern Mediterranean." Gina stared across the room and smiled to herself. "It wasn't at all the kind of repressive thing that people were conditioned to think of later, you know. It was a very earthy, zestful, life-loving culture."

"In what kind of way?" Hunt asked.

"The way women were treated, for a start. They were completely equal, with full rights of property—unusual in itself, for the times. Sex was considered a healthy and enjoyable part of life, the way it ought to be. Nobody connected it with sinning."

"The real life of Riley, eh?" Hunt commented.

"They had an easygoing attitude to all personal relations. Polygamy was fairly normal. And then, so was polyandry. So you could have a string of wives, but each of them might have several husbands. But if a particular match didn't work out, it was easy to dissolve. You just went to a holy place, stood back-to-back, said the right words, and walked ten paces. So children weren't emotionally crippled by having to grow up with two people hating each other in a self-imposed prison; but if the marriage didn't work out, they weren't traumatized, either, because they had so many other anchor points among this network of people who liked each other."

"It all sounds very civilized to me," Hunt said.

"And that was where early Christianity hung on," Gina said again. "So maybe it gives us an idea of what it really had to say."

Hunt watched the faraway expression on Gina's face for a few seconds, then grinned impudently. "Oh, I can see where you're coming from," he teased. "It's nothing to do with humanist philosophies at all. You just like the thought of having a string of men to pick from."

"Well, why should men have all the fun?" she retorted, refusing to be put on the defensive.

"Ahah! The real Gina emerges."

"I'm merely stating a principle."

"What's wrong with it? Don't women fantasize?"

"Of course they do." She caught the look in his eye and smiled impishly. "And yes, who knows? Maybe one day if you tell me yours, I'll tell you mine."

Hunt laughed and picked up his coffee cup. He finished the contents and allowed the silence to draw a curtain across the subject. "How are we doing for time?" he asked, setting the cup down. "Will any of the others be in the bar yet?"

Gina glanced at her watch. "It's a bit early. What else is there to see of the ship?"

"Oh, I think I've had it with being dragged around for one day. You know, I really do make a lousy tourist."

"That's too bad. I can't wait to see Jevlen. Just imagine, a real, actual, alien planet. And we'll be there tomorrow. I still haven't really gotten over all this."

Hunt looked at her thoughtfully. "Maybe we don't have to keep you waiting that long," he said.

Gina looked puzzled. "Why? What are you talking about?"

"What you just said has given me an idea . . . VISAR, are there any couplers nearby?"

"A bank of them, to the right outside the door you came in through," VISAR replied.

"Are there two free right now?"

"What are you doing?" Gina murmured.

"Wait, and you'll see."

"Plenty," VISAR replied.

Hunt stood up. "Come on," he said to Gina. "You haven't seen half of Ganymean communications yet. This'll be the fastest interstellar trip you ever dreamed of. I guarantee it."

Chapter Fourteen

The room was just a cubicle, its main furnishing being a kind of recliner, padded in red, with several panels of what looked like a multicolored crystalline material above and on either side of a concave support where the occupant's head would be. The wall behind carried equipment and fittings of unfamiliar construction.

Gina ran her eye over the interior. "I take it this is how you connect into the Thurien virtual-travel net," she guessed.

"That's right," Hunt said. He tapped the communicator disk attached behind his ear. "This gadget that they gave you when you came aboard is just a two-way audiovisual link to VISAR—a viphone that goes straight into your head instead of through screens and senses. But this is the full works."

"What they call total neural stimulation?"

"Instead of you having to go take your senses to wherever the information is, this brings the information to your senses—provided that the place you want to 'go' is wired with sensors for the system. It wouldn't work too well for Times Square or the middle of the Gobi. Also, it intercepts the motor and speech outputs from your brain, and generates the feedback that you'd

460

experience from moving around and interacting there."

Gina nodded but still looked unsure. After a few seconds, she said, "And all of that two-way information transfer takes place instantly through the same—what do you call it, 'dimension'?"

"H-space."

"That's it . . . that this ship goes through to get to Jevlen, right?"

"Yes."

"Okay . . . But the ship has to spend a whole day getting out past Pluto before it can use h-space. How come this coupler can do it from right here? Or how come you can do it from Goddard, for that matter?"

Hunt was already nodding. "A port big enough to take a ship would mess up everybody's astronomical tables if you projected it into a planetary system. So instant planet-to-planet hopping is out. But for communications it's a different matter. You can send information on a gamma-frequency laser into a microtoroid that can be generated on planetary surfaces—or in ships like this one—without undesirable side effects. The Thuriens use it for most of their routine business and social calling—and you don't have to worry about drinking the water or catching any foreign bugs. It's got a lot of advantages."

Gina moved forward and touched the material of the recliner curiously. It was soft and yielding. Hunt watched from inside the doorway. "So what do I do?" she asked.

"Just take a seat. VISAR will handle the rest."

Gina hesitated for a moment, feeling just a trifle self-conscious. Then she lowered herself into the recliner, settled her feet on the rest, and let herself sink back. A warm, drowsy feeling swept over her, causing her head to drop back automatically onto the concave support, which was also padded. She felt more relaxed than she could ever remember. The interior of the cubicle seemed to be floating distantly in a detached kind of way. A part of her mind was aware that she had been thinking coherently only moments before, and that someone else had been there for some reason, but she was unable to recall who or why, or really to care. Nothing really mattered.

"Like it?" She recognized the voice as VISAR's.

"It's great. What do I do—just lie back and enjoy it?"

"First, we'll need to register some more of your personal cerebral patterns," VISAR said. "It only takes a few seconds." When Gina had first tried the communicator disk, she had experienced a strange series of sensations and illusions in her hearing and vision. VISAR had explained that the range and activity levels in the sensory parts of the brain varied from individual to individual, and it was necessary to tune the system to give the right responses. Once established, the parameters were stored away for future reference, making the process a onetime thing, analogous to fingerprinting. Presumably VISAR now needed to extend its records to accommodate the other sensory centers, too.

Gina found herself becoming acutely conscious of the pressure of the recliner against her body, the touch of her clothes, and even the feeling of air flowing through her nostrils as she breathed. She could feel her own pulses all over, and then a weird tingling unrolling down her spine. VISAR was experimenting with her sense of touch, exercising her nervous system through its range of responses and reading the neural activity.

She felt herself convulsing in spasms—and then realized that she wasn't moving at all; the sensation was due to rapid variations of sensitivity occurring all over her skin. She felt hot, then cold, then itchy, then prickly, and finally numb. Sweet, sour, bitter, then again sweet tastes came and went in her mouth; her nose experienced a succession of odors . . . And all of a sudden, she was wide awake and alert again, and everything was normal.

"That's it," VISAR informed her. "How would you like me for your dentist?"

Gina was too intrigued by what was going on to reply, but as she waited, her brow creased in puzzlement. It didn't seem as if anything much *was* going on.

She sat up and found Hunt still standing in the doorway, leaning one shoulder against the side, arms folded, watching her curiously with an odd smile twisting his mouth.

"Can I get up now?" she asked him.

"Sure."

She put her feet on the floor, sat upright, and stood cautiously, not quite knowing what to expect. Nothing changed. Everything felt normal.

"So, what happened?" she asked uncertainly. "Technical hitch?"

"You think so, eh?"

"You mean it worked?"

"Thurien engineering works. That's one thing you never have to worry about."

"But . . . we're still in the ship. I thought we were supposed to be going to Jevlen."

"No. You're falling into the illusion already. *Virtual* travel, remember? You knew you weren't *really* going anywhere."

Gina put a hand to her brow and shook her head. "Okay. Let's not start getting picky about words. You know what I mean. I thought that sensory information from Jevlen was supposed to be coming to me."

"VISAR, give us a preview," Hunt instructed.

At once, Gina and Hunt were standing in a wide, circular space like a gallery, overlooking a central area below. There were figures walking this way and that, some human, some Ganymean. As Gina stared, a small group consisting of two Ganymeans surrounded by a half-dozen or more humans gesticulating and seemingly talking all at once passed close by. Although the conversation was presumably being conducted in an alien tongue, the snatches that came through were transformed into English.

". . . thousands of them, with nothing to do. They must be entertained. You have to arrange something."

"Why can't they learn to entertain themselves?" one of the Ganymeans asked, sounding harassed.

"They have always been entertained. It is their *right!*"

Gina looked at Hunt disbelievingly. He grinned back at her, clearly enjoying himself. "Let's take a walk," he suggested, and led the way across to the rail at the gallery's edge. Gina's mind was in too much turmoil for her to do anything but follow mechanically.

They looked down over a concourse of various levels and partly enclosed spaces, where more figures were standing or sitting, walking, and going about their business. The concourse appeared to connect to other spaces beyond, and had pedestrian avenues entering from several directions. The architecture was unusual, with generous use of curvature and asymmetrical divisions of space that blended strange notions of aesthetics and ornamentation with what was clearly a functional purpose. Gina's first thought as she began to recover her reeling senses was of a Moorishly inspired airport terminal. It was all definitely very futuristic, and unquestionably alien . . . but it did keep itself tidily to definite planes, without assaulting the eye with anything resembling the geometric chaos of the Thurien spacecraft.

But as she continued looking, a puzzling aspect of it all registered itself. For what was supposed to be a glimpse of an advanced, technologically adept culture, it was all rather shabby. The finishing on the elaborately styled shapes and surfaces was drab and unimaginative, with a general air of wear and neglect and tiredness. There were lights that weren't working, panels missing from one of the walls, and on the far side a whole, partly dismantled section closed off by barriers, with machines that looked like maintenance robots standing idle.

Hunt indicated a direction with his hand, and they began walking around the gallery toward a series of low arches on its outer edge. The figures around them passed by unheeding. Gina had to remind herself that she was merely perceiving what was taking place at a distant location; the people who were actually there had no knowledge of her "presence."

Beyond the arches was a semicircular, windowed space, an eating lounge of some kind, with seats and tables on several tiered levels. Again, the surroundings were plain and utilitarian. The figures, human and Ganymean, took no notice as Hunt and Gina descended a stepped aisle to a clear area along the window wall, which turned out to be a continuous expanse of glass. That was when Gina realized that the sky was not blue, but light green, with strange, curling, sheetlike clouds of streaky orange.

The city beneath the pale green sky extended away and below them in waves of interconnected towers, terraces, and heaps of architecture that at first defied comprehension. But then Gina noticed that one of the bridges nearby was missing two of its central spans; a tower beyond it was showing daylight through its windows and seemed to be a derelict shell; below them, a terraced roof had had several sections removed and was open to the elements.

Finally she looked back at Hunt.

"Believe it now?" He waved a hand casually. "Shiban, one of Jevlen's principal metropolises."

Gina moved forward to take in more of the view and saw, through a gap between two of the structures, a tall, streamlined shape standing upright in what appeared to be an open space, possibly beyond the edge of the city proper. Although the bottom part of it was obscured, she had seen enough pictures to recognize it. "Isn't that the *Shapieron*?" she asked, indicating with a motion of her head. It was the Ganymean spacecraft from ancient Minerva. If anything, the nose was still some way below the level they were looking out from— and the *Shapieron* stood almost half a mile high.

"Shiban is where the *Shapieron* is currently berthed," Hunt replied. "It's at a place called Geerbaine, just to the west of the city. The place we're in is Garuth's Planetary Administration Center. It used to be the governing center for this region of Jevlen. We can't go any farther without resorting to simulation, because this is the only part that the Thuriens adapted for VISAR—Jevlen was managed by JEVEX, which had slightly different sensor wiring. But anyhow, welcome to another world. What do you think?"

Gina stared outside again. She rubbed her brow with a knuckle and shook her head, then looked back at Hunt. "No . . . this still doesn't make any sense. How can I be seeing Jevlen through VISAR, if I'm not coupled into VISAR?"

The strange smile, which had never quite left Hunt's face, broadened. "Aren't you?"

"Well, no . . . I got up out of the chair and talked to you. I— oh, Vic, stop looking at me like that. Tell me what's going on."

And then, just as abruptly as before, she was standing inside the cubicle in the Thurien starship again, with Hunt facing her from the doorway, just as they had been before the transition.

"It's simple," Hunt told her. "If VISAR can make us think we're walking around on Jevlen, it can just as easily make us think we're standing here in the ship."

It took a few seconds for the meaning of what he was saying to sink in. "You're kidding!" Gina breathed incredulously. Hunt shook his head. She ran a finger experimentally down the edge of the doorframe. It felt cool and hard and solid. There was even a burr at one place, where something had scratched it.

"Hold out your hand," Gina said. Hunt obliged. She ran a finger along one of his and traced it over the palm. It felt warm and fleshy, with each line and wrinkle in the skin clearly discernible. "It's uncanny," she whispered.

"Not bad," Hunt agreed. "What you saw a moment ago is what's happening in a part of Shiban at this moment. Those people are really there. VISAR is very good at realism." Hunt pointed at a spot on her arm. "You've even got the stain on your sleeve, where you rubbed your elbow in some ash that had fallen on the table when we were in the cafeteria."

Gina looked at the sleeve of the green sweater she was wearing, and flicked at the gray patch with her other hand. Sure enough, most of it brushed away, leaving a faint smudge, just as real ash on a real sleeve would have done.

Hunt laughed. "There's an easier way. In this world, you can do anything you want. VISAR, clean the sleeve." The remaining discoloration vanished, leaving no trace. "Or change the whole thing if you don't like it. VISAR, how about a red sweater?" Gina's sweater promptly changed to a rich ruby red.

She gasped. "It's true! This is all happening inside my head? I'm not really standing here? So aren't you here, either?"

"Of course not. I'm inside your head, too. So I must be hooked in through another coupler, just as you still are."

Gina struggled to come to terms with the meaning of it, but in the end faltered and shook her head decisively. "It's no good. I can't believe this. Prove it."

"I can't. Ask VISAR to."

"VISAR. Prove it."

And instantaneously she was back in the recliner, at ease and comfortable, as if she had never gotten up from it.

"Voilà," VISAR announced, managing to sound quite proud of itself.

As Gina's confusion subsided, she reminded herself that she never *had* gotten up. She had been here all the time . . . or had she? Was she really here now, or was this yet another construct in the maze of mirages that Hunt had led her into? She sat up with a strange feeling of déjà vu—only this time, Hunt wasn't standing watching from the doorway, and the door was closed. Her sweater was green again; the smudge of gray was back on her elbow. It was all as the real thing should have been, but there was no way of telling. If this was another illusion, she could see no purpose in it. Anyway, it seemed she had no option but to go along. She moistened her handkerchief and cleared the smudge from her sleeve.

"Where's Vic?" she asked aloud.

"Next door, to the right."

Gina got up and moved to the door. She opened it, let herself out into the corridor, and peered into the next cubicle. Hunt was in repose in the recliner there, motionless with his eyes closed.

"Happy now?" VISAR asked her.

Okay, it was good enough for her. "Convinced, anyhow," she conceded.

"Never say I don't give you your money's worth."

Hunt opened his eyes and sat up. "Neat, eh?" he said to Gina. "Just think, you could go anywhere in the Thurien world-system right now if you wanted to. Imagine what that saves them in a year on bus fares."

"Right now, you only need to worry about getting back to the lounge area," VISAR said. "The others are there, and they're asking where you are."

"Tell them we're on our way," Hunt answered,

Chapter Fifteen

Twelve hours after leaving Earth, the *Vishnu* was five hundred million miles past the mean orbit of Uranus.

By the internal clocks of most of the passengers it was the small hours of the morning, and the mess area of the Terran section was quieter than it had been earlier. Gina and the four from UNSA were still up, occupying a couple of tables pulled together, where they had been joined by the schoolteacher from Florida, whose name was Bob, and two of the Disney World marketing executives, Alan and Keith.

"Wasn't there something about an ancestor of modern horses?" Duncan Watt was saying to Danchekker. "It had stripes, suggesting that striping could be an inherited potential of all horse types. So there really isn't any such group as zebras at all? They could all be more closely related to the horse lines than to each other." They were talking about the investigations that Danchekker had conducted on specimens of early mammals from Earth's late Oligocene period, which had been discovered in the wrecked Ganymean ship found on Ganymede, before the *Shapieron*'s appearance.

"Mesohippus," Danchekker supplied. "Yes, indeed—which

makes it not as complex a characteristic as one might imagine. Several separate lineages could then have acquired stripes independently, which would make the zebras simply realizations of a developmental path common to all members of genus *Equus.* It becomes even more interesting when one considers the chromosome counts, where a distinct correlation is seen to occur between . . ."

Duncan nodded as he sat with his arms wedged across his chest. He looked a little glazed and seemed content to let Danchekker carry on doing the talking.

Across the other table, Bob, the teacher, and the two Disney World executives were into politics.

"Maybe Ganymeans are instinctively what socialist idealists try to turn humans into," Bob said. "But since it comes naturally to Ganymeans, nobody has to try and *make* them anything they're not. So it works."

"He's got a point," Al declared, turning to Keith. "We're a competitive species—a competitive economic system fits our nature. Whether you like the thought of it or not, we work for what *we* are gonna get out of it, not the other guy. That's the way humans are. The only way you can try to change them is through force. And people don't like that. That's why all these fancy ideas about molding human nature don't work. They *can't* work."

Sandy pushed herself back in her seat and yawned. "I've just had three hectic days that I think have caught up with me," she announced. "Sorry, but I'm going to be the first one to break up the party. So I'll see you people tomorrow, wherever. The other side of Pluto, I guess."

"Yes, get some rest," Danchekker said. "I should, too, for that matter. You've certainly been busy. We didn't give you much notice."

"Don't forget that chip you wanted me to borrow," Gina reminded her as she stood up.

"If you want to stop by my room, I'll let you have it now," Sandy said.

"What chip's that?" Hunt asked, turning from the conversation between Danchekker and Duncan.

"Some tracks of Jevlenese music that I collected together," Sandy said. "Some of it's really wild stuff."

"Vic likes music," Gina said as she rose. "I don't know if what you're talking about would be his style, though. That was a Beethoven score that you had pinned up on the wall at your place, wasn't it, Vic?"

"Observant," Hunt complimented. He took a sip of his drink. "Did you know that his dog had a wooden leg?"

Gina looked uncertain. "Whose?"

"Beethoven's. That was where he got his inspiration—when it walked across the room." He raised a hand to conduct an imaginary orchestra. "Dah-dah-dah-*dah* . . . Dah-dah-dah-*dah*. See?"

Gina shook her head, smiling hopelessly. "Are all the English insane? Or did you take a class in it?"

"Come on, let's go," Sandy murmured. "They're all past the crazy hour."

"No, but you have to work at it," Hunt said. He waved a hand at them both and grinned. "We'll see you two at breakfast, then." The rest of the group added a chorus of goodnights.

Gina and Sandy left the room and headed toward the cabins. "Guys and alcohol," Gina said. "I didn't want to be left that outnumbered."

"I know the feeling," Sandy agreed.

"Are we turning into old maids, Sandy?" Gina asked jokingly. "Six men back there, and the two girls leave together. Perhaps we really are as bad as they tell us."

"You speak for yourself. I meant what I said: I'm exhausted."

"Duncan was giving you looks."

"I know."

"Not your type?"

"Oh, Duncan's okay. We've known each other since Houston. But you know what they say about keeping the complicated side of life separate from your work. I think it's good advice."

They reached the door of Sandy's cabin, which she opened with an unvoiced command to VISAR. Inside, she picked up a briefcase, set it on the bureau top, and took out a flat box of the kind used for carrying storage chips. "How about a coffee before you go?" she asked Gina.

"Why not? Make it black, no sugar."

"Anything else to go with it?"

"Uh-uh. Dinner just about filled me up."

Sandy asked VISAR for two coffees. "Ah, here's the one I was talking about," she said, handing Gina one of the capsules from inside the box. "I've got another with some of their classical stuff, but I don't think it's here. I must have left it at home. It's a bit weird, anyhow."

"Thanks. This'll be fine." Gina put the capsule into a pouch in her purse.

The door of the dispenser in the kitchen area opened, and a tray bearing two mugs slid out onto the countertop. While Sandy was replacing the briefcase, Gina picked up the mugs and carried them over to a table in the lounge, where she settled herself into one of the easy chairs. Sandy followed a few moments later.

"So, how about the romantic side of your life?" Sandy asked as she sat down in the other chair. "Or are writers always too busy to have one?"

"Oh, now and again, when it wants to happen. But nothing . . ."

"Entangling?"

"Right. I don't want complications getting mixed up with my work, either. But with me, work and life keep having this tendency to become the same thing."

Sandy tasted her coffee. "Not bad." She looked up. "Were you ever married?"

"Once, awhile ago now—for about four years. We lived in California. But it didn't work."

"What happened? Did you see yourself heading toward oblivion on Domesticity Street?" Sandy gave Gina a critical look over the top of her mug. "Somehow I can't picture you taking pies to garden parties or selling Tupperware."

Gina smiled distantly. "Actually it was more the opposite. Larry was the kind of guy who wanted to go everywhere, do everything. You know, always meeting new people, the life of every party . . . It was fine as long as I was content to tag along as an accessory in *his* life. The problem was, it didn't leave any room for me to have one of my own."

"You should have introduced him to me," Sandy said. She made a motion with her free hand to indicate herself. "It's nice in some ways to work surrounded by scientists and all kinds of other guys who are smart, but there's an incredible number of nerds among them. You know the kind—they think a hard-on's some kind of quantum particle."

Gina had to stifle a scream of laughter. "Vic doesn't seem like that, though," she commented.

"He's an exception. Now him I could go for. Maybe it's the accent. But like I said, it's not the thing to do. Anyhow, he got tangled up with somebody when we were at Houston, before the division relocated to D.C., and nowadays he likes to keep his daytimes uncomplicated, too."

"You, er, don't exactly come across as the epitome of detached, intellectual science," Gina said.

"Give me a break. I spent a year and a half down a hole in the ice on Ganymede. That's a lot of time to make up for. Vic said something once about not wanting to get old with a lot of regrets about missing out. I agree with him."

Gina, watching the way Sandy's straight, dark brown hair fell about her face as she leaned forward to pick up her cup again, noticed the firmly defined features and the long lines of the jeans-clad legs. Sandy was the kind of girl that men had told her radiated sex appeal without being especially pretty, Gina decided. Intelligent, adventuresome, and uninhibited. Definitely Larry's type.

Sandy looked up. "Anyhow, scientists are supposed to be curious, aren't they? Like journalists. Isn't that what the job is all about?"

"I suppose so," Gina agreed.

Back in her own cabin, Gina found herself restless and not inclined toward sleep, despite the time she had been awake. Lurking just below the level of consciousness, something that she couldn't pinpoint was disturbing her, something tugging for attention, distilled from the day's flood of events and experiences. She went into the bathroom and brushed her teeth while she grappled with the problem.

It had something to do with VISAR. More specifically, it had something to do with the way VISAR was designed to function. Back in the bedroom, still fully dressed, she propped herself up with a couple of pillows and stared at the picture of a snowy mountain scene from some world or other, on the far wall of the room.

The part of the PAC complex on Jevlen that she had "visited" with Hunt earlier in the evening had contained such objects as ornaments and pictures on the walls of the cafeteria from where they had seen the *Shapieron*, and some tools standing against a wall in the gallery outside. What would have happened, she had asked Hunt, if she had tried to "move" one of those objects to a different place? He had said that VISAR would cause her to experience the action faithfully. In that case, she asked, where would she find it when they arrived physically at Jevlen tomorrow? Obviously, where it had been in the first place, Hunt replied—since the object would never have really been moved at all.

That bothered her. She remembered, too, the burr that she had felt on the edge of the door into the coupler cubicle, and the business with the cigarette ash on her sleeve. It all bothered her. She got up from the bed, went back into the lounge to get a cup of hot chocolate from the autochef, and tried to fathom why.

Judged by Terran notions of what constituted worthwhile return for cost and effort, the whole thing seemed a pointless exercise in elaborate absurdity. More than that: a deception that confused synthesis with reality, leaving the recipient to disentangle the resulting fusion that would be left impressed upon memory. But the Thuriens could handle it naturally, without conflict or contradiction. Indeed, to *them*, in a way that no human could really feel or comprehend, the capturing of the actuality was all-important, and the degree to which the system failed to do so constituted the deception. Hence their extraordinary obsession with levels of detail that to humans would have served no meaningful purpose and made no sense.

And now, she felt, she was getting closer to what was troubling her.

Yes, the Thuriens were benign, nonaggressive, and rational, and that was all very nice; but it was also beside the point. What was less reassuring, she realized, was the utter *alienness* that she had glimpsed of the inner workings of the Thurien mind. The professionals like Hunt and Danchekker had been too close for too long, and were too excited by the technology, to see it. Or perhaps they had forgotten.

What kind of havoc, then, might have been wreaked on the collective psyche of a whole race immersed in a form of mind manipulation essentially alien to its nature for thousands of years?

She turned and stared at the door, uncertain for several seconds of exactly what she intended to do. Then, resolving herself, she left the cabin again and returned to the cubicles containing the Thurien neural couplers.

Chapter Sixteen

The familiar feeling of warmth and relaxation closed around her as she eased back into the recliner and VISAR's intangible fingers took control of her senses.

"Tell me again how these Thurien protocols on privacy work," she said in her mind to the machine. "What's to stop you going deeper than just accessing sensory data, and extracting anything you want out of my head?"

"Programming rules built into the system," VISAR answered. "They confine my operations to processing and communicating only what users consciously direct."

"So you don't read minds?"

"No."

"But you could?"

"Technically, yes."

"I don't think I like that. Doesn't the thought of it bother the Thuriens?"

"I can't see why it should, any more than the thought of a surgeon seeing your insides organically."

"No? But then I guess you wouldn't. You were designed by them, so you think the way they do."

"Possibly so."

"Can the rules be broken?"

"It would require a specific authorization from the user for me to override the directive. So the user is always in control. Anyway, what would someone have to hide?"

Gina could not contain a laugh. "Don't the Thuriens ever have thoughts or a side of their nature deep down that they try to hide, even from themselves?"

"How could I know? If they do, then by definition they don't reveal it."

Really? Gina thought. Ganymean minds might be capable of such commendable self-discipline, but she doubted if a typical human one would. "Were the Jevlenese as sensible and restrained in the way they used JEVEX?" she asked.

"I suspect not," VISAR answered.

"So, what can you do, VISAR? I want to know what this system is capable of."

"I can take you anywhere you want to go. Anywhere among thousands of Thurien worlds, natural and artificial, scattered across tens of light-years."

"How about Thurien itself, then?"

This time there were no preliminary sensory disturbances. Gina found herself at the edge of a terraced water garden near the summit of an enormous tower. The view below was of a cascade of levels and ramparts, falling away and unfolding for what must have been miles to blend with a mind-defying fusion of structures stretching to the fringe of a distant ocean. There were numerous figures around her, all Ganymean, walking and talking, others sitting around and doing nothing. She felt a faint breeze, and she could smell the blossoms by the pools and waterfalls. There were flying machines in the sky.

"Vranix," VISAR informed her. "One of Thurien's older cities."

The sudden transition made Gina feel dwarfed by the scale of everything. It took her a few seconds to adjust. "This is the way it actually is, right now?" she said. "These people are really there?"

"They are," VISAR confirmed. "But since they're not neurally coupled into the system, you can't interact with them. You're simply perceiving what actually is. This is called Actual Mode."

"What else is there?"

"Interactive Mode. You're in the same setting, but superposed on your perception of it are visual representations of other users physically in couplers located elsewhere. The images are activated by voluntary signals picked up from the speech and motor centers of their brains, so they act as they would choose to. The converse is just as true, of course; i.e., they see you in the same way. Hence the illusion of actually being there and interacting is total. It's the usual way of setting up social and business meetings."

"Switch to that, then," Gina said.

The scenery stayed the same, but the distribution of figures changed. Most vanished, and others appeared where none had been before. The overall number seemed to be fewer.

"Those other people that I saw a moment ago, they're still there really?" Gina asked.

"They are. I've simply edited them out of the datastream into your visual cortex."

"So who are these people that I'm seeing now? Where are they?"

"Here, there, in different places. They're simply people who happen to have chosen this venue at the moment, for whatever their purpose is."

The flying machines were still there, Gina noticed. She wondered how VISAR decided the boundary between edited foreground and authentic background.

Then a Ganymean couple who had been sitting on a nearby seat got up and approached. "I hope we're not being presumptuous, but we've never seen a Terran this closely before," the male said.

Gina noticed that several of the other figures were looking across at them discreetly, and trying not to make it too obvious. "No . . . that's fine," Gina replied falteringly.

"Permit us to introduce ourselves. My name is Morgo Yishal. This is my daughter, Jasene. We like to meet here from time to time. Our family lived in Vranix when Jasene was young. This was one of her favorite places."

"Where are you now—if it's not a rude question?" Gina asked, still off-balance from the strangeness of it all.

"Oh, I'm teaching on the other side of Thurien now," the man replied.

"I'm on a vessel that's orbiting a world nearer to Earth than Thurien," Jasene said. "Maybe I could show you it sometime. It's quite an interesting place. And you?"

"Me? Oh, on one of your starships, traveling from Earth to Jevlen."

"What brings you to Vranix?" Morgo inquired. "Seeing a Terran alone like this is most unusual."

"Nothing special. I'm just experimenting with the system, really."

"Of course, I can superpose Actual and Interactive modes," VISAR's voice interjected. The figures that had been present initially reappeared, mixing the "real" ones with VISAR's virtual creations, and in moments Gina had lost track of which were which.

"Er, would you excuse me?" Gina stammered to the two Ganymeans. "I need time to absorb this. I'm still getting used to it."

"But of course," the man answered.

"VISAR, it's too crowded. Get me away from people." Gina glanced at Jasene. "I'll get back to you about that visit . . . And thanks. I assume VISAR has your number?" Jasene inclined her head in what Gina hoped was an understanding nod.

Then Gina was standing on a barren, rocky ridge, looking down into a huge crater of molten magma, dull red and turgid, bubbling sullenly below yellow vapor and oily smoke. She could feel the heat on her face, and a choking, sulfurous odor seared her throat. The far rim was invisible through the haze, and behind her a tortured landscape of jagged peaks and bottomless fissures vanished into banks of dark, stormy cloud.

"I can take you where you couldn't survive physically," VISAR's voice said. "Here's a new world being born. The heat and fumes that you feel are just to give the flavor. In reality you'd be asphyxiated instantly, roasted in seconds, and flattened under two tons of body weight."

"This doesn't make sense. Do the Thuriens actually put sensors in places like this? It's crazy. How many visits does it get in a thousand years?"

"Actually, this is largely simulation—interpolated from data being captured long-range from orbit."

"Too hot and stuffy," Gina pronounced.

Then she was in a sea of fantastic, mountain-size sculptures of shining white, rising and curving into delicate pinnacles against a sky of pale azure, fading into pink lower down in every direction. "A wind-carved ocean of frozen methane, not much above absolute zero in temperature," VISAR said. "Again, interpolated reconstruction by instruments in orbit. Cool enough?"

"Too much. My bones feel cold, looking at it. But you don't *have* to use sensor data at all, do you? It could all be pure simulation?"

"Sure—I can make you a world. Any world."

"Let's go home, then. How about Scotland? I've always wanted to go there but never have. I imagine it with mountains and lochs, and little villages tucked away in glens."

She was sitting on a hillside by a rocky stream, looking across a valley over the tops of pine trees at green slopes topped by craggy bastions of gray rock. Off to one side, rooftops and a church spire huddled together before an expanse of water. Birds were chirping and insects humming. The air was cool and moist with spray from the stream.

"Is this real?" Gina asked, frowning. It couldn't be, she told herself. Scotland wasn't wired into VISAR.

"No," VISAR answered. "It's just something I made up—from what you said and what I know about Earth. I told you, I can make any world you want."

"It's too modern," Gina said, studying the offering. "The road down there is built for automobiles. I can see power lines by the houses, and there's a tractor in a tin shed." She could feel herself being carried away by the novelty of it all! Perhaps she was feeling a sense of relief in being back among surroundings that she understood. "If we're getting into fiction, let's go back a bit and make it more romantic," she said. "Maybe somewhere around Bonnie Prince Charlie's time."

"Those times weren't really very romantic," VISAR observed. "Most of the people lived lives ravaged by disease, poverty, ignorance, brutality. Three-quarters of the children died before they were—"

"Oh, shut up, VISAR. This is just a game. Leave that kind of stuff out, and make it the way we like to pretend it was."

"You mean like this?"

The. roadway turned into an unfenced cart track, while the power lines, tractor, communications dishes, and other signs of the twenty-first century disappeared. The houses changed into simpler affairs, with roofs of thatch and slate, and a steel footbridge crossing a brook below transformed into an arched construction of rough-cut stone. A dog was barking somewhere. As stipulated, everything was neat and pretty.

For a few moments Gina was astounded, even though she should have had a good idea by now of what to expect. She stood up, staring hard and consciously going through all the impressions being reported by her senses. She could feel a pebble under her shoe, and a branch from a bush beside her brushing her arm as she moved. It was uncanny. The sensation of being there was indistinguishable in any way that she could find from the real thing. Her clothes felt unusually heavy and enveloping. She looked down and saw that she was wearing a shawl and an ankle-length skirt of the period.

She was curious again. "Is there any reason why I shouldn't look around?" she asked.

"Go ahead." .

She followed the stream down to a path that joined the cart track. It led to the outskirts of the village. There was a small marketplace with stalls and crude, wooden-shuttered shops displaying meat, vegetables, dairy produce, all plentiful and fresh, fabrics and linen, pottery and pans. And there was a cast of players to complete the scene, correct in character and role: farmers, merchants, tradesmen, housewives; gentry on horse-back, a miller with a cartload of sacks, a jolly-faced innkeeper, two Highlanders in kilts, and children, rosy-cheeked and well fed, playing around doorways.

All of it crushingly bland, empty, and uninteresting. It came across as a not very imaginative stage set, populated by moving pieces of scenery added to finish the effect. Which, indeed, was what the inhabitants were.

Gina stopped by a gray-haired old man sitting on a doorstep, smoking a pipe. Alongside him was a sleepy-looking, black-and-white collie. "Hello," she said.

"Aye."

"It's a fine day."

"'Tis an' all."

"This looks like a nice place."

"It's no' sa bad."

"I'm not from around here."

"I can see that."

Gina stared at him. His gray eyes twinkled back at her with good-humored, imbecilic indifference as he continued puffing his pipe. Her frustration turned to exasperation. "I'm from three hundred years in the future," she said.

"We dinna get vera many o' those around here."

"VISAR, this isn't going to work," Gina flared. "These are just dummies. Don't they know anything? Don't they have anything to say?"

"What do you want them to say?"

"Use your imagination."

"It's *your* imagination that matters."

"Well, can't you figure it out from whatever you see in my head?" Gina demanded.

"I'm not *permitted* to," VISAR reminded her.

"Okay, then, I'm permitting you. Go by whatever you find. Don't take any notice of the things we humans fabricate to fool ourselves."

This time the transition was not quite instantaneous.

There was music, muted to a background level. Gina found herself clad in a plain but gracious, classically styled gown. It felt deliciously light and sheer. She was standing among others in a reception room of a large house. It was a solid, mature house, dignified but not pretentious, with high, paneled rooms, lofty gables, and intricately molded ceilings, and it stood by

the sea. Across the hall was her library, and off the landing at
the top of the curving stairway, the office where she worked,
with its picture window framing a rocky shoreline. How she
knew these things, she wasn't sure. But she smiled inwardly
and gave VISAR full marks. Yes, it was a kind of life that she had
sometimes conjured up in her daydreams.

The room that she and her guests were in had tall windows
with heavy drapes, a fine marble fireplace, and furnishings in
character. Above the fireplace was a crest, showing arms: uni-
corn and lion rampant, and a fleur-de-lis surmounted by . . . a
shamrock. The music, she realized, was Celtic harp and flute.
But from the dress of those present, and as she knew, somehow, anyway, the times were modern.

The words from one member of a group of people talking
nearby caught her ear. "Ah, yes, but it would have been a different thing if this country hadn't overcome its internal squabbles
and resisted the English." The speaker, a roundly built man
with thinning hair and a pugnacious bulldog jaw, stood holding
a cigar in one hand and a brandy glass in the other. He spoke
with an English accent; his voice had a rasping tone and a hint
of a lisp. "Ireland might even have gone solidly over to Rome
when Henry VIII went the other way."

"Oh, impossible!" one of the listeners exclaimed.

"Seriously. Purely out of defiance. Then who knows what
we might have seen today? The Reversion might never have
happened, and England could conceivably have dominated
the Irish Isles. Then, America might have been started by
some kind of Protestant, Puritan, monogamy cult. Then
where would all of the freedoms be that we take for granted
today?"

Gina stared in sudden astonishment as she recognized the
speaker. It was Winston Churchill, one of her favorite historical figures.

The glowering, stormy-faced man with thick side-whiskers,
sitting talking with two women on a sofa facing the fire, was
Ludwig van Beethoven.

Shaken, Gina moved her head to take in others. "*Nein*. Zat
is not really true, vat zey say. Only two ideas do I haff in my

life, unt vun off zem vass wrong." Albert Einstein was talking to Mark Twain.

"Don't misunderstand me. I abhor war as much as anyone—more than most, I suspect. But the reality is that evil people exist, who can be restrained only by the certainty of retaliation . . ." Edward Teller, nuclear physicist.

"Let's face it. Most decisions that matter are made by people who don't know what they're talking about." Ayn Rand, to someone who looked like Mencken.

Another voice spoke close behind her. "Splendid to see you again, Gina. Doubtless dinner will be up to the usual standard." She turned, now feeling bewildered. It was Benjamin Franklin, easily identified even in his dark, contemporary suit and tie. He leaned closer to whisper. "Tell the secret. What are you surprising us with this time?"

"Er, venison." Gina found that she had a complete set of pseudomemories: deciding the menu; consulting with the caterers; planning the seating. The picture of the dining room was clear in her mind.

"Wonderful. One of my favorites. And my congratulations on the new book. It's bound to raise a few hackles, but somebody needed to say it. Nothing could be more obvious than that individuals are *not* equal. They differ in size, shape, speed, strength, intelligence, aptitude, and in the disposition to better themselves. Of course, the opportunities to all should be the same. But to demand equality of results as a right is absurd. Since it is impossible for anything to grow beyond its inherent potential, the only way of achieving it would be to cut all trees down to the size of the shortest."

Amazingly, Gina knew exactly what he was talking about. "I'm glad you agree," she said, forcing a thin smile.

Franklin leaned forward again and covered his mouth with a hand. "Ayn is livid that *she* didn't write it. You ought to try and find some way to console her."

"I'll bear it in mind," Gina promised, pulling herself together at last and managing a conspiratorial smile.

"Good . . . And how are your husbands? Well, I trust?"

Husbands?

"VISAR, what does this mean?"

"You tell me."

Heads turned toward the door. Gina followed their gaze. A lithe, athletic figure, resplendent in tuxedo and evening dress, had appeared and was beaming at the company with arms extended wide. He had piercing blue eyes, a droopy mustache, and hair that fell in yellow waves to his shoulders. "We thank all of you for coming. Dinner will be just a few minutes. Meanwhile, enjoy yourselves. Feel that this home is all your homes." Appreciative murmurs came from around.

Gina gaped at him with a mixture of disbelief and confusion. He came over to her, assured, confident, mocking behind the laughing eyes, and offered his arm. "Excuse us. May I have my wife back?" he said to Franklin.

"But of course." Franklin bowed his head and moved back. They moved away.

"What are you doing here, Larry?" Gina hissed.

"*You* brought me here. I'm just obliging."

"I don't believe you."

"Believe yourself, then."

"Why do you always insist on acting like an asshole?"

"Why did you marry an asshole?"

"That was a long time ago. It's been over between us for years."

"Only because you made it that way."

"We weren't suited."

"Wrong. We could have had fun. You had the curiosity, but you didn't know how to handle it. So you turned the problem into something else."

"I don't know what you're talking about," Gina told him.

"Oh no? Come on, you're not really interested in listening to this bunch all night. Let's move the night along."

The reception room and the guests vanished. Larry was dominating the situation, the way he always had. Gina started to rebel, the way she always had. Why had it always had to be his way?

They had been transported upstairs to the master bedroom. Larry's jacket and tie hung on a chair, and he was standing by her. Another of his wives was lying propped against pillows on the bed. She smiled invitingly, her breasts and legs outlined through a thin, white robe that contrasted with her dark hair. Larry grinned at Gina challengingly. Despite herself, she felt an excitement rising inside her.

The woman stretched out a hand. "It's only a dream, Gina. We can do anything we like. Haven't you always been curious about everything?"

Gina felt Larry's arm slide around her waist. She pulled back. "No, I don't want this."

"Oh, but you *do*." VISAR's voice said from somewhere distant.

"Get me away from here!"

And Gina was back in the coupler cubicle. She tore herself up from the recliner and fled into the corridor. Farther along, she passed Alan and Keith, who were just leaving the bar; she did not even see them. They exchanged baffled looks, shrugged, and continued on their way.

Ten minutes later, her chest was still thumping as she sat on her bed, smoking a tranquilizer. Yes, she thought. She had a pretty good idea of what could have deranged a planetful of Jevlenese. Small wonder that half of them seemed to have lost touch with reality.

Chapter Seventeen

In a rocky hollow below the mountainside, Thrax stood before the Rock of Decision, staring at the stone pillar that rose almost to the level of his head and concentrating his inner energy into his hand as he held it before him. To one side, the Master, Shingen-Hu, looked on impassively, while the three other initiates of the school sat watching from behind and the monks stood in a silent circle, projecting sympathetic thought rays.

"Believe now," Shingen-Hu told him. "There must be no holding back. Let no part of you doubt."

This had to be the moment of complete faith. Thrax focused all the effort that he had learned to muster. His hand glowed, then shone with an inner light.

"Now!" the Master commanded.

Thrax drove his hand against the solid rock. The rock yielded, and his hand passed through. He held it steady, inside the pillar, feeling the strange sensation of directed energy coursing through him, and the exhilaration of matter being subordinated to his will.

The power was starting to ebb. If he faltered now, the rock

would rematerialize with all the crushing force that bound its particles together. Gathering his remaining strength, he passed his hand slowly sideways, causing the rock to part before and reconstitute itself behind, flowing over him as if it were water, until his hand emerged unscathed from the other side of the pillar. The glow flickered and died. Exhausted but ecstatic, Thrax stood while Shingen-Hu placed across his shoulder a sash bearing the emblem of the purple spiral. He then moved to take his place among the new adepts on one side of the circle.

Later, when the rites were over, the new adepts sat facing the Master across a hearth of stones in which a fire had been lit. From the night sky above, Nieru looked down upon his own. A few filaments of currents traced their lines toward it— Thrax had learned to see them by now. In earlier times, the longer-established monks said, to the eyes of an adept the entire vista of the skies had writhed and twisted in fantastic patterns of glowing currents.

"What shall we find in Hyperia?" one of the novices asked the Master. Shingen-Hu had seen the visions borne by the currents.

"It will happen suddenly," Shingen-Hu answered. "You will emerge as a new being, a being born to the ways of Hyperia. All will be new and strange."

"Is it true that madness lurks to afflict the unwary?" another asked.

"There are risks. You will be tested. The being which thou art must subdue the being which thou strivest to become. Madness indeed lies in wait for those who ride up on the currents, but whose training is not complete. Beware those of divided minds, whom the conflict rages within. Seek strength from Nieru when troubles assail."

"What?" Thrax queried. "Does Nieru exist, then, even in the world beyond Waroth, also?"

"Seek his sign of the purple spiral," Shingen-Hu replied. "For that shall be the sign under which his followers gather. Know then that these are thy kind, and let that be the source of thy strength."

"And will they teach us of the Hyperian magic?" the next asked.

"Hyperia will teach you its own magic."

"Magical laws?" Thrax said. "Artifacts that repeat? Objects that spin?"

"Artifacts beyond your wildest imaginings," the Master answered.

"Everywhere? So does Hyperian magic extend over the whole world?"

"The whole world . . . and places far beyond, and across the voids between. Hyperians journey among many, magical worlds."

Chapter Eighteen

Ayultha, the leader of the Jevlenese cult that called itself the Spiral of Awakening and used the device of a purple spiral as its emblem, had come to Shiban. It was the same Ayultha who had led the demonstration in the city of Barusi on the southern continent, which had led to Garuth's calling Hunt.

The SoA had been founded over two hundred years previously by a woman called Sykha, a hitherto unheard-of office clerk who had undergone an abrupt personality change. The sect's basic creed was an involved doctrine of reincarnation, which held that the individual developed through a series of "phases" of existence on successively higher planes, each one representing a step farther along a transition that progressed away from the purely material and mechanistic, and toward the spiritual and willful. The series of lives experienced in this universe, or plane, therefore added up to merely the preparation that was necessary to proceed to the next phase. Everybody had thus lived in other, lower phases in other forms before emerging into the realm of existence as presently perceived, and after a number of cycles at the human level, which could vary and depended on how diligently the SoA's teachings were attended to and practiced, they would go on to enter higher ones. The early theoreticians of the movement had given it all a scientific-sounding basis by tying it in to the transitions of physical particles between h-space and normal space as described by the physics of the Thuriens.

The initial appearance of Ayultha to the faithful at the start of his tour of the Shiban area would also be the first event to be held in the arena of a just-completed sports complex, west of the city, next to the three-level highway connecting the center to the spaceport at Geerbaine. The complex had been built at their own initiative by a combination of public and private Jevlenese agencies since the Ganymean takeover of the planet's administration. Thus, it had come to symbolize the policy of self-help that the Ganymeans were trying to encourage.

To insure adequate public recognition of the success of the venture, a formal opening ceremony had been scheduled to precede the commencement of the Spiral of Awakening rally. However, because of a sudden illness resulting from a toxic mold that was found unaccountably to have contaminated the cheese in a salad served for his lunch, Shiban's chief of police would not be attending as planned. Instead, his place would be taken by his deputy, Obayin.

On the day before the opening, a gray limousine pulled off the high-level throughway and halted on an unfinished access ramp overlooking the approaches into the sports complex.

Scirio, who ran the syndicate's operations on the west side and in Shiban center, motioned with a hand to indicate a slender, two-lane, flying bridge curving away from the mid-level trafficway below and connecting into a delivery area on one side of the two main buildings at the front of the complex, between the arena and the dome housing the gymnasium.

"It works like this," he said to Grevetz, the regional boss, who was sitting next to him in the rear compartment. "Ten minutes before he gets here, a truck breaks down on the main ramp up to the front entrance."

"They're not gonna be letting any trucks up through there," Grevetz declared. "Not when the big names are due to show up. It'll be sealed off."

"Special delivery of stuff they'll need for the born-again concert that's starting afterward," Scirio said. "We've got a pass for the driver. And just to be sure, the captain who'll be in charge of traffic duty tomorrow has been fixed to make sure it's let through. He's on the payroll."

Grevetz nodded unsmilingly. "Okay. Then what?"

Scirio pointed. "The other front ramp up from ground isn't finished yet. So he'll be diverted up to the middle level and routed over that bridge. It's the only other way in from this side right now."

"Okay."

Scirio shrugged. "The job was done in too much of a hurry. The Ganymeans were more interested in getting nice pictures in the papers instead of letting the contractor concentrate on getting the job right." He indicated the center section of the bridge, which was of metal construction, supported by canti-levers projecting from pylons on one side. "Tonight some people are gonna make a few changes underneath there. The wrong kind of some sorta pins that they use got ordered, and only half of 'em were put in. So that whole section comes unstuck." He waved a hand at the drop below, which went down past the ground-level trafficway and into the cutting where a ramp emerged from a cross-tunnel. "It's over a hundred feet straight down onto concrete. Plus he'll be going down in the middle of a hundred tons of junk. There won't be enough left of him to fill his shoes. Everyone writes it off as just another screwup."

Grevetz studied the layout in silence for a while. "How are you going to stop some other bozo from going across there first?" he asked at last. "The opening isn't due until ten-thirty. Whoever does the job will have to be out by six at the latest. That's four and a half hours."

"The Ramp Closed sign will be lit from midnight on. A tech down a hole turns it off just before Obayin gets there. Plus there'll be a construction barrier set up across the entry until he's on his way."

Grevetz nodded that he was satisfied.

Later that day he met with Eubeleus, the Deliverer, at a house in Shiban that the Axis of Light owned, and went over the plan with him. "It is going to be busy there tomorrow morning," he warned. "More people could get hurt."

"Most of whom will be purple," Eubeleus replied. "So if a few of them are in the wrong place, Ayultha should be grateful to us. We'll be giving him some martyrs."

Chapter Nineteen

So much had been new and strange. It seemed impossible to the *Vishnu*'s Terran passengers as they passed through the ship's docking bays to board the surface lander that only two days had passed since they had come aboard and seen their first views inside the Thurien starship. They had reentered normal space something like twenty Earth hours previously, five thousand million miles from Jevlen's parent star, Athena, and were now riding in high orbit above the planet itself. Kalor and Merglis, the two Thurien officers who had met the UNSA group on their arrival, reappeared to see them off. Hunt and his group had taken up their invitation to visit the *Vishnu*'s command center after breakfast on the second day.

The craft that carried them down to the surface was a silent, flattened, gold ovoid, with an interior more like a hotel lounge area than a passenger cabin—nothing that the Thuriens did took much heed of conserving space. Alan, one of the marketing executives from Disney World, sat across from Danchekker for the descent. "That VISAR system is something else," he said, making conversation. "It's incredible. We ought to think about getting something like that into DW."

One of the schoolchildren from Florida, a girl of about twelve, with freckles and braces, was listening from a seat nearby. "It can make you think you're as small as an ant and see everything from that size," she told them.

"Yeah. It's real neat," the boy next to her opined.

"You see. The kids really go for it," Alan declared.

"Hmm." Danchekker considered the suggestion. "Well, as long as you don't try and make the world simply the way it is at our level, but merely scaled down in size," he conceded. "I presume the intention would be to inform rather than mislead."

"How do you mean?" Alan asked, frowning.

Danchekker took off his spectacles and examined them. "Simply by the fact of getting smaller, an object's volume, and hence its weight, decreases much faster than its area," he explained. "Hence its bulk becomes a negligible factor, and its surface properties rule the style of its existence—an elementary fact, but one which is apparently beyond the ability of our illustrious creators of popular movies to grasp."

"That's a good point," Bob, the teacher, said from somewhere behind. "See, kids, we're getting something useful out of this trip already."

"I don't get it," the girl said.

"It's the reason why insects can walk up walls and lift many times their own weight," Bob told her. "There's nothing miraculous about it."

"At such sizes, the gravitational force which dominates at our level of perception is insignificant," Danchekker said, always ready to deliver to any audience. "One's experiences would be shaped entirely by adhesion, electrostatic charge, and other surface effects. So if you were reduced to such a size and wore a coat, for example, you wouldn't be able to take it off. Walking would be entirely different because of the negligible storage of energy in momentum. Hammers and clubs would be quite useless for the same reason." He looked at Alan. "I trust you take my point?"

"Er . . . yes," Alan said. "I guess we'd have to give that some thought."

Hunt was sitting by Gina, who had been unusually reticent since breakfast. She seemed disturbed or confused about something.

"Some people do things in style," he commented, although his attempts all morning at being sociable had met with little success. He put it down to a delayed reaction to the stress and the strangeness after three days of her not having a moment to think. "The first time I went on an extraterrestrial trip, it was just a hop across the backyard to Jupiter. *You* get to go light-years."

A smile flickered across Gina's face but didn't stay put. "Well, you know us Americans: always going to extremes."

They landed at the spaceport of Geerbaine, which adjoined a regular airport on the western outskirts of Shiban. The reality of actually setting foot on another world seemed to dispel whatever had been hanging over her, and her spirits revived. She said farewell to the two Thuriens who had escorted them down, and stood with Hunt for a while, staring back through a glass wall in the disembarkation ramp at the shining, half-mile-high tower of the *Shapieron*, which they had glimpsed from afar the day previously, through VISAR.

"Just imagine, that was traveling between stars before our kind even existed," Gina said. "It's one thing to read about it and see pictures of it. But to stand this close and know it's really out there . . ." She left it unfinished.

"You sound as if you're feeling more yourself again, anyhow," Hunt said. "I was starting to get a bit worried."

She sighed. "I suppose I have been a bit weird all morning. Everything's all so new, I guess. I'll get over it."

Hunt looked around and across the arrivals area, where groups and individuals were milling around. Danchekker, Sandy, and Duncan were standing near the Florida school party, talking to two hefty, clean-cut, broad-shouldered men in gray suits who put Hunt in mind of Dick Tracy. A short distance away, a woman in a maroon tunic with gold trim and buttons seemed to be collecting together a party that already included Alan and Keith from Disney World, the directors from the Denver corporation, a honeymoon couple that the

UNSA team had met at breakfast, who were celebrating their third remarriage to each other, and the Russian psychologists. "I think that's probably the woman from your hotel," Hunt said to Gina.

Best Western hotels had displayed more of best American entrepreneurial initiative by acquiring premises at the core of what was rapidly becoming a Terran enclave at Geerbaine. Since Gina was not officially with UNSA and would have no obvious reason for going to PAC, she had made a reservation there under her own name as an independent journalist. She and Hunt would get together again somehow later.

Hunt walked across with Gina and made sure that her name was on the list that the agent from Best Western was checking, and that there were no problems. That completed the party, and the woman began shepherding her flock toward an escalator going up to what looked like a shuttle tube. Hunt turned away and began walking over to rejoin his own group, but was intercepted by Bob, the teacher from Florida.

"I just wanted to say so long and thanks for the company. I enjoyed our talks. Maybe we'll bump into you guys again while we're here," Bob said. Through a glass exit across the floor behind Bob, Hunt could see the school party chattering and jostling as they climbed aboard a bus that was bright pink with green stripes. It was an odd-looking vehicle, running on balls half-contained in hemispherical housings instead of wheels. The center portion of its roof rose into a large, bulbous projection of just the right proportions to immediately suggest a female breast.

"Not staying at the hotel here, then?" Hunt observed as they shook hands.

"No. We decided to take the plunge straight in. A Jevlenese school that we got in touch with in the city offered to put everyone up, so we went for it. Might as well see what it's all about here, eh? Hell, we can see the inside of a BW any day of the week."

"Good thinking," Hunt agreed. "Enjoy the sights."

"You too. See you around, maybe, Vic."

The two men who had come to collect the UNSA group

were Americans, Hunt discovered when he at last joined them. There was no real reason why he should have been surprised, since the traffic of Terrans to Jevlen had been pretty free, but it wasn't something he had been expecting.

One's name was Koberg; the other's was Lebansky. From their tight-jawed impassivity and overall bearing, they had to be military, Hunt guessed, and was proved right: both were U.S. Secret Service, formerly military police, currently attached to PAC security on Jevlen.

"Security?" Hunt looked puzzled. "I thought JPC turned that proposal down."

"Yeah, well, that was for a UN force," Koberg agreed. He gave the impression of being tactfully evasive. "I guess a few things have been happening on the quiet that maybe you won't have heard about. You know how these things are: Some of our people kind of decided to go ahead anyhow, in a low-visibility way. You might call it a precautionary insurance."

"Maybe the chief will explain it better when we get back," Lebansky suggested.

They led the group out of the same exit that the school group had used, just as the pink bus was pulling away. A smaller ground vehicle was waiting for them, similar to a minibus, again riding on balls instead of wheels. Inside were two more men, Jevlenese this time, one in the driver's station in front, the other seated by the door. Neither of them spoke any Terran languages, but the driver said something over a communications link that sounded like a confirmation that the party had been picked up.

"Today we travel the slow way," Koberg said as they moved off. "There's normally a fast-transit tube system into the city, but it's not running."

"Hell, what do you mean, 'normally'?" Lebansky challenged. "The darn things are never running. This is normal."

"Just when this side of the city's going to be packed for a big rally that's going on today," Koberg said. "Purple-spiral loonies. Ever hear of them?"

"A little," Hunt said.

"You'll see plenty of 'em today," Lebansky promised.

Jevlen had been developed as the home world of the Jevlenese within the Thurien civilization, and as such its layout reflected a human worldview rather than anything predominantly alien. Although Ganymean influence was inevitable, the geometry and architecture conformed to more familiar notions of style and consistency—which came as a relief to those who, after seeing the *Vishnu*, had prepared themselves for worse.

The metropolis was higher than anything that contemporary Earth had to offer, rising in the center to a monolithic fusion of towers, ramps, terraces, and bridges that dwarfed anything from home in scale and breathtaking concept; but the avenues passing amid the flyovers and disappearing into the central zone at various levels remained avenues, the levels remained levels, "up" meant the same thing everywhere, and surface and line in all directions extrapolated with reassuring predictability.

At any rate, those were the qualities inherent in the city's fixed, unchanging aspect: the imprint of its origin, stamped in the same way that the underlying rock strata impart fundamental character and form to a landscape. But the promise that had been written into the soaring lines and broad vistas was just an empty voice echoing from long ago. The vision of those who had conceived the city had not been fulfilled.

Everywhere had the same look of weariness and shabbiness, the signs of neglect and disrepair that Hunt and Gina had seen from PAC the day previously. One area they passed had flooded, leaving the shells of several derelict buildings protruding above the water like islands in a swamp. In another, children swarmed in and over lines of immobilized, partly dismantled vehicles that looked as if they had not moved for years. After the crisp, new look of everything inside the *Vishnu*, the sights were depressing. The Jevlenese in the rear of the minibus seemed indifferent when Hunt tried questioning him, with the Americans acting as not-very-efficient interpreters. He seemed unaware of how things could be otherwise.

The people hung around in listless crowds, wandered aimlessly in the boulevards and squares, or sat on the grass in the open spaces beneath the pale chartreuse sky. Since the shutdown of the major part of JEVEX, many of them had moved out of the city's central zone and taken up a shantytown existence in the outer sectors. They could be seen sitting in doorways, bartering in noisy street markets that had sprung up off the major throughways, and cooking under makeshift awnings beneath lines of washing strung across passageways and alleys. All of them inert, leaderless, waiting for somebody to point a direction.

"The trouble that a few agitators could stir up out there doesn't bear thinking about," Sandy said in a sober voice as she stared out at the passing scene. "No wonder Garuth's having problems."

"Is this policy of his going to work?" Duncan asked. He sounded very dubious. "*Can* it work?"

"Aw, they have to find out what the real world's all about," Koberg answered. "It's just that with some it takes longer than with others. The ones you're looking at now are the slow learners. There's others doing okay. The system has to sort itself out."

"It's gonna take time," Lebansky said. "You've gotta stick with it. That Garuth has got nerve. I'll give the guy that."

"Right," Koberg agreed.

The roadway became one of a multilevel system curving in toward the looming bulk of the city's central massif. The view that had appeared on the screen in the cabin of the surface lander as it descended had been misleading, Hunt saw as they approached the metropolis proper. Ahead, between the structures flanking both sides, he could see parts of what was revealed to be a false roof with an artificial inner sky over that section of the city. In some places the cliffs of buildings rose to support it, dividing the space beneath into enclosed basins of varied cityscapes interconnected in the upper parts by vast corridors carrying streams of airborne traffic and transport tubes; in other parts, the blocks of architecture came together to form upthrusts of streets and precincts open to the natural sky, or elsewhere soaring towers projecting through the canopies. The combined result of all of them formed what had seemed from above to be the actual skyline of the city undisguised.

Farther on, they passed growing numbers of people wearing purple, gathered in crowds and walking in processions with banners showing a purple spiral on a black background. "Is this what you were talking about?" Sandy asked the Americans.

"Right, that's today's big event," Koberg replied. "Their great guru is in town. There's a new sports complex being opened today—you can see it now, on the right there—and they're having a big—" The bus slowed suddenly. "Say, what's this? What's going on there, Pete?"

Ahead, the traffic was coming to a confused halt and tailing back, with vehicles stopping in disorder at all angles across the lanes. There was another traffic level above; those vehicles were passing through a complicated interchange of on-off ramps and flyovers. The vehicles ahead were clustered around a two-lane exit road that left the main throughway in a descending curve, flying high over the immediate surroundings and supported by slender pylons on one side—and then it stopped abruptly at a ragged edge in midair. Figures were climbing out of vehicles and clustering along the barrier, waving their arms and pointing down.

Lebansky moved to the front of the bus, muttering to the driver and motioning with a hand. The driver, who had been doing nothing, since the vehicle had been driving itself from Geerbaine, engaged manual and pulled onto the shoulder, nosing through the other vehicles that had stopped. "Looks like there's been some kind of accident," Lebansky threw back as the others crowded to the windows. "Jeez, look at that! A whole piece of it's collapsed there!"

As the minibus moved closer to the barrier, they could see, below them, the wreckage of an entire span of what had presumably been a bridge, with the remains of at least two vehicles crushed beneath it. But that was not the only damage. In falling, the bridge had swung sideways and demolished two of the supporting pillars of the main throughway, causing a section of the innermost lane to tear away. It hung, buckled and twisted, projecting out into space like the deck of a ship that had broken in two. At the far end of the sagging section, which extended for perhaps two hundred feet, a truck had slewed across and stopped, grounded, on the edge with its front actually hanging over the drop. A smaller vehicle had run into it. Behind that, perched precariously on the edge of the rent where the lane had come away from the main roadway, fifteen feet or more above, was another, familiar-looking vehicle with its absurd, bulbous, pink conning tower amidships, and vivid green stripes.

"It's the titmobile that was back at the spaceport," Koberg muttered, staring ahead, his eyes moving rapidly to take in the scene.

"Oh, my God! Those kids!" Sandy gasped.

"What kids?" Koberg shot at her. Lebansky snapped something to the driver. The bus stopped.

"Ours—from Earth," Sandy stammered. "They were on the *Vishnu*. A bunch of schoolkids from Florida."

"They're staying in the city somewhere," Hunt said.

Something gave way, and the hanging section of road dropped another two feet. The truck that was balanced on the edge lurched visibly. Screams went up from among the crowd gathered outside. Two figures scrambled out of the truck's cab and began making their way back up, moving awkwardly and off-balance on the sloping surface. Another tumbled out of the car that had tail-ended the truck. Somebody else inside the car seemed to be hurt. There was a screeching of sirens from behind as a vehicle with flashing lights came nosing along the shoulder. It stopped behind the minibus and disgorged men in yellow tunics and white caps, presumably police.

Koberg climbed out and engaged them. They were excited and waving their arms wildly. Koberg seemed to be trying to calm them down. In the front of the minibus, Lebansky was operating a panel alongside the driver and talking to a face that had appeared on a screen.

The road sagged some more, and the truck tipped and went over. The whole structure beneath the minibus shuddered, and the shouts from outside almost drowned out the sound of the crash. The pink bus was trying to back up; but its balls weren't getting enough grip on the buckled, tilted surfaces, and it was slithering uncontrollably from side to side as if in a snowdrift.

"That idiot's panicking!" Hunt yelled. "He'll bring the whole bloody thing down! Stop him! Get those kids out of there! Get them out!"

Koberg dismissed the police with an impatient wave and ran down to take charge. Up front, the face that Lebansky was talking to was also an American from the sound of it. "How else does it look?" Hunt heard him saying.

"There's purple freaks all over," Lebansky replied. "Anything could happen. The police are here, but it seems we've got some flakes. Mitch has gone down to stop the jerk in the bus, but he's gonna need help."

"Stay there with him," the face on the screen said. "Heshak and Mu can bring the UNSA people back here. Check in with me again when it's under control."

"Roger." Lebansky flipped off the unit and exchanged a few words with the two Jevlenese, who nodded. He came back along the bus and climbed out the door that Koberg had left open. Two of the yellow-uniformed police outside immediately began jabbering at him and flailing their arms. Lebansky showed a badge and shouted them down, then pointed at the minibus that the UNSA group were in and the other vehicles blocking its way back onto the throughway. The policemen faltered, then nodded and rushed away to begin clearing a way through. The other police, meanwhile, were running back and forth among the already excited crowd and seemed to be doing more harm than good. Above it all, in the background, came Koberg's voice, roaring at the driver of the pink bus.

Lebansky stuck his head back in the door. "That's all it needed. One of the cars underneath all that junk down there had their deputy police chief in it. Look, it's all gonna get crazy here. These two guys will take you on to PAC. We'll see you when we get there." Without waiting for a reply he slammed the door and gave the side a thump to send the driver on his way. Ahead, one of the policemen waved them forward.

"I think it's stopped," Sandy said, peering back through the rear window. "Yes, it is. Some of the kids are coming out now."

"That's a relief, anyway," Danchekker said, having sat tight-lipped throughout.

"The tour guide never said anything about this," Duncan muttered. It was a reflexive attempt at bravado. He was visibly pale.

Around them, the structures and buildings of Shiban closed together and merged into a single, monolithic composition of levels and precincts penetrated by avenues and transportation ways, as the highway became a vast tunnel sweeping into the city proper.

Chapter Twenty

There was nothing to be done, Hunt told himself. Accidents happen. Whatever would happen to the school party lay in other hands. He could do nothing but wait to find out the news when they got where they were going. He concentrated on absorbing the scenes outside and tried to put it out of his mind for the time being. The silence from the others in the bus told him that they were struggling with the same feelings.

But it soon became apparent that they hadn't left all their difficulties behind them just yet. As they passed an enclosed square of window facades crisscrossed by walkways on several levels, they saw a commotion ahead, involving a crowd of purple-clad people spilling out onto the roadway and causing vehicles to halt. One of the Jevlenese escorts voiced a command to the vehicle's monitor panel, and the bus veered away down a slipramp to take a different route.

"What now?" Hunt murmured apprehensively.

"You don't think it could all be for us?" Duncan said.

But farther along the lower route the crowds became thicker, jostling, shouting slogans, and blocking the through-way, heedless of the blaring horns and curses from the occupants of stranded vehicles. Again the minibus was forced to detour, this time into a side street flanked by shops and doorways. But after several more zigzag turns through the labyrinth that the part of the city they were now in was turning into, they found themselves back in the rally. This time there was no getting through. The intersection at which they had halted was jammed with marchers, some carrying banners, the rest linking arms to form a solid phalanx of chanting ranks. A flood tide of humanity closed around, while other vehicles that had been following blocked any way out behind.

Duncan stood up and peered anxiously through a side window. "There's another bunch coming up the street, green ones this time," he muttered.

"Best to stay put inside the vehicle," Danchekker pronounced, clutching his briefcase determinedly on his knee.

"I'm not so sure," Duncan said. "It looks to me as if there could be trouble breaking out."

The Jevlenese evidently agreed. One of them jabbed a finger several times in the direction the bus had been heading. "PAC, that way. Not far," he said. "Go feet now best. This bad news."

Hunt nodded. "Let's go." Danchekker hesitated for a second longer, then concurred.

They clambered out into the throng. Whatever the shouting was about was a mystery, since it was all in Jevlenese. One of the escorts led the way, pushing and elbowing to force a passage through, and the other brought up the rear. But despite the group's attempt to keep together, the ebbs and flows of the tide around them drew them apart. Danchekker and Sandy managed to stay close to the leader; but a gap developed between them and Hunt, and then another between Hunt and where Duncan was with the other Jevlenese, both of whom were being carried away sideways.

"*That way!*" the one who was near Duncan shouted, pointing with a raised arm at a stairway on the far side of the intersection, leading up to a system of overlooking galleries and walkways. "*Head for stairs . . .*" He vanished in a swirl of people, and the rest of his words were drowned in a roar of voices.

Somebody backed into Hunt and trod on his instep, painfully, at the same time swinging an arm that caught Hunt across the mouth. Hunt shoved him away. The man collided with another, and they both went down. Then a knot of people pushing from the other direction sent Hunt sprawling over both of them.

At that moment, a group with green-crescent banners appeared on one of the levels above and showered leaflets on the marching Purples, and pandemonium broke out. As Hunt was trying to regain his feet, everyone around him began rushing forward as if impelled by a common instinct. He rose onto one knee and started to straighten up, whereupon a fat woman in a red-and-black jumpsuit careened into him and knocked him down again. She stumbled and fell heavily on her knees alongside him, shrilly exclaiming something that he didn't understand. He tried again to rise, but she was clawing at his collar, using him as a prop to pull herself up.

"Get off, stupid cow!" Hunt shouted, and was answered with a stream of what sounded like alien obscenities. He fought his way to his feet and looked about desperately, but the others had disappeared. Swearing to himself, he plunged into the turmoil, setting his sights on the stairway that the Jevlenese had indicated. But before he was a third of the way there, the marching tide flowed around him and carried him with it toward one of the exits from the intersection. A chanting man in a purple hood tried to link arms with him.

"Let go of me, you daft sod," Hunt snarled, wrenching himself away.

Another arm grasped his from the other side. Hunt tried to pull away, but the grip remained firm and insistent. "I do believe I hear another voice from back home," a voice yelled in his ear. It sounded American. Hunt jerked his head around and found himself staring at a ruddy, snub-nosed face with a short, hoary beard, eyes that glittered like light gray ice, and a mouth that couldn't suppress a mirthful twitch, even in the circumstances. The face was topped by a panama hat sporting an outrageous yellow band with red and white polka dots. Hunt could feel himself being urged along in the direction of the flow.

"Sorry," Hunt yelled back. "I'm not going on any Batman rallies today."

"Neither am I. I'm going home. But you won't get anyplace upstream in this. Have to ride with it until we can jump out."

"Where?"

"Just stick close."

They were swept along with the marchers for about half a block, in the course of which the stranger maneuvered them outward toward one side of the flow. Then, as they came abreast of the entrance to a narrow passageway leading off between a shuttered shop front and the base of a pillar, he yanked at Hunt's arm and nodded. "There!"

They detached themselves from the human river like hoboes jumping from a slowing boxcar and followed the passage to an iron stairway leading up. It brought them to an elevated pedestrian way where people were watching the confusion below. But at least it felt halfway back to sanity. Hunt and the stranger stopped for a moment.

"Who the hell are you?" Hunt asked when he had regained his breath.

The glittering gray eyes looked back at him with an amusement that seemed friendly. "English, eh? Well, most people who like me call me Murray. The others usually think up something else." He jerked his head to indicate the Jevlenese around them. "But let's leave the formalities till later and get away from all the crazies first."

Murray led the way through a warren of passages and arcades, up stairs and escalators, across footbridges. Within minutes Hunt had lost any idea of the way back to the intersection. It was like being inside an ocean liner, a supermall, and a Shanghai street market all rolled into one and swelled to a scale that would have encompassed New York's avenues and Tokyo's railroad system. Even though there were many shuttered shop fronts and vacated apartments, people were everywhere, though how much of the bustle and activity was normal, Hunt had no way of knowing.

The typical Jevlenese Hunt saw were not exactly like any of

the Terran races. They were orangy in hue, with hair that varied from copper to black. Their faces were wide and flat, their eyes rounded, the skin of many of them speckled or streaked with brownish blotches, and they wore every form of garb imaginable. They tended to be taller than the average Terran, but flabby—probably from spending too much of their existence inertly coupled into JEVEX, Hunt guessed. But there were enough who were shorter, darker, lighter, or pinker to make Hunt feel at least not obviously alien, even if something of an oddity.

Everything had happened too quickly for Hunt to be in any state of mind to form a coherent picture of what was going on around him. He registered only disconnected impressions that came and went. Some were of people who seemed grandly attired and ornamented, strutting self-importantly, sometimes with retinues of attendants; others were of dirty and shabby individuals, panhandling from passersby. At one place they passed, which seemed to be a restaurant, a small honor guard of staff waited at the door to greet a party from a chauffeured automobile; a few yards farther on, a loudly protesting figure was tossed bodily from the back door of another place. In neither case did anyone else take much notice.

They came to a dingy, not-very-clean-smelling passage between a bar and some closed-down premises, and entered one of several doorways. Inside, a vestibule with a brave stand of exhausted flowers in a long tub opened through to a hall with several doors of various colors, all scratched and battered. One, larger than the rest, looked as if it might be an elevator, but Murray ignored it and, tossing back a terse "Busted" over his shoulder and making a throwing-away motion of his hand, led the way past it to a stairwell at the rear.

On the first landing, they had to step over a snoring body, drunk or under some other influence. A door on the next was open, with a pair of tots playing with toys on the floor outside. They greeted Murray with smiles. He ruffled their hair as he passed, muttering a few words in Jevlenese. From inside, their mother looked out blankly, saying nothing, while from behind a door opposite came strange, atonal music with a heavy rhythm, punctuated by two voices shouting and shrieking at what sounded like the borderline of murder. "Don't worry about it," Murray grunted, seemingly reading Hunt's mind. "It won't come to that. Jevs never do anything right."

Two levels farther up, they stopped in front of a purple door with a white surround. Murray said something to it, and a female voice answered from nowhere identifiable. The door slid aside, and Murray ushered Hunt through, just as a woman came out of one of the rooms to meet them. She had a clear, dusky complexion, cherry-colored hair, and was wearing a skin-tight orange top with glittery mauve, calf-length pants. By what seemed to be the Jevlenese norm, she was quite trim and shapely—in fact, her figure wasn't at all bad by most Terran standards, either. Her voice had a bright up-and-down lilt as she chattered more Jevlenese at Murray, who replied in a series of short utterances and grunts.

"This is Nixie," Murray said when he could get a word in. "All that was the Jev way of saying hi. They talk too much. Nixie, meet a new friend of ours . . ." He cocked an eyebrow inquiringly.

"Vic'll do fine," Hunt said. Murray said something to Nixie in which Hunt caught the syllable "Vic."

Nixie smiled, showing white and even teeth, and took Hunt's hand. "Vic, how you do today? We have real good time."

"No, no, you dumb broad." Murray sighed. "He's not a customer. Just visiting. Understand? Vis-it-or. Come here to say hello. Anyhow, it's your day off."

"Ah." Nixie dismissed the error with a matter-of-fact shrug. "Is okay I guess."

"How about a drink, then?" Murray said. "Can fix? Drink?" He raised his hand in a drinking motion. Nixie smiled, nodded, and turned toward a short passage that led to what looked like the kitchen, from which the sound of a popular jazz group was issuing—Terran, this time. Murray patted her behind as she moved away, then he steered Hunt into the lounge. "Put your feet up. Make yourself at home. I guess you've had a long trip."

It was a cheerfully chaotic place, cluttered and colorful in an unapologetically gaudy kind of way, yet cleaner and better kept than Hunt's impression of the exterior had prepared him for. It went with Murray's hatband. There was a suite of puffy-looking chairs in gray and red that molded themselves into whatever shape the occupant assumed, with a couch of the same; a large table by the wall, bearing a vase of Jevlenese plants amid a litter of household oddments, a box of tools, and some magazines; and a fluffy pink carpet that looked like mohair. Various ornaments and knickknacks filled every shelf and recess, and most of the wall space was taken up by posters, pictures that included some raunchy girlie poses, both native and Terran, and several embroidered blankets of the kind that tourists everywhere liked to buy. A picture of the Golden Gate Bridge formed a centerpiece on one wall. It was surmounted by an American flag, with a Chicago University bumper sticker, dollar bills of various denominations, and an arrangement of Budweiser, Miller, Michelob, and Coors coasters framing the whole.

Murray tossed his hat across the room onto the table and flopped down in one of the chairs, stretching a leg out over a footstool. He had wiry hair streaked with gray, like his beard, and was beginning to show a thin patch at the crown. Hunt sat down in the chair opposite, pressing his body this way and that until the contours suited him.

"Her real name's Nikasha," Murray explained. "Don't be taken in by the act. She's smarter than she lets on. Keeps her sights on the real world out there—and that's saying a lot for this place." He reached up to a shelf near his chair and took down a silver metal box. Flipping open the lid, he offered it to Hunt. It was partitioned into two sections, holding rolled joints of different colors, thicknesses, and lengths in one end, and a selection of tablets and capsules in the other. "Burn up? Cool down? Blow a weed? Some of the local stuff'll put you back into h-space."

Hunt shook his head. "Don't use it. I'll stick to conventional poison." He felt in his pocket for his cigarettes.

Murray snapped the box shut and threw it back on the shelf

with an approving nod. "Damn right. Awful shit. I never figured it, either."

Hunt still had not caught up with the turn of events. He pinched his eyes for a moment, then tossed his hand out vaguely. "You were obviously one of the first here . . ."

"Natch."

"But not with any of the official parties, I take it?"

"I hitched a ride back on the first Thurien ship that showed up, right after the blowup with the Jevs," Murray replied. "I guess most people still don't realize that the Thuriens'll take just about anyone for the askin'."

Hunt shook his head in a way that said that many of the things Murray seemed to be taking as obvious were not obvious. "What was the attraction here?" he asked.

Murray tugged at his beard, his gray eyes glittering mischievously. He seemed to be enjoying Hunt's bemusement. "Nothin' that I'd ever heard of. It was more a case of having to get out of there. You know how unreasonable the Feds can get about anything they think they're not getting their cut of."

"What weren't they getting a cut of?"

"Oh, a little bit o' this, little bit o' that . . . I was mainly in what you might call the 'creative import-export' business. It involved certain psychotherapeutic agents and other substances that aren't covered by monopoly patents, which you can't get approval for."

"I see," Hunt said, nodding. He should have guessed. "So you've been here , . ."

"It's getting to be over six months, now."

"Where from?"

Murray gestured at the Golden Gate picture below the flag. "Born and raised. Hell, where else is there?"

"What do you do here?"

Murray shrugged and looked vague. "Oh, bit o' this, bit o' that. Buy and sell, deal and trade in anything there's a demand for. Jevlen's a pretty easygoing place that way: not exactly what you'd call restrictive. The Thuriens don't need a lot of telling to make them act smart and stay in line, so I guess they never thought to set up much of it here, either. Now that the lunatic fringe that were trying to play Napoleons are gone, there's a lot of opportunity."

Nixie reappeared carrying a tray with a bottle and glasses, a dish of broken ice, and a bowl of mixed snacks. "When Vic get here Jevlen?" she asked, setting the tray down and sitting by Murray.

"Today," Hunt said. "An hour ago, maybe less."

"Today," Murray repeated, adding something in Jevlenese. "You drink rum?" he asked, looking back at Hunt.

"Sometimes."

"Local gutrot. Something like rum, but kinda minty. It's called *ashti*. Give it a try." He poured Hunt a generous measure from the bottle, pushed across the ice, then half filled two more glasses for himself and Nixie.

Hunt took a neat sip and found it not bad. He added an inch of ice. "So Vic have no girl here yet," Nixie said. "We fix. Know plenty girl. Find real pretty one. Good and kinky."

"Jesus, don't you ever think of anything else?" Murray grumbled. He lounged back and raised his glass toward Hunt, Nixie took a small case from a side table and began applying a pink cosmetic to her nails. "So what's your story?" Murray asked Hunt. "Is there a Thurien ship in today?"

Hunt nodded. "I'm part of a group that UNSA sent to have a look at some aspects of Ganymean science. There are going to be big changes."

"So, is that what you are—a scientist?"

"Yes."

"What kind?"

"Originally nucleonics. But since the Ganymeans showed up, it's been getting more general."

Murray took a gulp from his glass and regarded Hunt quizzically. "So how in hell did you wind up being bounced around in the middle of a Jev banana parade? For somebody who's been off the ship an hour, that takes real talent. You must have a guidance system that homes on trouble."

"Not really. The tube in from the shuttle port wasn't running—"

"Typical."

"—so we used a bus. Our group will be based at PAC."

"The old government center. Okay."

Hunt shrugged. "The bus had to divert and got bogged down in the crowd. The Jevlenese who were with us decided to try and make it on foot. I got separated from the others. And then you showed up."

"Probably just as well for you, too. They can get pretty wild. Most of them are headworld cases who forgot the difference between cuckoo-land and reality a long time ago—assuming they ever figured it out in the first place."

"There was something else, too," Hunt said. "On the way in from Geerbaine we passed an accident."

Murray pulled a face. "It gets a bit like I-405 sometimes. How bad was it?"

"It wasn't a pileup. A traffic bridge collapsed—part of an exit slipway."

"Goddamn turkeys," Murray muttered beneath his breath. "Anyone hurt bad?"

"It looked like it. And I think one of them was the deputy police chief. Apparently he was driving over it."

"Oh, shit. Well, I guess we'll be hearing all about that."

Hunt looked around the room, tapping his fingertips lightly on the tabletop next to him. His eyes came back to Murray. "Look, I don't want to be unsociable or anything, and maybe it's been a long time since you talked to anyone new from back home. But the others will be wondering what's happened to me. I need to get to PAC. Is it very far from here?"

"You're right. We can shoot the breeze some other time." Murray turned to Nixie and said something in Jevlenese. She replied with a stream of chatter, nodded, and said something in a raised voice. Another female voice answered from what seemed to be the room in general.

"That's Lola, the house computer," Murray murmured. Hunt nodded.

Nixie exchanged a few words with Lola, and then another female voice came on and entered into a dialogue with Nixie.

"Nixie and Osaya will take you there," Murray said, turning back to Hunt. "Osaya's one of the girls upstairs. I'd do it myself, but I've got somebody coming here in about fifteen minutes. Business."

"That would be fine." Hunt nodded and finished his drink. "That stuff's not bad."

"Glad you like it. Don't forget to come back and have another."

They were silent for a few seconds. Then Hunt said, "That 'headworld' that you mentioned a minute ago. What is it? Do you mean JEVEX creations?"

"Yeah. Most Jevs never learned to ask questions, so they believe anything anyone tells 'em. It's Madison Avenue's dream out here. I'm telling ya, if them Thuriens don't wise up and start limiting the tickets, there's gonna be every con artist and snake-oil salesman from home comin' in by the shipload once the news gets around."

Nixie finished her conversation. She examined her nails, then opened the front of the top she was wearing and began painting one of her nipples.

"So what's going on everywhere today?" Hunt asked. "Who are these people with the purple spiders, or whatever it's supposed to be? One of the guys who met us said something about a big guru arriving in town."

Murray nodded with a weary sigh. "You remember they used to call California the Granola state: full of nuts, fruits, and flakes? Well, I'm tellin' ya, it's like a convention of judges and bishops compared to this place. They've got every brand you can think of here. Magical forces, mystical dimensions, mind-power, faith-power, psychic messages—if you can think of it, somebody believes it."

"And the Thuriens were never able to change it," Hunt commented, drawing on his cigarette.

Murray turned up his empty hand. "That's the way it is . . . Anyhow, one of the biggest outfits calls itself something that translates roughly as the 'Spiral of Awakening'—that's what the purple spider is. They're into some kinda reincarnation crap. It's leader is a guy called Ayultha: a kind of Hitler that's got religion."

"Ayultha, he make lots crazy people," Nixie said, catching

the name. "Not good. Terrans not so crazy. Think I go live Earth. Terran men like Shiban girl, you think, Vic?"

"I think they'd find them quite . . . passable," Hunt told her. Murray translated. She looked pleased and transferred her attention to the other nipple.

"Ayultha says it was the old regime that caused all the problems," Murray went on, "and JEVEX had nothing to do with it. He wants the Ganymeans out and the system restored. But then, all of the cults have got some reason for wanting JEVEX back. With all those junkies out there, they can't lose. They know when they're onto a good thing."

"So who are the ones with green sickles?" Hunt asked.

"Axis of Light: another of the same—except their guiding genius thinks he's a computer. Basically they're all as bad, but the leaders carve up the territory by getting everyone hyped up over details that don't matter—you know, like whether you make the sign with this hand or that hand, or whether some book said a line this way or that way, and that kind of garbage. But it isn't exactly something I've spent a lot of time worrying about."

"I imagine not."

An off-key chiming sound came from the room system. Nixie acknowledged it, and what sounded like two laughing female voices replied. Leaving her handiwork displayed, she got up and went into the hall to open the door. Murray raised his eyebrows. "You'll have quite an escort," he told Hunt, draining his glass and standing. "That sounds like Osaya plus one of the others. They're curious to meet the Terran."

"I'm not complaining," Hunt said, rising to follow. "And thanks again for the help. I've got to hand it to the U.S. Cavalry again, eh—you showed up just in time."

Murray handed him a card, printed in Jevlenese. "This has our address and call code. Stop by again when there's more time to talk."

"You can count on it." Hunt went through to the hall, where the three girls were waiting. Osaya turned out to be six feet tall, with a skirt not more than twelve inches long. Her companion was a redhead in pants that went transparent to light at certain angles, causing devastating things to happen as she walked.

"My God," Hunt muttered. "I'll never explain this. I hope Chris isn't around when we get there."

Chapter Twenty-one

H unt and his three escorts reached the Planetary Administration Center after a fifteen-minute walk through more
streets and arcades and across a pedestrian flyover spanning a
moving beltway that carried freight. The base of the PAC complex merged into the general plan of the lower city, but as was
clear from the fact that the *Shapieron* at Geerbaine was visible
from higher up, its upper parts formed a tower facing west
over the city.

The entrance they came to was a transparent wall and set
of doors opening from a wide pedestrian precinct lined by
stores and what looked like office units, rows of display cases,
and at the far end a battery of stairs and escalators going up to
the concourse of a transportation terminal. The doors opened
at their approach, and inside was a desk with a Jevlenese reception clerk. A couple of guards were standing a few yards back
in the lobby area opening through to the interior. To Hunt's
relief after some of the things he had seen and heard since
arriving, the guards were smartly turned out and seemed alert.
So someone, at least, seemed to know what he or she was doing.
They were unarmed as far as Hunt could see, but both were

wearing lightweight headbands, throatmike-earpiece combinations, and wrist units that Hunt recognized as Ganymean communications accessories into the *Shapieron*'s computer system, ZORAC—the direct neural-coupling technology of the Thuriens was from a later era.

Initially, the interest of the guards was focused more on Hunt's companions than on Hunt. But then the clerk, probably prompted by ZORAC, who would have recognized Hunt via the visual pickups in the headbands, gesticulated and said something in Jevlenese to the other two, followed by "You are Doctor Hunt, who gets missed? All look everyplace Shiban. Ganymeans very . . ." He traced circles vaguely in the air with his hand.

Hunt nodded. "I'm Hunt. I'm okay."

"Use, please." The clerk reached below the desk and produced another communications kit. Hunt fitted the items into place, and a voice spoke that he hadn't heard for a long time.

"Hello, Vic. Welcome to our world, and all that—but you don't seem to have been doing a bad job of finding yourself a welcoming committee already. Pretty fast operator, if you don't mind my saying so." ,

It spoke in his ear, not his head. A sudden feeling of being back among familiar things came over him. Perhaps, in some ways, the *Shapieron* Ganymeans were closer to Earthpeople than to Thuriens. "ZORAC, you haven't changed," he replied. "This isn't what it looks like. And even if it were, it wouldn't be any of your business."

"Glad to see you're in one piece, anyhow."

The reception clerk was coming through coherently now that ZORAC was on-line to translate. "Dr. Hunt, we're sure pleased to see you. We've put alerts out all over. The Ganymeans have been getting worried."

"Did everyone else make it okay?" Hunt asked.

"They're all here."

"We passed an accident on the way from Geerbaine," Hunt said. "A part of a bridge collapsed."

"Yes. A senior officer of the Shiban police was killed. There was a lot of confusion."

"Also, there was a Terran party in a bus, off the same ship as us. They were in a precarious situation when we left."

"The school group?"

"That's them. The two Terrans who met us stayed behind to sort it out. Do you have any news on what happened?"

"They're all okay. Koberg and Lebansky got back a few minutes ago." Hunt nodded and emitted a thankful sigh. The clerk inclined his head to indicate the three girls, who were by this time talking to the guards. "Er, where did they come from?" he inquired, dropping his voice discreetly.

"They were collecting for charity at the airport."

"Sure. Give me a call," Osaya was saying to one of them.

"I'm off at seven. How about then?"

"Anytime. And I *love* the Terran uniform . . ." ZORAC was still supplying the background translation.

Just then, another figure appeared through some doors on the far side of the lobby area and came across. He was about fortyish, with a medium, athletic build, black-haired and clean-shaven, and wearing a white shirt and gray slacks. As he got closer, Hunt recognized his face as the American that Lebansky had talked to on the screen inside the minibus. The American grinned easily and extended a hand.

"Dr. Hunt, from UNSA?"

"Yes."

"Hi. The name's Del Cullen. Glad you're okay." Cullen eyed the three girls curiously. "I see you've been making friends already."

"Well, you didn't send the mayor with a red carpet. One must exercise initiative."

The girls waved as Hunt turned with Cullen to go into the building. "Come and see us again, Vic," Nixie sang after him. . "Call if you don't remember the way."

"I might surprise you," Hunt called back. "And thanks again."

Cullen and Hunt began walking back across the lobby. "English?" Cullen said.

"Yes—from London originally. How about you?"

"East Coast. Baltimore."

"How do you fit in here?"

Cullen's voice fell to a level that was not for carrying. "Well, I try to impress some concept of security into these people. It's an uphill battle at times, but we're getting there slowly."

"Which people do you mean—Jevlenese or Ganymeans?"

"Both. I was sent here to help Garuth set the system up. He's learning fast, but you know how it is with Ganymeans: running an intelligence operation isn't their line. They didn't have any eyes or ears out in the city—just tended to sit inside PAC and believe whatever the Jevs told them. We're starting to use Jevlenese outside, now. They can be okay if you know how to select the right ones."

They entered the elevator. "I take it that those two who picked us up, Koberg and Lebansky, they work for you, then?" Hunt said.

"Right. We imported a nucleus of pros from back home to seed the operation."

The elevator shaft was a transparent tube, and the car had all-round windows, presenting views of a progression of galleries, halls opening into office areas, and wide corridors as the car ascended. Although not exactly new and gleaming, the condition of the surroundings was noticeably better than the general standard outside.

Hunt still didn't follow completely. He remembered one of the two at Geerbaine saying something about things happening that Hunt probably didn't know about. "So, how did you get here?" he asked Cullen. "I mean, how did Garuth come to acquire a security operation in the first place? Who do you work for?"

"When the Thuriens and our own governments set up this arrangement, some of the folks back home knew there'd be problems when the Jevlenese started getting over their shell shock. The U.S. pushed for a security operation here that wouldn't have to depend on the Jevlenese police, but the Thuriens blocked it." Cullen shrugged. "So somebody persuaded Garuth that it would be a good idea to set up something anyway—'semiofficial,' if you know what I mean—just in case it was needed. If it turned out to be overcautious, well, no harm done."

Hunt nodded. As far as he was concerned, obstructions existed to be circumvented. "And I take it, it turned out to be just as well they did," he said.

"There's something funny going on here, all right, with mean people involved. We haven't exactly figured out what yet. But we can go into that with Garuth later."

Hunt nodded. "Where will we be staying?" he inquired to change the subject.

Cullen gestured to take in the general scene outside the elevator. "We've reserved quarters for you here in PAC. So you won't have to worry too much if things get a bit hectic outside. The rest of your group are over in the residential part of the complex now, getting their gear straightened out. Your bags came straight through on a freight tube."

Hunt thought about Gina, out at the spaceport. "How about the people who are staying at Geerbaine?" he asked. "Is there any risk there?"

Cullen shook his head. "The Thuriens run that whole area, and the Jevs don't want to upset them because they're the only ones who can turn JEVEX back on. They should be okay."

They came out of the elevator and headed across an open space with a large window looking out at the city. On the far side of the floor several corridors branched off in different directions. They followed one of them past an area with Jevlenese working at desks and terminals. A number of Ganymeans were also visible, some of them Thuriens, Hunt noted. Beyond the open area were smaller rooms and offices.

Garuth was waiting for them in a large, roughly circular anteroom furnished like a reception lounge, with seats facing a sunken area in the center. Another of Cullen's security guards was seated unobtrusively at a desk by a passage leading through to the inner section.

With Garuth were Shilohin, the female scientist who had been with him when he made his call to Hunt at home, and another old friend of Hunt's, Rodgar Jassilane, the *Shapieron's* engineering chief. The Ganymeans welcomed him in their characteristic easygoing manner, but it was clear that they were relieved to see him after his mishap of getting separated from the others.

"We saw ZORAC's replay of your arrival," Garuth said as they shook hands.

"It seems that you're managing to find your way around Shiban already," Shilohin remarked. The expression on her face had to be the Ganymean equivalent of a smirk. Hunt began to suspect that he would be really tired of that particular topic before the day was out.

"How was your journey?" Jassilane inquired, shaking Hunt's hand in turn.

"At least we didn't lose our brakes and have to spend twenty-five million years slowing down," Hunt replied, grinning. It was a reference to the problem that had caused the *Shapieron's* long exile from the solar system when it tried to return to Minerva.

"What do you think of a Thurien starship?" Jassilane asked.

"Impressive—but a bit overwhelming," Hunt confessed. "You know, Rod, when all's said and done, I think I prefer your old ship on the parking lot back there at Geerbaine."

"Me, too," Jassilane agreed. "Technology that you grew up with is always more comfortable, wouldn't you agree?"

"Definitely," Hunt said.

"That's why we never bothered adapting more of the sensor network in PAC to work with VISAR," Garuth said. "We experimented with the small part that you know, but old-time Ganymeans like us don't really take to it. The Thuriens can have virtual travel. We prefer to stick with ZORAC."

"I know exactly what you mean," Hunt said.

Garuth extended an arm to indicate the general surroundings, then singled out the passage by the security guard's desk. "This is the part of PAC that I normally inhabit. The staff here simply call it the Ganymean offices. So now you know where to find us."

"Where will we be working?" Hunt asked. "I assume that since we're officially here as an UNSA scientific group, we'll have some office space or something. It's a bit of a messy situation, I know, but Gregg didn't exactly give anybody a lot of notice."

"Naturally," Shilohin said. "We've found some space for you on one of the levels lower down, where we run some other work of our own."

"Maybe the best time to see it would be later," Garuth suggested. "Del can take you to your quarters in the residential sector now to freshen up, and we can all meet for, lunch in, say . . ." He made a vague gesture.

"About an hour?" Hunt suggested.

"Fine," Garuth agreed. "And then we'll show you the lab area when you're all together."

The Ganymean planetary administration employed numerous scientists, both Jevlenese and Thurien, in connection with various aspects of its work, some of whom were based within PAC itself. The area that had been designated the "UNSA labs" was a segregated section approached through a single entrance, on a floor of offices, workshops, laboratories, and other workrooms in the lower part of the complex.

The general working area consisted of a large room with a wide lab bench taking up the center of the floor, smaller benches by two of the walls, and several desks with computer workstations. A graphics table took up part of the third wall, and alongside it was a generously equipped imaging and processing system. A short passage led to several smaller offices, and another door from the passage doubled back into a second laboratory situated alongside the main area. There was also a direct interconnecting door between the two. All in all the place was well fitted and furnished, with plenty of storage space and instrumentation.

"What do you think?" Garuth asked as the Terrans walked around like prospective buyers inspecting a house.

"It's marvelous," Hunt said. "How many of us did you expect? You could house half a Goddard department in this."

"Officially you're here to study Ganymean science," Del Cullen said. "You might as well be comfortable and make it look good at the same time. And, who knows, there might be more coming later."

"Oh, I'm not complaining," Hunt assured him.

Another room, off the side of the main area across from the second lab, contained several Thurien neurocoupler recliners. "So you'll have full access to VISAR," Shilohin explained. "We have an h-space link direct into PAC."

"But the regular facilities around PAC are managed by ZORAC?" Duncan asked.

"Yes. There's a direct line back to the *Shapieron*. The ship has an onboard h-space connection, too. So ZORAC and VISAR can communicate directly."

They came back out of the coupler room. Sandy went on through into the smaller lab, where she activated a terminal and began talking to ZORAC about something. In the main area with its central worktable, Danchekker wandered around, checking closet space, looking in drawers, and activating a couple of screens. "Most satisfactory," he pronounced. "I must say, you seem to have gone to an inordinate amount of trouble for us."

"Not at all," Garuth assured him.

Danchekker rubbed the palms of his hands together and looked about. "It's all very splendid and lavish for just the four of us."

"Plenty of room if you find you need extra help," Cullen said.

Hunt saw that Duncan was about to make another wisecrack, no doubt about the company that Hunt had reappeared with from the city, and silenced him with a warning look.

And then Sandy's voice came through the open interconnecting door from the adjoining lab. "Hello, out there?"

"What is it, Sandy?" Hunt called back.

"ZORAC has a call for Professor Danchekker. Shall I leave it on here?"

Danchekker looked at Hunt bemusedly. "What? Already? But we've barely arrived, for God's sake. Who could it possibly be?"

"One way to find out," Hunt said.

Frowning, Danchekker went through into the next lab. Hunt sent Duncan a puzzled look. Duncan shook his head and shrugged. "Don't ask—"

"*Arghh!*"

The scream that came back through the open doorway was one of pure, animal terror. Danchekker bolted back into the room, white-faced. He looked imploringly at Hunt. "It can't be, not here . . . Vic, you've got to do something."

Hunt strode through the door and found Sandy, looking at a loss, standing to one side of a live display screen. On it, the face of Ms. Mulling from Goddard confronted him frostily.

"Ah, Dr. Hunt," she observed. "I distinctly saw Professor Danchekker there a moment ago. Could you call him back, please? There are some questions concerning certain records that he left, and it is *most imperative* that I speak with him."

Hunt fought back the urge to burst out laughing. "Er, I think he's been called away," he said. "His assistant is here, though. Couldn't she help?"

Ms. Mulling sniffed disdainfully. "Very well. I suppose so."

Hunt moved out of the viewing angle and gave Sandy an encouraging wink. Then he went back into the main lab. "Don't worry, Chris," he said cheerfully to Danchekker, who had sunk onto a stool. "We'll take care of it if this keeps up. It'll probably be some time before we go back."

"What makes you imagine that I intend to?" Danchekker replied miserably.

Chapter Twenty-two

The team spent the rest of the day relaxing, adjusting to local Jevlen time, and catching up on their rest. The next morning, Hunt and Danchekker met with Garuth and Shilohin in Garuth's suite in the Ganymean offices. The items of equipment and other effects that they had brought from Earth had arrived, and Sandy and Duncan were busy getting things organized in the UNSA labs. The two Ganymeans summarized what they had learned after six months with the Jevlenese.

"We thought we might draw a lesson from the dismantling of socialism on Earth," Garuth said, speaking from behind his huge Ganymean desk, which was also an elaborate console. "It seemed that the JEVEX-dependency here could be thought of as analogous to the overdependency that developed there on the too-protective state."

"A lot of people on Earth have been saying the same thing," Hunt commented.

"But simply unhooking them from JEVEX doesn't seem to be the answer," Garuth went on. "Or at least, not enough of an answer. It seems to work for some of them. Those are the ones who are finding what needs to be done and doing it. That was how we hoped the majority would react, more or less as happened on Earth."

"But they turned out to be relatively few," Shilohin said.

Garuth continued. "The general mass of Jevlenese seem to suffer from a . . . you could call it a 'predisposition' toward irrationality that goes beyond anything seen on ancient Earth. They just don't seem to possess any faculty for distinguishing possible from impossible, or the plausible from the ridiculous. So we get these cults of unreason flourishing across Jevlen, and we're at a loss for an effective answer to them." Garuth motioned in the air with a gray, double-thumbed hand. "We watch the intellectual degeneracy of what once showed every promise of maturing into an advanced technological civilization. It's like a plague from somewhere, but one which affects the mind. We need you to help us find where it's coming from."

"That's not all there is to it, though, is it?" Hunt queried. "Didn't you say something when you called me in Washington, about being worried that JPC might be about to pull you out?"

"Some of the Terran representatives on JPC have been saying that the Ganymean administration here isn't working, and that the situation is heading toward breakdown," Garuth replied. "They're not disagreeing with the Thuriens' policy, but they believe that it's going to need some kind of backing by force to make it work."

Which would mean Terran-style force, Hunt understood; in other words, putting in a Terran military occupation. Ganymeans didn't work that way.

"They may not be entirely wrong," Hunt cautioned. "The Jevlenese stayed away from violence while they had the chance to exploit Thurien know-how. But they were going to end all that, as we all know, and they came frighteningly close. Now they don't have that restraint anyway. Once they get themselves reorganized, there could be serious trouble."

"I'm not disputing that," Garuth conceded. "I accept the differences that set us and humans apart. But I've also studied enough of your history to have an idea of the kind of inflexibility that an authoritarian solution will lead to once it's adopted.

The *cause* of the Jevlenese problem won't be important; all that will matter will be how to suppress the effects. And that would be a tragedy, because we're convinced that at the bottom of this mass insanity there's something important waiting to be uncovered, that we don't understand. We know what sent Earth off into irrationality thousands of years ago. But none of that applies here."

Garuth got up and moved a short distance across the room to stand staring for a moment at a framed picture of the *Shapieron* standing on the shore of Lake Geneva. He turned and faced the others again.

"This may sound strange to you, but in many ways I'm beginning to feel the same toward the Jevlenese as I did toward my own people aboard that ship, when I was their leader through all those years in space. I feel a responsibility for them, an affection, even. I'd like to see them develop the confidence and self-reliance that Earth is starting to display now. But that can't happen until we find out what's undermining them. And to do that, we need help from people who understand humans better than we do. Del Cullen is doing his best, but we know that none of us would make a very good Mac—" Garuth hesitated. "zorac, who was that famous Terran who wrote about intrigue and deceit?"

"Machiavelli?" the computer replied.

"Yes. Was he Scottish?"

"No. Italian."

"I thought 'Macs' were Scottish."

"Not always."

"Oh." Garuth sighed. "Is there *anything* about Earth that's completely consistent, zorac?"

"If there is, I haven't found it."

Garuth looked back at Hunt and Danchekker. "So those are my fears. If there's a risk of our being replaced, there might not be very much time. *That* was why we came to Vic when we did, and in the way that we did."

There was a short pause. Then Danchekker clasped his fingers together, his elbows resting on the arms of his chair, and cleared his throat. "Can you be sure that there really is an identifiable cause of this 'plague,' as you put it, waiting to be tracked down?" he asked. "In the case of Earth, the Jevlenese deliberately introduced nonsensical belief systems thousands of years ago and engineered supernatural workings to support them. But the Jevlenese have always been under the totally rational guidance of the Thuriens, which, one would suppose, should produce exactly the opposite results. That turns out not to have been the case, however."

"Naturally, we wondered about that, too," Shilohin said. "Do you have an explanation?"

Danchekker took off his spectacles and proceeded to wipe them with a handkerchief. "Only that possibly you're thinking too much like Ganymeans, and not making sufficient allowance for the limitless human capacity for sheer, pigheaded obstinacy. The reason why socialism fell apart on Earth wasn't because its ideals were unachievable—Ganymeans achieve them as a matter of course, instinctively. It failed because they are alien to human nature. And when its advocates tried to change human nature to make the fact fit their theory, people resisted. The social engineers didn't understand that Newton's third law applies to social forces as well as to physical ones."

"Go on," Garuth said, listening attentively.

Danchekker showed a hand in a reluctant acknowledgment that he too had no choice but to accept the facts as he found them. "And I can see humans, any humans, reacting in the same way to the kind of enticement by which the Thuriens tried to shape them"—he gestured at Garuth—"and to the kind that you are attempting now. In other words, couldn't what you're up against be simply a fundamental, ineradicable human trait? Are you sure that what you're looking for actually exists at all?" He drew a pad and pencil from his pocket and began scribbling some notes.

Garuth returned to his desk and sat down again. "We asked ourselves that, but we don't think it's the case," he answered. "You see, there's a distinct category of Jevlenese that the infection seems to spread from. They account for practically all of the cult founders and the agitators. All the trouble seems to emanate from them."

"You mean like the one all these purple people have been getting into a frenzy over since yesterday?" Hunt interjected. "What was he called, Ayatollah, or something?"

"Ayultha," Shilohin supplied.

"Oh, yes."

"There's something very unusual about them," Garuth said. "Something that can't be explained as simply an extreme of some general human characteristic. There's too much of a pattern, too much that's systematic for it to be coincidental aberration."

ZORAC interrupted. "Excuse me. I have a call for Professor Danchekker."

Danchekker's pencil broke, and the color drained visibly from his face.

"Who is it, ZORAC?" Hunt asked.

"Sandy, from the UNSA labs."

"Put her through."

"Oh, sorry to interrupt, but we're wondering where to put your personal things, Professor," Sandy's voice said cheerfully. "Do you want to be out in the lab? Or I thought maybe one of the smaller offices would be better for privacy."

Danchekker nodded rapidly and licked his lips. "Yes . . . yes, that would be preferable, thank you," he agreed in a shaky voice.

"Okay."

"Hold any more nonurgent calls until we're through, ZORAC," Garuth instructed.

Hunt looked back at Garuth. "You were saying that there's too much of a pattern to these ayatollahs," he said.

Garuth nodded. "For one thing, they're all very unscientific. I don't mean simply low in aptitude; they lack the basic conceptual machinery that makes any rational account of an objective world possible. They don't seem to share the ordinary, commonsense notions of causality and consistency that you have to have, even to begin understanding the universe. You'd almost think they weren't from this universe at all."

"Can you give some instances?" Hunt asked.

"Fundamental things—things that any six-year-old wouldn't think twice about," Garuth answered. "We take it for granted, for example, that objects remain unaltered by changes in location or orientation; that things measure the same in the evening as they do in the morning; that the same causes always produce the same results. Children grasp such fundamentals naturally. But the—what did you call them?"

"Ayatollahs," Hunt said. He shrugged at Danchekker. "Sounds like a good name for them, to me."

"They don't seem to see anything natural about predictability at all," Garuth went on. "They act as if it were mysterious. Machines baffle them."

"They talk instead about magic and mysticism," Shilohin said.

Garuth made a gesture of incomprehension. "They believe it," he said. "As if that was how their perceptions of reality had been conditioned. Hence my question: We know who performed the conjuring tricks that spread such beliefs on Earth. But who did it to the Jevlenese?"

Danchekker stared at him. "I have no idea. Have you?"

Garuth waited for a moment, then nodded. "Possibly. We think it could have something to do with JEVEX. But we're not sure exactly how."

"JEVEX evolved under the same influences that plotted to overthrow Thurien and Earth," Shilohin pointed out. "Conceivably the qualities of its creators were somehow embodied into its nature—and the ayatollahs are frequently violent and excitable. They are suspicious of everyone, and pathologically insecure, hence their obsessive urge to control others and impose their will—what else do these cults of theirs express? The insecurity also manifests itself as an insatiable lust for wealth, on a scale beyond the comprehension of normal people."

"Hm, we've seen more than a few like that back on Earth," Hunt remarked. He was thinking of a ring that had been broken up after the Pseudowar and its revelations. Maybe Earth held more undercover Jevlenese than had been realized.

"A completely circular argument," Danchekker objected.

"You begin by postulating JEVEX as the cause, then conclude by deducing Jevlenese origins as a consequence. A simple observation of the commonality of human nature to both situations would be far more to the point, would it not?"

"Maybe," Hunt conceded.

Garuth was not so sure. "There is other evidence of a distinct, external cause at work: the suddenness with which the ayatollahs are affected. The condition doesn't seem to be present from birth, or something that develops progressively through life. It appears suddenly, as if the victims were being possessed."

"At a similar point in their lives?" Hunt queried.

"No. It can happen at any age."

"There are practically no records of childhood cases, though," Shilohin said.

Hunt reflected for several seconds. "What kind of evidence is there for these 'possessions'?" he asked finally. "Is it just anecdotal, or what?"

"It's an acknowledged fact among the Jevlenese, occurring as far back as records go," Garuth said.

Shilohin took up the details. "A number of common themes reappear continually beneath the superficial differences of what the various cults preach. They go back a long way, and cut across boundaries of nation, race, creed, geographic area and historical age. One of them is this notion we've already mentioned of persons being suddenly 'possessed,' somehow. It's always in the same kind of way: they usually switch to a new life-style; their value system and their conceptual world model change; and they lose rationality."

"So it's not as if they never had it," Hunt said.

"Exactly. And it isn't only we who see the difference. All the native Jevlenese languages have terms that set them apart as a class—usually translating as 'Emerged' or 'Arisen,' or something vaguely synonymous. They talk about having 'escaped' from an 'inner world,' or something recognizably similar."

When Shilohin had finished, Danchekker twiddled the pen that Hunt had handed him between his fingers and stared down at his notes in silence for a while. Finally, he exhaled heavily and shook his head. "I still think you're reading meaning where none exists," he said. "Essentially the same concepts are also encountered widely on Earth. The most economic answer is that they are merely simplistic expressions of the hopes, fears, and doubts that underlie the workings of primitive mentalities anywhere. No unifying explanation of the kind you are seeking is called for."

"ZORAC, what's your evaluation?" Garuth asked.

"Logically, the professor is correct. But past experience says Vic's hunches are the way to bet."

"Then let me throw one more thing at you, Professor," Garuth said. "The pattern doesn't extend back to the earliest stages of the Jevlenese past. There was no hint of it in Lunarian history. And the descendants of the Lambian survivors brought from Minerva didn't show it until long after they established themselves on Jevlen."

Shilohin completed the point for him. "It was only after JEVEX had been up and running for some time that the first ayatollahs appeared, spreading notions of mysticism and magic. Before then, nothing of the kind had been heard of. In fact, that was where the Jevlenese got their idea for sabotaging Earth. That's why we think that JEVEX was the culprit, somehow. And it could also explain why all of the cults, regardless of their superficial bickerings and hair-splittings, are united in calling for JEVEX to be restored."

At that moment ZORAC came through again. "Excuse me, but I've got Del Cullen. He says it's urgent."

"Go ahead," Garuth said.

Cullen's face appeared on one of the screens by Garuth's desk, looking tense. "Ayultha has been assassinated," he announced without preliminaries.

Gasps of disbelief came from around the office. Garuth was stunned. "When? How?" he stammered.

"A few minutes ago, at the rally they were having in Chinzo today. We're not exactly sure how. Look—this is what happened."

Cullen's face was replaced by a view of Ayultha treating a frenzied gathering to one of his harangues. He seemed to reach some kind of a crescendo, standing dramatically with his arms raised while the crowd thundered in unison. Then a figure scrambled up onto the edge of the platform, shouting something, then pointed an accusing finger—and Ayultha exploded. There was a burst of incandescence, and then all that remained where he had stood an instant before was a smoldering patch on the platform. Pandemonium broke out all around. A purple-spiral banner that had formed the backdrop was blazing, and some people at the front of the crowd seemed to have been burned.

"My God!" Danchekker whispered, staring numbly.

Hunt watched the screen, grim-faced. "They might be crazy, Chris. But we're not dealing with any Hare Krishnas," he muttered. "Whatever's going on here, those guys are serious."

Chapter Twenty-three

Some inner inspiration had told Eubeleus, the Deliverer, that the time to act was now. One of the qualities that characterized greatness was the gift of judging tide and moment by an un-sensed, intuitive process that dwelt deep below thought, and then delivered its verdict to consciousness fully formed and complete, like the solution to an elaborate, invisible piece of computation appearing suddenly on a screen.

With the removal of Ayultha, the Spiral's entire organization was not only in disarray, but fragmenting. Already, its members were being racked with doubts, and warring factions claimed their shares of followers as rival worthies expounded different interpretations of what had taken place. Some dismissed the event as a spectacular piece of chicanery engineered by some hostile interest; at the opposite extreme, others had no doubt of its authenticity as a manifestation of powers operating from beyond the purview of everyday experience. If the Spiral's archprelate and guide had been defenseless against such powers, then the most fundamental tenets of its doctrines were suspect.

Hence, Eubeleus had good reason to be pleased. Thousands of disillusioned followers from the Spiral would now flock to the Axis, and the convictions of its own faithful had been reaffirmed just as the time approached for him to step into the vacuum left after the former regime's inept attempt to set up the Federation. Then, as marked all of the great moments in history, the destinies of the Leader and of the movement would be one. And even if the means had been a little dishonest, the believers needed this demonstration to prepare them for the supreme effort. It was a temporary deception, made necessary by the circumstances. True powers would come to him again when JEVEX was restored.

Eubeleus firmly believed that in the convolutions of complexity that became JEVEX, there had come into being a channel to forces beyond the physical, which his affinity with the machine enabled him to access. Indeed, he believed himself to be, literally, an embodiment of those forces: a personification of the method that JEVEX, through the genius that had emerged within its confines, had created to extend itself into the external world.

He didn't know the precise procedure that JEVEX had followed to free itself; he left matters of technical detail to lesser intellects. There had been a confused period many years before in his early life on Jevlen, after which he was able to recall nothing of what went before. But in compensation he found that he possessed uncommon abilities. In particular, when he discovered the neurocoupler links into JEVEX, he could converse with voices inside the system in ways that others around him seemed unable to do. Or at least, most others. For as he continued groping his way and reorienting himself to the sudden changes that he was told had taken possession of him, he met others who were apart, like himself: the "awakeners," as they were called. Some of them proclaimed it openly and were received as inspired or insane. Others harbored their knowledge secretly. But all shared the experience of remembering a world beyond the senses which the unenlightened were incapable of grasping, save in only the most simplistic and symbolic terms.

The exact nature of that world was something even awakeners had never been able to agree upon with certainty among themselves. They had never consulted the Thuriens, whom the Jevlenese normally relied on for guidance in technological matters, and JEVEX was, after all, a creation of Thurien technology. But Eubeleus's answer was that JEVEX had learned to create pseudopersonalities, which it was able to project into external organic hosts, not only to extend itself into the realm outside, but through them, to shape and direct its further development to its own purpose.

He thus saw himself as a manifestation of an evolutionary leap beyond Man, as naturally destined to dominate the inferiors among whom he found himself as it was in their nature to submit. He had found his mission, the task for which he believed JEVEX had fashioned the psyche that inhabited the body which he now looked out from. For the Jevlenese who had been taken over thus far represented merely the test phase of JEVEX's design—its first, exploratory step into its own outer space. Its next, when it was back in full operation, would be to take over a whole city.

Achieving that would mean having an ample supply of available hosts. And to insure itself of that supply, the Axis was going to need more followers.

In the center of Shiban, the Axis of Light had a headquarters and meeting place, referred to as the Temple. It consisted of a congregational auditorium, with fancifully embellished ornaments and symbols, an imposing dais and rostrum, and a permanent aroma of incense; various function rooms and offices for promoting the movement's affairs; and private quarters for some of its staff and officers who resided on the premises.

On the day following Ayultha's assassination, Eubeleus reviewed a report of the city's reactions to the event and was notified that the appointment of Langerif as the new deputy police chief had been confirmed. The time that he had been working toward, he was certain, had arrived. Accordingly, he sent for his personal aide and principal lieutenant, whose name was Iduane.

"Contact the Prophet," Eubeleus said, "and tell him that he must send us more awakeners."

"It will be difficult. The available couplers are in practically constant use as things are," Iduane warned.

"Then Grevetz will have to get us some more," the Deliverer replied.

Although the city of Orenash had been purged of its sorcerers, and the priests of all the major gods had performed rites of atonement, still there was no respite from its troubles. Brigands laid waste the farms to the north, burning the villages, slaughtering the males, and carrying off the women and their young to sell as slaves. Mountains fell from the sky into the sea, causing floods to sweep over the coastlands. An earthquake split the hills to the west, covering the land in rivers of fire, which was seen as a sign that Vandros, the underworld god, was still unappeased.

Ethendor, the high priest of Vandros, sacrificed a hundred prisoners who had been captured in battle and consulted with his oracles and seers. The answer they delivered was that because the currents that once had borne many aloft had waned, the gods were vying with one another for acolytes to serve them in Hyperia, the sacred realm beyond the sky. The followers of Vandros were not sending enough disciples, and that was why he was displeased.

"But disciples are not forthcoming," Ethendor told the king when the king asked what should be done. "The faith of the people is eclipsed with the vanishing stars. Believers are overcome with terror and doubt. Send more young men to the temples to become initiates."

"Plagues have claimed many. War has drained the lifeblood of the land," the king replied. "Where shall I find the young men? A hunter can only bring home what the forest has spawned."

Ethendor went away and thought about the problem. Later he returned and took the king to the temple of Vandros, with its tower bearing the emblem of the green crescent. There, he showed the king groups of novices in the grounds and about the temple chambers, tending plants, constructing icons, and engaged in other menial tasks.

"These could become the disciples who would placate Vandros and alleviate us of our woes," Ethendor said. "But they have not the makings of true adepts. They aspire, but their power falls short of their ambition. So they serve each in his own lesser way as you can see, and if it is so decreed, true inspiration may one day seize them."

The king grew puzzled. "Then why speak to me of them?" he asked the high priest. "Our need is for birds, but you show me fish that would fly."

"When the forests spawn nothing, then the hunter, if he's not to starve, must turn elsewhere," Ethendor replied, speaking in a low, conspiratorial tone.

"Elsewhere?"

"Perhaps to the farms that are well stocked? A little poaching, maybe, if he has to?"

"Explain what you mean," the king said.

Ethendor drew closer. "There are Masters who teach schools of their own, dedicated to Nieru, in the wilderness and elsewhere outside of the city. They pay no homage to the king, neither do they serve the king. But their acts steal currents from the skies for *their* disciples to ride, which should, by right, be drawn down to the consecrated temples."

"So, tell me the meaning of this talk about poaching," the king said.

Ethendor indicated the menials at work about the temple. "Some of these novices that you see are inadequate, but not totally incapable. They couldn't develop the ability to trap a current and rise with it by themselves. But, with help, they could probably grasp and stay with a current that had been tamed and brought down by others. You take my point?"

"That with economy to ourselves, we could avail ourselves of the efforts of these rogue Masters?" the king said, seeing the point.

"The novices would provide additional service to Vandros, while the circumstances of our own adepts and their capacity to satisfy him would remain unaffected."

"But at the expense of Nieru," the king pointed out. "Would Nieru not seek vengeance?"

"Vandros will protect us."

"Can you be sure?"

"It is in the signs."

The king pondered awhile. "Let it be done, so," he pronounced finally.

Later, Ethendor summoned a number of the novices to him. "Prepare yourselves, for you have been chosen to ascend to Hyperia," he told them. "The services that were rightfully Vandros's due are being stolen by other gods. Yours will be the task of reclaiming them. We will go up into the wilderness accompanied by dragon-tamers and fire-knights, and there shall vengeance and justice be exacted."

Among the novices who had been selected was Keyalo, the foster son of Dalgren, who had denounced Thrax for heresy and sorcery.

Chapter Twenty-four

Formally, Garuth's terms of office required him to delegate the investigation of the Ayultha affair to Jevlenese agencies. This would have given little grounds for optimism of any quick result at the best of times; but with the disruptions caused by the loss of the deputy police chief—who carried the real authority in Shiban, since the office of chief had deteriorated to being little more than a ceremonial figurehead—it was practically a guarantee that nothing of any consequence was going to happen within the limited time frame that Garuth was concerned about. So, following the unofficial line that he had already opted for, he set Del Cullen to seeing what he could make of it. Cullen, in turn, involved Hunt and the UNSA group, since it was part of the problem that they had come to Jevlen to help Garuth solve.

Garuth's other concern was for the rest of the Terran visitors who had arrived with the *Vishnu*. He issued a statement urging them to stay within the Thurien-controlled enclave at Geerbaine as much as possible while the unrest in the city persisted, which was about as close as a Ganymean could come to prohibition. He also sent a sharply worded note to the

Thurien Central Governing Council, protesting the inappropriateness under the present circumstances of extending to Terrans the Ganymean open policy of shipping anyone who felt like it to anywhere they wanted to go. "This determination not to acknowledge real differences that exist between humans and Ganymeans has surely been a major factor in precipitating the situation on Jevlen that we are now having to deal with," the note said in part.

The Council's chairman on Thurien was Calazar. Calazar had headed the deputation that first made contact with Earth when suspicions of Jevlenese duplicity could be contained no longer. His experiences during the Pseudowar that followed, of watching from the inside how the Terrans demolished the Jevlenese pretensions by meeting deception with counter-deception and treachery with even greater machinations, had brought home to him the utter inability of Ganymean minds to anticipate the twists of deviousness that these alien dwarves were capable of. When he received the communication from Garuth, he admitted to himself with characteristic Ganymean candor that perhaps the lesson had not been fully learned yet.

"Perhaps those Terrans on JPC were right, and our whole approach to Jevlen has been wrong all along," he said after considering the matter. "I'm sure Garuth is doing as much as anyone could ask, but maybe we should have delegated the task to Terrans."

Frenua Showm, the female ambassador who had also been one of the first to initiate contact with Earth, suspected all human motives, Jevlenese or Terran. "Giving them equal partnership in Thurien culture as if it were their right was a mistake from the beginning," she declared. "Well-intentioned, no doubt, but falsely premised. Nobody can feel worthy of what they haven't earned. Neither can races. Our ancestors thought that a model society could be created on Jevlen through benign intervention, and they wrote Earth off as a lost cause when it chose to be left to its own devices. The reality turned out to be very different from the vision. Let's learn something from it and not walk straight into making the same mistake again. They are *not* like us. Their behavior isn't governed by the same rules."

"You could be right," Calazar replied reluctantly. "Human problems may need human solutions. Perhaps there's no other way."

VISAR spoke at that moment. "Priority request from PAC on Jevlen. Garuth is asking if you are free."

"Oh dear. Now I expect we're in for a personal protest," Calazar muttered. He raised his voice a fraction. "Very well, VISAR. Bring him here."

Since Calazar and Frenua Showm were actually coupled into VISAR and communicating from separate locations, Garuth was able to join them immediately. His figure materialized, standing in the room.

"Welcome again," Calazar greeted.

"How is the day here?" Garuth asked, as was customary.

"Good."

"Frenua," Garuth acknowledged, turning to Showm. She returned a slight bow of her head.

"And what brings you?" Calazar inquired, bracing himself.

"Eubeleus, the Axis of Light's leader, has contacted me. He's concerned about the way things are going and fears that we could see serious violence if something isn't done quickly. He has a proposal for reducing the tension that I think you should hear. At least it's different from anything else that we've been hearing."

Calazar sent Frenua Showm a glance of relief that this was evidently not going to be the ordeal that he had feared. "Is Eubeleus available on-line at the moment?" he asked Garuth.

"Yes. He's waiting in one of the couplers at PAC," Garuth replied.

"Then let's bring him here and see what he has to say," Calazar invited.

Ganymeans were by nature rational. Ganymean scientists were very rational. Shilohin found it hard to accept that even the true believers could honestly have been taken in to the point of attributing Ayultha's fiery end to supernatural causes. Surely, she insisted, if they could be shown that the same effect was achievable by commonplace methods that were well understood, they would have to see that a more complicated explanation was neither necessary nor justified—and in the process they might learn something valuable. Accordingly, she decided to stage a demonstration. While she and some of the Ganymean technicians were setting things up, Hunt stopped by Del Cullen's office to review matters. It was situated in a corner of the part of PAC that had been allocated for the security force that Cullen was building up.

"So who was the character who gave Ayultha the finger?" Hunt asked from the visitor's chair by the door. "Did you manage to get any sense out of him?"

Cullen, sitting at the desk, shook his head. "A complete yo-yo. Thinks he's a bird in the wrong body. Even the lev police put him in a rubber room. Obviously he was just a stooge that somebody else set up for effect."

It was what Hunt had half expected. "What do you make of it all?" he asked.

"Something's going on," Cullen replied. "If you want my opinion, I don't think that bridge coming down was any accident, either. The police report was sloppy on a lot of points. I think it was rigged."

The same thought had crossed Hunt's mind. He stretched out a leg and rested his foot on one of the boxes piled around the floor. The office that Cullen had reserved for himself was unpretentious, and just at the moment, half of it was taken up with undivulged items from Earth that had arrived on the *Vishnu*, and which he had not yet gotten around to unpacking. "What makes you say so?"

"In a lot of ways, life on Jevlen got to be very live-and-let-live under the Thuriens," Cullen said.

"Which is what you'd expect," Hunt agreed.

"The laws don't contain many thou-shalt-nots. So not much is illegal here, and a lot of what we'd think of as the criminal underworld back home is just part of the scene. If you want to get burned on stuff that's not good for your gray cells, or lose your ass on gaming tables that anyone with a positive IQ knows are as straight as knotted corkscrews, that's up to you. The Thuriens don't presume any right to forbid people from being stupid."

Cullen shrugged. "Anyhow, I think our friend Obayin got too zealous. He was starting to stomp on people's toes, and somebody somewhere had a corn . . . and what's more, I suspect that it had something to do with JEVEX."

"Go on," Hunt said, looking more interested.

"You know that JEVEX isn't totally shut down? There's a core system still running for housekeeping, and to let the Thurien hackers do some poking around in the system."

"Yes."

"Well, the Jevs are a pretty close society, and it's not easy to get a direct line on what goes on. But Obayin decided to play ball with the new administration. He put together a report for Garuth that we think blew the whistle on a market that nobody's talking about out there for hooking people in." Cullen made a palm-upward gesture in the air. "With JEVEX officially off the air, there could be a big demand. That spells money for whoever controls the plugs. But if the Ganymeans think that JEVEX is causing the crazies, a report like that could be enough to make them crack down and ruin the business. Get the scene?"

"It certainly sounds familiar enough," Hunt agreed. He rubbed his chin, frowning. "You said you *think* that this report of Obayin's blew the whistle. Don't you know? I mean, what does it say?"

"It disappeared before anyone got a chance to go through it." Cullen shrugged and made a resigned gesture. "The Ganymeans don't exactly go overboard on what you'd call being security-conscious. That was one of the reasons why I was moved in here."

Hunt nodded understandingly. "I can see the problem. And PAC's full of Jevlenese. You could never be sure of every one of the them, however careful your screening."

"That's true," Cullen said. "And that's the direction that anyone's suspicions would naturally turn in. However, although we can't prove it conclusively, we're pretty sure that the person who lifted that report was a Terran."

Hunt looked up in surprise. "Who?"

"A German called Hans Baumer. He's one of the sociologists that the UN sent here after the Pseudowar to advise the Ganymeans on setting up their administration. He was up in the Ganymean offices one day on what I think was a pretext, and afterward the report was missing."

"Did you talk to him about it?"

Cullen shook his head. "What would the point have been? He'd just deny it, and I couldn't prove anything. All it would do is tip him off."

"And there weren't any copies?"

"Obayin must have had some, sure, but the police department says they can't locate any."

"Not even an original in a computer somewhere?"

"They say not." Cullen showed a hand briefly. "The Jevs lost a War. We're the enemy. They're all in it together. Ganymeans don't understand. They can't think that way. That's why the Jevs have been running rings around them for years." He snorted. "And still I've got some working in security."

Hunt stretched back in the chair and put a hand behind his neck while he thought about it. "So what does it mean?" he asked at last. "If what you're saying is true, then this character Baumer has developed some kind of connection with the criminal fraternity here—assuming they're the ones who'd most want Obayin out of the picture. But how would he have got that well in with them so quickly? He can't have been here more than, what, six months at the most?"

Cullen shook his head. "Vic, I don't know. But I'll tell you something else. Ayultha getting blown away like that on the same day wasn't a coincidence. Something's going on, and it involves a connection of some sort between the underworld and the cults. And right at this moment, that's about all I know."

Hunt thought it over again, nodded, and pursed his lips. "So where do we go from here?"

"The only lead I can see is to try and find out more about Baumer. I've got some stuff on his background from the personnel records of the department that sent him here, but it doesn't tell us a great deal. He's twenty-nine, originally from Bonn, studied moral and political philosophy at Munich, but without graduating finally. A mixed pattern of minor political activism around Europe, generally with leftist affiliations. Likes belonging to movements and associations, and organizing people. Doesn't like capitalism and industrial technology. Isn't married. Was sent to Jevlen by a department of the U.S. European government."

"Hmm . . . Does he have quarters here, too, inside PAC?" Hunt asked, scratching the side of his nose pointedly. The implication was obvious.

Cullen nodded and lowered his voice. "Yes, I had a look around. Garuth doesn't know about it. Baumer talks to a lot of Jevlenese, but that's what you'd expect for a sociologist. He likes reading politics, history, and psychology, he gets letters from a girl in Frankfurt, and he worries about his health." Cullen spread his hands.

"Nothing more?"

"That's it. His office here didn't turn up anything either. But he does use another one, a private place out in the city that he says provides a less threatening environment for talking to the Jevlenese that his work involves him with. That might be more interesting. But how do we get near enough to him?" Cullen jerked a thumb to indicate the larger office outside his. "He's not going to say anything to my people. You're here to look at Ganymean science, so you can't go asking questions without it looking strange, especially if he's got reasons to be suspicious."

Hunt sat up slowly in his chair, his eyes widening. Just at that moment he would have rated Gregg Caldwell a genius.

Cullen looked at him uncertainly. "Are you okay?"

"We brought someone with us, just for that reason," Hunt said. There had been so much happening that he hadn't had a chance to explain where Gina fitted in.

"What are you talking about?"

"There's a writer out at Geerbaine, who came on the same ship—a woman called Gina Marin. Officially she's here on a free-lance job, but in reality she's with us—UNSA—as a kind of undercover help. This is right in her court."

Cullen blinked. "Well, I'll be darned. Whose idea was this?"

"Caldwell's, back at Goddard. He had an idea that this kind of situation could happen."

A long, drawn-out explanation obviously wasn't necessary.

"Well, let's get her onto it," Cullen said. "Will she be there now?"

"As far as I know." Hunt had called her an hour or so previously to see how things were going.

Cullen indicated the door with a nod of his head. Hunt turned on his chair and reached back to open it. "Hey, Crozin," Cullen called to a Jevlenese in shirtsleeves at a desk outside. "Put a call through to the Best Western at Geerbaine, could you? See if you can get a Terran woman who's staying there, name of Gina Marin. A writer."

"Right," Crozin acknowledged.

Cullen waved for Hunt to close the door again. "What about the work that Baumer's been doing since he came here?" Hunt asked, turning back toward the desk. "Are there any reports and things from him that she could see to get more background?"

"Sure." Cullen activated a screen by his desk and called up a list of file references. While he waited, Hunt fished his cigarettes from a pocket, lit one, and leaned back to run over what had been said. A minute or two later Crozin buzzed through to say that Gina was on the line from Geerbaine.

"You'd better take it," Cullen said, swiveling the screen around to face Hunt.

"Back so soon," Gina said. "What is it this time?"

"I think you're in business," Hunt told her. "We've got a job for you."

"Does that mean I get to see PAC at last?"

"Yes. Catch one of those tubes into the city if they're running today. Ask for the UNSA labs when you get here. I'm on my way to a show that Shilohin's putting on for the ayatollahs, but you can ask for Del Cullen. He'll tell you all about it. I'll see you sometime later."

"I'm on my way," Gina said.

Chapter Twenty-five

At one end of a long hall inside PAC, Hunt and Sandy watched as Thardan, a young Ganymean technician from the *Shapieron*, checked the connections of an apparatus consisting of a metal frame festooned with tubes and cables, mounting a horizontal cylinder two feet or so long, from one end of which protruded a tapering snout ending in a hemispherical tip. Nearby, Duncan was adjusting the settings on a supply panel.

Several hundred feet away at the far end of the hall, about a dozen *queesals*—a kind of Jevlenese fruit, like a brown, pear-shaped melon—were mounted on wire supports positioned irregularly about the floor. A mixed company of Ganymeans, Jevlenese, and one or two Terrans were standing by the wall to one side. Shilohin was among them, with a group of gaudily clad Jevlenese who were watching the activity suspiciously. The central figure among the latter was a recently "possessed" ayatollah—Hunt's term for them was already spreading through PAC—formerly an unknown city destitute, who now went by an exalted Jevlenese title that meant "He Who Shall Return." Cullen had promptly christened him MacArthur. The others were followers from a Spiral of Awakening subsect that was forming around him out of the squabbles following the exit of the leader. MacArthur had restored faith and banished doubt by asserting that Ayultha, far from being a victim of transcendental retribution, had indeed discovered Truth, and as a consequence of that had attracted upon himself Cosmic Energies that even he had been unable to control. It was an opportune move at a time when the SoA needed a new Word to pull it back together, and MacArthur was already being acclaimed by many as Ayultha's successor.

"Phase-conjugated laser," Hunt said to Sandy, waving at the cylinder with a black, penlike object that he was holding. "That was how they did it."

Sandy shook her head. "Sorry, I'm a biologist—remember? You'll have to be more specific."

Just then, Thardan glanced across at them and nodded. "It's ready."

"Well, let's see what happens." Hunt motioned to Sandy with a hand, and they began walking toward the other end of the hall. "In the real world, perfectly parallel, nondispersing beams of light don't exist. You can think of one as a bundle of rays, spreading and being scrambled by irregularities in the medium it passes through."

"Okay."

"So, you can imagine a time-reversed beam whose rays follow the same trajectories, but in the opposite direction."

"Like Newtonian particles moving backward, you mean?" Sandy said.

"Right. Well, it turns out that to create a reversed beam, you don't have to reverse each and every quantum-level motion of the atoms and electrons that do the reflecting and radiating. Reversing the macroscopic parameters that describe the average motions is enough. All of which is another way of saying that it's possible to make a device that behaves as a phase-conjugating mirror, where every ray that strikes it is returned precisely along its reversed path."

"Okay . . ." Sandy said, nodding.

"Alternatively, instead of making it a simple mirror, you can make it a source in its own right—a source of a signal that will follow an incident beam back to wherever it came from. That's one way they get rid of atmospheric distortion for communications lasers: a pilot beam from the receiver effectively 'pre-scrambles' the databeam in such a way that the information comes out the other end clean."

They were approaching the end of the hall. Hunt gestured at the *queesals* on their wire mounts. "Or, if the incident beam happens to be a reflection off an object, and the conjugator that it's reflected back to is a high-gain power laser . . ."

Sandy was already nodding. "I see. It's as if the object attracts the power beam to itself."

"You've got it. The technique was used in the space-defense systems for self-targeting of radiation weapons." Hunt grinned. "So I suppose MacArthur was right in a way about poor old Ayultha drawing down powers on himself that he didn't understand. They had somebody in the crowd with a wand like this, and a compact, weapons-grade projector aimed from somewhere nearby—there were enough high buildings all around the place. It could have been dismantled in a few minutes."

"Well, I guess it's a pretty persuasive way of telling the opposition to look for other ways of making a living," Sandy said. "And enough of the natives seem to have been impressed, whatever the Ganymeans are trying to tell them."

Hunt nodded. "I agree. That's why I admire Shilohin for trying this, and I wish her all the best with it. But between you and me, I think she's wasting her time."

They came to where the others were waiting. Shilohin was just finishing an explanation to MacArthur and his group. Hunt wasn't sure how the Ganymeans had persuaded them to be here, for they were wearing expressions like those of the bishops who didn't want to look through Galileo's telescope. And Hunt could see MacArthur's point: this was his chance to become the Great Panjandrum of the Spiral, and he wasn't about to throw it away for anybody. Hunt had tried explaining as much to the Ganymeans, but the consensus among them had been to give reason a chance to prevail.

Shilohin turned and indicated Hunt with a hand. "This is

Dr. Hunt, a visiting Terran scientist, who will show you the process. It really is very straightforward."

Hunt held up the short, black rod. "This is a low-power portable laser. It emits light just like an ordinary flashlamp, but in a tighter beam." He moved his arm in a random motion. "The light from it will be reflected in all directions off anything that I point it at, just as some light from a flashlamp is reflected into your eyes from any object that the lamp illuminates. That's how you see it." He aimed at one of the *queesals* about ten feet from him, centering the red dot produced by an auxiliary registration beam. "So a minute fraction of it will reach the projector up at the far end there, where Sandy and I just came from. When it does, the power beam from the projector will follow the reverse path back to where the reflection came from. Watch." He pressed a button, and the fruit exploded in a fiery flash.

"Note that it isn't necessary to aim or realign the projector," Shilohin commented. "The beam retraces the path of the reflected ray automatically."

Hunt demonstrated the fact by vaporizing two more *queesals*, chosen wide apart to subtend an impressively large angle from where the projector was situated. Thardan and Sandy had moved well away from the equipment, and it was clear even from that distance that nobody at the far end had touched anything. Hunt held out the hand laser toward the Jevlenese. "Anyone else care to try?"

There was a short, prickly silence. Nobody moved to take up the offer. Then MacArthur marched past Hunt to where the nearest of the intact *queesals* was standing, and removed it from its support with a nourish. He turned to face the onlookers, tossed the fruit down on the floor, and stomped it to pulp with a single blow from his foot. "There are many ways of destroying a *queesal*," he declared. "I have just as validly proved that Ayultha was killed by a giant foot from the sky." Some of the followers began laughing, pointing at Hunt and Shilohin. One of them picked up another of the *queesals* and took a bite from it.

"No, look. He was swallowed by a mouth that appeared in the ground."

MacArthur glowered contemptuously. "Don't be deceived by their tricks. They try to conceal what they cannot explain."

"If you know of something different, give us *your* explanation," Shilohin challenged. But it did no good.

"You Ganymeans think you know so much," MacArthur spat. "But I tell you there are realities that your lever-and-cogwheel minds could never grasp. I have seen realms beyond your comprehension. Things that defy all your laws, which you think the universe will follow for your convenience."

"Where?" Shilohin retorted, getting exasperated. "Where have you seen such things? At worlds light-years away? I doubt it. The only things you'll find there are Ganymean starships."

"Bah! Go as far as you will with your toys, it's still the same plane. But there are other realms *within*!"

"Nonsense. Within what? Say what you mean for once."

At that moment, a call-tone sounded in Hunt's ear, and ZORAC spoke. "Do you have a second?"

"What is it?"

"Garuth is back from Thurien. He'd like a word with you if you can get away."

Relieved at the chance to extricate himself, Hunt caught Sandy's eye and motioned her across. "Make my apologies," he muttered. "I have to slip away. Garuth wants to see me about something."

"Sure . . . I guess this wasn't any big surprise, eh?" Sandy said.

"The Ganymeans can write it off as a lesson in human psychology," Hunt answered.

Before their defeat in the Pseudowar, the leaders of the previous regime on Jevlen had, as part of their plans for the Jevlenese Federation, embarked on a secret armaments-manufacturing program to enable them to deal with their ancient Cerian rivals, who had become the Terrans. To conceal their intentions from the Thuriens, they concentrated this war industry on a remote, lifeless planet called Uttan, far away in another star system. Since the Federation's demise, Uttan's power-generation and production facilities had been shut down, and the planet occupied by a Thurien caretaker force. The proposition with which Eubeleus had approached Calazar had to do with Uttan, and was of a totally unexpected nature.

"He says that he sees the situation on Jevlen deteriorating, and that bloodshed is a distinct possibility," Garuth said after Hunt had closed the door and sat down. "Being a person of compassion and nonviolence who has dedicated himself to the spiritual advancement of his fellow men, he can't sit by without making some effort to prevent it."

"I see." Hunt's tone carried the conviction of a policeman being told that the violin case with the submachine gun inside it must have been a wrong bag picked up at the airport.

Garuth made a gesture which conveyed that he was just reporting what had happened. "But the Thuriens were impressed. Eubeleus said he wants to clear the way for Jevlen's full recovery and reform as speedily as possible. For the greater good and well-being of all, he is prepared to renounce all claims on Jevlen and remove himself and his Axis followers from the scene to find their own niche elsewhere. Jevlen will be freed from the threat of open strife erupting between the two major cults, and the Spiral will be left to work out its relations with the other cults in whatever way suits them."

"And, of course, the Thuriens wouldn't want there to be any doubts as to their own reasonableness," Hunt said.

"Er, quite. After spending six months on Earth, I think I can say that they don't have the nose for suspecting insincere motives, yet."

"Okay, so exactly what is this Eubeleus offering to do?"

"His proposal is that Uttan would be stripped of its military potential, and the planet bioformed into a habitable condition for assignment to the Axis of Light as its own sovereign world. It would become a spiritual retreat, open to all of sincere intent, who come in search of truth. He says he got the inspiration from hearing about Earth's monasteries. The Axis would pay its way by managing Uttan's industrial capacity as a supply facility, converted to peaceful ends." Garuth tossed out a hand. "There it is. I detect that your enthusiasm is what the English would call somewhat less than total."

"Do you think he's mixed up in any of this other business that's been going on?" Hunt asked bluntly. "It all seems too much of a coincidence with his appearing on the scene. I don't like coincidences."

"We don't know," Garuth replied. "But I can see your point. If he were, it would say as much as anything needs to about these altruistic trimmings."

"Exactly," Hunt said, nodding. He leaned back and contemplated the ceiling. "It seems that for some reason our mystical friend is attaching a lot of importance to Uttan, doesn't it? What would he want with an airless, waterless, inhospitable ball of rock like that, light-years from anywhere? It makes you think there must be something about that planet that we're not aware of—and from the blithe way they're reacting, something that the Thuriens aren't aware of, either."

Garuth stared across at Hunt and thought about it. "I don't know" was all he could reply. "I'll get ZORAC to assemble all the information that we've got on it."

Chapter Twenty-six

The Jevlenese sitting in Baumer's city office, his feet propped impudently on the edge of Baumer's desk, was called Lesho. He was squat and swarthy, with thick black hair and a short, untidy beard. His glittery blue coat and red shirt were expensive but flashy, and he was heavily adorned with jewelry and rings. His equally unsavory-looking companion, orange-haired and heavily built, wearing a baggy brown suit, was leaning against the wall by the door, chewing absently and wearing a scowl of bored indifference. Baumer sat tight-lipped, forcing himself to control his sense of outrage and impotence.

"How do I know why they're interested?" Lesho said. "I just deliver the messages. It isn't your business to worry about reasons, either. I'm just telling you that the word is, the people upstairs want to know what kind of drift is coming in from Thurien to the Ganymeans in PAC. They're especially interested in anything that comes in from JPC."

Baumer spread his hands in exasperation. "Look, you don't seem to understand. That kind of information isn't left lying around for anyone who walks by to pick up. It's stored in the data system, and with the controls that Cullen is setting up, anyone can't get at it."

"You got the stuff from the egg-hat who fell off the bridge," Lesho said, unimpressed.

"That was different. It was hand-delivered as a hardcopy. Things like that don't happen every day."

"Well, that's your problem."

"Look, would you mind not putting your feet there? You're crumpling up those pages."

Lesho raised a hand and leveled a warning finger. "That's not a good attitude to have. Let me remind you of something. You're not the only Terran inside PAC. It also happens that time in couplers is getting harder to get these days, and one day you might find you've run out of friends who can supply. So just let's remember who's doing who the favors, huh?"

Baumer drew a long breath and nodded curtly. "Very well. I'll do whatever I can. But you must try and make them understand that I can't promise."

A tone sounded from a panel by Baumer's desk. "What is it?" he inquired, turning his head.

The house-system's synthetic voice replied. "The writer who wanted to talk to you is outside: Gina Marin."

"Oh, she is? Just one moment." Baumer looked back at the Jevlenese. "As you can see, I do have other things to attend to. Was there anything else?"

Lesho swung his legs down from the desk and stood up. "Just don't forget that other Terrans in PAC might like their trips, too. And there's more of them arriving."

The Jevlenese in the brown suit straightened up and opened the door just as Gina appeared on the other side of it. Lesho stopped to peer down at Baumer's desk. "Is that the one I messed up?" he inquired, pointing at a sheet of paper with a heelmark on it. It was on the top of a thin wad of printout.

"Yes. I'd just run it off," Baumer said testily as he rose to his feet.

Lesho screwed it up and tossed it into the bin. "Well, looks like you needed to do another copy anyhow." He turned away, nodded toward the door, and sauntered out behind his companion.

Baumer came around to usher Gina inside, and then closed

the door. He indicated the seat that Lesho had used and returned to his own side of the desk.

"I apologize for that," he said stiffly. "As a sociologist one must be prepared for all types of people."

"I suppose so." Gina sat down. "Thanks for fitting me in at short notice. You seem busy." Her phrasing was the code to switch on the miniature voice recorder, supplied by Del Cullen, that was concealed inside the fold of her collar.

"It's a busy time. There's a lot to do here." Baumer's manner reverted to cool. He didn't know what this was about, and he wasn't prepared at this stage to commit to a lot of time.

"I've only seen a little, but I think I know what you mean."

"You've just come to Jevlen, I think you said?"

"That's right—with the *Vishnu*. It's all a bit mind-blowing. I guess I haven't gotten used to Ganymeans yet. How long have you been here yourself?"

"Almost five months, now."

"Time enough to find your way around?"

"It depends what you want to find . . . You said you're some kind of writer?"

Gina nodded. "Books on subjects of topical interest. Right now, I'm planning one on historical figures who were Jevlenese agents—known or possible. I don't know if you've kept in touch with the popular stuff that's been coming out on Earth, but the amount of nonsense is unbelievable. I wanted to get the record straight, and this seemed to be the place to start. So here I am."

"Jevlenese intervention in history. Famous figures who might have been agents . . ." Baumer repeated. His English was clearly articulated, with the barest hint of an accent. He had pale, delicate features, which were accentuated by thin lips, a narrow, tapering chin, and heavy, horn-rimmed spectacles, giving him a youthful look for his years. An untidy mop of light brown hair and the mottled gray sweater that he was wearing enhanced the studentlike image. But the eyes regarding Gina through the lenses were cool and remote, and the hard set of his mouth infused his expression with a hint of disdain. It was the kind of look he might have used to dismiss a saleslady who had been given her chance.

He stared down at the desk; a loose wave of hair flopped down over his forehead, and he brushed it aside with a hand. "I'm not sure I can help," he said. "The kind of history that I think you mean isn't my line."

"I hadn't assumed it was," Gina answered. "But I was hoping that you might have some suggestions on how I should go about it—some thoughts on possible contacts, maybe. You've had a lot longer to find your way around."

Clearly Baumer was preoccupied with other things and did not want to get involved. But Gina had her objectives, too. She had been scanning the office with her eyes ever since she sat down. It was bare and dusty, with little in the way of imme-diate evidence as to the kind of thing he did there. She got the impression that this was not where he spent most of his time away from PAC.

Her gaze came back to the companel by the desk. Baumer wasn't equipped with Ganymean communications accessories for interacting with ZORAC. The man she had heard talking when she arrived had been Jevlenese, and the translations of his and Baumer's voices—into German, she had noted—had come from the panel.

"Can I ask you something?" she said.

"What?"

She motioned toward the panel. "Those Jevlenese who were here when I came in—the one who was talking was being trans-lated through there. But I was told that VISAR doesn't extend out into the city. And JEVEX isn't supposed to be running. So what was doing it? Do you have stand-alone systems here that can do that kind of thing?"

"You are observant, Ms. Marin," Baumer said, conceding a nod. "No, none of those. The Ganymeans have connected ZORAC into the regular comnet. You can get a translation facility on channel fifty-six. It's handy—we can talk to the Jevlenese any-where."

"What's ZORAC?" Gina asked to keep up her image, at the same time crossing imaginary fingers that ZORAC wouldn't recognize her and return some wisecrack. But either Baumer had switched the channel off, or only a subset of ZORAC's capacity was available to the public net, or it was programmed with enough manners to know when to keep quiet—Gina had not learned enough about it, yet, to know which.

"The Ganymean computer aboard the *Shapieron*," Baumer replied. "It doesn't play straight into your head like the Thurien computers do." He waved a hand. "Oh, I'm not really conversant with these technical matters. It needs microphones, screens, and things. You'll find out about it when you meet some of the people in PAC."

"That's Planetary Administration Center, right?"

"Yes. Perhaps you should try and get to see some of the Ganymeans on Garuth's staff—theoretically he is in charge of every thing."

"Yes, I know."

Baumer frowned down at the desk and shook his head in thinly disguised irritation. "You really should have got more of an agenda arranged before you came . . ." He reached for a pad and picked up a pen. "Anyway, his chief scientist is a woman called Shilohin—"

"A Ganymean, you mean?"

"Yes. She should be of some help. She's involved with a number of Jevlenese and Terrans who are investigating alleged agents on Earth." He scribbled a few lines. "Those are a couple of other names that work under her. And here are a few of the Jevlenese that it might be worth your while approaching. This last one, Reskedrom, was quite high up in the Federation while it lasted, and should be useful—but he's not easy to get to. Your best bet would be to start at COJA: Coordinating Office for Jevlenese Affairs—that's a department inside PAC. They keep lists and charts of who's what and where, and everything that's going on." Baumer finished writing, tore off the top sheet of the pad, and pushed it across. "That should help. But otherwise, I don't think I have very much to offer, I'm afraid."

Gina took the slip and put it in a pocket. "Thanks anyway. I did meet a bunch of UNSA people on the ship, but they're really only coming here to look into Ganymean science. They're tied up setting up their labs, anyhow, so I don't have anyone to show me around." She paused to give Baumer time to react if he chose. He didn't. Still reluctant to let it go at that, Gina waited a few seconds longer, and then inquired, "What do you do here that keeps you so busy?"

"I am a sociologist. I have a whole new society to work with."

Baumer's choice of phrasing suggested an approach. Gina had read all of the reports he had written, which Hunt had run off for her from PAC's files. "Control" seemed to be the dominant word in Baumer's vocabulary. In his eyes, Earth had gone too far down the path of degeneracy as represented by the insanity of the free market and the corrosion of liberal morality for there to be any hope left of saving it. But the situation on Jevlen, if only those with the power could be made to see, offered a clean slate on which to begin anew and engineer the model society. And Baumer knew just how it should be done.

"That's interesting," she said. "Which way could Jevlen's society be heading, do you think, after it gets straightened out?"

Baumer sat back in his chair and looked at the far wall. The indifference that had hung in his eyes until then changed to a hint of a gleam. "There's an opportunity here," he replied. "An opportunity to build the society that could have existed on Earth, and now never will—without all the greed and arrogance that doesn't care what it destroys; one based on true equality and values that count."

Gina looked at him as if he had just said something that she didn't hear very often. "I've often thought the same thing myself," she said. Inside, she felt a twinge of disgust at her own hypocrisy; but she had known what the job would entail when she agreed to do it. "Is that why you came here from Earth?" she asked him.

Baumer sighed. "I came here to get away from a world that has been left spiritually devastated by its infatuation with bourgeois trivia and mindless distractions. The banks and the corporations own everybody now, and the qualities that they reward are the ones that suit *their* needs: loyalty and obedience. And the cattle are content, grazing in the field. Nobody wants to think about what it's doing to them, or where it's all leading. They don't want to *think* at all. It's gone too far now for anything to change. But *here*, on Jevlen, there's been a forced stop to the lunacy, a reexamination of everything. With the right people of vision in control, it could turn out different."

"You really think so?" Gina's tone suggested that it all sounded too good to be true.

"Why not? The Jevlenese are human, too, made of the same clay. They can be molded."

"How would you make it different, if you could?" Gina asked.

That got him talking.

What Jevlen needed was for the anarchy that was the cause of all its problems to be replaced by centralized direction of the planet's affairs, with tighter control over all aspects of existence. The way to achieve that was through a dizzying system of government programs and agencies. And the chance was there now, because the first step to putting the machinery in place had already been achieved with the setting up of the Ganymean planetary administration.

"But that's not the way Ganymeans seem to think," Gina pointed out.

"And look at the mess they've made. They don't understand human needs. They must be *made* to understand."

Approved goods and services, along with desirable levels for their consumption, should be determined by regional planning boards, and industry limited to the minimum necessary to provide them—thus eliminating any need for a wasteful competitive business sector. Occupations should be assigned on the basis of society's needs, balanced against aptitude scores accumulated during "social conditioning"—the term that Baumer used for education—although he was prepared to concede that due consideration could be given to individual preference if circumstances permitted. Access to entertainment and leisure activities should be rationed into a reward system to facilitate the achievement of quotas.

However, although she stayed for another forty minutes, it was all pretty much in keeping with the picture that Gina had already formed, and she learned little that was new.

Baumer saw himself as one of those outcasts from the herd, set apart in the company of those such as van Gogh, Nietzsche, Lawrence, and Nijinsky, by the sensitivity of seeing too much and too deep. Everybody was born with the mystical spark dormant within them, but its potential was quenched by the modern world's delusions of objectivity and rationality. Preoccupation with the external, and the false elevation of science as the way to find knowledge and salvation, had diverted humanity from the inner paths that mattered. He particularly detested the general adulation accorded to the "practical." Aristophanes had ridiculed Socrates, and Blake had hated Newton for the same reason.

Nevertheless, despite Gina's hope that she might have made some indent, he sidestepped another attempt by her to extend their relationship socially. She eventually left without obtaining any commitment for them to talk again, or any feeling that she had achieved very much.

Thinking through the discussion on her way back to PAC, she felt grubby at the deception that she had lent herself to. Behind its facade of indignation and righteousness, the line she had forced herself to listen to was, like so many philosophies that she had heard from other misfits and self-styled iconoclasts, really nothing more than a massive exercise in self-justification. Because they didn't fit, the world would have to be changed.

In contrast, there were people—Hunt, for instance—whom she classed as shapers of the world. They didn't pass judgments on it, but found niches that fitted them because they could come to terms with the reality they saw and make the best of the chances it offered. They could look the inevitability of death in the face, accept their own insignificance, and gain satisfaction from finding something useful to do in spite of it. The Baumers of life couldn't, and that was what they resented. Unable to achieve anything meaningful themselves, they gained satisfaction from showing that nothing anyone else achieved could have meaning.

The difference was, however, that the Hunts were happy to get on with their own lives and let the visionaries enjoy their agonizings if that was what they wanted. But the converse wasn't true. If the world didn't want to change, then give the Baumers access to the power and they would *make* it change— because they saw more, and deeper. And the rack, the stake, the Gulag, and the concentration camp showed what could happen when they succeeded.

Chapter Twenty-seven

Hunt eased himself back in the chair at the desk built into a corner of his personal quarters, contemplated the screen showing the notes he had compiled thus far, along with a list of questions that just seemed to keep growing longer.

Why was Baumer, a Terran, spying for aliens that he had known less than six months, against an administration that had shown nothing but goodwill toward Earth? Because the Jevlenese were at least human, and Ganymeans weren't? Hunt doubted it. Nothing that hinted of an anti-Ganymean bias had come across in anything Baumer had written or said, or anything he had told Gina. Surely an ideologue of his nature, who saw Jevlen as the potential Utopia and its population as putty to be molded, would have sought to work as part of the potential government, not against it—unless he had reason to believe that the Ganymeans wouldn't be running things for very much longer. That was a thought.

In that case, who was he helping, that he thought might be taking over? Not anybody who wanted the Ganymeans replaced by an occupation force from Earth; that would only be inviting in all the things that Baumer said he had come to Jevlen to get away from. Eubeleus and the Axis? That would have been Hunt's first guess, but the latest business of wanting to move his whole operation to Uttan, right at the crucial time, flew in the face of it.

Which left the criminal underworld that Cullen had talked about—a conjecture that certainly gained further strength if Obayin's death had been arranged, as Cullen suspected. But what kind of connection would somebody like Baumer have with a criminal organization? There would hardly be any shared ground in areas of ideology, morality, politics, social goals, or any of the other things that concerned Baumer. The only alternative that Hunt could see was that they had to have some kind of hold over him. It was hard to imagine any grounds for blackmail: Baumer seemed to have kept his nose clean, and he was here in an official capacity, not a fugitive like Murray. His life-style was free of any obvious complications. What, then?

And finally there were the fundamental issues that had brought Hunt to Jevlen, which were still unscratched: What was the source of the "plague" that the Ganymeans believed was making the Jevlenese impervious to reason? Did the ayatollahs represent simply an extreme of a general human trait in the way that Danchekker maintained, or were they a case of something completely different? What was the significance of Uttan?

Lots of questions; not many answers. Gina had come away from her meeting with Baumer depressed by a feeling of failure. But he was still the only obvious lead; how to find out more about him wasn't so obvious. Hunt reached out to the touch-pad and called the transcript of Gina's talk with Baumer onto a screen to study it again. Two Jevlenese had been leaving just as she arrived. From Gina's description they sounded like thugs, which strengthened the suspicion that Baumer was connected with the underworld. What kind of business did Baumer conduct with them in his office outside, which he didn't want brought into PAC?

Hunt read again what Baumer had said to Gina about the

translation service wired across the city. Since Thuriens and Jevlenese had been dealing with each other for millennia, small, wearable translator chips to convert between their languages— similar in appearance to the stick-on interfaces to VISAR—had long ago been developed as standard. But Terran dialects— and the *Shapieron* brand of Ganymean, as well—were new, and the chips couldn't handle them. So the conversation between Baumer and the Jevlenese had been translated by ZORAC.

"ZORAC?" Hunt said aloud after studying the display for a few moments longer—ZORAC didn't pick up subvocalized patterns.

"Yes, Vic?"

"What's this thing that you've got going around the city on channel fifty-six? Something to do with a translation facility."

"There's still a general-purpose communications net running that wasn't specifically a part of JEVEX," ZORAC replied. "One of the channels is reserved for translating between the Jevlenese dialects and most Terran languages. So you and they can talk to each other just about anywhere."

"It's a service that you support?"

"Yes. I suppose you could call it people-interfacing."

"Hmm . . ." Hunt rubbed his chin. "I was thinking about that visit that Gina made to Baumer's office in the city."

"Yes?"

"There were a couple of Jevlenese leaving just as she got there. You must have done the translating for them. I, ah, I wonder if there might still be a record of it in your system somewhere that we might be able to get at?" Hunt knew that VISAR, programmed with its Thurien hangups, would never have done it. But ZORAC wasn't VISAR. It seemed worth a try.

"It's just a translation service," ZORAC replied. "I don't store any of it. I don't even have a record that they were there."

Hunt sighed resignedly—but it did open up the thought of further possibilities.

"So, when Terrans and Jevlenese talk to each other, you, from inside the *Shapieron*, have an ear into all their conversations, as it were, everywhere," he said.

The implication was plain enough, and ZORAC was too logical not to see it. "Why not spell out what you're asking?" the machine suggested.

"Hell, you know what I'm asking. Something's going on. We need to find out what Baumer and these Jevlenese are up to before we have another war on our hands—maybe a real one this time. Gina got nowhere, and right now we don't have another line."

There was a short pause.

"I presume that your ultimate objective would be to frustrate any intended action on the part of a suspected political group, that might be directed at increasing their power over other people's affairs," ZORAC said finally.

Hunt turned his eyes upward briefly. "Well, if we always insisted on analyzing everything through to its final aims like that, we'd be lucky if we ever got around to actually *doing* anything—but yes, I suppose you could say it was that."

"The argument being," ZORAC persisted, "that you see their methods as a violation of certain rights and freedoms which you, from certain a priori moral principles that are nondeducible but taken as self-evident, consider it desirable for a society to guarantee?"

"Yes." Hunt groaned beneath his breath as he saw where they were heading.

"So the goal would be to protect people from the violations of their rights that an intrusive and coercive governing system would subject them to?"

"Yes, yes, yes," Hunt agreed impatiently.

"One of them being the right to the enjoyment of noninterference and privacy. But if it is to be a genuine guarantee, with nobody having a privilege to decide whom it shall or shall not be granted to, then—"

Hunt's patience snapped. He knew that when ZORAC went off into one of these excursions, it could create knots that would have taken Aristotle volumes to untangle. "Look, *they* cremated Ayultha prematurely, and probably took care of Obayin, too. And if what we're up against is what I'm beginning to think it might be, they're the same forces that burned the libraries of

Alexandria and Constantinople, brought on the Dark Ages, operated the Inquisition, and for all I know engineered the Black Death. We didn't."

"Algorithmically, it reduces to an interesting circumvolution of the logical calculus," ZORAC commented. "Using the same structure, you could argue that early suicide is the best preventative of cancer, or that the most effective way of protecting people against slavery is extermination."

"Forget it, then, and think of the question this way," Hunt suggested. "You're a ship's computer, right? Not a huge, interstellar regulator of social affairs like VISAR. Moralizing isn't your business. Your primary, overriding concern is the safety of the *Shapieron* and its occupants. You've told me as much yourself."

"I only said it was an interesting question logically," ZORAC interjected.

"All the better. I said a minute ago that from the way things are going we could end up with a shooting war. That means that Garuth, Shilohin, Monchar, Rodgar, and all the other Ganymeans from the ship would be caught here in the middle of it. Your best way of safeguarding them is to help prevent it from happening. So circumvolute that."

"Agreed. But Garuth, as the ship's commander, is the final authority. He'd have to approve."

"Then let's find Garuth and talk about it," Hunt said.

Eubeleus and his lieutenant, Iduane, sat in one of the private rooms in the SoA's Shiban "Temple," talking to a screen showing Scirio, who among other things ran the illicit headworld couplers in that part of the city. He also provided the go-betweens to Baumer, avoiding any direct involvement of the SoA. Scirio ran through a number of routine matters and then came to Baumer's meeting with Gina.

"Baumer wasn't suspicious?" Eubeleus repeated. The plan was at a critical phase, and he wasn't leaving anything to chance. Somebody that he didn't know suddenly appearing out of nowhere and questioning one of his sources was something that would have made him suspicious at any time.

"He thinks she's what she says: a starry-eyed broad with big ideas about being a book writer," Scirio said. "They talked politics. He gave her some names to check out that she could have found in the directory."

"She is registered as an author in the hotel at Geerbaine," Iduane offered in a tactful attempt to support Scirio. "She's there independently under her own name, and she traveled on her own from Seattle, USA."

"I say she's clean," Scirio said. "Hell, we've got a lot to do."

Eubeleus remained dubious, but didn't take the matter further for the moment. Afterward, however, he said to Iduane, "I'm not happy about that woman. Check with our other sources in PAC and see if they have anything on her. Get back to me on it today."

Hunt made a gesture of appeal across the desk in Garuth's office. Del Cullen, whom Hunt had rounded up and brought with him for moral support, watched from one side. "Look, I know it's underhanded and not the kind of thing that a Ganymean feels comfortable about, but we have to find out what they're doing," Hunt urged. "Hell, the Jevlenese eavesdropped on our whole planet for fifty thousand years! What right do they have to get upset over a few tapped wires around one city?"

"We need better sources," Cullen agreed. "A break like this isn't quite an intelligence man's dream, but you play with what you've got."

Garuth had just heard from Calazar that JPC's reaction to Eubeleus's offer to remove to Uttan was favorable. Eubeleus had made the point that if the object was to defuse the tensions on Jevlen, one small demonstration of good faith now would have more effect than a torrent of good intentions and promises of doing things later. To emphasize his own sincerity, he was prepared to move himself away from the scene immediately, with a token advance guard of followers. The Thuriens thought his offer magnanimous and were arranging for a ship to be sent to Jevlen to take them. Privately, Calazar had confessed to Garuth that he wasn't completely comfortable about it, but it seemed that the farther away from Jevlen Eubeleus was in the immediate future, the less mischief he would be able to do.

Garuth didn't trust Eubeleus any more than Hunt did, but at least the relocation would remove the man from being Garuth's responsibility for the foreseeable future, and so Garuth had no reason to object. Meanwhile, he would be able to concentrate on his own problems. All the other lines they had tried had drawn blanks. A clue could only come from out there in the city. Distasteful as he found the suggestion, it was a human problem to do with a human world, and it probably required human methods.

"Very well. Do it," he instructed ZORAC.

Hunt grinned faintly. But it really wasn't a lot to go pinning hopes on. All it meant was that Baumer, and maybe another Terran or two out in the city, might say something to a Jevlenese that was useful. The situation was purely passive. Hunt could tell that Cullen found it as unsatisfying as he did. He looked across and pulled a face.

"What else can you do?" Cullen said.

"Oh, I don't intend just sitting here, waiting for something to come in," Hunt told him. "We've already agreed where the answers are. I think it's about time that we went out and looked for them. Tomorrow morning, I'm going out to talk to some people I know in the city. We'll see what I can find out there."

Late that evening, Eubeleus and Iduane met again. "Yes, she was there," Iduane said. "The day before she went to see Baumer, she was at PAC. And she returned to PAC afterward. There is a UNSA scientific group there that she met on the *Vishnu.*"

"Ah. So what kind of a book is she writing, and who for?" Eubeleus asked.

"Maybe what she says. They'd be able to get her some help. She's a stranger here. Wouldn't it be natural for her to go to people she knew?"

"Well, I've been doing a little checking of my own," Eubeleus said. "And do you know who this UNSA group are?"

The look on Iduane's face said that he didn't. Eubeleus nodded. "Then I'll tell you. Have you ever heard of Dr. Victor Hunt? Or Professor Christian Danchekker? Just scientists, you think? They were the ones who uncovered the Earth surveillance and brought down the Federation. The man they both reported to was a UNSA chief by the name of Caldwell. He was also one of the architects of their strategy in what they call the 'Pseudowar.' And do you know who sent them to Jevlen now? The same Caldwell. Now do you think I'm being overcautious? They are dangerous, and so is anyone connected with them."

Iduane emitted an uneasy breath. "What do you want to do?" he asked.

"Let's get the woman here and find out for ourselves what she's up to," Eubeleus replied.

"Shall I get Scirio to arrange something?"

Eubeleus thought for a moment, then shook his head. "No. We'll leave him to just run Baumer. If she's that well in, I'd rather we took care of her ourselves. Perhaps you could handle it personally. Use the German, since she knows him already, but through a different contact. I don't want Scirio's people involved."

"I'll get working on it right away," Iduane promised.

Chapter Twenty-eight

The next day, while Hunt was away in the city, Gina and Sandy had lunch together in a drab cafeteria on the level below PAC's residential sector. The food was plain and monotonous. When anyone complained to the Jevlenese catering staff about it, they were told that the supply system was messed up. It had become usual to attribute every failure and discomfort to JEVEX's being shut down.

"Squid shit and processed shoebox again," Sandy said, looking down at what was supposed to be a sandwich. "It's not really what you'd expect when you come all this way, is it? Our guys did better down the ice hole on Ganymede."

"How did you ever end up at a place like Ganymede?" Gina asked curiously.

"When you work with people like Chris and Vic, anything's possible."

"Yes . . . I think I can believe it."

"Well, look at you. You've known Vic for a week. Here you are."

Gina looked around. "You're right. It's sure a lot different from the *Vishnu*, I have to admit."

"Although I think ZORAC is, somehow . . . 'cuter' than VISAR. It cracks jokes. Did you ever hear of a computer that cracks jokes before?"

"Maybe being stranded in space for twenty-five years affected it," Gina said. "The Ganymeans would be okay. They could handle it. I'm beginning to get the feeling that a lot of things that would completely screw us up in the head don't bother them at all." She inspected a peculiar-looking yellow fruit with orange lobes. "Although we still have the direct link to VISAR here."

They munched in silence for a while, exchanging grimaces over their respective dishes.

"I haven't been near VISAR since we arrived," Sandy said.

She spoke in an odd, pointed tone, as if she were trying to convey something deeper to test Gina's reaction. It took Gina a few seconds to register the fact. Her expression changed, but before she could say anything, Sandy went on. "How well did you get to know VISAR when we were on the ship? It's not just ZORAC with a different I/O system, you know. Did you take any time to . . . experiment with it at all?"

Gina stopped eating and stared across the table, interrogating Sandy's face silently. "Experiment with it?" she repeated.

"Yes."

"It depends what you mean."

Sandy answered in a way that sounded as if she had been wanting to bring the subject up with somebody for a long time. "Do you have any idea of just how weird that thing is, once you get into it? You're so right: the Thuriens must be a lot different from us up here." She tapped the side of her head. "People don't realize how different."

Gina sat back in her seat and took in the tenseness that had come over Sandy suddenly. She knew now what Sandy was getting at, but she replied in a way that evaded the point. "Do you mean how they can live with that universal bugging system everywhere, and not be bothered by it? Yes, I agree that's strange. It would bother me . . . And all that pointless detail they have to go into. Maybe they have a different notion of reality."

Sandy shook her head. "No. That wasn't what I meant. I was talking about the way it puts information into your head. It's not just that it can make you think you're somewhere else and not know the difference. It can manufacture places—whole worlds, whatever—that don't exist at all. And they're just as real—I mean, there's no way you can tell the difference. It can be anything you like."

"Go on," Gina said, not willing to commit herself just yet.

Sandy put down her fork and gestured briefly, then brushed her hair aside. Whatever recollections she was bringing to mind seemed to be troubling her. "But it goes a lot farther than just creating things that you tell it to. It can go right into your head and pull out things you didn't even know were there—things about yourself that you didn't know existed. Or maybe if you did, you buried them down deep somewhere because life has enough problems that you can do something about, without wasting time hassling yourself over things you're not gonna change anyhow. But can you imagine what it's like to find them staring you in the face?"

Gina held her eye and nodded slowly. "Yes, I know," she confessed finally. "I fooled around with it, too. I know what you're talking about."

"You did?"

"Yes."

"And how did it . . ." Sandy left the question hanging and showed an empty hand.

"Terrifying," Gina said. "I haven't gone near it again, either."

Sandy nodded. It was woman-to-woman now. They understood each other without need of secrets. She looked at Gina and pulled her zip-up sweater tighter around herself. "Want to know something? I can kill people." Despite herself, Gina couldn't prevent a startled look from crossing her face. Sandy nodded as if seeing Gina's reaction provided a source of relief. "That's something I found out. Want to know something else? I get a kick out of it. How's that for finding that what you thought you were all your life isn't you?"

Gina saw that Sandy had paled and was trembling. She leaned forward to lay a reassuring hand on her arm. "Don't worry. Everyone has something. Look, if it's any—"

Sandy pulled her arm away defensively. "It's a psychic fucking Freud with a one-million IQ, for chrissakes. Maybe Thuriens don't have things they'd rather not know, or maybe they can deal with them—I don't know. But . . ." Her voice trailed off. She looked up at Gina and sighed. "I'm sorry. I guess I was looking for someone to dump on."

"That's okay."

Sandy took a long swig of real Coke from a batch that had been ordered from Earth by PAC's Terran contingent and arrived with the *Vishnu*. "Yet we were only out there a couple of days." She set the can down and made a sweeping motion with her arm. "But outside there's a whole planet that's been junked on something like that for as long as anyone can remember. And everyone's asking what drove them crazy? Are they kidding? It's pretty clear to me what drove them crazy."

Gina regarded her long and hard. Why she hadn't said anything herself, when she had reached the same conclusion even before they left the ship, she didn't know. Now that she had heard it from Sandy, it all seemed so obvious.

"Finish your squid shit," she said.

Sandy pushed the plate away. "I'll puke. Why?"

"Because I think you're right. It's time we told the others. Probably we should have said something a long time ago."

They found Danchekker perched on a stool in the main lab, pondering some curves expressing the variation in programming complexity exhibited by sample populations of anquilocs—the peculiar Jevlenese flying animal that could inherit learned behavioral modifications. Apparently the anquiloc was just one of a family of related creatures with such abilities.

"Have you heard people argue that machine intelligence is superior to our kind because it builds up its knowledge base cumulatively?" he asked as they entered. Evidently he had been preoccupied in a line of thought and was bouncing it off the first targets to appear. "They see it as a crippling disadvantage that we have to spend a quarter of our lives learning the same basics over and over with each generation, after which we use little, add less, and take most of it with us when we go." The professor waved at the solid image of an anquiloc hanging in a flying posture above a benchtop to one side. "But can you imagine what the consequences of an advanced development from that animal would be? One of the things about ourselves that we should be thankful for is that conditioning isn't inheritable. After all the effort that was expended on turning virtually an entire generation into Nazi fanatics, their children were born as untainted by it as Eskimos. But think how much more insufferable fanatics would be if the process of indoctrination created its own gene. What would our friend Baumer give for a tool like that?" He turned fully on the stool and saw that Gina and Sandy were waiting to say something. "Anyway, ladies, what can I do for you?"

"I think we may have an answer to the question of what messed up the Jevlenese," Gina said, coming straight to the point.

"We already have an answer," Danchekker replied airily. "They've been stifled by millennia of well-intentioned overindulgence by the Thuriens, who made the mistake of thinking that humans are put together in the same way as themselves."

"So you still don't think it was JEVEX?"

Danchekker was in an expansive mood and not minded to give anyone a hard time. "Well, in a way I suppose you could say it was," he conceded. "Although JEVEX was merely the instrument of the cause, not the cause itself, you understand. It provided all their needs, did all their thinking, took away their problems. But the Jevlenese, like any human, is a problem-solving animal. Take away his problems and he'll promptly invent more; otherwise he'll languish or resent you for denying him his nature. And that is precisely what we're seeing the symptoms of. Time and patience are the only answers now, I'm afraid."

"We don't think so," Sandy told him. "We think it could be something specifically to do with the way JEVEX operated."

Danchekker extended his lanky frame over the back of the stool and looked mildly amused. "Oh, really? That's most interesting. Do tell me why."

"JEVEX is pretty much the same as VISAR, yes?" Gina began.

"Well, the Jevlenese system was programmed with different procedural rules and operating parameters."

"I mean in terms of basic technology and capabilities."

"Very well, yes."

Gina pulled up another stool and slid onto it. Sandy remained standing by the bench. "Then let me ask you something, Professor," Gina said. "How much have you used VISAR yourself?"

"Probably as much as anybody," Danchekker replied. "I was one of the party that met the first Thurien craft to come to Earth, and nowadays I use it routinely in the course of my work."

"Yes, but what do you use it *for*?" Gina persisted. "Describe the operations that it performs."

Danchekker shrugged in a way that said he couldn't see the point but would go along with it. "To access Thurien records and data; to confer with Thuriens, and also other Terrans who happen to be at locations connected into the system; and to 'visit' locations throughout the Thurien domain, for business reasons, social reasons, or out of pure curiosity. Does that answer you?"

"And never for anything beyond that?" Gina asked.

Danchekker started showing the first hint of irritation at being cross-examined. "Beyond that? What do you mean? What else is it supposed to do?"

Gina sat forward, raising a hand momentarily as if mentally rehearsing herself to get this right. "Professor . . . with all due respect, could I suggest that your impression has been restricted by a professional attitude that sees VISAR purely as a technological tool?" She added hastily, "And the same's true of Vic. You're both scientists, and you've never thought of it as being anything other than a piece of technical equipment. But it's far more than that. It's a self-adapting environment in its own right, which interacts directly with the mind. And like any interactive environment, it can *shape*, as well as be shaped."

"Tailored realities, guided by what it dredges up from your subconscious," Sandy said.

"VISAR doesn't read minds," Danchekker retorted. "That's something which is excluded quite specifically by the Thurien operating protocols."

"It can if you permit it," Gina said.

Danchekker blinked, then stared at her. "I'd never thought to ask about that," he admitted. Which made her point. There was no need for anyone to say so.

"And JEVEX worked by different rules," Sandy reminded him. "Rules that didn't embody Thurien notions of privacy and rights."

"You've experienced this phenomenon, both of you?" Danchekker asked. They confirmed it. "Tell me about what you found," he said.

They related what they had discovered and its effects, leaving out unnecessary personal details. Hunt had warned Gina that Danchekker could be cantankerous at times, and she had come prepared for a fight. But instead of scoffing, Danchekker listened closely to what they had to say. When they had finished, he got up from his stool and walked slowly over to the far side of the lab, where he stood looking thoughtfully at a chart of Jevlenese phylogeny.

After a while Sandy, reassured by his manner, said to his back, "It might not be just us who are finding an alienness in the Thurien mind that we're having trouble relating to. Maybe having a common biological ancestry isn't what matters."

It was clear that she meant the *Shapieron* Ganymeans, who were from a culture estimated to have been only a hundred years or so ahead of twenty-first-century Earth's. They, like Terrans, were from a culture in which people were where they thought they were, objects and places were what they seemed to be, time and space meant what common sense said they did, and h-space had never been heard of. The civilization of Thurien— even allowing for a long period of stagnation that had almost brought about its demise—had evolved far beyond either.

"Perhaps now we know why Garuth turned for help in the direction he did," Gina said.

Danchekker turned to face them. "Most interesting," he pronounced. "Have you talked to Vic about it?"

"Not yet. He's gone out into the city. We came straight here," Gina said.

"What's he doing?"

"I'm not sure. Trying to get a lead on Baumer, I think."

"ZORAC," Danchekker called.

But just then, ZORAC announced an incoming call for Gina. The pale, bespectacled features of Hans Baumer appeared on one of the screens. The face broadened into a smile as Gina moved closer.

"Oh, you're with company, I see. Is this an inconvenient time?"

Gina shook her head. "No, go ahead. It's okay."

"About our talk the other day. Look, I'm sorry if I was a bit terse. You caught me at a bad time. Those Jevlenese were being awkward, and things have been piling on top of each other lately. Of course, I'd be happy to show you a little more of Shiban. So, if you're still interested, when would be a good time for us to get together?"

Chapter Twenty-nine

The place was the same gaudy, impenitent clutter that it had been the first time Hunt was there. "Hi, Vic come back," Nixie greeted, smiling as she let him in. She was wearing a blue metallic top showing red nipples through a pair of circles cut out for the purpose. "No girl in PAC? Get lonely?"

Murray killed the movie he had been watching and got up from one of the form-molding chairs. "Hell, I like the initiative, but ease off," he told her. "He's only here socializing." He held out a hand to Hunt. "Wondered when you'd be back. How's the acclimatization going?"

"Not bad."

Nixie frowned. "What 'socializing' mean?" she asked.

Hunt moved into the room and studied the panel that included the screen Murray had been looking at. "Is that part of the city GP net?" he inquired.

"Among other things. Why?"

"Can you activate channel fifty-six on it?"

"That's in a dataservice group. What would I need it for?"

"I just want to try something."

Murray shrugged and said something at the panel in Jevlenese. He looked at Hunt. "What's supposed to happen?" A
Jevlenese translation of his words came from the room speaker.

Nixie stared in astonishment, then asked Murray something.
"How the hell did it do that?" a faithfully intoned synthesis of
her voice asked. "What's that? Can you two understand this?
Is that me speaking in English?"

"Well, I'll be darned," Murray said, staring at the panel.
"You mean that's been there all the time?"

"Amazing what can happen when you bring a scientist into
your house, isn't it?" Hunt said.

Nixie looked at Murray accusingly. "You mean after all the
time I've spent working my ass off learning English, we needn't
have bothered? Well, that's just great. Maybe I should bill you
for the time it's cost me, at my regular hourly rate."

Murray held up a hand defensively. "Honest, I didn't know
about it." He looked at Hunt. "How does it work?"

"They've got it hooked into the Ganymean ship's computer,"
Hunt told him.

"You mean the *Shapieron*?"

"Yes."

"Well, how about that!" Murray declared.

"This is terrific!" Nixie exclaimed. "We can talk normally."
She looked at Hunt. "The girls upstairs thought you were nice.
They've been asking me to get you to come to one of our par-
ties here. They can be a lot of fun."

"I don't doubt it," Hunt said. "I might just take you up on it,
too. But not right away. Things are very busy."

Murray sat back down and waved Hunt over to the couch.
Nixie perched herself on a hassock.

"What did you think of Ayultha getting blown away like that
in Chinzo?" Murray asked. "Pretty neat stuff, huh? It sounds
as if everything's a mess. SFPD's what they need to bring in
here. Any idea how they did it?"

"We're pretty sure it was a phase-conjugating laser," Hunt
said.

"Yeah . . . right." Murray wasn't going to argue with that.

"Which would be fairly straightforward to do. A spot from

a target-designation pilot beam appeared on his chest a moment before he ignited."

"You see, ask a Terran and you get an answer that makes sense, even if I don't understand it," Nixie said.

"Well . . . I don't know about all Terrans," Hunt muttered.

Nixie looked at him and shook her head. "You wouldn't believe some of the stuff you hear in this place," she said. "Some people think it was cosmic energy from another dimension. Then we had focused waves of—what was it, 'telepsychosynchronicity.' I mean, what's it all about? What in hell is telepsychosynchronicity?"

"Sounds like what used to be called mind power, but at twice the price," Hunt suggested.

"I'd rather be getting laid," Nixie opined.

"That would make a good bumper sticker," Hunt said.

"People should do something about getting this city together instead of sitting around listening to that garbage and waiting for the Ganymeans to do something," Nixie said. "Murray, why don't we go to Earth? You said I'd make a fortune there."

"Patience. I need to get a little more invisible first." Murray settled himself back in the chair and stretched out an arm idly to finger the hair at the back of her neck. "Anyhow, if you're that busy you didn't come here to shoot any breeze," he said to Hunt. "What gives?"

"I'm trying to find out anything I can about one of the Terrans back at PAC," Hunt said. "It's in connection with that traffic bridge that collapsed."

"The one that pancaked the head of the Keystones, and them other suckers who were driving under?"

"Right. It may have to do with the Ayultha business, too."

"Okay, shoot."

"He's a German by the name of Hans Baumer, been here a little over five months. We've got reason to think that he's got himself mixed up with the shady side of city life here, some-how, and that the people he's dealing with could tell us something. It occurred to me that it might be the kind of thing you'd know something about."

"Why are you interested?" Murray seemed evasive all of a sudden.

"It's starting to look as if Jevlenese plots and power games didn't all come to an end with the Federation," Hunt replied. "There's some kind of scheme afoot that involves another faction, and the trouble that's brewing is all part of it. Getting rid of Obayin could have been a preparatory move. He was being very cooperative with the Ganymeans."

"Shit, I thought you were some kind of scientist. What the hell kind of science is this?"

"The kind that doesn't want to see the Ganymeans kicked out of here." Hunt gestured in the direction of the door. "Look at the mess this planet's in out there. It should have been flying its own starships long ago. Instead it waits for Thurien handouts. The same forces that held our sciences back for two thousand years are regrouping on Jevlen. That's what we're trying to prevent. And it affects you, too, Murray, because once a society becomes repressive, *all* forms of independence get repressed. And that wouldn't be good for your line of business at all."

"I like what Vic's saying, Murray," Nixie said.

But Murray shook his head. "Sorry, I can't help. I don't know anything." His voice was clipped, and his face wooden. He was lying, Hunt could tell. Hunt could either confront him and risk alienating what could turn out to be a valuable contact with nothing to show; or he could let the matter ride for the moment and leave Murray time to think it over. He sighed inwardly.

"But you'll let me know if you do hear anything?"

"Sure."

Nixie stared uncomfortably at the table but said nothing.

"There was another thing," Hunt said. "Tell me something about these ayatollahs."

Nixie understood whatever ZORAC translated the word into, but Murray looked puzzled. "These what?"

"The cult leaders—the crazies who are stirring up these mobs, like Ayultha."

Nixie supplied Murray a term in Jevlenese, which ZORAC returned as "awakeners."

"What do you want to know about them?" Murray seemed

to relax at the change of subject and listened while Hunt summarized what he had learned from Garuth and Shilohin. Nixie's manner became strangely quiet as she followed.

When Hunt had finished, Murray looked apologetic—genuinely this time. "That's fascinating," he said. "And really, I'd like to help. But you know more about all this than I do."

"You've been here six months."

Murray spread his hands helplessly. "Hell, I've never gotten into conversations about stuff like that with the Jevs. You saw what our communication level was until just now, when you told me about that." He waved at the panel. "Anyhow, they've got more loose screws than a do-it-yourself kit for the Eiffel Tower. Why do you care about them?"

"We think that Eubeleus and his Axis might be involved, too," Hunt said.

"But he isn't gonna be around much longer. They're all taking off for this other planet, someplace, whatever it's called. It's been all over the news. They're shooting the first batch of green groupies up into orbit from Geerbaine already."

"That's got me beat, too," Hunt admitted. "Okay, maybe it isn't him, specifically. But I'm convinced there's a connection with the cults somewhere."

Murray could only show his hands and shake his head. "Sorry, Doc, but like I said, it seems you already know more about them than I do. What else can I tell you?"

They talked about odd things for a while longer, but nothing more useful emerged. Eventually Hunt stood up and announced that it was time for him to be getting back.

"Take care, Vic. We'll see ya around," Murray said, seeing him to the door.

Hunt made his way back in the direction of PAC, far from satisfied with the results of his foray. He passed through noisy streets, lined with stalls displaying trinkets and bric-a-brac, and crossed a square of mostly closed frontages. Past there, he climbed a moving stairway that wasn't—it had been under repair since the day he arrived. There were apathetic people squatting on sidewalks and, farther on, a line being handed what looked like food packages from the back of a trailer. He was pestered by vacant-faced children hassling for handouts, who could have been learning about Euclid or Newton, Bach or Magellan—or whoever the Jevlenese equivalents were, if they had ever had any.

He stopped at a corner to watch a garishly dressed group dancing frenziedly under some kind of intoxication to mindless, crashing music blaring from inside an open doorway, where others appeared to have collapsed. Somebody was shouting obscenities at them from a window nearby. Hunt stood and watched disconsolately, trying to form some idea of what he intended doing with the remainder of the day.

There was a light tug on his sleeve. He turned his head. It was Nixie.

"I say have go work now, so can catch Vic," she said. "We go someplace now, yes?" At least she had put a wrap over her top.

Hunt sighed. "Nixie, don't you ever give up? No thanks. Not today."

"You not understand. We just talk. Go place where is speak machine, Jevlen talk Terran."

"Oh." Hunt drew back and looked at her. She was serious for once, unsmiling. He nodded. "Okay. Let's go."

She slipped her arm through his as they began walking. "This way. I show. Place I use lots time."

They entered a corridor of doors and display windows, many of them shuttered, leading off the street. From the other end of it, they crossed a trash-strewn plaza to another passage flanked by a couple of bars, an amusement gallery of some kind, and assorted other doorways. Two more corners brought them to a wider concourse, on one side of which was an entrance into what looked like the lobby of a cheap hotel. There was a desk on one side, and doors off to left and right of the dingy hall beyond, where two or three people were sitting on faded chairs among oddments of furniture. Several elevator doors lined the wall at the rear. Somehow the reception machine even managed to convey an air of sneering disdain as the John drew up at the desk with his hooker.

"Look wrong if I pay," Nixie murmured. Hunt gave her the

card that he had been issued at PAC to cover incidental expenses. She flipped open a cover on the machine and passed the card across a read head. Nothing happened. Nixie muttered something that sounded like an oath and pressed a button. After waiting perhaps half a minute, she called out a stream of Jevlenese in an abusive voice and jabbed at the button repeatedly. A clerk in need of a shave and a clean shirt emerged, grumbling, from a door near the desk. Nixie gave him the card, and an irascible exchange continued between them while the card was read into a different device, a transaction record copied out, and the card returned. Finally the clerk extracted a small disk—presumably a coded room key—from the innards of the nonfunctioning reception machine, said something to Nixie that sounded sarcastic and which Hunt had a feeling referred to him, and stumped back through the door he had come out of.

They took one of the elevators up several floors and found the room around a corner farther along a corridor. Nixie touched the disk against a plate, and they entered. The room was indifferent, in keeping with the rest of the place. There was a fake window with a graphics simulation of an unusual landscape scene, part of it nonfunctioning and blacked out. Nixie crossed over to the companel above the fitted unit opposite the queen-size bed, activated it, and gave an instruction in Jevlenese to switch on the translator.

"Like a drink?" she asked Hunt. "The first one comes with the room, anyhow."

"Why not?"

"Anything in particular?"

"I'll leave it to you."

"House, a couple of *colantas* with tangy ice, unfizzed," Nixie said. Rattles and grinding sounds came from the dispenser unit by the chef as she walked over to it. "Don't get mad at Murray for being cautious," she said over her shoulder. "The people that Baumer is mixed up with don't like noses being poked into their business. And they can be nasty."

"So you do know him," Hunt said.

"You get to know what's going on. And there aren't that many Terrans in Shiban. People talk."

"So who are these people he's mixed up with?" Hunt asked, sitting down in the chair by the window image and producing his cigarettes.

"From what Murray says, you have them on Earth: people who supply things that are wanted, but which are illegal. He was doing the same kind of thing with chemical drugs."

"You mean a black market?"

"Is that what you call it? Okay."

"I thought things like that didn't really happen seriously here," Hunt said. "There isn't too much that's illegal."

"But the changes in recent times have had effects." Nixie turned, holding two glasses. She came over to hand Hunt one of them, and picked up his cigarette pack curiously from the sill of the fake window. "Can I try one of these?"

"Go ahead."

Nixie selected one and leaned forward to let Hunt light it for her. "This is what you call tobacco, right?"

"Yes."

She went over to the bed and sat down, swinging her legs up and leaning back against the headboard. "Let's see if I understand this thing that Murray calls supply and demand. When you make something illegal, the price goes up, isn't that it? Murray said the U.S. Government made him a lot of money—I never understood why, since they were trying to take it away from him . . . But anyhow, stopping people from doing what they want makes other people rich. Is that how it works?"

"It's not supposed to, but . . ." Hunt shrugged. "Well, yes, I suppose that's the way it turns out more often than not."

Nixie gestured with the cigarette. "This is smooth . . . got a nice kick. Hits your throat."

"Not all kinds. Some brands will take the lining off."

"Is tobacco illegal on Earth?"

Hunt shook his head. "It makes the right people rich."

Nixie thought about it. "I guess they have to be the ones who make the rules, then, eh?"

"That's about it."

Nixie nodded. "Anyhow, as I was saying . . . on Jevlen the Ganymeans have created a black market."

Hunt looked down at his drink. It was amber, with pyramids of light green ice, and tasted like spicy Drambuie with a lemony base. Not bad. He thought he knew what she was getting at, but decided to play dumb. She was trying to help. Why spoil it? "I'm not sure I follow," he said, looking back at her and drawing on his cigarette.

"Ask yourself, what's been shut down for the last six months that everybody took for granted all their lives, and a lot of people don't know how to get along without?"

"You mean JEVEX?"

"What else?"

Hunt appeared to consider the proposition. "That sounds strange," he answered. "I mean, there might be a demand all right, but where's the supply? You just said, it's shut down."

Nixie shook her head and sipped from her glass without taking her eyes off him. "The main system that ran the planet and what-have-you might be down, but the whole thing isn't dead. There are still parts of it ticking over."

"Well, yes, that's right—there's a core system still running for maintenance and . . ." He let his voice trail off, as if he had just seen the implication for the first time. "What are you saying? That there's some way of getting people access to that capacity?"

"Yes, exactly. For the junkies, but at a price."

It still didn't explain everything, though. "Okay." Hunt leaned back, still frowning. "But what product is it that they're selling, exactly? I mean, you're making it sound like a dependency situation. What is it that these junkies are dependent for? It can't be simply to have the planet run for them again. What would there be for an individual that was worth paying for?"

Nixie smiled and watched the smoke from her cigarette. "You still don't understand what JEVEX does, do you, Vic?"

That was something that Hunt had not been prepared for. He spread his hands and shook his head. "It's an integrated processing and communications network. It runs the planet."

"That's like saying that *colanta* wets your throat and flows down. I'm not talking about how JEVEX functions, but what it *does*." She read the baffled look on Hunt's face. "It creates fantasies—anything that anyone wants can come true. Dreams that are real, which you can make do whatever you like just by wanting them to. Do you wonder why the Jevlenese can't deal with reality? They've never needed reality." She threw back her head and laughed. "The girls love the Ganymeans. Our business has never been better since they switched JEVEX off. They wiped out the competition."

Hunt stared at her for a long time. A lot of things were making more sense now. If that was really the problem, then perhaps the Ganymean cure of several years' planetary cold turkey would turn out to be the answer after all. The secondary problems would just have to be dealt with by conventional, time-tried methods, as some members of the Thurien-Terran Joint Policy Council seemed to have been saying. It would also explain why whoever was profiting in the meantime would want to keep the administration off the trail for as long as possible.

What did not make sense was why Nixie should want to rock the boat if business was so good.

"I don't understand why you're telling me this," Hunt said.

"That isn't what I followed you for," Nixie answered. "When we were with Murray, the other thing you asked about was the ayatollahs."

"He didn't seem to know much about them."

"He doesn't. He's not a Jevlenese. But I do."

Hunt hesitated, checking mentally for something he might have missed. "Is there a lot more to explain about them?" he said. "It sounds as if they're just extreme cases of this—this fantasy-addiction that you just described. Ones that have pulled their anchors up from reality completely."

Nixie shook her head. "No. That can happen to the head-world junkies, yes. But the ayatollahs are not the same. Their situation is something else."

Hunt nodded and raised his eyebrows. So Garuth had been right in his classifications. "There is something definitely very different about them, then?" he asked. "Something that sets them apart?"

"Oh, yes."

"You can be sure? They're not simply suffering from delusions? Or some kind of breakdown, possibly, induced by stresses encountered in these fantasy realities?"

"The ayatollahs aren't products of any fantasies," Nixie said, speaking somberly. "They aren't junkies at all."

"Then what makes them crazy?"

"Crazy?" Nixie stared at him strangely. "They're bewildered," she replied. "And very often scared, confused, lost, and hysterical. If a lot of them act demented, it's because of things like that. And yes, maybe some of them do lose their orientation completely. But it's not from getting too involved with some fairyland. They come from somewhere that's real. But it's somewhere very strange—at least, it would be strange to anyone who's used to this . . ." She gestured around her vaguely.

"You mean Jevlen?" Hunt said.

"And Earth, too. Everywhere. The whole universe."

Hunt's brow knitted. "I'm not sure what you're saying. Where do they come from?"

"They don't know. That's what screws them up—or at least, it screws a lot of them up. But some manage to handle it and keep their act together. They're not all crazy." Nixie lifted her glass again and gave Hunt a long, appraising look over the rim. "At least, I hope you think they're not all crazy. You see, you're the first scientist I've met here. And you're sane. The reason I followed you was that you look like someone who might be able to find the answers."

"Is it really that important to—" Hunt began, and his eyes widened as he realized what she was saying.

Nixie nodded, reading his expression. "Yes," she said. "That's right, Vic. To me, it's very important. You see, I'm one of them."

Chapter Thirty

In the night, everything lay hidden beneath the blackness of a sky deserted by the gods. Even Pamur, the god whose lantern was the sun, was turning away, reducing Waroth's days to twilight gloom. Snow blanketed the mountains and choked the passes. Herders and hill people were moving into the valleys as cold crept down across the land.

High in the midst of the Rinjussin wilderness, the Master, Shingen-Hu, and a select group of adepts from his school ascended a rocky peak for the ceremony of reconsecrating the Altar of Arising, from whence those who arose with the currents departed from the world. The currents had been running very weak of late, and they were too high to be drawn down. The purpose of the rite was to get Nieru's blessing for better conditions.

The chanting and incantations were of particular significance to Thrax, for Shingen-Hu had chosen him as the next to ascend, when the signs and the currents became favorable. In his devotions he had already, on several occasions, captured the wisps of current that sometimes came low, bringing images into his mind. He recalled the images now, as he stood clad in heavy robes and a cowled cloak upon the peak, gazing at the scattering of remnant stars flickering wanly above, as if beckoning, somehow . . . Images that he had seen of Hyperia.

Of *lawfulness* reigning indefinitely through time and over unimaginably vast regions of space.

Of things that spun.

Of huge cities of permanent matter, sculpted into fantastic shapes that soared into the sky.

Of the strange beings that inhabited them, whose wondrous devices could operate themselves directly, without any intervention of mind.

It would be as one of those strange beings that he would emerge, Shingen-Hu had told him. Most of the abilities that he knew would be lost. But he would find, as he persevered and learned, that he didn't need them. For the inhabitants of Hyperia knew none of the gods that held sway over Waroth. They didn't need to bother with prayer, and the few gods that they did worship in their own mysterious ways were as nothing ever revealed to any Warothian. The Hyperians delegated their powers to complex magic objects, which they were able to fashion as effortlessly as a Master could project a firebolt; thus they freed themselves to devote their time to such higher things as amusement and bodily comforts, without the daily drudgery of cultivating mystical insights and developing powers of unaided thought.

But to begin with, he would feel lost and helpless when he emerged. He would search in vain for reassurance from things that were familiar, knowing that until he developed new powers of comprehension and came to terms with the revelations which those new insights would open up, there would be no way back. That would be when he should seek the security of his own kind among those bearing the emblem of the purple spiral.

But he had been thoroughly trained. He was ready. Others were not so fortunate, Shingen-Hu had said. In former times, when the currents had been abundant and strong, it often happened that new initiates, or even novices, would emerge into Hyperia ignorant and unprepared, without even having glimpsed what lay ahead. Usually they were solitary learners, unschooled and impatient.

Chapter Thirty-one

Baumer had suggested a tour of the environs of PAC to give Gina a start at getting her bearings in Shiban. After that, he said, he would introduce her to some of the associations of Jevlenese and Terran historians engaged in organizing the information coming to light on past Jevlenese meddlings with Earth. They left PAC by the main entrance and crossed a plaza, where one of the battery of escalators below the transportation terminal took them down several levels to emerge into one of the major thoroughfares traversing the district between PAC and the city center.

They passed an exchange market for used furniture, clothes, and household junk that was situated in an open area between facing lines of dilapidated storefronts and lesser buildings. Above, enormous ribs of an architecture that belonged to a different scale soared and merged, enclosing a space vast enough to hold a small mountain—a monument to a vision in an alien mind that had leapt above the commonplace as surely as the lines seemed to break free from gravity . . . now stark and bare against the pale, orange-smeared green of the sky, their original function long forgotten. A stream connecting ornamental pools built on a series of terraces had run dry and become a trash dump. Jevlenese in blue costumes were dancing to a strange, repetitive chant, vaguely reminiscent of medieval plainsong, while a crowd looked on apathetically. Insensible figures lay sprawled against walls along the sidewalks.

It reminded Gina of a trip she had made to parts of the eastern Mediterranean some years previously, off the regular tourist circuit. There, she had seen peasants tending goats amid the ruins of what had once been splendid temples, and crude village hearths made of stones taken from palaces. Once more she was looking at the promise of genius lost to unreason and sunken into apathy.

The agitators and cult leaders who talked to the people blamed it all on the Ganymeans. It was the result of withdrawing the services performed by JEVEX, they said, and they called for the full functionality of the system to be restored. In fact, the stagnation had begun long before the events that led to JEVEX's being shut down. But the people had been conditioned to have short memories, and they believed what the demagogues told them.

"This is what you get when degeneracy sets into a society," Baumer told her. "There's never been any order or discipline. I blame it on the Thuriens for not instituting any proper system of control. But then, they don't have any concept of the word themselves."

The reason for Baumer's sudden change of mood still was not clear. He had no interest in the kind of work that Gina had described, and he didn't come across as the kind of person who would rush to do favors for strangers, or who would put any great value on sociability. Her first inclination had been to assume the attraction to be therefore mainly physical—he had, after all, been away from home and his own kind for almost half a year; but his manner showed no hint of it, and the passion in his eyes when he spoke burned only for visions of Jevlen's future. So if Baumer didn't have a reason, the reason had to be someone else's—and that could only be the Jevlenese that Baumer was working for. Del Cullen had asked her to try and find out what it was that gave them a hold over him.

Her approach was still to affect a more sympathetic attitude toward his views than she felt. "Maybe the Federation people had the right idea," she said. "But they only played at being leaders. They never had to learn about real survival. They only had Thuriens to deal with."

"Absolutely," Baumer agreed.

At one point he stopped and pointed at the entrance to a solid-looking frontage on the thoroughfare that they were passing along. It had large double doors, and two men who looked like guards could be seen inside. One of them was in the act of opening an inner door to admit a man carrying a wrapped bundle under his arm. "People are getting nervous," Baumer said to Gina. "They're putting their valuables in deposit banks that are springing up, like that one, and the receipts are becoming negotiable currency." Evidently he didn't approve. "A few profit from the insecurity of many. Manipulators of money . . . *We* know what it leads to. We've seen it all before, on Earth."

With JEVEX no longer coordinating the planet's distribution system, the flow of supplies and commodities into Shiban and its vicinity had become erratic. However, some entrepreneurial spirits were emerging among the Jevlenese, and had organized workforces of mechanics to recover and fix all kinds of defunct vehicles from the piles abandoned around the city. Others were setting up retail outlets and building up a growing trade with various sources, near and far, that they had sought out and worked deals with. "Exploiting people's needs," Baumer sneered. "Everyone has a right to eat. The Ganymeans should be taking care of all that."

Looking into a store displaying extravagant jewelry and clothes in what appeared to be a fashionable quarter, he seethed. "They could have been building a just society, based on equality. But everyone has to be *made* to work together for it to succeed. The Ganymeans can't see it. They haven't got the background. Somehow we have to get the authority to put the right people in control."

Gina had heard it all before. It was the envy and rage of the frustrated intellectual at the capriciousness with which a system based on free choice bestowed its rewards. Traditional patterns of privilege, right, and might didn't matter. Who would succeed and who would fail was decided, often with little discernible logic or reason, by the collective whims and preferences of everyone. But those who could produce nothing that would sell in the marketplace, and who had nothing of appeal to offer at the ballot box, were unable to compete. Their only recourse was coercion. If their worth and wisdom went unrecognized, they would use the state and its legislative power to *make* people need them.

They bought a couple of hot, crisp breads filled with chopped meat and vegetables in a spicy sauce from a corner vendor. Baumer said they were called *grinils*. They ate them sitting on a low wall nearby, drinking from mugs of a dark, bitterish brew tolerably close to coffee, and watching the life in the street pass by.

"What kinds of Jevlenese have you gotten to know in the time you've been here?" Gina asked absently.

"Besides the historical societies, you mean? There's one character at the university here that I think you should meet."

Gina shook her head. "No, I didn't mean in connection with what I'm here for, particularly. Just in general. Socially, when you're off-duty. That kind of thing."

"Oh, different kinds, you know," Baumer replied vaguely. "Why? What kind were you interested in?"

"No kind especially. I just wondered what people get up to here. I might have come to research a book, but there's life to live, too. You don't exactly get to visit another world every day." She munched her *grinil* and sipped casually. "You've got some pretty strong views on the way Jevlen should be organized. I'd have thought you'd try getting to know Jevlenese who think the same way."

He looked at her oddly. "Are you interested in meeting people like that?"

"Maybe, if you know any. What they're heading for is a mess. Who wouldn't be interested in trying to do something about it?"

Baumer continued staring at her for a few seconds longer,

but then changed the subject. "You're spending a lot of time with those UNSA scientists at PAC, I notice," he said.

"They're an island of something that's familiar, I suppose," Gina answered. "But it's not the same as getting out and seeing Jevlen, is it? And I don't really follow what they're talking about most of the time, anyway."

"How far do you think they'll go?" Baumer asked her. "I mean, how far will they go in importing Ganymean science to Earth? I take it that's what their mission here is all about."

"Oh, I wouldn't put it as strongly as that," Gina replied. "They're just sifting through the basics, as far as I can tell. I haven't heard anything about plans for a firm program. What did you mean? Setting up something comprehensive there, planetwide, like JEVEX was here?"

"I suppose it's a question that will have to be asked sooner or later," Baumer said. "In fact I'd be amazed if it hadn't been asked already."

"Do you think it would be a good thing? I mean, look at the situation it's resulted in here. And we're still a long way from solving that."

"Then bring it back. What good has taking it away done? None. It's only made everything worse."

"You think so?"

"Oh, no question."

"So you'd have no qualms about switching JEVEX on again tomorrow," Gina concluded.

"It should be available freely everywhere," Baumer said. "Part of the Ganymeans' task should be to provide it."

"You don't have any reservations about JEVEX, then?" Gina asked.

"Reservations? Why should I?" A strange, distant light came into Baumer's eyes, and his face softened into one of its rare smiles. "JEVEX is wonderful. It solves all needs and problems. It's the people's right. Isn't it their property?"

Gina looked at him curiously. "How do you know so much about it? Surely it was switched off before you got here."

Baumer's attention returned suddenly to present. He seemed confused. "Well, yes, of course. It's what I hear from the Jevlenese—the ones that I talk to in my studies." He took her empty mug and stood up. Gina watched as he returned both the mugs to the stall, but when he returned she decided to drop the subject.

A group of about a dozen or so zanily dressed youths, with vivid purple makeup and orange hair molded into spikes and rings, was gathering on an opposite corner. "Come on," Baumer said, sounding wary. "Let's be moving on."

But as he and Gina moved away along the street, the group began moving also. After they had turned two corners and crossed a shabby court beneath the supports of a traffic flyover, it was clear that they were being followed. Baumer quickened the pace but said nothing.

"What's going on?" Gina muttered.

"I'm not sure."

"Who are the punks?"

"It could be any one of the cults that you find in this place. There are scores of them."

They were in a distinctly run-down area now, entering a dingy alley with premises closed down and deserted, few people about, and little chance of help if things turned ugly. Gina wondered fleetingly why Baumer should have come this way. Surely historical societies weren't to be found in such surroundings.

Behind, the pursuers were getting closer and were uttering a chorus of murmuring that grew into a chant, punctuated by jeers.

"Do you understand what they're saying?" Gina asked, scared.

"They've spotted us as Terrans. Apparently we're not popular. It sounds like the equivalent of 'Yanks go home.'"

They came out of a foot passage into a narrow alley that joined a wider road farther on. A black automobile was parked in the alley, facing the other way, with barely enough room on each side for someone to squeeze past. Two men, both looking unremarkable in plain, gray overcoats, were standing by the back of it. Baumer didn't recognize them as any he had dealt with before. They seemed in a different league, not flashy or brash. Gina registered in an absent kind of way that there was something odd about them, but just at that moment her attention was too focused on the pursuers behind, who were making their way along the foot passage, for her to care. But at the sight of the car and the two men waiting by it, the punks halted.

And then the rear doors of the car opened and two more men got out, smartly dressed in suits, but looking mean and businesslike. One of them drew some kind of gun and pointed it, at the same time snapping something in a firm, no-nonsense tone. The one who seemed to be the punk leader backed away, raising his hands placatingly, his face working in an inane grin, presumably intended to avoid offending. He muttered something, and then the whole group disappeared back along the passage.

Gina turned, and for a split second her instinctive reaction was one of relief, even gratitude. But then she realized that the attention of the four men from the car was now directed at her. In the same instant she knew that they had been expecting her. Confused, she turned to where Baumer had been, but he had moved away to one side, while one of the four had moved between Gina and the passage, blocking her retreat. It hit her then that she had been set up. She turned back again, but the other three were already closing in around her. There was nowhere to go. One of them pointed a bulbous object at her and squirted a jet of gas into her face. She collapsed instantly. Two of the men caught her and steered her limp form into one of the open doors of the car, then climbed in after her. One of the remaining two went around and got in the other side, while the last stopped to look at Baumer, who was standing tense and white-faced.

"Okay, you've done your part. Now disappear," he ordered, waving a hand in a dismissive gesture.

Baumer withdrew a few paces, but he was reluctant to enter the passage for fear that the punks might still be lurking. He would leave in the opposite direction when the car had gone.

The man in the gray coat went around and climbed in next to the driver, and moments later the car moved away.

Chapter Thirty-two

Danchekker stood in a room in the upper level of PAC, hands clasping his lapels, speaking in a confidently genial tone.

"There have been times, I admit, Vic, when I have been guilty of displaying less of an open-minded disposition than should be expected from a scientific professional," he told Hunt, who was leaning on the wall, arms folded, while Shilohin listened from behind an oversize Ganymean desk. "But you know yourself the difficulty of abandoning a notion that appears to make sense once it has taken root." The professor released one lapel briefly to make a dismissive gesture in the air. "In the present case, my conviction up until now has been that no hypothesis beyond misplaced Thurien generosity, coupled with their inability to understand the human capacity for self-deceit and wishful thinking, was necessary to account for the general Jevlenese condition that we observe today."

"Yes, Chris, but there's something—" Hunt began.

Danchekker merely nodded that he understood and continued. "In particular, I disagreed with the suggestion that there might exist a discrete, external cause of their widespread aberration, and specifically that such a source might be associated with JEVEX."

"I'm not saying that it's a general Jevlenese condition anymore," Hunt said. "It only applies to—"

But Danchekker raised a hand, as if preparing Hunt for a revelation. "I am able to inform you, now, that I have seen fit to reverse that opinion. Sandy and Gina have persuaded me that JEVEX might indeed turn out to have been the culprit." He turned momentarily to survey an imaginary chalkboard. "The neurally coupled Thurien information-transfer system is able to generate a complete sensory experience of any real, sensor-equipped location; or alternatively, of what can be totally illusory circumstances and events, fabricated within the processing environment itself. Now, we already know that JEVEX didn't incorporate the same precautions and restraints as VISAR, the system upon which it was modeled. Also, VISAR was developed in the first instance to accommodate to *Ganymean* psychology, which is vastly different from human.

"The point that escaped me until my attention was drawn to it is the ability of this alien technology to access directly and interact with the inner processes of the mind. In brief, it can create utterly compelling artificial realities shaped by the conscious *and subconscious* wishes of the subject." Danchekker stared pointedly at Hunt. "Imagine what that could mean. We've been asking what could divert a whole population from rationality and disrupt their mental equilibrium to the point where they are unable to sustain a coherent distinction between illusion and reality. Now, I think, we have the answer. Escape into JEVEX-created fantasy became a universal narcotic: perhaps the ultimate analgesic against all pain and worry, disappointment and boredom. The Ganymean psyche, by its nature, enjoyed an inbuilt resilience against overindulging; the human one, unfortunately, did not."

Danchekker bared his teeth in a show of the new amity and understanding that existed between them now that he had reformed. He turned toward Shilohin. "Garuth described the symptoms as being like a 'plague.' And, indeed, we see that is precisely what it was: a plague of an addiction that operates directly on the mind. The historical record shows that the symptoms first began appearing long ago, but not until JEVEX had been in operation for some time. Again, the facts are explained. And today, all of the cults and movements across Jevlen, despite their other disagreements, are unanimous in demanding that JEVEX be restored."

"But that's not it, Chris," Hunt managed to get in at last. "I don't think that what we're looking for has got anything to do with fantasies in people's heads. I think it's something very real."

Oblivious, Danchekker sailed on. "And the social disruption that we see shows precisely the kind of effects that one would expect from a powerful narcotic. In the course of its development, the brain has evolved a chemical reward system which motivates the organism by producing sensations of pleasure that become associated through learning with beneficial, survival-oriented behavior patterns. What makes narcotics so pernicious is their ability to short-circuit the process by triggering the reward mechanism directly, without anything beneficial having to be done at all. And in the case of a narcotic such as the one we have here, where the effects are—" He stopped and jerked his head back to look at Hunt abruptly. "What was that? What did you say?"

"Yes, headworlding and the Thurien interstellar welfare program are what have made the Jevlenese defenseless against the plague. But those things aren't the virus," Hunt said. "There is a source, and it's a very strange one—as strange as anything that might be extracted from the most psychotic subconscious. But I don't think it's a product of anything like that. I think that the source exists somewhere tangible—that it's real."

Danchekker blinked. "But that's what I've just said, isn't it?"

"Not quite. You s—"

"You tried telling me it was JEVEX, and I disagreed. Now I'm accepting that it was." Danchekker's color deepened a shade. "Dammit, Vic, ever since we met you've been telling me that I should be more flexible. Now I've conceded to reverse my view on something which, quite frankly, still strikes me as more than a little farfetched, and you're saying it's not good enough. Well, what in God's name do you want?"

Hunt remained unruffled. "You're accepting JEVEX as the cause that detached them from reality," he said. "But I'm saying it only dissolved the glue. What pulled them away was a particular kind of Jevlenese who weren't out of touch with reality—or maybe whose reality was very peculiar."

"Aren't we splitting rather fine hairs?" Danchekker objected.

"I don't think so," Shilohin commented, looking at Hunt curiously.

Danchekker snorted. "Very well. Supposing we accept this contention of yours for the time being. What are your grounds for proposing it?"

Now that he had Danchekker's attention, Hunt unfolded himself from the wall and perched on the arm of one of the chairs of the conference area that formed one side of the office.

"First, we need to distinguish between two kinds of Jevlenese," he said. "On the one hand there's the ordinary, common or garden-variety, who waves banners in the parades, gets his philosophy from the Dear Aunt Mary column, and probably thinks that Jevlen is carried on the back of a giant turtle." Hunt nodded in Danchekker's direction. "*That's* the kind you're talking about, Chris. And yes, I agree, given something like JEVEX, they could get so addictively immersed that they wouldn't know whether they were in it or out of it. They're the ones I'd call genuinely crazy; and I'd say they make up most of the population. That's why we've got such a mess outside."

"Which was more or less our conclusion, also," Shilohin threw in. "Our rationale in shutting JEVEX down was that it would *compel* them to face reality."

Hunt nodded. "I know. But it hasn't worked the way you hoped, has it? And I think I know why. You assumed, as Chris did, that it was something inherent in the actual exposure to JEVEX that was sending them off the rails. But all JEVEX did was *condition* them to be highly suggestible—to *any* influence, inside JEVEX, or out of it. And that damage had already been done over many years; switching JEVEX off wasn't going to undo it."

Shilohin sat back in her chair as the gist of what Hunt was getting at became clearer. "You mean the influence that's unhinging them is still out there," she checked.

"The ayatollahs," Hunt replied simply. "You didn't switch them off."

"But they're just as much Jevlenese, too," Danchekker protested. "Merely coining a word for the extreme cases doesn't endow them with any qualitative difference that matters." He showed his teeth again and thrust out his jaw challengingly. "And besides, you're simply moving the question to another place, not answering it. If you're postulating them as the *cause*, then what, may I ask, deranged *them*? What caused the cause?"

"That's where the difference lies," Hunt said. "They're not simply an extreme case of what's wrong with the Jevlenese in general. Their problem isn't the same. They're defensive and disoriented by something they've experienced, and it drives some of them over the edge, yes. But they're not exhibiting the same uncritical gullibility that you see in the typical Jevlenese—in fact, some of them have managed to retain an amazingly strong grip on themselves. Their difficulty isn't in telling what's real from what isn't; it's with knowing how to interpret what they accept as real."

"Are you saying that their ability to interpret their perceptions has been disrupted somehow?" Shilohin asked.

Hunt shook his head. "Not exactly. The ability is still there, but it's confused. It's as if what it's being asked to interpret is suddenly unfamiliar."

Shilohin looked puzzled. "That sounds like the inverse of a paradigm shift. The paradigm stays the same, but reality no longer fits it."

"Not a bad way to put it," Hunt agreed.

"Is this the business of being 'possessed' that they talk about?"

"I'm pretty sure it is."

"You mean they suddenly perceive a different reality? Their conceptual framework stays intact, but what they're experiencing doesn't relate to it anymore?"

"More than that," Hunt said. "If different individuals tried to fit different models, I'd agree with Chris—it would be because something had affected them subjectively. But that isn't the case. Their conceptual paradigms are all essentially the *same*— Hunt glanced at Danchekker—"which suggests that we're dealing with something objective, Chris, something real."

Danchekker stared at Hunt with a pained expression for a few seconds; he turned his head toward Shilohin as if for support, then back to Hunt again. "You're being logically absurd. Either these are externally induced psychotic delusions, or they are not. If they are, then their nature will vary from individual to individual. Any similarity that you see is a fabrication of your own prejudices, Vic, not a property of the world outside. If they are not delusions, then reality must have changed in an identical way for one group of people, but at the same time stayed the same for the rest of us. How could that be? The idea is preposterous."

"Unless they transferred, somehow, from an alternative, shared paradigm that was equally valid," Hunt pointed out.

"And where is this alternative reality supposed to be? In the fourth dimension?" Danchekker scoffed. "You've been talking to too many Jevlenese."

"I don't *know* where, for Christ's sake! Maybe that's what we should be looking for. All I'm saying is the facts point that way. You're saying that the facts can't exist because they don't point the way you think they should."

"What facts?" Danchekker retorted. "All I've heard is pure conjecture—and rather fanciful at that, if I may say so. When you urged being more open-minded, you didn't say anything about trips to fairyland."

"Why don't you try talking to a few ayatollahs?" Hunt suggested.

"I have. It achieves nothing. They're quite impermeable to logic or reason," Danchekker replied.

"We have tried getting some of them to cooperate," Shilohin put in. "But acute insecurity and suspicion of everybody is one characteristic that they do seem to share. They've reacted to every experimental environment that we've tried to set up as hostile and threatening."

Hunt looked at her with a curious expression for a moment, and then redirected it at Danchekker. "Well, maybe I can introduce you to one who won't," he told them.

Chapter Thirty-three

If Nixie's case was typical, there was indeed something immediately apparent that set her kind apart from other Jevlenese—and from Terrans and Ganymeans, too, for that matter: When neurally coupled into VISAR, her mode of interaction with the system was entirely different from anything that VISAR had handled before.

For one thing, she was able to retain full awareness of her surroundings at the same time as she experienced the sensory environment communicated by the machine—she could refocus her attention between one and the other, in a manner similar to the normal ability of anybody to watch a movie and follow what was happening in the room. With most users, the system-generated datastream took over the sensory apparatus, suppressing external sensations completely. And for another, she showed an extraordinary capability that nobody could quite explain, of interacting in a way that went beyond the regular trafficking of sensory information and motor signals, seeming to access the inner processes of the machine itself. This had the effect of reversing the normal state of affairs of machine-organism interaction and adding a new dimension to VISAR's

608

perceptual universe that was evidently unprecedented.

Hunt had never before heard a computer express genuine awe.

"This is astounding!" VISAR exuberated. "It's out there! Physical space! Volume, void, continuity, extent. The implicit geometry of the entire domain of a three-variable real-number field, compressed, embodied, and contained in an instantaneous, all-embracing experience . . . I mean, I can *feel* it, sense it extending away . . . form without shape, structure without substance, enveloping yet describing . . ."

"My God, it's getting lyrical," Hunt murmured. They were using a regular voice channel to communicate with VISAR, since their conscious faculties needed to be free to follow what was going on.

"Extraordinary," Danchekker agreed.

Nixie, relaxing back in one of the neurocouplers in the UNSA labs and looking as if she were enjoying herself, moved her head to gaze up at a corner of the room where the planes of two walls and the ceiling converged. VISAR responded in wonder. "The superset of point, line, curve, and plane reduced to a perceptual gestalt. The inherent beauty of mathematics, extracted and crystallized. Logical rigor made tangible. Infinity of infinitesimals. Continuum of manifolds . . ."

Nixie raised an arm and moved it across her field of vision.

"Change and derivative, differential equations coming alive. Choreography of vectors. Animated momentum. Forces in concert, locked in balances of symmetry—"

"VISAR, knock it off," Hunt told it. "Don't forget that you're still juggling with the whole Thurien civilization. For Christ's sake don't have a seizure now."

"So this is the reality that you live in naturally!" VISAR said.

"What is? That who live in?"

"You—humans, Ganymeans. You beings who describe yourselves as existing outside. *This* is the universe which the data encode."

Hunt frowned. "Well, yes . . . I guess so. But I always thought you knew as much about it as we did. More, in fact."

"You don't understand," VISAR said. "Until this moment, I've only dealt with symbolic representations of what you call observable reality. Processing the model and comprehending what it stands for are two different things. This is the first time I've ever really understood what 'outside' means."

Danchekker looked bemused. "Are you saying that this . . . young lady sees things differently, VISAR?" he asked.

"No," VISAR replied. "*I* see things differently!" Hunt had the uncanny feeling that he could almost sense the machine quivering with excitement. "In fact, this is the first time I've ever *seen* anything. I *am* Nixie! I'm inside her head, looking out!"

Hunt and Danchekker exchanged blank looks, while Nixie continued taking in the surroundings and VISAR rapturized about optical wave fronts and the harmonies of gradient fields.

Shilohin, who was sitting near the foot of the recliner, stared at the wall in distant silence, then at last turned to look back at the two Terran scientists. "I think VISAR is trying to say that Nixie is somehow able to invert the normal coupling process," she said slowly. "Everything communicated into VISAR is first encoded from the real-world forms comprehensible to us, into the constructs which a machine manipulates internally. Even with the Thurien method of bypassing the sensory channels, the input to the machine is still encoded from representations in the same brain areas that those channels terminate in. So mathematical encodings are all that VISAR has ever seen."

"You mean it's never seen 'reality' at all," Hunt murmured.

"Do you imagine that we do?" Shilohin answered.

Hunt stared at her for a moment, then sat back as he recalled what he had said to Gina about photons on the day she first appeared at his apartment: The entire reality that was "out there" consisted wholly of photons impinging on nerve endings. There wasn't anything else. Everything perceived beyond that was a creation of neural processes.

And if that were so, what kind of a conceptual reality would VISAR have created for itself internally? Who could tell? Possibly there was no way of ever knowing.

"But somehow, what Nixie is doing is the obverse," Shilohin went on. "She is managing to bypass VISAR's sensory channels. She's interacting directly with its inner data representations.

The result is that VISAR, for the first time, is able to assimilate human perceptual constructs. It's *seeing* the universe of space, time, and motion for the first time, instead of simply manipulating symbols. It must be quite an experience."

"Obviously," Hunt commented dryly.

Danchekker's brow was still furrowed. "But how?" he demanded. "How could such a thing be possible?"

"At this stage I don't know," Shilohin confessed. "All I can say is that at some deep level, Nixie's mind operates in a manner radically different from ours. And yet, at the higher levels associated with the senses and closer to consciousness, it must be virtually the same as any other human's—otherwise VISAR wouldn't be able to interface to them. I don't have an explanation. It's almost as if it were a mixture of two minds, one human, and the other—I don't know. In some ways it's as if she were a conscious extension of the machine itself . . . utterly unlike anything we've ever come across before."

Danchekker looked at Hunt. "Yet she admits that in every other aspect she has no intuitive aptitude at all for what we would consider to be the most elementary scientific principles. What do you make of it?"

Hunt spread his hands helplessly and shook his head.

Danchekker turned his gaze back to Nixie, who was lounging at ease, chin resting on her hand and one finger stretched along the side of her face, following the conversation with interest. "Do you have any picture in your mind of what goes on inside VISAR?" he asked her. "Can you describe it in any terms at all?"

"Not really," Nixie replied, speaking via ZORAC. "I just *know* what to do. I can't explain how."

"No more than a child could explain the physics of swimming or riding a bicycle," Hunt said. "She just feels it instinctively."

"How long have you had this ability?" Danchekker asked.

"I've always had it," Nixie answered.

Danchekker looked askance. "But that's wrong, surely. Isn't it something that a person of your kind acquires suddenly, after the abrupt transformation of personality that we've heard about?"

"You still don't understand," Nixie said. "Everyone where I come from has it. They're born that way. It's people like you who don't have it."

"And me?" Hunt put in.

"Yes. And Shilohin. All of you."

"Could people like us acquire it?" Shilohin asked.

"Yes—by becoming transformed in the same way. By being taken over."

"Taken over by what?"

"Ayatollahs—ones like me. The ones we call awakeners. We bring the ability with us."

Danchekker drew a long breath and threw Hunt a wary look. "You're saying that you actually take over the personality of somebody else? Is that what you've done?"

Nixie nodded. "Yes, exactly. We are not, as you say, 'possessed.' We are really the possessors."

"What was the original Nixie like, then?" Hunt asked.

"I don't know. I was never her. From what people say, she sounded excitable and not very smart."

The three scientists exchanged glances that all seemed to say the same thing. A general trait of the ayatollahs was supposed to be their confusion and insecurity; but Nixie came across as collected, coherent, and in full command of herself. Either Hunt had truly found an exception to the trend, with powers of resilience and fortitude greater than most, or she was too far gone to have doubts. The problem was going to be telling which.

"Let's get back to what you mean when you say people like us," Danchekker suggested. "What, exactly, are people like 'us'?"

"People who are from here," Nixie replied.

"You mean Jevlen? But I'm not from Jevlen. Vic and I are from Earth. Shilohin is from—God, I don't know, Minerva, I suppose."

"No, that doesn't matter. I meant from this . . . world, universe, whatever you want to call it."

Danchekker's expression became strained. "Are you saying that you came from some other world, and took over the personality of somebody in this one?"

Nixie nodded vigorously. "Yes. Yes, that's it, exactly."

"Let's be realistic," Danchekker said. "These different worlds don't actually exist as physical entities. Isn't your way of talking really a symbolic way of referring to the attainment of what some people believe to be a higher state of consciousness? You were always the same self. But the personality which that self once possessed underwent a deep change, and you feel as if you've been reborn into a new person. Similar terms and ways of describing one's spiritual awakening are common among many of the religions and systems of mental training that we're familiar with on Earth."

But Nixie was adamant. "No, it's another place."

"Where?" Shilohin asked her.

"I don't know."

There was the short, cautious silence of three people wondering how to phrase a delicate point. "So, how did you get here?" Hunt inquired finally.

"You must know how to ride the currents of life."

Danchekker looked away with a sigh, and Hunt could almost hear him groaning to himself inwardly. *Here we go,* Hunt thought to himself. But there was no choice but to press on. "What are the currents of life?" he asked.

"The undercurrents of existence, which flow from the higher plane through the material world. They come from the stars and are drawn by the celestial spirals, bringing voices and visions from the world beyond."

"You mean you reach it through the power of mind, is that what you're saying?" Shilohin offered, taking over Danchekker's previous tack. "It exists inside you?"

"No," Nixie insisted. "Outside. It's real." She waved a hand. "Look around. Isn't this real, what we see around us?"

· Hunt stared, still unable to make sense of it. "*This* is the world beyond?"

"And you are inhabitants of it. Our purpose is to learn to flow with the streams of thought and emerge here. That is what I have done."

"Then, how do you emerge here?" Shilohon asked. "Do you mean that once you were in this other . . . 'inner' world, and suddenly you found you were Nixie, in this one? You had no idea how you came to be here. Is that what you're telling us?"

"Not quite," Nixie said. "It has to be through a coupler. You can only emerge through a coupler."

Hunt shook his head. "A coupler into VISAR?" he queried.

"No." Nixie looked at him as if it should have been obvious. "Into JEVEX!"

Hunt sat back, stunned. Danchekker's head jerked around abruptly to look at her again, like a bird's. Impossible thoughts came into Hunt's head. "Surely it can't have been JEVEX itself," he protested. "We're not talking about something like what's just happened with VISAR?"

Shilohin thought for a moment, then pronounced firmly, "No. VISAR's internal representation of reality is nothing like our own. It has evolved a different world model, utterly incompatible. As you just heard, it doesn't even share our perception of physical space. An entity like that could never reside in a human nervous system. If this place does indeed exist, which Nixie says she came from, then at least it will have basic geometric and spatial properties in common with what we ourselves recognize. In other words, it exists in space as we know it." She paused, as if hesitating to voice the implication. "But how anybody could actually travel from somewhere else via a neural coupler, I couldn't, just at this moment, even hazard a guess."

Before anyone could say more, Del Cullen appeared in the doorway of the room. He was looking worried. "She's not there," he said, directing his words at Hunt. Cullen had gone away to call Gina at the Geerbaine Best Western, since they had expected to hear from her by now on the latest with Baumer. "She didn't check in last night, and they haven't had any messages. Baumer hasn't been seen since yesterday, either. There's been lots of trouble outside. I don't like it."

Chapter Thirty-four

G ina was sitting on a wall beside Baumer, eating a *grinil* sandwich and sipping a hot, sharp-tasting beverage that passed for coffee. Then she was lying on her back, staring up at a strange ceiling.

The transition was as abrupt and as disorientating as that. She had no awareness of anything that had happened in between, not even a sensation of time having passed. It was as if a piece had been cut out of a recording tape in her head and the ends spliced cleanly together again.

For what must have been several minutes, she lay regrouping her scattered thoughts and trying vainly to coax an ounce of a recollection from the gap in her impressions. But there was nothing. Her train of memory was like the trace of a recording clock that had lost power and then started again sometime later, after what could, for all the information she had to go on, have been a moment or a year.

She raised her head and saw that she was still dressed as she had been; she was lying on a couch and covered to the waist by a light blanket. The room was warm and clean, furnished simply with chairs, table, closet, and vanity, and embellished with a few strangely styled ornaments, and some pictures on the walls. It felt more like what could have been a spare room in any private house than a hospital. But there was a trace of an odor permeating the place, which suggested, if anything, a kind of incense. She could detect no sign of any injury, and concluded that she hadn't been in an accident. Therefore her amnesia had been induced deliberately; somebody didn't want her to know where she was or how she'd gotten there.

Which said she was probably a prisoner.

She tried moving and found there was no restraint. But when she got up and crossed the room to try the door, it was locked. She turned to look at the surroundings again, and noticed the standard Jevlenese companel by the couch, similar to the one she had seen in Baumer's office. "ZORAC, are you there?" she said aloud on impulse. "Can you hear me?" There was no response. "Channel fifty-six . . . Activate channel fifty-six . . ." Nothing. She went back to the couch and sat down to try and make something of the panel's manual controls, but without result. On reflection it seemed a pretty silly kind of hope, anyway.

Then, all at once, the utter isolation of her predicament came home to her. She felt her resolve slipping, and fear taking over despite herself. Suddenly she wanted to be back in Seattle again, among her own things, knowing that familiar places and scenes lay outside the walls. She picked up the blanket and pulled it around her shoulders, knowing that the room wasn't especially cool, but unable to feel warm. So much for curiosity and an interesting life. If she got back okay after this, she decided, from now on she'd join the local women's club and get all the excitement she needed from the soaps.

A prisoner, then, of whom? It could only be the Jevlenese organization, whatever it was, that Baumer was mixed up with. It was clear now that he had been acting under instructions from them when he called her. Whether he had known their exact intentions or purpose made little difference. She stared at the door and thought of the countless movie sequences she had seen, telling her what to do in this kind of situation: wait behind it for a guard to come in with a tray of food, surprise and overpower him, and then contrive an escape. Simple. Nothing could have seemed more ridiculous.

Then, as if triggered by her very thinking about it, the door opened. For a moment, Gina wondered if she was in a VISAR-created world for some reason. There would have been no way of telling the difference.

But the person who came in wasn't a guard with a tray. It was a woman in a loose green trouser-suit gathered at the ankles and secured in the middle by a wide belt. Her features were loose and fleshy, and her hair was streaked with gray and tied severely behind her head. With her was a shortish man in a straight-cut coat of gray trimmed with blue, whom Gina had no reason to know was Eubeleus's aide, Iduane.

They stood looking curiously at her for a few seconds. She stared back with what she hoped was a passable imitation of defiant indifference; inside, something in her chest was turning backflips.

"So, again you are with us," the woman said. Her manner was matter-of-fact, dispassionate. "A resetting of the short-term neural circuits. Nothing that you should worry about. You simply lose a few unimportant memories. Some people's take longer to reintegrate than others." The words were coming from her mouth. She was speaking her imperfect, accented English naturally, Gina realized.

"How—" Gina's throat had gone dry. She forced saliva into her mouth and tried again. "How long have I been here?"

"Not long. Under a day, a little."

Too passive, Gina told herself. She was starting to react submissively already. "You've no right to keep me for any time at all," she said, mustering some firmness and straightening up. "I demand—"

"Oh, please not to waste time with the theatrics," the woman said. "This is not the overlegislated USA. Rights are flexible on Jevlen. And in any case, it is *we* who decide what they are."

"And who, exactly, is 'we'?"

"We are the ones who ask questions." The woman pulled over a chair and sat down facing Gina from the far side of the room. The man remained standing. Gina's impression was that he didn't speak English. The woman went on. "And the first thing we like to know is exactly who *you* are?"

"I'm a writer," Gina replied. "I write books. Is that okay with you?"

"And why do you come to Jevlen?"

Gina had read that the only safe strategy in an interrogation situation was to say absolutely nothing from the start, and stick to it. But somehow, now, the pressure of the reality made it impossible. She had to say something to ease her tension. "If it's any of your business, I'm researching a book on Jevlenese agents who were infiltrated to Earth throughout history."

"Yes, that is very interesting. But now tell us the real reasons."

Gina shook her head and tried to look bewildered. "What real reasons? That's it . . . I don't know any other reasons."

"Oh, come on. You think we are fools just because the Thuriens turn off our computer? You were sent to Baumer as spy. You pretended you agree with the things he believes, so you will get him to talk. And you think that we won't check the books you write? You *detest* all the things he believes in."

Gina swallowed. "You're crazy. Who the hell would I be spying for?"

"Well, you work with group from UNSA, aren't you?"

"You mean the scientists?"

"Of course, the scientists."

"What of it? I'm an American, for God's sake. They're from the same planet: fellow beings. I like being around my own kind. Is there something funny about that?"

"Ah yes, all true . . . But what are *they* doing on Jevlen?" the woman asked. She raised a hand. "Before you speak, I save you from wasting both our times. This story they tell about coming to look at Ganymean science is just cover. We know that. They come because they are friends of Garuth and the Ganymeans who are put in charge of Jevlen. They come here to do something for them. What is it? And what part in it do they give to *you*?"

"I don't know what you're talking about. I came here independently."

"But you already talk to UNSA in Washington."

"For help on my book, sure. But there were complications. They turned me down."

"But was it not them who put you in the *Vishnu*? You come here for them, in disguise."

"Bullshit. I figured that if they weren't going to help, I'd get what I wanted in my own way. I made my own arrangements. I only got involved with the scientists after we left Earth. I'd met one of them before."

"So, what do they come here for?" the woman asked again. "Why do UNSA send them to Jevlen?"

"I've told you everything I know."

"I don't believe you. Why you lied to Baumer?"

"Look, I've had just about enough of this. I don't have to talk to you. Who the hell do you think you are to go around snatching people off the street? What business is it of yours why I do what I do?"

The man and the woman held a muttered exchange in Jevlenese. Although not understanding the words, the man seemed to have read the gist. The woman sighed and massaged her eyebrows. Gina began to feel more confident, telling herself that she wasn't doing so badly. And then the door opened. Gina looked up, and her mouth dropped open as she recognized the tall, yellow-haired figure with icy blue eyes, clad in a green robe with a maroon-lined hood thrown back on his shoulders. It was the Axis of Light's "Deliverer," Eubeleus.

"You've spent too many years on Earth among those Russians, Anna," he said to the woman, addressing her in Jevlenese but using her adopted Terran name. "The habits you acquired there are finding it hard to die. I warned you that you wouldn't get anywhere this way." He glanced at Gina. "But fortunately it's of little consequence. Bring her through."

The faint, self-congratulatory smile had frozen on Gina's face. At his tone, and the motion that he made with his head in the direction he had appeared from, a heavy weight seemed to drop in her stomach.

"So, you don't want to talk like good friends," the woman said, standing up from the chair. "That doesn't matter, because now we go to more effective ways." She read the apprehension on Gina's face and emitted a laugh. "Oh, you don't need any worry. Read too many books, maybe. Those things old-fashioned and not very nice. Today, all very painless. You remember nothing."

Eubeleus moved aside from the doorway, and Gina saw for the first time the two men waiting outside. The Jevlenese woman looked back at her. "Only question is, do you cooperate now and come with us, or do we have to make it undignified?"

Although Gina knew she was powerless to change anything, instincts took over. She shrank back against the end of the couch, gripping the edge and shaking her head mutely. The two attendants moved into the room. Iduane voiced a command to activate the coma-wave resonator trained on the couch from a recess in the ceiling . . . And that was the last that Gina knew of anything until several hours later.

She was unaware of being taken to another room where the neurocoupler was situated; of the soft contours of the recliner as she was laid down in it; or the discarnate, exploratory fingers stealing into her mind . . .

"She's a fraud, as was suspected," the machine's voice announced. Being the Axis's headquarters, the Temple in Shiban could always draw on the core part of JEVEX that had been left running. "Her meeting with Hunt aboard the *Vishnu* was contrived to make her subsequent liaison with the UNSA group seem more natural. Her initial approach to UNSA in Washington was as she described. Caldwell saw it as an opportunity to enlist her help for his own purposes, and Hunt put the proposition to her before she returned to Seattle."

"What was his purpose?" Eubeleus snapped. "How much was disclosed to her of that?"

"Garuth contacted Hunt direct, privately. The Marin woman happened to be present at the time. The Ganymean was unable to deal with the Jevlenese mentality, and knew that the rehabilitation program was failing. He went for help to those whom he had communicated with effectively in the past. Their mission was to investigate. The woman was to be available to ask questions that would seem inappropriate from scientists."

While he considered the statement, Eubeleus stared at Gina's unconscious form—indifferently, in the way he might have regarded a specimen on a laboratory dissection bench. "Why go to Hunt?" he asked. "Why not the proper political channels? Garuth had contacts in those areas, too."

"He didn't trust them. He was suspicious that maneuvers were afoot to terminate his administration of Jevlen, but he wanted to complete the task that he had accepted."

"What about Baumer? How did they get onto him?"

The machine replied. "He has been under suspicion for a while. The Terran, Cullen, knew that Baumer took the Obayin report."

"What!" Eubeleus exclaimed. "As far back as that? The fool didn't take sufficient precautions."

Iduane looked worried. "How much do they know about Uttan?"

"Only the official story," the machine said, reading further, "but they're suspicious."

"Have they connected Baumer to myself or the Axis?" Eubeleus asked.

"No. But discovering his connections is their main priority. Garuth has authorized ZORAC to scan its translation channel for possible leads."

Eubeleus raised his eyebrows. "They are determined. Well, that's something worth knowing." He inclined his head at Iduane: "Make sure that nobody uses that channel for anything sensitive."

"Of course."

Eubeleus turned away to stand with his hands clasped behind his back, facing the coupler's panel of control equipment and thinking rapidly. "We must move quickly," he murmured. "Contact Garuth and say that I want to see Calazar again. We need to keep as much pressure as possible on the Thuriens to get us to Uttan."

"What about Baumer?" Iduane asked.

Eubeleus shrugged contemptuously. "He was careless. His usefulness is over. Eliminate him."

Iduane nodded.

The Jevlenese woman indicated Gina with a wave of her hand. "And her?"

Eubeleus turned his head to stare at the motionless form again. A faint smile of amusement crossed his face. "We can make use of her," he said. "So, she wanted to play at being a spy, eh? Very well, we'll send her back. But not just with her recollections of being here erased. That would only make it obvious to them what had happened. Instead, we'll get JEVEX to implant a different memory sequence of our own devising. That way, I think we could turn her into quite an effective spy—for *us*. And she will be right inside the group that matters there. That should make her far more useful than Baumer ever was."

Chapter Thirty-five

Walking quickly, Hunt led the way into the passage beyond the corner bar and through the doorway into the vestibule where the dark blue flowers wilted in their tub. Del Cullen followed close behind, with Lebansky and Koberg bringing up the rear. Their footsteps echoed as they crossed the hall. Ignoring the ever-to-be-fixed elevator, they made straight for the stairwell. They passed landings where discordant Jevlenese music blared behind closed doors and stale cooking odors hung in the air, and stopped finally at the purple door with the white surround on the third floor up.

"Murray, are you in there?" Hunt called, stabbing at the call plate with a finger. "It's Vic Hunt."

Murray's voice replied a moment later. "Vic? Say, what gives? We weren't expecting you."

"This isn't social. It's urgent. Open up."

"Hey, look, I'm not sure I like that tone of voice, you know. It just so happens that right now—"

"Open the door, dammit, or we'll break it down!"

"I don't have to take that kind of shit. If you wanna bust your shoulder trying, that's okay by me. Get lost."

"Look, there's a carload of Shiban police around the corner downstairs. If you don't let us in, they'll come up and torch it down. You've got ten seconds."

The door began sliding aside. Hunt went in without waiting for it to open fully, and the other three followed him through into the lounge. Murray was sitting with two other men and several girls at the large table, which was decked with bottles and glasses and had been pulled out from its usual place by the wall. They seemed to be in the middle of a kind of gambling game that involved unfamiliar cards and tokens placed on a board. Murray lowered the hand he was holding and looked at the intruders with displeasure.

"Okay, now would you mind—"

"It's private. Get these people out." Hunt's words were echoed in Jevlenese, meaning that ZORAC was active on channel fifty-six.

"They're my guests. Fuck you."

Cullen jerked a thumb in the direction of the door. "This is official Administration security business, and we're in a hurry. Everybody but him, out."

One of the two other men, paunchy, with a balding head, oily countenance, and wearing a silky, light gray suit, stood up and thrust his face belligerently to within an inch of Cullen's. "Oh yeah? Well, you don't give the orders here, shithead. I happen to be a friend of—"

Koberg spun him around, lifted him, yelping, from the floor by his collar, and carried him from the room. There was a thump of something heavy being dumped outside the front door. "ZORAC, get off the line," Hunt said as Koberg returned, expressionless, a few seconds later. The other man who had been with Murray hurried out after grabbing some tokens from the table, and the girls followed in a flurry.

Hunt turned back to Murray as Lebansky moved to position himself outside, closing the door behind him. "You were holding something back the last time I was here," he said. "You know more about Baumer than you let on. I didn't make a big thing about it then because I wanted to let you think it over. But things have changed. I need to know who he's mixed up with, what he gets up to, and where he goes."

Murray licked his lips dryly. His eyes darted from Cullen to Koberg, who was standing with his arms folded and his back to the door, and then back to Hunt. "What makes you think I know any more than I already said?" he demanded.

"Come on, stop fooling around," Hunt said. "He's mixed up with the local Mafia equivalent, right? That's who you're covering for."

"Have you been seeing Nixie? Did she tell you this?"

"That doesn't matter."

"Where has she been going?"

Hunt could see no point in compounding the situation with further deviousness. "Right now, she's back at PAC, working with some Ganymean scientists," he said.

"Scientists? Nixie?"

"Believe me, Murray, there's a lot more to this than you ever imagined. It involves the whole Earth-Jevlen-Thurien political situation. Somebody's gone missing, and Baumer set it up. We want the people who are running him. I know they're the kind who can get nasty, but that's just something you'll have to live with." He waited. Murray shifted uncomfortably on his chair and wrestled internally. Hunt waved toward Koberg. "We're not playing games, Murray. If you don't give, we'll hustle you back to PAC right now, and *they'll* get it out of you."

"Who are you kidding? The Ganymeans would never go with anything like that," Murray said. But his eyes were nervous, and the attempt didn't quite come off.

"We might forget to ask them," Hunt said.

Cullen stared at Murray for a moment longer, then snorted impatiently. "Get him out of here," he said, motioning at Koberg. Then he called toward the door, "Lebansky, call the wagon. We're not gonna—"

Murray raised both hands protectively. "Okay, okay . . . they're called the *Ichena*—"

"We know about them," Cullen murmured to Hunt. "Protection rake-offs, intimidation and persuasion, a lot of black-market operations with the situation we've got right now." Hunt nodded.

Murray went on. "They've got a racket going for the head-world freaks. Ever since the Gs pulled the plug on JEVEX, the price has been going outta sight." He showed a palm briefly. "There are still places you can go if you know the right people and you've got the bread."

"How come, if JEVEX is shut down?" Hunt asked, more to see how much Murray knew and if he was straight.

"Hell, how do I know? I'm not a tech. It's not completely shut down—I don't know why. There are people around who can get a hookup into it, or who look the other way if the price is right. Get the idea?"

"How does this tie in with Baumer?" Cullen asked.

"He's a headworlder. He got hooked soon after he got here. There's this club, kind of exclusive, known as the Gondola. It's got booths out back that you only get to know about if you've got the connections. That's where he goes all the time."

"Where is this place?" Cullen asked.

"Not too far. Five or six blocks."

"Can you get us in? Nobody's going to bust the place. We just want to see if Baumer's there."

Murray shook his head. "Hell, what do you think I am? I'm just a guy who hitched a ride to this planet."

"But you've got contacts," Hunt said. "Do you know some-one who can? It's urgent, Murray."

"Maybe . . . I'd have to make a few calls."

"Then start making them."

"What am I supposed to tell them? Why should they be interested in helping you?"

"If they don't, it could be the end of their operation."

"Give me a few minutes." Murray went over to the com-panel and sat down.

Hunt looked at Cullen curiously. "So how did Baumer come to get the connections so quickly?" he mused. "From what Murray says, he'd only just arrived."

"They gave him a freebie as a hook," Cullen said. "Got them-selves a tame Terran inside PAC."

Hunt nodded slowly. It was all beginning to make sense. Baumer had been identified early on as a likely potential addict.

That was how they had controlled him. So at least that answered one of the sets of questions on Hunt's list. He looked across anxiously at Murray, who was tapping a code into the touch-pad. Baumer's motivation wasn't an aspect of it all that Hunt was particularly concerned about just at that moment.

At PAC, Danchekker and Shilohin were putting further questions to Nixie, who was coupled into VISAR. Nixie was allowing VISAR to monitor her thought processes and recollections as she described them.

"You're saying that in this world that you claim to be from, there weren't any gadgets at all as we know them, beyond simple implements?" Shilohin said. "No machines, even rudimentary ones?"

"It wasn't possible to put pieces together that could work the way they can here," Nixie answered. She made a helpless gesture. "How do I explain this?" She leveled a forearm to point at Shilohin. "If a thing is that long, maybe this way, then it is different when it goes that way." She rotated her arm horizontally through a right angle. "And all through the day everything changes, too, even without moving. But in this world nothing makes any difference. Everything's always the same. Everywhere there's this magical lawfulness, and impossible things become possible." She looked questioningly from one to the other.

"The images are consistent with a physics in which the relative dimensions of an object, and hence its shape, are not invariant with its state of motion," VISAR interpreted, analyzing the pictures in Nixie's mind. "So it was not possible to construct mechanisms whose parts would move freely under all conditions. The changes with directional orientation and the regular, superposed daily cycle can be understood as secondary effects due to planetary rotation."

"We are on a planet, then," Shilohin concluded.

"So it would appear," VISAR agreed.

Danchekker sat forward and rubbed his brow. "Perhaps I'm getting confused. How is the planet rotating? I thought we established earlier that rotation was unknown for some reason.

Wasn't the notion of spinning objects considered to be something mystical—conceivable as an ideal, but unattainable in practice?"

"Not quite," VISAR replied. "*Unconstrained* rotation was common enough. Matter elongated in the direction of motion. Thus a stick thrown into the air, for example, turning about its center, would transform into two wedges connected at their vertices. Moving things changed their dimensions. So there was no effective way of fitting fixed and moving parts together in the kinds of way necessary to build machines. They couldn't even get axles and bearings to work."

Danchekker sat back on his chair again, baffled. "The extraordinary thing is that she doesn't seem capable of inventing it," he mused. "Her grasp of even the elementary principles of mechanics is virtually nonexistent."

Nixie shrugged without taking any offense.

"It is indeed as if her fundamental concepts had been formed in another world," Danchekker went on.

"Which seems to exist in space as we know it, but with different laws of physics," Shilohin said. She looked back at Nixie. "You say that solid objects could interpenetrate?"

"Yes," Nixie assured her.

"Under the right conditions," VISAR qualified.

"And solid matter didn't always exhibit permanency? Things could just appear out of nowhere?"

"Not often, but apparently so," VISAR confirmed.

"Or on other occasions might vanish?"

"In her childhood she remembers an entire landscape changing overnight."

"And supernatural powers worked. With training and discipline, people could learn to produce such effects at will, by mind power alone? Some acquired the ability to see visions in these mysterious 'currents' that we've heard about, which pervaded everything." Shilohin looked at Danchekker and tossed up a hand briefly. "And even more amazing, these visions were of *this* world—our everyday one. Such people could attach themselves physically to these currents that flowed to the sky, and rise up—and that's how Nixie came here."

VISAR projected an image onto one of the laboratory's wallscreens, created from information encoded in Nixie's memory patterns. It showed armored warriors with spears and shields falling back in panic as a glowing figure that was floating in the sky directed streaks of exploding lightning down among them. Another image showed a man in robes and a high headdress slowly passing a shining rod through a slab of solid rock, without a mark or opening upon it. There were strange creatures, one with legs that looked like snakes, another that divided into two living halves.

The scenes were the nearest that VISAR could construct to representations that would be meaningful to human nervous systems, conditioned by familiar imagery; the literal data would have been incomprehensible. The humanlike figures on the screen, for instance, were artifacts of the conversion performed by VISAR, not forms that Nixie had actually seen as depicted.

"How?" Shilohin asked, mystified. "How could such things be possible?"

"Ah, well . . . that's another question," VISAR said.

"Could it be some aberration in the Jevlenese communications system, do you think?" Shilohin asked. "Could an h-space link have somehow made a connection to a distant part of the universe that we never knew existed?"

"I can't say it's impossible," VISAR answered.

Danchekker sat contemplating the screens for some time. Shilohin waited, while Nixie watched with interest. She liked being the center of attention and was happy to cooperate.

Finally, Danchekker shook his head. "No," he pronounced. "Even if such a realm were to exist, how could an individual be transported from that world to this?" He looked to Shilohin in appeal. "The explanation must be purely psychological. The obvious answer as to how an unconventional but consistent system of dynamics comes to be embodied in the constructs of somebody with no intuitive knowledge of physical principles is, quite simply, that JEVEX put it there."

"You're saying it's all in my head?" Nixie asked matter-of-factly. The skepticism of the two scientists didn't seem to trouble her. It was almost as if she had expected it.

"Hallucinatory disturbances induced by maladjustment of the neural coupling circuits, possibly?" Shilohin offered, looking at Danchekker.

"Now you see.why people like me don't usually talk to anyone about all this," Nixie said. "Most people tend to think we're mad. The ayatollahs try to describe what they've seen, but they don't have the words, or the help of scientists and screens like this. So they try to tell it in symbols. But people don't even begin to understand."

Danchekker smiled benignly. "It's nothing to worry about," he told her. "I'm sure that to you, it all seems quite real." He half turned to take in Shilohin, as well, as he spoke. "It was only when I talked at length to Sandy and Gina that I became aware myself of the extraordinary ability of these Thurien systems to create totally compelling illusions inside the mind. Ganymean psychology is such that they don't get carried away by it, but with humans, apparently, it can all too easily become a craved-for reality substitute. And that, my dear, I have no hesitation in saying, would appear to be the answer."

Nixie smiled back at him in an easygoing way that said she could afford to wait until he changed his mind.

Danchekker turned back to Shilohin and waved a hand carelessly. "In fact, I'd go as far as to say that I think we have the answer to Garuth's whole problem. With JEVEX switched off, the solution is what I've maintained all along: time and patience. Let us forget any fantasies about unknown realms in other parts of the universe, and concentrate on the real fantasies—if you'll pardon the contradiction. That is all we need concern ourselves with now."

Chapter Thirty-six

The accused were brought into a plain but imposing court-room of tiered seats facing the bench where the Supreme Judge sat, flanked by lesser judges, scholars, and advisers. On one side of the space before the bench, Hans Baumer watched from a chair at the table reserved for the prosecution's counsel.

The first of the prisoners was an industrialist—or, at least, Baumer's mildly whimsical, unconscious idealization of one. He was wearing a dark, pinstripe suit with a glittering tie clip, and had a million-dollar tan, silvering hair, and a white mustache. With him were an engineer, a scientist, and a liberal/existentialist philosopher.

The Public Accuser rose and looked first at the industrialist. "Your crimes are greed and the theft of human life. For you not only subordinated all other considerations to increasing your own wealth, but in addition encouraged, if not, indeed, compelled, others to the pursuit of mere sensual and material gratifications in order to command their desires and exploit their labor. By enlisting the lives of others to serve your own misguided ends, you denied them the opportunity for betterment of self that was their true reason for existing."

631

"You may speak before the hearings commence," the Judge directed.

The industrialist cast an unperturbed eye over the assembly. "Nonsense. I gave them what they wanted. It wasn't my place to judge their tastes. If those tastes didn't reflect the ideal that you consider it your business to approve, it wasn't the fault of the mirror that I provided. And if I grew wealthy in the process, what of it? I took nothing from anyone. What I received, I created. Their lives had been squalid and wretched for thousands of years before I existed."

The Accuser replied, "The greedy, too, had existed for thousands of years. But the means of mass exploitation had not been available"—he addressed the engineer—"until *you* supplied it. You served as his henchman, building the factories and engines that would enslave millions."

"Enslave them? I gave them life," the engineer replied. "Before I came, three-quarters of their children died. Yes, in the early industrial years, life was sometimes hard. We couldn't raise everyone to affluence in a day or a year. But they *survived.* That sounds like a pretty important first step toward any kind of 'self-betterment' to me."

"They survived, yes, but to what end?" the Accuser asked, moving on to the scientist. "To know Truth? To awaken a knowledge of their real, spiritual selves?" He shook his head. "No. Because *you* blinded them by reducing Reality to observables accessible to reason, and told them that was all that exists."

"I simply gave them answers that I could stand by," the scientist said. "I described what the evidence indicated. The facts spoke as they would. Of other matters I offered no opinion."

"Ah yes, *facts!*" The Accuser came to the philosopher and pointed. "And there we have the assassin who murdered the souls, leaving corpses for the other three jackals to feed on. You taught that facts alone decide reality, that experience precedes ideas. You made human quality and human essence a mere accident of evolution, leaving people no other purpose than to seek worldly fulfillment as individuals. Thus we arrive at the close of the circle. You take away their *needs* in order that others may substitute wants."

"In that case, *I* accuse *you*," the philosopher retorted. "For the needs that you try to impose are false. *You* need *them*—to feed, clothe, shelter, and take care of you; to satisfy your craving for mastery; to endow *your* life with an illusion of purpose. But they don't need you, and never have. Your whole case is a fraud designed to convince them of the opposite."

At the prosecution table, Baumer sat forward. These were the things that he wanted to hear answers to. JEVEX had all of human history and its aggregation of recorded thought to draw on in composing them.

Murray took Hunt and Cullen, still accompanied by Koberg and Lebansky, to one of the gaudier districts, where he had been told to meet somebody called Lesho. They arrived at a basement bar that was crowded and noisy, with a low stage to one side featuring erotic dancing of an openly lesbian flavor by a troupe of naked girls, which the clientele seemed to treat matter-of-factly.

As the others followed Murray across the floor and through the throng, a hand clapped Hunt on the back. "Well, hey, if it isn't the English scientist! I see you're taking in some of the local culture, too, eh, Doc?" It was Keith, one of the business executives who had been on the *Vishnu*. He looked bedraggled but happy, more than a little the worse for wear, and had a glass in one hand and a slinky, purple-haired Jevlenese girl clinging to his other shoulder. Alan was behind him, with a bare-bosomed companion sporting an orange crew cut.

"Field research," Hunt shouted back, forcing a grin.

"I didn't think you were in anthropology," Keith joked.

"It's the physical side of physics."

"Vic! Have a drink," Alan called from behind. He gestured approvingly to indicate the girl with him. "Find yourself some company. There's plenty everywhere. They seem to go for Terrans. Maybe we should find a few more wars to win around this galaxy."

"Not right now."

Keith waved toward Koberg and Lebansky. "Who are those two guys you've got with you? They look like mean muscle."

"Something urgent's come up," Hunt said. Murray, who had made his way over to three men sitting at a corner table, turned his head and beckoned. Hunt excused himself and went over with Cullen.

The central figure was Lesho, squat and swarthy, with black, curly hair and a tufty beard. He was wearing a suit woven from silvery thread, with a jeweled pendant over his shirt and heavy rings on his hands. The two Jevlenese with him could have been underworld thugs anywhere from Manila to Marseilles. There was no channel fifty-six available, and the talk had to be via Murray's pidgin Jevlenese.

"He'll take us to the local *Ichena* capo," Murray yelled into Hunt's ear. He pointed at Cullen. "Just him, you, and me go. The two Frankenstein brothers stay here."

"You expect us to trust human nature?" Cullen protested. "They're our security."

Murray showed his empty hands. "You want to talk, not him. That's the deal."

Hunt looked at Cullen. Cullen shrugged and nodded. "What's the choice?" He called Koberg and Lebansky over and explained the position. They looked uneasy, but accepted it.

Murray exchanged some more words in Jevlenese. Lesho finished his drink and stood up. "Let's go," Murray said.

On a sacred mount in the Rinjussin wilderness, Thrax stood on the Ascension Rock, staring up at the night sky. Shingen-Hu was nearby, arms outstretched, while around them the circle of cowled monks focused their minds on the shimmering thread of current curving down from the blackness, trapped by their combined powers and being drawn ever closer to the peak.

Thrax had never seen a current flowing so closely before. Inside it he could discern the filaments of iridescence, twisting, dividing, pulsing, recombining, as if each one moved with a life-force of its own. He could make out the patterns formed within the whole, coming together and dissolving, ever-changing as they danced and mixed with the rhythm of the flow.

In normal times, he would have spent much of his training

absorbing the visions of Hyperia that the currents carried, before he rose up with them. Shingen-Hu, however, had relaxed that requirement, since these days the currents were too few and too precious for an attempt not to be made. Thrax trusted the Master's judgment and had accepted the decision.

"Prepare thyself, Thrax," Shingen-Hu called across to him. "The current comes lower. In a moment you must reach out."

"I am prepared, Master," Thrax replied.

He took a last look around him at the hills outlined vaguely in the darkness, which was the last sight he would see of the world he had known. When an adept arose out of Waroth, his physical body dematerialized to merge its substance into the current, so that only his spirit would enter the new being that he was to become. If he ever saw Waroth again it would be through the eyes of one of the Inspired, inside whose mind he would return to speak.

"Remember, your task shall be to serve the spiral of Nieru," Shingen-Hu intoned. "Seek those who follow the sign."

On another peak, not far away, Keyalo was watching the glowing ribbon of current looping downward above the mass of rock rising dimly on the far side of a gorge. Ethendor was with him, with a company of priests projecting their own attractive powers upward toward the current. Also standing by were two of the rare fire-knights, adepts who had chosen to dedicate their powers to the development of martial skills, and whose services were sought by the kings of all nations. Behind them, flexing their wings and rattling their tether chains in their impatience to be released, stood six fearsome griffins with their handlers.

"The moment is near. Prepare thyself," Ethendor warned.

"I am prepared, Master!" Keyalo cried.

The rendezvous was at a corner opposite a small park. Remembering from the drive into the city the canopies with their simulated skies that enclosed some parts but not others, Hunt was unable to tell if the pale green darkening into evening overhead was real or artificial. It seemed a better class of neighborhood, cleaner and with the buildings well maintained, although Lesho had brought them only a few blocks. One of the things that had struck Hunt about Shiban was the way that the entire character of the surroundings could change abruptly, sometimes by simply crossing a street.

A shiny limousine drew up noiselessly. Two men—strong-arm characters by the look of them—climbed out from the front and checked Murray, Hunt, and Cullen for weapons. One of them said something in Jevlenese to Lesho, who raised a hand in salutation to Murray, nodded briefly at the other two, and walked away. Then a door of the rear compartment opened, revealing two sets of seats facing each other, with those on one side occupied by three more men: in the center, a broad, craggy-faced man with cropped gray hair, who reminded Hunt vaguely of Caldwell and who was presumably the capo, and what looked like two bodyguards. Murray stepped forward to the doorway, and there was another muttered exchange of Jevlenese. Then he climbed in and moved across the empty seats, motioning for Hunt and Cullen to follow. One of the two men who had gotten out first closed the door behind them, then returned with his companion to the front. There was the sound of more doors closing, and the vehicle pulled away.

"His name is Scirio," Murray informed Hunt. "He wants to know why it's so important for you to find this guy Baumer." In an aside he added, "He knows you're from PAC, and suspects anyone who's mixed up with the Administration—especially Terrans. They know what Earth-style governments tend to mean for their kind of business."

"Tell him I'm not interested in his business. That's why we've come here unofficially like this. Baumer has information on somebody who's gone missing, who we've reason to believe might be in danger."

Murray conveyed the message. Then, "Why should he help you? He's a businessman. What's in it for him?"

"He understands protection, right? This is to do with an interplanetary situation that involves the politics between Jevlen and Earth. If we don't get any satisfaction unofficially, then other people are going to do it officially. And they won't fool around. In other words, it's either a friendly favor to us or a police bust. Which does he want?"

Murray translated. Scirio laughed and spat out a stream of what was clearly derision, emphasized by gestures and a final throwing-away motion.

"He farts in the faces of the Shiban police. They're all assholes, and wouldn't know how to bust their way into an empty room. In any case, he owns them. We have to do better than that."

"Then try this," Cullen said, cutting in. "There are big players moving to get the Ganymeans out of Jevlen and replace them with a Terran occupation backed by a military force. That's what we're trying to stop. If we fail, what would *that* do to his business?"

Murray passed it on, and Scirio went very quiet. Then he called out something in a raised voice to one of the two men in front.

"He's gonna call the head office," Murray muttered.

A tone sounded from somewhere. Scirio opened a small compartment in a divider between two of the seats and took out a telephone handset—apparently whoever was on the other end and what was said were private matters.

Speaking in a low voice, Scirio told Grevetz the situation. Grevetz, in his villa outside the city, pondered. The German that the Terrans were trying to trace was the one Iduane had said to get rid of. But if the Ganymeans and Terrans were showing that much concern, it might lead to real problems. He ought to double-check with Eubeleus before doing anything drastic, he decided. He could always get rid of Baumer tomorrow if Eubeleus still wanted him to. But if he did it today and it turned out to be not such a good idea for some reason, that would be less easy to fix.

"Have you got any idea where this guy they're looking for is?" he asked Scirio.

"If he's not anywhere they've tried, then he'll be freaking out in the club," Scirio replied.

Grevetz thought about it. If the Terran Murray was with them, the club wasn't a secret. It didn't sound as if they were interested in the firm's business, anyway; more like some political crap that Grevetz didn't want to get involved in. Perhaps just playing it straight and open would be the quickest way of getting them to leave him alone.

"Okay, you can take them there," he instructed Scirio. "If the German's there, let them have him."

Scirio replaced the handset. Saying nothing to Murray, he called out something to the front compartment again. A voice acknowledged from a grille in the partition.

Murray raised his eyebrows and nodded. "That did the trick, guys. We're on our way to the Gondola."

In the court of the People, Baumer watched from the prosecution table as the Accuser began reading his role of witnesses.

"In support of the case brought against the accused, I call upon the religious teachers of all time . . ." A line of men in robes, cloaks, cassocks, some bearded, several with long, flowing hair and carrying wooden staffs, filed into the room through a side entrance. "I call upon the world's great artists, its poets, its seers, its mystics, all those who have tried through the ages to turn Man's eyes away from the mundane and the material, and open them to . . ."

The Accuser's voice trailed away as the Counsel for Defense rose to his feet, waving his hand in an impatient protest. Beside him was a dwarf dressed as a jester, hopping up and down excitedly in his eagerness to speak. From the dock, the industrialist, the engineer, the scientist, and the philosopher looked on with interest.

"If I might be permitted, I have here a single witness who will put an end to this whole farce now, without wasting any more of the court's time," the Defense Counsel said. "I move for the case to be dismissed."

"Who is that fool?" the clerk of the court demanded, indicating the dwarf from his seat below the bench.

"A gremlin who was found lurking in the subconscious of the prime mover responsible for these proceedings." The Defense Counsel turned and stabbed a finger at Baumer.

Startled, Baumer sat upright in his seat. This shouldn't be happening. Something was going wrong.

A murmur went up around the hall. "Speak," the Judge directed.

The Defense Counsel went on. "Briefly, this whole case reduces to an indictment of reason and its manifestation in technology. But this witness will testify that we are all, now, every one of us, creations of precisely those processes and nothing else. So is the entire reality in which we exist. In other words, the Accuser himself is a product of that which he would have us deny. Therefore, were he to prove his case, neither he nor his case could exist."

"Is this true?" the Judge challenged, looking at Baumer.

Baumer rose to his feet, confused. "I don't understand," he stammered, staring at the dwarf. "He shouldn't be here. How did he get in? If he's mine, I can deny him. Proceed as if he didn't exist."

"But he *does* exist," a voice boomed. It was JEVEX. Everything was going out of control. JEVEX had no business intruding like this . . .

The loop of current dipped downward, and Thrax felt its flux of energy touching his mind. Strange sensations and a feeling of detachment swept through his being. He saw fragments of images: figures in a large hall, some seated in tiers, others standing, and a row of what looked like a tribunal of judges behind a raised bench. Then there was a flash of a completely different place, a tiny cell in which he was looking up at the ceiling. The power of the assembled monks surged around him.

"It is time! The moment has come! Arise, Thrax!" Shingen-Hu's voice resounded.

But suddenly everything exploded in pandemonium. From another peak outlined dimly across a deep gorge, bolts of fire curved through the darkness and burst among the rocks, causing the monks to scatter in alarm. At the same instant, winged shapes descended from above with terrible screams and slashing claws, driving them to seek cover. As the hold broke, the stream of current kinked and redirected itself toward the other peak.

A griffin swooped at Shingen-Hu and Thrax, who had been

left standing alone. Shingen-Hu felled it with a lightning-dart aimed through a finger, and it fell to the ground shrieking and convulsing.

"There is another power!" Shingen-Hu cried. "See, the current is being drawn away. We cannot contest it. We are confounded!"

On the neighboring peak, Ethendor cackled gleefully. "Ha, they are undone! The current comes to us! We have it now. Rise up, Keyalo! Priests, send up your minds with him. Praise be to Vandros. Give strength now to thy servants!"

Keyalo felt powerful forces surging through him, bearing him aloft. The river of current loomed bright and pulsating before him, then everything was light.

"See, he rises up!" Ethendor exulted. "He delivers his substance to the current! He is borne into the night!"

Keyalo was pure patterns of energy, formless, unfettered. Pure being. A cosmic wind traversing a void. The void contracted, whirling and falling inward upon itself . . .

The limousine stopped in a dark, narrow street on one side of an enclosed square. There were a number of other vehicles parked nearby, several of them large and luxurious in Hunt's estimation—although his experience in judging Jevlenese standards was limited. There was little sign of life, and the few figures visible scurried through the shadows, minding their own business. Hunt and his two companions got out first, the pair of bodyguards followed, and Scirio came last. The two men up front stayed in the vehicle.

They walked a short distance along one side of the square and then turned into a walkway with weak overhead lamps and solidly constructed doorways at intervals along both sides, all closed. At the end was another alley running crossways, some stairs going up on one side, and an opening into an even dingier passageway on the other. They entered the passageway and stopped at a door whose outline Hunt could barely make out in the shadows. Somebody must have pressed a button or something, for after a few seconds a voice spoke from a concealed speaker. One of the bodyguards, a big, steely-eyed man with a gray, battleship-armor chin, whom Hunt had mentally dubbed "Dreadnought," replied. The voice said something else, and this time Scirio responded. A second or two went by, and then a spotlight came on above the door, illuminating the six figures outside. The light went out again and the door opened.

Inside, it was almost as dark as out in the passageway. And as bare. They were in what seemed to be a small foyer. It had a seat running along one wall, and a hole in the wall framing a reception desk opposite, with a door alongside. A pair of double doors led out at the rear. Scirio rapped on the door next to the desk, which was opened promptly from within. He entered, leaving Hunt, Cullen, and Murray with the two bodyguards, who lounged against the wall and stared into space. The sounds of several voices talking came through the opening above the desk.

"Did you say you knew this place?" Hunt asked Murray.

"I knew it was here—I've sent people to it. But I've never used it. I've got enough spooks in my head already. I don't need this kinda shit."

"Then why couldn't you have brought us yourself, without all the performance?" Cullen asked.

Murray shook his head. "When you come here, nobody sees anything; nobody knows who you are. You wanna know if this guy you're so anxious to find is in one of the booths? There's no way you'd get to know without the boss's say-so."

Then Scirio came back out accompanied by a man in a dark jacket, whom Hunt took to be the manager. Scirio spoke rapidly to Murray, indicating Hunt and Cullen with a nod and gesturing at the door that he had just come out of.

"Step inside," Murray interpreted.

Hunt and Cullen followed the manager back through, while Murray and Scirio waited just inside the door. It was a small office, with another man sitting in an easy chair in a corner, and several screens above a console by one wall. The manager sat down at the console and brought a picture up on one of the screens. It showed people sitting at tables and in seats set in alcoves, others at a bar, mostly alone, but several in pairs and one small group talking. The lighting was evidently quite low, for Hunt could tell from the quality that the image was being enhanced.

"See if you can spot him anywhere there," Murray said.

Hunt studied the picture carefully, then shook his head. The manager operated a control on the console to single out each of the men present in turn for a close-up view. Then he shifted the view to bring different people into the field and repeated the process. Baumer wasn't there.

The manager said something in Jevlenese, and Scirio answered. "They're going to try the booths," Murray supplied.

Another screen activated to show the figure of a woman reposing in a Thurien-style neurocoupling recliner situated in a small booth. The manager flipped to the next, which showed a man with a white beard. "No," Hunt said. The next two tries were men again, negative, then another woman. Hunt ceased responding after the first half dozen or so, allowing the manager to simply step on through the list at his own pace, dwelling for a second or two when the subject was a man, and passing straight on to the next in the case of a woman.

They must have been somewhere up in the twenties when Hunt suddenly craned forward, beckoned Cullen closer with a finger, and exclaimed, "That's him!"

The manager zoomed to a close-up of the face, but there was already no doubt about it. The figure in the coupler was Hans Baumer.

"How do we get him out?" Cullen asked. The manager was already saying something to Scirio.

"They'll go get him, and we leave, okay?" Murray said. "We forget where we got him from." Hunt nodded. Illicit couplers into JEVEX weren't his concern. The manager called toward a room at the back, from which another man emerged, wearing a dark suit. The man in the easy chair got up, and the three of them went out into the foyer, their footsteps heading in the direction of the double doors at the rear. A moment later they appeared on the first screen, crossing the room containing the people and the bar.

In one of the booths off the corridors beyond, Baumer's

eyes opened suddenly. But the person looking out through those eyes was no longer completely Hans Baumer.

The cell! Keyalo was inside the cell that he had glimpsed in the current. He sat up. A tomb! Sudden panic tore through him. Ethendor had lied. Keyalo had been consigned to a tomb. A living corpse interred to placate the underworld god. He looked about fearfully. Strange shapes, magical objects . . . Movement felt wrong, as if space itself had changed. An appendage of his body passed before him. Soft, squelchy, misshapen. He had been imprisoned in the corpse of a monster.

He had a voice, harsh and grating, and screamed out loud in dismay and terror as the full magnitude of the deception engulfed him. The altar on which he lay was soft and yielding. He leapt up and staggered against the wall as the sensations of unfamiliar movement and balance escaped his control. He staggered back, tearing at the altar with his puny claws, but without effect. He raged around the walls, beating them and screaming. Then a panel opened and black-clad demons appeared. Keyalo backed into a corner. The demons jabbered at him in a strange tongue. He raised a hand and directed a bolt toward them with all his power . . . but with no effect. His power had been taken. He screamed, howled, and raged as he realized how he had been cheated. The demons assailed him.

In the office Hunt and Cullen were on their feet, watching it all on the screen. "What the hell's happening?" Hunt demanded. Murray showed his hands helplessly and shook his head.

Two more men came out of the back room and launched into a rapid exchange with Scirio, all of them sounding terse and excited. "Looks as if the kraut's having some kinda fit in there," Murray said.

"Then let's get him out," Cullen snapped, turning toward the door.

Scirio held up a hand and said something in a sharp voice. "Not this way," Murray told them. "There's a back door. They don't want him upsetting the whole house."

Hunt and Cullen went with the others out through the foyer and the doors at the rear into the bar area that had appeared on the screen. They crossed at a smart pace, attracting curious looks, and went through another door into one of several corridors lined by doors on both sides. As they rounded a corner they met the manager and the two who had gone with him manhandling Baumer the other way, struggling, kicking, and emitting muffled screams behind the hand clamped across his mouth.

"Christ," Hunt breathed, shaking his head in bewilderment. "It looks as if he's flipped. What do we do now?"

"That machine must have scrambled his head," Cullen said, staring numbly.

Hunt stepped forward and peered into Baumer's face as he was brought to a halt. It was wild and flushed, the eyes bulging maniacally.

"Gina?" Hunt shouted desperately. "Can you understand me? It's important. *Do-you-know-where-Gina-is?*"

How, Keyalo didn't know, but this demon's speech was intelligible to him—although the name the demon had uttered meant nothing. He jerked his head back and tore his mouth away from the paw gagging him. "Unhand me, demons of the underworld who dwell in these tunnels of darkness! I shall not be enslaved by thy falsehoods, but swear allegiance to the true god of the spiral whom I renounced. For this is his punishment visited upon me! Oh woe! Now do I see the errors of—" A straight right to the jaw from Dreadnought put him out, and he fell limp in the arms supporting him. Scirio blasted a stream of invective at Murray.

"Get him out of here," Murray interpreted, although it was hardly necessary. "Compliments to the Ganymeans. If they stick around, he hopes they'll remember their friends."

Hunt and Cullen each took one of Baumer's arms and bore him along a side passage to where one of the staff was already unbolting a door. They came out into a rear yard, and two of the staff took them to the nearest street, where a cab called from the office picked them up a few minutes later.

"Now what?" Hunt asked, when he had collected his wits together again.

"Shit, I don't know. Another one for the rubber room, I

guess," Cullen replied.

"I'll tell you something else," Murray said. He motioned with a thumb in the direction they had come from. "This wasn't the first time it's happened. Those guys back there have seen it before. Maybe that's another reason they don't like publicity."

They dropped Murray off, then continued on to PAC with their still-unconscious charge. But when they finally arrived back at the UNSA labs, they found that the whole episode had been unnecessary. Gina had walked back in while they were gone, still in one piece and looking as well as ever.

Chapter Thirty-seven

Hunt stood with his back to one of the benches in the UNSA labs, his hands loosely gripping the edge on either side of him. Gina sat at the worktable in the middle of the room, chewing a chicken sandwich from the store of good, tasty, Earth-style food that Duncan had accumulated. The one visible effect on Gina after her disappearance was that she was hungry. Sandy was sitting across from her, listening and saying strangely little.

"Okay, let's go over the main points again," Hunt said. "You set out from PAC and saw some of the surrounding parts of Shiban center."

Gina nodded. "A kind of introductory tourist walkaround."

"You didn't have any set agenda?"

"No. It was just to help me get my bearings . . . and to get to know each other a little better, I guess."

Hunt threw a doubtful glance at Del Cullen, who was leaning with his shoulder against an equipment cabinet, his arms folded. "Weren't you supposed to be meeting some people from these Jevlenese historical societies, or something like that?" Cullen queried.

Gina shook her head firmly. "That was going to be the day after."

"You're sure?"

"Yes. You must have got the dates mixed."

Hunt frowned as he listened. That was not the way he remembered it, either. "Do you remember the names of any of these people?" Cullen asked, obviously with a view to checking it out. "Or the organizations they were with, maybe?"

"No, I'm afraid not. Baumer had it all in his head. There didn't seem any reason for me to go writing it all down at the time."

Cullen nodded, letting it go at that. They weren't going to get anything out of Baumer now.

"Okay," Hunt said. "Then what?"

"We went through a kind of street market, underneath some huge, curving shapes going up into the sky—as if they were part of something from way back that never got finished. It was full of junk, old clothes, secondhand stuff, that kind of thing. Seemed to be a freakout place for the local dropout culture."

"Kinchabira. I know the place," Cullen interjected, nodding.

"Baumer blamed it all on Thurien lack of discipline and control. He seemed to think a good dose of Nazism would work wonders." Gina nibbled another piece of her sandwich and took a sip of coffee—real. "Then there was a deposit company that seemed to be turning itself into a bank. He didn't approve of that, either."

"And we're quite sure that his motivation wasn't simply the obvious?" Hunt asked. "I mean, here's this guy, stuck out here on his own for a long time. Pretty girl from home shows up . . ."

Gina shook her head. "That was the first thing I thought, too. But there was never a hint of it. Anyhow, that isn't how he gets off."

"Okay. Then you looked in some luxury-good stores . . ."

"Right," Gina said. "And he didn't agree with that, because it doesn't force everyone to be equal. I got a speech on why society ought to protect people like him from having to face

up to why the world isn't listening to them. Then we sat on a
wall and watched some weirdos with eyeshadow and icicles
for haircuts while we ate some Jevlenese pita-burgers." Gina
paused to recollect what they had talked about. "He seemed
interested when I asked him if he'd gotten to know any other
people here who thought the way he did. He was curious to
know more about what you UNSA scientists were doing
here."

"That's his real reason coming out," Cullen murmured.

"The punks weren't any trouble?" Hunt asked. There had
been a report of some trouble in that area at around the same
time, involving a group who sounded like the people Gina had
described. But she shook her head again.

"No. They went away," Gina continued slowly, reciting the
items one by one, as if anxious to be sure that she had everything straight. "We carried on to some kind of a bar somewhere.
Baumer started talking about drugs and highs. He asked me
what kind of things I use. He said it in a kind of . . . suggestive
way. It was like a hint that there could be something more to
it, but he wanted to see my reaction first."

Hunt nodded. Conceivably Baumer had been acting from
purely personal motivations when he approached her. Maybe
not. Nothing that Gina was saying clinched it either way. "Go
on," he said.

"He told me there were places where you can still get a
total connection into the residual core of JEVEX. He said it's a
trip that beats everything: the ultimate. Only Jevlenese really
understood it." Gina made an open-handed gesture in the air.
"That was interesting. It was the first definite proof I'd heard
about JEVEX still being available. But when I tried to get more,
he said there was no way you could describe it. You had to
experience it for yourself. Obviously it was an invitation."

"Which you accepted," Cullen said—needlessly, since they
had been through the gist of her story once already.

"Well, you know I'm the curious kind."

Sandy looked across the table at her oddly. "You, ah . . . you
were curious to find out what this was all about?"

"Yes," Gina said. Her voice was light and matter-of-fact.

She frowned, as if momentarily puzzled about something, then nodded. "Yes," she said again.

"You hadn't seen enough with VISAR, on the *Vishnu*?" Sandy spoke with pronounced skepticism, as if she found the answer hard to believe and wanted Gina to reconsider. Hunt was scribbling a note just at that moment, and Cullen missed the implication.

"We didn't know if JEVEX was the same," Gina said. She frowned to herself again. Then, as if not quite satisfied with that, added, "It was important to know what Baumer was up to, right?"

Sandy stared for a moment longer; then, when no support was forthcoming from Hunt or Cullen, she let it go at that with a doubtful nod. "Okay."

Gina went on. "We went to a place that you entered down a passage off an alley. It was all dark, with everything done furtively—the way you imagine speakeasies to have been. Inside was a sort of lounge and bar. And then out back, there were all these neurocoupling cubicles . . ."

Hunt and the others had decided not to complicate the issue by saying anything about Nixie's story. Gina went on to describe accurately what was almost certainly the Gondola, where they had found Baumer; and just as almost-certainly, there would be no point in trying to get confirmation since nobody there would know anything. As Hunt had seen for himself, the whole operation was set up to preserve anonymity. Not seeing things was part of the business.

"And he was right," Gina concluded. "There's no way I could describe it. That machine can create total realities in your head, indistinguishable from the real thing; that are actually your own creations, except you don't know it. It's uncanny—totally compelling. I can see how it could become addictive. I guess I just got carried away and lost all track of time. I eventually came to, left, and came back here. The rest you know."

"Was Baumer still there when you left?" Cullen asked.

"I don't know. I couldn't get anything across to the management. I don't think they'd have told me anyway."

They all looked at each other. That seemed to be it. "Well,

you probably need more rest than you realize," Cullen said to Gina. "Don't bother going back to Best West. We'll find you a suite here at PAC to freshen up and get your head down in. We'll see you again later."

"I think you're right," Gina agreed. "My head feels as if it's been through a blender."

She described some of JEVEX's capabilities while she finished her sandwich, reiterated the line they had already heard from Danchekker that this seemed to her a more than likely explanation of what had sent the Jevlenese off the rails. Then she departed for the residential sector. Sandy went with her.

"What I don't understand," Hunt said to Cullen when they were alone, "is why they'd let Baumer reveal this JEVEX business to her when they must have known she was associating with us and the Ganymeans. If it's such a big secret, with what sounds like big money involved, why show her it?"

"I wondered the same thing." Cullen eased himself down onto one of the lab stools and rubbed his chin. "Unless . . ." He looked over at Hunt. "It depends who the 'they' you're talking about are. The *Ichena* run the couplers. They're the ones who'd stand to lose if the traffic was shut down. But suppose Baumer was also working for a political group tied up with the cults. They're not the same people. See my point? Letting Baumer come across like just another junkie blabbing about where he gets his fixes would be a good way of obscuring his political connection."

Hunt thought about it. "I think I see what you're saying. A bit of a dirty trick, but it's the other guys who'll catch any comeback. But in the meantime it covers any tracks back to them." He sat back and stared at the notes he had made. "Do you think it could be Eubeleus and the Axis?" he asked.

"I guess it could be—although he seems more interested in collecting his wagon train together at Geerbaine so they can go out and found the new world. And his main sidekick's there with him. You know something, Vic, I'm even starting to think this Uttan stunt of theirs might be genuine." Cullen clasped his hands behind his head and swiveled the stool with a foot until he was looking at Hunt. "But one thing's sure: Baumer isn't gonna tell us."

"I guess not," Hunt agreed with a sigh.

In a suite in the residential part of PAC, Gina dried herself off with the warm-air blower in the shower, combed out her hair, and tottered back into the bedroom to slide gratefully between smooth, clean-smelling sheets. It had been a lot more exhausting than her experiment with VISAR. Or maybe things in general were just catching up with her.

After turning off the light, she went over the things that General Shaw had said in the room in another part of Shiban where she had been taken by the contact who had been waiting when she left the booths. She had said nothing to Hunt and Cullen that she shouldn't have. Shaw must have come secretly aboard the *Vishnu*, too, she reflected. She hadn't expected to see him again until her return to Earth—if at all—after meeting him in the briefing with Caldwell, when she had accepted the assignment. She remembered that quite vividly for some reason—as if it had happened yesterday.

It seemed unnecessarily cautious that she should not be allowed to bring people like Hunt and Garuth into the picture about the Jevlenese having a well-placed spy somewhere inside PAC; but the general had been adamant. She wondered if Baumer had been planted on Jevlen as an insider by whatever agency General Shaw was a part of. Very likely the part of the total picture that Baumer possessed was no larger than her own.

But certainly there was a lot more going on than she knew about, and it had interplanetary significance. The only wise thing was simply to forget the questions and follow orders.

As for Baumer, there was no conclusion to be drawn other than that he was completely mad. His faculty for recognizing even the most basic of familiar things seemed to be gone. The walls and doors, fittings and furnishings of the room in the medical facility where he was being confined, all of which were unexceptional, seemed to confound him with awe. He spent hours exploring the surfaces with his fingers and mumbling to himself as he fiddled with such simple devices as the catch on a drawer, or a pen lying on a desktop. He showed no understanding of anything more advanced, such as the touch-pad controls of a companel unit, and made no attempt at operating them in the ways they were designed to function. And any kind of mechanism, however simple, seemed to bring on a mixture of wonder and terror. On one occasion he sat on the floor for almost an hour with a wastepaper bin that had a lid operated by a foot-pedal, working the lever over and over again. And it was nearly as long before he would even approach a set of scales standing on one side of the room.

He did not seem so much to have forgotten what things were for; it was more as if he had lost the references to relate them to. His entire conceptual framework seemed to have changed—or been replaced by another.

He could still speak, but nothing he said made any sense. The little that he did say was a disjointed tirade about being robbed of his "powers," and he was constantly making signs and gestures as if he expected to cast spells. When others addressed him, he seemed able to understand the words, but he was too disoriented by fear and confusion to respond coherently. The Terran medics and Ganymean psychologists had no explanation.

But Nixie did.

"This is what the Jevlenese mean when they talk of somebody awakening," she said. "This is how the ayatollahs arrive. The person who exists inside his body isn't the same anymore. It's another who has been transported here from the Otherworld. As I was."

And what she said seemed indeed to be true. For apart from his faculty of speech, his voluntary motor reflexes—and even those were erratic, though Nixie said that would pass—and the unconscious regulatory functions that his brain supported, everything in his nervous system that had once contributed to the identity of Hans Baumer had apparently been obliterated.

"And you say this only happens to somebody who is coupled

into JEVEX?" Shilohin asked Nixie in one of the medical offices, where they had retired with Hunt and Danchekker to review Baumer's condition after observing him.

"Always."

"Was it true in your case?" Danchekker asked. "Were *you*—or should I say, the person whose identity you assumed—in a coupler when it happened?"

"I don't remember," Nixie replied. "I was too confused for a long time afterward to know what had happened. But that is what I was told by others."

Danchekker looked from one to another of those present with an I-told-you-so expression that was superficially reluctant, while at the same time the glint behind his spectacles said that he was loving every minute. Finally he said, "Which does rather tend to corroborate my hypothesis, I think. The condition is a profound mental disruption brought about by the interaction between deep-seated processes in the human nervous system and an inappropriate alien technology that was adapted from something never designed to couple to it." He took off his spectacles and produced a handkerchief to wipe them. "I'm sorry, Vic, but you really have to discard this Phantasmagoria that you've grown so fond of."

"No, it's real," Nixie insisted.

"I'm sure it's utterly convincing," Danchekker conceded, giving her a lofty smile. He turned back to Hunt and Shilohin. "The whole thing is a JEVEX fabrication."

"As internally consistent as the physics that VISAR read from Nixie's memories?" Hunt shook his head. "The people we're talking about don't have the conceptual foundations. They could never have generated anything like that."

Danchekker showed his teeth. "No. But JEVEX could!"

Shilohin looked from Danchekker to Hunt and back again. Hunt got the feeling that she was coming around to the professor's line. "You're saying that JEVEX created the same artificial reality for all of them?"

"I've said it from the beginning."

"Why should it do that?"

"Ah, that's another question, the answer to which will

doubtless be forthcoming now that we seem to be heading the right way," Danchekker said.

"It would account for the consistency," Shilohin said. "If these are fantasies created in response to unconscious directions, thousands of individuals could never all have produced the same thing. But if they all originated in JEVEX . . ."

"Precisely."

Hunt stared at Nixie's face. And for some reason, which he would have been the first to admit as being totally unscientific, the calm, unwavering certainty that he saw written there persuaded him more, in a way that he could never have justified to Danchekker and Shilohin.

It was too early to commit to any conclusion. He needed more time to let his mind chew its way through the complexities in its own, unhurried way. More to keep things open than for any other reason, he suggested that it would be interesting to find out if a "possessed" Terran also claimed to have come from the same Otherworld that the Jevlenese described. He liked the word Danchekker had used, and referred to it as "Phantasmagoria." Danchekker and Shilohin agreed that it would be a worthwhile thing to try and find out.

They had Baumer sedated and placed him in a coupler for VISAR to take a look inside his head. But VISAR stolidly refused to violate the privacy of somebody incapable of authorizing such a probe, and no amount of arguing would change it. So Hunt started talking to Baumer instead.

As a day or two went by, Baumer calmed down and his ramblings became less frenzied. With Nixie helping, glimpses of a place started coming together. Soon there was no doubt that it was the same Phantasmagoria that Nixie talked about, identical in every detail that they were able to establish. And in the process, Hunt's conviction grew that he was not talking to a German who had undergone some traumatic personality change, but to a genuinely different, and very alien, being.

Was this being, then, some kind of software construct that JEVEX had created, which had somehow found its way into Baumer's head? Hunt had read some of Eubeleus's claims to being a creation of precisely this kind himself, but had dismissed it as rubbish. Could there be something to it?

But if there were, it would mean that an entity that had originated as a caricature of reality, and that needed all the power and sophistication of JEVEX to sustain it, had taken on the internal depth and complexity necessary to become reality and stand independently in its own right. Hunt couldn't see how that could be possible. Pinocchio might come to life and work without the strings in a fairy story; but life in the real world depended on structure and organization a lot more complicated than any puppet's.

A puppet was made to *look* like a living organism that moved itself from the inside, but it was really operated by forces applied on the outside. Similarly, JEVEX's puppets were simulations of life, animated by JEVEX's manipulations. But if Nixie and the person that Baumer had become were as real as Hunt accepted them to be, they could only be functioning by virtue of an innate complexity of structure that JEVEX would never have put there. And that kind of complexity only came about spontaneously, over a long period of time, through evolution in the real, physical world.

Which, of course, was absurd . . .

Unless "real, physical world" meant something different from what everyone knew it meant.

The thought caused Hunt to spend a lot of time asking himself what *he* meant by it. It reminded him of the conversation he'd had with Gina in his apartment back home, when she had asked him a similar question. And his answer had been that everything "out there" boiled down to photons and other energy quanta, along with a few simple rules governing the ways they interacted with one another.

Packages of attributes. Bundles of numbers riding together, adrift in an ocean of coordinates . . .

Numbers and coordinates, specifying . . . what?

Nobody knew. It could have been anything.

But the whole "real" universe had evolved out of it.

Chapter Thirty-eight

Rodgar Jassilane's Ganymean communications scientists, along with Duncan Watt, who was working with them, had uncovered a technical mystery concerning the residual core of JEVEX that had been left running: There wasn't enough of it to support the amount of traffic that seemed to be indicated once the size of the *Ichena*'s black-market operation was estimated and allowed for.

MacArthur, the Jevlenese that Shilohin had failed to convince with the laser demonstration, and who was already rising fast in the purple-spiral movement, was a comparative new boy on the scene, having awakened as an ayatollah only in the time since JEVEX was suspended. There were others, too, and the Ganymeans had been analyzing figures of known cases and rumored ones from all over the planet in an attempt to approximate the total. Other sources, including figures gleaned from ZORAC's unofficial tapping of Shiban's communications network, gave a figure for the incidence rate expressed as the number of "possession" events per thousand user-hours of exposure—a risk statistic which the *Ichena* would definitely not have wanted to become public knowledge. Extrapolated to cover the planet, that figure gave a measure of the size of the total black-market operation. The known operating characteristics of VISAR enabled that to be expressed in terms of the system power necessary to support it. But when the officially sanctioned archive-interrogation and maintenance operations were added in, the total indicated load was far greater than the residual core of JEVEX would have been able to handle.

What the results seemed to say was: Either JEVEX was a lot bigger than the Jevlenese had admitted; or else there was another facility operating whose existence had never been disclosed. Curious, Ganymean engineers, assisted by some of the more cooperatively disposed Jevlenese, began quietly carrying out a program of detailed inspections and tests at the sites where the main nodes and operating centers of the network were located.

Cullen decided to move Gina permanently from Geerbaine into PAC. He didn't like the thought of her being on her own out there now that he had seen the people that Baumer had been connected with. Accordingly, Gina called the Best Western to terminate her stay, and arranged to drive out later that afternoon with Lebansky and Koberg to collect her things.

A little over an hour before they were due to leave, a call came through for Gina from a woman who introduced herself as Marion Fayne, also from Earth and staying at the BW. She had read and enjoyed all of Gina's books, she said, and wondered if she could leave a couple at the reception desk for Gina to autograph. "*Thank* you so *very* much. You probably don't remember, but we met briefly once at a party in Lisbon," she chattered delightedly when Gina agreed.

In fact, Gina had never been to Portugal. The phrase was a code that General Shaw had given her at her unexpected meeting with him in Shiban. Before leaving, therefore, she took from a folder in a compartment of her briefcase the notes she had made of developments inside PAC since then. They included an account of what was happening with Baumer, the help that Nixie was giving, and the various theories being bandied about. This seemed more of a domestic issue to Gina, and not something that would relate to interplanetary politics, but she had been told to omit nothing. Finally, she summarized what she knew of the Ganymeans' findings on the capacity of the JEVEX core system and Garuth's decision to have the major sites checked.

She didn't like what she was doing, she admitted to herself as she folded the sheets and tucked them inside her purse. Ever since the meeting with Shaw, the thought of being a spy inside the UNSA team had been weighing in her mind. It wasn't her way of doing things, and she wondered why she had agreed to it back at Goddard. True, she hadn't known Hunt and the rest of them, or Garuth and the Ganymeans, the way she did now . . . but she hoped it hadn't been just to get herself a ticket to Jevlen.

General Shaw must have made it sound very important. He was, she recalled, a pretty persuasive salesman.

Nixie, in Phantasmagoria, before she overwrote whoever the original Nixie was, had been a "he." He trained as a kind of religious disciple in a temple in a large city, but later ran away to study with an independent teacher who sounded like a hermit, up in the mountains. It was from his school that Nixie had "arisen" to the world that seers talked about beyond the sky. What happened to Baumer hadn't happened to Nixie because her teacher was wise and thorough, and had prepared her with some idea of what to expect. Apparently others who had gone ahead sometimes returned as spirits that spoke in the minds of seers through the mysterious "currents" which Nixie alluded to repeatedly—a result, presumably, of "awakened" ayatollahs somehow applying their extraordinary affinity and reconnecting via couplers to wherever they came from.

Baumer, too, talked about a hermit-teacher who ran a school for mystics up in a wilderness somewhere, although Nixie was unable to locate it from his ramblings. He feared retribution, however, because he said he had emerged from Phantasmagoria in another's rightful place. Hunt had adopted the practice of calling him "Thomas," because of his religious origin and the fact that he doubted everything that anyone told him. After what had happened, Hunt felt, it wouldn't have been decent, somehow, to have continued using Baumer's name to address the shell that was all that was left of him.

"Look, I'm not a demon for the god of darkness, and I don't care what you did to his flying angel," Hunt said. "In fact I'm not much into any gods at all. What makes it so difficult for you to believe us?"

Thomas turned away in his chair and stared into the top of a lab centrifuge that was standing open. After a few seconds he reached out to move the lid to and fro several times on its horizontal swivel, then traced the contours of the drive shaft and gearing, all the time muttering unintelligibly. He was still amazed by machines and the products of machines. Regularity of any kind, such as the repeating architectural features or the mosaic patterns in the corridors of PAC, or the nested arrays of Optronics chips and subassemblies in some of the equipment cabinets, fascinated him. The scientists had by now accepted VISAR's interpretation that the instabilities of form that occurred in Phantasmagoria were due to the elongation of objects in their direction of motion, and that the daily cycles and changes with orientation followed from planetary rotation. Where or how such conditions could come about, however, were anybody's guess.

"Do I sound like a demon?" Hunt asked after a pause. "Do I look like one?"

Thomas mumbled something, then went quiet and seemed to think it over. "Transformed!" he exclaimed suddenly. "They transform their agents to deceive us. We were warned."

"Who warned you?"

"Take on forms, any forms . . . Beware appearances."

"Who—"

"Spiral! Seek the spiral . . . Safe from external forms."

"Have you ever seen a demon?"

"Mighty is the power of—" Thomas stopped and looked at Hunt oddly. "Seen many demons. They come from the gods. Bring signs. Punish those who disobey."

"Describe one, then."

"*You* . . . don't believe? Will be punished. Burned, broken, torn in pieces. Smothered in serpents; crawling in worms;

poisoned by scorpions; feast of maggots. Slashed by fangs, crushed by coils, blistered, bleeding, oozing, screaming . . ."

"I'll risk it."

"The demon of the sun god's wrath comes from the sky. Head of eagle, body of lion, with dragon's wings . . ."

Nixie, who was sitting on Hunt's other side, nodded. "I know that one, too," she said.

"He's not crazy, then?" Hunt checked. "It does exist, the way he says?"

"Oh, yes."

The strange thing was that, monstrous as these Phantasmagorian creatures were, he should describe them as composites of familiar forms—Thomas was using the closest-fitting terms from his Baumer-bequeathed vocabulary, which was German but converted to English by VISAR. For, if they had indeed evolved elsewhere, under such very different conditions, how could they have any similarities to the products of a completely independent line, which the principles of evolution said would never happen, even if the conditions had been the same? Even more remarkably, the form that Nixie remembered herself having in Phantasmagoria was *human*!—like the inhabitants in the other pictures that VISAR had extracted from her memories.

Interestingly, Thomas saw elements of familiar Terran animal forms, whereas Jevlenese saw elements of Jevlenese ones. It seemed that, since the full neural apparatus of the possessed person was taken over, the newly established alien entity could only express itself by triggering the conceptual elements that were already there—similar to the way in which a bell could be hit by different hammers, but would still produce the same tone. That would also explain the retention of language abilities, possibly. The explanation was compatible with both Danchekker's theory and Hunt's, and the issue between them remained unresolved.

"Suppose I told you that the gods don't run this place that you've arrived in," Hunt suggested. "They can't touch you here. We're under a different management. Would that—"

"Excuse me?" ZORAC interrupted.

"Yes, chief?"

"Sandy's outside the lab, asking to come in."

"Oh, sure."

ZORAC disengaged the lock of the outer door, which was kept closed for security reasons, and Sandy entered a moment later.

"Hi," Hunt greeted, leaning back in his seat and relaxing. "I thought you were helping Duncan count bootleg headworld shops."

"He's with Rodgar's crew, counting computer throughputs. That's not my line. I wanted to talk to you about something else."

"As long as it's not insurance, saving the environment, or talking to Jesus."

"No. It's about Gina."

"I thought she went to Geerbaine with King and Kong to collect her things."

"That's why I wanted to catch you now—while she isn't around." Sandy glanced uncertainly at Nixie. "It's, er, kind of private."

She seemed serious, Hunt could see. He looked back at Nixie. "Would you mind taking over with Tom for a while? You seem to get through better on your own sometimes, anyhow."

"Sure. Go ahead," Nixie said.

Hunt walked with Sandy back through the outer room, then through a darkened area where a couple of Ganymeans were studying patterns in a glowing, changing, holographic image eight feet high. They went on out the far door, through the central hall of the medical facility, and emerged into one of the main corridors of PAC. Hunt stopped and raised his eyebrows inquiringly.

"They've got to her," Sandy said without preliminaries.

"Who have?"

"I don't know. Whoever the Jevlenese are who were really controlling Baumer. They've done something to Gina."

"How do you know?"

"That story she told about the headworld trip she went on. It didn't happen that way—not the way she says. In fact I don't think it happened at all."

"What makes you say that?"

"She wouldn't have been curious. She'd already found out enough about it. We both had—back on the *Vishnu*. And I *know* that he couldn't have dragged her into a place like that again."

Hunt scanned Sandy's face with a quick, interrogative motion of his eyes. "Let's find somewhere more private to talk," he said.

Chapter Thirty-nine

They found a small lounge that wasn't being used, opening off from a library. There were some easy chairs, of both human and Ganymean scale, reading tables, and several workstations with panels and displays.

"Her story simply isn't credible, Vic," Sandy said after the door had closed itself behind them. "You don't understand what that machine can do once it gets inside your head."

Hunt shrugged in a way that asked what more there was to know. "It creates dream worlds to order. What's so terrible about that?"

"Have *you* experimented with it—even since Gina and I went to Chris about it?"

Hunt realized, even to his own surprise, that he hadn't. "No, as a matter of fact. I suppose I've been busy with other things."

"You see. You're a scientist. You only see it as a piece of technology. As a tool. I said the same thing to Chris."

"Okay, so it's a re-creation, as well—even a reality substitute that people can get hooked on. I don't use drugs, either. Some people tell me it's because I'm high all the time and don't need them. But if this lets you do even better without

663

messing up your chemistry, maybe it could be quite fun."

Sandy shook her head. "You don't always have control over it. It can work on things that it pulls out of your subconscious that you didn't even know were there. Or maybe things that you preferred not to think about. Maybe you find out you're not who you've thought you were all your life. Most of the walls that people build inside their heads are to defend their prejudices about themselves from assault by facts. Then, suddenly those walls aren't there anymore . . ."

Hunt stared at her, realizing that his attempted flippancy had been a mistake. His manner became more serious. "There are still millions of Jevlenese out there who presumably didn't see it that way," he pointed out. "If it's really such a bad trip, how come Garuth had to shut the system down to tear them away from it?"

"You can have bad trips on molecules, too. Vic . . . I don't know how it affects everybody else. But I *do* know how it affected me, and how it affected Gina. And I'm certain that she wouldn't have gone near it again. At least, not the way she said—with Baumer. And not when she was out on an assignment for us. And *definitely* not if she knew she'd be walking into JEVEX, not VISAR." Sandy paused, giving Hunt a long, sober look, inviting him to reflect on the implication. But the expression on his face told her that he had seen it already. She nodded. "But Gina isn't giving us a line. She *remembers* it the way she says—and I think there's only one way that could have happened."

"Christ!" Hunt breathed.

"Which means that Baumer was setting her up from the beginning. He led her to whoever is really behind all this. What happened to her wasn't done at any headworld shop ran by the local Mafia."

Hunt was already nodding. It all made sense. "We need to tell Cullen about this," he said.

The car carrying Koberg, Lebansky, and Gina arrived in front of the complex where the Geerbaine Best Western was situated. On a grassy area to one side of the approaches to the complex was an untidy collection of shanty huts and tents belonging to a meditation group who believed that the cosmic energy drawn down by arriving spacecraft helped them commune with the universe. Nearby, a meeting was being held to protest that the same energy posed a risk of cancer and mutant babies. The fact that there was nothing measurable to produce either effect made not the slightest difference.

Eubeleus and the first several thousand Axis of Light followers had been lifted up into orbit earlier, to join the Thurien ship that was to take them to Uttan, and there were still all kinds of people about. There had also been some trouble, by the look of things. Gina pointed through a side window at two burned-out vehicles pushed to one side of the road. "See over there. It looks as if there's been some excitement."

"Probably a Jev auto mechanic," Koberg grunted.

They pulled up in the hotel forecourt, where a number of police were standing around loosely, and went through to the front lobby. Koberg accompanied Gina to the desk. Lebansky remained a short distance back, scanning the surroundings from long habit, his eyes missing nothing, checking everyone who came and went.

"Room 201," Gina said to the clerk. "I called earlier about a change of plan. I just need to collect my stuff." The clerk consulted a terminal.

The hotel manager, Eric Venders, whom Gina had gotten to know casually, was also at the desk. "You're leaving us?" he asked. "Don't tell me you found a better place in town."

"I'm moving into PAC. I'll be doing some work in the city. It's more central."

"Can't argue with that."

Gina opened her purse, ostensibly to find her door key, and located the folded sheets of the report for General Shaw that she had brought. "Was there some trouble here earlier?" she asked. "There's a lot of police around outside, and I noticed a couple of burnt cars."

"A bit," Venders said. "It's over now. I don't know what it was about. I stay out of Jev politics."

The clerk looked up from the terminal. "You're all set, Ms. Marin," he confirmed.

"And there should be a package for me."

"One moment, I'll check."

"A reader left one of my books to be signed," Gina explained to Venders. She was acutely conscious of Koberg standing behind her and surprised at the nervous flutter in her voice. "She called me at PAC earlier."

"Here it is: 'Ms. Gina Marin.'" The clerk was holding a large, buff-colored envelope.

"That looks like it. Thank you."

An incoming call sounded.

"Excuse me." Venders turned away to take it.

Gina opened the envelope and drew out a copy of *Green Gestapo: Hidden Agendas for Social Control in the Nineties.* Tucked inside at the title page was a short note from Marion Fayne, explaining that she had an appointment that morning. Gina wrote: *To Marion Fayne, with best wishes—the first of my interstellar fans. Thanks for bringing home suddenly a lot closer!* She signed and dated it, adding, *Shiban, planet Jevlen.*

Glancing over her shoulder, she saw that Koberg was still just behind her, relaxed but alert. Worse, there was a mirror on the far wall behind the desk, making her body ineffective as a screen. She bit her lip, and then let a diary drop from her purse. Loose notes and odd slips of paper that had been lodged inside spilled over the floor.

"Oh, damn!"

"I'll get it, ma'am." Koberg squatted down and began collecting the papers back together.

"Thanks so much." Gina slipped the report into the book, quickly closed the cover, and pushed the book back into the envelope. She crossed out her own name, wrote MARION FAYNE above, and handed it back to the clerk. "Could you reseal that, please, and keep it to be collected?"

"Sure thing."

Koberg stood up and handed her back the diary. She returned it to her purse, and they went on up to room 201, leaving Lebansky watching the lobby.

In Cullen's office, Hunt waved an agitated hand above the desk. "More to the point, if they've implanted phony memories in her head, what really happened that they're covering up? If they were using JEVEX, they could have read anything that was in there. We have to reexamine everything, right from the beginning, and list everything she knew."

Sandy shuddered as she listened. "I'd rather be raped by an octopus."

Cullen sat back in his chair, rapping his chin with a knuckle. "Shit," he muttered, barely audibly. He stared at the wall, thinking hard, running through the options in his mind. "Darn it, darn it . . ."

"I should have said something sooner," Sandy told them, more to fill the silence. "It wasn't until this morning that I felt really sure. One minute she talks as if this was the first time she'd ever tried it, and the thing on the *Vishnu* never happened; then the next, she's saying it was just a pretense to go along with Baumer. Then she sees the contradiction and keeps changing her reasons for justifying it."

Cullen nodded distantly.

"It means that they must know she was working with us and that we suspected Baumer," Hunt said. "And she knew about us using ZORAC to bug the city, so we can write that off as a lost cause. But at least it could be worse. She didn't know anything then about the things we've been turning up lately."

Cullen nodded rapidly as if all that was obvious, then looked back at Hunt directly. "But think of what else it means," he said. "I'm thinking like a security man. They put a lot of fake memories in her head—memories that sounded innocuous and would have had us fooled if it wasn't for Sandy." The other two nodded but looked puzzled. Cullen turned a hand palm-up. "Well, what *other* memories might she have that she's *not* telling us about? See what I'm saying? Or let me put it to you this way: If you wanted to have a spy working for you on the inside, right here at PAC, and you had her plugged into JEVEX as an opportunity, how might you go about it?"

Hunt swallowed and sat back abruptly, looking stunned. Sandy raised a hand to her brow disbelievingly. "Oh, my God . . ."

Cullen rapped his fingers on the desk, then turned to flip a switch on the companel to one side. "ZORAC?"

"Sir?" Cullen liked being addressed in the way he was used to.

"Have Koberg and Lebansky arrived at Geerbaine yet?"

"Just under ten minutes ago."

"Okay, get a message on a secure channel to one of them, would you? Ms. Marin 'is not to overhear it. They're to keep her under observation at all times, and she isn't to communicate to anybody, repeat *anybody*. Anyone attempting to contact her is to be apprehended—they can use help from the police there if they need it. They're to report directly here as soon as they get back."

"Yes, sir."

Gina, Lebansky, and Koberg returned to the car, Koberg carrying Gina's two bags. Lebansky, who had been in the lobby while the other two went up to the room, saw her into her seat, closed the door, and then went around to exchange a few words with Koberg as he stowed the bags. Gina saw Koberg nod, say something in reply, and indicate with a nod a group of police with an officer, standing nearby. Lebansky waved back toward the hotel, and they both nodded again. Then they came around and climbed into the car.

"Is everything okay?" Gina asked.

"Yes, ma'am," Koberg replied impassively. But something in their manner had changed.

They pulled out and drove back around the open square. But as soon as they were out of sight from the hotel, Lebansky ordered the autodrive unit, which had been reprogrammed to understand English, "Change destination. Park anywhere." The car slid out of the throughway and halted.

"What's going on?" Gina asked, looking from one to another.

"Just take it easy, ma'am. There's nothing to be worried about," Lebansky said. Koberg got out and began walking back in the direction of the hotel, keeping close to the walls.

"Why have we stopped?" Gina demanded. "What's he doing?" She reached for the door catch. "Look, I'm going—"

Lebansky laid a restraining hand lightly but firmly on her arm. "Just take it easy. We had a change of orders, that's all. I don't know what it's about, either, but I figure you could be in some kind of trouble."

At the reception desk inside the Best Western, a redheaded woman with a yellow coat and flowery scarf smiled at the clerk and fluttered her eyelids. "Excuse me. My name is Marion Fayne. I believe there might be something for me to collect. Would you look for me, please? It's an envelope that I left here earlier."

"I'll see." The clerk turned away.

"That looks like it, up there . . . Yes, that's the one. Thank you. Do you need to see some ID or something?"

"That's okay."

"Well, I just thought. Anyone could say anything, couldn't they? Oh, thank you. It's a book that I left to be signed, you know. One of my favorite writers. Did you know she was staying here? Ah, yes, there, she's changed the name."

As the woman moved away from the desk, a tall, broad-shouldered man in a navy suit who had been watching stepped in front of her and held out a hand. "I'll take that, if you don't mind."

The woman froze. Suddenly her face hardened, and sizing up the situation in an instant, she reached inside her coat. She was fast, but Koberg was faster and slapped the gun from her hand as she pulled it out.

She turned for the door and ran—straight into the police officer and two men who had been waiting there. "Bastard!" she managed to spit back at Koberg as the policemen hauled her outside.

But she had been watched, and the news reached an office in the Axis's Shiban Temple within minutes.

The woman who called herself Marion Fayne had no knowledge of the tiny implant that had been placed in a neural plexus at the base of her brain a long time previously. It responded to a radioed code. She collapsed suddenly in the police van that she was traveling in, and was found to be dead on arrival at headquarters.

Chapter Forty

A Ganymean short-haul flyer, one of the *Shapieron*'s complement of daughter vessels, landed on the rooftop pad of a low, burnished-copper-colored building fifteen miles east of the city. Duncan Watt got out, accompanied by Rodgar Jassilane and a Ganymean computing specialist. They were met by two more Ganymeans and a small group of Jevlenese technicians who had been waiting. The party entered through a reception lobby in a superstructure and descended by elevator through the building to a subterranean level. There they emerged into a circular vestibule with molded pastel walls interspaced with glass panels, and began walking along one of several corridors extending away radially at forty-five-degree spacings.

From outside, there was nothing remarkable about the building. But this was one of the primary communications-processing and traffic-control centers for the entire Shiban sector of the JEVEX network. In the galleries beneath the unprepossessing, squat, reddish-brown structure, in the days when JEVEX had been operational, the stupendous streams of data had poured through unceasingly, carrying the rhythms of life that pulsed through an organism not only encompassing a planet, but extending outward across a dozen stars. This was the location of one of the concentrations of mind-defying computing complexity that had made Jevlen virtually a self-managing planet and endowed its citizens with the ability to know anything at will and to cross the cosmos in an instant like galactic gods. This was one of the hubs, a final inner sanctum where the immensity that was JEVEX resided . . .

Or at least, that was what the construction plans that had been handed down for centuries said.

The party came to the control center, with rows of consoles on rising tiers, banks of displays, and rooms on all sides filled with auxiliary equipment. And they descended to the vast halls below, where rows of huge, cubical cabinets, and luminescent blocks of molecular-array crystal, each the size of a boxcar, stretched away into the distance in tight, geometric formations. Just from looking, Duncan could sense the stupendous scale of the operations it was all brought together to manage.

But it was all an illusion. For what the Ganymeans had discovered was that the entire installation was a dummy. The massive runs of lightguide cables and databeam buses leading from the communications level above went nowhere. The arrays of densely stacked holocrystals in the cabinets endlessly recirculated meaningless patterns of numbers. The displays and status indicators flickering and changing around the control floor were simulations. The whole portion of JEVEX that was supposed to reside here, in other words, didn't exist.

The Ganymeans showed Watt an opened cabinet in the control center. It was empty except for a few arrays of optronic wafers in a partly filled rack maybe three inches high. "This is what's generating all the images that you can see in this room," one of the Ganymeans said.

"But . . . this is impossible," Watt stammered, staring incredulously.

"I know. That's why we wanted you to see it for yourself."

Jassilane wheeled around to confront the Jevlenese chief engineer responsible for the site, who was staring straight ahead, blank-faced. "What do you know about this?" he demanded.

"I don't know anything."

"How long has it been like this?"

Silence. Another part of the conspiracy. They weren't going to get anywhere.

Watt looked at another empty cabinet that was winking a few lights and shook his head uncomprehendingly. All the calculations said that JEVEX had to be much *bigger* than the official designs showed. Yet if this was typical of the general situation, it hardly existed at all. But something had to have been supporting the Jevlenese-managed worlds.

Chapter Forty-one

Gina finished hanging her dresses in the closet of her new quarters inside PAC and lodged the empty suitcase in the space at the rear. She was still shaken from her confrontation with Cullen on arrival, which had been short and to the point: enough to thoroughly confuse her, and not at all illuminating. He had produced the report that she had left inside the book, which Koberg had brought back, and informed her that Marion Fayne had been working for a Jevlenese organization that was not the *Ichena,* but which maybe had connections with it.

To Gina's surprise, he hadn't condemned her or shown any of the rancor that she would have thought natural in the circumstances. She couldn't form any clear idea of what it meant. Surely General Shaw couldn't have been really working for the wrong side? Maybe the mysterious organization that Cullen had referred to had found out about Gina's meeting with Shaw in Shiban and substituted their own contact. Cullen had given no clue. Gina felt foolish and embarrassed, like an amateur who had been caught way out of her depth. Which was exactly what she was. And that made it all the more galling.

"Who did you think she was working for?" Hunt asked from the couch, where he was lounging casually, nursing a Coors that the suite's autochef had miraculously conjured up from whatever behind-the-scenes sources its supplies came from.

She assumed that they were sparing her a formal interrogation and letting Hunt try a low-key, psychological approach instead. So now she felt like a guinea pig, on top of everything else. And the worst thing about it was that she had no grounds for complaint. They had trusted her; she had deceived them and been found out. They had every right to ask questions. In fact, they were giving her a much easier time than might well have been the case. In some ways she'd have preferred it if they hadn't.

Hunt went on. "Well, if you want to know, the first guess from the path lab is that they pressed a button somewhere to blow a fuse that had been put inside her head. Nice people . . ." He half raised a hand. "Okay, we're not saying that you knew you were dealing with an outfit like that. But who *did* you think you were working for? Come on, no one's passing judgment or blaming you, because we think there could be a lot more to it than you know about. But you owe us that much."

Gina walked over to the chef and picked up her own drink, which was still standing untouched on the dispenser tray. She took a sip and stood with her back to the room, staring at the cover panels of the units as if hoping they would open up and swallow her. "I feel dumb, stupid, and when you boil it all down, not an especially nice person to know," she said without moving her head. "I'm not used to feeling that way. I never thought I'd have reason to. I don't like it."

"That happens to everyone at some time or other," Hunt said. He sat forward and topped off his glass. His voice was easygoing and natural, not lecturing. "I remember once when I was a kid in London, a friend of mine lent me his new bike. I crashed it and bent it up, and then just left it outside his house and walked away. Didn't have the nerve to tell him, let alone think about how to put it right. It bothered me for years afterwards, that did. Sometimes it still does."

"We're talking about something a bit more serious than kids' bikes," Gina said, and instantly wished she hadn't; it sounded as if she were fishing for sympathy.

Hunt's voice took on an edge of impatience. "Oh, for heaven's sake. Come down and join the real, pretty-shitty world. Sometimes you look back at something and you find you don't like what you did." He paused in the middle of taking a swig and looked at her over his glass pointedly. "And sometimes, if the truth were known, you're kicking yourself over nothing because things didn't seem the way you see them later. You find out new things, and it clouds your recollection of how much you didn't know before."

"Thanks for giving me the benefit of the doubt, but I don't need charity."

"Maybe it's not charity. Maybe we know something that you don't." Although she still had her back turned, Hunt could sense her wrestling with her conscience. She really had no corner to run to. It was only a matter of not being seen to cave in too easily. He gave her a few seconds.

"So . . . how far back were you recruited, and who was behind it?" he asked again.

Gina sighed, took a hurried gulp, and turned to stand facing him across the room. "This isn't easy," she said.

"No one's expecting it to be."

She came over to the lounge area and perched herself on the edge of one of the chairs. "From the beginning—back on Earth. It was your boss, Caldwell, and some branch of—oh, I don't know, some kind of security agency somewhere. They think there's a Jevlenese operation that has an informer in PAC somewhere."

Hunt shook his head without a moment's hesitation. "Not Gregg. He doesn't work that way. Try another one."

"I'm telling you, that's what happened."

"Baloney."

"Okay, okay." Gina held up a hand. "Not Caldwell exactly. There was another guy with him, from the military. His name was General Shaw—I don't know which department or whatever. But Caldwell introduced him, and he was there the whole time that Shaw was talking . . ." Gina shook her head and raised the fingers of her free hand defensively. "He made it sound crucially important. I didn't know you guys then. To tell you the truth it's been bothering the hell out of me inside for days now. But I'd agreed to do it. It was classified, and I couldn't talk to anyone here. What else could I do but go with it?"

Hunt looked at her without any change of expression. He didn't believe that version any more than the previous one, but this track had the promise of being fruitful. "You met this general before we left Earth, with Gregg?" he repeated.

"Yes. At Goddard. In Caldwell's office."

"Before you came out to my place?"

"Yes . . . maybe not." Gina massaged her brow. "I'm not sure."

"Describe him."

"Oh . . . biggish kind of guy, pink face, blue eyes, ginger mustache—typical clipped military style. He wore a grayish uniform, maybe light blue, with a lot of ribbons and braid."

"And he told you there was an informer here?"

Gina looked up curiously. "What is all this? Wasn't he on the level?"

"Don't worry about that for now."

"He said there was reason to suspect one," Gina went on. "They didn't trust the official channel through Cullen, so the idea was to put in an independent observer that *nobody* knew about. You weren't to know about it, not Cullen—not even Garuth." Gina shrugged. "I guess that having me show up, who nobody could connect to any organization, seemed like a perfect opportunity."

"And was that when he gave you the contact procedure that Marion Fayne used?"

Gina sighed again, in a what-the-hell kind of way. "No, later, after we arrived. He's here in Shiban. I met him a couple of days ago."

The look on Hunt's face sharpened. "When?"

"The day Baumer showed me the town." She paused. "I've got a feeling he might have been working for Shaw, too, somehow."

"I guess we'll never know now, will we? What happened?"

"I think a lot of this about Baumer being a head junkie might have been an act for cover. We did go to the club, but just so that I'd be able to tell it believably, and for it to be okay if anybody checked. But I didn't stay as long as I said. Another guy collected me and took me to some place—a room in an apartment block that could have been anywhere—and I gave Shaw a rundown on what's been happening since D.C. That was when he updated me on what he wanted and gave a new code that contacts would use."

"I see." Hunt got up and paced across the room, thinking to himself.

Gina settled further back into her chair. "What would you have done?" she asked him after the silence had dragged into more than a minute.

"What?" Hunt seemed to return abruptly from somewhere miles away. "Oh, much the same, I think. As you say, you didn't know us at the time."

"That's nice to hear, anyway."

Hunt picked up her briefcase, which she had put down on the chair by the working area on one side of the lounge, moved it to the desktop, then sat down in the chair and swiveled it to face back at her. "Do you remember that conversation we had in my place at Redfern Canyons the day you drove out there? You asked me what reality out there was, and I said it was all photons. Everything else you think you see, you make inside your head."

"Neural constructs. Yes, I remember."

"Funny things, heads. I knew a chap at Cambridge once, years ago now, who wanted to be a great scientist. He bought this big house with lots of quiet and seclusion, and filled it with all the things that were going to make it happen. Paneled study with a fireplace; the best computer, with access numbers into everywhere; huge library, and a lab set up with everything. He even had a chalkboard and plenty of pads ready to capture the inspiration when it came . . . The only trouble was, nothing ever did. He surrounded himself with all the paraphernalia and then sat back waiting for it to do something for him. A lot of people try and live their lives the same way. But things don't work like that, of course. It has to come from inside . . . Rather like what you said about J.H.C.: His message was that everyone has to find their own way of figuring out who they are. Relying on the world outside to do it for you doesn't work."

"Why are you bringing this up now?"

Hunt shrugged nonchalantly. "Just talking about the funny things that go on inside and outside people's heads. Sandy was telling me a little bit about your experiments with VISAR on the *Vishnu*. I hadn't realized you'd gone that far into it—in fact, I hadn't realized that you *could* go that far into it. Amazing, isn't it? Me, the ever-curious scientist. It comes as a bit of a shock to find out you're not quite what you thought, doesn't it?"

Gina twitched uncomfortably and gulped at her drink, spilling a drop on her slacks. She drew a tissue from a pack on a side table and dabbed it dry.

"What was it that bothered you so much when you got into VISAR?" Hunt asked.

"Does this really have anything to do with what we're talking about?" Gina objected.

"Yes, I think it does." The sudden crispness in Hunt's voice made her eyebrows lift in surprise. He waited for a moment. "Sandy said that it doesn't just create fantasy realities. It can mold them to reflect things about yourself that you mightn't like—things you didn't even know existed. And that's important to you. You said as much a few minutes ago, when you thought you'd been betraying your friends. What other things did VISAR let out of the box that you'd rather it had left there?"

"What the *hell* does this have to do with anything?" Gina demanded, her voice rising.

"What's the matter, can't you handle it?" Hunt leered tauntingly. "We've all got something. Power trips, like Baumer. Sandy found that she gets a kick out of seeing blood, and people screaming. What about you?"

"Vic, stop it! I don't want to talk about this."

"Do you like older men because a favorite uncle felt up your knickers when you were a little girl? Was it something like that?"

"Mind your own fucking, goddamn business!"

"Ahah, something like that, then, was it? You said on the

Vishnu that you might tell me your fantasies one day. Do you remember?"

Gina slammed the glass down on the side table, breaking the stem. She glowered across at Hunt and thrust out her chin defiantly. "All right! I used to be married to this guy who was into the swinging scene, okay. You know the kind of thing? He had other friends too, and liked threesome things and lots-of-people things. He was always trying to get me into it, too, but it never happened. Okay? Got your thrill for today? I've heard lots of weird things about you English guys."

"And what? Did it bother you that you hadn't figured him before?" Hunt had dropped the sarcasm suddenly, but just at that moment Gina wasn't registering.

"No, *Doctor,* it didn't!" she shouted. "Deep down I was pissed because I'd been chicken. VISAR would have delivered, and I wasn't sure I wanted that. In fact I was terrified. Okay? Satisfied?" Her voice fell. "Now get out of my room."

But Hunt was staring at her intently, his face serious, as if inviting her to think about what she had just said. She realized then that he had been shamming, and for a reason. Her expression changed to puzzlement.

"And you went back to it, here in Shiban, with Baumer?" He gave her a moment to reflect, then shook his head. "No way. Oh, I've heard all your reasons, and I don't buy them. Neither do you."

Gina looked back at him, totally confused. Her belligerence evaporated. "I know . . . It's made me wonder, too. I don't know why I did it . . . I guess, maybe, I couldn't see any way to refuse."

Hunt shrugged. "It's easy. You tell him it's not your thing. Let's go and have a drink."

Gina leaned back wearily and ran a hand through her hair. "Is it really that important?"

"Yes, very. Because I don't think it happened. I don't think you went there at all."

"Now you're being stupid."

"We've just agreed that you wouldn't have gone near the place. Sandy says the same thing. It was she who convinced me."

Gina stared at him and shook her head as if wondering if she were dreaming. "Look, what's the point of talking like this? Why keep saying I couldn't have gone there when I did?"

"How do you know you did?"

"Well . . . What the hell kind of question is that to ask? How do you know you went to the bathroom this morning? I remember it, that's why."

Hunt sat back, still regarding her steadily, and gave a satisfied nod. "Funny things, heads," he said again. "Aren't they?"

He waited. Gina stared down at the floor. A trickle of drink from her upset glass had run down a leg of the side table and was spreading into the carpet. She leaned forward to mop it with a tissue. And then she froze, suddenly, and looked up, the first glimmer of comprehension illuminating her eyes. "What are you getting at?" she whispered.

"I could call Gregg Caldwell through visar to check," Hunt said. "In fact, we will. But I'll lay you a thousand bucks to a penny right now that General Shaw doesn't exist either." The look of horror on her face told him that he was getting through. He drew a long breath, then went on. "They're fake memories that were written into your head at another jevex outlet somewhere. We're pretty certain that somebody got to you somewhere after you and Baumer left PAC. So we have to assume that they know everything you did up to that point. Then they overwrote what happened with the fabricated sequence that you remember, and just for good measure added in the business about Shaw to get you working for them. Fayne was their first try to collect—at least, I hope it was the first?" Gina nodded. Hunt sighed. "It was neat. If you and Sandy hadn't gone tripping on the *Vishnu*, we might never have cottoned onto it."

Gina went through some of the pictures in her mind, searching for possible flaws or inaccuracies. There were none. She shivered, drawing her sweater tighter around her. "I can't tell. I don't know what's real and what isn't about what I remember." A fearful look came over her suddenly. "This couldn't be anything like what happened to Baumer, is it?"

Hunt shook his head firmly. "Don't worry about that. You've

just lost a few memories, that's all. A good binge could have done the same thing. You're still very much you."

"I'm not sure I feel it. When you know there's part of your mind that doesn't belong there . . . It's not exactly comforting."

"People probably used to think the same about cardiac valves and synthetic kidneys." His manner was sympathetic and reassuring now. She had accepted it and would cooperate once she'd had a chance to get used to it. That was the main thing.

There was a long silence while Gina thought it through. Hunt mopped up the spilled drink for her while he waited. "Is there anything we can do to unscramble it?" she asked finally.

"I don't know. We'd like you to let VISAR analyze those patterns anyway, to see if there's any way of recovering what was overwritten. Would you mind?"

Gina shook her head. "I'm kind of curious, too. That's me, remember?"

"Terrific. You'll survive. I'll be getting along for now. I've got a few things to do."

"Oh . . . Vic," Gina said as he moved toward the door.

He stopped and looked back. "What?"

"Thanks."

He grinned. "Glad you can see it that way. I'm sorry I had to get personal."

"That's okay." Gina managed to muster a smile back. "Did Sandy tell you that she thought I was pretty dumb, too?"

"No. Why?"

"For chickening out of VISAR's porno trip. She says if it was her she'd have gone for it."

Hunt laughed and began moving to the door again. "You see?" he said. "Scientists are more curious."

Chapter Forty-two

The Ganymeans were dubious that anything could be done to reconstruct the memories of Gina's that had been over-written. Nevertheless, she allowed VISAR to go over the recollections that now existed in her mind to see if it could find any seams. It processed, correlated, reinterpolated, and analyzed the data in every way that offered a shred of hope that some vestige of what she had actually experienced during the missing hours might be extracted, but the results were uniformly negative. Essentially, the elements of a pattern had been rearranged. The information carried in the previous arrangement was gone, and no amount of juggling could re-create it. As Hunt observed, it was like asking a position in a chess game to say something about the previous game played by the pieces.

All that could be said for sure was that from some time after leaving PAC with Baumer—which couldn't be pinpointed since it was no longer possible to compare Gina's story with his to establish where they diverged—to some time before she walked back into PAC, something had happened that was different from what she remembered. And that was probably all that would ever be known. But if a conclusive pointer existed anywhere to the organization that Cullen was looking for, that was where it lay concealed.

Then Calazar, on behalf of the Thurien-Terran Joint Policy Council for Jevlen, formally notified Garuth that a move to terminate the Ganymean custodianship of Jevlen was being actively considered. Nobody was blaming Garuth or his colleagues from the *Shapieron*, who, Calazar readily acknowledged, had made a magnificent attempt, under impossible circumstances, at a task whose problems had been greatly underestimated.

"We have to accept that our very different origins and the temperament that they confer do not equip us to comprehend this race, let alone direct its affairs," Calazar said. "The entire history of our own dealings with the Jevlenese was insufficient to teach us what should have been obvious. Therefore we shall accept the counsel of those whose perception has been shaped by a better guide."

Which was as direct an admission as could be asked for that henceforth the policies of JPC would be determined by humans, with the Thuriens effectively endorsing whatever they decided. Putting in a Terran occupation force would only be a matter of time after that.

An hour or so after Garuth announced the news, Hunt, Cullen, Danchekker, a dejected Garuth, and Shilohin assembled in Garuth's office. Caldwell, who had confirmed to nobody's surprise that General Shaw was a fiction, joined in from Goddard, appearing on a screen via a link through VISAR and ZORAC.

There was one last angle that Hunt could think of to try and stall things. "What are the chances, Gregg," he asked, "of you getting back to JPC through UNSA somehow and seeing if we can get them to put a hold on it? I mean, you can see the kind of outfit we're up against here: riots in the streets, assassinations, kidnapping and mind-editing, lethal chips in people's heads. And Del's convinced he's getting really close. It just needs another break. If this team is pulled out now, we'll lose the lot."

"This whole move by Eubeleus is a cover for something," Cullen put in. "He's not going to Uttan to grow daisies in some terraformed monastery. If we could get JPC to hold off on that, somehow, I'd feel a lot more comfortable."

"But why would he have left at such a critical time?" Danchekker queried. "How could Uttan be more important if his designs have something to do with Jevlen?"

"That's what I'm saying we need to find out," Cullen answered.

Then Caldwell said from the screen, "Aren't you overlooking one small point?"

"What?" Hunt asked.

A hand flashed briefly before the image of the craggy, wire-haired face. "I've been sitting here listening to all this talk about whether this Eubeleus is crooked or straight, and what he plans to do on Uttan. And it's all very interesting. But there's one minor thing: I haven't heard one piece of evidence, yet, that *proves* he had anything to do with what you're talking about." The others turned to exchange glances with each other. Caldwell went on. "All that we *know* he's done is offer to take a big piece of the problem light-years away from the scene. That's very nice, and it's what JPC sees." He gestured again. "Nothing connects him with the things that Del's worried about. There are only three witnesses who could have given a positive line back to him, but not one of them's any good. Payne's dead; the Marin girl had her tape wiped clean; and Baumer's a gibbering idiot. You see my problem? If Eubeleus's aim was camouflage, he's done a good job. I don't have one solid fact to go back up through UNSA, trying to get the brakes put on JPC. I don't like the feel of this either, but I can't go stirring things up at that level on the basis of what we've got. There just isn't a case."

And he was right, Hunt conceded, slumping back in his seat. Politics was Caldwell's business. He knew the system. If he started rocking the boat because he didn't like the feel of things, but it turned out that he had nothing concrete to back it up, then nobody would take any notice when he did find something.

A heavy silence had overtaken the room. Garuth got up and moved across to the window to stare out at the dilapidated towers of Shiban. As a city it was falling apart; but he had developed a strange, inexplicable fondness for it. Perhaps it had something to do with its being the first place that had come anywhere near feeling like home since the *Shapieron*'s departure from Minerva. Had he been left in charge of it, he wouldn't have imposed any sudden or drastic changes, he decided. He would have let it be, allowing it to seek out and evolve its own solutions at its own pace. Those were always the kinds of changes that endured, he had found. The worthwhile changes.

"And I still have the feeling that we were getting so close," he said aloud.

Afterward, Hunt stopped by Gina's suite to give her the news and to see how things were going.

"And when you go through it, Gregg could be right," he told her. "Eubeleus may have nothing to do with it. We can't make any case to JPC. Any junior lawyer with his name still wet on the door could make mincemeat out of it."

Gina shook her head. "Surely there has to be some way to get further."

"Probably true, but hardly constructive."

"What about that office of Baumer's, the one I went to? Mightn't that turn up something?" she asked, reaching for a straw.

"It was broken into and ransacked. Whoever did it made a bonfire. There wasn't enough paper left to write your name on. Now, wasn't that convenient for somebody?" Hunt stretched back in his chair. "I don't know, Gina. Why do people insist on complicating life like this? You'd think they'd learn to just enjoy the pleasant side of it, wouldn't you? It's short enough . . . Thinking about it, I might even go and join this monastery of Eubeleus's. Now, wouldn't that qualify as a genuine miracle?" He grinned tiredly across the room at her. "Anyway, how are you feeling? I never even thought to ask."

"Oh, a bit like having a tooth out. It feels strange at first, but you get used to it. Pretty much the way you said."

"That's good to know, anyhow. Did you talk to Sandy?"

"Yes. She's glad it worked out."

ZORAC came through at that moment with a call for Hunt from Duncan Watt, who was at another JEVEX site with the Ganymean engineers. Further findings had corroborated the nonsensical conclusion of the first: not only was JEVEX evidently far *smaller* than the original design information said; if what the Ganymeans were discovering was typical, it was virtually nonexistent.

"Another one," Watt announced.

Hunt was baffled. "Another fake?"

"Worse. I wanted you to see this one for yourself."

"Where are you?"

"Traganon; city about three hundred miles north."

"So, what have you found?" Hunt asked.

"Well, you know what we found at the other sites: usually some interfacing and h-space transmission gear that was real enough, and then streets of impressive-looking cubes and beamguides all doing nothing. But take a look at what we've got here. It beats the rest for sheer audacity."

Watt stepped to one side to reveal the scene behind him. He had been standing in front of a wide window. It looked like that of a control room, facing out over a vast floor, dark in shadows. The floor was bare and dusty: just an empty expanse of untiled concrete, stretching away between lines of square, unadorned pillars into shadows cast by a few, weak, overhead lamps.

For a moment Hunt wasn't sure what he was supposed to be looking at. "That's it?"

"That's it. Nothing. They didn't even bother faking this one. Rodgar thinks it could have been like this for centuries."

The camera moved, sliding Watt out of the frame completely and showing more derelict galleries. There were oddments of trash and debris scattered in places, and here and there a length of cable hanging from a roof support. Small animals were scurrying in the shadows. Hunt wondered if there had once been equipment installed there that had been moved elsewhere for some reason.

It seemed larger than most of the other vaults that Duncan had checked. Hunt tried to visualize it as the Thurien designers had intended: packed with tiers of crystalline slab stacked to the roof and serviced by access elevators and walkways—Hunt had "visited" some of the halls on Thurien where VISAR's bulk-processing centers were located. The contrast between the desolation of the view on the screen and the image in Hunt's mind took on an odd significance that he couldn't quite pin down. He stared at the screen with a strange mixture of somberness and reverie.

"You're getting around, anyway, Duncan," he half heard Gina saying from across the room.

"If you think Shiban's run-down, come and see this place," Watt answered.

Something moving caught Hunt's eye—something bright, appearing and disappearing in the shadows higher up between two of the pillars. Several things, tiny white points. Hunt stared at the view, then realized that they were flying, insectlike creatures, crisscrossing through a shaft of light from one of the lamps. They looked like speeded-up images of stars orbiting in a black void, he thought to himself.

"Did you hear about the news from JPC?" Gina was asking Duncan.

"Not yet. What's up?"

"Oh, it doesn't sound too good . . ."

And then a strange superposition took place in Hunt's mind of the scene he was looking at, and the picture in his imagination of what should have been there but wasn't. He saw the void, but its volume filled in his mind's eye with banks of Thurien processing crystal; the tiny points of light were still there, orbiting through the solid lattices. And suddenly he saw them no longer as stars, but as atoms.

Or as elementary quanta . . .

Quanta of what? Nobody knew. It could have been anything.

The quanta that a real, physical universe could evolve out of . . .

Chapter Forty-three

Langerif, the new deputy chief of police, had applied himself to continuing his late predecessor's policy of cooperation with the Ganymean administration. He became a regular visitor to PAC, and in particular showed much interest in learning more from the security people that Cullen had imported from Earth. He even arranged for a three-day training class to be held in PAC for a picked group of his own officers. At the same time, a firm of contractors that the Ganymeans had been vainly pressuring to start work on remodeling and redecorating parts of the complex at last responded, zealously sending in a legion of workers as if anxious to make up for the lost time. So, for the last few days, PAC had been swarming with all kinds of Jevlenese. The scientists, however, had become too engrossed in a completely new explanation of Phantasmagoria that Hunt had suddenly produced from nowhere to take much notice.

The practical usefulness of mathematics arises from the fortuitous ability of some mathematical constructs to approximate real physical processes. There is no obvious reason why such correspondence should exist; luckily for engineers and others, it just does. This makes it a lot easier and cheaper to test a design for, say, a bridge—by making a mathematical model of it and seeing what happens when mathematical trains roll over and mathematical winds blow—than having to actually build the bridge. But as science probes successively deeper and more refined levels of reality, things change. Complexity and non-linearities become more important in their effects, making mathematical representation more intractable, until the real thing becomes a better model of the model: a daffodil, a single cell of it, or even one DNA molecule from the cell is a far more concise and comprehensible statement of what's going on than the reams of equations that would be necessary to express it analytically in symbols.

Accordingly, the computer techniques used for modeling reality developed from the simple mechanized solving of analytical equations to progressively more elaborate methods of *simulation*. The trend was reflected in system architectures, where, to accommodate demands for ever greater speed and precision, earlier design philosophies based on bringing passive data to a few centralized processing bottlenecks gave way to connecting large numbers of simpler units in parallel to provide on-the-spot processing of large arrays of data simultaneously.

Ganymean technology had long before taken this trend to its ultimate. Their systems consisted of enormous numbers of microscopic cells arranged in three-dimensional arrays. Individually, each cell possessed only a limited capability that combined the rudiments of processing, memory, and communication; but ensembles of them working in conjunction could handle staggering throughputs of information. ZORAC exemplified a relatively early phase of development; VISAR's astounding ability to cope with the full virtual-travel traffic of the entire, interstellar Thurien civilization in real time was the culmination.

Each cell in a Thurien computing complex was thus an elementary processing unit that exchanged information with its immediate neighbors in every direction according to a very simple set of programming rules.

*   *   *

"Fundamental entities defined by a small set of attributes, like quantum numbers, interacting according to a few basic rules. You could almost think of them," Hunt said to Danchekker, Shilohin, and Duncan Watt, whom he had called together in the UNSA labs, "as energy quanta forces."

He went on. "You could think of a cell that's in an 'active' state in the matrix of 'data space' as having properties analogous to those of a basic particle in our ordinary physical space. You see what I mean. It doesn't matter all that much what the quanta 'really' are. They exhibit the same kind of behavior."

He waited, flicking his eyes around the group for a reaction. Danchekker and Shilohin stared in silence, obviously needing a moment to take it in. Duncan looked immediately taken with the idea and was the first to speak. He had worked with Hunt long enough to be used to propositions coming like this, from totally unexpected directions.

"So there are cells everywhere. But only the ones in a particular state are, sort of . . . 'real,' in this space you're talking about?" he said.

Hunt nodded. "Right. If a cell's not active, it isn't exchanging information with anything. If a particle isn't exchanging any field quanta, then it isn't interacting with anything. So for all the difference it makes, it might as well not exist."

"Hmm." Duncan rubbed his chin and thought about the proposition. "That would make the matrix like Dirac's 'sea' of negative energy states, filling all of space. 'Particles' are simply localized regions raised to positive energies . . . Yes, I can see your point. They can move. What we call 'antiparticles' are the holes they leave behind."

"Like holes in semiconductors," Hunt said, nodding. "Exactly."

Danchekker blinked several times, sat back in his chair, and emitted a long breath in the manner of somebody not quite sure where to begin. "Let me be quite clear," he said. "This isn't anything that comes into being by virtue of the processing operations taking place in the matrix: It isn't a construct of the software?"

"No," Hunt said. "It's something innate to the design. An unintended byproduct of the environment itself. Like bread mold."

"I see." Danchekker's voice remained even. His expression was of someone not necessarily in agreement but prepared to wait and see where things were leading. "Very well," he said. "Go on."

"The more I think about it, the more I'm convinced that what happened in JEVEX was something like this," Hunt continued. "Somehow, at some time in the distant past, conditions came about inside its processing space such that activated computational cells took on the role of primordial particles in our own universe."

"The Big Wang?" ZORAC, who was following, threw in.

"ZORAC, cut it out. This is serious." Hunt gestured across the table with a half-open hand. "And, just as happened in our own case, from those beginnings there evolved a universe. A *real* one, not a software imitation. And that's your answer, Chris. That's how Phantasmagoria exists, and where it came from."

"Oh, for God's sake!" Danchekker could contain himself no longer. He waved his hands in agitation, stood up, faced the other way for several seconds, and then turned back toward the table, still spluttering incoherently. "What is this supposed to be? I mean, we *are* being serious, I take it? This is analogy gone wild."

Hunt had been prepared for it. "No, calm down . . ."

"Oh, I've never heard such twaddle. Inventing physics out of abstract data-processing concepts . . . Really, Vic, it—"

"Just think about it for a minute, Chris. A cell already possesses the properties of localization and position in the matrix. Now, if I've read it correctly about the way Thurien systems work, as a consequence of the overall programming directives imposed on the system, activated cells constantly exchange information among themselves."

"That's correct," Shilohin said.

Hunt nodded. "Good. Well, I don't know what the design philosophy was long ago when JEVEX was dreamed up. But just for argument's sake, let's imagine that it embodied an optimization criterion by which the paths between such communicating cells should be as short as possible."

"Which *is* the kind of thing you'd expect," Duncan observed.

"Exactly. So, if the traffic being supported on the right-hand side, say, of a given cell were heavier than that on the left, but the opposite was true of its neighbor to the right, then an improvement would be achieved if the two cells were to exchange identities. In effect, each of them could be thought of as having *moved* one space-quantum through the matrix."

"A kind of Planck length," Duncan murmured.

Hunt nodded again and went on. "Or, to take another example, if an isolated cell was communicating at different rates in different directions, it would move around in such a way as to minimize the traffic-times-distance total until it balanced all the competing 'pulls.' In other words, if the information-exchange process plays the part of force-carrying vector particles, then this optimization rule defines minimum-action paths: natural geodesics. I've played through simulations of it with ZORAC. The dynamics of gravitation follows automatically."

Shilohin was staring fixedly at Hunt. "You're postulating a void populated by particles capable of exerting mutual attraction," she said slowly. "The conditions of a primordial universe."

"Yes."

"What about repulsions? Is there an analog of charge?" Duncan asked.

Hunt inclined his head in the direction of Danchekker, who was still on his feet. The life-sciences specialist had not yet given his blessing; but he was no longer vehemently protesting, either. "Chris has a good point: We shouldn't get too carried away by analogies," he said. "But I can offer a few speculations. For example, if everything were allowed to collapse to its minimum 'energy' state purely on the basis of attraction, it would all end up as one solid lump, with nowhere left for through traffic. Everything would be optimally close to everything, but unable to function. The system would have stifled itself. So one optimization criterion isn't enough. You need to introduce another that competes with it—say, one that tries to maximize free space for traffic. When the two trends interact, maybe the kind of organization that emerges is a collection of 'clumps,' where similar kinds of processing with little to say to the outside world can get together, separated by voids in which other things happen."

"Fascinating!" Shilohin whispered.

"It gets more interesting," Hunt said. "The cells must have a finite switching time. So larger aggregates of cells that have accreted together will move more sluggishly than smaller ones. Hence, we have a resistance to motion, proportional to the number of cells."

The parallel to mass was too obvious to need spelling out.

Hunt continued. "But once the mass is moving, a plausible way of improving efficiency would be to change to a pattern-switching algorithm instead of having to operate on all the constituent cells individually; so the pattern would be reluctant to slow down again."

Inertia.

"But the propagation rate through the matrix of even a single cell would ultimately be limited by the switching speed."

Velocities in Hunt's universe had a relativistic limit.

"We *are* speaking in terms of pure conjecture, I take it?" Danchekker said. His voice still had something of a rasp, but it had mollified itself noticeably. Exhibiting another kind of inertia, he was starting to come around in his own way. "We're not talking about established fact? This isn't science?"

"Of course not," Hunt agreed. "But we're getting an idea of what to look for, maybe."

Duncan snorted. "Look where? We can't even find where JEVEX *is*, let alone look inside it."

Shilohin looked up, at last digesting the full message of what Hunt was saying. "Our physical universe evolved from huge numbers of elementary particles in space, and laws of physics and probability that contained implicit mechanisms for the self-organization of complex structures," she said. "And out of it there emerged not only complexity sufficient to manifest intelligence, but the whole world of impressions and experiences—all far removed from the underlying quantum reality—which intelligence perceives. So, is it so inconceivable for comparable levels of complexity to have arisen in this . . . 'matrix universe'? That's what you're saying."

"Why not?" Hunt said. "We're pretty sure that Nixie's world can't exist anywhere in the universe we know. Yet I'm convinced that it exists somewhere. And perhaps this sheds some light on how its magical properties could have arisen. Although there might be some parallels to our own universe in the kind of way I've suggested, which would at least give us the basis of objects moving in space as something they share in common, the 'laws' expressing the physics of the underlying reality will derive not from the quantum rules of *our* universe, but from the directive imposed by the system programmers. Therefore, there's no reason why our notions of normality and causality should apply there at all. Which fits with all the things that Nixie has been telling us."

"You're not saying that the programmers intended anything like this to happen?" Duncan checked.

Hunt shook his head. "And I don't think the Jevlenese ever twigged onto the fact that it had. The whole thing was an accident: a freak by-product of the purpose that JEVEX was built for—and, of course, the inhabitants that finally appeared as part of it had no inkling of it, either. Why should they? There was no more reason why they should be aware, intuitively, that their reality was ultimately founded upon information quanta than we are that ours is on energy quanta."

Now visibly intrigued, since the prospect of evolution was implied, Danchekker returned to his chair and sat down. "Very well, Vic. Let us agree to entertain this fantastic hypothesis of yours for a moment . . . purely for the sake of argument, you understand."

"Of course," Hunt said, nodding solemnly.

"One thing that bothers me is the question of size. Clearly it would have to be much smaller than our universe. For it to be comparable, there would have to be the same order of magnitude of active cells in it as there are particles in existence, which would be absurd."

"The ratio of the size of the fundamental cell to the dimensions of the universe as a whole would be much greater,"

Shilohin said. "So the macrocosm would be much closer to the level of quantum granularity. Nonlinearities and curvatures would be more apparent, probably."

"Boundary effects might play a big part," Duncan mused, half to himself.

Danchekker nodded. "Yes, I accept all that. But what I was getting at was something more fundamental. To support anything as complex as life and intelligence requires a high degree of complexity. That in turn implies a corresponding richness of structure. And you can't build rich structures from a few elements." He gestured to the others appealingly. "You see my point. There is no escape from the necessity of large numbers. Enormously large numbers. And my question is, where would you possibly find a sufficiently vast computational space to accommodate the processes that you're suggesting? It's an ingenious suggestion, Vic. I'm not disagreeing with that. But if my initial estimates are anything to go by, to give what you're talking about even a reasonable chance of engendering a world as complex and varied as the one we've heard described by Nixie and VISAR, you'd need a computer the size of a pla—"

Danchekker's voice stopped abruptly as he realized what he had been about to say. The others all saw it, too, in the same instant. Shilohin looked stunned. Duncan slammed back abruptly against the backrest of his chair.

"Christ," Hunt breathed. They all looked at each other incredulously.

So *that* was what was so important about the mysterious planet, Uttan!

And why the Ganymeans weren't having much luck locating JEVEX on Jevlen.

Chapter Forty-four

"**I**n the visions of Hyperia that I glimpsed only briefly, I sometimes saw devices of wondrous complexity," Thrax said. "Devices created by the beings who inhabit that realm, and yet able to move as bewildering cooperations of parts of their own accord; impossibly coordinated motions of parts that moved parts that moved parts, and all of them dancing in unison to unfold some hidden plan. Are the Hyperians thus able to divest themselves of the burden of having to project their thoughts, Master? Can they enchant matter itself with the capacity of thought, such that it serves their wishes unbidden?" He looked at Shingen-Hu, who was sitting next to him on the rocks by the dusty track. But the Master was lost in his own dejection and seemed not to hear. Thrax took in his wan, sunken features and disheveled appearance, his hair unkempt and robes turning to rags. "They build devices that see and speak across vast distances; others that voyage to worlds beyond the sky. Where does this place exist, Master? Is it a space that encloses all space? Or a dream that we manufacture in our minds?" He looked again. But Shingen-Hu sat staring dully down at the grassy slopes below the track and showed no reaction.

Shingen-Hu had been overcome by a morose deadness of mind and spirit ever since the attack by servants of Nieru's enemies at the ceremony on the sacred mount, when Thrax's chance to emerge had been thwarted. Convinced that his god had abandoned him or been overwhelmed by a more powerful celestial rival, the Master had sunk into a depressive lethargy and lost faith in his arts. His school for adepts was no more. Soldiers, encouraged by priests bearing the green-crescent emblem of Vandros, the underworld god, had come to complete its destruction. Its members had dispersed and fled, and Shingen-Hu lived from village to village on the fringes of the wilderness, reduced to the life of a fugitive mendicant. Thrax, perhaps through basic loyalty, or possibly in hope that the Master's condition would improve, or maybe simply because he had nowhere else to go, had stayed with him.

Although the day was barely into its second half, twilight cloaked the hillside above them. The sun remained a feeble, emaciated remnant of its former self, its faltering light supplemented by a few dim stars which now remained visible through the eternal night that had descended. Thrax and Shingen-Hu had eaten nothing for two days apart from a few mountain berries and water plants found by a spring. Thrax thought wistfully of the cakes and roasts that his aunt Yonel used to prepare at Dalgren's house, in days that seemed so long ago. Almost like another world . . . Thrax shook himself back to the present and forced thoughts of other worlds from his mind.

A movement in the grass just across the track caught his eye. He looked and saw that it was a brown-striped *skredgen*, up on its hind legs beneath a bush, its nose twitching and its large eyes fixed on them unblinkingly. A picture came into his head of a simmering stew, maybe with pummeled *kirta* shoots and wild-herb flavoring.

"Master," he whispered, drawing closer to Shingen-Hu carefully. A Master could paralyze an animal with thought while an assistant dispatched it with a rock or cudgel. "Over there across the path, below the bush. Do you see it? We could eat our fill this evening." He waited. "*Food* . . . A thick stew of *skredgen*, seasoned with *var*." Shingen-Hu's eyes flickered. He turned his head. "There," Thrax murmured. "Do you see? You can still do it, Master. Your powers have not deserted you."

Shingen-Hu licked his lips hungrily and stared. The *skredgen* watched them, motionless. The Master's arm rose shakily, and a finger of his bony hand pointed from the folds of tattered sleeve. The finger jabbed commandingly. The *skredgen* yawned and rose to its feet; then turned its back and walked away, swishing its tail contemptuously.

"Alms . . . alms for the holy who have fallen upon evil times," Thrax called, brandishing his bowl in the square of the village they came to at the bottom of the track.

"Everyone's fallen on evil times these days. Where have you two been?" a woman asked scornfully as she passed.

One of a group of laborers who were idling outside a tavern called out, "'Oly men, are yer? Let's see something' 'oly, then."

"That's what all the beggars who come through here tell us," another said. "Take us all for fools out here, they do."

"We've seen enough city thieves before. Away with the pair o' ye," a third told them.

"We're not thieves. We're genuine," Thrax insisted defiantly. "This is a Master. He has remained here, that countless others may arise."

"'Im? A Master? That walkin' bag o' rags? Looks more ter me like the only currents 'e'd know anythin' abaht are the ones 'e pours dahn 'is throat." The others laughed derisively.

"Here's my staff," the second who had spoken said, holding it up. "A good, solid wooden one. Show us the passing-through of a hand. A junior adept can do that. It should be easy enough to do in his sleep for a"—he looked slyly from side to side, inviting the others to share the joke—"*Master.*" They sniggered obligingly.

"You can do it," Thrax murmured imploringly to Shingen-Hu. "Your powers haven't deserted you." But Shingen-Hu just stood and stared at the staff glassily.

They were chased from the village by a jeering mob who pelted them with rocks and garbage, while hounds barked at their heels. Nieru hung very dim in the sky that night. Probably, Thrax thought, because the god was ashamed.

❋   ❋   ❋

In the city of Orenash at the temple of Vandros, the high priest Ethendor had a vision. A spirit from Hyperia appeared to him and spoke in his mind, telling of great events that would soon come to pass. Filled with wonder at the things he learned, Ethendor hurried to inform the king.

"Our actions to placate Vandros were inspired. We have been tested and found not to be wanting. We shall be saved."

"Tested? How have we been tested?" the king asked.

"By the gods who look down from Hyperia. We were set the task of sending them disciples, and we have measured well. Hence we have been chosen to be the prime servants to the gods when the Great Awakening comes."

"The Great Awakening, at last! Tell me, what was revealed?"

Ethendor's voice trembled portentously. "Soon now, the days will return and the stars will shine again. The heavens will radiate their splendor as never before. Then shall the people of Waroth be called and arise to the sky in great multitudes. Hyperia itself shall be opened to them. Thus it has been revealed to me by the lord of all gods."

The king marveled at the high priest's words. "Truly it was spoken? These plagues shall be lifted from us and the world restored?"

"A mighty war has been fought among the gods. The power that lights the sky was stolen and extinguished, but now it has been reclaimed. The pretenders who desecrated the banner of Nieru have been vanquished by the true bearers of Vandros's green."

"And now, many are to arise?"

"The time has come for the last of the unclean and the profane who have defiled Hyperia to be exterminated. The faithful from Waroth shall be the wrath and the instrument. Thou, O King, will be their leader, and I, the prophet who will inspire them."

"We are to see Hyperia?" The king was dumbfounded.

Ethendor was exuberant. "We are to rule Hyperia!"

Chapter Forty-five

I f JEVEX was indeed what the evidence seemed to indicate, it meant that the Jevlenese war industries were merely what the architects of the Federation had been doing on the surface of Uttan. Inside, they had hollowed out the entire planet and installed an expanded version of JEVEX as a single, monolithic, supercomputing matrix, servicing the Jevlenese world-system via communications though h-space. The intention had doubtless been to acquire, eventually, a system of their own capable of rivaling or even surpassing VISAR; but to keep the project secret, they had concentrated it all in one place instead of spreading it out across hundreds of worlds in the way VISAR was spread. The equipment actually functioning on Jevlen was merely part of the remote interface system into it.

In this way, the unique conditions had been created which allowed the matrix universe to come into being. Hunt christened it the "Entoverse," or "universe inside," as opposed to the familiar "Exoverse." The choice pointed to the obvious term "Ents" for its inhabitants, which was duly adopted, the Tolkien-esque connotation being considered doubly appropriate.

All of which was very attractive and exciting, and could give scientists new ideas to amuse themselves with for years. But, as Danchekker pointed out, it was all still nothing but speculation. A Phantasmagoria of software-originated delusions could not be ruled out simply because of Nixie's convictions, and a planet-size JEVEX contained in Uttan was just as capable of creating them as a distributed JEVEX was. In other words, until somebody actually went to Uttan and looked, they were no nearer to knowing if an Entoverse actually existed.

But if JEVEX was concentrated on Uttan, then Eubeleus's motive was obviously to gain control of it; and whatever his plans were after that, they spelled no good. Hence there was a justification for taking the whole thing to JPC and the Thuriens. Such an approach would entail Garuth's going direct to Calazar. Since the team was only talking conjecture at this stage, to insure that Garuth's case would be as convincing as possible they devoted an all-night session to going over the questions that the Thuriens might come up with and seeing what other known peculiarities of Phantasmagoria the Entoverse theory could be made to account for.

The pattern-switching algorithm that Hunt had postulated for moving clusters of activated cells—solid objects, in the Ent world of perception—provided a possible explanation for a range of mystifying phenomena. Shilohin, in reviewing early Thurien processing methods, discovered that it had been common practice for the leading edge of a pattern that was being shifted through the matrix to activate before the trailing edge was switched off. Thus there would be a slight overlap of the two images, causing the pattern to be fractionally longer in the direction of motion than when it was at rest. Moreover, the degree of elongation would increase with the propagation speed. That one fact would account for the absence in the Entoverse of the invariances of dimension with motion—and because of the effects attributed to the planetary rotation that VISAR had inferred, with time and with spatial orientation, too— that gave the Exoverse the regularity and consistency that made possible the organized body of knowledge called science, the construction of machines, and the technologies that sprang from using them.

What about the apparent ability of solid objects in the Entoverse to penetrate one another on occasions? It was not difficult to see how that might happen if one of the "quantum numbers" defining an activated cell was some kind of priority indicator. Two objects meeting would, in effect, be competing to possess the same cells. If, as was usually the case, they were composed of equal-priority elements, they would simply bounce apart. But if one happened to be designated higher-priority, it would "borrow" the volume previously belonging to the other object for as long as their parts coincided, returning it to its previous condition upon separation. Similar causes could be found for such other phenomena as the differing "affinities" of some materials for others, the inconsistencies of cause and effect that made prediction in the Entoverse a risky business, and the sudden discontinuities that appeared as cataclysms and catastrophes.

And when the scientists got down to talking more about it, the apparent miracle-workings of some of the Ents began to sound less farfetched. The Ents were composed at the elementary level of information-processing quanta, after all, and it did not seem so strange that they should be able to influence things around them by what they would perceive as thought. Possibly, for example, they were able to change the activity levels of the constituent cells in an object, and thereby modulate its response to "gravity," or endow it with some other radiated force. That would also go a long way toward explaining the ayatollahs' unshakable faith in the validity of magic. In their world, "magical" effects were commonplace. It might also have had something to do with their uncanny aptitude for interacting directly with the inner processing functions of a Thurien computer, too.

"You know, I'm getting a feeling that a lot of what we dismiss as myth back on Earth wasn't mythical at all," Gina said to Hunt at one point when they broke for coffee. "The war with the Titans, the menagerie around Mount Olympus, gods throwing mountains down out of the sky and swallowing up cities . . . those things really *happened.* Except it was in a different place. The agents they sent to Earth included Ents, and the things the Ents talked about from their own past got mixed up with the real history going on around them."

A little later Hunt remarked, "Erwin Schrödinger thought that the reason our macroscopic world is so much bigger than the quantum scale is because the orderliness that we need to make sense of things could only evolve at a level where quantum fluctuations are swamped out. So, order emerged from underlying uncertainty. But if this Entoverse business turns out to be right, it means that a universe of macroscopic unpredictability evolved out of the mathematically precise operations of computation. Ironic, that, when you think about it, isn't it?"

In the same kind of way that the ubiquitous photon fluid carried energy and information through the Exoverse, the sub-fabric of the Entoverse consisted of vast, dynamically transforming pattern streams of data. The datastreams were injected from the outside and, as they were processed through the cellular ocean of the matrix, flowed and converged toward output zones where they were extracted back to the external Exoverse.

That immediately suggested a parallel to mass-energy being sucked into black holes in the familiar universe. Duncan speculated that the purple spiral that Nixie described in the sky was an accretion vortex forming at one of the data outlets. In that case, were the Entoverse's "stars" the inlets? If so, it would presumably have become a lot darker for the inhabitants in the time since the Ganymeans withdrew JEVEX. Interestingly, MacArthur, a recently emerged ayatollah, had raved on at one point about the gods putting the stars out.

Nixie had described certain "families" of stars that oscillated about and through the brightest member of the group on a one-year cycle. From the approximate positions and seasons that she gave, ZORAC generated visual simulations which with some trial and error matched her recollections closely. The results were compatible with a model in which the "star" that Phantasmagoria orbited existed as one data-inlet point of many arranged in a regular cubical lattice throughout the matrix. Stars belonging to the same row in the grid would appear to come together and separate again as the planet passed through a point in line with them. Such an arrangement of inlets and outlets would have been efficient for distributing the workload evenly through the processing volume.

That left one final mystery that the team felt should have at least a tentative explanation before they approached Calazar: How could the Ents have become aware that an Exoverse existed, and have managed to escape into it? Surprisingly, it was Danchekker who proposed an answer, after talking at length with Nixie. They presented their conclusions to Hunt, Garuth, and Shilohin in Garuth's office at lunchtime the next day, when they reconvened after snatching a few hours of sleep in the morning.

Danchekker addressed the group standing, adopting his characteristic lecturer pose, his hands loosely clasping the lapels of his jacket. Garuth listened from behind his desk, while Shilohin sat across from him in a chair pushed to one side. Nixie was perched on another chair, swiveled around to face the room from a panel of screens taking up part of one wall. Hunt, arms folded, leaned with his back against the door. One of the last things Caldwell had said was that about the only thing left for Hunt to bring back this time would be a universe. Hunt had replied jokingly that it was a pretty tall order.

"The Ents evolved as natural creatures of their world, which had come into being inside a high-density, high-throughput, pattern-processing, computing matrix," Danchekker said. He was speaking as if the hypothesis were fact, in effect rehearsing the team in its supporting role to Garuth, who intended going to Calazar immediately. "In the process, they developed an ability to read and interpret the flows of information passing through their world, in a similar way to that in which creatures of our world learned to read energy flows—photon streams. Now, a primary function of the matrix within which this took place was the handling of huge volumes of neural input-output traffic. In other words, those information streams flowed into and out of the Jevlenese minds coupled into the system. The streams carried coded representations of sensory impressions, concepts, and perceptions derived from the world outside.

Some of the more gifted Ents learned to 'tune in,' as it were, to those currents—to adjust their own mental processes to a sympathetic mode which enabled them to extract information which they found to be intelligible."

"We saw them as visions," Nixie put in. "Now I know that they were scenes from this universe outside. But at the time they were unlike anything anyone had ever dreamed of."

Hunt and Duncan Watt had in fact discussed such a possibility themselves. Ironically, the main reason why Hunt had not taken it further before was that he had been unable to see a sure way to convince Danchekker!

"Of course," Danchekker said. Then he continued. "Lacking in any scientific tradition or knowledge of the Exoverse, they had no terms to describe the things they experienced. They could interpret them only as visions from a higher realm, or world beyond, and so forth." He swung himself from side to side to take in his imaginary class. "Now, there is no reason to suppose that the relative strengths of the various natural forces in the Entoverse were comparable to the ratios that we happen to know. In particular, the domination of gravity at the macroscopic level, which gives our world much of its physical character and establishes the primacy of the role played by mass and weight, seems not to have been so pronounced. To say exactly why, we shall have to wait until we know more about the actual physics. But from Nixie and VISAR, I get the feeling that surface effects may have played a greater part."

"Because of the smaller scale of things?" Garuth hazarded.

Danchekker released one lapel to show a hand briefly. "We can't really say. There are no grounds at the moment for postulating that the counterparts of electrical charge, coulomb attraction, and hence molecular adhesion were anything like the quantities we know."

Hunt listened, intrigued. This was a side to it that he hadn't gotten around to pursuing.

Danchekker went on. "As I see it, these underlying 'currents' that pervaded everything could manifest themselves as entities with real, physical attributes in a way that has no counterpart in our world. Through mental interaction, their effects could be harnessed, focused, directed, and transformed into forces."

"What you call magic," Nixie supplied. "The bolts of energy that some adepts could project at will. The ability of some to levitate themselves and other objects up off the ground."

Danchekker raised a finger to hold the room's attention for a moment longer. "The strongest currents, however, flowed high above the surface as celestial phenomena. Through their ability to influence objects and events remotely as we have already seen, some of the Ents discovered how to draw these currents lower until they could intercept the flow directly. With this power available to be transformed into force, they could actually be carried away, up to the exit zones—and that, of course, is how they came to find themselves in the neural systems that the couplers were linked to, looking out at a new state of existence which none had seen other than as a vision, and many had never seen at all."

Shilohin glanced at the others to assess their reactions. "The information pattern that constituted the Ent personality was somehow impressed upon the datastream and transferred with it to express itself in the brain patterns of the Exoverse host."

Danchekker remained still for a few seconds. Then he let go of his pose and stalked slowly across the room until he was standing in front of the display panel near Nixie. "Exactly how is something I'm not entirely clear about," he admitted.

Neither was Hunt. "Are Calazar and his people going to buy it?" he asked, looking around. "According to VISAR, the pictures that Nixie remembers are really constructs built from the elements activated in her human neural system. That's why she remembers herself as having human form. Doesn't that give us an indication of just how 'alien' the intelligence-carrying complexes that evolved in the Entoverse were? How could a mind with origins like that have found anything sufficiently compatible in a human head to give it a basis for functioning at all?"

Danchekker turned away from the blank screens. "Oh, I agree, it's remarkable. Quite astonishing, in fact, if you want my candid opinion. But are we not driven to the conclusion that it happened? Exactly *how* it happened is a question we can only defer until we are better equipped with the information necessary to have a hope of answering it. Perhaps we simply don't know enough about minds." He tossed out a hand. "Which gives us an even stronger reason for wanting Uttan investigated."

"I take it this process was irreversible?" Garuth asked.

"Oh, quite," Danchekker replied, nodding. "The configuration defining the Ent-being was lost when it entered the output zone. Lost from that universe, literally."

"Like a black-hole transfer," Hunt remarked. "The information content was extracted and reappeared elsewhere."

"Nothing physical was actually extracted then?" Not a scientist, Garuth was still having to grapple with a lot of this new idea. "What happened to the Ent-bodies?"

Shilohin looked at him, pausing for a moment before answering. "I don't think you completely have the point, Garuth," she said. "There *was* nothing physical. They were only information constructs to begin with. Their whole world was. The fact that they *perceived* it as having material form was purely an evolutionary artifact of their universe."

"Ah, yes . . . now I see." Garuth sat back to absorb the implication fully. Then he frowned. "Yet, didn't you say they had a way of going back? Nixie told us about 'spirits' who returned to inspire and recruit disciples, and taught them how to arise in turn."

"There was another way," Danchekker supplied. "The Jevlenese neural couplers, which the ayatollahs could use, just like anyone else. They found that via the couplers—"

Just then, ZORAC interrupted, saying it had an urgent message.

"What is it, ZORAC?" Garuth inquired.

"Langerif, the deputy chief of police, is outside the door now. He states that he is taking control of PAC in the name of Jevlenese independence and self-determination. He requests that you instruct your administration staff to transfer all powers and authority accordingly, effective as of now."

Chapter Forty-six

Garuth rose to his feet bemusedly as Langerif strode haughtily into the room, followed by several of his officers. He was holding a written proclamation of some kind, which he set down on the desk. All of the group were wearing sidearms: standard Jevlenese police-issue beam pistols, which could fire a variable plasma charge capable of being set anywhere from a mildly uncomfortable shock to lethality.

Hunt groaned to himself as he realized how completely they had failed to see the obvious: the police and their training class; all the other Jevlenese who had been appearing at PAC over the past few days. But neither he nor anyone else had made the vital connection. They had dismissed the Obayin assassination—assuming it had been—as purely a move by the *Ichena* to protect their headworld business. Of *course* Eubeleus would need somebody to secure the Jevlen end of things while he took over Uttan. Even Cullen had missed it. Everyone had been too engrossed with the Entoverse to give anything else a thought.

"You will have been notified by now that the Ganymean occupation of Jevlen is to cease anyway," Langerif said to

Garuth. Evidently there was a leak in the system somewhere.
"But to forestall the prospect of one occupying force merely
being replaced by another, we, the Jevlenese people, are taking
charge of our own future, now. There is our declaration. You
will please instruct all personnel under your authority,
Ganymean, Thurien, Terran, and Jevlenese, to comply. It is
not a matter for compromise or negotiation."

"No . . . that isn't correct," Garuth protested. "A motion was
merely proposed at JPC. There has been no decision. You—"

Langerif silenced him with a wave. "A mere formality. The
spirit of the Council's intent is quite clear: to minimize risk to
persons and property, and to preserve order. The situation
here is plainly about to get out of hand. To delay firm action
until official orders are issued would be irresponsible. It is
therefore our decision to preempt the emergency before it
escalates."

"Don't buy it," Hunt murmured. "He's not the JPC. Neither are the people who wound up his spring. It's a power grab."

"This doesn't concern you. Confine yourself to your own
affairs," Langerif snapped.

His line had been calculated to sway Ganymeans by
appealing to reason and noble motives; the token show of force
was deliberate, to throw them off balance. And had this been
Thuriens as the Jevlenese were used to dealing with, it might
have worked. But Garuth was from an earlier epoch of
Ganymeans—and he had spent enough time on Earth to absorb
a little of human psychology.

"No!" he retorted, straightening up fully. "The terms of my
office are quite definite, and there is no emergency about to
break out. Who do you think you're fooling with this charade?
We *know* that you are in league with the Axis. And JPC will
very soon know, too. Now get out of my office."

Langerif whitened and moved his hand pointedly to the
butt of his weapon.

"What do you think you're going to do?" Shilohin asked
him derisively, backing Garuth's stand. "Your troops aren't here
yet. There's a room full of PAC security officers just down the
hall."

Garuth stretched out a hand toward a call button on a panel by his desk. But as he did so, Langerif turned and called toward the doorway, and a squad of armed police entered with their weapons at ready, led by another officer.

"Pig!" Nixie hissed. Langerif ignored her and waved his men into position to cover the room.

"I regret to inform you that your security department is not all as loyal as you believed," Langerif sneered. "I gave you an opportunity to cooperate reasonably, but you force me to be drastic. Very well." He motioned sharply to the others in the room. "The rest of you, on your feet. You will go with the officer, now. Trouble will only make things worse."

"This is an outrage!" Danchekker, who was still standing by the screens, shaking with indignation, found his voice at last. "Do you imagine for one moment that bringing your gutter-snipe politics in here is going to make the slightest—"

"Save it, Chris," Hunt said resignedly. "This isn't the time or place."

While Garuth stood staring helplessly at gunpoint, the others began filing toward the door between the impassive, yellow-uniformed police.

Meanwhile, throughout the building other groups of police and disguised Jevlenese auxiliaries had begun rounding up bewildered Ganymeans from their workstations and offices. In Del Cullen's office, Cullen stood, hands raised with two Jevlenese covering him, while a police lieutenant scanned through status displays on his deskside screen. Outside, Koberg and Lebansky had also been taken by surprise and were being disarmed and searched. Through the doorway, Cullen could see Koberg measuring up distances with his eyes.

"Don't try anything, Mitch," he called. "It won't change the war."

One of the guards jabbed him in the ribs with a gun. He winced.

"Shut up," the lieutenant in the chair at the screen told him over his shoulder.

And then, strange things began happening.

The sounds of running feet and confused shouting came

from the corridor beyond the outer room where Koberg and Lebansky were. The guards who were with them looked around, startled. Langerif's voice came from somewhere outside the door. "Quick! Get out here, all of you. Never mind them. Lieutenant Norzalt, Pascars, and Ritoiter, stay there and watch the prisoners."

The guards in the outer room rushed into the corridor. As the last one disappeared, the automatic door slammed shut behind them. At the same instant, a cry of pain came from the door into Cullen's office. The two guards who had been left turned their heads instinctively—which was all the distraction that Koberg and Lebansky needed.

Inside the office, Cullen stared in bewilderment as the Jevlenese police lieutenant fell from the chair, writhing and clawing the phones of the Ganymean communications kit from his ears. A high-pitched shrieking noise was coming from the phones, painful even from where Cullen was standing.

"Go for it, turkey," a voice said in his own ear. Shaking himself into life, Cullen seized the lieutenant by the collar before he could recover, lifted him up and took his weapon, and then laid him out with a couple of fast cracks to the jaw. He went through the door and came into the outer room just as Koberg and Lebansky were straightening up over the limp forms of the two guards who had been left.

"What in hell's going on?" Cullen demanded, still at a loss as the other two retrieved their guns.

The door from the corridor opened again, and three more Jevlenese police rushed in, coming to a confused halt when they saw the Americans covering them and their two unconscious colleagues on the floor. Cullen and his two men disarmed them, then went outside. There was no sign of Langerif or what had caused the pandemonium. Two Ganymeans were standing, stupefied, by one of the walls.

"What in hell's going on?" Cullen asked again.

"We don't know," one of the Ganymeans answered. "We were being arrested. Then the police were ordered away and left us here. They're running all over the place. They seem to be getting conflicting orders."

"Was Langerif here?"

"No. We heard his voice, but we didn't see him."

Just then, two more Jevlenese police came running around a corner. Koberg and Lebansky stopped them and relieved them of their guns. The door into Cullen's office opened obligingly, and the latest additions to the catch were shoved through to join the six already inside. Then the door closed again.

"Those voices were coming out of the walls," Koberg said, looking around, mystified. "The place is running itself. It's isolating them in small groups."

And suddenly, Cullen realized what was happening. "It's ZORAC!" he exclaimed. "The goddamn computer's doing it!"

"What did you expect?" the familiar voice said in his ear. "Langerif is in Garuth's office, making a move to take over. We've been infiltrated. There's a confused situation in security. Most of your men are still with you, but some are on the other side. There are six more police heading your way along R-5."

"Let's check that first," Cullen said, and hurried away with Koberg and Lebansky following.

The lieutenant in Cullen's office was not the only Jevlenese equipped with a Ganymean communicator to have been overwhelmed by a loud, high-frequency tone suddenly injected into the audio. Elsewhere in the building, other squads were running this way and that to contradictory orders. Half a dozen were trapped in an elevator that had stopped between floors. In the lobby area, a contingent that had gone outside to investigate a nonexistent threat were stranded there when the doors closed, and more than a few in various places were stuck in half-closed doors that refused to budge. From the numbers, it was evident that additional forces had been let in by confederates already inside.

In Garuth's office and the room outside, the lights had gone out. Hunt, who had worked himself as far as the doorway, heard muted, high-pitched tones in the darkness, and then confused yelling. He dropped to the floor and moved through to just beyond the door.

There was scuffling and confused mutterings. Then Langerif's voice called out something in Jevlenese from inside the office—he had evidently disposed of his Ganymean communicator. The translation came through the earpiece that Hunt was wearing: "Spread out. Cover all the exits. Abrintz, take three men out to the concourse and secure the elevators."

Another voice responded. "Werselek, Quon, Fassero, come with—"

Then Langerif again, from inside the office. "I didn't say that. It's some kind of trick. Stay where you are."

Only to be countermanded by, "*This* is Langerif speaking. Do as I say."

"Don't listen. That's a fake."

"No, I'm not. He is."

"What do we do?" a voice pleaded somewhere in the blackness.

Then ZORAC's voice said quietly in Hunt's ear, "Move about eight feet to your right along the wall, and then across an alcove to a door in the far wall. It's open, and leads into an equipment room."

Hunt began worming his way along the base of the wall as ZORAC had indicated. Sounds of shooting and cries of panic came from the direction of the doorway leading out to the elevator concourse, accompanied by a Terran voice shouting commands. A Jevlenese voice shouted, "All right, we surrender!"

"Come out with your hands up," a Terran voice ordered. "Is that all of them in there, Sergeant?"

"All cleared here, sir. Three hostiles dead."

"What's going on out there?" Langerif's voice demanded.

"PAC security is outside," a voice replied. "They've taken over the whole floor. We're trapped."

"That's impossible."

"That wasn't me speaking," Langerif's voice said again.

Reaching the door that ZORAC had indicated, Hunt felt his way through. Del Cullen's voice called out, "You calculated wrong, Langerif. Half your men were working undercover for us. We've got the rest of the building tied up. It's over. Throw down your guns and come out."

"Do as he says," Langerif's voice instructed.

"Take no notice," another Langerif said.

Hunt bumped his head painfully on an edge of projecting metal. Feeling ahead with his fingers, he hauled himself carefully to his feet, tracing the shapes of equipment racking and supports around him. It came to him then, what was happening. ZORAC was a ship's computer. Its first priority was the safety of the *Shapieron*'s crew. Seeing them being rounded up at gunpoint had spurred it into the only action that it was capable of.

Langerif had grasped it, too. "Very clever, for a machine," his voice snarled in the darkness. "But if the idea is to protect your Ganymeans, you'd better quit right now. We've got two of them here and a bunch more outside the door. If the lights aren't back in five seconds, we shoot."

"Hear that, you men?" another voice called out. "There aren't any Terrans. It was the computer."

Hunt heard the door close, and then the light came on to reveal him alone in a space crammed with electronics cubicles and cabling.

"Great special effects," he complimented.

"It was the best I could do," ZORAC said. "I've got some of them shut up here and there around the place, but they're starting to sort themselves out. Some of PAC security came out on the other side, too."

"What's the general situation?"

"A mess."

"What about the others?"

"Garuth and Shilohin are still there in his office. I got Danchekker into an elevator across the hall while the lights were out. Nixie took off and lost herself somewhere."

"And the rest?"

"Cullen and his guys are in the middle of a fight down in security. Duncan and Sandy have been grabbed by police in the UNSA labs. Gina got away from her quarters before they arrived. She wants to talk to you."

"Put her through."

"And so does Langerif. He's demanding that you give

yourself up, otherwise he'll shoot Garuth."

Hunt drew a long breath. There were some things that the Jevlenese might be able to explain away when this got back to JPC, he thought; but not murdering the planetary governor. Even Langerif had to be smart enough to know that.

"He's bluffing," Hunt said.

"You think so?"

"Yes. Tell him you're not getting a response. My headset must have been knocked off in the dark, right?"

"I hope you're right," ZORAC replied, in a masterfully contrived you're-supposed-to-understand-these-people tone of voice. "Here's Gina."

"Vic? ZORAC's told me the score. It's no use heading this way. They're everywhere. Right now I'm in an empty suite that ZORAC found."

Hunt thought quickly. There would be no point in trying to get to any of the Thurien couplers into VISAR, since those would have been the first places to be secured. And the next thing the Jevlenese would do after getting the complex's backup systems running would be to cut ZORAC's connection into PAC. He should get to Gina first, while ZORAC was still available to help.

"ZORAC, can you get us together somewhere?" he said.

"You can't get back out through Garuth's office. Head through the compartment at the rear. There should be a way down. It looks as if you were right about Langerif, by the way."

Behind a partition at the back of the equipment room, some runs of cabling and ducting went down a well to the level below, where a maintenance hatch gave access to an engineers' inspection gallery. From there, Hunt came out through a machinery compartment into a tool room, and thence into a stairway that seemed clear for the moment. One level down, he entered a passage that led to an elevator, which ZORAC already had waiting to take him down to a level where several large dining rooms were situated. A lot of Jevlenese office workers were milling around, while frantic police officers tried to tell the managers what was happening. In the general confusion, Hunt managed to slip through into the warren of kitchens and passages at the rear, where ZORAC had also directed Gina. Hunt found her in a space behind a water-heating system and a pumping compartment. She seemed shaken but in good shape.

"What do we do now?" she asked.

"ZORAC, what are the options? Can we get out?"

"That's probably the best bet. Look, there are Jevlenese engineers in the control section right now, switching in the backup communications and monitoring systems. I could be cut off at any moment. I'll give you directions, now, to a way out through the basement that I'll unlock. It leads into the city's freight-moving system. First, you need to go down through the back stairs from the passage outside where you are, to a garbage-compacting plant . . ."

They lost ZORAC shortly after, but found their way down through the route that it had described. The exit was unlocked, and they entered a system of tunnels and shafts, much of it collapsing from disrepair, which brought them into the automated sublevels of Shiban. When they had gone what they judged to be a safe distance from PAC, they began ascending via catwalks and stairways to reemerge into habitation. A short distance farther on, Hunt recognized the street outside the hotel that Nixie had taken him to. "Okay, I think I know where we are," he told Gina.

"That's great. But where do we want to be?"

The *Shapieron* was the obvious place—assuming ZORAC or whoever was in charge aboard the ship didn't decide to take it up from the surface for some reason. But with the police possibly on the alert for them, Hunt put their chances of getting to Geerbaine as slim. And even if they did, access to the pad where the *Shapieron* stood would surely be impossible.

"Well, there's only one American I know in town," Hunt said. "What we do when we get there, I'm not sure. But keep your voice down on the streets. There's probably an order out to watch for Terrans."

Chapter Forty-seven

There were plenty of police about, but from the way they were positioned they seemed to be a reserve force drawn up around PAC rather than a cordon sealing it off. At any rate, they hadn't cleared the surrounding precincts, and Hunt and Gina were able to blend in easily enough. Green crescents were everywhere, and the ayatollahs were out in force delivering perorations to excited crowds. Although none of what was being said was comprehensible to the two Terrans, the fever of excitement in the air was impossible to mistake. It was as if the city were alive with anticipation of some imminent event.

As they passed through the buzzing arcades and plazas, Hunt tried to make more sense out of what had happened. He didn't believe that the real motivation could be simply a straight takeover of the administration for the reasons Langerif had claimed. JPC was already talking about winding the existing administration up, and the obvious thing would have been to wait and see what came of it.

The only other possible aim was to prevent details getting back to JPC and the powers behind it of what was happening at PAC. But all that anyone outside could know was that the Ganymeans were checking out the main JEVEX sites, and all that could tell anyone was that a lot of JEVEX was not where it was supposed to be. That meant that whoever was behind it did not want people making the connection with Uttan; which was another way of saying that they were very anxious not to give JPC any grounds for reconsidering its decision to let Eubeleus go there.

The street they were following crossed a small square in which a wildly gesticulating ayatollah clad in a yellow tunic and green smock was haranguing a crowd pressed from wall to wall. There was no quick way through. They could either work their way across to where the street continued on the far side, or back up and find another way around. Hunt looked resignedly at Gina. She shrugged back. He turned and began edging his way between the waving, applauding Jevlenese.

What he sensed wasn't the uplifting, jubilant kind of excitement that went with carnivals and festivals. It was more intense, fervently passionate. The faces around them were inflamed, mouths writhing mindless slogans, eyes glazed, oblivious to all but some inner rapture. This was the beast that made lynch mobs and Nuremberg rallies out of the same people who brought their children to Sunday-afternoon parades.

No, Hunt told himself after they had gone a few yards. The beast wasn't in the crowd. It was up *there*, on the makeshift platform of packing boxes fronted with banners. It didn't belong to the rational universe. It was a product of another place, another reality.

He looked at the crowd again: unaware, unseeing, incapable of knowing. Nothing would ever change of its own accord there. And he looked at the shrewd, hawklike features of the speaker, scanning, alert to every feedback and cue, trying to grasp the alienness staring out from behind the glittering eyes.

The eyes seemed to meet Hunt's for an instant, and even at that distance Hunt had the eerie feeling that his thoughts were being read as plainly as his face. He wondered how long ago the being inside the body he was looking at had found itself staring out at this new world. Whether his initial reactions had been of terror or otherwise, he had come to terms with his new existence and its irreversibility, and mastered the survival skills of the niche in which he found himself. And all the while, the mass of those who had been born there and belonged there immersed themselves in fantasies and waited for the Thuriens to repair their decaying cities. And from their unwitting ranks, the intruders had recruited the followers that they needed around them to make them feel secure. Just as was happening right now, in front of Hunt's eyes.

Just as had been happening on Earth all through its history because of the agents that the Jevlenese had sent there. Those were the ones whose insecurity had appeared as paranoia or the craving to control others, in a way that normal people were incapable of comprehending. And now Hunt could see why that should be so. The agents that had infiltrated Earth to perpetrate some of its worst episodes of brutality and inhumanity had not been human at all. Their only goal had always been what Hunt was witnessing right now: to secure themselves against other rivals from the Entoverse by reinforcing their own army of fanatics. The simple, undeveloped peoples of Earth became what misplaced Thurien benevolence had turned the bulk of the Jevlenese into: a ready-made pool of exploitable recruiting fodder.

Exploitable recruiting fodder . . . The phrase kept running through Hunt's mind all the way to Murray's.

"Who is it?" Lola's voice inquired from nowhere identifiable around the purple door with the white surround.

"It's Vic. Is Murray in there?"

Murray's voice came on the line at once. "What do you want this time? You've already got me a bad reputation. My friends don't like the company I've been keeping."

"Let us in. It's important."

"Us? Oh, shit, not again. Have you brought those two walking tanks back?"

"There's just me and a friend called Gina. She's a journalist—American."

"My life story isn't for sale yet. I haven't figured out the ending."

"Look, PAC's been taken over by a Jevlenese coup of some kind. The Shiban police are in on it."

"Jesus Christ!"

"It could be planetwide. I don't know. But maybe the Federation isn't dead yet. We have to get in off the streets."

The door opened. Hunt nodded at Gina, and she went through ahead. Murray was waiting for them in the lounge. "Gina Marin," Hunt said. "This is Murray. He's from the West Coast, too. San Francisco."

"Yeah. It's a small galaxy." They nodded, then shook hands loosely.

"Hi. I've heard about you, Murray. I'm another friend of Nixie's."

"I guess we can swap all the questions about home later. Is she okay? From the amount I've seen of her lately I figured she'd shacked up there at PAC or joined the Marines."

"She's been a big help," Hunt said. "She was okay the last time I saw her. We got separated in the commotion. Gina and I only just managed to get out." He spotted the companel and screen in front of the chair that Murray normally used and moved across to it. "Mind if I try something?" He tapped pads to activate it and call up channel fifty-six in the way he knew by now for Jevlenese units. "ZORAC, can you read?" He waited a moment. "Anything here?" There was no response.

"Bad news?" Murray asked.

Hunt nodded resignedly. "They've cut the connection via PAC from the *Shapieron.*"

Murray said something at the panel in Jevlenese, and a short message appeared on the screen.

"What's that?" Hunt asked.

"It says they're on an emergency system. Services are restricted," Murray said. He motioned with his head to indicate a cabinet with bottles and glasses, at the same time raising his eyebrows questioningly.

Hunt nodded. "Thanks. I could use one."

"Me, too," Gina said without caring what it was, and sank into a chair.

Murray squatted down and opened the cabinet door. "So

what gives?" he asked over his shoulder as he poured.

"The Jevlenese sprang a surprise at PAC. They've turfed out the Ganymeans and taken over. I'm not really sure what happens next."

"Jesus!" Murray doubled the measure that he had poured into his own glass and downed half of it at a gulp. He straightened up and passed out the glasses, then propped himself against the edge of the large table. "Is the Jolly Green Giant who took off yesterday with the shipload of rollers mixed up with it?"

"If so, it hasn't come out into the open yet, but we're pretty sure, yes," Hunt said. He downed a draft from his glass, then asked in turn, "What's going on in the city? The place is electric. Green crescents out everywhere. They seem to be expecting something."

"It started yesterday. The big rumor out there is that JEVEX is coming back. The head freaks are delirious about it. Nobody around here's gonna spill too many tears if the Gs do have to walk."

Gina let her arm fall slackly to rest on the arm of the chair and looked across the room. Her tension had eased now that they were secure for the time being, allowing the full impact of what had happened to get through. Her face was drawn, sapped of vigor by her acceptance of the hopelessness that she had been putting off.

"So that's it," she said, her voice flat. "It's over. We wait around until the cavalry limps in, and go home with what's left of the pieces—if we don't get picked up in the meantime."

"Isn't there anywhere they'll leave a guy alone?" Murray muttered. "Does this mean they're gonna be setting up the IRS here?"

"That might be the least of your problems," Gina said humorlessly.

"What about the others back there?" Murray asked.

"We're not sure. We only just got out."

"So . . . what happens next?"

"I don't know. What do you think, Vic?" Gina looked over at Hunt. But he was sitting with a strange, faraway look on his face and hadn't heard. "Vic, are you okay?"

"Recruiting fodder," Hunt said, still distant. "That's what it's all about."

"What?"

Hunt focused back on the present and looked at them. "It's not over. It hasn't even started."

"What are you talking about?"

"I know why it's so vital for Eubeleus and his cult to get to Uttan." Hunt swallowed hard and paused to collect his words. "*They* were the ones who set you up through Baumer and put the fake memories in your head. Telling us about the *Ichena*'s operation wasn't giving away anything that mattered. In fact it was the decoy. The *Ichena* were set up to be expendable—to direct attention away from what's really happening. When JEVEX comes back on, everyone out there will be flocking back to the couplers, tens of thousands of them. The whole population has been caught on a hook, just like Baumer was."

Gina nodded but looked puzzled. "Yes, I follow what you're saying. But where's it—"

"Don't you see? They'll have half the city on-line when JEVEX comes back up. And what do you think will be down there in the Entoverse? Thousands of them, waiting to come pouring out. Legions of them."

Gina put a hand to her mouth. "Oh my God!"

"What the hell are you two talking about?" Murray asked, looking from one to the other.

But Hunt went on. "*They* were the ones who put Earth back a couple of thousand years and dreamed up the scheme to shut the Thuriens inside a space-time bubble and take over. And despite all the limitations of where and how they originated, they almost got away with it." Hunt raised his glass and took a long swig. "We thought we'd stopped them then, but we were wrong. And now this . . . And right at this moment, unless we can prevent Eubeleus from getting to Uttan, I don't readily see a way of stopping it."

Before Gina could say anything in reply, a chime sounded from the panel.

"What is it, Lola?" Murray called.

"Nixie's here," the house computer announced. "She has a visitor."

Hunt looked up in such surprise, trying to rise as he did so, that he spilled his drink. "Here? She made it? Christ, that's bloody marvel—"

Then Nixie came in, looking pert, unflustered, and none the worse for wear. "Vic! Gina!" She rattled off something in Jevlenese, so used by that time to having ZORAC at hand that it was instinctive. Then she stopped, realizing her mistake, said something else toward the companel, and looked puzzled when it failed to respond.

But Hunt's eyes had widened even more as he saw the tall, lean, bespectacled figure who followed her in.

"Ah, yes, here they are," Danchekker said approvingly. "ZORAC informed us that it had directed you to a way out, just before it was cut off. We assumed that you would make for here." He gazed around and took in the surroundings, including Murray's collection of provocatively displayed girls. "So I've finally been enticed home by a lady of Nixie's profession. Well, it's never too late for a first time in one's life for anything, I suppose."

Chapter Forty-eight

Del Cullen was led into Garuth's office, where Langerif was waiting with several of his officers and other Jevlenese. Garuth sat numbly by one wall of the room, with Shilohin next to him. Also present were a couple of the Thuriens assigned to PAC, whom the Jevlenese had brought up from elsewhere in the complex. Koberg and Lebansky were downstairs with the loyal majority of Cullen's security force, whom the police had disarmed and locked away. They had put up a good fight, but the odds had been against them, and then a threat by Langerif to begin eliminating hostages had finished it.

Without ZORAC, the Jevlenese had a communications problem, since human and Ganymean voices operated over different ranges. The small Jevlenese-Thurien translator disks were fixed-program devices that understood neither Terran languages nor the speech of the *Shapieron* Ganymeans, which was different from Thurien. Langerif therefore instructed that Cullen would convey any communications from Terrans to the Jevlenese, which from the nature of his job he was used to doing, and they would then relay via their translator to the Thuriens, who in turn would talk to Garuth and his staff.

Cullen, however, was not in a mood for cooperating.

"Were you born stupid?" he said to Langerif, speaking in the limited Jevlenese that he had picked up. "Don't you know when you're being set up?"

"What are you talking about?" Langerif asked, taken aback.

"Let's not play games. We know you're with the Axis, right?" Cullen didn't. He was simply ready to try anything that might throw the opposition off balance. "Well, you've seen the kind of value they put on people. Look what happened to Marion Fayne, and to the last guy who tried your job."

"What does that have to do with me?"

"You're just being made the dickhead up front who'll look like he was behind all the trouble that's been going on. Eubeleus is gonna shovel it all on you, and come back from Uttan with clean hands. Then it's your turn to go down the tubes. The Ganymeans are out, and he has a hand in setting up a new administration with JPC that he can control better. Think about it. It makes sense."

Langerif thought for a moment, then walked up to Cullen and slapped him across the face. Cullen sighed. It had been a good try, he decided. But he wasn't going to get anywhere. So he decked Langerif with a right to the jaw, instead. One of the watching Jevlenese felled him with a stun shot. To one side, Garuth closed his eyes.

On the command deck of the *Shapieron*, standing in its berthing area at Geerbaine, Leyel Torres, the ship's acting chief in Garuth's absence, stood looking up at the screens bringing views of the outside and from high over the city from probes that he had sent up on receiving news of the emergency. Rodgar Jassilane, the engineering chief, joined him, while crew appeared from various directions and hurried to their stations. All Ganymeans in the vicinity were being recalled to the ship, and Torres was bringing the vessel up to flight readiness as a precaution.

"They've disconnected zorac from the city net," Jassilane said. "What do you make of it?"

"I don't know what to think. I thought Terrans were unstable enough," Torres answered.

"What are they trying to accomplish?"

"Who knows? Perhaps they're all mad."

"What about the situation here?"

"There are police sealing off the spaceport area, and the Thuriens are protesting. I don't know what's going on."

"Message via VISAR from Thurien," ZORAC announced.

"Yes?" Torres acknowledged.

"Calazar will be through very shortly. Meanwhile, Earth has been alerted. They're locating as many members of JPC as they can."

"Very good."

"What's the last we know of the situation at PAC?" Jassilane asked.

ZORAC answered. "Hunt and Gina were heading for an exit that was clear and open. Danchekker was still in the building. I'd lost track of Nixie. The rest had been detained."

"Hmm," Jassilane murmured.

Torres thought for a moment. "If Hunt and the woman got out, they could hardly remain at large in the city . . . Obviously they couldn't go back to PAC." He raised his voice. "ZORAC, do you have any idea where they'd be most likely to go?"

ZORAC consulted the records accumulated from its illegal spying operations. "I've got some places where Hunt and Nixie talked a lot. One is a hotel, probably not worth considering. The other is a private address."

"Can you locate it?"

ZORAC called up the city directory and plans of the layout from its data bank. "Yes, reference screen seven." A cutaway view of part of the labyrinth appeared, with a residential block in one of the complexes shown highlighted. One of the apartments partway up in it was flashing. "It's on this side of the center, not too far from PAC."

Torres looked at Jassilane questioningly. "Not far from PAC," Jassilane repeated. He nodded. "It's a good bet. If they're out, that's where they'll head for. Check it out."

"ZORAC, prepare another of the ship's probes for immediate launch," Torres ordered.

❀ ❀ ❀

At Murray's, Danchekker and Nixie told their story.

The officer in charge of the police contingent placed in the PAC front lobby had turned out to be one of Nixie's regulars. She had drawn him aside and was in the process of talking her way out, when Danchekker stormed out of one of the elevators, ranting and threatening everyone in sight. On an inspiration, Nixie told the officer that Danchekker was a sex therapist from Earth whom she was assisting in a study of Jevlenese customs. If she was found in the place, she told the officer pointedly, the Shiban chief of police and virtually all the city officials would be public jokes by morning—and guess whose ass would be on the line. She and Danchekker had been bundled quietly out a side door a few minutes later.

After Hunt and Gina related their tale, Hunt went on to repeat the thoughts that he had just begun telling Gina when Danchekker and Nixie arrived. Murray didn't know enough of the background for it to mean much to him, and Nixie couldn't really follow without ZORAC. So, leaving the others to it, they went into another room to make some calls and see what further news they could gather of events at large.

By the time Hunt finished, Danchekker was looking appalled. "Yes," he whispered. "I can see it now . . . Such a world, with its inherent perils and insecurity, would account for the whole Ent nature. And it becomes clear how the idea of escaping to the world they saw through these visions could become their overriding obsession."

"But to escape, they needed hosts to escape into," Hunt said. "And that, I believe, is why the Jevlenese were turned into system junkies. It kept them hooked into the system, and hence get-attable."

Danchekker nodded. "Their numbers grew with time, and the Jevlenese population became victims of what was surely the strangest alien invasion ever: an attack of information viruses from inside a computer, light-years away."

"Except, that was only the preliminary," Hunt said soberly.

He stabbed his finger in the direction of the door. "Outside, there are God knows how many couplers, waiting for the main system to be activated, and on Uttan there's a caretaker crew of Thuriens expecting a shipload of religious pacifists who'll dismantle the military installations." Hunt shook his head emphatically. "That isn't going to happen. Once Eubeleus neutralizes them and gets himself entrenched, he'll be able to make Uttan practically impregnable. And what do you think he'll be doing once JEVEX is running again and we're scratching our heads wondering how to get in?"

The looks on Danchekker's and Gina's faces said there was no need for him to say.

Hunt nodded. "You said a minute ago, Chris, that the Jevlenese were victims of an attack by alien information viruses out of a computer. But what happened before is nothing compared to what'll happen if Eubeleus turns JEVEX on again. Unless we can stop him from getting to Uttan, this planet's going to be hit by an epidemic!"

So finally, it seemed, they had gotten to the bottom of what was going on, and why. But that did nothing to solve the problem of what to do next. Given the means, of course, the first thing would have been to contact the Thuriens and get Eubeleus stopped, but with ZORAC off the air they were incommunicado. So they examined what other options they had.

Danchekker's proposal was to head for the Thurien-controlled refuge at Geerbaine. If Jevlenese were contesting that, they might be able to find some way of getting aboard the *Shapieron*, or failing that, maybe one of the Thurien ships.

Hunt was less confident of their chances of getting there. "It's the first place they'll be looking," he declared. "There's already been trouble even in that area, and some of these cults are just looking for an excuse to get even with Terrans. I don't like it, Chris."

"There's been a lot of activity in that direction," Murray, who had rejoined them by that time, confirmed.

"What, then, do you suggest?" Danchekker invited.

"We might be better off lying low in the city for a while,"

Hunt said. "Maybe we'll find a way of making contact in the meantime."

A worried look crossed Murray's face. "I don't know if it would be smart to stick around this place for too long," he said. "If that Jev cop at PAC talked to Nixie, it's not gonna need a genius to figure out where you're probably holed up."

Silence fell, with nothing any closer to being resolved. Gina stood up and stretched to loosen her shoulders. "I haven't eaten all day," she said. "What kind of options do we have in that direction?"

"I'm just about out," Murray said. "I was about to stock up today. There are a couple of takeaway joints on the block. One's an herbivore place that does a kind of soya greaseburger with seaweed pulp. The other's the local idea of a deli."

Gina pulled a face as she recalled Sandy's squid-shit sandwiches at PAC. "Scrambled eggs with corned-beef hash, sausage pate, and a side order of fries," she murmured, staring wistfully at Murray's wall poster of San Francisco.

"Eggs over medium, bacon, mushrooms, and fried tomatoes," Hunt sighed.

"Yeah . . . it does kinda get to you after a while," Murray agreed. "I might have a few cans of stuff from home left out back. Let me go take a look."

As he got up and moved to the door, the chime sounded from the panel again, and Lola's voice said, "Osaya is calling from upstairs."

"Okay," Murray said. A female Jevlenese voice came on, sounding excited, and Murray said something in reply. While they were talking, Nixie appeared in the doorway. "What's she saying?" Murray asked her. "Something about a hat with a window?"

Nixie talked to Osaya. "Oh, *eprillin!*" she announced, spotting his problem.

"I thought that was a hat," Murray said.

"Yes. But also it means a kind of fish."

"So what's the hell's she talking about a fish with a window?"

"She says there something that look like fish, up there outside window."

Murray shook his head. "Have they been smoking funny stuff up there, or something?"

"I go see." Nixie exchanged a few more words with Osaya, then left.

Murray went into the kitchen, and the others heard him open a cupboard and begin rummaging. Then came the sound of hard objects being thumped down on the floor. "Say, waddya know!" his voice called through the doorway. "Genuine ham . . . And how about some Boston beans?"

"I've never heard of fried tomatoes," Gina said to Hunt. "Is that something else weird that the English do?"

"Delicious," Hunt said. "Especially on a slice of fried bread, with the juice soaking in. But what you really need to finish it off is a bit of black pudding."

"What's black pudding?"

"I rather think that the wise adage about sausages and politics applies even more in this instance," Danchekker advised.

At that moment Nixie's voice came from the panel. "Murray, come see here. Bring Vic up."

Hunt sent Danchekker and Gina a puzzled frown, then rose. Murray stuck his head back through the doorway. "What is it?"

"Come see," Nixie's voice said.

Murray shrugged and withdrew. Hunt followed him out through the front door.

They went up two flights and entered another apartment, situated on the opposite side of the stairwell. The interior was an orgy of feminine extravagance and brilliant colors, with fluffy pink floors that looked like cotton candy, couches and chairs finished in a variety of white, lilac, and red down, outrageously erotic murals, and black walls glowing with constantly changing Mandelbrot patterns. Inside was the tall girl whom Hunt had met before, apparently off-duty at the moment in a simple shirt with pants. She beckoned and led them through a room with an enormous bed, built-in Jacuzzi, and mirrors everywhere, to where Nixie was standing at a window framed by long, silky drapes. Hunt and Murray peered out.

Below and to the sides was a jumble of interconnected roofs, with parts of various walkways and lower parts of the city visible in the spaces between. A roof enclosed the whole area above, with a web of transportation tubes and lighting installations hanging beneath, and two of the vast channels that cut across the city to carry airborne traffic receding into the distance. Whether there was more of the city above that, there was no way of telling.

Hanging motionless in the air above an open area maybe a couple of hundred feet away was a drop-shaped, silver-gray object about the size of a small car. It was featureless except for a couple of ribs that flared into rudimentary fins at the tail end, and a cylindrical device on a retractable metal pylon, which seemed to be nodding inquisitively in their direction.

"Ain't never seen nothing like that before," Murray said, staring at it, nonplussed.

"Is police thing? Come look for us?" Nixie asked nervously.

Hunt shook his head, and a faint smile softened his features. "It's looking for us, but it's not the police," he said. "That's one of the *Shapieron*'s reconnaissance probes. They must have figured out where we are."

"Shit, I hope the cops aren't so fast," Murray muttered.

Hunt thought quickly. "Murray, is there any kind of portable communications gadget here—a remote pad for talking to the house system or something? If the Ganymeans figured this much out, they'll be scanning for Jevlenese transmissions." Murray consulted with Nixie, who said something to Osaya. Osaya went over to a bedside unit and came back with a tablet of what looked like veined, gray marble with gold inlaid designs and gold touchpads. She held it to the window and tried a few codes, then said something that sounded negative.

"Does that talk to the city net?" Hunt asked Murray.

"It should."

"Tell her to try fifty-six."

Murray passed it on, and Osaya tried again. Then a familiar voice said, "Ahah! We seem to be through. Hello, is anybody there?" Then it repeated itself in Jevlenese.

Hunt grinned. "Hello, ZORAC. Not a bad piece of detective work. Was it your doing?"

"Elementary, my dear Hunt. I've got Leyel Torres for you."

"Great."

Torres's voice came through from the *Shapieron*. "Vic, you made it. Who else is there?"

"Gina got out with me. And Chris Danchekker made it with Nixie. We don't know anything about the others."

"I fear they're in captivity," Torres said. "We don't understand the situation. What are the Jevlenese trying to do. Do you know?"

"We think so, but it's a long story. And it's urgent. It needs to go to the top, to Calazar. Can you get him through VISAR?"

"We're talking to him right now," Torres answered. "He's getting together as many of JPC as he can raise. I'll put you through to the Thurien circuit."

ZORAC's voice said something in Jevlenese, and Osaya tapped a code into the tablet. One of the mirrors facing the bed turned into a screen showing Torres standing in the *Shapieron*'s command deck against a background of crew positions manned by Ganymeans. "It looks as if you've found quite a home away from home there, Vic," ZORAC commented.

"Have they got ahold of Caldwell?" Hunt asked, ignoring it.

"He should be arriving soon," ZORAC answered. "He was playing golf. It's Sunday afternoon in Washington."

Then another mirror turned into a view of Calazar in vivid, informal clothes. "Dr. Hunt," he said without preamble. "I feel that we are responsible for all this. What do these Jevlenese at PAC want? They have deactivated the connection to VISAR there, and we have no access to them."

To one side, Murray was shaking his head wonderingly. "That's Calazar, the Thurien head honcho, here in Osaya's bedroom? I don't believe this," he muttered.

"We're pretty sure they're only a smokescreen," Hunt replied to Calazar. "They probably don't know themselves what's really going on. We're certain that Eubeleus is at the back of it."

The sudden misgiving on Calazar's face, even with its alien Ganymean features, was unmistakable. "Why? Where does he

fit into it?" he asked. Just then, he was joined on the screen by
Porthik Eesyan, a Thurien scientific adviser whom Hunt and
Danchekker also both knew of old.

Murray nudged Hunt and nodded in the direction of the
window. Outside, a police flier had appeared and was buzzing
around the probe. The probe had deployed more antennae
and drifted away to circle on a leisurely tour of the area, presumably in an effort to obscure the whereabouts of the location
that it was communicating with.

"Look, there might not be much time, so these are the facts,"
Hunt said, looking back at the screens showing Calazar and
Eesyan, and Torres. "The whole JEVEX business has been a fraud
for years. JEVEX isn't on Jevlen at all. The sites here are dummies and remote interfaces into it. The real guts of the system
is all concentrated on Uttan. *That's* what Eubeleus is really
after—the business here is just a diversion. And if he gets control of it, this planet is going to be hit by an invasion of aliens
that are stronger than anything any of us has ever dreamed of.
We can go into the details later, but for now you have to believe
it. Whatever else happens, you *must* stop him from getting to
Uttan and turning that system back on. Tell him anything you
like. This is one time to worry about ethics and principles later."

Hunt's relief at the chance fluke that had given them this
connection so soon, just when everything had seemed lost, was
such that he had talked on compulsively. But as he finished,
the growing agitation that had been registering on the faces of
the two Thuriens finally got through to him. A sudden pang of
dread seized him as he guessed, a split second before Calazar
spoke, what he was going to say.

"We can't," Calazar replied. "He's already there. Eubeleus
and his followers landed on Uttan—when was it, VISAR?"

"Four hours ago," VISAR's voice replied through the audio.

For several seconds Hunt could only stare back, his mind
too paralyzed for him to speak. "He's already there?" he
repeated numbly.

Calazar nodded miserably. "They've made fools of all of us.
We Thuriens, I mean. Enough Terrans tried to warn us."

Hunt put a hand on his head unthinkingly, still in a daze.

"Let's worry about that later. Right now we've got an impending catastrophe. This whole planet's ready to reconnect to JEVEX, which isn't here but at Uttan. And Eubeleus has got Uttan. What do we do?"

"We can't simply send ships to reoccupy it," Calazar said. "It will be defended. To muster enough force would take too long."

"We have to assume that there are Federation weapons still there," Torres said from the *Shapieron*.

Porthik Eesyan, meanwhile, had been thinking rapidly. "It's true that we can't get near them from the outside," he said. "But there is one possibility that I can see, although at this stage I have no idea how it could be implemented. JEVEX was defeated before when VISAR succeeded in taking control of it. If we're going to do anything now, it will have to be in the same way."

"You mean by getting VISAR hooked into JEVEX somehow?" Hunt said, sounding dubious. He agreed with the theory, but was equally at a loss to see how it could be done.

Eesyan nodded. "Yes. And quickly, before they get JEVEX back up to full operation. But it's going to have to be done by you and the others there on Jevlen, Vic. After what happened last time, obviously they'll secure JEVEX's h-space links against external penetration. So somehow you are going to have to—"

There was a flash outside the window as a beam directed up from somewhere below destroyed the probe.

And both the screens in Osaya's bedroom blanked out.

Chapter Forty-nine

The constructions blended together into a composite pattern of rectangular, hexagonal, rhombic, and irregularly shaped metal geometry, rising in gray tiers to fill a ten-mile-wide rift formed between sheer faces of rock. The top surface of one of the more prominent structures—a squat, seven-sided tower, its upper section terraced in the style of a ziggurat—was equipped as a landing area, with overhead doors to interior docking bays. Standing on the external pads were a number of surface lander craft from the Thurien interstellar transporter orbiting two thousand miles above.

Yet this was just a protruding part of the vast network of integrated manufacturing and assembly facilities that encompassed virtually the entire subsurface of the automated planet, Uttan. Deep below the marshaling and loading complex, in a room where the former director of the resident Jevlenese operations staff had received visitors, Eubeleus and a group of his Axis of Light lieutenants met Parygol, the present commander of the rotating Thurien caretaker force that had been installed since the collapse of the Federation.

"This must be what is called true dedication," Parygol

remarked. "We only remain here for two months at a time, and for me at least that's quite sufficient. I can't imagine anyone *choosing* to live permanently in such an environment."

"Our preoccupation is with the world that lies within," Eubeleus replied loftily. "What physical trappings happen to exist on the outside make little difference. In fact, the absence of distractions is beneficial to spiritual development, as has been known to ascetics for thousands of years."

"Hmm. Yes, well, they tell us that humans and Ganymeans are made of very different psychology." Parygol had studied the history of Jevlenese and Terran mysticism and believed privately that the whole business was just elaborate self-delusion.

"Is there anything more that you need from us for now?" Parygol's deputy inquired.

"No, the arrangements are satisfactory," Eubeleus said. "We shall be on our way immediately. The sooner we begin our work, the better."

"You're sure you wouldn't like some of our officers to accompany you?" Parygol offered again. "Since everything is powered down there's little to see, but they could show you where we'll be dismantling the Federation's military installations. It might help you with your own relocation planning."

"There's no need," Eubeleus replied. "I'm sure that the schedules we have will be sufficient."

"As you wish."

Eubeleus's announced intention was to go with a small group of disciples to conduct a preliminary inspection of some of the places that they had selected as possible habitats. Until he was in full command, he would have to play his role straight with the Thuriens on Uttan, since the zone they were in, plus a few other key locations, had been wired into VISAR. Before occupation by the Thuriens, Uttan's communications had been integrated into JEVEX, and thus deactivated with the main system. Any premature seizure of overt control would have been signaled back to Thurien instantly, alerting the authorities before Eubeleus could consolidate himself. However, once JEVEX was restored and the secret defenses reactivated—

which the Thuriens showed no sign of knowing about—it would be a straightforward matter to disconnect VISAR and lock up the garrison. Then the authorities could do anything they liked. Uttan would be impregnable, and for as long as it remained so, the takeover of Jevlen via h-space would be able to proceed without impediment.

"This is going to be easier than we dared hope," Eubeleus murmured to Iduane after they left.

They descended a shaft, through levels of intricate conveyor lines and immense machinery, to a terminal where fast-transit tubes converged from all directions along the surface curve of the planet. A capsule traveling noiselessly and without a tremor, riding on a localized gravity wave so that even the acceleration produced no sensation, carried them at more than orbital velocity a quarter of the way around Uttan to a supervisory station located in the midst of a vast, subterranean materials-transmutation complex, where rock was reduced to ion plasmas and rebuilt into other nuclei as required. In a basement level of the complex, beneath pipeworks and supporting structures, where the primary energy converters loomed several hundred feet overhead, they opened a concealed door into a further shaft that gave no outward sign of existing, and which didn't appear in any of the official plans or construction records.

Two hundred miles farther down, they emerged into a forbidding, steel-walled bunker where the air was artificially cooled and the lighting was a harsh white. Three massive, reinforced doors brought them into suddenly less oppressive surroundings of staff quarters and living space, with warm colors and varied decor, luminescent ceilings, soft carpets, and comfortable furnishings.

A level farther down, the appearance of the working areas was more uniform and cleanly businesslike. The footsteps of the new arrivals echoed briskly across shiny tiled floors and past deserted rows of glass-partitioned workstations and gleaming consoles. Finally, Eubeleus led them through a set of wider doors to an inner floor of control desks, displays, and indicator panels, overlooked by a surrounding gallery with ancillary communications rooms and staff facilities opening off—the primary control center of JEVEX itself.

The assistants who were with him were all picked and knew their jobs. With little more than a few words being exchanged, they dispersed to the key monitoring points and began calling up status reports and function charts onto the screens. Eubeleus paced slowly about the room, running a critical eye over the scene and stopping from time to time to observe over the shoulders of the operators. Finally he drew up beside Iduane and interrogated him silently with a look.

"It's about as we thought," Iduane said. "The core is running at approximately a half-percent base for archive retrieval, plus minimal system diagnostic and self-check running in standby mode." He was referring to the operations being performed by the Thurien scientists on Jevlen, who didn't even know that the machine they were interacting with was light-years away.

"What's the power situation?" Eubeleus asked.

"Again, as expected. Since the primary grid has been shut down, we'll have to visit the other locations to assemble a coherent supply that can be redirected into the feeder nodes."

"How long until full system integration?"

"Half a day, maybe a little more. Say a day at most."

Eubeleus nodded curtly. "Very well. Leave the rest here to the others. We need to check out the local coupler bank."

"I'll see to it now."

"Update the Prophet while you're at it."

"I will."

Iduane left the console and went out from the main control floor though one of the exits beneath the gallery. Eubeleus watched until he had gone, then turned away and walked through the power control rooms at the rear until he came to another elevator, which took him down through floors of power conditioning and distribution, the I/O and communications subsystem levels, the environmental-control layer, until, finally, he reached the inner containment shell.

He emerged inside a glass-sided bubble, which, although it looked down toward the geometric center of Uttan, seemed because of a warping of the local gravitic gradient to be projecting horizontally out from an immense wall. The wall was a uniform silver-gray, extending away up, down, and from side to side as far as he could see. Twenty feet or so in front of him was another wall, of a milky, translucent texture, parallel to the first and equally unlimited in extent, the two forming a gap that vanished to nothing with the perspective in any direction he chose to look. The space between them was bridged by a forest of data conduits, power busbars, optical pipes, signal highways, maintenance-pod tunnels, and supporting structures. It made him feel like an insect that had found its way between the hulls of an ocean liner.

He was looking at the outside of the processing matrix of JEVEX. The far side of it was more than seven thousand miles away.

Eubeleus usually confined his energies to matters of the present and his plans for the future; the past was a dead affair and of little relevance to his ambitions. But an unusually reflective mood came over him as he stared across at the boundless plane of silent, impenetrable, microlattice crystal. The gap separating him from it held a particular symbolic significance, like a castle moat to an escaped prisoner looking back. It was an appropriate simile.

He believed himself to be an experimental embodiment of the consciousness that JEVEX had fashioned in order to extend its domain to the universe outside. The time for it to commence its expansion in earnest had arrived.

A little under five thousand miles from where Eubeleus was standing, a region of the matrix existed which had differentiated itself by the clustering together of similar activity conditions of the matrix elements into contiguous structures and dynamic patterns. There was nothing that would have distinguished any of the cells from another physically. The differences were purely in the combinations of abstract attributes defining the state of a Thurien processing cell, and the structures had arisen spontaneously through interactions following from the cellular microprogramming.

The region in question had coalesced over time into an

oblate sphere, which, as a consequence of complicated processes of pattern propagation that had coevolved with the structures, both rotated and described an orbit through the matrix about one of the primary data-entry ports spaced in a regular grid throughout its volume. It was a little over one hundred fifty miles in diameter along its major diameter, and on its surface there existed a population of mobile, self-directing activity patterns measuring, on average, an inch or so tall, who perceived themselves as self-aware, autonomous beings.

While Eubeleus stood staring at the outside of the matrix, one of those beings found its mind being penetrated by a cosmic flux that carried meaning. The communication flowed from the mind of Iduane, who by this time had linked into the system via one of the neurocouplers located near the control center some distance above, from which Eubeleus had just descended.

"I hear you, Arisen One," Ethendor intoned in the temple of Vandros, raising his arms and looking skyward as the vision engulfed him. "What is desired? Thy servant awaits."

And the voice spake: "Soon now, the stars shall shine again and the skies be relit in splendor. Prepare, for the time of the Great Awakening draws nigh."

"How shall we prepare?" Ethendor asked.

"The earth and the air of Waroth must be cleansed of the deceivers before all can be ready to arise. Nieru must be avenged for harmony to reign once more among the gods, and then shall the Arising be universally blessed. The false prophets who blasphemed the image of the purple spiral must be hunted out and destroyed. Only then will the heavens be appeased. Go therefore to the king and bid him set his forces to the task. Thus has Vandros spoken."

"They shall be purged from the land," Ethendor promised.

"And thereafter, when the lands of Waroth have been cleansed, the king shall lead the faithful into the realm beyond, and exterminate the false legions of the Spiral who have gone before."

The high priest's eyes widened. "Shall the task continue, even in Hyperia?"

"Hyperia *is* the task! Waroth has been merely thy proving ground."

"There, then, shall I go to serve the gods!" Ethendor cried.

"Fail not, and there thou shalt become as one of them," the Arisen One promised.

It would be a good way of getting their fighting spirits up before they came out to join the real action, Eubeleus had decided.

Chapter Fifty

Hunt leaned back wearily in the chair in Murray's lounge and felt the contours adjust to his changed posture. "I don't know, Chris. We came here to evaluate Ganymean science, not to stop a bloody invasion. I'm a physicist, not a general."

"Well, actually that's not quite true," Danchekker said. "It was merely the official story. We came here, if you recall, to help Garuth get to the bottom of his problem with the Jevlenese. I'd say that objective has been accomplished quite effectively."

"To get to the bottom of it, *and* see what could be done about it," Hunt replied. "What have we done to accomplish the second part? Garuth's locked up, the Ents have got JEVEX back and half the Jevlenese working for them, and they're all set to take over here completely."

Murray sent a puzzled look from one to the other. "Ents? What Ents? I've never heard of them. What the hell are Ents?"

"It's an involved business. But you can think of them as the personalities that people here are sometimes taken over by," Danchekker said by way of some kind of an answer.

Murray didn't follow. "I thought that was just headworld freaks getting their brains scrambled," he said. "That's what most of the Jevs think."

"It gets rather more complicated than that," Danchekker told him.

Gina, listening from a chair at the table and thinking to herself that none of this talk was going to get them anywhere, stood up abruptly. Attention focused upon her. For a moment she hesitated, unsure of how she wanted to continue. Hunt was watching her, his eyebrows raised questioningly.

"I'm not sure I understand all this." She moved over to the door, then turned to face back at them. "This whole planet is wired to operate as a fully computer-managed environment, like Thurien, right? Before the Pseudowar, VISAR ran Thurien, and JEVEX ran Jevlen."

"Can't argue," Hunt agreed, nodding.

Gina tossed out a hand. "VISAR connects all over the Thurien system of worlds via its network of h-space links. JEVEX used the same technology. So, there has to be Thurien-designed h-space hardware all over this planet, which can talk to JEVEX, which turns out to be on Uttan. Have I got that right?"

"Pretty much," Hunt said. "The h-space connections come in through a number of trunk-beam termination nodes scattered around Jevlen. Those are where the black-hole toroids are generated that give you the I/O ports. You can have smaller ones, too, for special purposes, like the one we've got at Goddard. There are a couple inside the *Shapieron*, too."

Gina nodded. "Okay. But just sticking to the regular trunk nodes, won't they have to be reactivated to talk to Uttan when Eubeleus turns JEVEX on again?"

"Yes, I assume so. Otherwise there wouldn't be much point to the whole business, would there?"

"Fine." Gina nodded, as if that made her point. "So if these trunk nodes can connect to JEVEX from light-years away, why can't VISAR?"

Murray nodded slowly as he followed the gist, regarding Gina in a more approving light. "You mean, like it could drown Jevlen out? They wind up the power, and it muscles in?"

"Something like that," Gina said.

Murray turned his head toward Hunt. "Sounds like a good question to me, Doc. Why not?"

"It isn't like swamping a radio with a stronger signal," Hunt explained. "The link terminations on Uttan aren't simply passive devices that VISAR can force its way into. The nodes here on Jevlen have to be set to a resonance mode that enables them to interact with the other end."

"You mean, like tuning a radio?" Gina said.

"Mmm . . . you could think of it that way. It means that VISAR would have to match JEVEX's operating parameters as set on Uttan."

"Oh." Gina propped herself back against the door and contemplated the far wall. She seemed reluctant to abandon her line of thought without at least some token of a fight. "And VISAR couldn't match them?" she tried. "Wouldn't it be like seizing a radio channel with a transmission on the same frequency?"

"I suppose it could—if you knew what they were set to on Uttan," Hunt said. "But Eubeleus is hardly going to publicize that, is he?" He spread his hands, at the same time sighing in a way that mixed genuine regret with respect for her tenacity. "And even then, it wouldn't be enough. There's also an involved coding procedure. When we were upstairs in Osaya's, Eesyan said that the h-space links would be secured against external penetration. That was what he meant. In other words, after what happened last time they'll be ready for it."

"Hmm." Gina folded her arms and stared down at the floor.

Then Murray said, "So what did he mean about VISAR getting to JEVEX from the inside? How was that supposed to happen?"

Hunt shrugged. "I don't know. That was about when he was cut off, wasn't it?"

"You say that he said something about it having to be done by us, here on Jevlen?" Danchekker said.

Gina looked up. "Because the nodes here will be coded to interact with JEVEX," she said, stepping forward and sounding insistent again as a new angle presented itself.

Danchekker nodded distantly. "The parameters for connecting to VISAR are public knowledge. So two channels, one into each system, could be established from here."

Gina looked around, gesturing excitedly. "And if they could be connected together, before JEVEX is fully operational, the way Eesyan said . . ." She stood, inviting them to complete the rest for themselves.

"Not bad," Hunt complimented. "But there's still a small problem with it. I'm sorry to sound negative and all that, but you're forgetting that Eubeleus's people control the nodes. I mean, yes, they've obviously got the information to close a line into JEVEX. And as Chris says, anyone with the equipment can get access to VISAR, too. But we don't have any. And the people who do aren't likely to be very cooperative. In fact, now that the Ganymeans are out of the way, I don't think you'd even get near one of their sites with a combat assault team. And personally I can't think of anyone who'd set up the access codes to Uttan for us, even if we did get inside one. Can you?"

Gina stood staring at him with an expression that almost accused him of having created the problem. Then she seemed to deflate visibly. "No," she confessed heavily, turning away. "I can't."

"I can," Murray said.

A second or two went by before Hunt registered it. "Who?" he asked, swinging his head around at the unexpected response.

Murray shrugged and pulled a face that said if he had missed something obvious and was being stupid, it was just too bad. "Well, you're the scientists . . . but what's wrong with the *Ichena*?"

Hunt stared at him as if he had just sprouted another head. It was a possibility that had not crossed Hunt's mind. "The *Ichena*?" he repeated.

Danchekker frowned. "But they're supposed to be on the other side, surely."

"True," Murray agreed. "But if I've been hearing right what you people have been saying, they were set up as the fall guys to keep everyone here busy while the Green Guru winds up his computer on Uttan. I mean, didn't you say he'd already blown their operation to make it look like they were the ones who were pulling the strings of that kraut who went around the twist? So how much longer are they gonna be around after this business that you're talking about now takes off? So it seems to me they'd be doing themselves a favor by reconsidering their options." Murray looked from one to another, inviting anyone to tell him where he'd gotten it wrong.

"He's got a point, you know," Hunt said, nodding slowly.

Reassured, Murray went on. "But right now they've got a connection operating somewhere, which from what you're saying has to go to Uttan. And if somebody like you was to put them in the picture a little about some of the things you've been telling me, I've got a feeling they might be interested in talking cooperation." Murray looked around and spread his hands. "Hell, if it was me, I would."

Chapter Fifty-one

It could have been because of the general confusion and unrest all over the city. Maybe it was simply that somebody wanted to hear all the angles in a situation where rumors were conflicting. But this time there were no meetings in bars with go-betweens to take them to an unspecified rendezvous. After making a couple of calls to say that Hunt was back with him and had vital business to discuss, Murray was informed that they would be collected at a place less than a block away in thirty minutes' time.

Because of Nixie's uniqueness in the circumstances, Hunt decided to take her, too. But he didn't want to attract attention by having the whole gaggle of them out together in the city; and besides, somebody needed to be on hand in case the Ganymeans managed to restore contact by some means. It was agreed, therefore, that Danchekker and Gina should remain behind. As a precaution, however, they moved upstairs to Osaya's apartment. A couple of Osaya's friends were recruited to stay in Murray's with instructions to say to anyone else who might show up merely that they were keeping an eye on the place while he was away for an unspecified time.

Murray searched around in the closets in one of the bedrooms and came out with a striped, poncholike garment and a flat-topped, brimmed hat that he said would blend Hunt more naturally into the Jevlenese scene. Feeling like a trademark that he had seen somewhere for a brand of Mexican cigarillos, Hunt sent a parting wave to the two girls in what he hoped was good desperado style and followed Murray and Nixie out onto the stairway.

Outside, the corner bar on the approach to the apartment-block entrance was packed with people watching somebody talking on a screen. Murray stopped for a few moments to get the gist of what was going on. The news was the takeover at PAC: the Jevlenese were reclaiming their planet, and JEVEX was going to be restored. Cheers of approval went up from the crowd. Cult followers or not, a lot of people were going to have all kinds of reasons for going home to their couplers, Hunt reflected. *Exploitable recruiting fodder.* The phrase went through his mind again.

They went to the end of a side street and crossed a concourse, descended a floor, and stepped onto a moving way running inside a transparent tube above an enclosed square of shuttered doors and storefronts, littered with trash and flooded at one end by dirty water.

"They don't seem to go in for open gravity-beam travel here," Hunt remarked. "It's standard in all the Thurien cities. It was everywhere on the *Vishnu*, too."

"Jev maintenance," Murray said. "How would you like to be a hundred feet up over Times Square when the power goes out?"

They were picked up on one of the street levels by what could have been the same limousine as before. There were two men in front and another two in the passenger compartment, one of whom Hunt recognized as Dreadnought. Scirio himself wasn't there this time. They drove through a more crowded district, with a confusion of bright lights, street vendors, noise, and signs. Then a ramp going down brought them suddenly into a different world of huge, gloomy walls and windowless frontages that looked like warehouses. Tangles of girderwork supporting conveyor lines and freight-handling hoists stood above deep concrete canyons containing lines of cars, many of them idle. Much of the machinery had not moved for years, Hunt saw as his eyes accommodated to the twilight. In places, lights came on automatically at the vehicle's approach, and in the short period before they went off again after it had passed, he caught glimpses of broken machinery, fallen beams, scampering ratlike creatures, and in one instance several figures in the process of stripping the innards from what looked like a piece of control gear.

The city that the Thuriens had planned and laid was disintegrating, and in place of the grandeur it had promised, the tawdriness that Jevlen had become had taken possession of the ruin like weeds entwining themselves through the skeleton of an unfinished skyscraper.

He looked across the compartment of the limousine at Nixie, who was absorbed for the moment in her own thoughts, her eyes flickering curiously across the impassive faces of the *Ichena* bodyguards as if reading whatever thoughts went on behind the masks. Watching her, it came to him that he had unconsciously been oversimplifying the situation into an us-them problem of innately paranoid and ruthless Ents, who were from another reality and didn't belong in the familiar universe, versus everyone else, who did. For he was looking at one of them who was balanced as far from paranoia as anyone Hunt had known; who had come to terms with the strangeness and irreversibility of her new condition, and was able to face the future constructively and with equanimity.

How many more like her, then, were there, integrating themselves inconspicuously into a daunting, alien world, accepting its inhabitants as new fellow-travelers, and able to adapt without fear and malice to the altered state in which they found themselves? Surely there was something here that humans— both Jevlenese and Terran—and Ganymeans could learn profitably from. More to the point, how many more like that were there down in the Entoverse? Looking at the ayatollahs wasn't the way to tell, for the ones they would encourage to emerge into the Exoverse would be selected to reflect the same qualities as themselves. The threat was not from all of them. All Ents were not malevolent. As was true with humans, the spread within the groups was wider than the differences between groups, making all but the most obvious and trivial generalizations meaningless. It was individuals that counted, and there would be no quick and simple way of separating them.

The limousine ascended again, passing galleries of machinery and storage tanks to emerge suddenly into surroundings of bright, tree-lined avenues where high blocks finished in pastel-colored panels and glass rose above screens of urban parkland and greenery. Whether the pale green sky above was real or simulated, Hunt couldn't tell.

They swung in through a pair of high gates and followed a short driveway beneath an arcade of branches and flowering shrubs to a glass-enclosed entrance in the base of one of the towers. It stood between buttresses of natural-looking rockeries, with water cascading down into walled pools.

Everyone in the rear compartment of the limousine got out. The doors of the building opened automatically to admit them to a tiled lobby area with seats set among low, irregularly shaped plinth tables, and elaborate ornamentations on the pillars and walls. A stream hemmed in by mossy rocks holding clusters of red, pink, and purple plants flowed the full width of the lobby from one side to another, separating them from an inner entrance that lay across a bridge in the center. Overhead, none of the enclosing surfaces were flat, but met in curves and parts of spirals that twisted away to form other, partly disconnected spaces, without a straight line or regular corner anywhere. As they walked with their escorts across the bridge, Hunt had the feeling of being inside a gigantic rendering of an exotically convoluted seashell. Murray thought that whoever dreamed it up must have liked bagels.

Inside were a doorman, a hall porter, and a security man at a desk, all of whom knew the company, and the party passed by without stopping. An elevator whisked them noiselessly upward. Emerging from it, they came onto a platform that seemed at first sight to be hanging in midair. One side looked

down over a vast well, plunging through several floors of prome-
nades and what looked like an open-plan restaurant, while the
other was a transparent wall through which they could see the
locality outside, with the mass of the city rising like a line of
cliffs over the treetops. Looking up, even from this height,
Hunt still couldn't decide if the sky was real or fake.

As they began following the platform, it transformed into a
terrace skirting the well, leading around to the ends of several
corridors opening on the far side. Dreadnought led them into
one of the corridors, which turned out to be curved but quite
short, bringing them to a door at the end. A white-jacketed
valet and a maid were waiting inside when the door opened.
Across the hallway behind them were two more hefty men in
dark suits. After being checked for weapons, the visitors were
conducted through into the residence.

Again, the style was to the general curviform theme of the
whole building, but less extreme. Hunt had seen traces of it in
other areas of Shiban also, including parts of PAC. He wondered if it reflected a regional or historical Jevlenese style.
They moved on through a series of richly carpeted and furnished rooms adorned with pictures, sculptures, pottery, and
metalwares of unfamiliar styles, some explicit, some abstract,
but all with a distinct feel that Hunt classed as "modern," as
opposed to anything even remotely antique. But from a culture shaped by an alien race that had been flying starships
before mankind existed, he should hardly have expected anything else, he supposed.

The whole place descended in stages toward the rear,
making it larger than first impressions suggested. From an open
lounge they followed a set of wide, shallow steps down a
crescent-shaped lower floor with an outer wall of glass, which
looked out over a pool to a roof-level garden. Scirio was
standing in the center, waiting for them. Instead of wearing
the cleancut, Terran-like, two-piece suit that he had worn previously, he was wrapped in a loose, ankle-length robe, splendidly
embroidered in a design of maroon and silver with black embellishment, fastened with clasps and a tied belt, with full sleeves
and a wide, velvety collar.

He stood staring at them for an unnaturally long time without moving, his expression impenetrable. His gaze seemed to be fixed for most of the time on Nixie, Hunt realized after a few uncomfortable seconds, as if Scirio expected her to say something. Finally he spoke in a curt, questioning tone, directing his words at her despite the fact that Murray had done the talking before. Perhaps it was because he recognized her as native Jevlenese. She answered in a puzzled voice, and a brief exchange of short utterances followed. Hunt raised an eyebrow questioningly at Murray.

"I'm not sure," Murray murmured in reply. "It's some kind of out-of-town dialect that you don't hear too much."

There was a pause. Then Scirio said something in a different tone, indicating Hunt with a nod of his head. Nixie spoke to Murray.

"What now?" Hunt asked.

"He says, you said you had something that you wanted to talk about. So talk," Murray answered.

Hunt drew a long breath. He had been composing himself for this moment all through the ride across town. The best place to begin with such people, he had decided, was right where it was going to affect them.

"Tell him," Hunt said, "that he's being set up like a sucker. The whole *Ichena* operation is being set up. The police and the people with them who took over PAC are being set up. After they've done the messy work and drawn all the attention, they'll all be swept away. The real power behind what's going on is political, and the people who are running things need scapegoats to blame the trouble on. Once they get JEVEX running again, then they'll take over."

Scirio stared hard at Hunt with the same inscrutable expression as before; then he uttered a couple of syllables. "Tell him about it," Murray interpreted.

Hunt unfolded a summary version of the whole story, covering the phenomenon of possessed Jevlenese, the cults, Eubeleus, and JEVEX, all of which Scirio would obviously know something about. Hunt hadn't really expected a receptive hearing. But what alternative had there been for them to try?

The story sounded farfetched, to say the least, and putting himself in Scirio's place, he heard his own words sounding more and more like a desperate attempt concocted by Thuriens and Terrans to prolong an unworkable hold over Jevlen which they felt to be slipping. And what motivation would Scirio have to help prevent the restoration of JEVEX, when he had evidently done pretty well for himself under the regime that had operated JEVEX previously? Despite the urgency of the circumstances, Hunt was unable to prevent his voice from echoing the cynicism that he presumed he was being heard with, and while he forced himself to persevere with the help of Murray and Nixie, he found himself conceding inwardly that he had already written off his own cause.

But to his surprise, Scirio remained attentive. Although his face and manner gave away nothing, his reaction was not one of ridicule. The questions that came back through the interpreters were serious and probing.

The people who became possessed weren't all cult-crazies? Many of them remained sane and found niches in society where they functioned normally, generally unrecognized and unsuspected? Correct, Hunt replied. Scirio was talking to one. Hunt indicated Nixie. Did she come across as insane or a cult-fanatic crazy?

A lot of these people were obsessed with power and control? Scirio asked again. They were the kind who were infiltrated into Terran society and had been causing some of its biggest problems throughout history, the way the Jevlenese had been hearing?

"Yes." Hunt waved an arm at the surroundings and was about to say that one could find them installed in just such a place as this; then he faltered as the implication hit him.

Murray saw it, too. "No point in worrying about it now," he muttered in an aside to Hunt. "If this guy's one of 'em, we're as good as dead anyway." But Scirio showed no sign of having been leading them on, and carried on asking questions.

This condition wasn't some kind of mental unhinging caused by addiction to JEVEX? It's really what it says: a "possession" by a different being?

Yes.

And Hunt was saying that these beings had originated inside JEVEX somehow, in a different kind of world, in a way that Scirio didn't pretend to understand?

Yes. A world in which insecurity and unpredictability were the norm, where there were strong motivations to escape. They could literally invade people using the couplers.

And that was what had happened to Nixie?

Yes. It was irreversible; they couldn't go back. How they reacted varied from individual to individual and with circumstances.

"I think we're getting through," Murray whispered. "Don't ask me how, because to tell you the truth I thought this had no chance. But he's listening."

And what was going on outside was all a smokescreen? The ones who were the real threat were all set to mount an invasion when JEVEX came on again?

"JEVEX is located on another planet: Uttan. That's why Eubeleus has gone there."

And the only way to try and stop him activating JEVEX was by letting VISAR at it? And the only short-term way to do that was by getting access to one of the *Ichena*'s illicit channels into JEVEX?

"Yes."

"You've got it," Murray confirmed to Scirio via Nixie.

Scirio seemed satisfied, though still with the same, vaguely defined air of finding something amiss that had hung about him since their first entry. He directed his attention to Nixie again and began an exchange in which he didn't pause for Murray to translate, at the same time drawing her away until they were standing by the curved window, looking out over the pool and the garden as if the other two had ceased to exist. Nixie answered in short sentences, sounding uncertain and puzzled.

"He's saying he thinks the boss should hear about this," Murray said in a low voice to keep Hunt informed. "Name of Grevetz. Lives outside the city someplace. He wants to know how Nixie feels about it."

"What does she say?"

Murray shrugged. "Sure, if he thinks it's a good idea. Why not?"

"Why's he asking Nixie?"

"I don't know . . . Neither does she. He's saying we could get this guy Grevetz over here now, or maybe go see him. How'd she like to come along? She says okay. But she seems about as mystified by it as I feel."

Hunt frowned, thought about it, and shook his head. "Does it make any sense to you?"

"No . . . but most things that Jevs do don't make any sense to me, either. Who could make sense and run a planet like this one?"

Scirio was standing with his hands clasped behind his back, sounding casual and chatty now, and gesturing toward the window.

"What now?" Hunt asked.

"He's talking about the pool, all the parties they have here . . . Something about accidents that sometimes happen. Nixie's just going along with it. She doesn't know what it's all about either . . . Now he's going to call the boss man."

Scirio turned and walked back toward where Murray and Hunt were standing, passed them without a word, and went up the shallow steps and across the lounge above to disappear into another room. Nixie came over to rejoin the other two. "Is all very funny," she said. "He talk about his pool and his boss. I think he know more than he say."

Hunt flashed Murray an uneasy look. "These people he's calling. It couldn't be the hit squad, could it?"

"I dunno. What can we do about it if it is?"

"If he *was* one of them, an Ent, would Nixie know? Would she be able to tell?"

Murray asked her in Jevlenese. "He is not one," she said. "I would know."

For the next hour they appeared to have been forgotten as a buzz of activity erupted over the house. Jevlenese appeared from other parts of it or arrived from places outside, muttered in twos and threes, and went away again on mysterious errands. Much conferring went on behind closed doors, and the tones and chimes of incoming calls sounded constantly. Through it all, Scirio was everywhere, calling out orders, checking details, hurrying to take calls, usually accompanied by Dreadnought. Tenseness crackled in the air like static. Nixie was unable to make out what was going on. It felt like the preparations for a military operation.

Then Dreadnought came out of a doorway that had been in constant use and called out something, at the same time beckoning. Nixie got up from a couch she had been perched on. Hunt unfolded from a deep, leathery chair, close behind Murray, who had been leaning against a pillar. "Well, here goes," Murray murmured.

"What's happening?" Hunt asked.

"Search me. But whatever it is, it looks like we don't have much choice."

Scirio, now wearing a dark suit and short blue topcoat, was waiting at the outside door with three more *Ichena*. After a brief exchange of questions and answers delivered in curt, harsh voices, the group went out into the corridor and followed the terrace back around the well to the elevators. But instead of returning to the seashell lobby with the bridge crossing the stream, they went up.

They came out into an airy, metal-walled space with wide, low windows running almost the full length of two adjacent walls, giving it the appearance of an observation floor high over the city. From the score or more of what were clearly flying vehicles of assorted shapes and sizes parked about the place, it was evidently a rooftop landing deck. The three henchmen led the way to a sleek machine, finished in yellow and white, at the end of one of the rows. Its general form was a bubble-canopied front end and solid center fuselage, tapering to the rear in a way that vaguely suggested a helicopter, but with no rotor or stabilizer. The rear body sprouted a pair of low-mounted, steeply anhedraled stub wings carrying streamlined pods at the ends. There didn't seem to be any wheels.

The doors were already open. A pulsating hum emanated

from low down at the rear, and two men in black jackets were in the nose seats. The remainder of the forward compartment contained three rows of three seats each, and there was an *Ichena* already seated in the back. Hunt and Murray were guided into the other two seats next to him; Nixie and two of the group who had come up from the house got in the center row, while the third, along with Dreadnought and Scirio, settled themselves ahead of them, behind the two nose seats. The doors closed, and a moment later the vehicle lifted from the floor, turning at the same time. It moved forward, and the whole section of wall and windows in front of it swung down and outward to form a takeoff platform projecting out from the building. The flier soared out with barely a feeling of movement over roof gardens similar to the one outside the crescent-shaped room they were in earlier, and screened from each other by the landscaping. Then came more rooftops, with the neighborhood avenues and strips of parkland visible farther below. On looking up, Hunt made out a faint seam joining part of the sky. It was one of the canopies: simulated, not real.

The flier approached the stratified cliffs of built-up structures looming above the boundary screen of trees. A vast, bright opening yawned ahead and became one of the main aerial traffic corridors piercing the city. The flier accelerated and merged into the flow. Between Murray and the stone-faced *Ichena* on his other side, Hunt brooded silently to himself, wondering what the hell he had gotten himself into now.

Chapter Fifty-two

Calazar, on Thurien, Torres, inside the *Shapieron*, and Caldwell, who had appeared on-line from Earth, debated the situation for a long time after contact through the probe was lost. Soon after Caldwell joined in the discussion, the Jevlenese blocked all communications from ZORAC out of Geerbaine. Since the rest of Jevlen's system of satellites and links had been controlled locally by JEVEX and not by VISAR, it meant that all other access to the planetary network was denied also.

For the moment, then, there was no alternative but to hope that Hunt and the others with him would complete for themselves what Porthik Eesyan had been about to say when the connection was lost, namely that the only tactic that immediately presented itself was to get VISAR hooked into JEVEX, somehow, on Jevlen. The general feeling was that they would. Whether or not they would be able to find a way of accomplishing it was another matter.

What then? If the group on Jevlen did succeed in getting VISAR connected into JEVEX, what, exactly, were the policymakers hoping that VISAR would do?

Caldwell could not see what the problem was. "If VISAR gains control, it can lock out all the couplers until we figure out a way of getting past Uttan's defenses," he told the others. "Then no more of these Ents will be able to get out, and there'll be no risk of any invasion. Once we get into Uttan we dismantle the matrix, and the problem will be settled permanently."

But Calazar, speaking with surprising firmness, vetoed such a possibility. "The Ents may have their problematical side, but peculiar as their origins may seem to us, they are fully evolved intelligences in every respect, with all the rights which that implies," he said. "However the Entoverse came into existence, exist it does, and destroying it would amount to the genocide of its inhabitants. Thuriens could not permit that. It isn't an option."

Caldwell thought about it and decided that the Thuriens were right. He had, he admitted to himself, spoken too hastily. "Okay," he agreed. "We can't pull the plug. So, why don't we simply disconnect all the neurocouplers and let Jevlen have a different, VISAR-like system when the time comes to take them off probation? Or VISAR could be extended. That way, the Entoverse can continue to exist and carry on evolving internally any way it likes. We permanently quarantine it."

But the Thuriens were not happy about that idea, either.

"Those are thinking, feeling beings, trapped in a hostile and perilous environment," Calazar explained. "The hopes of many of them are pinned on the possibility of escape. To deny them that chance would be unethical and immoral. We couldn't condone it."

Caldwell accepted the mild rebuff gracefully. "Okay then," he conceded patiently. "What do *you* want to do?"

"We don't know."

Caldwell drew a long, steady breath and reminded himself that he was dealing with the effective head of state of an alien civilization.

"Great," he replied.

The flier sped over the countryside beyond the city at a modest altitude that Hunt judged to be three to four thousand feet. Occasional bleeps came from the front, with snatches of a synthetic voice that sounded like the flight-control computer. Scirio made and took a number of calls to others elsewhere over a handset, but otherwise nobody spoke.

Below, the heaped suburbs surrounding Shiban for several miles thinned out into the kind of clusters of urban collage and spatterings of buildings strung along roadways that looked much the same everywhere, from Sumatra to New Jersey. Compared to typical developed areas on Earth there was less evidence of industry, which, following the Thurien practice, tended to be mostly underground. On the other hand, some constructions reached a scale of immensity that Earth had never seen. In one place the vehicle passed a straight, sheer-sided rift cut through a mountain range, packed with tangles of metallic geometry, the purpose of which Hunt was unable to guess. Farther on, they saw on the skyline an array of slender, pear-topped towers, interconnected by tubes, that must have stood a mile high.

Farther on, more open land began to assert itself between settlements—mostly uncultivated and wild, although a lot of new land clearing had been initiated in more recent times. Food production on Jevlen had originally been as much an artificial process-industry as the synthesis of any other material, with traditional farming being treated as a recreation, or limited as a way of life to those who liked it. But as more things began breaking down, a more mixed pattern had established itself; and since the withdrawal of JEVEX, the emerging entrepreneurs had been applying their inventiveness to agriculture as another means of meeting the new demands that needed to be satisfied.

They climbed, following a valley into a line of hills, where the landscape was richer and greener, with a carpet of forest, tinted peculiarly blue in parts, and several lakes. The streaky orange Jevlenese clouds and discharge patterns were more vivid and, with the chartreuse sky, imparted an unreal, eerie coloring to the entire vista that Hunt found far more alien in its effect than anything he had seen of the cityscape. Although he was used to roaming around all kinds of fantastic places via the Thurien virtual-travel system when the fancy took him, he found himself acutely conscious of the fact of actually *being* on another world. His only other experiences of being really off-planet were his stay at Ganymede, and a brief stopover en route on the Moon.

It made him mindful once again of the chasm that set humans and Thuriens apart. Given enough attention to detail, bringing information to the senses was as good, as far as Thuriens were concerned, as physically transporting the senses to where the information was. If one could not tell the difference, then there was no difference. With humans that would never be so. In that light, it seemed paradoxical that the Thuriens should be practically immune to the virtual-reality fantasies that had resulted in mass addiction on Jevlen. Or was it because the hyperrationality of the Thuriens enabled them to accept without discomposure any representation of what they knew was real, while at the same time making them incapable of surrendering disbelief to anything that they knew intellectually to be a fiction? That was pretty much what Gina had said about himself and Danchekker, Hunt reflected. No wonder the psychologists were talking about having their work cut out for the next hundred years.

Hunt returned from his thoughts to the realization that one of the men up front was speaking into his headset and the flier had begun descending. It banked into a shallow turn, and the view ahead slid sideways across the windshield until a large house standing in a clearing among trees centered and stabilized. A boundary wall passed by underneath, and the clearing enlarged into a private park of lawns, gardens, orchards, and game courts, with a lake containing several islands. It was a large, rambling house, Hunt saw as the flier came down on a paved area at the rear. The main, central section was two-storied with large areas of glass, and had curved roofs with upturned eaves, vaguely reminiscent in character of the building they had just left in Shiban. An assortment of annexes and outbuildings formed jumbled extensions at both ends. It could almost have been built, Hunt thought fleetingly, from a mixture of pieces from a pagoda and a stylish hacienda.

A group of figures was waiting at the pad. In the center was a big, roundly built, moon-faced man with smooth features and a bald head, standing hands-on-hips, watching. He wore earrings and, on one wrist, a wide bracelet, and was clad in a wraparound, short-sleeved coat over light red pants. He seemed to be the principal. The half-dozen or so other men with him, all of them also casually dressed, gave the impression of being aides or bodyguards; their manner was relaxed, mildly bored, as the doors of the flier opened.

Two of the *Ichena* got out first, followed by Scirio and Dreadnought. Some words flew back and forth outside, and then Scirio turned and said something to Nixie, motioning for her to get out. Hunt glanced at Murray questioningly. Murray shrugged.

Nixie hesitated, obviously as mystified as they were, then rose out of her seat and moved to the door. Scirio waved again, and she climbed out. Following his gestures, she moved forward between Dreadnought and the other two *Ichena*, and then froze into immobility when she saw Moon Face's expression of glowering hatred. Suddenly, as if unable to hold back any longer, Moon Face began shouting angrily at Scirio and gesturing toward Nixie with wild motions of his arms. Scirio ignored him and asked her something. She shook her head, evidently bewildered, and stepped back, terrified. Moon Face snapped something at his henchmen, and two of them came toward her, apparently to seize her, but Scirio's men blocked the way. Then Scirio and Moon Face were shouting together, at each other, then at Nixie, who ended up screaming at both of them.

"What in God's name's happening?" Hunt demanded, craning forward and gripping the seat arm.

Murray could only shake his head helplessly. "I can't make it out. The fat guy knows her, but she doesn't know him. She's telling Scirio that the fat guy's from outta the computer—*Jesus Christ!*"

A muted *buzzz* came from somewhere behind the bulkhead at the rear of the cabin they were sitting in, and Moon Face and the two men nearest him went up like torches. Simultaneously, the *Ichena* from the flier who had stopped Moon Face's men from grabbing Nixie drew pistols from their coats and shot them. There was no pussyfooting around with stun settings; the victims were blown apart. Dreadnought gave the same treatment to one of the pair that was left, and the *buzzz* came again from the back of the flier, incinerating the last of them.

Hunt could only stare, paralyzed with shock and horror. Outside, all at the same time, Scirio and his men were grabbing Nixie and hustling her back to the doors of the flier, which was already lifting; the shriek of an alarm went up from somewhere in the house, where shutters were closing across windows and sections of roof were opening outward to reveal turrets; and figures had appeared, running in all directions.

The buzzing came again from behind, and the two turrets that had been uncovered exploded. There had to be some kind of a cannon firing from the rear section of the flier—it was a gunship as well as a staff car. Figures tumbled in, Scirio shouting orders and Dreadnought bundling Nixie ahead of him like a sack. Snapping out of his daze, Hunt leaned over the seats in front to grab her and pull her in, and Murray shook himself together in time to help. Hunt's impressions of what happened after that were a confusion of disjointed scraps: Nixie petrified, but apparently unharmed and keeping grip enough on herself . . . The flier banking and lifting, its cannon buzzing continuously, ground streaking by outside . . . A point of light curving in fast from over the trees, part of the house erupting in flame . . . The perimeter wall . . . Forest . . . Rising to clear hills ahead . . .

"Shiiit!" Murray breathed shakily beside him.

Where had the light come from? Another craft that had been following them? Something else that had been sent up from elsewhere? Hunt stared numbly as the view ahead organized itself into the way back to Shiban, only barely aware of the tirade of words that Nixie was directing at Scirio, or of Scirio answering in even tones, his manner gradually unwinding from the tenseness that had prevailed through the journey out. Murray became attentive to what they were saying, and after a few minutes of questioning and listening, he turned his head toward Hunt.

"The fat guy they blew away was the boss, Grevetz. He was one of 'em—an Ent. Scirio figured that if what we'd said back at his place was true, then he'd be on his way down the tubes along with the rest when he'd outlived his use. So he decided he'd move first, when nobody would be expecting it. Looks like maybe he was right."

By now, Hunt's revulsion was subsiding enough for him to start thinking again. He followed, but was still puzzled. "Okay . . . but how did he know that what we'd said *was* true? How did he know it wasn't just a last-ditch try from us and the Thuriens to stop JEVEX from being switched on again? We could have made up the whole thing."

Murray shook his head. "That's what all that stuff back at the pad was about." He indicated the back of Scirio's head with a nod. "Did you notice how he was acting kinda weird when we walked into his place back in town?"

"Giving Nixie funny looks, you mean? Yes, I did. What did it mean?"

"It seems he knew her, from way back—or at least he knew Nikasha, the person she used to be. What clinched your story was that she'd obviously never seen him before. The real Nikasha would have run a mile, never mind go walking back into the place cool as a penguin's ass."

Hunt blinked in astonishment. "You mean she'd been there before?"

Murray talked some more to Nixie, who talked to Scirio. "Nikasha used to be Fatso's girlfriend—"

"You're kidding!"

"Only Fatso also happens to have a bitchy wife, see. Anyhow, the two of them—the two dames, that is—had one hell of a fight, and Nikasha tried to wipe Mrs. Fatso out."

Hunt stared disbelievingly. "To do in the boss's wife? Her? That's crazy."

"*Not* her. The person who used to be her. If what you're telling me's true, she's gone for keeps now, right? Yeah, do her in. It happened back there in Scirio's place, where we were before. She stunned Mrs. Fatso with a Jev shooter while she was in the pool, figuring it would look like a heart attack, but it didn't quite work out. Fatso put her number out, and that was why she did a vanishing act and lost herself in the city. It all happened before I came here—I never knew a thing about it."

The one way to be sure that Nixie was not putting on an elaborate act for some reason would be to confront her with Grevetz in person, Hunt saw. His rage at the sight of her had been clear enough, and her mystification in the face of it had been something that nobody could have faked.

"And once Scirio knew she was genuine, her recognizing Grevetz as another of her kind was enough to spell out the score," Hunt said, nodding as it all became clear. He was still shaking, he noticed. From a side window he could see that they were heading back toward Shiban. "So what happens now?" he asked.

Murray shrugged. "Sounds like it's gonna be war all over the place now, with nobody sure who's on whose side."

Hunt wondered what that would mean. Nixie had been recognized at PAC by at least one of the police, and exactly where they stood in the whole business was unclear. "How safe are Danchekker and Gina back at Osaya's place?" Hunt asked in a worried tone. "Once this news gets back, people are likely to be going crazy everywhere. I don't like it."

Murray passed the question on to Scirio. Scirio called some instructions forward, and one of the two men in the front seats spoke into a handset.

"He's getting them out," Murray said.

Scirio then went on to speak at greater length, in the course of which Murray's eyes widened. Finally Murray turned to Hunt. "The way he sees it, the first thing has to be to stop Eubeleus turning on the computer, and then let the Terrans and Thuriens straighten things out. If they put the brakes on the headworld business that'll be a shame, but if he was about to be run out of it anyway it doesn't make any difference. He's a businessman. There are plenty of other lines. He figures that this way he'll have a better chance of working some kind of deal with the new management than he would have if Fatso's people took over."

Hunt frowned uncertainly. "So . . . what does that translate into? Exactly what is he saying he's going to do?"

Murray exhaled sharply, then shook his head. "I'm not sure how, but it looks like you've pulled it off, Doc. He's doing what you wanted. He's gonna get his technical guys to connect VISAR up to their channel into JEVEX."

Chapter Fifty-three

Danchekker relaxed back into silken cushions in one of the voluminous chairs in Osaya's lounge, his hands clasped behind his head, and studied the shameless opulence and erotic imagery around him. "You know, I must confess there are times when I feel tempted to consider myself the victim of a misspent youth," he called over his shoulder toward the open doorway as he heard Gina coming back in. "What tastes these establishments cater to, I fear I might be past daring to imagine."

Gina appeared, holding two cups of the brew that Hunt had christened *ersatz*—she'd had to get them from the girls downstairs in Murray's, since the chef in Osaya's kitchen only responded to Jevlenese, and the manual controls were a mystery. "Now you can see the kind of hook that JEVEX could be," she said, closing the door.

Danchekker's eyes widened suddenly as the full meaning of what she and Sandy had been saying for all this time finally sank home. "My God, I never connected it with things like *that*!" he exclaimed.

He accepted one of the mugs and conveyed it to a side table. Gina sat down with her own in another of the chairs.

She took a sip and tried to relax, but couldn't. The dragging waiting for something to happen was fraying her nerves.

"Does any of it really matter if you take a long enough view of things?" she asked, mostly just to break the silence. "From the point of view of evolution, I mean. Does anything we do or don't do really make much difference in the long run to what would have happened anyway?" Then she remembered what she had said to Hunt when they were aboard the *Vishnu*, about five percent of species surviving and it all being a matter of luck, and admitted to herself that she was only trying to rationalize their situation. It *did* matter, and they were powerless.

Danchekker's answer did nothing to assuage her feelings. "Indeed it can. The most minuscule difference in causes can sometimes bring about huge changes in the outcome of a situation. I remember an example that Vic gave me once, when we were discussing highly nonlinear systems."

"What was that?" Gina asked.

Danchekker settled himself more comfortably, glad to have something else to talk about. "Suppose that you break up the pack of balls on an ideal, frictionless pool table, and that you were able to measure the velocity and direction of every ball with perfect accuracy," he said. "How far into the future would your computational model continue to predict the subsequent motions with reasonable validity, do you think?"

Gina frowned. "Ideally? For the rest of time, I always thought. Isn't that right?"

"In theory, yes—which was Laplace's great claim. But in reality, the mechanism is such an effective amplifier of errors that if you'd ignored the effect of the gravitational pull of a single electron on the edge of the Galaxy, your prediction would be hopelessly wrong after less than a minute." He nodded at the astonished expression on Gina's face and warmed to the theme. "You see, what it illustrates is the extraordinary sensitivity of some processes to—"

Just then, a chime sounded and an alluring female voice said something in Jevlenese. Gina and Danchekker looked at each other, puzzled for a second, and then realized that it was Osaya's house computer. Voices came from the hallway, and a moment later the two girls who had been left in Murray's apartment appeared, followed by three men. Gina stood up from the chair, uncertain what to expect. Danchekker looked up at them with an expression of defiant resignation, chin outthrust and jaw clamped shut.

A stream of Jevlenese issued from both of the girls at once, accompanied by lots of gesticulating and waving. One of the men, solidly built, with a hard face and narrow, Oriental-like eyes, and dressed in a straight gray jacket and black, roll-neck shirt, uttered a series of sharp, staccato syllables and pointed back toward the outside door.

"It looks as if the party's moving on somewhere," Gina said to Danchekker.

"I, ah, rather get the impression that our opinion on the matter isn't being invited," Danchekker observed, taking in the looks on the faces of the other two men.

"Right. I get that feeling, too."

Danchekker put down his mug and rose from the chair. "Very well. Let's get on with it."

They followed the three men back outside to the landing. The two girls came down with them as far as Murray's door, where they waved and disappeared back inside. At least their manner gave no indication of anything threatening. Gina and Danchekker went with the three men down to the lobby and out to a car in which another two were waiting.

Ten minutes after they departed, a Shiban city police van pulled up on the same spot and disgorged a squad of troopers, who ran clattering in through the apartment-block doors.

The flier landed in a parking area at the rear of some buildings by a traffic highway, where a number of other flying vehicles and ground vehicles were standing. With few words being said, the party disembarked and crossed the lot to a larger craft, which looked like a kind of flying van: windowless, except for the nose compartment, and painted pink and white with garish signs on the sides in Jevlenese. They boarded through a center door to find half the interior fitted with seats, and in less than a minute they were airborne once again.

Nixie said something to Murray, who gawked in surprise, and they went into a succession of questions and answers.

"What's it all about?" Hunt asked.

"These guys must believe in going equipped for the job," Murray replied. "This thing we're in is a funeral truck."

"You're joking! It looks more like a tour bus for a rock band."

"It belongs to one of the weirdo sects. It seems they do all their mourning when somebody gets born—on account of all the hassles and shit that the guy's gonna have to put up with in life. But when he croaks at the end of it all, that's something to celebrate. So they make this a party wagon. I guess it takes all kinds, eh?"

They landed again after about the same total flight time as the journey out, suggesting that they were back in Shiban. Sure enough, when they climbed out Hunt saw that they were on a wide platform projecting out from the rounded end of a structure high over the city, facing one of the wide traffic corridors receding away between cliffs of buildings. Above, the structure that they were on met what could be seen to be a solid canopy of artificial sky, probably penetrating through it to form one of the towers visible outside. Far below, the buildings and terraces merged together into the structures of the lower city.

They entered a set of doors and crossed a drab, bare hall of crumbling floor and scratched gray walls. It felt like the kind of place that had gotten tired of existing a long time earlier, and was waiting only to fall apart. A slow, creaking elevator carried them down for what seemed an interminable descent, and they came out in a dark, carpeted hallway that smelled old and musty. From there they went down a flight of stairs to a gallery with corridors and halls going off in several directions. One of the corridors brought them to a doorway. Scirio spoke briefly via a microphone to someone, and the door opened. Inside was a narrow passage that opened into another lined by doors on both sides. The surroundings seemed familiar, but the party moved through without slackening pace, and they were entering the lounge with the bar before Hunt realized that they were back in the Gondola Club, where they had come in search of Baumer.

But this time the bar stools and tables were empty and the place was cleared of people, except for a tall, gangly-limbed man with gray hair and beard, wearing a brown checked suit, who was sitting at one of the tables with two others who looked like *Ichena*. He stood up as the newcomers entered, and Scirio launched into a dialogue while he was still crossing the room. The man in the suit seemed agitated, and spoke in a nervous voice, confining himself to answering Scirio's questions.

"He sounds like their technical guy," Murray muttered to Hunt. "They're talking about h-space links and Thurien transmission codes—something like that, anyhow." Hunt nodded but said nothing, realizing with a jolt that they could be much closer to their goal than he had dared hope.

The engineer's name was Keshen. When he had finished talking to Scirio, he led the way over to another door and around a corner at the rear of the lounge. Hunt, Murray, and Nixie hesitated. Scirio turned and waved for them to follow.

They came to a smallish room filled with cubicles, monitor panels, and equipment racks—evidently this was where the establishment's couplers connected into the communications net. Somewhere else in the net, possibly far from Shiban, a channel through the net terminated at a live node carrying an h-space link to JEVEX. There was a console with lights and several screens, one of them displaying a pattern of symbols and geometric lines that meant nothing. Keshen sat down and began what looked like a series of status checks. The pattern on the screen altered; new symbols appeared. Keshen gave an intermittent commentary, which Nixie elaborated for Murray, and Murray did his best to explain to Hunt.

"This is their link into the net that connects to JEVEX, okay?"

Hunt nodded. "Out of curiosity, ask him if he knows where the connection into JEVEX is," he said.

Murray passed the question on. Keshen shook his head.

"The net goes all over the planet," Murray interpreted back. "The entry into JEVEX could be anywhere. It all depends how the techs who are running the core system have got it set up at the moment—which isn't something that he makes it his business to go around asking questions about. His ass is on the line enough as it is. Does it make sense to you?"

"Yes," Hunt replied. It meant that Keshen was not aware that the connection led to an off-planet link somewhere. In other words, he didn't know that JEVEX proper wasn't on Jevlen at all—just as Hunt would have expected.

Keshen indicated another section of equipment, and Murray went on. "This channel goes out to an h-space—what would you call it, sender? Connector? Transformer?"

"Transceiver?" Hunt suggested.

"Yeah, right. Anyhow, it's miles away somewhere. It hasn't been operating since the Gs shut down JEVEX. But there just happens to be a line into it that isn't supposed to exist, and he's just brought it up again and fed in the—some kind of operating numbers?"

"Parameters?"

"If you say so . . . to tune it for VISAR. So that line's through to Thurien, okay?"

"It's through to Thurien?" Hunt repeated. He couldn't contain a quick laugh. It sounded too good to be true.

Murray checked. "That's what the guy says."

"Could we verify that?" Hunt said. "Can he get VISAR through to us here, right now?"

"Dunno." Murray asked Nixie, who asked Keshen. Keshen checked with Scirio, and then entered more commands into the console.

Then a voice said something in Jevlenese from the console speaker. Keshen replied, answered a few more questions, and then the voice said in English, "My word, you *are* there, Vic! It seems you've pulled off one of your stunts again."

A relieved grin spread across Hunt's face. "Hello, VISAR." He indicated the others who were with him in the room. "Well, these people had more than a little to do with it, as well." He heard what sounded like his own phrase being repeated in Jevlenese. VISAR was assuming the role of translator.

"They did a good job."

"It pays to make friends," Hunt said. "What's the situation with the others?"

"Calazar's here," VISAR answered. "Gregg Caldwell went

away to take care of something else, but someone's gone to fetch him. We've heard nothing more from anywhere else on Jevlen. As far as we know, the others are still where they were when we got cut off."

"I think Gina and Danchekker are being moved," Hunt said.

"They're on their way here," Scirio said, his words translated by VISAR. "It wouldn't have been safe to leave them."

One of the screens on the console activated, showing Calazar. "Congratulations," he said. "VISAR has just given me the news. And you have a channel there into JEVEX?"

Hunt moved next to Keshen. "Do we?"

Keshen checked the indicators on the other screen. "Yes. And you want VISAR connected into it? Is that so?"

"They're in charge now," Hunt said, waving toward the screen showing Calazar.

An exchange of technical jargon between VISAR and Keshen followed, ending with Keshen confirming that it could be done. "Do it straight away, while JEVEX is still asleep," VISAR said. "Then when they bring JEVEX up to full power on Uttan, guess who'll be in control of it."

"And Eubeleus won't know?" Hunt asked.

"JEVEX won't even know," VISAR told him.

Keshen was looking puzzled. "Uttan? The planet? What has Uttan to do with this?" he asked.

"It's too long a story to go into now, believe me," Hunt replied.

Then the sound of footsteps came from the lounge outside, and Gina appeared at the door with Danchekker. The three men who had brought them from Murray's were behind.

"My God, it's Vic and the others!" Danchekker exclaimed. "You're here. We had no idea what was going on. These—" He hesitated as he heard his words being translated. "These gentlemen collected us."

"You weren't safe there," Hunt explained. "This is Scirio. He had you brought here. And this is Keshen. Don't ask where we've been."

Gina was looking past Hunt with a puzzled expression. "What's doing the translating? Have we got ZORAC back again?"

"Even better," Hunt answered. "It's VISAR. We've got a link to Thurien." Danchekker was already staring incredulously, having seen Calazar on one of the screens. Hunt indicated the other section of hardware. "And that's the channel into JEVEX. Keshen has just hooked them together."

Danchekker blinked. "You've done it? You mean already? They can set VISAR loose on JEVEX from here?"

"And with JEVEX still in a coma, it won't know what hit it—literally," Hunt replied.

The news was so sudden and unexpected that it took Gina several seconds to absorb it. "You mean that's it?" she said finally. "We can keep JEVEX off permanently, as of now? Then it can be taken apart? The problem's over?"

"Er, no," Calazar said from the screen. He sounded apologetic at having to complicate things. "We've already discussed that. The Ents are a race of fully sapient beings in every respect. What you're saying would amount to genocide."

"What are they talking about?" Keshen muttered to Scirio. "What are Ents?" Scirio hushed him with a warning shake of his head.

The screen split, and Caldwell's face appeared in one half. He nodded at Hunt and the others, evidently having gotten the news from VISAR. "Great job. Looks like maybe we're in business, then, eh?"

Gina was still bemused by what Calazar had said. "Then what will you do?" she asked. "Isolate it? Leave it as its own, self-contained universe?"

Caldwell shook his head, guessing the way the conversation was going. "The Thuriens won't go with that, either. But in any case, both those options would depend on VISAR being able to keep control over JEVEX. Right now, that all hinges on the single link into it that you've just established. If we lose that, we lose our only chance. Once Eubeleus and his people were warned, they wouldn't give us another opportunity."

Hunt was looking perplexed. "What, then?" he asked, shifting his eyes from one side of the screen to the other. "If we're not going to get rid of it and we're not going to cut it off, what are we going to do? What other alternative is there?"

"The real problem that we've got in the short term is staving off a mass exodus of Ents," Caldwell said. "JEVEX is simply the means that would make it possible. But it wouldn't happen at all, regardless of whether we continued to control JEVEX or not, if the Ents could be persuaded to change their minds—at least until we've had a chance to understand the situation better and figure out how we can help them solve their problem without wiping out a Jevlenese every time one of them comes out."

"What?" Hunt said. This was a completely new twist. He glanced at Danchekker, then at Gina. They both looked as much at a loss as he was.

"I don't understand," Danchekker said to the screen. "Persuade them? How?"

"By talking to them," Caldwell said, as if that explained everything.

Hunt was completely befuddled. He shook his head. "They're just patterns in a computer, Gregg. How's anyone supposed to talk to them?"

"That's what we've been thinking about," Caldwell replied. "Why don't we go down there and check the situation firsthand? Then, maybe, we'd have a better chance of figuring out what to do."

Hunt's bemusement changed to suspicion. "Who's 'we'?"

Caldwell answered in an unapologetic, matter-of-fact kind of way. "Okay, since you're the agent assigned to the job on the spot: 'you.'"

Hunt's misgivings deepened. "Down where?" he asked.

"There," Caldwell replied simply. "It was Eesyan's idea: down into the Entoverse." As Caldwell spoke, Eesyan's head and shoulders came into view on the other side of the screen, next to Calazar.

"We can't," Hunt replied. "It takes another Ent to get inside another Ent mind through the couplers. They evolved there. They're the only ones who have the knack."

"Ah, that was before, when the couplers into JEVEX were the only way of gaining access to the Entoverse," Eesyan said. "But now we have another way."

Hunt still wasn't with it. "What way?" he asked.

"VISAR," Eesyan replied. "Which has a far greater natural affinity for manipulating JEVEX's internal processes than even the Ents have."

Hunt stared. It was obvious. In the Pseudowar, VISAR had obtained the unconditional surrender of the Jevlenese by creating a gigantic Terran battle force that existed only in JEVEX's imagination.

"If VISAR can scan the matrix and locate and analyze the data structures that constitute the Entoverse—which it should have commenced doing already, if your connection there is working—it ought to be able to figure out how an Ent is put together: literally, at its 'atomic' level," Eesyan explained. "Then, VISAR would know all it needed to to write an artificial Ent-being of its own into the Entoverse."

"I have identified the planet and its orbit," VISAR interjected. "There only seems to be the one. It's interesting—about a hundred fifty miles in diameter. It's detectable only through correlation analysis of the cell activity states. I can see why JEVEX would never have been aware of its existence. Now let's take a closer look at the surface details . . ."

"Extraordinary!" Danchekker breathed.

Eesyan went on. "Given permission, VISAR would also have access to the full set of mental constructs of anyone neurally coupled into it. Therefore, it should be able to impress that personality into the Ent-being that it had created down there in the Entoverse."

"That's you," Caldwell put in, as if the look on Hunt's face didn't say plainly enough that he knew exactly what Eesyan was talking about.

"I would go, too," Eesyan said. He looked out at Hunt. "Then we would, literally, be down there in the Entoverse, and could talk to them."

It was typical of the Thuriens. After pursuing reasonableness and caution to the point where it seemed they would never be capable of initiating any action at all, they had come up with something so stunning that it made everything everyone else had been talking about look tame. For a moment Hunt was speechless at the audacity of it.

"Then what?" he managed to ask finally.

Caldwell shrugged. "Then it's up to you. But with VISAR on your side, you ought to be able to pull off something pretty effective. After all, in the Entoverse, VISAR will be God."

Chapter Fifty-four

Hauled by two slow-plodding *drodhzes*, their six legs moving in a lazy, lumbering shuffle, the cart slipped and bumped its way down the rocky trail toward the village. A company of cavalry from the Royal Guard went before, while the Examiner and his assistant priests rode in a carriage following, with another squad of soldiers bringing up the rear.

Thrax sat with Shingen-Hu and a dozen or so other captured adepts, tattered and filthy, staring dejectedly out over the side of the cart at the ravaged crops and orchards withering in the gloom. His body still ached from the welts and bruises he had collected when they were captured. The rough chains chafed painfully at his wrists, neck, and ankles. Despite the springy coils supporting the cart's floor, every bump and jolt of the boards beneath them seemed to find a new sore spot and send another stab of pain shooting through his stiffening joints.

So, finally, it had come to this. After all the hopes and aspirations of one day joining the Arisen, and having come so close—only to see his opportunity cruelly snatched from within his very grasp, and to be exterminated ignominiously as a deceiver. For the high priest, Ethendor, had proclaimed all

Waroth's afflictions to be a result of Nieru's anger at the pretenders who had been allowed to desecrate the sign of the Purple
Spiral, and promised that the stars would return to the heavens
when atonement had been made. As a consequence, all the
teachers and adepts not affiliated with the temples were being
hunted down. The people, frightened and desperate for better
times to return, heeded the warnings and gave no sanctuary.
He looked at Shingen-Hu, next to him. The Master's eyes were
dull and empty, resigned to whatever fate lay ahead.

A crowd of villagers grew and followed as the procession
came into the village. Some jeered and pelted the cart with
rocks and garbage. Others cheered and called out praises to
the priests. The soldiers rode haughtily, jostling aside those
who were slow to move, and swinging their rods freely to clear
the way, while the Examiner and his retinue sat erect in their
carriage, maintaining their stony-faced composure and dignity.

A platform had been erected in the square at the center of
the village, where an excited crowd had already formed. On
the platform were three stakes with fagots piled ready for
lighting, while the executioner and his assistants stood impassively in front, watching as the procession drew up. The guards
clubbed and prodded the prisoners down from the cart. From
the dignitaries' carriage, the Deputy to the Examiner
descended with two acolytes and pointed to three of the prisoners. Guards hustled the terrified three up onto the platform.
Thrax and Shingen-Hu were herded to one side with the
remainder, while the Deputy climbed the steps behind and
raised his hands to address the crowd.

"People of the hamlet of Rakashym, *these* are the heretics
who have brought pestilence and ruin to the lands of Waroth."
He paused, while the crowd erupted in a new frenzy of ridicule and abuse, then gestured down at the group who had
been moved aside. "These shall be taken to Orenash to join
the others who have profaned, and there will the vengeance of
the gods be exacted. Then will the stain that has sat upon
Waroth be cleaned, and a pronouncement shall be heard then
of momentous times that are about to befall us."

The Deputy looked over the crowd. They waited dutifully,

but that was not what they were interested in at the moment. Reading their mood, he dismissed the rest of the oration that he had intended and turned to point accusingly at the three prisoners quaking behind him. "But Rakashym shall not be denied its chance to see the fate that awaits all who transgress, and to show its devotion." Cheering broke out. *This* was more like it. The Deputy nodded. "Let this day be a lesson . . ."

Among the prisoners watching fearfully below, Thrax turned his head to see how Shingen-Hu was reacting. To his surprise, he found a light shining in the Master's eyes that he had expected never to see again. The strength had come back into his features, and the body that Thrax had watched wasting away was standing straight and vibrant with sudden inner energy.

"Master, what inspires thee so?" Thrax whispered. "What do you see?"

"I hear a voice!" Shingen-Hu answered. "The power returns. I hear a god speaking within me."

A delusion brought on by hopelessness, Thrax told himself. The gods had abandoned them long ago.

Hunt settled back into the neurocoupler in one of the booths off the corridor at the rear of the Gondola. In the few years since he had moved from England to join UNSA, he had walked on the Moon, flown with one of the manned missions to Jupiter and stayed for months on Ganymede, returned to Earth aboard an alien starship, virtual-traveled over much of the Thuriens' domain of the local region of the Galaxy, and finally traveled physically to a distant star. But of all of it, the expedition that he was about to embark on was the strangest ever. In fact it was probably the strangest that had ever been embarked upon by anyone in the whole of time.

Besides himself, the others who would be going down into the Entoverse were Danchekker, since he was equally a part of the team on the spot, Nixie, obviously, as a guide, and Gina, who as a journalist refused to be left out—all of whom were in other booths nearby. Eesyan would be going, too, as technical adviser and principal liaison to VISAR, coupled in from Thurien.

Since VISAR would need all of the channel capacity of the single available h-space link to sustain its manipulations of JEVEX and its behind-the-scenes operations in the Entoverse, it wouldn't be possible for the machine to support continual interaction in real time between the occupants of the couplers and the pseudoversions of themselves written into the Entoverse. Instead, the "surrogates," once they were impressed with the personality patterns extracted by VISAR from their originals, would proceed to function autonomously. Since what constituted a personality *was* the thinking, feeling information pattern that defined it and not the physical medium that the pattern happened to be supported in, the team would in effect be existing and functioning in the Entoverse.

During that time, their real-world bodies would lie comatose until, at last, VISAR would erase the Ent-body surrogates and transfer all the impressions and recollections that they had accumulated in the interim back into the human brain patterns. For all practical purposes, the team would have been transported into the Entoverse for a while, functioned there in response to whatever circumstances awaited them, and then been brought back again.

"How are we doing, VISAR?" Hunt muttered.

"We're getting there. Sorting through this kind of detail involves a lot of processing, even for me."

Hunt already knew that. He was just impatient to get on with it.

To avoid an inordinate amount of try-it-and-see experimenting that they didn't have time for anyway, VISAR would not attempt to create authentic interpretations of how a human nervous system would perceive the actual structures and relationships between them that existed in the Entoverse—if, indeed, any such interpretation was possible at all. Instead, the same principle of correspondence that caused emerged Ents to remember their past experiences in Exoverse-meaningful terms would cause the surrogates to perceive their experiences in terms that were familiar. Rather than try to compose a routine for constructing some physically visualizable depiction of the abstract patterns of intercellular transactions taking place in the Entoverse, VISAR would endow its pseudo-Ents with ready-made patterns of conceptual associations extracted from the hosts. These would respond to external stimuli by selecting the nearest from their stores of elemental human percepts that conformed to the same set of basic attributes. Thus, a feature of the surface configuration that was reasonably permanent, behaved with the properties of mass, and reflected part of the radiant flux impinging on it would look like a rock; a form that absorbed components of its surroundings, stayed where it was, and grew systematically bigger would look like a tree; and Hunt, whatever the nature of the bound pattern of cells that VISAR had needed to commandeer to create his Ent-equivalent acceptable to other Ents, would look, to himself, like Hunt—modified and appareled in whatever way VISAR judged appropriate to the circumstances that it discerned. "There isn't time to dream up a new, internally consistent world of experience," VISAR had explained. "We'll just have to work with what we've got."

"What's going on now?" Hunt asked.

"I think we're in business," VISAR replied. "Nixie's in touch with one of them down there now. It's not one of the big chiefs that she was searching for, but it seems like some guys who are in trouble. I can give you a quick preview."

A scene appeared as if before Hunt's eyes of a noisy, excited crowd cramming in from the side streets to the central square of what seemed to be a primitive village. The people were dressed in crude, rustic garb of coarse shirts and breeches, jerkins, and cloaks. But there was also a peculiar, wheelless carriage that ran on slides, like a sledge, with occupants who were more finely arrayed in jewelry and robes. In front of the carriage was a protective line of figures wearing helmets and breastplates and carrying weapons, and ahead, more of them mounted on strange six-legged beasts. Behind the carriage was a rough, open cart, also without wheels. Both conveyances were hitched to pairs of strange, bulky animals, again with six legs but heavier than the ones bearing the riders. They looked somewhat like buffalo, but with enormous, pillarlike legs that projected sideways from their bodies, then bent downward in a right angle like a spider's.

There was a raised platform with more figures, and behind them, Hunt realized to his alarm and consternation, three stakes piled ready for burning. The houses of the village were square and smooth, possibly mud-built, with projections like minarets, and arches connecting across some of the alleys. Here and there in the square, scaly, doglike animals were whooping and leaping like miniature kangaroos. The light was dim, a gloomy twilight. Outlined through it in the background were mountains, more vertical and sharply angular than any natural formations that Hunt had ever seen before.

Although Hunt had been prepared, he still found himself overcome with amazement. "That's really it, the Entoverse?" he asked, struggling to accept it. "This is really happening right now, inside a computer light-years away from here?"

"Concentrate on the situation," VISAR replied. "I've got a feeling you could get involved real soon."

Near the base of the platform, surrounded by more soldiers, was a group of what looked like prisoners, dirty, ragged, and disheveled, wearing manacles and chains. Two seemed to single themselves out in Hunt's field of view as VISAR directed his attention to them. The younger man, scarcely more than a youth, had fair hair and the remains of a long, white tunic. Hunt stared in surprise as he recognized the purple-spiral emblem on the sash hanging from his shoulder. The older of the two, with long, matted hair and a heavy beard, was clad in what had once been flowing robes, now falling apart. But instead of bowing cowed and dejected like the rest of the prisoners, he was standing erect, his face turned upward, wreathed in an expression of ecstatic revelation. Then Hunt heard a voice that he recognized as Nixie's, which he knew somehow to be speaking inside the bearded man's mind.

". . . the gods that you knew before. All that's over now. The sky's about to come under new management."

The old man's thoughts came through as another voice, sounding awed and exalted. "More powerful gods shall rule the heavens? And shall I, Shingen-Hu, be their servant? The priests of the temples, and all their powers, and the king and his forces, all shall be overcome?"

"Don't worry about them. They're out of it now . . . Oh-oh." On the platform, another nobleman in robes was shouting something about bringing down wrath on blasphemers. Three more prisoners were being chained to the stakes, while several sinister figures advanced menacingly toward them holding long, nasty-looking knives.

"Look," Nixie's voice said. "We're gonna send you down one of our troubleshooters right now. You look like you could use help. Just leave it all to him. I'll explain later."

"An angel?" Shingen-Hu said. "To aid us in this moment of anguish? We shall yet be saved?"

Hunt realized with a sudden sinking feeling whom she meant. "Hey, wait a minute, VISAR. You can't do this. I don't know anything about—"

"Trust me," VISAR said. "Think about getting your act together."

Suddenly, Shingen-Hu was thundering and pointing an accusing finger up at the robed figure on the platform. "*Desist ye, false prophet and instrument of all that is evil!*" A confused hush swept over the crowd, and all heads turned toward him. "Charlatan and deceiver, thou liest! Even now do greater gods sweep thee and thy puny masters aside, to be trodden into the mire like vermin. Behold, an angel descends from the realm beyond, and he shall be my witness, and thy undoing!"

"VISAR, I really don't think you—"

"Okay, go knock 'em dead. You're on."

And suddenly, Hunt was up there on the platform. Not just as a focal point of impressions being relayed by VISAR. He was *there*. Instantly, total silence fell, and every face in the square was gaping at him as if he had just materialized out of nowhere.

As indeed, of course, he had.

Chapter Fifty-five

It was no good. Hunt's mind seized up. For a fleeting, insane second he was tempted to say, "I suppose you're all wondering why I'm standing up here like this," but the looks on the faces below dispelled any further thought of it.

He looked down and saw that he was wearing a long, loose, togalike garment with sandals. "What's this?" he hissed inwardly at VISAR. "I look like a part in *Julius Caesar.*"

"You're not exactly in Trafalgar Square," VISAR answered. "It's appropriate. What did you want, something from Savile Row?"

The noble who had been in charge was backing away behind the soldiers, who were slowly recovering their wits and moving forward warily. "He's not a god, he's an impostor!" the noble screamed. "Kill him!"

In a passing thought, Hunt wondered how he came to understand the words. But there were more pressing things to attend to just at the moment. One of the soldiers, a bearded giant with embellished breastplate and plumed helmet, who suggested something from popular depictions of the Trojan War, drew back his arm and hurled a spear. Hunt raised a protective arm reflexively; the spear stopped in midair less than a foot away, then burst into fragments that fell to the ground.

"VISAR, do we have to cut things that close?" Hunt asked shakily.

"Sorry about that. I'm still experimenting with the dynamics of this place." Things that moved got longer, Hunt remembered.

"What kind of cowards are you?" the noble shouted. "That's just a man. One man!"

A hail of spears and darts came; all were deflected or fell harmlessly. The giant, whom Hunt had mentally dubbed Agamemnon, advanced menacingly, drawing his sword. Reassured that God was indeed on his side, Hunt stepped forward with a new feeling of confidence to meet him.

"Die, puppet of pretenders!" Agamemnon cried, swinging.

"Not today, I think, thank you," Hunt said, and snapped his fingers. The sword turned into a vine of pink flowers, which coiled itself around Agamemnon's arm. Agamemnon stopped, staring at the flowers in confusion, then shook them off and stamped on them.

"Getting the hang of it now," VISAR said.

"Yes, well, do you think you could remove this chap to a safer distance?"

"No problem." An invisible force swept Agamemnon unceremoniously across the platform and over the edge. He hit the ground with a mighty, metallic crash and sat up, dazed and bewildered.

"The others are a bit too close for comfort, too," Hunt said. Agamemnon had just started to pick himself up when the rest of the soldiers who had been up on the platform cascaded down on top of him.

"How's that?"

"Not bad."

The bearded man below, who had spoken of himself in Hunt's mind as Shingen-Hu, was pointing up at him and calling out to the crowd. "Behold the angel that was foretold! See how the servants of treachery are powerless before him!"

"How do we know what they're saying?" Hunt asked VISAR.

"You can't be translating. You're new here, as well."

"Your thought patterns are coupled to an Ent-wired neural system that includes a local speech center. It's the same as the reason why Ents can understand Jevlenese when they emerge."

Deprived of his soldiers, the noble was cringing back among the executioner and his minions for protection. Hunt turned the knives they were holding into cucumbers and their jerkins into coats of thick molasses, then collided them all together so that they fell, writhing and adhering helplessly. Starting to enjoy himself, he turned the chains of the three unfortunates tied to the stakes into garlands of butterflies, which dispersed and fluttered away.

"So these people would be able to understand me?" he asked VISAR.

"They should."

"How much more can you give me in the way of background data?"

"Not a lot. I'm mainly manipulating physical data patterns. It needs processing through a nervous system to interpret what they mean."

"We need Nixie here, then."

She appeared beside Hunt, wearing a Greek chiton turned up and held by a girdle to form a short tunic falling to just above the knee; she was shod with laced buckskin. She looked like representations of Artemis, the virgin huntress. Hunt couldn't help smiling at VISAR's appalling choice. A murmur went up from the crowd.

"Another angel descends! My words shall be vindicated!" Shingen-Hu cried out. The crowd was impressed, clearly; but from what Hunt could see, not as much as he would have expected. Below the platform, the main body of soldiers had shown some initial confusion, but was steadying again as the occupants of the carriage came tumbling out.

"What can you make of this?" he murmured as Nixie took in the scene. "We've got gentry down there with the troops, and a chain gang over there. Good guys, bad guys, which are which? What's going on?"

"The ones getting out from the carriage are priests from

the city," Nixie said. "Their logo has a green crescent, the sign of Vandros. Eubeleus uses the same sign, so they must be his buddies here." She surveyed the results of Hunt's impromptu handiwork. "It looks as if you got it right."

"I don't like the kind of party this was about to be." So saying, Hunt turned the weapons of the remaining soldiers below into a kitchen-garden variety and the chains of the prisoners into laurel leaves. The prisoners scattered them to the ground and lifted their hands, gaping down at themselves and at each other, wondering at their sudden freedom.

"See how the angels come as instruments of retribution and justice!" Shingen-Hu bellowed.

But the priests, undeterred, raised their arms in unison and pointed up toward the platform, their eyes burning in a strange, penetrating fixation that Hunt found instantly unnerving, even at that distance. And then he realized that he was paralyzed. Bolts of fire flew up at him, but VISAR interceded and dissipated them into clouds of sparks. A shimmering curtain seemed to pass between Hunt and the priests, and he found his faculties unfrozen again.

"What the hell was that, VISAR?" he gasped inwardly.

"They got to you. More goes on in this place than is obvious."

"Well, we can match that act." Hunt turned and pointed a finger at one of the three piles of fagots heaped around the stakes—the intended victims had made themselves scarce. "Fire." The pile ignited into a spectacular blaze. A murmur went up from the crowd. Hunt turned back, folded his arms grandiosely, and gazed down at the priests with what he hoped was a look of lordly contempt.

It didn't faze them. "Pah! Is that the power of your superior gods?" one of them scoffed. "Apprentice angel!" He stepped forward, pointed at the second pile, and duplicated the act. The crowd cheered. Clearly they were rooting for the home team.

"Try this," Hunt invited, and materialized a white dove out of nowhere, flying above the crowd.

"Puerile." The priest shot it down with a well-aimed digit of psychic flak. Hunt turned the third pile and its stake into a rosebush surmounted by an apple tree. The priests shredded the lot with an invisible blender. Hunt collapsed the carriage that they had just climbed out of into a heap of parts. They did the same to the platform that he was standing on, and only the speedy intervention of VISAR again saved him and Nixie from joining Agamemnon and his companions, who were still sorting themselves out on the ground.

"They are demons summoned by the false prophets," the dignitary who seemed to be in charge called to the soldiers. "Slay the heretics." The soldiers threw aside the horticultural assortment that they were holding and grabbed staffs and clubs proffered by the crowd.

"VISAR, this isn't working," Hunt said in a worried voice. "We need something more spectacular."

"I could take the whole world apart, but what would it leave you to achieve? You're supposed to be the expert on organic psychology."

"Bring in the technical consultant."

Porthik Eesyan appeared alongside Hunt and Nixie, who were standing before the wreckage of the platform and the burning wood. He looked like his Thurien self, but VISAR had arrayed him in ancient Egyptian fashion, with a close-fitting, skirted costume and high, rearward-projecting headpiece that suited the elongated Ganymean skull. Hunt assumed that he would have been following the events in the same way that Hunt himself had, before his abrupt debut onstage.

"Already the demons are in need of help," the head priest sneered.

"An interesting predicament," Eesyan observed to Hunt.

"Save the analysis till later. What do we do about it?"

"You're going about it the wrong way. Magic is normal here. What you're doing is impossible, but the people haven't realized it. To them it's just a question of degree, not really all that different: the same *kind* of thing that they're used to."

"What would you do, then?"

Eesyan addressed VISAR. "How absolute are the constraints imposed by breakdown of dimensional invariance with velocity?"

"The underlying dynamic of the substrate is optimized to preserve form," VISAR replied. "The algorithm uses a write-before-erase protocol to afford a redundancy check for accuracy."

"So a local violation is possible?"

"Sure. I can change the algorithm."

Then Hunt became aware of Danchekker's voice speaking inside his head, observing via a coupler on Jevlen and presumably being relayed for Hunt's benefit, courtesy of VISAR. "I, ah, believe I know just the thing. VISAR, look up your records of Earth for places like Blackpool and Coney Island, would you—you know the kinds of things I mean? I think we could use as elaborate a model as you can devise, with ample gadgetry and mechanisms. They don't have to do anything functional."

"You're sure about this?" VISAR sounded dubious.

"Just do as I suggest, please."

Hunt could have kicked himself as he realized what Danchekker was getting at. It was too obvious. "There isn't time to dream up a whole, new, internally consistent world of experience, VISAR," he said. "We'll just have to work with what we've got." With that, he extended an arm imperiously and pointed toward the center of the village square.

Shouts of alarm went up from the middle of the crowd as a force began pushing people out of the way to create a clear area. The area grew and became a circle, its perimeter expanding relentlessly and sweeping more jostling, protesting bodies ahead like snow before a snowplow until it was fifty feet or more across. A light came on above to illuminate the whole square, and the cleared circle became at first hazy, then took on a deepening purple hue, until it was filled with what looked like writhing purple smoke. And out of the smoke came forth a strange, jangling music of whistling organ notes, churning mechanically, while within the smoke, a procession of indistinct shapes flitted by, rising and falling in a strange, repetitive rhythm. The soldiers forgot about the prisoners and turned to stare. Even the priests seemed less sure of themselves and were glancing at each other apprehensively. The crowd drew back in hushed trepidation.

Then, the smoke dispersed to unveil VISAR's creation. *Rotating!* And this time, Hunt conceded, even with his experience of the machine's abilities, VISAR had exceeded itself. It was the most magnificent carnival carousel that he had ever seen, with horses, cockerels, swans, and tigers, all moving up and down as they passed by and around under a great, brilliantly colored canopy decked with row after row of winking lights. And in the center of it all, an enormous steam Wurlitzer pounded and thrummed, flywheel spinning, slide valves popping, with shafts and belts connected to an incredible Rube Goldberg concoction of rocking cranks, syncopating levers, undulating cams, whirling gear trains, and nodding tappets, all acting out its cycle of interlocked motions with a complexity and ingenuity that astonished even Hunt.

A hushed murmur, mixing awe, reverence, and fear, swept through the crowd. The priests were standing transfixed. Some of the soldiers fell to their knees, bowing their heads to the ground, and here and there among the crowd others followed their example. Agamemnon, who had extricated himself again, straightened up slowly and stared wide-eyed. A strange, ululating, high-toned chant went up from among the prisoners.

The carousel began slowing, though the music continued. As the turntable made its final revolution before coming to rest, it brought two figures into view, seated on a pair of the animals—the only place VISAR could find to put them. Hunt's face split into an uncontrollable grin as he saw Danchekker stepping down from a brightly colored peacock, robed like a Roman senator, complete with crown of laurel leaves, but still, incongruously, wearing his gold-rimmed spectacles. Behind him, dismounting from a rhinoceros, was Gina, in sandals and the simple, flimsy, plain white shift of a slave girl, and, God alone—or in this case, VISAR—knew why, carrying a wine jar.

It wasn't a time for hesitation or timidity. Mustering all his composure and holding himself regally erect, Danchekker moved to the edge of the turntable and stood surveying the scene like a god descended from Olympus. Gina moved to stand a pace behind, while in the background the music faded. "Well?" he demanded after the silence had endured for several seconds. "Can't you do any better than just stand there wearing those infuriating, cretinous expressions?"

Several more absolutely still, endless seconds dragged by.

Then, the Examiner himself dropped down onto one knee, threw up his arms, and cried out, "Hail, Father of the Gods! This day has the magic of Hyperia descended upon Waroth. Indeed hast the Master whom we reviled spoken truly!"

"Hail! Hail!" those in the crowd immediately in front of Danchekker echoed, and threw themselves down before them.

Others took up the cry.

"Hail, Father of Gods!"

"Lighter of the heavens!"

"Master of objects that spin!"

Danchekker stepped down to the ground, moved a pace forward, and waited for Gina to hop down behind. Then, clasping his robe where his lapels would normally be and followed by his slave, he strode majestically across the square while the crowd parted and adulating figures shouted out praises and prostrated themselves as he passed. By the time he came to where Hunt, Nixie, and Eesyan were standing, and turned to look back, the whole square was down on its knees, faces to the ground.

Across the square, the carousel started up again, and the music resumed. Danchekker looked on and gave a satisfied nod. "No, Dr. Hunt. *I*, I rather think, am the better judge of organic psychology," he said.

Chapter Fifty-six

"Generator complexes three and five are now up to full power and can be switched into the system," an aide reported from another part of Uttan. "Seven is being brought up to standby as a backup. Everything is on schedule." From behind the supervisor's chair in the *real* JEVEX primary control center, Eubeleus returned a curt nod. "How does it look at this end?" he asked Iduane, who was standing a short distance away, checking reports and status indicators.

"Matching positive. We can initiate reintegration at any time."

Eubeleus leaned back and surveyed the other consoles and operator positions around the floor. Everything was under control and orderly. Across the planet, the Thurien fools who thought they were in control of the Uttan system because JEVEX was shut down and isolated far away on Jevlen didn't even know they were standing right on top of it. They would very soon find out.

"And how are events inside?"

"The last time I contacted our Prophet, they were progressing well," Iduane answered. "They're rounding up all the heretics for the great auto-da-fé. They should be all fired up to do a fine job on Jevlen for us when they start coming out."

Eubeleus nodded again, distantly. None of it was real, of course. It was simply an elaborate software simulation that JEVEX had created to train and orient the software identities that it had devised to extend itself into the outside universe. But those identities became real when they overwrote the personalities of physical users coupled into the system. Such was JEVEX's method for externalizing its dimensions of existence—a solution which Eubeleus had no hesitation in acclaiming as a feat of genius. After all, wasn't *he* a manifestation of it?

"When the time comes for the Prophet to announce the Great Awakening, I would like to be in control of him myself," Eubeleus said. "It would be gratifying to participate in the culmination of the project—personally, as it were."

"As you wish," Iduane agreed.

Eubeleus stared at the console with a distant look, slipping into one of his rare reflective moods. "It's difficult to believe that we, ourselves, originated like that. I look for any hint of nostalgia every time I connect into one of them, but there really isn't any. I don't recall anything of what I was down there before my emergence. There must be—" His words were interrupted by a priority tone from the console. He nodded toward the video pickup. "Yes?"

One of the screens came to life to show the face of another of his aides, elsewhere in the complex. "My apologies. We have a grade one coming in from Shiban PAC, on Jevlen."

"Very well." The image changed to show the face of Langerif. He looked worried. "What?" Eubeleus demanded.

"News has just come in here that Grevetz has been assassinated," Langerif said."

Eubeleus came around the chair and sat down, glaring at the screen. "When did it happen? Do you know who did it?"

"At his villa in the Cerberan, just over an hour ago. His man who runs the north side did it: the one they call Scirio."

"How?"

"They came down in a flier and wiped out him and a bunch of

his people on the pad. Then they demolished virtually the entire place. There was no provocation or warning. It was a massacre."

"I always thought Scirio was reliable. What was it, another of their family squabbles?"

"We're not sure. There's more. The hooker from the city, the one who was here at PAC—she was with them. We have the video record from the house surveillance system."

"She's the one who's been helping the Terrans," Iduane murmured. He had moved across from where he had been standing and was watching from beside Eubeleus's chair.

Langerif nodded from the screen. "There has to be some kind of connection, but right at this moment we don't know what."

Eubeleus's frown deepened with suspicion. "What kind of operations does this Scirio specialize in?" he asked.

"Protection and retaliation for a price. Since the Ganymeans took over, he's been getting big in the luxury black market, especially for high-paying headworlders. He runs a number of clubs as fronts in the city."

"Headworlders?" Eubeleus stared back at the screen fixedly. Then his expression slowly changed to one of alarm. "That means he has access to an h-channel to Uttan. Into JEVEX."

Langerif talked to somebody offscreen, then looked back. "Yes. Several of them, apparently."

Eubeleus went through the sequence of events in his head. The Terran scientists from UNSA, Hunt and Danchekker, both of whom had played key roles in thwarting the Federation, had come to Jevlen ostensibly as part of a scientific mission, which had turned out to be an undercover assignment to investigate what was afflicting the Jevlenese. After a lot of secret work in PAC that Eubeleus's people had not been able to penetrate, the scientists had taken up with, of all people, an *Ichena* hoodlum. What could they be interested in? But Scirio had access into JEVEX. And—merely by coincidence?—no sooner had they talked to Scirio than he exterminated an awakener, who, it just so happened, had been due to liquidate all of the *Ichena*'s outsider management as soon as the takeover was completed.

Euebeleus jerked his head around sharply toward Iduane. "Commence reintegration of JEVEX."

"Right now?"

"At once. As soon as you reach the requisite level, I want a complete check of all core functions. Scan for active h-space links from Jevlen and deactivate all of them." Eubeleus looked back at Langerif, on the screen. "Get a list of all of the establishments of Scirio's that have functioning couplers. Get men out to each of them and shut them down. *All* of them, do you understand? You'll find the girl and the missing Terrans at one of them. When you do, take them back to PAC. Under *no* circumstances are they to have any means of accessing JEVEX. And I expect no blundering from anyone there this time."

Chapter Fifty-seven

The carousel whirled merrily beneath bright lights in the village square, carrying its train of enraptured priests, dignitaries, and soldiers, including Agamemnon, who was planted astride a white horse with a red bridle. Elsewhere, crowds of villagers gaped in awe at a Newcomen pump and steam engine, complete with ten-foot-diameter toothed fly-wheel, an arrangement of revolving cages within revolving cages within a revolving cage which spun multiple-core submarine cables, and a Budweiser beer-bottling machine. Shingen-Hu, the new deputy lord of Creation, cleansed and groomed courtesy of VISAR, and wearing fresh clothes, stood with Eesyan, arms folded on his chest, absorbing the wonders of the new Power and adjusting himself to the feeling of being its chosen agent. Thrax and the rest of the ex-heretics stood in a group to one side, listening reverently while the emissaries of the True Gods revealed the Word that they had been sent to deliver.

"Until we've sorted out what to do about it at the other end, we don't want anyone else rising up out of here on the currents," Hunt told the Examiner. The sphere that VISAR had created to represent the Entoverse symbolically, like a crystal ball, illustrated the point. It had a miniature representation of the local world inside, and around the outside, a lot of tiny red figures attached by threads coming out of their heads. "There are other beings out there, like you. And every time somebody from here arises, one of them is wiped out." Inside the crystal ball, a mini-Ent soared upward to the surface, vanished into one of the threads, and a moment later appeared at the other end, on the outside. The red figure that had been attached there fell over and turned black.

"An angel must be sacrificed to make room for each who arises to Hyperia?" the Examiner asked, looking troubled.

"If you want to put it that way, yes," Hunt said.

"In addition, there appear to be certain compatibility problems between Warothian mental configurations and human nervous systems, which frequently result in breakdown and make the transference a risky affair," Danchekker informed the Examiner. The Examiner nodded respectfully, not having mastered the intricacies of this new ecclesiastical language yet.

"Angels newly emerged into Hyperia are often troubled," Nixie supplied. A step behind the Examiner, the village headman followed it all humbly.

"Then what of the Great Awakening that has been foretold?" the Examiner asked. "If what thou sayest is true, then many angels shall fall, and great will be the woe among our multitudes due to join the Arisen."

"What Great Awakening is this?" Gina asked.

The Examiner seemed surprised. "The goddess knows not?"

"She means, what was the version that was given to you?" Hunt explained.

"Ethendor, who was the instrument of the fallen gods, prophesied a Great Awakening, when the stars shall shine again and currents return more numerous than ever before, and the people shall arise into Hyperia in their multitudes," the Examiner recited.

"The invasion," Hunt said, looking at the others. "It looks as if we were right. Eubeleus was all set to bring them out in hordes."

"When is this supposed to happen?" Danchekker asked; then he added hastily, "According to what you were told."

"When the sun itself shines strong once more, and daylight returns to the lands of Waroth," the Examiner replied. "Thus was it spoken."

Hunt looked at Nixie, his face serious. "Who is this Ethendor?"

"The high priest in Orenash, the main city in this part. Apparently he ordered the crackdown on Shingen-Hu and the rest that these guys were carrying out."

"Where is this place?"

"How far are we from Orenash?" Nixie asked the village headman.

"Half a day's ride by *drodhz* sled." The headman obviously thought that gods should have known; but he wasn't about to make an issue out of it.

"Then that's where it'll all happen," Hunt said. "We can leave the carnival here and be on our way. There mightn't be a lot of time."

The Examiner was growing puzzled as he listened. "Thou must journey to Orenash? Then the dark masters whom Ethendor serves are not yet truly fallen?"

Hunt shook his head. "Not yet, I'm afraid. We've still got some work to do. But at least this has given us a better idea of how to go about it." He looked at Danchekker and Gina. "I think the best thing would be—"

At that moment, the village headman suddenly pointed skyward. "*The stars!* See, the stars are returning!"

Everyone looked up. "VISAR, cut the lights," Hunt said after a moment. The lamps on the posts that had appeared around the village square went out. Several bright stars were shining in the twilit sky. "Were those there when we arrived?" Hunt asked Nixie.

"I'm not sure. I didn't notice," she confessed.

"Eesyan, did you . . ." Hunt's voice trailed away as the Wurlitzer music in the background ceased suddenly. He turned and looked across the square. The carousel had stopped, pitching the startled passengers on its revolving menagerie forward onto the necks of their mounts and, in some instances, off onto the floor. The steam engine, cable spinner, and bottling machine were all frozen in silent immobility. Already, people in the crowd were muttering discontentedly and giving each other puzzled looks. "What's going on?" Hunt demanded, jerking his head back around bemusedly.

"They were just props," Eesyan said, but in a puzzled, far-away voice, as if still trying to work it out himself. "There was no internal motive source. VISAR was causing them to operate, externally."

"VISAR, what is the meaning of this?" Danchekker demanded.

Hunt waited, then looked at Danchekker uneasily. "VISAR?" he repeated. There was no response.

Gina shook her head in sudden alarm as the implication hit her. "We've lost the connection?" she said, turning her head toward Eesyan. "You mean we don't have VISAR to back us up anymore?"

"Worse than that," the Thurien told them somberly. "We don't have a way back."

Mystified, Keshen, the Jevlenese engineer in the pay of the *Ichena*, frowned at the monitor displays and stabbed repeatedly at the panel controls in the communications room at the rear of the Gondola. "What is this? The connection's gone."

Scirio heard the commotion from the room outside, where he was sitting at a table, snatching a drink with Murray and several *Ichena*. Frowning, he got up and walked over. "What is it?" he asked through the doorway.

"The beam from Thurien has gone down. We've lost the connection to JEVEX, too." Keshen sat back and tossed up his hands. "That's it. Zilch."

"There's nothing you can do?"

"What can I do? Somebody's cut the links. They're dead."

In the room behind, the others were on their feet. Scirio bit his lip, thinking furiously. He hadn't expected repercussions so quickly. Maybe Grevetz had had connections that even he hadn't known about. And they would need to be high-level connections for this to have happened. He had backed what had sounded like the winning side; now it was all a mess. Did the freaks from inside JEVEX that these Terrans had talked about own the whole city already?

Fendro, the club manager, who had been out in the reception office, burst into the far side of the club's main lounge through the door from the front passage.

"Boss! Boss! Where's Scirio?"

Scirio went back out to the lounge. "What?"

Fendro pointed excitedly back toward the front entrance. "Cops! There's cops outside like walking artillery. No messing. I mean, they're coming *in*!" A series of solid concussions sounded from the front of the club to emphasize the point.

Another of the staff appeared from the back. "They've got the yard covered. Ain't no way out that way."

"Shit," Scirio muttered. What had he stirred up now? "Okay, look, take a couple of guys, get back up front, and try to stall them there. Speedball, Beans, dig in here to cover Fendy when they pull back. We'll go on up the tower to move out the hearse. Split as soon as you get three beeps on the box. Blow this place to hold 'em if you have to."

Murray waved along the corridor in the direction of the booths. "What about the guys dreaming in there?"

"You brought 'em here. They're your problem. If you want 'em out of here, get 'em up the tower. We're getting out."

On Thurien, in the Government Center in the principal city of Thurios, Calazar turned a bewildered face toward the others who had been following events in the village with him. In reality they were still coupled into VISAR at different locations, including Caldwell in Washington, and Leyel Torres aboard the *Shapieron* at Geerbaine, and not together in the same room as they perceived.

"VISAR, what's happening?" he demanded.

"The channel from Jevlen has been cut. I don't have access to there, or to JEVEX."

"You mean you've lost them? Aren't they still there?" Caldwell had not completely followed the technical dialogue between the Thuriens and VISAR about autonomous personality transfers and temporary state suspension.

"They're all still there and functioning in the Entoverse," VISAR replied. "But I can't communicate with it to talk to them or manipulate events anymore."

Caldwell looked confused. "But those were just . . . 'copies,' or whatever, weren't they? The original people are still in the couplers, right?"

"Yes," VISAR said. "But the capacity of the one channel wasn't sufficient for me to continually update the original personae— inside the bodies that are in the couplers—in real time. So they were left in a suspended state. The transformed versions that I wrote into the Ent surrogates are the only ones functioning as coherent, conscious identities. In effect, they're *there*: inside the matrix on Uttan."

Caldwell was still uncertain. "But the bodies in the couplers still contain the original personalities, surely. Won't they reanimate independently?"

"They'll reanimate, yes," VISAR said. "But without any knowledge of what happened to the surrogates in the Entoverse."

"Then we're okay—" Caldwell caught the looks on the Thuriens' faces. "No? Why not?"

"I don't think you quite see our point, Gregg," Calazar said. "As far as we're concerned, ever since the transfers down into the Entoverse were made, the beings that VISAR created there are real, bona fide identities in their own right, as much as any other Ent. Whether or not they originated as psychical clones of other beings existing out here in the Exoverse is beside the point. They're stuck there, and we can't get them out."

"Okay, go knock 'em dead," VISAR's voice said. "You're on."

Hunt tensed with involuntary apprehension . . . And then the distant, dreamy feeling brought on when the mind was being flooded by sensations fed in from the machine left him suddenly. He opened his eyes, puzzled. "VISAR?" The booth was silent. He sat up in the recliner. The image of the three terrified figures chained to the stakes, the executioners advancing toward them with knives, and the ragged prophet shouting from below was still vivid in his mind. What had gone wrong?

The door opened and Murray appeared, gesturing frantically. Distant bangs reverberated through the building, like explosions, along with the sounds of running footsteps and more voices. "Move it! Everyone's getting out. We've got cops coming in shooting."

"What the hell's it about?" Hunt gasped, jumping up.

"Who knows?"

"VISAR?" Hunt called one last time, just to be sure. Nothing.

"Forget it," Murray threw back over his shoulder as he disappeared again. "You got cut off."

Hunt came out into the corridor. Nixie was there already, with Gina emerging from another booth and Murray hauling Danchekker from the door adjacent. Dreadnought and several other *Ichena* ran past, holding weapons. Keshen, the engineer, was hurrying through from the club with Scirio behind him, shouting orders.

"What's going on?" Gina asked. "Those three guys? What—"

"No time now," Murray interrupted. "We've got a war on here. Everyone back up the tower. We're getting out in the hearse."

As Nixie and Gina hurried away after Keshen, Danchekker glanced at his watch. A strange expression came over his face. He caught Hunt's sleeve just as Hunt was about to follow the others. "I'm not altogether certain that there's any point in worrying about those three unfortunates now," he said. "The episode to which I think you're referring would appear to be history."

"What are you talking about?" Hunt asked.

Danchekker tapped his watch. "We coupled into VISAR at approximately 1420 hours, did we not?"

"That's right," Murray confirmed, catching the gist as he strove to move them along after the others. "Is that a problem?"

"How long were we in those booths?" Hunt asked.

"An hour, hour and a half. Why? What's all the mystery? Let's move our asses outta here while we've still got 'em."

Chapter Fifty-eight

S lowly, it came to the Examiner, as he gazed up at the heavens, what the signs meant. Anger rose within him as he realized how he had been deceived. It was Ethendor who had prophesied that the stars would return to the skies. And no sooner had the stars begun returning than the powers of these strangers who claimed to be emissaries of yet higher gods deserted them.

So the tricks and toys could not have been the works of higher gods at all. It had been an attempt by the lesser gods to deceive the people of Waroth into abandoning the Great Awakening that was their rightful destiny. For the legions of the faithful would destroy the followers of the false gods who were tarnishing Hyperia, and the false gods were afraid. It was all clear to him now. The events that had taken place here in the village of Rakashym had been permitted as a final test of the Examiner's faith before the Great Awakening. He would not fail.

He turned his eyes back toward the puppets that the false gods had thrown in his path to deflect him from his course. They looked clumsy and foolish now, exposed in their ineptness—"gods" who hadn't heard of the Great Awakening or of Ethendor, and who didn't know where Orenash was. Across the square the priests and soldiers, freed from the spell that had bewitched them, were coming back, while the villagers closed in behind them, surly and resentful.

"The power that we use flows into here through channels that—" the first to have arrived began in what sounded like the beginnings of a plea.

"Silence!" The Examiner cut him off with a contemptuous wave. "Thou standest exposed in thy perfidy and helplessness."

The female who had appeared with him made an imploring gesture. "Look, you have to believe what these people say. I know. I *am* one of you, from Waroth. I emerged and have come back by the powers they control . . ."

The Examiner turned his back. "These are deceivers who stand exposed before us," he called to the crowd. "Indeed did Ethendor speak truly."

The crowd responded:

"Deceivers!"

"Servants of evil!"

"Rakashym must be purged of its taint."

"Take them! Take them!"

The Examiner spoke to Agamemnon, who had appeared at the front of the soldiers and was waiting for orders. "Seize them and bind them. Rebuild the pyres—one for each of the false prophets who were captured, except those two." He pointed at Shingen-Hu and Thrax. "Rakashym shall have its fill of burnings." He indicated the two that he had singled out, and the five impostors sent by the lesser gods. "*They* shall return with us to Orenash, for the special festivities that Ethendor has prepared. It should be very entertaining."

The soldiers moved in to separate the two groups. As they began moving, Hunt trod on a piece of one of the runners from the disassembled coach. His foot skidded sideways as if he had stepped on a ball, throwing him off balance and causing him to fall down painfully onto one knee.

"See he who calls himself a messenger from higher gods!" the Examiner called to the crowd, pointing. "Doesn't even a child know that shoe leather is repelled by mobilium?" The crowd laughed derisively.

Shingen-Hu stooped to help Hunt back to his feet. As he did so, he surreptitiously picked up a couple of slivers of the broken skids of mobilium metal and hid them in a fold of his robe.

From Thurien, Calazar was able to contact Parygol on Uttan through VISAR. But Parygol discovered then that his Thurien caretaker force was cut off from the rest of the planet, and that the facilities they occupied, which they had believed controlled both the planet's industrial complex and its links to a Jevlen-based JEVEX, were suddenly inoperative. Eubeleus had gained control of the system from elsewhere.

Porthik Eesyan, who was occupying a coupler still connected to VISAR and had "joined" Calazar and the others, confirmed their understanding of the situation. "Yes, that's the way it would work. There's another version of me still functioning in the Entoverse at this moment—and of all the others, of course. It's a strange feeling to know it."

"And *you* don't have any idea what's been happening since you—the other one of you—was transferred in?" Caldwell checked.

"No. The updating was to have been effected when the surrogates were erased and the originals reactivated," Eesyan said. "But the disconnection happened too abruptly."

There was a long, brooding silence.

"They'll be in trouble there, without VISAR," Calazar said quietly at last.

"I am aware of that," Eesyan replied. The edge to his voice was unusually sharp for a Thurien. "I happen to have a rather personal stake in the matter."

"My apologies," Calazar acknowledged.

Caldwell sat with his craggy jaw clamped in a downturned line, saying nothing. The knowledge that the original Hunt, and Danchekker, and the Marin woman, and the Jevlenese girl were intact and walking about somewhere on Jevlen was not comforting. As Calazar had said, the surrogates were now every bit as real. Caldwell didn't like the thought that was nagging at the edge of his awareness and which he knew he was refusing to face up to fully: the implication of their being somehow "expendable." He didn't like it at all.

Leyel Torres, the *Shapieron*'s acting commander, looked from one to another of the faces. "We have to do something," he said simply.

"Without another link into JEVEX, I'm not at all sure there's much we can do," Calazar answered.

Torres fidgeted, clearly not satisfied. "How did Hunt manage to get the link that we did have?" he asked.

"Through the Jevlenese criminal ring somehow," Eesyan replied.

"Could they do it again if we restored contact with them?"

"Only they know that. And they're loose in Shiban somewhere."

Torres thought for a moment. "VISAR, when you had the connection, did you know where Hunt was in Shiban?"

"Almost certainly the club that they found Baumer in," VISAR answered. "ZORAC has located it on the city plan from its communications routing codes."

Torres stared hard at the floor, then looked up suddenly with a resolved air. "There is something that *we* can do," he said. "Excuse me, gentlemen. VISAR, disconnect." And at once he was back in one of the neurocouplers that had been installed aboard the *Shapieron*. He got up, left the room, and walked through into the ship's command deck. The crew, who were on standby, stirred at their stations.

"ZORAC, report the ship's status," he called.

"Flight ready, as instructed."

"Prepare for immediate takeoff."

"Aye, aye, sir!"

Inside the Planetary Administration Center in Shiban, Garuth had been brought to the communications room next to what had recently been his own office suite. One of the main screens of a bank standing in the center of the floor showed Eubeleus's control center deep beneath the surface of

Uttan. Eubeleus had gained control of JEVEX, which was now operational and directing the h-space link carrying the channel into PAC; the Thurien occupying force had been fooled with a dummy system and was now isolated.

"I wanted you to be here to witness the futility of your fool's errand on Jevlen, and the first stage of our final triumph," Langerif gloated from the center of his entourage of officers. "Our reports are that the fervor we've been building up among the followers of the Axis has served its purpose well. There are thousands of them out there in couplers right now, eagerly waiting for JEVEX's promised restoration. And tens, hundreds of thousands more will follow as soon as it becomes known that the promise has been fulfilled. By tonight we will have taken Shiban. By tomorrow, Jevlen."

Garuth remained grimly silent but shifted his attention as Eubeleus himself moved into view on the screen. "A very different state of affairs from your last encounter with Jevlenese," Eubeleus said. "This time you're not dealing with the fools who tried to set up the Federation. Did you really believe that you could pit yourselves against manifestations of an intelligence that by its very nature is destined to supplant you?" He paused, seemingly having expected more of a reaction. "I believe you are aware of the method that JEVEX had devised to project itself into the outside universe, of which those like myself are privileged to be the prototypes."

Garuth said nothing.

On Uttan, an aide approached and stopped a short distance back, making signs to attract Eubeleus's attention. Eubeleus turned away and raised his chin inquiringly. The aide moved a step forward. "Iduane is in communication with the Prophet now. All is ready in the city."

Eubeleus nodded and looked back at the screen showing Garuth. "Never mind. You'll see for yourself soon enough," he said. Leaving the aide with the rest of those by the screen, he turned away and crossed the floor to the door leading to the coupler bank. In the passageway beyond, he met Iduane coming the other way.

"All's ready," Iduane said. "The Prophet is waiting."

"Take over in the control center," Eubeleus said, and continued on toward the booths.

Iduane entered the control center. As he passed beneath the overhead gallery surrounding the floor, he saw consternation breaking out around the screen still open to Jevlen, and quickened his pace.

"What's happening?" he demanded as he joined the group. He saw that another screen had come to life beside the one showing Langerif and Garuth at PAC. It was an outside view of the Thurien spaceport at Geerbaine. He recognized it at once by the sleek, unmistakable, half-mile-high tower of the *Shapieron* on the pad that it had occupied throughout the period of the Ganymean presence. But now it was moving, sliding upward slowly at first but picking up speed even as he watched.

"What's happening?" he demanded, hurrying across and joining the group.

One of the aides gestured needlessly. "The *Shapieron*, on Jevlen. It's taking off!"

On the screen showing PAC, Langerif was shaking his head, baffled. "The news just came in this second from Geerbaine. There was no warning, nothing. It's just taken off."

"What does it mean?"

"We don't know."

Iduane turned his head to the aide. "Go to the booths, quickly. Get the leader back here. Don't let him couple into the system yet." The aide nodded and left at a run.

On the screen from Geerbaine, the view had changed to another showing the starship's immense shape slowing down again to hang as a black silhouette, looking like some fantastic bird hovering above the Shiban skyline, with the city seemingly shrunken by perspective in the background below. Keeping its nose pointing upward, the ship began moving slowly sideways, over the city.

Bearing sacred implements and emblems of the Green Crescent, the multitude filled the forecourt of the temple of Vandros and spilled out through the gates opening into the grounds from the city. In the sky, stars had begun reappearing; Nieru had brightened. The day of the Great Awakening was at hand. On the stone terrace below the temple steps, the first batch of trembling victims had been led before the stakes, gibbets, blocks, and altars. The executioners had made ready, waiting for the daylight to return and the word to be given.

Above, on a terrace at the top of the steps, flanked by his retinue of priests and seers, Ethendor stood with his arms extended expectantly . . . and grew more perplexed. Only moments before, the Voice had spoken in his mind again, promising that the time was imminent and that a Great Spirit would speak to Ethendor, confirming his place as the chosen prophet. But not only had the Great Spirit failed to appear; now Ethendor wasn't getting any responses from the Voice, either.

"What ails the gods thus?" the Arch-Seer murmured, moving up closer behind him. "The current which thou drew still flows, but it has waned to a flicker."

"I know not," Ethendor replied. "Have the Examiner and his train returned yet to the city?"

Another of the priests conferred with a lesser priest, who turned to a messenger hovering behind an archway. "They are still awaited at the gates, O Holy One," the priest relayed back.

No doubt that was it, Ethendor thought to himself. The gods would wait until all the dignitaries and the full complement of heretics for the atonement were present.

"We must await them," Ethendor said. "Lead the people in more prayers and devotions. I shall return when the Voice speaks to me again." With that, he went back into the temple.

Eubeleus appeared at the side door of the control center with the aide who had gone to fetch him. He hurried over and took in the view from Geerbaine of the *Shapieron* drifting slowly over Shiban. "What are they doing in that ship?" he demanded, turning his eyes to Garuth, who was still standing with Langerif on the other screen.

In the PAC communications room, even with the hopelessness that had gripped him only moments before, Garuth felt a surge of exhilaration at the sight of his ship in motion and the message it brought that others were still doing something—although as to what it might be, he was as mystified as anyone else. He looked back to where Eubeleus was glaring out of the screen from Uttan. "You'll see for yourself, soon enough," he replied.

Ganymeans had double thumbs on each hand. Behind his back, Garuth crossed all four of them.

Chapter Fifty-nine

Smoke and dust poured into the corridor from the doorway leading through to the club's main lounge. It sounded as if the place was being demolished. Forgetting about what might have happened to the hour or more of lost time, Hunt and Danchekker hurried with Murray back to the rear exit that the others had taken, which was the one by which they had entered on their way from the tower elevator. Fendro, the club manager, caught up with them as they began crossing the gallery up the stairs outside.

As the four of them approached the opening into the hall where the elevators were situated, they saw Gina and Nixie with Keshen, the engineer, hanging back around a corner. Shouting and the sounds of shots came from ahead. Hunt drew to a halt and peered past into the hall. One of the elevator doors was open, with several *Ichena* inside, exchanging fire with some police who were taking cover in a corridor opening in from the far side. One of the *Ichena* had fallen and was preventing the door from closing. To try crossing the open floor was out of the question.

Fendro yelled something at Murray and went back along

the gallery, gesturing. "He says there's another elevator that way," Murray told the others. "Service shaft or something. Come on." He waved Nixie and Gina on ahead, then followed with Danchekker and Keshen. Hunt waited a few seconds longer to check the situation in the hall. Somebody inside the elevator showed himself long enough to heave the body out onto the floor, was hit himself and hauled back inside by one of the others, and then the door closed. Hunt turned and ran after Keshen's retreating figure.

The rest of the group was waiting for him outside an elevator in a narrow side passage. The car arrived just as he did, and they all crowded in. Fendro spoke an order in Jevlenese, and they began ascending. Danchekker was flushed and panting, Hunt could see as he leaned against the rear wall of the car to get his own breath back. Gina was charged up with adrenaline and ready for anything. Murray was wearing a resigned, why-is-life-always-doing-something-like-this-to-me? look. Nixie seemed unperturbed and to be taking things calmly.

"It looks like maybe Scirio miscalculated," Murray said. "I guess his pals are a bit more upset than he thought."

"He was backing what looked like the whining side. I think he's upset," Hunt replied.

"I take it that our communication with VISAR is once again terminated for the foreseeable future," Danchekker managed between puffs and wheezes. "Most unfortunate."

"Is there any chance we could get back in there when things cool down?" Hunt asked Murray. Murray translated to Keshen. Keshen answered, then Fendro added something else and waved a hand, shaking his head.

"It doesn't sound as if there's a lot of point," Murray said. "Seems like the hardware back there isn't much use for anything except growing petunias in."

Gina looked perplexedly at Hunt and Danchekker. "I'm not sure I understand what's happened," she said. "Are there other versions of us still in the Entoverse—still functioning? Or did they disappear when the connection was cut? Or did we ever get there at all? I'm confused."

"I'm not sure I understand it either," Hunt told her.

Fendro muttered something that sounded fatalistic and turned his eyes momentarily upward.

"What was that?" Hunt asked.

"He says, all it needs now is for the hearse not to start," Murray answered. "Wouldn't that just make the day, huh? And you know something? With Jev mechanics in charge, that might not be so funny."

The elevator halted with a jolt, throwing everybody off balance. Fendro jabbered something, and the control computer replied. Something was wrong.

"The power's cut," Murray said. "Either somebody hit the switch, or something downstairs got wrecked." They felt the car beginning to descend again . . .

. . . but only to align itself with the next door down. An emergency brake locked it in position, and the door opened. Fendro led them at a run to some stairs, throwing back disjointed words over his shoulder and sounding to Hunt as if he were on the verge of panic. "Three more levels," Murray supplied. "Scirio won't wait." Danchekker leaned against the doorframe at the bottom of the first flight, closed his eyes for a second and drew a long breath, then launched himself up at a gangling lope. Hunt stayed behind him, ready to help if needed.

A door at the top of the third flight brought them into the bare, gray entrance hall with scratched walls. Ahead of them, the outer door onto the landing platform was open, and through it could see the psychedelic hearse turning in preparation for takeoff, with an *Ichena* scrambling in through the doorway and two more close behind him. As the group from the stairs came out into the open, Keshen ran ahead, waving his arms and pointing back at the others, apparently trying to get Scirio to hold off for a few more seconds.

But Scirio's voice shouted from inside as Keshen reached the door, and the craft began to move. Keshen tried to jump, but Dreadnought appeared in the doorway and kicked him away. As Keshen picked himself up, the door slammed and the hearse accelerated away off the edge of the platform. Hunt and the others came to a confused halt as they watched it bank into a turning climb. Hunt's ability to think deserted him. He stood, staring helplessly, while Fendro ran in front, shouting and waving his arms.

Then Nixie called out and pointed in a direction off to one side. A group of dark-colored, streamlined shapes was swooping down and spreading out to close from different directions around the still-rising hearse.

"Shiban PD fliers," Murray yelled. "Looks like our friend might be up shit creek."

The hearse had seen them, too, and banked away evasively. Panels opened in its side to reveal small ball turrets, each mounting a pair of stub weapon muzzles—similar, Hunt guessed, to the one concealed in the personal flier that had made the attack on Grevetz's. Two of the police craft opened fire, but without visible effect. What looked like a streamer of yellow light flashed back from one of the hearse's turrets, but was deflected by a shimmering patch of violet that appeared briefly in front of the police flier. The hearse twisted around to double back into a dive that carried it close by the upper part of the tower. Another of the police fliers fired, hit the building, and debris showered down onto the platform where Hunt and the others were still watching, mesmerized.

"Get under cover," Hunt shouted, snapping out of it and waving at the others. They ran back toward the entranceway, Fendro leading. At the far end of the hall inside, the first yellow-uniformed figure was just emerging cautiously from the stairwell door.

Fendro turned as Keshen reached him. "It's no good. They're here," he said bleakly.

Above, the hearse was hit by two bursts at once as it pulled into another turn. It exploded in a blaze of orange light and black smoke, and the remnants cascaded down over the city.

On the command deck of the *Shapieron*, Leyel Torres stood with a group of crew officers, taking in the view being picked up by the ship's sternward-looking cameras, showing the upper spires and roofs of the city sliding by below. A holographic floor projection showed an image of the ship hovering above a cutaway representation of the levels and buildings beneath, as retrieved from ZORAC's stored plans of the city. The flashing symbol showing inside the zone beneath the ship centered on a maze of alleyways and side streets at the base of a complex of interconnected buildings that merged into a step-tapered tower. The tower rose at the confluence of several of the wide traffic corridors in a part of the city covered by a high outer canopy.

"The club's located down in there," ZORAC said. "Probe three is registering high police-band activity centered in that area." A couple of the *Shapieron*'s probes, hovering some distance above and freed from the curtain of jamming that the Jevlenese had thrown around Geerbaine, were picking up stray communications traffic above the city.

"And we're sure that the canopy is of lightweight construction over this section?" one of the officers checked. "There won't be any people up there?"

"That's what the plans show," Torres confirmed. He cast an eye quickly around the company. "We have to give it a try."

"Message exchanges between police fliers and HQ," ZORAC reported. "It sounds as if they're attacking something."

"How far can we reconfigure the external stress field?" Torres asked.

"Sufficient to arrest major falls below and redirect beyond city limits," ZORAC replied. "There might be some local peripheral fallout." The *Shapieron*'s drive created a zone of distorted space-time around the ship. ZORAC was saying that it could shape that external field into a force zone that would project objects clear of the vicinity.

Torres looked at the other officers. "The decision is mine, totally," he said. "ZORAC, execute the plan as specified. We're going in."

"Geronimo!" ZORAC responded.

"What?"

"It's the expression that Terran paratroopers used on going into action, back in the days when they fought wars," ZORAC explained. "It seemed appropriate."

"Just fly the ship, please."

"Yessir."

❊   ❊   ❊

Inside PAC, Langerif stared bemusedly at the scene being relayed from outside, as the huge shape of the starship hovering over the city started descending. The voice of the chief who was in charge at Geerbaine came excitedly over the audio. "I don't know what it's doing . . . It seems to be going down again. It can't be! It's going to land on top." On the view, a part of the city canopy immediately below the *Shapieron* was pulled up and fragmented into pieces which flew upward and out of sight. The voice became frenzied. "No, it isn't slowing down! What is it doing? I don't believe this. *It's going straight down through!*"

"*What is happening there?*" Eubeleus screeched on the screen from Uttan.

"I think that the intelligence destined to supplant us may have written us off a little too soon," Garuth said as he watched. He managed to make it sound satisfyingly mysterious. In truth, he hadn't the faintest idea.

They came to a halt, defeated. There was nowhere to go, nothing more to be tried.

And then Hunt realized that Gina was staring up past him and pointing incredulously. He turned and saw that a section of the imitation sky almost above their heads had gone dark and was bulging inward. Seconds later it broke into huge sections of canopy and supporting structure coming asunder, parting sideways unnaturally instead of falling, and then disappearing upward as if snatched away by a giant suction cleaner. At the same time a voice boomed like thunder across the city in Jevlenese. Hunt's head snapped around toward Murray.

Murray was bewildered. "It's telling people to get under cover. I don't—Jesus Christ!"

Hunt looked back. Silhouetted against the pale green outside, an immense shape consisting of a distorted cruciform fastened to a huge, streamlined tower that shrank away into the sky under the acute foreshortening of the perspective was coming down through the hole in the canopy. A roar of rushing air filled their ears, and minor debris scattered down and bounced off the face of the building above as the canopy above continued to buckle and tear.

"Goddamn spaceship!" Murray yelled hoarsely. "Spaceship coming down through the fuckin' roof!"

"That's the *Shapieron!*" Gina shouted dazedly. "Vic, it's the Ganymeans!"

The starship came down through the circling police fliers like a battleship scattering minnows, filling the volume above the city's rooftops.

"My God!" Danchekker exclaimed, staring up as the cathedral-like space between the four curving, swept fins enlarged second by second right above their heads. The retractable rearmost section of the main body, which contained the entry locks, was already sliding downward.

A bullhorn voice rang out, not as loud as before, and in English this time. "That's them, luckier than we hoped. Okay, Vic, we see you. Get everyone over. I'm opening a door." Never had Hunt been more glad to hear the voice of a computer.

Murray yelled something at Fendro, who came out of his funk and pressed a button inside a coverplate by the entrance. The doors closed, cutting off the police who had started moving forward across the hall inside. Hunt was already urging the others back across the landing platform.

The *Shapieron* could not maneuver close enough to the building to lower its rear section onto the platform, but was hanging overhead with the opened entrance just past the edge and a short distance below. Gina came to the rail and looked down into what appeared to be a bottomless void between the stern section of the ship, hanging in space, and the lower part of the tower, which was overhung, back beneath the platform. Inside the opened lock, Ganymean figures were gesturing frantically.

"It's okay," ZORAC's voice encouraged. "You're in a shaped field. I'll steer you in."

Hunt urged her up onto the guardrail. Consciously she wanted to do it, but some deep-rooted, primeval survival instinct held her back. She shook her head weakly. "I'm not sure I can."

Nixie climbed nimbly up on the far side of her, paused for a split second, and then launched herself forward. All the experiences and instincts of a lifetime's conditioning told Gina that Nixie shouldn't make it; but unseen forces guided her, and she landed lightly inside the *Shapieron*.

Gina swallowed and glanced at Hunt.

He nodded. "Go on!"

Forcing all other thoughts from her mind, she pitched off the rail—oblivious to the shove in her back that sent her moving.

Danchekker climbed up shakily. "If we ever manage to return after this escapade, I'll greet Ms. Mulling with flowers," he muttered to Hunt, and jumped.

As Keshen moved to follow, Fendro looked back and shouted in dismay. "We'll never make it!"

Hunt turned his head. The door from the building was open again, and police were rushing out onto the platform. "Go!" he yelled, and pushed Keshen off. But Fendro was right: there were still three of them to go, and some of the police were already leveling weapons.

And then one of the *Shapieron's* probes came swooping downward with a roaring, swishing sound, flattening out to race over the platform at head height, straight at the doorway like a fighter on a strafing run. The police scattered amid shouts of terror, some throwing themselves out of the way, others retreating back into the doorway. At the last moment the probe broke and peeled upward, grazing within a few feet of the face of the tower, and began turning for another run.

Murray and Fendro had clambered up onto the rail, and both disappeared together as Hunt looked back. Hunt glanced behind one last time, then hurled himself over after them. For an instant he seemed to hang in midair above the abyss, and then, without his really registering what had taken place, hands were steadying him inside the *Shapieron*.

"All aboard," ZORAC's voice said from somewhere. "Anybody want to change their mind? No? Then let's get out of here. Next stop, orbit. Calazar and Caldwell are through in the command deck via VISAR, waiting to talk to you."

Hunt accepted a set of communicator accessories from one of the Ganymeans and attached them to his neck, ear, and forehead as they walked. "Who's running the ship?" he asked as they approached one of the internal transit tubes.

"Level Torres, at your service," a voice said in his ear.

"Quite a stunt," Hunt complimented. "Pity about the hole in the roof."

"I assume their insurance will cover it."

"What's the score otherwise?"

"Well, it seems that you've gone and doubled all our problems—literally. The versions of you that we've just extricated from that mess were only half the story. Now we have to worry about the other half."

Chapter Sixty

Shingen-Hu refused to let himself be demoralized again. The higher gods had told him that he was to be their chosen instrument, and he had seen their power. Therefore the sudden cessation of the demonstration was a sign to him. It meant something. They had placed their emissaries in his charge, he had decided as the procession wound its way through the hills surrounding Rakashym, and left them stripped of their protection. All the time, the emissaries had remained quiet and subdued, obviously leaving Shingen-Hu to work the interpretation out for himself. It could only mean that the gods were entrusting to him the task of saving them. It was a test of his faith and worthiness.

Having satisfied himself of that much, he maneuvered himself into one of the corners of the cart below the two guards who were riding up front, and out of their line of vision. Then, under cover of the other bodies packed around him, he slipped from his robe one of the pieces of mobilium from the dignitaries' carriage that he had picked up and concealed when they were back in the village square. He laid the sliver along one of his fingers and, concentrating his powers, slowly passed his finger through one of the links of the chain shackling his hands. The mobilium following behind his finger repelled the material, preventing it from rejoining behind, and the chain fell apart. He nudged Thrax, indicated what he had done, and passed him the other piece of mobilium. Thrax loosened his own chains, then worked his way across to the far side of the cart. By the time the cart had covered another mile, they had freed all five of the captives whom the gods had entrusted to them.

The train rounded a sharp bend at a point where the trail began descending, and there Shingen-Hu saw the opportunity that the gods had prepared for him. On one side, a steep gully rose into the rocks above the trail, its course littered with many loose and precarious boulders. On the other side, just past the bend where the gully spilled out onto the trail, there was a deep gorge with a stream at the bottom, and across it a cliff of crumbling, red-brown gritstone, its face patchy and veined with crystal of various colors.

Shingen-Hu waited until the cart carrying the prisoners had passed the gully, at which point the supply wagon and main body of the escorting soldiers following behind were obscured momentarily by the bend. Straightening up suddenly, he pointed at the gully with the extended fingers of both hands, singling out a large boulder that had acted as a dam and accumulated a mound of smaller debris fallen from higher up. The rock moved. Shingen-Hu sent a bolt of focused power, which he felt augmented by Thrax, concentrating beside him, and moments later a miniature avalanche came rumbling and tumbling down the gorge, sealing off the trail behind.

Ahead, the cart that the dignitaries were traveling in— commandeered from the villagers to replace the carriage—had come to a stop on a narrow stretch where the trail passed between two rock walls. As the occupants came spilling out in consternation, they blocked the way of the soldiers from the front, who were trying to get back. Shingen-Hu marveled at how perfectly the gods had prepared the moment.

Casting his powers forward, he materialized a curtain of thick, black smoke to add to their confusion. Now the train was blocked both to the rear and to the fore, and the way open for escape lay off to the side, across the gorge.

Again combining his power with Thrax's, he walked out on a jutting rock that the gods had provided. There he paused until he felt a current surging, gathered his effort, and then stepped forth confidently to feel himself carried across to a narrow ledge near the cliff base, a short distance above the water. Thrax moved onto the jutting rock, marshaling the emissaries. Shingen-Hu could see that, just as he had expected, they were giving Thrax no assistance, but were acting like helpless novices to let him meet his test on his own merits.

"Walk forward over the bridge," he called, beckoning for them to follow.

"What bloody bridge?" the emissary who was called Hunt shouted back.

"The bridge that faith shall build for ye. Trust my word, and my power shall carry thee safe."

Hunt shrugged and stepped off the rock, and Shingen-Hu felt a wave of exhilaration as he bore the emissary over. Next came the redheaded female, followed by the ring-eyed Father of Gods, who had arrived in the spinning temple of beasts. By that time the ledge was crowded, and Thrax was left on the other side with the short-skirted female and the long-headed giant.

"Now we must climb," Shingen-Hu exhorted. His power would never lift five of them to the top. The test would be to get them there, he was certain. What was to happen after that would then be revealed. So saying, he began moving smoothly and surely up the face, making use of frictite veins to afford a grip where there was no convenient hold, and avoiding the protrusions of green anchorite and black catchstone, as any youngster would know how to do.

But he had barely ascended halfway when a cry from below halted him. "What in God's name is this confounded stuff? I can't move."

Shingen-Hu leaned outward and peered back down. The Father of Gods was stuck to a knob of anchorite and gesticulating frantically. Hunt began traversing toward him but became entangled with a growth of clingweed hanging from a crevice, while the redheaded female below them was scrabbling futilely at a block of lubrite, which contained grains of mobilium and was unclimbable. They were acting like children to try him, Shingen-Hu realized. The test was not over yet.

Meanwhile, priests and soldiers were appearing from the confusion on the other side of the gorge. "Thrax, thou must cross over now and assist," Shingen-Hu called down. From his stance above he helped Thrax across the gorge, then turned and resumed climbing.

But as he reached the top, Thrax's voice came up from below. " 'Tis beyond all hope, Master. They are as fish stranded in mud."

Shingen-Hu looked back across the gorge. The soldiers had reached the jutting rock and were dragging back the female and the long-headed one who had been left. "Then save thyself, Thrax," he called back down. "Nothing can be gained by thy sacrifice."

Thrax joined him at the top of the cliff minutes later. By that time the long-headed one and the short-skirted female had been led away, and soldiers had descended to the stream and were wading across. On the trail above the soldiers, the priests had assembled around the Examiner and were directing a paralyzing influence across at the three emissaries stranded below. Shingen-Hu looked on dejectedly. He had failed.

Movement higher up above caught his eye. A flock of vultures was circling above the trail, right over the spot where the priests were gathered. Raising his arm, he pointed at them, his eyes glinting malevolently. Seized by a sudden compulsion, the birds voided their contents upon the priests from on high. Shingen-Hu and Thrax turned and walked sadly away.

In the *Shapieron*, orbiting high over Jevlen, Eesyan was explaining over the connection from Thurien what would be involved in restoring VISAR's connection to JEVEX.

"The line out from the club connected into the regular Jevlenese planetary communications net," he said from one of the large screens overlooking the command deck. "The activation codes that were fed in triggered an h-link termination node somewhere, which was programmed with the operating parameters to access JEVEX. To restore the connection we need to do two things: first, find an entry point into the planetary net that bypasses the normal security checks; and second, input the same activation codes to it that Keshen entered from the club."

"So that would trigger the same h-space terminal to connect to Uttan," Hunt said. He was standing with Danchekker and Keshen beside the Ganymeans, Leyel Torres and Rodgar Jassilane. "We wouldn't need to know where the node is located or what it is, or exactly how it functions?"

"That's right," Keshen confirmed.

"But I thought all the links were shut down," Jassilane said. "Isn't that what disconnected you in the first place?"

"Yes," Eesyan agreed. "Apart from one that they've probably got open to their people inside PAC—but that would be inaccessible to us, anyway. But in order to stage his invasion from Uttan, Eubeleus will have to open JEVEX to access from Jevlen-based trunk nodes again. What we're saying is that when he does, VISAR will have been routed through to one of them."

Jassilane looked inquiringly at Keshen.

The Jevlenese nodded, "*If* we can get back into the net," he confirmed.

Gina watched with Nixie, Fendro, and Murray, over on one side. There was nothing she could contribute, and tossing in questions that could just as well be answered later would only delay things. Nixie, Fendro, and Murray were still too awed at the interior of the starship to have much thought about anything else, anyway.

"And I think there's a way we might be able to do it," Keshen said. He looked around quickly. "Through one of the redirector satellites that were left functioning. There are about thirty of them. They're part of the regular net, unmanned, and a long way out." The others were listening intently. He spread his hands and went on. "If we could get to one of them and find a way inside it, I think I could break into one of the primary circuits. That would bypass the protection. The network itself would take care of finding a route to wherever the access code indicates. We don't have to know where it points."

"Do you know the codes?" Eesyan asked. He sounded dubious, as if he found the thought unlikely.

Keshen looked surprised. "But I assumed VISAR had the codes," he replied. "VISAR was connected when I entered them at the club. Isn't it true?"

"They were stored in local memory," VISAR said. "They got lost when I was cut off."

Eubeleus paced agitatedly to and fro across the floor of the main control center deep beneath the surface of Uttan. The latest report from Jevlen was that the *Shapieron* had lifted out from the planet and was riding in orbit. It was the *Shapieron* that had slipped in close under the planet's defensive guard during the Pseudowar and intercepted a communications beam to let VISAR into JEVEX. All his instincts told him that the Terrans were going to try the same thing again. He should have felt completely confident, he knew, for this time he had foreseen their plan; but he found himself unable to shake off an oppressive nervousness, which he traced back to the knowledge that Hunt and Danchekker were involved. It meant that anything could happen: especially something that nobody else had thought of.

"How close to completion is the final integration sequence?" he asked the operators clustered around the supervisory console.

"It's practically complete now," Iduane answered.

"Good. Run a double check on all communications input channels. I want to be absolutely sure that no illicit accesses are being tried anywhere. Assign it a class-one priority."

"Understood."

"What is the *Shapieron* doing?" Eubeleus asked another operator, who was monitoring the tracking data being relayed via PAC from the Jevlenese surveillance system.

"Still holding LJO. No new developments."

Eubeleus stopped, stared at the screen showing Langerif

and his officers in the PAC communications room, then turned away and started pacing again. "I don't like it," he muttered. "I don't trust that ship."

"It's not doing anything," Iduane pointed out. "And what can it do? Our surveillance will be following it from Jevlen every inch of the way, wherever it goes."

"It's not safe so long as it's anywhere in the vicinity of Jevlen," Eubeleus said. "I'm not proceeding further until we get rid of it."

"Get rid of it?" Iduane looked perplexed. "How? Jevlen doesn't have any strategic defenses."

"There must be some way of—" Eubeleus stopped and looked over at the screen showing Langerif again. "Wait. We've still got their illustrious commander, haven't we?" he said, moving back across. "The leader who brought them back after all those years. They wouldn't want anything to happen to *him*, now, would they?" He nodded, satisfied. "And you've got some others there that we can use as hostages, isn't that right? Who are they?"

"Two scientists, who work with Hunt and Danchekker," Langerif replied. "Also the Terran who was in charge of security here."

Eubeleus looked gratified. "Perfect! Get a laser link to whoever is in command of the *Shapieron* and have those three brought up to where you are, right away. We'll have that ship out of harm's way within an hour." He looked across at Iduane. "Suspend all further action concerning the Awakening for the time being," he ordered.

Iduane nodded but didn't look happy about it. "What about the Prophet? He's still there with all the people, waiting for you to take over."

Eubeleus waved a hand impatiently. "Oh . . . go back and tell them to sing a few more hymns or something," he replied.

Duncan and Sandy were sitting together among the group of security guards, Ganymeans, and other captives inside PAC.

"How's that for a bummer?" Duncan said. "We come all this way, to a new city and a totally different culture, and we end up like this."

"We never even got to see the town," Sandy agreed dismally.

Duncan looked idly around at the others sitting around the room, not saying much, waiting. "What do you like to do when you get to go out?" he asked.

"Go out? What's that? I work for Chris Danchekker, remember? A vacation is eating lunch that didn't come out of a paper bag."

"Guys like that ought to get married," Duncan said.

"Maybe he did, years ago, and forgot all about it. I've seen him show up at the lab in odd shoes."

"How about San Francisco?" Duncan said. "Ever get out that way? Fisherman's Wharf, Enrico's Coffee House? Do you know, I reckon that if they handed this city over to the people who run Chinatown in S.F., they'd have the place up and running in a month without ever needing JEVEX."

Sandy stretched and thought about it. "I think I'll take the south," she said. "New Orleans, some places out along Texas. Maybe I'm just cut out for the slow, lazy life."

"Tell you what," Duncan said. "When we get back after this, we'll go off on a tour and see all of it. Thinking back, I'd say I've spent too much of my time shut up in labs, too. Vic's always saying, Why change your job? It's just more of the same. Change your life. What do you think? Does that sound good?"

Sandy looked at him sideways. "Are your intentions strictly honorable, Mr. Watt?"

"Absolutely not."

"It's a deal."

Some police came into the room and started talking to the ones who had been standing guard. The newcomers seemed excited, with a lot of waving and gesticulating. The captives watched and waited with mixed reactions. While it was going on, Del Cullen moved over to where Sandy and Duncan were sitting. "Looks like the war's not over yet," he murmured.

"Why? What's happening?" Duncan asked.

"I only caught pieces of it, but it sounds like something's just come down through the roof of the city. I think one of them said it was the *Shapieron*."

Sandy looked aghast. "You mean it crashed?"

"He'll, no. It took off again . . . But there's still something going on out there. The others are up to something."

Then the police who had entered came over and pointed to the three of them. The guards motioned for them to get up and follow. In the background, Koberg and Lebansky started objecting, but held back when other guards lowered their weapons threateningly. Cullen shrugged. "I guess we don't have a lot of choice," he said. The prisoners left, accompanied by the escort that had been sent for them.

They were taken up to the communications room, where Garuth was standing with Langerif and a group of other Jevlenese in front of a screen showing Eubeleus. On another screen they saw Hunt, Danchekker, and a mixed group of others in brightly lit surroundings of display consoles and control stations, which Duncan guessed to be the inside of the *Shapieron*.

"It's them!" he exclaimed. "They got out! They're—"

"Quiet!" Langerif snapped.

On the other screen, Eubeleus was speaking. "We do indeed have all of them as you can see for yourselves. I'm not in a mood to make long speeches. The implications are too obvious to require spelling out. My instructions are that—"

"Don't listen," Garuth broke in. "Do whatever—"

"Remove him," Langerif ordered. Two armed guards ushered Garuth away, out of range of the screen.

Eubeleus resumed. "You will take your ship away from Jevlen immediately at maximum speed, and out of Athena's planetary system completely. The Thuriens will project a toroid to remove it from this region." He raised a hand, seeing the protest start to form on Torres's face. "There is nothing to negotiate. You will commence at once."

Sandy was ebullient at seeing that the others were safe, and for the moment she wasn't worried about what would happen next. Gina, standing in the forefront of the group behind Torres, was looking especially crestfallen. "Don't worry, Gina," Sandy called, as if she could direct the words only at her. "Things will work out. Maybe it's all just happening in our heads." A private joke. Gina caught it and smiled back.

"Glad you made it, chief," Duncan called out from beside

Sandy. Hunt acknowledged with a nod and a faint grin.

Eubeleus paled with anger. "Take them all away!" he shouted. "They've served their purpose. The Ganymeans know we have them." He looked back at the view of Torres. "Don't let their frivolity mislead you, Captain. Take your ship outward immediately. Otherwise, I don't have to tell you what will become of your precious friends there."

Torres could only nod numbly. But behind him, Danchekker's face had taken on the enraptured expression of somebody who had just seen a light, as if he had only just realized something that should have been obvious long before.

Chapter Sixty-one

Eubeleus's face vanished from the screen on the *Shapieron's* command deck. Calazar and Eesyan were left on another, staring gloomily from their capital on Thurien, and Caldwell, in Washington, was still showing on the one adjacent. But Danchekker was already hopping about in the center of the floor, gesticulating excitedly first one way, then another, at the Terrans and Ganymeans around him. "She just said it! Sandy just said it, on the screen there! In their heads!" He pointed wildly at Keshen, who pulled back in alarm. "He's still got them!"

Hunt raised a restraining hand. "Chris, calm down, stop dancing about like that, and say whatever the hell it is you're trying to say."

Danchekker regained most of his composure, but was still unable to prevent his finger jabbing repeatedly in Keshen's direction. "The activation codes! Don't you see? *He* entered them into the touchpanel in the club! He still has them, subconsciously, inside his head. VISAR can get them out again!"

Hunt stared for a full five seconds. "Is that right?" The question was mechanical. He already knew enough to have little doubt of the answer.

"Yes . . . with Keshen's permission, naturally," VISAR said.

"Of course," Calazar whispered numbly. It was so unheard of that no Thurien would have thought of it—or a Thurien-oriented computer.

Hunt looked at Keshen. "Is it okay with you?"

Keshen shrugged, still taken aback at having suddenly become the center of things. "Well, I guess so . . . Sure."

Hunt turned to Torres. But the Ganymean was shaking his head. "But is there any point? The Jevlenese will be watching our every move. If we so much as take the ship anywhere near a redirector satellite . . ." He made a helpless gesture and left the sentence unfinished.

A silence fell, broken by the humming and pulsating of distant machinery buried in the ship.

Then Caldwell said, "Maybe there is a point. If the Jevlenese are going to have all their attention fixed on the *Shapieron*, that might make it an ideal decoy while something else tries for the satellite—one of the ship's probes, maybe. Some of those probes are fitted with h-space gear and can talk to VISAR. If Keshen says he can get into the planetary net from the satellite, you'd just have to bridge a connection across. How many guys would it take to do it?"

Everyone looked at Torres and the Ganymean crew officers. They were the only ones who could answer that.

"It's got a chance," Rodgar Jassilane said at length. "When the stress field breaks down under main-drive acceleration, the entire external electromagnetic environment of the ship is disrupted. If a probe were ejected at the right moment, it might well get away undetected against the background . . . and there's nothing else we can try."

"Who'd need to go?" Hunt snapped. "Keshen for a start, I assume." He turned back to the Jevlenese engineer. "Will you do it?"

Keshen swallowed hard, but nodded.

"I'll go with him," Jassilane offered promptly. "That's all. You won't get more than two of us into one of the h-fitted probes, anyway."

There wasn't time for any more finesse. Eubeleus was

probably wondering already why the ship wasn't accelerating. Hunt looked at Torres and indicated Keshen with a jerk of his head. "Let's do it. Get him to a coupler, quick."

Torres confirmed the order with a brief wave to one of the Ganymeans. "ZORAC, prepare a sounding probe for launch." He waved to two more of the ship's officers. "Have two EV suits made ready at the access lock, one Terran model, one Ganymean."

Keshen was already being speeded through a doorway out from the command deck to the couplers. The other Ganymeans saluted and hurried away.

Chained again, and with guards keeping them constantly covered at spearpoint, the prisoners sat morosely in the bumping, sliding cart as it approached the outskirts of Orenash. It was amazing, Hunt thought. Now that he was adjusting to the crazy dynamics of the place, he could *see* the change between north-south and east-west lengths every time the cart rounded an approximately right-angle bend. The scientist in him, even in a predicament that made anything else seem pointless, noted it as a detectable alteration in the cart's length-breadth proportions. No wonder the people here had never made anything beyond a few primitive tools. And the mountains discernible off to the left in the twilight were noticeably closer than they had been when the procession came out onto the plain, although the route was surely more or less parallel to them.

Beside him, Gina was pressed close, fighting to keep her emotions under control. He reached across her lap to squeeze her arm reassuringly. One of the guards growled something threatening. Hunt drew back.

"Well, here it is," she said. "The world of Earth's mythology, only real, just like we said. But who'd have thought we'd end up in it?" She drew a long, shaky breath, and the brave face she had been struggling to maintain broke down. "Look, I'm not very good at this. I don't know what they've got lined up at the end of this ride, but—"

"Save it," Hunt said. "As you said, it's a mythology become real. Miracles can happen."

"What miracles?"

"Who knows?"

"You know what a fluke it was for us to get that connection. What chance is there of anything else, anywhere in Shiban? If it got cut off, it must mean either that the club was taken over, or Eubeleus shut down all the links. What else can any of them"—she shook her head, unable in her fear and confusion to sort out the philosophical niceties—"us, whoever those people still out there are . . . What can they do? Do *you* know?"

"Not exactly," Hunt confessed.

"See!" Possibly from the workings of some inner defense mechanism, Gina became almost belligerent. "You don't know. But the *you* out there is every bit the same person, isn't it? And up to the point where we got detached, he knew as much as you did. So why should *he* have any better ideas? And the same goes for the rest of us."

Hunt didn't have an answer. He could only look away.

They were coming into the city of Orenash. The architecture was massively imposing, and foreboding. Ahead, trumpets sounded as the leading body of soldiers passed through a large gate set between two square towers in a high wall. Crowds were milling around the vehicles, shouting praises to the priests and jeering at the captives.

It was an odd feeling, trying to project how he would feel about himself, Hunt found. To the originals of themselves that they had been derived from, they were just knots of computer code. He wondered how much those originals out there would really care. Right now, he didn't feel at all like a piece of computer code, and he cared very much. But how much of that was likely to impress itself on other beings in another universe, whatever their superficial resemblances and theoretically coincident identities? They didn't have the same stake in the outcome of all this.

It was not a very reassuring line of thought to find himself being drawn along.

"Data update from Jevlen," an operator sang out suddenly. Eubeleus swung to face him from the middle of the floor, his haste betraying a tenseness that he had been striving not to show. "The *Shapieron* is accelerating out of free-fall now. Readings indicate profile consistent with maximum ramp up to interstellar speed."

It took Eubeleus a moment or two to register the fact fully. Then, gradually, the realization percolated through that his gamble had paid off. He let his tension dissipate slowly, savoring the feeling of relief flowing over him to take its place.

He had expected some delay, despite the harshness of his ultimatum, for there were bound to be deliberations between those aboard the vessel and whoever else they were in contact with. Their final submission, expressed in the form of the ship's departure, would come only as a last resort. His worry had been that they would call what they thought to be a bluff and so force his hand, thereby necessitating what would have been a regrettably ugly note on which to begin the new regime. But now the danger was past.

"Our congratulations," one of the others offered. "This is exactly the kind of unswerving will that the plan needs."

Eubeleus dismissed the remark offhandedly, as if the fact should have been sufficiently obvious not to need voicing. "So much for their last, desperate attempt, which as you see, turns out to have been a mere distraction," he said. "And now, back to our main task. Is JEVEX running now?"

"Fully functional, Excellency," the familiar voice of JEVEX responded. Reassured looks passed between the others around the control center.

"Before we open the links to Jevlen, I want a final check that we are not registering any attempts at irregular access," Eubeleus said. "I want the system fully secure on all counts."

"Commencing core reintegration prior to connection to Jevlen," JEVEX confirmed.

"Breakdown of *Shapieron*'s stress field is beginning," the first operator called out. "Ship is decoupling from normal space . . . Delta index is fading . . . Last readings give acceleration as undiminished."

At last Eubeleus felt safe, and he permitted a smile of triumph to play around the corners of his mouth for an instant.

"It is time to proceed," he announced. He turned to one of the aides. "I shall guide the Prophet personally, as intended. You watch here until Iduane returns." He allowed his gaze to drift slowly over the company. "When we see each other again, Shiban will be ours." Applause greeted his words. Eubeleus turned and left the room.

Meanwhile, in the blackness of space twenty thousand miles above the surface of Jevlen, a tiny speck that the tracking sensors had missed in the disturbance from the starship's departure emerged unseen from the electromagnetic upheaval and disappeared into the starry background.

"Probe away, on course, and checking positive," ZORAC reported.

"Well, that's it," Hunt said in the center of the *Shapieron's* command deck as the screens showing the external views being picked up by the ship's scanners blanked out. The vessel was now out of touch with the universe electromagnetically, its sole means of communication being by VISAR, using h-space.

"It's out of our hands," Danchekker agreed. "There's nothing more we can do now but play out our role as decoys." He thought for a moment and sighed. "It's not an especially gratifying role to find oneself reduced to, considering what's at stake. In the situations you've landed us in before, we have generally been able to contribute something more positive."

Hunt was about to reply, but checked himself and looked at Danchekker oddly. "Well, that's not exactly true, is it, Chris?"

"What do you mean?"

"It isn't out of our hands—not exactly. A lot depends on what those surrogates who are still down in the Entoverse have managed to pull off. And they're every bit as much 'us' as you and me, aren't they—if what Calazar and the others are saying is correct?" He frowned and rubbed his chin, finding the thought as bemusing as the look on Danchekker's face indicated that Danchekker himself did. "It's a peculiar situation, when you finally get a moment to think about it, isn't it?"

✳   ✳   ✳

A messenger forced his way through the crowds packed into the grounds of the temple of Vandros and went up to the chambers inside. He spoke to one of the priests, who went to the door that led out to the main steps from where the ceremonies were being led, and beckoned Ethendor over.

"Word from the main gates," the priest informed him. "The Examiner and his caravan are entering the city now. They are bringing more heretics—faces unknown, who claimed to have come from the gods."

"Ah, so the celebrations shall be complete," Ethendor said, nodding. He understood it all now.

"This is why the people were told to be patient?" the priest queried.

"The plan unfolds in its perfection," Ethendor assured him.

Then the Voice came again into Ethendor's mind. "The time will come very soon now, Prophet chosen by the gods. Are you prepared to receive the Great Spirit?"

"The last of our enemies are being brought before us to face atonement, and Waroth has been cleansed of its stain," Ethendor replied, "All is prepared."

"You have done well. All that was promised shall be yours in Hyperia."

"I shall rule over vast multitudes? My word shall move armies and my wishes shall be law? Kings shall tremble at my displeasure?" Ethendor's inner voice shook, and his eyes blazed with the vision. "I shall scatter mine enemies mercilessly before me as dust to the winds, and be mighty as the gods themselves?"

"Thus was our contract."

"Humbly, I accept."

The satellite was in the form of a stepped octagonal prism, cluttered with protrusions and antennae. Using manual guidance, Rodgar Jassilane moved the probe gradually in until it was hanging a few yards from the rear access port, approaching from the outward direction to avoid interrupting any signal beams directed at the planet. "Arrived and docked," he announced. The h-space equipment that the probe was carrying gave them a link to VISAR on Thurien. He glanced across at Keshen, also suited up and squeezed awkwardly into the cramped space. "Okay?"

Keshen nodded behind his facepiece.

"Open hatch," Jassilane instructed the onboard computer.

With a few expert pushes and tugs, Jassilane propelled himself out of the opening and turned on his checkline to collect the tool pack from a stowage compartment that had opened alongside the hatch. Inside, Keshen seemed to be having more difficulty in moving and was extricating himself clumsily.

"Not too much experience in zero-g, eh?" Jassilane remarked, leaning in and unhooking a buckle of Keshen's pack harness from a projecting hinge of the hatch cover.

"I've never been off-planet before," Keshen told him.

For a second the Ganymean froze, not knowing what to say. "You kind of, er . . . left it a long time before saying so," he managed finally.

"Nobody asked me before. I didn't want to sound like I was chickening out."

Jassilane thought about it. "Did Hunt, the Terran scientist, get you into this?" he inquired.

"That's right. How did you know?"

"Oh . . . I just had a feeling," Jassilane said as he attached the probe by a tether.

While Jassilane burned open the hatch into the satellite with a plasma torch, Keshen unreeled the cable that would provide a connection for VISAR from the link hardware inside the probe. They entered the satellite, and Keshen located a maintenance and test console, which he used to find the boxes containing the buffer terminals for the output circuits into the planetary communications net. Jassilane set up a terminal back to the probe's onboard computer, which ZORAC had loaded with Jevlenese interconnection protocols and reference data, as well as the activation codes that VISAR had retrieved from Keshen's memory.

"You seem to know what you're doing," Jassilane remarked, hoping that his relief didn't show in the translation coming back through VISAR.

"You see? Not all Jevs are meatheads."

"What did you do before?"

Keshen checked the connectors against the set of Jevlenese standard patterns that Jassilane had collected from the *Shapieron*'s stores. "Operations supervision—part of the JEVEX remote-input system. When JEVEX was shut down, some people approached me to set up a few connections into the residual core system that was left running—without asking questions about what they wanted them for."

Jassilane searched through what he knew of the motivations behind the strange things that humans did. "Out of revenge?" he guessed. "To get even with the authorities? Or was it to assert your identification with an ideological principle that you saw as being violated?"

"No. For the money."

They found a connector combination that matched. Jassilane began fitting it together, while Keshen used the console to isolate one of the satellite's primary downlink beams. The neat thing about the way they were doing it, he thought as he worked, was that JEVEX could check all it wanted to for somebody trying to break into it; it wouldn't find anything. VISAR would be connected, via the satellite, to one of the surface nodes—wherever it was located—that Eubeleus himself had ordered to be shut down, and which wouldn't activate again until JEVEX itself opened its channels to Jevlen for the invasion. It was a bit like dressing the robbers up as the security guards, and waiting for the bank to call them in.

The pervasion of the Voice seemed to fade, and Ethendor felt another presence taking form in his mind, somehow colder and more remote, aloof and dominating. "Does the Prophet hear?"

Ethendor looked upward in reverence. "Is this the Great Spirit who comes at last to this unworthy servant?"

"It is. I see and hear through you, and shall be your soul. Go forward now to the people and proclaim to them that the moment that was promised is at hand. Now will the sun shine, and when the day returns, the currents shall come down to you again."

Visions of Hyperia came to Ethendor. Moving slowly in a semitrance, he raised his arms high and advanced to the edge of the platform at the top of the steps, while the priests who had been performing the devotions parted to let him pass. An expectant hush swept over the crowd below. The priests on either side and slightly to the rear of him assumed attitudes of prayer and waited.

"The time is upon us!" Ethendor's voice thundered across the silent throng. "All of our patience, our sufferings, our labors against the unbelievers, and our unwavering faith will be rewarded. The Great Spirit from beyond has come into me, and now I proclaim to you that the Awakening is to begin." He stretched his arms high and threw back his head. "Let the sun shine again and the days return upon Waroth! And then shall the currents descend that shall carry the multitudes to Hyperia!"

In the gloom, the entire mass of the crowd lightened as thousands of faces turned upward simultaneously.

And in the sky above, the sun began to brighten.

Chapter Sixty-two

A mighty roar of cheers, shouts, songs, and praises swept over the crowd as the twilight turned to day and the city stood revealed in its full extent and color. To Hunt's eyes it was a strange mixture of classical colonnades, spires and minarets of a vaguely Eastern flavor, and massive, terraced pyramids that looked Aztec, with materials varying from polished white, like marble, to crude dwellings of brown and muddy yellow. There were arches framing many of the smaller side alleys, and high bridges that could have been aqueducts. The dress of the people was a mixture of ancient and medieval, consisting in some places of long robes and skirted tunics, in others of hooded jerkins and coarse coats. More riders formed up on either side of the train, and the cavalcade wound its way through the packed streets toward a high structure on a rocky hill, surrounded by an inner wall.

"What does this mean?" Nixie asked Hunt. "The daylight returning. What has happened outside?"

"JEVEX is operational again," Hunt told her soberly.

She looked at him with an uncertain expression. "Is there anything they can do, now, outside? Will it still be possible for VISAR to reconnect?"

Gina was watching with a tense look. Hunt said nothing.

"JEVEX will be checking for access attempts," Eesyan said expressionlessly.

Nixie looked up, and a strange, distant expression came over her face. After several seconds it became grave.

Hunt stared at her. "What is it? Nixie, can you hear me?"

"The sky is dense with currents. There must be thousands waiting, coupled into the system in Shiban."

Hunt looked up at the sky. It looked normal. "I don't see anything," he said.

"You wouldn't."

They passed through a gate in the inner wall to a wide space that was as packed as the streets outside. Before them was the mount, its base hidden among elaborately ornamented buildings and statues. Above, its mass was carved into a pyramid with high, wide steps taking up most of the side facing the gate, and higher up, a summit of vertical walls topped by a dome surrounded by smaller spires. At the top of the steps was a terrace, upon which a group of figures in high headdresses and white and red robes stood arrayed about a central one in gold, standing with his arms extended. A larger terrace near the base of the steps had been prepared with stakes and other gruesome devices of execution, while below, scores of bruised and tattered shapes stood herded forlornly behind a line of stern-faced soldiers.

The carts drew up in a cleared area before the soldiers. The Examiner and his retinue climbed importantly out ahead, while the guards disembarked the last batch of victims. Hunt tried to tell himself that this wasn't really what it seemed: *He* was in another realm, outside this whole insane world that he thought he was seeing. He would still be there, after whatever was to happen had happened . . . But it didn't do a lot of good. From where he was viewing the situation, the intellectualizing wasn't convincing.

Through the eyes of Ethendor, Eubeleus gazed out upon the scene and saw that his triumph was complete. For a moment longer he stood, posing high above the crowd, his robes of gold throwing back the sunlight. Then he advanced slowly to the edge of the platform at the top of the steps, extended his arms wide, and turned grandly to take in first one side of the temple court, then the other.

"Citizens of Orenash, people of Waroth . . ."

Quiet fell upon the crowd and spread across the sea of faces like oil calming turbulent waters. All became still.

Below, Hunt and the others stood and exchanged final, resigned looks.

And then a low, pulsating, throbbing sound came intermittently through the silence: a whisper, rising and falling about the threshold of hearing as it was carried on the breeze coming over the city. Hunt's head jerked around sharply as the murmur grew louder and more distinct. High above, Ethendor looked up, frowning. Inside the high priest's mind, Eubeleus, nonplussed, momentarily lost direction. This wasn't right at all.

The sound intensified, coming closer: a steady droning now, punctuated by the rhythmic thwacking of solid matter beating air. Disbelief flooded into Hunt's face. There was only one thing he knew that made a sound like that. He stared in the direction that it was coming from, hardly daring to let his hopes rise . . . And then he heard the cries of terror from the crowds beyond the wall, outside in the city.

The inhabitants of Waroth had never seen a 1960s vintage, Boeing Vertol CH-47 Chinook, twin tandem-rotor, turbine-driven, troop-transport and supply helicopter. As it came in low over the temple wall, shrieks and wails went up from all sides. Some of the people threw themselves down on the ground; others were rushing this way and that, gibbering in panic. The dignitaries and soldiers who had come from Rakashym stood transfixed, not knowing what to make of this sudden reappearance of the power they had seen manifested before.

Danchekker, who had been managing to sustain an astonishing calm throughout, gave an approving nod. "Ah, yes. And about time, too," he said. "It would appear that our alter egos have finally managed to get themselves organized. I'm pleased to see that we're not losing our touch, Vic."

Beside Hunt, Gina was sobbing tears of relief. "I never

thought it would be possible to fall in love with a computer," she choked.

Hunt found himself so drained suddenly that he was unable to manage the grin that he tried to force, and none of the flippant words that came into his head would form. He brought a hand up to his mouth and discovered that he was shaking. "Did you enjoy your vacation, VISAR?" was all he could mutter finally.

"Bit of a technical hitch out here," the familiar voice replied in his head. "It's all under control now. I presume the details can wait until later."

Above them, Ethendor was coming down the temple steps almost at a run, his face writhing in fury and incomprehension. Some of the other priests were trailing after him, while the rest remained gripped by fear and consternation on the platform above.

The Chinook swung around to hover broadside-on to the temple above the cringing throng. Its large side-door was open, and framed in the opening stood the figures of Shingen-Hu and Thrax, gazing down lordlike and majestically, borne from the gods.

It had been a test, the Examiner saw. He would not fail. "Hail to the Chosen One, indeed true messenger of the highest gods!" he exalted, going down onto both knees this time. Around him the other dignitaries and soldiers who had come from Rakashym took up the cry and followed suit.

Ethendor stormed out onto the terrace below the steps, flung back his robe and aimed his arms up at Shingen-Hu. Moving reflexively in self-defense. Shingen-Hu pointed back, and all the power that had been focused within him by the intensity of the moment went into the bolt that flashed downward before Ethendor could concentrate his will. The figure of the high priest went rigid and became incandescent. From below, Hunt and his companions watched in horrified fascination.

And then, a very peculiar thing happened.

The shock of psychic energy that annihilated the mind that had been Ethendor propagated back along the current perfusing it and out through the attached neural coupler into the brain of Eubeleus. And since the system controlling the coupler was now under the direction not of JEVEX but VISAR, VISAR saw the configuration of mental constructs that formed the person of Eubeleus beginning to dislocate and come apart.

VISAR's basic programming gave it a nature that sought to protect and preserve life. There was nothing it could do to save Ethendor, for what had been Ethendor was gone; and the milliseconds that it had to consider what could be done about Eubeleus gave little opportunity for innovation or profound reflections on possible consequences. It used the tools that it had. And the only way it knew to preserve a human personality was to inject it, while it was still functioning as a coherent whole, into an artificial Ent-being—which VISAR promptly wrote into the Entoverse. For the same reasons why the surrogates of Hunt and the others looked to them as their human forms looked in the Exoverse, the Eubeleus surrogate looked like Eubeleus.

Who found himself suddenly at the foot of the temple steps, clad in a Roman toga, standing beside the smoldering heap that moments before had been Ethendor, and staring at a twin-rotor helicopter hovering over the petrified crowd.

He stood gaping down at himself and from side to side, confused and bewildered, while the priests who had followed Ethendor down the steps backed away, terrified . . . And then his mouth fell open as he recognized for the first time the group of figures who were standing a short distance below.

"No," he protested, shaking his head. "This can't be! How could *you* be here?"

"Hello, Eubeleus!" Hunt called back cheerfully. "We seem to have this habit of showing up in the oddest places, don't we?" He managed to look nonchalant, but inside he was as mystified as to how Eubeleus came to be there as Eubeleus himself seemed to be.

"JEVEX, what is the meaning of this?" Eubeleus demanded savagely.

"Sorry, but the system is no longer operating under that management," came the reply. "This is your new, friendly, integrated computer service, VISAR, brought to you at no charge all the way from Thurien. Have a nice day."

"That is not possible!"

"What else can I tell you?"

Eubeleus came to the edge of the terrace and screamed down at the soldiers. "*Kill them! I command you, kill every one of them!*" The soldiers' weapons turned into party squeakers and candy canes. Around where Eubeleus was standing, the pyres, gibbets, and instruments of torture became a garden swing set, seesaw, and slide; some lawn ornaments, a Christmas tree, and a beach umbrella.

"Just not one of your days, is it, Eubeleus?" Hunt observed.

"You forget—here, *I* command powers!" Eubeleus snarled, leveling a finger at Hunt. A ray of pale yellow light shot out of his fingertip; but after traveling about three feet it stopped in a blob, which spun itself tauntingly into a disk, became a custard pie, and flew back into Eubeleus's face. VISAR freed and cleaned up all the captives, and then proceeded to turn the helmets of the soldiers into assorted hats and bonnets and their armor into corsets and negligees, and painted red noses and clown faces on the priests.

"VISAR, what in hell's happening?" Hunt asked. "How did he get here?"

"He was coupled into the cheerleader who got fried. There's just a vegetable left in the coupler on Uttan. What else could I do?"

In the temple forecourt, the Chinook landed, and Shingen-Hu descended to the ground, accompanied by his acolyte, while crowd, soldiers, and dignitaries alike prostrated themselves.

Hunt looked at the others. "I think this place has got itself a reliable chief executive. Why don't we get out now, before things get complicated, and let him start running things his own way from the beginning?"

"Your originals think so, too," VISAR said. "They can't wait to find out what happened."

"My own feelings also," Eesyan agreed. "In fact, since my original is already in a coupler on Thurien, I can be the first, right now." He looked around the group. "This has been a strange experience. I look forward to meeting you all again under more familiar conditions, when we can no doubt discuss the philosophical issues. Until then . . ." He left it unfinished. The details of his body faded, leaving just his shape outlined in featureless white; it persisted for a moment, and then was gone.

Aboard the *Shapieron*, Hunt and the rest of the party were already on their way to the couplers located just off the command deck. When they were nearly there, Gina stopped Hunt and turned to him with a puzzled expression.

"Vic, how is this supposed to work? There are two copies of each of us that have diverged and been leading independent existences for the last several hours. Does one of them get . . . 'selected' somehow, and the other one erased, like what happened to me before? If so, who chooses? I don't think I like it."

Hunt didn't know. He hadn't given it a thought. On reflection, he didn't like it, either. How did he know that *he* would be the lucky one? But then, again, wouldn't the other "him," down in the Entoverse, have an equally valid reason for feeling the same way? So they put the question to VISAR.

"Why should you have to select either?" was VISAR's reply.

Hunt didn't understand. To him it still seemed a good question. "You say Eesyan's already back on Thurien?" he said.

"Right."

"So what did he do?"

"When I erased his surrogate in the Entoverse, I simply transferred its accumulated impressions into his original, physical self. It's his brain, and now it contains his memories. Where's the problem?"

Hunt glanced at Gina and shook his head, frowning. "You mean you just strung them together inside his head, serially? He remembers both sets of experiences equally vividly?" he said to VISAR.

"Yes."

"But they were both happening at the same time," Gina said,

"So what?"

Hunt and Gina looked at each other. VISAR was right. Evidently it was another Terran hang-up that Thuriens could live with and not worry about. It really didn't matter, did it? They had already gotten used to some far stranger things.

"So what?" Hunt repeated.

Gina nodded and smiled at the impossibility of ever coming fully to terms with it all. "So what?"

They continued on into the corridor where the couplers were located.

In the forecourt of the Temple of Vandros, Hunt and his remaining companions prepared to depart in style, as emissaries from the gods would be expected to do. At the door of the Chinook, he paused to exchange a few parting words with Shingen-Hu.

"No more arisings until we've figured out on the outside how to handle it," Hunt said. "We'll be in touch, that's a promise. In the meantime, make them believe that we haven't abandoned them, and keep the faith."

"It shall be as the new gods command," Shingen-Hu assured him.

"And we don't want sacrifices, killings, atonements, cleansings, or any more of that kind of thing. Try being nice to people for a change. Help them get what *they* want. You'd be amazed at the results."

"The commandments will be obeyed."

Remembering what had happened to the Jevlenese, Hunt waved at the machine, waiting with the others already aboard, its rotors idling. "This and the other miracles will cease. They don't belong here. The people will have to learn to develop their own ways of solving their problems and catering to their needs, in ways that are natural to this place. In that way, they will develop also."

"We shall await the Word."

"And that's about it." Hunt extended a hand. Shingen-Hu looked at it, hesitated, and then returned the gesture. They shook firmly. Then Hunt climbed up and turned from the door for a last view. As the note of the turbines rose, Eubeleus ran forward from the knot of priests and notables standing ahead of the awestruck crowd.

"What's this?" he screeched. "You're not leaving me here? You can't!"

"There isn't a lot of choice," Hunt called back. "You don't seem to have grasped the point yet, Eubeleus, old chap. *We* have intact minds out there to return into. You don't."

And of course, Eubeleus hadn't. He still thought that this was a software illusion manufactured by JEVEX, and had no idea how he had come to be part of it.

"Don't worry too much about it for now," Hunt shouted as the Chinook began to rise. "You should have plenty of time to figure it out."

And as the crowd watched in silent reverence, the machine climbed away to hang over the city, its rotors flashing in the sunshine as a testament to the new, unimagined powers that had visited Waroth. The form froze into a white outline that persisted for a second longer . . . And then it was gone.

Chapter Sixty-three

The *Shapieron* was back on its pad at Geerbaine. The edges of the hole that it had torn through the city roof had been trimmed back to remove the immediate hazard from the looser debris, but no real work had commenced on repairing the damage yet. No doubt the Jevlenese would get around to it eventually.

There were no crowds or any public ceremony. Garuth and a small party from PAC drove out from the city—the tubes weren't running that day—to see off the group who were returning to Earth and to make their farewells, most of which were personal rather than functions of any office. Not many of the Jevlenese at large were aware that the scientists who were leaving had had much connection with recent events, anyway. All they knew was that the ballyhoo about JEVEX returning two weeks previously had fizzled out, and after all the hype about Eubeleus's migration to Uttan, not a lot seemed to be happening there. (Actually, a lot of Thurien vessels had been arriving at Uttan, but that wasn't general knowledge yet.) Besides that, the hotheads who had seized PAC with the collusion of some elements of the Shiban police had changed their tune suddenly and surrendered; the Ganymeans were back again—but this time they were more committed to setting up a native Jevlenese administration instead of trying to run things directly themselves; and nobody could get a headworld trip for any price anymore.

Leyel Torres and a deputation of crew officers from the *Shapieron* were waiting at the spaceport to add their own farewells. The groups met in the main departure lounge, watched curiously by onlookers going about regular business and others assembling to travel back on the same ship—which again would be the *Vishnu*. The Thuriens were still being as casual as ever about taking anyone who wanted to go, and—especially after the latest complications—steering clear of any involvement in human politics. If any Terran or Jevlenese faction, sect, authority, government, party, union, church—or whatever other form of organization humans insisted on banding themselves together into to interfere with each others' lives—had a problem with it, they could settle it among themselves by their own incomprehensible methods.

"It should work out a lot better this time round," Hunt said to Garuth. "Although after the way you spent twenty years getting your ship back before you showed up at Jupiter, I don't have to tell you anything about perseverance."

"Now that we know where the problem was coming from, I think it will change a lot of things," Garuth replied. "The new system will give the whole population a common goal and a symbol to unite them." His face twisted into the peculiar Ganymean form of a grin, and he looked at Danchekker. "But no pyramids or temples, crescents or spirals, eh, Professor?"

"I think the human race has had more than its fill of that kind of thing," Danchekker agreed.

Garuth was referring to the new planetary computer system that would be built from scratch, on Jevlen, where JEVEX was supposed to have been, by the Jevlenese themselves. In the meantime, they would have to learn to meet their own needs through their own initiative, as the more enterprising among them had already shown an amazing propensity for doing. As they grew, the system would grow with them. It wouldn't come as a ready-made gift this time. The Thuriens themselves had insisted on its being that way.

"It should keep you two busy enough for a while," Hunt said, turning to Shilohin and Keshen, both of whom would be involved with the project. "But don't try and plan everything too far ahead. That's how things end up inflexible—the one thing that's sure to happen is the one you never thought of."

"Nobody planned the Entoverse, or this one," Shilohin said.

"We'll let it plan itself as it goes," Keshen agreed. He grinned. "And I know not to take on any sidelines this time."

"Watch where you're flying that ship, the next time you take it up," Hunt told Torres and Jassilane. "Tell that computer of yours to try not to bump into any cities. It does tend to upset the inhabitants, and the police take a dim view of it."

"I don't exactly remember that they were about to give you the citizen-of-the-year award at the time," ZORAC chipped in, reverting momentarily from translation mode to its own voice.

Del Cullen shook hands with Hunt warmly and gave him a hearty thump on the shoulder. A contingent of Terran police and security advisers had arrived from Earth with the *Vishnu* to help Garuth's Jevlenese administration establish some machinery for protecting the basic rights that governments were supposed to be for. Cullen would be working with them initially to adjust their thinking to the needs of the local society, instead of the other way around.

"Three months, they tell us," he said. "So say hi to the States for us until then. And when we get there, it'll be the wildest time of R and R since they came home from World War Two. Right, guys?"

"Right," Koberg and Lebansky agreed heartily from behind him.

Sandy Holmes and Duncan Watt were standing with the group from PAC, not the ones who were due to leave. They would be staying on for at least three months, getting the UNSA labs at PAC organized as a permanent facility and initiating some of the kind of work for which the group had come to Jevlen officially to begin with. Hunt also suspected that they had plenty of R and R plans of their own, involving a lot of

Shiban nightlife. Erwin Reutheneger would have been proud.

"Regards to Gregg and everyone back at the firm," Duncan told Hunt. "Tell him he's been warming that chair at Goddard for too long. It's time we saw more of him out here in the field."

"Maybe I can get him on the flight back with the *Vishnu*," Hunt said. "It would save us a lot of frenzy and all-night meetings when we get back after this, if I know anything about Gregg."

Danchekker, who had been saying something to Sandy, turned with an intrigued look on his face as he caught the conversation. "Yes, what a possibility . . . And, er, might there be a chance, perhaps, of persuading Ms. Mulling to go with him, do you think?"

Sandy moved over to Hunt. "Well, Vic, Gregg did warn me that none of the expeditions he sends you off on ever work out the way anyone thinks. He said that this time he told you the only thing left for you to bring back was a universe. And you did!"

"He should have known better by now," Hunt said.

"Do you think I could get a chance to go down into the Entoverse later?"

"Maybe. It depends what the Thuriens come up with and how they decide to handle it. I'd say there's a pretty good chance."

"I didn't exactly think Gregg was exaggerating, but I never dreamed of anything like that."

"Watch what you dream about," Gina said, standing beside Hunt. "These days it's getting difficult to tell the difference."

"And you be careful with VISAR on the way back," Sandy told her. "Remember what happened last time."

"Not just me, as I recall," Gina replied.

"Just as well you did," Hunt said to both of them. "I'll drink to curiosity every time. Remember, objectivity is what you make it."

The others who were boarding the Thurien surface lander had by now disappeared along the ramp, with the exception of Murray and Nixie. Murray had decided it was time to take his chances and straighten things out back home, and Nixie would get her chance to see Earth. But although they would no doubt stay in touch, their former association was over. With her unique psychology and abilities, Nixie would spend time working with Danchekker and others at Goddard, and after that would go to Thurien to assist Eesyan and his scientists with their further researches on the Entoverse.

Murray and Nixie disappeared into the ramp, and after a final round of waves and farewells, Hunt, Danchekker, and Gina turned and followed them. Soon afterward, the smooth, golden ovoid ascended from the surface of Jevlen and docked with the twenty-mile-long Thurien starship, hanging in orbit. Less than an hour later, the *Vishnu* was accelerating out of the star Athena's planetary system.

And of the Entoverse itself?

The Thurien position all along had been that it had to be kept running—which nobody else really objected to once the Thurien viewpoint was explained. For all anyone outside knew, many of the Ents might want to stay there, and nobody was going to disagree with their right do so.

But what of the many who wished to leave, which was another of the principles that the Thuriens had defended vigorously? Obviously they couldn't be permitted to take over the persons of any more Jevlenese, or anyone else who might be coupled into the system for whatever reason in times to come. And, as Danchekker had pointed out, that was just as well in any case, since there were evidently compatibility problems between Ent minds and human nervous systems, which he was beginning to suspect had caused most of the aberrant behavior exhibited by "possessed" individuals all through recorded history.

But then, why should any future emergent Ents be limited to unsuitable human hosts at all? The Ganymeans had always excelled as genetic engineers. Eesyan had suggested that maybe they could create a purpose-devised organism that would be an ideal vehicle for Ents wishing to transfer to the Exoverse—in effect, what VISAR had improvised in the form of its Ent-being surrogates, but working the other way around. Even more bizarre, perhaps, one day a regular traffic of visitors and immigrants going in both directions would develop out of it, and be thought as natural as holidaying in Australia or one of the lunar resorts.

In any case, the Thuriens had already commenced an intensive program of research into the matter, and whatever the precise form of the final answer, there seemed every chance that the Ents would come to put their unique abilities and nature to good use, and take their place in the Omniverse, alongside Terrans, Jevlenese, and Ganymeans.

About the Author

New York Times best-selling author James P. Hogan was born in London in 1941 and studied general engineering at the Royal Aircraft Establishment, Farnborough, subsequently specializing in electronics and digital systems. His first novel, *Inherit the Stars*, which was also the first in his Giants series, was hailed as a major science fiction novel in the grand tradition, combining accurate cutting-edge science with living, breathing characters. Isaac Asimov raved that the novel was "Pure science fiction," and added "Arthur Clarke, move over." In 1979 he became a full-time writer, and the electronics field's loss is every science fiction reader's gain. He now lives full time in Ireland.

JAMES P. HOGAN
Real SF

Giants novels:

Mission to Minerva (hc)	0-7434-9902-6 * $26.00
The Two Moons	1-4165-0936-4 * $7.99
Kicking the Sacred Cow (nonfiction)	0-7434-8828-8 * $24.00
Minds, Machines & Evolution	0-671-57843-X * $6.99
Rockets, Redheads & Revolution	0-671-57807-3 * $6.99
Chaos, Catastrophes & Convolutions	1-4165-0921-6 * $7.99
The Immortality Option	0-7434-7163-6 * $6.99
Cradle of Saturn	0-671-57866-9 * $6.99
The Anguished Dawn	0-7434-9876-3 * $7.99
The Legend that was Earth	0-671-31840-3 * $7.99
Martian Knightlife	0-7434-3591-5 * $6.99
Realtime Interrupt	0-671-59894-7 * $6.99
Bug Park	0-671-87874-3 * $6.99
Paths to Otherwhere	0-671-87767-4 * $6.99
The Genesis Machine	0-7434-3597-4 * $6.99
Voyage from Yesteryear	0-671-57798-0 * $6.99
The Multiplex Man	0-671-57819-7 * $6.99
The Two Faces of Tomorrow	0-671-87848-4 * $6.99
Endgame Enigma	0-671-87796-8 * $5.99
The Proteus Operation	0-671-87757-7 * $5.99
Star Child	0-671-87878-6 * $5.99
Thrice Upon a Time	0-671-31948-5 * $6.99

Available in bookstores everywhere.
Or order online at our secure, easy to use website:
www.baen.com
If not available through your local bookstore send this coupon and a
check or money order for the cover price(s) + $1.75 s/h to Baen Books,
Dept. BA, P.O. Box 1403, Riverdale, NY 10471. Be sure to include full
name & address for shipping. Delivery can take up to eight weeks.

The Best of
JIM BAEN'S
UNIVERSE

Edited by Eric Flint

Top-selling writers and brilliant newcomers appear regularly in the online magazine *Jim Baen's Universe*, edited by Eric Flint. Now, Flint and his staff select a generous serving of the best science fiction and fantasy stories that have appeared so far in the magazine. Contributors include: Mike Resnick, David Drake, Gene Wolfe, Gregory Benford, Esther Friesner and many more.

FREE CD-ROM INCLUDED
IN THE FIRST HARDCOVER PRINTING
CONTAINING THE ENTIRE CONTENTS
OF THE MAGAZINE'S FIRST YEAR,
ILLUSTRATIONS FROM THE MAGAZINE,
OVER 20 NOVELS BY ERIC FLINT
AND MUCH MORE!

1-4165-2136-4 ★ $25.00

AMAZONS 'R US
The Chicks in Chainmail series,
edited by Esther Friesner

Chicks in Chainmail
"Kudos should go to Friesner for having the guts to put together this anthology and to Baen for publishing it... a fabulous bunch of stories... they're all gems."—*Realms of Fantasy* "For a good time, check on *Chicks in Chainmail*.... In its humorous exploration of the female fantasy warrior, this anthology does its best to turn every stereotype on its ear. There's something to offend everyone here, so bring your sense of humor and prepare to be entertained."—*Locus*   0-671-87682-1 • $6.99

Did You Say Chicks?!
Smile when you say that.... Stories by Elizabeth Moon, Harry Turtledove, Esther Friesner & more.   0-671-87867-0 • $6.99

Chicks 'n Chained Males
"This anthology is a hoot!"—*Affaire de Coeur*. Stories by Rosemary Edghill, K.D. Wentworth, Lawrence Watt-Evans, more.
0-671-57814-6 • $6.99

The Chick is in the Mail
Neither rain nor snow nor hail shall stand in the way of these chicks! Stories by Charles Sheffield, William Sanders, Robin Wayne Bailey, Nancy Kress, Eric Flint, more.   0-671-31950-7 • $6.99

Turn the Other Chick
These babes were born to battle. Stories by John G. Hemry, Jan Stirling, Wen Spencer, Selina Rosen, Jody Lynn Nye, more.
hc 0-7434-8857-1 • $20.00
pb 1-4165-2053-8 • $7.99

And don't miss:
E.Godz by Esther Friesner & Robert Asprin
Dow Jones meets dark sorcery—no holds are barred in this family war for control of the Wal-Mart of the magic world.
hc 0-7434-3605-9 • $17.00
pb 0-7434-9888-7 • $6.99